O9-BTJ-166

# More praise for Wilbur Smith and GOLDEN FOX:

"Wilbur Smith affords us fascinating glimpses into the grandeur of the African continent and into the political machinations of the government factions seeking control in Africa."
—*The Free Lance-Star* (Fredericksburg, VA)

"Reading African author Wilbur Smith is like riding a rhino bareback: You get wherever you're going *fast.*"
—*The Tampa Tribune & Times*

"A tale of romance, politics, and espionage . . . Enjoyable."
—*Times Record News* (Wichita Falls, TX)

"Smith is a writer of surpassing skill."
—*Kansas City Star*

Also by Wilbur Smith:

*The Courtneys:*
WHEN THE LION FEEDS*
THE SOUND OF THUNDER*
A SPARROW FALLS*

*The Courtneys of Africa:*
THE BURNING SHORE*
POWER OF THE SWORD*
RAGE*
A TIME TO DIE*

*The Ballantyne Novels:*
FLIGHT OF THE FALCON*
MEN OF MEN*
THE ANGELS WEEP*
THE LEOPARD HUNTS IN DARKNESS*

THE DARK OF THE SUN*
SHOUT AT THE DEVIL*
GOLD MINE
THE DIAMOND HUNTERS*
THE SUNBIRD*
EAGLE IN THE SKY
THE EYE OF THE TIGER
CRY WOLF
HUNGRY AS THE SEA
WILD JUSTICE
ELEPHANT SONG

*Published by Fawcett Books

# GOLDEN FOX

## Wilbur Smith

FAWCETT GOLD MEDAL • NEW YORK

Sale of this book without a front cover may be unauthorized. If this book is coverless, it may have been reported to the publisher as "unsold or destroyed" and neither the author nor the publisher may have received payment for it.

A Fawcett Gold Medal Book
Published by Ballantine Books
Copyright © 1990 by Wilbur Smith

All rights reserved under International and Pan-American Copyright Conventions. Published in the United States by Ballantine Books, a division of Random House, Inc., New York. Originally published in Great Britain by Macmillan London Ltd., in 1990 in the U.S. by Random House, Inc. in 1991.

Library of Congress Catalog Card Number: 90-39062

ISBN 0-449-14906-4

This edition published by arrangement with Random House, Inc.

Manufactured in the United States of America

First Ballantine Books Edition: December 1993

*This book is dedicated
to Danielle Antoinette,
who transformed my life into
a joyous adventure.*

# GOLDEN FOX

# 1

A cloud of butterflies rose into the sunlight, the breeze smeared them across the summer sky and a hundred thousand young faces shining with wonder turned upward to watch them drift overhead.

In the forefront of that vast concourse sat a girl, the girl he had been stalking for ten days now. A hunter studying his prey, he had come to know with a peculiar intimacy her every gesture and movement, the turn and lift of her head as something caught her attention, the way she cocked it to listen or tossed it in annoyance or impatience. Now in a new attitude she lifted her face to the glorious cloud of winged insects, and even at this distance he could see the sparkle of her teeth, and her lips formed a soft pink O of wonder.

On the high stage above her the figure in the white satin shirt held up yet another box and, laughing, shook from it a fresh burst of fluttering wings. Yellow and white and iridescent, they bore aloft, and the crowd gasped and "oohed" afresh.

One of the butterflies toppled and dived, and though a hundred hands were held out to catch it, it swerved and wobbled down to alight at last on the girl's upturned face. Even above the swelling murmur of the crowd, he heard the girl's happy cry of laughter, and he found himself smiling in sympathy with her.

She reached up to where it sat on her forehead and took it gently, almost reverently, in the cup of her hands. For a moment she held it close to her face, studying it with those indigo blue eyes he had come to know so well. Her expression was suddenly wistful and her lips moved as she whispered to it, but he could not hear the words.

Her sadness was fleeting. Then those lovely lips smiled again and she leaped to her feet and held both hands high above her head, standing on tiptoe. The butterfly hesitated, perched on her outstretched fingertips, pulsing its wings softly on the point of flight, and he heard her voice.

"Fly! Fly for me!" And those around her took up the cry. "Fly! Fly for peace!"

For a moment she had usurped the limelight, and all eyes were fastened on her rather than on the flamboyant figure in the center of the stage.

She was tall and lithe, her bare limbs tanned and glowing with health. She wore her skirt so short, in the fashion of the day, that as she reached upward the hem rose high above the circular creases where her cocky little buttocks joined her thighs in a froth of white lace.

For a moment, poised like that, she seemed to epitomize her generation, wild and free and fey, and he sensed the instant accord of spirit of all those who watched her. Even the man on the stage leaned forward to see her better. His lips, thick and livid as though stung by bees, split in a smile and he called out, "Peace!" His voice was magnified a thousand times by the great banks of amplifiers that rose high on each side of the stage.

The butterfly flew from her hands. She pressed all her fingers to her lips and blew a wide kiss after it as it fluttered aloft and was lost in the swirling cloud of insects.

The girl sank down onto the grass, and those seated close to her reached out to touch and embrace her.

On the stage Mick Jagger held his arms wide, commanding silence. Once he had it, he spoke into the microphone. Distorted by the amplifiers, his voice was slurred and incoherent; his accent was so thick that the watcher could barely understand the stumbling tribute he read out to the member of his band who only days previously had drowned in a swimming pool during a wild weekend party.

The whisper was that the victim had been almost comatose with drugs when he entered the water. It was a hero's death, for this was the age of drugs and sexual excess, of pot and Pill, of freedom and peace and overdosing.

Jagger ended his little speech. It had been so brief that it had not dulled the buoyant mood of the gathering. The electric guitars struck a discord, and Jagger hurled himself into "Honky Tonk Woman" with every fiber of his being. Within seconds he had a hundred thousand hearts racing in time to his, a hundred thousand young bodies jerking and pulsing, two hundred thousand arms held high, swaying like a field of wheat in a high wind.

The music was cosmic, brutal as an artillery bombardment;

2

painful to the ear, it penetrated the skull and seemed to numb and crush the brain. Swiftly it reduced the audience to a mindless frenzy, transformed the multitude into a single organism, like a gigantic amoeba that throbbed and undulated in the act of reproduction, fraught with a passion that was overtly sexual. From it rose the stench of dust and sweat, the sickly sweet odor of cannabis smoke and the heady overpowering musk of young bodies physically aroused.

The watcher was alone in the midst of the throng, isolated and detached, unmoved by the blasts of sound that swept over him. He studied the girl, awaiting his moment.

She swayed to the primeval rhythm, moved in time to the bodies that pressed close about her, but with a singular grace that set her apart. Her hair was glistening jet with highlights of ruby that glinted in the sun, piled on top of her head; but thick tresses of it had come down in smoky coils, enhancing the elegant line of her neck and the set of her head upon it, like a tulip on its stem.

Directly below the stage, an area had been cordoned off with a low picket fence, a tiny enclave for a privileged few. Marianne Faithfull, in a flowing caftan but with bare feet, sat here with the other wives and camp followers. Her beauty was remote and ethereal. Her eyes seemed dreamy and sightless as those of a blind woman, and her movements were slow and somnolent. Children crawled about her feet, guarded and protected by a phalanx of Hell's Angels.

In black Wehrmacht steel helmets, hung with chains and Nazi iron crosses, chest hair curling out from under vests of black leather studded with silver metal, steel-shod motorcycle boots, arms covered with intricate tattoos, they struck menacing poses, arms akimbo, billy clubs in their belts, their clenched fists heavy with sharp-edged steel rings. They surveyed the crowd with brooding insolent stares, watching for trouble, hoping for trouble.

The music pounded on and on, one hour and then another. The heat built up, and the smell of humanity was like that of an animal cage, for some of the audience, both men and women, hemmed in and reluctant to miss a moment of it, had urinated where they sat.

The watcher was disgusted by the decadence, the wild abandon and the gross indulgence of it all. It offended everything he believed in. His eyes felt gritty and sensitive, and his head ached, throbbing in time to the driving rhythm of the guitars. It was time to leave. Another day wasted, another day spent waiting

3

for the opportunity that never came. However, he was a hunter with all the patience of the predator. There would be other days; he was in no hurry. The moment must be exactly right for his purpose.

He began to move, working his way through the dense throng of bodies across the low knoll where he had stood, shouldering through them; they were in such a trance they seemed neither to see nor to feel him push past them.

He glanced back, and his eyes narrowed as he saw the girl speak to the boy beside her, smile and shake her head in response to his reply and rise to her feet. Then she also began to work her way through the crowd, stepping over the seated ranks, steadying herself with a hand on a shoulder, laughing an apology as she went.

The watcher changed direction, angling down the gentle slope to intercept her, the hunter's instinct warning him that unexpectedly the moment for which he had waited had arrived.

Behind the stage were the television trucks, row upon row of them, each as tall as a double-decker bus, parked so close together that there were only inches between them.

The girl moved back, circling the low picket fence, working her way around the side of the stage, trying to get clear of the throng; but it was so dense that it blocked her further progress, and her expression was desperate as she glanced around her, caught in the press of bodies.

Suddenly she turned directly toward the fence, pushed her way to it, and then with a swift athletic bound jumped over it and scuttled into the narrow space between two of the high television trucks. One of the Hell's Angels saw her dart away into the forbidden area, and he shouted and followed her at a run, twisting his shoulders to squeeze into the narrow passage down which she had disappeared. As he turned, the watcher got a flash of the grin on his face.

It took the watcher almost two minutes to force his way to the point on the fence where the girl had crossed. Somebody reached out to stop him, but he struck the hand away and went over, slipping into the space between the high steel sides of the parked trucks.

He moved sideways, the gap too narrow to accommodate the width of his shoulders, and he was level with the door of the driver's cab when he heard muffled cries of protest just ahead of him. The sound spurred him, and as he came around the side of the bonnet, he stopped for an instant as he took in what was happening just in front of him.

4

The Hell's Angel had caught the girl, and now he had her held against the front wing of the truck. He had one of her arms twisted up behind her back, almost at the level of her shoulder blades. She was facing him, but he was pressing her backward against the steel wing with his hips and his pot belly. He bent over her, trying to reach her mouth with his. The girl's back was arched, and she rolled her head violently from side to side, trying to avoid his mouth. He was laughing, his mouth wide open, flicking his tongue out at her, trying to force it into her mouth.

With his right hand he had hoisted her tiny skirt up to her waist, and his hairy fingers, stained with motorcycle grease, were hooked into the waistband of her lace panties. The girl was striking and clawing at him with her free hand, but he hunched his shoulders so that she could not reach his face with her nails, and her blows fell on studded black leather and thick shoulders padded with muscle and fat. The Angel's laughter was thick and guttural, and the lace of her panties tore with a sharp crackling sound as he forced them over her hips and down the smooth tanned thighs.

The watcher stepped forward and touched the Angel's shoulder, and the man froze and twisted his head around. His eyes were glazed, but they cleared instantly and he flung the girl sideways so viciously that she sprawled on the torn muddy grass between the trucks. The Angel reached for the club in his belt.

The watcher reached out and touched him again, under the ear, just below the rim of his steel helmet. He pressed with two fingers, and the Angel froze and stiffened. All his limbs went rigid, and he made a glottal cawing sound deep in his throat. His entire body convulsed and he collapsed in a heap and, like an epileptic, lay twitching and jerking spasmodically. The girl was on her knees, pulling up her torn underclothes and watching in fascinated horror. The watcher stepped over the sprawling Angel and lifted the girl to her feet without apparent effort.

"Come," he said softly. "Before his friends arrive."

Swiftly he led her away by the hand, and she followed as trustingly as a child.

Beyond the parked trucks was a maze of narrow pathways through the rhododendron bushes. As they ran down one of these paths, she asked breathlessly, "Did you kill him?"

"No." He did not even glance around. "He'll be on his feet again in less than five minutes."

"You flattened him. How did you do that? You hardly touched him."

5

He did not answer, but after the next bend in the path he stopped and turned back to face her.

"Are you all right?" he asked. She nodded jerkily without speaking.

He studied her, still holding her hand. He knew she was twenty-four years old, a young woman who had just experienced a violent attempted rape, but the gaze of her dark blue eyes was level and appraising. There were no tears, no hysterics, not even a tremor of those pink lips, and the hand in his was slim and firm and warm.

The psychiatrist's report on her, which he had studied, had been correct in at least this much: she was resilient and self-assured; already she was almost fully recovered from the attack. Then he saw the color mount softly in her cheeks and at the base of her long elegant throat, and her breath quickened perceptibly. She was experiencing another strong emotion.

"What's your name?" she asked, her eyes fastened on his with an intensity he recognized. On first encounter most women looked at him like that.

"Ramón," he replied.

"Ramón," she repeated softly, relishing the sound of it. God, he was beautiful. "Ramón who?"

"You won't believe it if I tell you." His English was perfect, too perfect. He must be foreign, she thought. But the voice matched his face, beautiful, deep and grave.

"Try me," she invited, and heard the catch in her own voice.

"Ramón de Santiago y Machado." He made it sound like music; it was impossibly romantic. It was the most beautiful name she had ever heard, perfect for that face and voice.

"We must go," he said.

She was still staring at him. "I can't run," she said. "Don't make me run."

"If you don't, you might end up as a mascot on the handlebars of a motorcycle."

She laughed, then bit her lower lip to stop herself.

"Don't do that," she protested. "Don't make me laugh. I need a loo. My condition is critical."

"Ah, so that's where you were headed when Prince Charming fell in love with you."

"I warned you, don't do that." With an effort she smothered her giggle, and he took pity on her.

"There is a public loo at the gate to the park. Can you make it that far?"

"I don't know."

6

"The alternative is the rhododendrons."

"No, thanks. No more public performances today.'

"Let's go, then." He took her arm.

They skirted the Serpentine, and Ramón glanced back. "Your boyfriend's ardor must have cooled," he said. "No sign of him. What a fickle fellow."

"Pity. I'd love to watch you do that trick of yours again. How much farther is it?"

"Here it is." They had reached the gate, and she dropped his arm and started for the small red brick building that nestled discreetly in the shrubbery beside the path; but at the door she hesitated.

"My name is Isabella, Isabella Courtney. But my friends call me Bella," she said over her shoulder, and darted through the doorway.

"Yes," he murmured softly, "I know."

Even while she was in the cubicle she could hear the music, barely muted by the distance and the brick walls, and then the clatter of a helicopter passing low over the roof, but it was unimportant. She was thinking about Ramón.

At the washbasins she studied herself in the mirror. Her hair was a mess; she tidied it quickly. Ramón's hair was thick and dark and wavy. He wore it long, but not too long. She wiped off her pale pink lipstick on a Kleenex and then repainted her mouth. Ramón's mouth was full but masculine, soft but strong; she wondered how it would taste.

She dropped the lipstick back into her bag and leaned close to the mirror to appraise her eyes. They didn't need drops. The whites were so clear they had a bluish sheen, like those of a healthy baby. She knew her eyes were her best feature, that Courtney blue, something between cornflower and sapphire. Ramón's eyes were green. They were the first thing that had struck her about him. That clear startling green, beautiful but— she searched for the adjective—deadly. That was it exactly. She didn't need the demonstration that had felled the Hell's Angel. One look at those eyes, and she had known he was a dangerous man. She felt the back of her neck prickle with a delicious thrill of fear and of anticipation. Perhaps this was the one, at last. Beside his image all the others seemed to pale and fade. Perhaps this was the one she had searched for for so long.

"Ramón de Santiago y Machado." She said it in a throaty purr, savoring the taste of it in her mouth, watching her lips form the words. Then she straightened up and turned to the doorway. She prevented herself from hurrying. Slowly, lan-

7

guidly, on the tall stiletto heels that made her hips roll as she walked and her bottom swing like a metronome, lace flashing under the abbreviated skirt, she went to the door.

She pouted slightly and let her long thick eyelashes droop over the blue as she stepped out into the slanting golden sunlight. Then she stopped dead.

He was gone. She caught her breath and felt the cold quick slide of her stomach, as though she had swallowed a stone. She looked around her in disbelief. "Ramón," she said uncertainly, and ran into the pathway. There were hundreds of others coming down the tarmac path towards her, the first escapees from the concert trying to avoid the human avalanche that would soon follow, but none of them was the elegant figure she sought.

"Ramón," she said, and hurried to the park gates. The traffic boomed down the Bayswater Road, and she looked frantically right and left. She was overcome with a sense of disbelief. He had gone and left her. It was beyond her experience. She had shown him that she wanted him—she couldn't possibly have made it plainer—and he had walked away.

Her next emotion was outrage. Nobody did that to Isabella Courtney, not ever. She felt slighted and insulted and very angry.

"Damn him," she said. "Damn the man."

Her anger lasted only seconds, then it slumped. She felt lost and bereft. It was an alien sensation for her.

"He can't just leave like that," she said aloud, and recognized in her own voice the self-pitying whine of a spoiled child, so she said it again differently, trying to recapture her anger, but it was unconvincing.

Behind her she heard a shout of raucous laughter, and she glanced back. A bunch of Hell's Angels was swaggering down the pathway, still a hundred yards away but coming directly toward her. She couldn't remain here.

The concert was over, the crowds were breaking up. The helicopter she had heard must have been coming in to pick up the Rolling Stones. There was little chance of her rejoining her friends now; they would be lost in the multitude. She looked around her just once more, swiftly but despairingly. Still no sign of that dark, wavy head of hair. She tossed her own head and lifted her chin.

"Who needs him anyway, damned dago?" she muttered furiously, and struck out down the pavement.

Behind her there was a chorus of whistles and catcalls, and

someone, one of the Angels, began calling the step for her. "Left, right, left—shake, rattle and roll."

She knew that her high heels were making her bottom waggle furiously. She hopped on one foot and then the other as she pulled off her shoes and then fled barefoot down the pavement. She had left her car at the embassy carpark in the Strand, so she had to take the Tube from Lancaster Gate station to reach it.

Her car was a brand-new Mini-Cooper, the very latest 1969 model. Shasa, her father, had given it to her for her birthday, and had had it customized for her by the same body shop that had done Anthony Armstrong-Jones's Mini. They had souped up its engine, upholstered it in white Connolly leather like a Rolls and resprayed it the same glitter silver as Shasa's new Aston Martin with her initials in gold leaf on the door. All the swinging set were driving Minis; there were more of them than Rollses or Bentleys parked outside Annabel's on a Saturday night.

Isabella threw her shoes into the tiny backseat and revved the engine until the needle went into the red; the tires squealed and left black smears on the ramp of the carpark. As she glanced back at them in the rearview mirror she felt a dark satanic pleasure.

She drove with abandon, protected from the wrath of the Metropolitan Police by her diplomatic plates. She wasn't really entitled to them, but Shasa had wangled them for her.

She beat her own record back to Highveld, the ambassador's residence in Chelsea. Shasa's official Bentley with its pennants on the wings was parked at the entrance, and Klonkie, the chauffeur, grinned and saluted her. Shasa had brought most of his own staff from Cape Town.

Isabella controlled her mood long enough to give Klonkie her sweetest smile and toss him the keys. "Put my car away for me, there's a dear, Klonkie." Shasa was tremendously strict about the way she treated the servants. She could take her moods out on anyone but them. "They are part of the family, Bella." And most of them had indeed been at Weltevreden, the family home at the Cape of Good Hope, since before she was born.

Shasa was at his desk in his study on the ground floor overlooking the garden. He had discarded his coat and tie, and the desk top was piled with official documents, but he tossed down his pen and swiveled his chair toward her as she came in. His face lit up at the sight of her.

Bella dropped into his lap and kissed him. "God," she murmured, "you are the most beautiful man in the world."

9

"Far be it from me to question your good judgment,"—Shasa Courtney smiled—"but may I ask what has brought this on?"

"Men are either boars or bores," she said. "All except you, of course."

"Ah! And what has young Roger done to arouse your ire? To me, he seemed fairly inoffensive, if not actually insipid."

Roger was the one who had escorted her to the concert. She had left him on the crowded lawn in front of the stage, but now it took her a moment to remember him.

"I'm off men for life," Isabella declared. "I shall probably hie me to a nunnery."

"Could you possibly eschew holy orders at least until tomorrow? I do need a hostess for dinner this evening, and we haven't yet arranged the seating."

"All done, long ago," she said. "Before I left for the concert."

"The menu?"

"Chef and I settled that last Friday. Don't panic, Papa. All your favorites: Coquilles St. Jacques and lamb from Camdeboo." Shasa served only lamb reared on his own farms in the Karroo. The desert scrub gave the flesh a distinctive herby flavor. All the embassy beef came from his extensive ranches in Rhodesia, and the wines from the vineyards of Weltevreden where for the last twenty years Shasa's German wine maker had labored with rare skill and dedication to raise the quality of the vintage to the point where Shasa would back it against nearly any of the second *crus* of Burgundy. His ambition was still to make a wine that could compare with those of some of the great and noble houses of the Côte d'Or.

When it came to transporting this fare from the Cape of Good Hope to London, Courtney shipping lines ran a weekly refrigerated vessel on the Atlantic route.

". . . *and* I picked up your dinner jacket from the cleaner's this morning, *and* I had Budds in Piccadilly Arcade make you three more dress shirts and a dozen new eye patches. Your others were all getting so tatty. I've thrown them out."

Still sitting in his lap, she adjusted his eye patch. Shasa had lost his left eye flying Hurricanes against the Italians in Abyssinia during the Second World War. The black silk eye patch gave him a dashing, piratical air.

Now Shasa smiled complacently. When he had first invited Isabella to come to London with him, she had only recently turned twenty-one years of age, and he had thought long and hard before foisting the onerous task of official embassy hostess onto one so young. He need not have worried. After all, she had been trained by her grandmother, added to which they had brought the chef and butler and half the staff from the Cape with them, so she had started with her own highly trained team.

In three years, Isabella had built up a reputation in diplomatic circles, and her invitations were sought after, except by those embassies whose countries no longer maintained relations with South Africa.

"Do you want me to cover for you while you sneak off with your Israeli pal for half an hour after dinner to build an atom bomb?"

"Bella!" Shasa frowned quickly. "You know I don't like remarks like that."

"Joke, Daddy. There is nobody to hear us."

"Even in private and in fun, Bella." Shasa shook his head severely. That had been uncomfortably close to the truth. The Israeli military attaché and Shasa had been involved in a court-ship dance for almost a year now, and they had gone far beyond the stage of flirtation already.

She kissed him, and his expression softened. "I must go and bath." She stood up from his lap. "The invitations are for eight-thirty. I'll come and do your tie for you at ten past." Shasa had tied his own bow for forty years, until Isabella had decided he was incapable of doing so.

Shasa's eyes dropped to her legs. "If your skirts get any shorter, mademoiselle, your belly button will be winking at the moon."

"You really must try not to be an old fogy. It's most unbe-coming in one of the swingingest papas of the twentieth cen-tury." She headed for the door, deliberately accentuating the movement of her lower body under the offending article of cloth-ing. Shasa sighed as the door closed.

"That's a load of dynamite with a very short fuse," he mur-mured. "Perhaps, in a way, it's a good thing we're going home."

In September, Shasa's three-year ambassadorial stint would be up. Isabella would once more go under the control and dis-cipline of Centaine Courtney-Malcomess, her grandmother. Shasa realized that his own efforts in that direction had been less than totally successful, and he would hand over the responsibil-ity with relief.

Thinking of their imminent return to Cape Town, Shasa glanced back down at the papers on his desk. The years in the London embassy had been a political penance for him. When the prime minister, Hendrik Verwoerd, had been assassinated

11

in 1966, Shasa had made a serious miscalculation and backed the wrong man to succeed to the premiership. The result of that mistake had been that once John Vorster had become prime minister, Shasa had been shunted into this political backwater; but, as so many times before, he had turned disaster into triumph.

Using all his gifts and natural abilities, his shrewd business acumen, his presence and good looks, his charm and powers of persuasion, he had done much to deflect from his homeland the building wrath and contempt of the world, particularly that of Britain's Labor government and her Commonwealth, most of whose members were nations headed by black or Asian premiers. John Vorster had taken these achievements into account. Before leaving South Africa, Shasa had been intimately concerned with Armscor, and Vorster had offered him the job of chairman of Armscor on his return home.

Armscor was, put simply, the largest industrial undertaking that had ever existed on the African continent. It was the country's answer to the arms boycott begun by America's President Dwight Eisenhower and now being extended rapidly by other nations in an attempt to leave South Africa defenseless and vulnerable. Armscor—Armaments Development and Production Corporation—was the entire defense industry of the country under single management, state sponsored to the extent of billions upon billions of dollars.

It was an enormous and exciting challenge, especially since the multifarious companies that made up the Courtney financial and business empire were being well managed. During the three years of his ambassadorial duties, Shasa had allowed the management and control to pass gradually, in an orderly fashion, into the hands of his son Garry Courtney. Garry was making an amazing success of it for one so young; but, then, Shasa had not been much older when he had become chairman of Courtney Enterprises.

Then, again, Garry had the day-to-day backing of his grandmother, Centaine Courtney-Malcomess, the founder and dowager empress of the empire. He also had, working under him, the management team of experts that Centaine and Shasa between them had meticulously assembled over the previous forty years.

This in no way detracted from Garry's achievements, not least of which was the fashion in which he had steered them all through the recent collapse of the Johannesburg stock exchange, which had stripped up to 60 percent of the value from some share prices. In some remarkable fashion that would have done credit to either Shasa or Centaine, Garry had anticipated the end of the wild bull run that had preceded the collapse. Far from being damaged or destroyed, Courtney Enterprises had come through the ordeal even more powerful and cash-liquid, and in a better position to take advantage of the bargains the market now was offering.

No—Shasa smiled and shook his head—Garry was doing great things, and it would be bitterly unfair to come in above him again. However, Shasa was still a young man, not much over fifty years of age. When he got home he would need something to keep his wits sharp and his juices flowing. The Armscor job was perfect.

Of course, he would keep his seat on the Courtney board, but he could devote most of his time and energy to Armscor. Many of the subcontracts could be steered in the direction of the Courtney companies. Both enterprises might benefit enormously from this mutual association, and Shasa would have the additional pleasure and comfort of warming his patriotic ardor at the fire of capitalistic rewards.

Isabella's remark that he had objected to earlier was directly related to his new appointment. He had used his diplomatic connections with the Israeli embassy to initiate and then pursue the idea of a joint nuclear project between the two states. Tonight he would be handing over another batch of documents to the Israeli attaché to be forwarded in the diplomatic bag to Tel Aviv.

He glanced at his wristwatch. He still had twenty minutes before he must go up to change for dinner, and he switched all his concentration back to the papers in front of him.

Nanny had laid out the Zandra Rhodes couture model and run Isabella's bath.

"You are late, Miss Bella. And I still have to do your hair." She was a Cape Colored, her Hottentot blood mixed with that of most of the world's seafaring nations.

"Don't fuss so, Nanny," Isabella protested, but Nanny swept her off to the bathroom with as little ceremony as she had when Isabella was five years old.

While Isabella sank chin-deep into the steaming foam with a luxurious sigh, Nanny gathered up her discarded clothes.

"Your dress is stained with grass, child, and your new panties are torn. What you been up to?" Nanny washed all Isabella's underclothes by hand; she would trust no laundry with them.

"I've been playing touch rugby with a Hell's Angel, Nanny. Our team won thirty-love."

"You'll get yourself in bad trouble. All the Courtneys got hot blood." Nanny held up the torn panties and examined them with heavy disapproval. "Long past time you were safely married."

"You've got a dirty mind. Now tell me what's been happening today. What about Klonkie's new girlfriend?" Isabella knew how to distract her.

Nanny was an inveterate gossip, and this was the time of day when she brought Isabella up to date on the doings and undoings of the entire household. While she chattered, Isabella made little murmurs of encouragement, but she was listening with only half her attention, and when she stood up to soap herself she examined her body in the steamy full-length mirror across the room.

"Do you think I'm getting fat, Nanny?"

"You are so skinny, that's why no boy married you yet," Nanny sniffed, and went through to the bedroom.

Isabella tried to be completely objective as she studied herself. Was there any way in which her body could be improved? Should her bosom be a little bigger? And did the tips point outwards at too acute an angle? Were her hips too wide or should her bottom be smaller? After critical relection, she shook her head. It all looked just about perfect from where she stood. "Ramón de Santiago y Machado," she whispered, "you will never know what you missed." Why did that make her feel so miserable?

"You are talking to yourself again, child." Nanny came back with a bath towel the size of a bed sheet and held it open for her. "Out you get, now. We are running out of time." She enveloped Isabella in the towel as she stepped out of the bath and vigorously began to rub her back dry. It was no good trying to convince Nanny that she could dry herself.

"Don't be so rough." Isabella had been making the same protest for twenty years, and Nanny ignored it.

"How many times have you been married, Nanny?"

"You know well that I been married four times, but I only been churched just once." Nanny looked at her with new attention. "Why you ask about marrying? Did you find something interesting, that's why the torn panties?"

"You vulgar old woman!" Isabella avoided her eyes and snatched up her Thai silk gown on the way to the bedroom.

She picked up the hairbrush and made one stroke through her hair before Nanny took it away from her.

"That's my job, child," she said firmly. Isabella sat down

and closed her eyes, giving herself up to the familiar comfort of having Nanny brush out her hair for her.

"Do you know, I think I'll have a baby just so you'll have someone else to fuss over, and get you off my back."

Nanny missed a stroke, taken by the attractions of that proposal. Then she said sternly, "You get yourself married first before we talk babies."

The Zandra Rhodes creation was an ethereal cloud of subtle color, spangled with sequins and seed pearls. Even Nanny nodded and looked complacent as Isabella pirouetted in front of her.

Isabella was halfway down the staircase on her way to a last-minute conference with Chef when a thought occurred to her and she stopped abruptly. The Spanish chargé d'affaires was one of tonight's dinner guests. It took only a second for her to rearrange the table seating in her mind.

"Yes, of course." The Spanish chargé nodded immediately when she mentioned the name. "An old Andalusian family. As I recall, the Marqués de Santiago y Machado left Spain and went to Cuba after the civil war. He had considerable sugar and tobacco interests on the island at one time, but I imagine Castro changed all that."

A marqués—the reply silenced Isabella for a moment. Her knowledge of Spanish nobility was less than elementary, but she imagined that a marqués ranked just below a duke.

"The Marquesa Isabella de Santiago y Machado." With awe she allowed herself to consider the prospect, and she saw again in her mind's eye those deadly green eyes. For a moment she had difficulty breathing, and her voice was still ragged as she asked, "How old is the marqués?"

"Oh, he would be getting on a little now. That is, if he is still alive. He must be in his late sixties or early seventies."

"He had a son, perhaps?"

"That I don't know." The chargé shook his head. "But it would be easy to find out. If you wish, I will make some inquiries for you."

"Oh, that would be so kind of you." Isabella laid her hand on his arm and gave him her most brilliant smile.

Marqués or not, you don't get away from Isabella Courtney that easily, she thought smugly.

# 2

"It took you almost two weeks to make contact, and then when you had at last done so you immediately allowed the subject to escape." The man seated at the head of the table stubbed out his cigarette in the overflowing ashtray in front of him and immediately lit another. The first two fingertips of his right hand were stained dark yellow, and the smoke from the oval Turkish cigarettes that he smoked incessantly had already tarred the air in the small room to a blue fog. "Was that in accordance with your orders?" he asked.

Ramón Machado shrugged lightly. "It was the only certain way of getting and holding her attention. You must realize that this woman is accustomed to male adulation. She has only to lift a finger and men come swarming about her. I think you must trust my judgment in this matter."

"You allowed her to get away." The older man knew he was repeating himself, but this fellow needled him.

He did not like him, nor did he know him well enough yet to trust him. Not that he ever fully trusted any one of his operatives. However, this one was too self-assured, too disrespectful. He had turned aside the rebuke with a shrug, where another might have cringed. He had blatantly set his own judgment above that of a superior officer.

Joe Cicero hooded his eyes. They were as opaque as puddles of old engine oil, startlingly black against the pallor of his skin and the silver-white hair that hung limply over his ears and forehead.

"Your orders were to make contact and to maintain it."

"With respect, Comrade Director, my orders were to inveigle myself into the woman's confidence, not to rush at her barking like a mad dog."

No, Joe Cicero did not like him. His attitude was offensive,

16

but that was not the only reason. He was a foreigner. Joe Cicero considered any non-Russian a foreigner. No matter what the concept of international socialism dictated, East Germans, Yugoslavs, Hungarians, Cubans and Poles—they were all foreigners to him. It infuriated him to have to pass on responsibility for so much of the section that he had headed for almost thirty years to others. Especially people like this.

Not only was Machado a foreigner, his very roots and origins were corrupt. He was no scion of the proletariat, not even of the despised bourgeoisie, but was a full member of that hated and outdated system of class and privilege, the aristocracy.

True, Machado disparaged and despised his origins and used his title now only to achieve his goals, but to Joe Cicero his bloodlines were tainted and his aristocratic manners and affectations were an insult to all he, Cicero, believed in.

Furthermore, he had been born in Spain, a fascist country historically ruled by a Catholic monarchy that was the enemy of the people, even more so now under the monstrous Franco, who had put down the communist revolution. He might call himself a Cuban socialist, but to Joe Cicero he stank of Spanish fascism and aristocracy.

"You let her get away," he persisted. "After all this time and money wasted." He realized he was being ponderous and heavy-handed, and he knew his powers were failing. The sickness was already slowing his wits.

Ramón smiled, that condescending smile Joe Cicero hated so much. "She's on the line, like a fish; she may swim and dive only until I am ready to reel her in."

Again he had contradicted his superior, and Joe Cicero considered his last but most poignant reason for his dislike of the man: Machado's youth and comeliness and health. They made him painfully aware of his own mortality, for Joe Cicero was dying.

Since childhood he had chain-smoked these rank Turkish cigarettes, and on his last visit to Moscow the doctors had finally diagnosed the cancer in his lungs and offered him treatment in one of the sanatoria reserved for officers of his seniority. Instead Joe Cicero had elected to continue in service, to see his department securely handed over to his successor. He had not then known that this Spaniard was to be that successor. If he had known, perhaps he might have chosen the sanatorium.

He felt tired now, and discouraged. His store of energy and enthusiasm was all used up, just as only a few years ago his hair had been jet black and dense and now was white, tinged only

17

with yellow like sun-dried seaweed, and he could not walk a dozen paces without wheezing and coughing like an asthmatic.

Recently he had been waking in the night, drenched by terrible night sweats, and while he lay awake in the darkness he fought for breath and was assailed with terrible doubts. Had it been worth it, a lifetime of dedicated, painstaking work? What did he have to show for it? What solid success had he achieved?

For almost thirty years he had served in the African department of the fourth directorate of the KGB. For the last ten of those years, he had been head of Station South, the division responsible for the African continent below the equator. Quite naturally, most of his attention and that of his department had been devoted to the most developed and richest country in the region, the Republic of South Africa.

The third man at the table was a South African. Up until now he had remained silent, but now he said softly, "I do not understand why we are spending so much time discussing this woman. Explain it to me." Both the white men at the table diverted their attention to him. When Raleigh Tabaka spoke, other men usually listened. He had about him a peculiar intensity, a charged air of purpose that held the attention of others.

All his life, Joe Cicero had worked with black Africans, the nationalist leaders of the forces of liberation and the socialist struggle. He had known them all, Jomo Kenyatta and Kenneth Kaunda, Kwame Nkrumah and Julius Nyerere. Some of them he had come to know intimately: men like Moses Gama, who had been sent to a martyr's death, and Nelson Mandela, who was still languishing in the prison of white racism.

Cicero placed Raleigh Tabaka in the forefront of that illustrious company. In fact, Raleigh had been Moses Gama's nephew, and Raleigh had been present the night the South African police had murdered his uncle. He seemed to have inherited Moses Gama's tremendous personality and force of character, and he had stepped squarely into the wide gap left by Gama. He was thirty years old, but already he was deputy director of Umkhonto we Sizwe, "The Spear of the Nation," the military wing of the African National Congress. Joe Cicero knew he had proved himself time and again in the field and in the councils of the ANC. He had the talent, the guts and the verve to rise as high as any other man in Africa.

Joe Cicero preferred him to the white Spanish aristocrat, but he recognized that despite their differences in color and lineage they were men cast in the same mold: hard, dangerous men, well versed in death and violence, adept in the subtle, shifting

18

world of political power and intrigue. These were the men to whom Joe Cicero must hand over the reins, and he resented them and hated them for it.

"The woman," he said heavily, "could be of extraordinary value if she is controlled and developed to her full potential, but I will let the marqués explain that to you. It is his case, and he has studied the subject fully."

Abruptly Ramón Machado's smile thinned, and his eyes turned flat and hostile.

"I would prefer the comrade director not to use that title," he said coldly. "Even in jest."

Joe Cicero had learned it was probably the only way he could penetrate the Spaniard's slick armor plating.

"I beg your pardon, comrade." Joe inclined his head in mock contrition. "But please do not let my little lapse interrupt your recitation."

Ramón Machado opened the loose-leaf binder that lay on the table in front of him, but he did not even glance at it. He knew every word it contained by heart.

"We have assigned the woman the case name Red Rose, and we have had our psychiatrists develop a detailed profile of her. The evaluation is that she is highly susceptible to skillful recruitment. She is uniquely placed to become an extremely valuable field operative."

Raleigh Tabaka leaned forward attentively. Ramón noted that he did not interject questions or comments at this stage, and he approved of that restraint. They had not yet worked together extensively; this was only their third meeting, and both of them were still evaluating each other.

"Red Rose can be placed in an emotional dilemma. On her father's side she is a member of the white ruling class in Southern Africa. Her father is just finishing a term as his country's ambassador to Britain, and he is about to return to take up an appointment as the chairman of the national armaments industry. He has enormous holdings in mining, land and finance; after the Oppenheimers and their Anglo-American Company, the family is probably the most wealthy and influential in southern Africa. In addition, the father had conduits to the very highest levels of the ruling racist regime. Most important, however, is the fact that the father dotes on Red Rose. She is able to obtain from him, with little effort, anything she sets her heart upon. This would include an entree to any level of government and any information of whatever classification, even that relating to his new appointment on the armaments corporation."

Raleigh Tabaka nodded. He knew the Courtney family and could find no fault with this assessment. "I have met Red Rose's mother, but she is on our side of the political fence," he murmured.

Ramón nodded. "Precisely. Shasa Courtney has been divorced from his wife, Tara, for seven years. She was an accomplice of your uncle, Moses Gama, in his bomb attack on the white racist parliament, for which he was imprisoned and subsequently murdered. She was also Gama's mistress and bore his bastard son. Tara Courtney fled from South Africa with Gama's child after the failure of the bomb plot. She lives now in London, where she is very active in the antiapartheid movement. She is also a member of the ANC, but she is not considered sufficiently competent or emotionally stable for any but junior rank and routine assignments. At present she operates a safe house for ANC personnel here in London and occasionally undertakes courier work or assists in the organization of rallies and demonstrations. Her real potential value lies in her influence over Red Rose."

"Yes," Raleigh agreed impatiently. "I know all about this, especially about her relationship to my uncle, but does she in fact have any influence over her daughter? It appears that Red Rose's sympathies lie heavily on her father's side?"

Again Ramón nodded. "At present this is the case. But apart from her mother, there is another member of the family who holds radical views: her brother Michael, who has a much greater influence on her. And there are other ways of turning her."

"What are those?" Tabaka asked.

"One of them is the honey trap," Joe Cicero said. "The marqués—forgive me, Comrade Machado—has made the initial contact to that end. The honey trap is one of his many specialties."

"You will keep me informed of progress." Raleigh stated. Neither of them replied immediately. Although Raleigh Tabaka was an executive of the ANC and a member of the Communist Party, he was not, unlike the other two, an officer of the Russian KGB. Joe Cicero, on the other hand, was a KGB officer first and foremost, although his promotion from colonel to colonel-general had been confirmed only a month previously, at the same time the Moscow clinic had diagnosed carcinoma of both his lungs. Joe Cicero suspected the promotion had been given to him merely to allow him to retire at a higher pension after a lifetime of loyal service to the department. Nevertheless, he was an officer in the ANC only after his loyalty to Mother Russia, his lines of allegiance were not diluted, and the ANC would receive only what information it was necessary for them to have.

Ramón Machado's lines of allegiance were also clear-cut. He had been born in Spain, and his title of nobility was Spanish, but his mother had been a Cuban woman, sloe-eyed and raven-haired. She had met Ramón's father when she was a young housekeeper on the Machado estates near Havana. After the marriage, the marqués had taken his beautiful commoner bride back to Spain.

During the Spanish Civil War, the marqués had opposed General Francisco Franco's Nationalists. Despite his noble background and inherited wealth, Ramón's father had been an enlightened and liberal man. He had joined the Republican army and commanded a battalion at the siege of Madrid, where he was severely wounded. After the war, the Machado family found the oppression and discrimination under the Franco regime intolerable. The marquesa had prevailed on her husband to take her and her young son back to her native island in the Caribbean. Although they had been stripped of most of their Spanish property and possessions, the family still owned the Cuban estates. However, the Machado family found that life under the dictatorship of Batista was no great improvement on that under Franco.

Ramón's mother was an aunt of the young left-wing student firebrand Fidel Castro and one of his avid admirers. She became active in the campaign of agitation and intrigue against the Batista régime, and young Ramón gleaned his own first political convictions from her and from her celebrated nephew.

After Fidel Castro was imprisoned for leading the gallant but abortive attack on the Santiago barracks on July 26, 1953, both Ramón's father and mother were arrested along with the rebels.

Ramón's mother died under interrogation in a police cell in Havana, and his father died in the same prison only a few weeks later of ill-treatment and a broken heart. Once again the family estates were confiscated, and Ramón's only inheritance was the derelict title of marqués, void of all property or fortune. At the time he was fourteen years old. The Castro family took him in and cared for him.

When Fidel Castro was released from prison under amnesty, Ramón went with him to Mexico, and at sixteen years of age was one of the first recruits to the Cuban army of liberation in exile.

It was in Mexico he first had learned how to exploit his extraordinary good looks and to develop his natural winning ways with women. By the age of seventeen his companions had nicknamed him "El Zorro Dorado," "The Golden Fox," and his reputation as an irresistible lover was established.

Up to the time of his father's arrest and death in Batista's prison, Ramón had been given the benefit of the finest education available to the only son of a wealthy aristocratic family. He had attended an exclusive preparatory school in England and spent two years at Harrow, so he spoke English like a native, as well as his own Spanish. During his school-days, he had demonstrated superior academic ability and had become proficient in the manners and pastimes of a young gentleman. He had a good seat on a horse, and could keep a straight bat and cast a salmon fly. He was also a phenomenal shot at Spanish red-legged partridge and Mexican white-winged dove. He could shoot and ride and dance and sing, and he was beautiful, and when he returned to Cuba with Fidel Castro and the eighty-two heroes on December 2, 1956, he proved his valor in the fighting that left most of the valiant band dead on the beaches.

He was with the survivors that escaped with Castro into the mountains. During the years of the guerrilla warfare that followed, El Zorro was sent down into the towns and villages to practice his arts on scores of women, young and not so young, beautiful and plain. In Ramón's arms they became enthusiastic daughters of the revolution. With every conquest he become more skilled and confident until his band of female recruits contributed significantly to the eventual triumph of the revolution and the overthrow of the Batista regime.

By this time Castro was fully aware of the potential value of his young relative and protégé, and once in power he rewarded him by sending him to further his education on the American mainland. While he studied political history and social anthropology at the University of Florida, Ramón used his amatory skills to infiltrate the band of Cuban exiles who, with the collusion of the American CIA, were planning a counter-revolution and an invasion of the island.

It was largely Ramón's intelligence that had pinpointed the time and place of the Bay of Pigs landing and resulted in the annihilation of the traitors. By this time, his extraordinary gifts had been recognized not only by his own countrymen but also by their allies.

After he graduated cum laude from the University of Florida and returned to Havana, the head of the KGB in Cuba prevailed upon Castro and the director of the DGA—the Cuban secret service—to send Ramón to Moscow for further training. While

22

in Russia, Ramón exceeded the estimates the KGB had made of his capabilities and his potential value. He was one of those remarkable creatures who could pass easily in any stratum of society, from the crude guerrilla camps of the jungle to the drawing rooms and private clubs of the most sophisticated capitals of the world.

With the knowledge and blessing of Fidel Castro, he was recruited into the KGB. Given his connections, it was only natural he should be appointed director of the joint committee coordinating Russian and Cuban interests in Africa.

In this job, Ramón made a special study of the African socialist liberation movements and was responsible for selecting the organizations that were to receive full Russian and Cuban backing. He initiated the policy under which Cuba came to act as a surrogate for Mother Russia in southern Africa, and he was soon responsible for the supply of arms and the training of African resistance groups. In that capacity, he became a member of the ANC.

In a very short time, he had visited all of the African countries under his jurisdiction, using his Spanish passport and his title, posing as a capitalist investor and merchant banker with credentials supplied by the Fourth Directorate. He was accepted without reservation by the white colonial administrations and received cordially and entertained by everyone from the governors of Portuguese Angola and Mozambique to the British governor-general of Rhodesia. He even dined with that notorious architect of apartheid, the South African leader, Hendrik Verwoerd.

When it became necessary to appoint a new station head for the African division to replace the ailing General Cicero, Ramón's qualifications and experience made him the natural choice.

So as he sat now in the back room of the Russian consulate in Bayswater Road with the man he was about to replace and this black African guerrilla leader, his loyalties were as clear-cut as those of his superior.

When Raleigh Tabaka said, "You will keep me informed of progress," he was being naïve. He would be informed only on a "need to know" basis. In Ramón's view and that of his government, the installation of this man and the organization he represented as the ruling élite in South Africa was merely one step along the road to the eventual goal of universal socialism throughout the length and breadth of the African continent.

"Naturally, you will be kept right up to date with this as with all other matters of joint interest," Ramón assured him in a tone

23

of such total sincerity that the black man settled more comfortably into his chair and returned Ramón's smile. Very few persons, male or female, were immune to his charms. It gave Ramón a solid sense of satisfaction to see his magic work on even such a tough and uncompromising subject as this one.

Raleigh Tabaka was fully aware of the white man's smug self-satisfaction, although no sign of it showed on his face. There had been that flat spot in the Cuban's otherwise clear green gaze. Only someone with Raleigh's developed powers of observation would have noticed that. Raleigh had worked with these whites from Russia and Cuba for many years now, and he had come to understand that in dealing with them only one principle was fixed and certain. They were never to be trusted, not in any circumstances or in even the smallest detail.

He had learned to fake acceptance, to give them false signals of compliance, such as the deliberate physical relaxation and the frank, trusting smile. However, he never forgot for one instant that they were white. Like most Africans, Raleigh was a natural racist and a tribalist. He hated these white men, who patronized and condescended to him across the conference table, with the same passion as he hated the white policemen who had fired the bullets at Sharpeville.

He had never forgotten for a single waking minute that dreadful day when under a blue African sky he had held in his arms the girl he loved, the lovely black maiden who was to be his wife. He had held her and watched her die, and then before her flesh cooled he had thrust his fingers deep into the bullet wounds in her chest and made his vow of vengeance.

The vow had been made not only against the assassins but against them all, every white face and every bloody white hand that had forced slavery and subjugation upon his tribe down the centuries. Hatred was the fuel on which Raleigh Tabaka's life ran.

As he watched the white faces across the table, he smiled and drew strength and resolve from his hatred. "So," he said, "you will take care of the woman, it is agreed. Now let us move on . . ."

"A moment." Ramón lifted a hand to restrain him and turned back to Joe Cicero. "If I am to proceed with Red Rose, there is the matter of the budget for the operation."

"We have already allocated two thousand British sterling—" General Cicero protested.

"Just sufficient for the preliminary stage. The budget will have to be upgraded. Red Rose is the daughter of a wealthy

24

capitalist, and to impress her I will have to maintain my role as a Spanish grandee.''

They argued for a few minutes more while Raleigh Tabaka tapped his pencil impatiently on the tabletop. The African division was the Cinderella of the Fourth Directorate, and every ruble had to be counted.

It was degrading, Raleigh thought as he listened to them haggle. They were more like a pair of old women selling pumpkins beside a dusty African road than two men planning the overthrow of an evil empire and the liberation of fifteen million oppressed black souls.

At last they agreed, and Raleigh found it difficult to conceal his disgust as he repeated, ''Can we move on to discuss my itinerary for the African tour?'' He had believed that this was the reason for today's meeting. ''Has the authorization been received from Moscow?''

The discussions went on into the afternoon. They ate a frugal lunch sent up from the consulate canteen as they worked, and the fog of Joe Cicero's cigarette smoke dulled the shaft of sunlight through the single high window. The room was a high-security unit on the top floor, regularly swept for electronic listening devices and safe from outside surveillance.

At last Joe Cicero closed the file in front of him and looked up. His dark eyes were bloodshot from the smoke and the strain. ''I think that covers all points for discussion—unless there is anything new?''

They shook their heads.

''As usual, Comrade Machado will leave first,'' said Joe Cicero. It was an elementary rule of procedure that they should never be seen in public in one another's company.

Ramón left the consulate by the entrance to the visa section, the busiest part of the building, where he would be less noticeable in the crowd of students and others applying for travel documents to the Soviet Union.

There was a bus stop directly outside the walled consulate. He took a number 88 bus but left it at the next stop and hurried through the Lancaster Gate entrance to Kensington Gardens. He lingered in the rose garden until he was certain he was not being followed and then crossed the park.

His flat was in a narrow side street off Kensington High Street. It had been rented specifically for the Red Rose operation and, although it contained only a single bedroom, the living room was spacious and the locality was fashionable.

During the two weeks that he had been in residence, Ramón

25

had managed to create an air of permanence. His personal chests had come from Cuba in the diplomatic bag. They had contained the few good pictures his father had left him and other small items of furnishing, including family photographs in silver frames of his parents and the family castle and estates in Andalusia when these had been in their heyday. The glassware and porcelain were incomplete sets, but they bore the Machado coat of arms: the stag and the boar rampant on either side of the quartered shield. His golf clubs were displayed casually in the corner of the tiny entrance hall, the plain leather Hermès bag was well used, the discreetly embossed coat of arms almost obscured by wear. From what he had learned about Red Rose, he knew that she would have an eye for such detail.

He glanced at the venerable gold Cartier, another family heirloom, which felt unfamiliar on his wrist. He would have to hurry. His growth of beard was heavy and dark. He shaved it off quickly but carefully, then showered and washed the stink of Joe Cicero's Turkish cigarettes out of his hair.

He checked himself automatically in the mirror as he went through to the bedroom. He had been in peak physical condition when he had returned from Russia three weeks previously. The refresher course for senior officers at the KGB training college on the shores of the Black Sea had honed his body and, although he had managed to take little physical exercise since then, the lack was not yet apparent. His body was still sleek and hard, his belly flat and his body hair crisp and curly black. The scrutiny he directed at his image was completely without vanity. Face and body were simply implements, tools to be used to accomplish the tasks that he was set. He had no illusions about the fleeting nature of his physical attributes, but he worked to prolong them in the same way a warrior cares for his weapons.

"Gym tomorrow," he promised himself. Ramón had the use of a martial arts studio in Bloomsbury run by a Hungarian refugee. Two hours of hard work a couple of times a week would maintain him in fit condition for the Red Rose operation.

His riding breeches were cavalry whipcord, and he wore a sage-colored Trevira woolen shirt with a green tie under his tweed hacking jacket. His riding boots fitted him like a second skin, with a supple gloss of dubbined leather that flexed into perfect creases over his ankles as he moved. No amount of craftsmanship or money, only years of loving attention, could achieve that effect.

He knew that Red Rose was a horsewoman; in her world horses were a major part of existence. She would recognize

26

those boots as a badge of membership of the same exclusive and elite group to which she belonged.

He checked his watch again; he had timed it nicely.

He locked the flat and went down into the street. The rain clouds that had threatened earlier in the afternoon had dispersed, and it had turned into a glorious summer evening. Even the elements seemed to conspire to assist him.

The riding stables were in a narrow mews behind the Guards' barracks. The stable manager recognized him. As Ramón signed the register he ran his eye down the immediately preceding entries and saw that his good fortune was persisting: Red Rose had signed for her mount twenty minutes previously.

He went down to the stalls, where the groom had the saddle on his mount. She was a bay filly that Ramón had chosen with care and for which he had paid five hundred pounds from his expense budget. However, she had been a bargain, and he knew that he would recoup the cost and probably make some profit whenever he chose to sell her. He checked the girth and harness, speaking softly to the filly, soothing her with hands and voice, then thanked the groom with a nod and went up into the saddle.

On this evening there were fifty or so other riders out in Rotten Row. Ramón walked the filly under the oaks, while groups of horsemen cantered past him in both directions. The girl was not among them.

As soon as the filly had warmed a little, he pressed her with his toes and she moved up into a trot. She had an elegant action and he rode her like a centaur, his superior horsemanship obvious even in that expert company. They made a striking pair, and more than a few of the women they passed turned in the saddle to look back after them.

At the Park Lane end of the row, Ramón turned and moved the filly up into an easy canter; galloping was forbidden. A hundred yards ahead, a group of four riders was coming toward him, two couples, young people well mounted and turned out. The girl stood out among them like a sunbird in a flock of sparrows.

From under her riding hat her hair undulated like the wings of a bird in flight and glistened in the buttery sunshine. When she laughed her teeth were very white, and her color was vivid from exercise and the wind in her face.

Ramón recognized the man riding beside her. He had been her companion on most of the occasions when he had observed Red Rose over the previous two weeks. Ramón had requested information on him from records. He was the second son of an

27

extremely wealthy family of brewers, an effete upper-class play-boy of the type known in London society as a "deb's delight" or "Hooray Henry," and he had been with her at the Rolling Stones concert four days before. Since then Red Rose had spent two evenings in his company, party-hopping around Knights-bridge and Chelsea. Ramón had noticed that she treated him with a type of amused condescension, as though he were an overaffectionate St. Bernard puppy. On no occasion when Ramón had followed them had she been alone in his company except when he drove her in his MG from one party to the next. Ramón was almost certain that they were not sleeping with each other, which was unusual in this summer of 1969, when sexual license was a raging epidemic.

He knew also that Isabella Courtney was not a simpering virgin. It was documented that in the three years that she had been living at Highveld, she had indulged in at least three explosive, if short-lived, liaisons.

As the gap between them closed, Ramón transferred his attention to the horse under him and leaned forward to pat her neck. "There, my darling." He spoke to her in Spanish, while from the corner of his eye he watched the girl. It was a trick he had of deflecting his gaze so that he seemed not to be looking but missed not the smallest detail.

They were almost past each other when he saw the girl's chin snap up and her eyes fly wide open, but he ignored her and rode on.

"Ramón!" Her cry was high and imperative. "Wait!"

He checked the filly, and glanced back with a little frown of annoyance. She had wheeled her own mount and was riding after him. He let his expression remain reserved and slightly frosty as though he resented her scraping acquaintance.

She drew up beside him, reining her horse down to a walk. "Don't you remember me? Isabella Courtney. You were my savior." Her smile was uncertain and awkward. Men always recognized her, no matter how fleeting or distant their last meeting. "At the concert in the park," she ended lamely.

"Ah!" Ramón allowed his smile to bloom at last. "The motorcycle mascot. Forgive me. You were dressed rather differently then."

"You didn't wait for me to thank you," she accused him. She suppressed the urge to laugh out loud with relief that he had recognized her at last.

"No thanks were necessary. Besides which, you had rather urgent business elsewhere, as I recall."

"Are you on our own?" She changed the subject quickly. "Why don't you join us? Let me introduce you to my friends."

"Oh, I don't want to impose myself."

"Please," she insisted. "You'll enjoy them; they are good fun."

Ramón bowed slightly in the saddle. "How can I refuse such a kind invitation from such a lovely lady?" he agreed. Isabella felt as though her chest were in a vise. She had difficulty breathing as she looked into those green eyes in the face of a dark angel.

The other three had reined in and were waiting for them. Even before she came up to him, she saw that Roger was already sulking, and it gave her a vindictive little pleasure to say, "Roger, may I introduce the Marqués de Santiago y Machado? Ramón, this is Roger Coates Grainger."

Ramón glanced at her quizzically. Only then did she realize that she had made a gaffe by using his title; he had not mentioned it at their first meeting.

However, her momentary discomfort was forgotten when she introduced Ramón to Harriet Beauchamp and saw how Harriet reacted to him. She actually licked her lips like the cat in the television advertisement for pet food. Harriet was Isabella's best friend in London, more out of symbiotic considerations than out of genuine mutual affection. Lady Harriet was Isabella's entrance ticket to the inner circles of London society. As the daughter of a belted earl, she was welcome where Isabella, despite her looks and family wealth, would have been considered a nouveau riche interloper with a funny accent. Harriet, on the other hand, had found that wherever Isabella Courtney was there swiftly assembled a superabundance of males. Beneath Harriet's plump, bland and colorless blond exterior flourished a ravenously amorous nature, and Isabella was happy to pass on her rejects to her.

Usually the arrangement worked perfectly, but Ramón was definitely no reject, not yet anyway, and smoothly Isabella interposed her horse between them, flashing a silent warning at Harriet. Harriet was enormously flattered. She knew she could never aspire to become Isabella's rival, but it was gratifying to be treated like one.

"Marqués?" Ramón murmured as they rode on. "You know considerably more about me than I do about you."

"Oh, I must have seen your photo in one of the slosh columns," Isabella suggested airily as she thought, God, don't let him think I have been that interested.

29

"Ah, *The Tatler*, of course . . ." Ramón nodded. His photograph had never appeared anywhere, except possibly in the files of the CIA and a few other intelligence agencies around the world.

"Yes, *The Tatler*, that's it." Gratefully Isabella jumped at the escape he offered her, then set herself out to captivate him, without making her interest too obvious or oppressive. It was easier than she had anticipated. Ramón had a relaxed charm, a savoir-faire that fitted in with their group. Soon all of them except Roger, who was still sulking monumentally, were chatting and laughing together as though they were old chums.

As the dusk gathered and they turned back toward the stables, Isabella kneed her mount closer to Harriet's and hissed at her, "Invite him to the party tonight!"

"Who?" Harriet opened her vacuous pansy eyes in feigned incomprehension.

"You know damned well *who*, you randy little witch. You've been rolling your eyes and ovaries at him for the last hour!"

Lady Harriet Beauchamp had the run of the family house in Belgravia during the week, when her parents were in the country. She put together some of the best bashes in town.

Tonight most of the cast of *Hair*, the current musical hit, turned up after the show. They were still in costume and stage makeup, and the four-piece Jamaican band that Harriet had hired burst into a calypso version of "Aquarius" to welcome them.

It bode fair to becoming one of the Harriet's more memorable parties. It was so crowded that those couples with serious business in mind took up to twenty minutes to get from the ballroom up the staircase to the bedrooms; even there they were forced to wait their turn. Isabella wondered sourly what Harriet's papa, the tenth earl, would think if he knew of the flow of traffic through his four-poster bed.

In the midst of all the gaiety and laughter, Isabella was determinedly insular. She had found a perch halfway up the sweeping marble staircase from which she could keep an eye on all arrivals at the front door, as well as on the action in the ballroom and the front drawing room, into which the dancing had overflowed.

She steadfastly refused to dance, despite an incessant string of invitations to do so. She had been so icily dismissive of Roger Coates-Grainger's ponderous attention and callow humor that, discouraged, he had wandered away to the champagne bar on the terrace. By now he was probably pissed out of his gourd, she thought with gloomy relish.

Such was the success of the evening that none of the guests could tear themselves away to move on to any other venue. All the traffic through the teak double front doors from the square was one way, and the noise and crush increased with every passing minute.

Another group arrived squealing and shouting tipsy greetings, and Isabella felt a fleeting lift of her spirits as she saw among them a head of dark wavy hair, but almost immediately she realized the man was too short, and when he turned so she could see his face, he was sallow and jowly. She actively hated him, whoever he was.

As a kind of masochistic penance she had made her single glass of champagne last all evening, and now the wine was flat and warm from her fingers on the stem. She looked around to find Roger and send him for another glass but saw that he was dancing with a tall thin girl with false eyelashes and a high penetrating giggle that carried even to where Isabella sat.

God, she's awful, Isabella thought. And Roger looks such a ponce, slobbering all over her like that.

She glanced at the ormolu and porcelain French clock above the door to the drawing room. The time was twenty minutes to one, and she sighed.

At half past noon today, Daddy was having an important lunch for a group of influential Conservative members of parliament and their wives. As usual, Isabella was to be hostess. She should get some sleep to be at her best, she thought, but still she lingered.

Where the hell is he? she thought bitterly. He promised he'd come, damn him. (Actually, he had said he would try to drop in later.) But we were getting on so well, it was as good as a promise.

She dismissed another invitation to dance without even looking up, and tasted the champagne. It was awful.

"I'm not going to wait a minute after one o'clock," she promised herself firmly. "And that is absolutely final."

Then abruptly her pulse checked, then raced away again. In her ears the music took on a sweeter, more cheerful note, the oppressive crowds and the noise seemed to recede, her dark mood evaporated miraculously, and she was borne up on a wave of excitement and wild anticipation.

There he was, standing in the front doorway. He was so tall he towered half a head above those around him. A single lock of hair had fallen onto his forehead like a question mark, and his expression was remote, almost contemptuous.

31

She wanted to shout his name: "Ramón, here I am!" But she restrained herself and set aside her glass without looking. It toppled over, and the girl on the step below her exclaimed as lukewarm champagne cascaded down her bare back. Isabella did not even hear her protest. She came to her feet in one fluid movement, and instantly Ramón's cool green gaze was on her.

They looked at each other over the heads of the swirling, gyrating dancers, and it was as though the two of them were completely alone. Neither of them smiled. It seemed to Isabella that this was a solemn moment. He had come, and in some vague way she sensed the significance of what was happening. She was certain that in that instant her life had changed. Nothing would ever be the same again.

She began to descend, and she did not stumble over the sprawling, embracing couples that clogged the staircase. They seemed to open before her, and her feet found their own way between them.

She was watching Ramón. He had not moved to meet her. He stood very still in the giddy throng. His stillness reminded her of one of the great predatory African cats, and she felt a tiny thrill of fear, an exhilaration of the blood as she went down to him.

When she stood before him, neither of them spoke. After a moment she lifted her tanned bare arms toward him, and as he took her to his chest she wound her arms around his neck. They danced, and she found every movement of his body transmitted to her own like a current of electricity.

The music was superfluous; they moved to a rhythm of their own. As she flattened her breasts against the hard rubbery muscle of his chest, she could feel his heart beating, and her own nipples swelled and hardened. She knew he could feel them pressing into him, for the beat of his heart quickened and the green of his eyes darkened as she stared up into them.

She arched her back, a slow, voluptuous movement that made the ridges of hard muscle stand proud along each side of her spine. His fingertips traced them down, moving lightly over the crests of her spine as though he were playing a musical instrument. She shivered under his touch and pressed her hips forward instinctively, welding them against his, and she felt his flesh harden and swell just as hers had done.

For her he was a great tree and she was the vine that entwined it, he was a rock and she the current of a tropical ocean that washed about it, he was a mountain peak and she was the cloud that softly enfolded it. Her body was light and free, she seemed

32

to float in his arms, and that was all of reality. They were alone in the universe, transported far beyond the natural laws of space and time; even gravity was suspended, and her feet no longer made contact with the earth.

He moved her toward the door, and she saw Roger mouthing something at her across the room. The tall girl was gone and he was flushed with outrage, but she left him caught helplessly in the press of bodies like a fish in a net.

They went down the front steps, and she took the key of the Mini-Cooper from her sequined evening bag and pressed it into Ramón's hand.

He drove very fast through the deserted streets, and she leaned as close to him as the bucket seats would allow and watched his face with such fierce concentration that she did not see or care where he was taking her. She did not think she could endure another moment without touching him, without feeling his hands on her body again. She found she was shivering once more.

Then, abruptly, he pulled up to the curb and parked the Mini. He came around to her side with long strides, and she knew his need was almost as great as her own. She clung to his arm, and she could not feel the ground beneath her feet as they crossed the pavement and went to the entrance of the red brick house in a row of similar buildings. He led her up the stairs to the second floor.

As soon as he closed the door of the flat he turned to her, and for the first time she felt his mouth on hers. His face was as rough as sharkskin with new beard, but his lips were soft and hot, sweet as ripe fruit, and his tongue was like a live thing deep in her mouth.

She felt something burst within her, and all reason and re-straint were washed away on the flood. There was a sound in her ears like a gale force wind over a turbulent sea, and a mad-ness descended on her.

She twisted out of his embrace and tore at her clothing in a frenzy of impatience, letting it fall around her feet on the pol-ished wooden floor of the small hallway. He stripped off his own clothing as swiftly, facing her, and she stared hungrily as every exquisite detail of his body was revealed.

She had never dreamed a man's body could be so beautiful. Where other men were gross and hairy, inflamed and knotted with veins, he was smooth and perfect. She felt she could stare at him forever, but at the same time she knew that if she did not instantly feel him against her she would scream aloud with frus-tration, and she flung herself naked against his naked chest.

She pressed hard to him, and his body was firm and sleek and hot. Yet the hair on his chest was unbearably harsh against the sensitive engorged tips of her breasts. She moaned and covered his lips with hers to prevent herself screaming out her desperate need.

He picked her up, and she felt herself weightless in his arms, and he carried her to the bed without breaking the clinging suction of their mouths, one upon the other.

As she came awake, Isabella was aware of an overwhelming sense of well-being. She felt as though she might burst with joy. Her body tingled as though every separate muscle and nerve had a life of its own.

For long moments, she could not understand what had happened to her. She lay with her eyes closed, clinging to the moment. She knew that such a magical sensation must be evanescent, but she did not want it ever to end. Then slowly she was aware of the male musk in her nostrils and the taste of his mouth that still lingered on her tongue. She felt the ache where he had been deep in her body and the heat of the pink rash his beard had raised on the sensitive skin around her lips. She savored it all, small pain transmuted into deep, fulfilling pleasure.

Then, with a sense of fresh wonder, the thought imploded into her consciousness: I'm in love! And she came fully awake. Her joy was almost delirious.

She sat up quickly, and the sheet dropped to her waist.

"Ramón," she said. The indentation of his head was impressed on the pillow beside hers. A single strand of dark body hair was coiled like a watch spring on the white sheet. She reached for it and discovered that the sheet was cool, the heat of his body long since dissipated. Her joy sank into despair.

"Ramón." She slipped from the bed and padded to the bathroom on bare feet. The door was ajar, and the bathroom was empty. Once again he had gone, and she stood naked in the middle of the floor and looked around her with dismay.

He was like a cat. His stealth was eerie, and a rash of tiny goose pimples arose around her nipples. She hugged herself and shivered.

Then she saw the note on the bedside table. It was a single sheet of expensive cream-colored paper embossed with his family crest. He had weighted it down with her key ring, the keys to her Mini. She snatched it up eagerly. There was no salutation.

34

You are an extraordinary woman, and yet when you sleep you look like a child, a beautiful innocent child. I could not bear to wake you. I could hardly bear to leave you, but I must.

If you can come to Málaga with me for the weekend, meet me here at nine tomorrow morning. You will need your passport, but do not bother with pajamas.

RAMÓN

She chuckled with delight and relief, all the lightness of her waking mood recaptured. She reread the note; the paper was smooth and cool as marble and had a sensuous feel under her fingertips. His skin had been as smooth, and her eyes turned dreamy and reflective as tiny disjointed episodes from the night before replayed in her mind.

He had been far beyond all her previous experience. With the others, even the most skilled and patient and perceptive of them, she had always been aware of their separate bodies, their divergent existences, the deliberate attempts to please and to reciprocate. With Ramón, there had been no division. It was almost as though he had taken over her mind as well as her body. They had blended into each other in some semidivine osmotic process; their flesh and their minds had become one.

So many times during the night, she had believed that they had reached the pinnacle together, only to discover that they were still on the foothills and that before them towered an alp and then another and another, each higher and more magnificent than the last. There had been no end to it, only at last the oblivion of sleep so deep it had been like dying, and a resurrection into this new charmed and joyous existence.

"I'm in love," she whispered in almost religious awe, and she looked down on her own body, amazed that such a frail vessel could contain so much happiness, such abundant emotion.

Then she noticed her wristwatch lying beside her car keys on the bedside table.

"Oh, my God!" she breathed. It was half past ten. "Daddy's lunch!" And she leaped to her feet and flew to the bathroom. On the washbasin, Ramón had placed a brand-new toothbrush still in its sealed plastic container for her, and this small kindness touched her out of all proportion.

She hummed the tune of "Faraway Places" through a mouthful of foaming toothpaste.

She decided there was just time for a quick bath, and as she lay in the hot water and thought about Ramón she found there was a great void in her body aching for him to fill it.

35

"Enough of that, girl," she laughed at herself. "With a wave of his magic wand, he has transformed you into a shameless little raver."

She jumped out of the bath and reached for the towel. It was still damp from his body, and she pressed a fold of it over her mouth and nose, inhaling the faint but distinctive aroma of his skin. It excited her all over again.

"Stop it!" she commanded herself in the steamy mirror. "You have to be at Trafalgar Square in a hour."

She was just about to let herself out of the flat when she exclaimed again, and darted back into the bathroom. She rummaged in her sequined handbag for the birth control pills in their calendar-marked pack and broke one out of its sealed compartment.

She placed the tiny white capsule on her tongue while she ran half a glass of water from the tap, then saluted her image in the mirror with the raised glass.

"To life, love and freedom," she said, "and to many happy returns." And she washed down the pill.

# 3

Blood sports did not revolt Isabella Courtney. Her father had always been a hunter, and the walls of Weltevreden, their home at the Cape of Good Hope, were decorated with trophies of the chase. Among the family assets was a safari company that owned a huge hunting concession in the Zambezi Valley. Only the previous year she had spent an idyllic fortnight in that enchanted wilderness with her elder brother, Sean Courtney, who was a licensed professional hunter and ran the outfit for Courtney Enterprises. On a number of occasions Isabella herself had ridden to hounds at Harriet Beauchamp's invitation. Isabella was a passable shot with the lovely little gold-engraved Holland & Holland 20-gauge shotgun her father had given her for her seventeenth birthday. With it she had shot snipe in the Okavango delta, sand grouse in the Karroo, duck and geese on the great Zambezi, grouse on the highland moors and pheasant, woodcock and partridge on some of the great English estates to which she and the ambassador had been invited.

She felt no offense at the sight of blood deliberately spilled, and in addition she had inherited her fair share of the family's gambling instinct, so the contest intrigued her.

This was the second day, and the original field of nearly three hundred contestants had been whittled down to two, for it was a "one miss and out" and a "winner take all" competition. The entrance fee was one thousand U.S. dollars a head, so there was well over a quarter of a million in the pot, and the tension was as hot and thick as minestrone soup as the American went to the plate.

He and Ramón Machado were the only two remaining contestants, and they had shot level for the last twenty-three rounds. Finally, to break the deadlock and decide the winner, the Spanish judges had decreed that double birds must be taken from now on.

The American was a full-time professional. He followed the circuit in Spain and Portugal and Mexico and South America, and until last year in Monaco. Now, however, tournaments had been banned in that tiny principality, after a mortally wounded pigeon had escaped from the stadium and winged its way over the palace walls, to crash at last onto Princess Grace's tea table, spraying the lace table cloth and the ladies' tea gowns with its blood. Prince Rainier had heard the screams halfway across his tiny realm, and that was the end of live pigeon-shooting tournaments in Monaco.

The American was Isabella's age, not yet twenty-five years old, but his income was reputed to be well over a hundred thousand dollars a year. He was shooting a 12-gauge "side by side" that had been made by the legendary gunsmith James Manton almost a century before. Of course, the weapon had been rebarreled and proofed to accommodate the longer modern cartridges and smokeless powders. However, the stock and action, complete with the engraved hammers, were original and retained the marvelous balance and pointability that old man Manton had built into it.

The young American took his stance on the plate, cocked the hammers, tucked the buttstock under his right armpit, and pointed the double muzzles just over the center of the semicircle

37

of five woven wicker baskets that were placed thirty yards from where he stood.

Each basket contained a live pigeon. They were feral birds of the type that live in flocks in the center of most large cities, big robust birds of variegated colors, bronze and blue and iridescent green, some of them with dark bands around their necks or patches of white in their wings.

To ensure a supply of birds, the shooting club had built a feeding shed on the premises, a structure containing trays that were replenished daily with crushed maize and enclosed by drop sides that could be released by remote control and trap the feeding birds within. Often a pigeon that escaped untouched from the killing ground would head straight back for the feeding shed. Many birds had been shot at numerous times before, and these were wily creatures that had learned subtle little tricks to disturb the aim of the marksmen. In addition, the bird handlers who loaded them into the baskets knew how to pluck a feather or two from wing or tail to make them fly an erratic, unpredictable course.

The baskets were operated by a random mechanism, with a delay of up to five seconds after the shooter had called "Pull" for the release of a bird. For a man with sweaty palms, a racing heart and tens of thousands of dollars at stake, five seconds could seem like all eternity.

The baskets were thirty yards out, and the effective range of a 12-gauge shotgun was generally reckoned to be forty yards. Thus the birds were released at almost extreme range, and in addition the retaining circle was a mere ten yards beyond the line of baskets.

The retaining circle was a low wooden wall, only eight inches high, painted white, which demarcated the boundary of the killing ground. To qualify as a hit, the carcass of the bird or, in the event of the blast of pellets tearing a bird into more than one piece, the largest portion of the carcass, calculated by weight, had to fall inside the low wooden wall. In this way, the shooter had to kill his bird as it rose from the release basket within the ten yards before it passed over the periphery of the killing ground.

The baskets were fanned out over a forty-five-degree arc in front of the shooter, and there was no indication as to which lid would fly open at the command "Pull" and no way to predict which direction the bird would take once it was released. It could cross either left or right, bear directly away, or sometimes—most disconcerting of all—race straight toward the gunner's face.

Added to all this, the pigeons were fast, noisy fliers that could jink and swerve in full flight, and now the judges had decided that instead of a single bird two pigeons would be released simultaneously.

The American braced himself at the plate, crouching a little, left foot leading slightly like a boxer, and Isabella reached for Ramón's hand and squeezed it lightly. They were sitting in the front bottom row of the covered grandstand in the padded leather chairs reserved for contestants and club officials.

"Pull!" said the American, his Texas twang ringing in the silence like a hammer on a steel anvil.

"Miss!" whispered Isabella. "Please miss!"

For a second and then another second, nothing happened. Then, with a crash, the lids of two of the baskets snapped open, numbers two and five, half left and full right from where the American stood. Both birds, hit by compressed-air jets from nozzles in the bottom of the baskets, launched into instant flight.

Number two went straight out, keeping low and going very fast. The American swung smoothly onto him, mounting the shotgun to his shoulder, and as it touched he fired. Five yards out from the basket, the silhouette of the pigeon was distorted by the rush of pellets. Its wing beats froze in midstroke, and it died instantaneously in the air and fell in a puff of feathers to hit well inside the ring and lie without further movement on the bright green turf.

The American swung onto the second bird. It had broken away toward his right, a glistening streak of burnished bronze, but at the sound of the first shot it jinked back inside the American's swing so swiftly he could not correct his aim in time. The shot was left of center, but only inches out. Instead of slicing into heart and brain, the blast of pellets from the fully choked barrel tore away the bird's right wing, and the horribly maimed creature tumbled and fluttered, streaming a trail of feathers through the air.

It struck only a foot inside the low white wooden wall, and a sigh went up from the watchers in the grandstand. Then, incredibly, the bird, one wing gone, pumped frantically with its remaining wing and found its feet. It tottered toward the wall, beating at the air ineffectually with one wing, uttering an agonized cawing sound in its puffed-out throat.

The spectators gasped and rose to their feet as one. In the center the American froze with the empty shotgun still mounted

39

to his shoulder. He was allowed only two cartridges. If he reloaded now and killed the bird with a third shot, he would be instantly disqualified and would forfeit the prize money.

The pigeon reached the barricade and leaped weakly at it. It struck the wood with its chest only an inch from the top and fell back, leaving a splash of brilliant ruby blood on the white paint.

Half the spectators screamed, "Die!" while those who had bet against the American screamed, "Go! Go for it, bird!"

The pigeon gathered itself groggily and leaped at the barrier once more. This time it reached the top and balanced there uncertainly, swaying back and forth.

Isabella was on her feet, howling wildly with the others, "Jump!" she pleaded. 'Don't—oh, please don't die, pigeon! Get over, please!"

Suddenly the dying bird stiffened into a convulsive rigor, its neck arched backwards, and it flopped from the wall and lay still and dead on the green lawn.

"Thank you!" Isabella breathed, and dropped back into her seat.

The pigeon had fallen forward and died outside the circle, and the loudspeakers above their heads boomed out the verdict in the Spanish phrases Isabella had come to understand so well in the past two days.

"One kill. One miss."

"My heart won't stand the strain." Isabella clutched her bosom in a theatrical gesture, and Ramón smiled at her with those cool green eyes.

"Look at you!" she cried. "The original ice man. Don't you even feel a thing?"

"Not outside your bed," he murmured.

Before she could find a suitable reply the loudspeakers interrupted her. "Next gun up! Number one hundred and ten!"

Ramón stood up, and while he adjusted the protectors over his ears his expression was still cold and remote. He had taught Isabella not to wish him luck, so she said nothing more as he moved to the long rack at the gate on which his was the only weapon still standing. He took it down, broke it open, placed it over the crook of his arm and walked out into the bright Iberian sunshine.

To Isabella he looked so beautiful and romantic. The sunlight sparkled in his hair, and the sleeveless shooting vest with suede leather shoulder patches was tailored to his lean torso, fitting so smoothly that the butt of the shotgun could not catch on a fold or tuck of cloth as he swung it up to mount.

**40**

At the plate he loaded the "under and over" barrels of the Perazzi 12-gauge and snapped the breeches closed. Only then did he glance back over his shoulder at Isabella, as he had done every time he had shot over the past two days. She had anticipated it, and now she held up both hands, clutching her own thumbs hard, and showed him her clenched fists.

Ramón turned back, and his whole body went still. Once again he reminded her of an African cat, that peculiar stillness of the wild leopard as it fixed on its prey. He did not crouch as the American had done but stood tall and lean and graceful, and said softly, "Pull!"

The birds bounded from the open baskets on wildly clattering wings, and Ramón mounted the gun with such elegant economy of movement that he seemed casual and unhurried.

When he had been in Mexico with his cousin Fidel Castro he had provided much of the funds of the embryo army of liberation's war chest with his shotgun expertise in the live pigeon rings of Guadalajara. So he also was a professional with the marvelous eye and reflexes needed for the job.

The first bird was going out obliquely, speeding for the wall on shining green wings, so he had to drop that one first. He took it cleanly with a charge of number-six shot from the fully choked bottom barrel, and it exploded in a puff of feathers like a burst pillow.

He turned for the other bird, pirouetting like a dancer. This pigeon was a veteran; it had been shot at a dozen times before, and it stayed low, at basket level. The handler had plucked its tail unevenly, and although it was going sixty miles an hour it slid to one side and wobbled in flight.

Instead of going for the wall, it came straight at Ramón's head, reducing the range to less than ten feet and, in doing so, making the shot many times more difficult. As it flashed toward his eyes, he had only a hundredth part of a second to react, and the extreme shortness of range would not give the charge of shot an opportunity to spread. It was as though he were firing a single ball, and an error of a mere fraction of a minute of angle would mean a miss.

He hit the pigeon squarely in the head with the full charge at point-blank range, and the bird disintegrated. Its body was blown away in a flurry of bloodied feathers, and only the two separate wings remained intact. They spiraled down and fell at Ramón's feet.

Isabella screamed wildly and jumped to her feet; then, with a single bound, she vaulted the barrier. Although the range master called sternly to her in unintelligible Spanish, she flouted range discipline and ran out in long denim-clad legs to throw her arms around Ramón's neck.

The crowd was already excited and volatile from the tensions of the contest. Now they laughed and applauded as Ramón and Isabella embraced in the center of the stadium. They made a splendid couple, almost impossibly handsome, both of them tall and athletic, shining with health and youthful vigor, and that spontaneous display of affection touched a chord in those who watched them.

They drove into the city in the Mercedes Isabella had hired at the airport. Ramón opened an account at the Banco de España in the main square and deposited the winner's check into it.

In a strange fashion, they shared a common attitude to money. Isabella seemed never even to consider price or value. Ramón had noticed that if a frock or a trinket took her fancy she never even bothered to ask the price. She merely flipped one of her vast collection of credit cards onto the counter, then signed the slip and crumpled her copy into her handbag without as much as glancing at it. When she emptied her handbag in the hotel room, she screwed the accumulated receipts into a ball and, still without reading them, tossed them disdainfully into the wastebasket or dropped them into the nearest ashtray for the chambermaid to dispose of.

As a convenience, she also carried a fist-sized wad of banknotes, crammed into her large leather shoulder bag. However, it was obvious that she had not concerned herself with the rate of exchange of sterling into Spanish pesetas. To pay for a cup of coffee or a glass of wine, she selected a bank note whose size and color she deemed appropriate to the occasion and dropped it onto the table, often leaving a waiter staring after her in speechless astonishment.

Ramón had a similar contempt for money. At one level he abhorred it as the symbol and the foundation of the capitalist system. He hated to be dictated to by the laws of economics and wealth he had dedicated his entire life to tearing down. He felt besmirched and demeaned when he had to wheedle and haggle with Moscow for the cash with which to perform his duties. Yet very early on in his career he had become aware of the particular approbation he earned from his superiors when he personally provided funds to finance his own operations.

In Mexico he had shot live pigeons. While at the University of Florida he had imported drugs from South America and sold them on campus. In France he had run weapons for the Algerians. In Italy he had smuggled currency and had arranged and executed four lucrative kidnappings. All the profits of these operations had meticulously been accounted for to Havana and Moscow. Their approval had been reflected in the rapid promotion he had enjoyed and the fact that a man of his age had been selected to replace General Cicero as head of a full section of the Fourth Directorate.

It had been quite obvious to Ramón from the outset that the paltry operating expenses General Cicero had allocated for the Red Rose project were totally inadequate. He had been obliged to make up the shortfall as expeditiously as possible, and of course this little jaunt to Spain also provided an ideal opportunity to begin the second phase of the operation.

That evening, to celebrate Ramón's win, they dined at a tiny seafood restaurant, jealously concealed from the tourist hordes in one of the back alleys. Isabella was the only foreigner among the dinner guests. The meal was an exquisite paella cooked in the classical tradition and accompanied by a wine from one of the estates that had once belonged to Ramón's family, and whose tiny production was never sold outside Spain. It was crisp and perfumed, and had a pale green luminosity in the candlelight.

"What happened to your family estates?" Isabella asked, after she had tasted and exclaimed over the wine.

"My father lost them all after Franco came to power." Ramón lowered his voice as he said it. "He was an antifascist from the very beginning."

Isabella nodded with approval and understanding. Her own father had fought against the fascists, and she subscribed to the comfortable and fashionable belief of her generation in the essential goodness of all mankind and the fervent if rather hazy ideal of universal peace, of which she was aware that fascism was the antithesis. She carried a "Ban the bomb" button in her handbag, although it would have been crass to wear it actually pinned on her clothing.

"Tell me about your father and your family," she invited him. She realized that, although she had been with him almost a week, she actually knew very little about him, apart from what the Spanish chargé had told her over the dinner table.

She listened with fascination as Ramón recounted a little of his family history. One of his ancestors had received the title after he had sailed with Columbus to the Caribbean in 1492, and Isabella was vastly impressed by the antiquity of his lineage.

43

"We go back as far as great-grandfather Sean Courtney," she said, deprecating her own ancestry. "And he died sometime in the nineteen-twenties." As she said it, she realized for the first time that if Ramón were the father, her own son might one day be able to boast of such distinguished bloodlines. Until that moment, she had been content simply to be with Ramón, but now, as she leaned close to him and watched his eyes in the candlelight, the horizons of her ambitions widened. She wanted him as she had never wanted anything in her life before.

"And so you see, Bella, despite all of this, I am not a rich man."

"Oh, yes, you are. I saw you pay over two hundred thousand dollars into your bank this afternoon," she told him gaily. "You can afford to buy me another bottle of wine, at the very least."

"If you didn't have to fly back to London tomorrow morning, I would have used some of that money to take you up to Granada. I could have accompanied you to the bullfight and shown you my family castle in the Sierra Nevada . . ."

"But you have to go back to London as well," she protested. "Don't you?"

"A few days—I could have managed a few days. Any sacrifice to be with you."

"You know, Ramón, I don't even know what you do. How do you earn your crust?"

"Merchant banking." He shrugged dismissively. "I work for a private bank, and I am responsible for African affairs. We arrange loans for developing companies in central and southern Africa."

By now Isabella's mind was accelerating up to racing speed. Ramón's lack of fortune was fully compensated for by his august origins, and he was a banker. There would certainly be a place for a merchant banker in the top ranks of Courtney Enterprises. It was all beginning to look marvelously exciting.

"I would like more than anything in this world to see your castle, Ramón darling," she whispered huskily, thinking, I wonder how much a castle would cost and if I could talk Garry into it. Her brother Garry, the chairman and financial head of Courtney Enterprises, was no more proof to Isabella's charms and wiles than any of the other male members of the family. Like most of the family, he was also a terrible snob. A marquesa needed a castle—he might just fall for it.

"What about your father?" Ramón asked. "I thought you promised you'd be back on Monday."

"You leave my father to me," she said firmly.

44

"Bella, this is the most ridiculous hour to wake an old man," Shasa protested as he answered her telephone call. "What time is it, in the name of all that's holy?"

"It's after six, and we have already been for a swim, and you are not old. You are young and beautiful, the most beautiful man I know," Isabella cooed over the international line.

"This sounds ominous," Shasa murmured. "The more extravagant the compliment, the more outrageous the request. What do you want, young lady? What are you up to now?"

"You really are an awful old cynic, Pater," said Isabella, tracing patterns in Ramón's chest hair with her forefinger. He was sprawling naked beside her on the double bed; his body was still sticky, damp and salty from their dip in the Mediterranean. "I just rang you to tell you how much I love you."

Shasa chuckled. "What a dutiful little mouse. I certainly trained you well." He lay back on the pillows and slipped his free arm around the shoulders of the woman who lay beside him. She sighed sleepily and wriggled closer to him, nuzzling against his chest.

"How is Harriet?" Shasa asked. Harriet Beauchamp had agreed to provide cover for Isabella's expedition to Spain.

"She's fine," Isabella assured him. "She's right here now. We have been having a wonderful time."

"Give her my love," Shasa ordered.

"Oh, I will," she agreed. Covering the mouthpiece, she leaned over and kissed Ramón full on the lips. "She sends her love back to you, Papa, but she refuses to catch the London plane this morning."

"Ah!" said Shasa. "Now we come to the true reason for all this filial consideration."

"It's not me, Daddy, it's Harriet. She wants to go up to Granada. There's a bullfight. She wants me to go with her." Isabella let her voice trail into silence.

"You and I are flying to Paris on Wednesday. Had you forgotten that? I'm addressing the Club Dimanche."

"Daddy, you speak so well; the French ladies adore you. I'm sure you don't really need me."

Shasa did not reply. He knew silence was the one sure way in which he could disconcert his wayward daughter. He covered the mouthpiece and asked the woman cuddled against him, "Kitty, can you come to Paris on Wednesday?"

She opened her eyes. "You know I'm leaving for the OAU conference in Ethiopia on Saturday."

"I'll have you back by then."

She raised herself on one elbow and looked down at him thoughtfully. "Get thou behind me, Satan."

"Daddy, are you still there?" Isabella's voice floated between them.

"So my own flesh and blood are determined to desert me, are they?" Shasa asked in his most injured tones. "All by myself in the least romantic city in the world?"

"I can't let Harriet down," Isabella explained. "I'll make it up to you, I promise."

"You'd better, young lady," Shasa warned her. "I shall remind you of your indebtedness at a future date."

"Granada will probably be deadly dull—and I'll miss you awfully, dear Papa," said Isabella contritely. She traced her forefinger down Ramón's body, past his navel and into the thick bush of hair below it; she twirled a dark curl around her fingertip.

"And I will be desolated without you, Bella," Shasa agreed. He dropped the handset of the telephone onto its cradle and pushed Kitty back gently onto the pillows.

"I said get thou behind me, Satan," she protested huskily. "Not get thou on top of me."

# 4

Isabella drove as fast and as well as any man he had known. Ramón lay back in the leather bucket seat of the hired Mercedes and studied her openly. She basked in his attention and every few minutes, when a straight section of road allowed it, she glanced sideways at him or reached across to touch his hand or his thigh.

Unlike many of the assignments he had been given over the years, Ramón did not find it difficult to act out his part with this woman. He sensed a strength in her, an untapped reservoir of courage and determination that intrigued him.

He recognized that she was as yet unfulfilled and restless,

dissatisfied with and rebellious against her easy, undemanding existence, ripe for excitement and challenge, searching for something, some cause to which to dedicate herself.

Physically she was immensely attractive, and he had no difficulty faking that tender concern toward her that is the hallmark of the accomplished lover. When he looked at her like this, it was a deliberate device. He knew the appeal of his gaze, that cold green contemplation like the stare of the serpent that mesmerizes a wild bird, and yet he enjoyed looking at her as at an exquisite work of art. Although he knew from her file that she had been with other men, he had learned in these last few days that the core of her being was still untouched, and there was a strange virginal quality about her that aroused him.

As with so many legendary male lovers, Ramón experienced that condition known as satyriasis. The name derived from those woodland godlings of Roman mythology that were half man and half goat and whose sexual appetite was insatiable. Although Ramón Machado was abnormally responsive to any woman, whether she was attractive to him or otherwise, it was unusual for him to be able to achieve orgasm. He was in most cases simply indefatigable, able to outlast a partner with even the most tardy libido and to drive a normal woman on and on until she at last screamed for mercy. Then he was able to continue at the very first indication that she wished to do so, and he was so sensitively attuned to feminine sexuality that he would usually recognize that indication before she did so herself.

However, this woman was one of those rare creatures who was able to bring him on without too much difficulty. With her he had already achieved true orgasm a number of times, and he knew he would again. It was, of course, essential to his plans that he do so.

Driving up from the coast on that sultry summer day, Isabella was as happy and exhilarated as she had ever been. She was in love. There was not the least shadow of doubt in her mind that this was the grand passion of her life. There had never been, and there could not conceivably be again, anyone to match him. She would never experience any emotion to exceed what she felt for him now. His presence beside her and those green eyes upon her made the sunlight brighter and the high dry air of the Sierras taste sweeter on her lips.

The wide plains and the mountains beyond were so like her own beloved land. They transported her back to the open horizons of the great Karroo, for there were the same lion-colored earth and sepia rockscapes. Looking upon them, her mood was carried upward even higher, and she laughed aloud with joy and had to strive hard to prevent herself crying out, "Oh, Ramón my darling, I love you. I love you with all my heart and with all my soul forever."

Even in her giddy exhilaration, she was determined he must say it first. That way she could be doubly certain that what she already knew was true—that he loved her as much as she loved him.

Ramón knew these mountains, and he directed her over dusty back roads to vistas of grandeur and beauty hidden far from the usual tourist routes. They stopped in one of the little villages, and he joked with the locals in their patois. He came away with a slab of pink *serrano* ham cured in the snow, a loaf of rough peasant bread and a goatskin full of sweet dark Malaga wine.

Beyond the village, they left the Mercedes parked beside an ancient stone bridge and followed the stream up through the olive groves into the foothills of the Sierra Nevada. While a bearded billy goat watched in astonishment from the cliff above, they plunged naked into a secret pool of the river. Then, still naked, they ate their picnic lunch seated on the smooth black rocks above the water.

Ramón demonstrated how to hold the wineskin at arm's length and direct a hissing jet into the back of his open mouth. When she tried, the wine spurted over her cheeks and dribbled from her chin, and at her request he licked the ruby droplets from her face and her taut white bosom. This was such fun they forgot about the rest of their lunch and made love, Isabella still perched on her rock and Ramón standing knee-deep in the pool facing her.

"You are incredible," she whispered. "My legs are like jelly. You'll probably have to carry me back to the car."

They spent so much of the afternoon beside the pool that the sun was at the tops of the mountains, turning the snows to incandescent gold, when they came into sight of the castle.

It was not as large or as grand as Isabella had expected it to be. It was simply a gaunt dark building high on the slopes above the higgledy-piggledy pink-tiled roofs of the village. As they approached, Isabella saw that part of the parapet had collapsed and that the grounds were overgrown and neglected.

"Who does it belong to now?" she asked.

"The state." Ramón shrugged. "There was talk some years ago of turning it into a tourist hotel, but nothing came of it."

The caretaker was an old man who remembered Ramón's family, and he led them through the ground-floor rooms. They were empty; all the furniture had been sold to pay the family debts, and the chandeliers were thick with dust and cobwebs. The walls of the hall were stained with rainwater from the leaks in the roof.

"It's so sad to see something once so lovely ruined by neglect," Isabella whispered. "Doesn't it make you sad, too?"

"Do you want to go?" he asked.

"Yes, I don't want to be sad today."

As they went down the hairpin track into the village, the last of the sunset on the mountaintops was so splendid that Isabella recaptured her bubbling mood.

At the inn in the village, the innkeeper recognized the family name. He ordered his two daughters up to change the bed linen in the front room and sent his wife back to her kitchen to prepare an Andalusian specialty for their dinner, *cocido Madrileño*, a stew of chicken and spicy little *chorizo* sausages on a bed of *cabello de angel*, noodles so fine they deserved their name of "angel's hair."

"In Spain, sherry is the drink of the people," Ramón explained to her as he filled her glass. It was cold enough here in the mountains to warrant a fire in the stone fireplace, and the light of the flames played over his features, making him even more improbably handsome.

"We always seem to be doing one of three things"—she contemplated the golden wine in her glass—"eating or drinking or . . ." She sipped the wine.

"Are you complaining?" he asked.

"Gloating, actually." She slanted her eyes at him. "Eat your *cocido* and drink your sherry, señor, you are going to need your strength."

She awoke with the sunlight streaming in through the open window and experienced a moment's dread that he had gone again. However, he was there beside her in the wide soft bed, watching her with that cool, enigmatic expression. She felt another moment's chill of doubt, but as she reached for him almost diffidently, she found that he was already hard and swollen for her.

"Oh God!" she whispered joyously. "You are incredible!" No man had ever wanted her as much as he did. He made her feel like the most desirable woman in the universe.

The innkeeper had laid a breakfast of purple figs and goat cheese for them in the walled courtyard. They sat under the trellised vines, and Isabella peeled the figs with her long painted

49

nails and placed the globules of succulent flesh between his lips. Her father was the only other man she had ever done that for.

When one of the daughters brought a pot of steaming coffee out to them, Ramón excused himself and went up to their bedroom. Through the tiny bathroom window, he could see Isabella sitting in the courtyard below and hear her voice and her laughter as she tried to make herself understood in her newly acquired Spanish.

Earlier he had watched her swallow a birth control pill as she stood beside him at the washbasin. She had made a silly little ritual of it, toasting him with the glass of water. "Many happy returns!" However, the pack of remaining pills was no longer in her toilet bag on the ledge above the basin.

He went back into the bedroom. The bed occupied almost the entire floor space, and their luggage was crammed into the curtained alcove beside the door. Isabella's big squashy leather shoulder bag was thrown carelessly on top of her suitcase.

He paused to listen again and heard her voice faintly through the open window. He took the bag to the bed and began to unpack it swiftly, laying out the contents in careful sequence so that he could repack them in exactly the same order. He had searched her sequined handbag and checked the brand of birth control pills she was using while she was still asleep on that first morning in the Kensington flat. Later he had discussed them with the doctor at the Cuban embassy.

"If the woman discontinues treatment before the tenth day of her cycle, she will almost certainly experience a fertility backlash effect and become considerably more susceptible to impregnation when she ovulates," the doctor had assured Ramón.

The slim pack of pills was in one of the compartments of her black crocodile-skin purse near the bottom of the bag. Once again Ramón straightened up to listen. There was no sound of voices from the courtyard, and he darted back to the window. He saw that Isabella still sat at the table and that the innkeeper's black cat now had all her attention. The supercilious creature had settled in her lap and was allowing her to tickle behind his ears.

Ramón stepped back into the bedroom. There were seven pills missing from the separate date-marked compartments in the packet. From his inside pocket Ramón slipped the identical packet the embassy doctor had provided him. He removed the first seven pills from their compartments and dropped them into the toilet bowl. Then he placed the two packages side by side and compared them. Now they were identical in every respect, except that the second package contained only aspirin tablets cunningly coated to resemble birth control pills.

He slipped the packet of placebo tablets into Isabella's purse and replaced her shoulder bag in the alcove. He pocketed the original package and flushed the toilet, making sure the seven pills were gone before he washed his hands and went down the narrow staircase to where Isabella waited in the courtyard.

In Granada, Ramón took her to the *corrida de toros* and exulted in the great good fortune that they were to be able to watch El Cordobes work.

Had not Ramón's father been a patron of this most famous of all matadors when he was a mere *novillero*, they would never have procured tickets to the performance at such short notice. As it was, two tickets were delivered to their hotel on the morning after their arrival. Not only were they seated at ringside directly to the right of the president's box, but before the spectacle they were invited to watch El Cordobes dress for the *corrida*.

Isabella had read Hemingway's *Death in the Afternoon*, and she realized the honor of that invitation. Nevertheless, she was unprepared for the depth of Ramón's respect as he greeted Manuel Benítez, El Cordobes, or for the semireligious solemnity of the ritual of dressing.

"You have to be Spanish to understand the bulls," Ramón told her as they took their reserved seats. Indeed, she had never seen him so moved and emotional. His involvement was so powerful and infectious that she found herself as wrought up as he.

The trumpets of the entry parade sent thrills down her spine, and the spectacle was magnificent: the horses, the costumes encrusted with silver and gold and seed pearls, the matadors strutting in their short embroidered jackets and skintight trousers that blatantly emphasized their buttocks and their bunched genitalia. Even the flaring coral pink and incarnadine satins of the capes glistened with the lubricious tones of intimate feminine flesh and served to underscore the essentially lascivious nature of the frenzy that descended upon the tiered ranks of spectators.

When the bull surged into the ring, horned head high, the great hump of its shoulders swollen with rage, white sand dashing from under its hoofs and its engorged scrotum swinging to the pounding rhythm of his charge, Isabella leaped to her feet and screamed with the crowd.

As El Cordobes performed the initial passes, Ramón gripped her arm and leaned close to her, describing and explaining the significance of each graceful evolution, from the pure elegance of the simple *verónica* to the more complicated *quite*. Through Ramón's eyes, she came to see it as the beginning of some movingly beautiful ritual, steeped in ancient tradition, which did not attempt to disguise its cruel and darkly tragic essence.

When the trumpets saluted the entrance of the picadors, Isabella moaned aloud and pressed her knuckles against her teeth, for she had been dreading the horses. She had read of the horror of the disemboweled horses with their entrails tangled about their legs. To calm her fears, Ramón pointed out to her the thick armor of compressed cotton and canvas and leather that protected them. In the end none of the horses was harmed even when the bull hooked viciously into their padded bodies and drove them up against the barriers.

The picador leaned down from the saddle and worked the steel into the bull's hump. Blood sprayed up in a roseate nimbus of light, then slicked down over the bull's shoulders so that its hide gleamed like metal in the sun.

Isabella shuddered with awful fascination, and Ramón murmured, "The blood is real, everything you see here is real, as real as life. This *is* life, my darling, with all life's beauty and cruelty and passion."

She understood it then, accepted it and allowed herself to be carried along on the flood.

El Cordobes took his own *banderillas*. He posed in the sunlight and held high the long darts wrapped in colored paper streamers. He called to the bull, and when it came he ran to meet it with light, dancing strides. As they came together, Isabella gasped, and then the master had planted the *banderillas* and pirouetted away. The bull dropped its head and bucked at the sting of the barbs high in its withers, but its momentum had carried it out of goring range.

The trumpets sounded the *tercio*, the hour of truth, and a new mood descended upon the stadium. El Cordobes and the bull engaged each other in the stately, intimate dance of death. With only the floating cape between them, the passes were so close and dangerous that the bright blood from the beast's shoulders smeared the matador's thighs as it swept by.

At last El Cordobes stood below the president's box and lifted his *montera* cap decorated with black silk pom-poms to ask permission to dedicate the bull. Isabella was overwhelmed when he came to where she sat and dedicated the bull to her beauty.

He tossed his *montera* up to her, turned and went back to face the bull.

In the center of the ring El Cordobes performed the final passes, each one more graceful and closer to the horns than the last. Each time the crowd erupted with one primeval voice, a great burst of sound that punctuated the aching silences in which each separate pass was performed.

In the end, he prepared for the kill directly below where Isabella sat. As he sighted the bull over the long silver blade, Ramón gripped Isabella's arm hard and whispered to her, "Look! He will take it *recibiendo*, the most dangerous manner of all!" When the bull made its last desperate rush, instead of running to meet it, El Cordobes stood foursquare and went in over the top of the horns. The bright point of the *estoque* severed the great artery of the heart, and the blood gushed up in a fountain.

On the return from the bullring to the hotel, neither of them spoke. They were entranced, caught up in a rapture that was mystic and semireligious. The cruelty and the blood, the tragic beauty of the spectacle had not wearied or jaded their emotions, but had enhanced them to the threshold of a kind of spiritual agony that cried out for release. Isabella sensed that Ramón's need was even greater and more uncontrollable than her own.

In their bedroom, whose double doors and wrought-iron balcony overlooked the gardens of the old Moorish palace, Ramón stood her in the center of the floor. While the blades of the old-fashioned fan on the high ceiling revolved overhead, he undressed her. It seemed that in doing so, he was performing another ritual as ancient as that of the *corrida*. When she was naked, he knelt at her feet, clasped her around the hips and buried his face in the dense, warm pillow of hair in the basin of her pelvis.

She caressed his head with a tenderness she had never felt for another human being, yet it was tinged with a great sadness and humility. She felt that a love like this was divine, and that she was not worthy of it. It was too great for any mortal being to bear.

At last he rose, took her up like a child in his arms and carried her to the bed. It was as though it had never happened before, as though he had broken through to such secret depths of her physical and spiritual being that even she had not suspected their existence.

The laws of time and space were redefined while she was in his arms. It lasted an instant and a flaming eternity. Like a comet she was transported through the full circle of the heavens. When she looked up into his green eyes, she knew with a lambent joy that his spirit was locked into hers as deeply as his flesh was entrapped within her throughout all that incredible odyssey. When she believed she could reach no higher, survive no longer, there was an outpouring within her, as hot and copious as a flood of volcanic lava.

As the last light of day faded and their room filled with shadows, she found she was so devastated that she could no longer speak or move; she had strength left only to weep, and while she wept with exhaustion and fulfillment sleep overcame her.

# 5

Her entire world was a brighter, more joyous place now that she had Ramón.

London, that most fascinating and vital of cities, transcended itself and became for her an earthly paradise. She saw it all through a shimmering golden mist of excitement. Each minute spent in his company was like a precious jewel set in that gold.

When Isabella and her father had come to London three years earlier, she had resumed her studies and gained her bachelor's degree. Surprised at her sudden studiousness, her father had encouraged her to enroll in the School of Oriental and African Studies at London University, and she had embarked on her doctoral thesis. She had chosen as her subject ''A Dispensation for Postcolonial Africa.'' Her thesis was advancing well, and she had hoped to complete most of it before her father's term as ambassador ended and they returned to Cape Town.

However, all that had been before Ramón entered her life. Since then she had become a shameless truant. In the weeks since they had returned from Spain, she had not visited her tutor once and had barely had time to open a book.

Rather than laboring on her thesis, she rose before dawn and slipped away to ride with Ramón in the park or to jog with him along the Embankment. Sometimes they worked out together in the shabby little gym in Bloomsbury run by a Hungarian expatriate who had fled his own country after the abortive uprising.

There Ramón began to instruct her in the mysteries of karate and self-defense, arts in which he was frighteningly adept. Sometimes they wandered hand in hand through the galleries and museums. They dreamed in front of the Turners in the Tate or disparaged the new acceptances at the Royal Academy. Always they ended up in the bed in Ramón's flat in Kensington. She didn't care to ask him how he was able to spend so much time with her instead of at his bank. She simply accepted it gratefully.

"You've turned me into a junkie," she accused him. "I have to have my regular fix."

Indeed, when he left London for eight days on some mysterious business for his bank, she moped and pined and truly sickened, even to the point of throwing up when she rose in the morning.

She kept half a dozen changes of clothing and a full range of perfumes and cosmetics at his flat and made it her duty to arrange the flowers and replenish the refrigerator daily. She was a talented cook, and she loved to prepare food for him.

She began to neglect her duties at the embassy. She wormed her way out of official invitations and often left the chef and his staff to work on their own. Her father taxed her with her changed behavior.

"You are never at home any more, Bella. I can't rely on you for a single thing. Nanny says that you slept in your bed only twice last week."

"Nanny is a little telltale—and a fibber."

"What's going on, young lady?"

"I'm over twenty-one years of age, Pater darling, and it was part of our agreement that I don't have to account to you for my private life."

"It was also part of our agreement that you show your face at my receptions once in a while."

"Cheer up, Papa." She kissed him. "We'll be going back to Cape Town in a few months' time. Then you won't have to fret about me any longer."

However, that evening she asked Ramón if he wouldn't come to a cocktail party Shasa was holding at the embassy in Trafalgar Square to welcome the celebrated South African author Alan Paton to London.

Ramón thought about it carefully for a full minute before he

55

shook his head. "It is not the right time to meet your father yet."

"Why not, darling?" Up to that moment it had not been important to her, but now his refusal piqued her.

"There are reasons." He was often so damnably mysterious. She wanted to draw him out, but she knew she was wasting her time. He was the only man she had ever met who could resist her. There was a lining of steel beneath that beautiful façade.

"Therein lies much of his appeal," she laughed at herself ruefully. It was not that she wanted to share him with any other person, not even her father. She was more than content to be entirely alone with him; their love was so totally engrossing that they avoided other people.

True, they occasionally dined at Les A or the White Elephant with Harriet or some of the myriad other acquaintances that Isabella had made over the past three years. Once or twice they went on with the party to dance at Annabel's, but mostly they sneaked away from the others to be alone. Ramón did not seem to have friends of his own or, if he did, he never invited her to meet them. It troubled her not at all.

On the weekends when she could wriggle out of the official ambassadorial arrangements, she and Ramón threw their overnight bags and tennis rackets into the back of the Mini-Cooper and escaped into the country. They were usually very late back to town on Sunday night.

At the beginning of August, they departed from their solitary habits and caught the train up to Scotland. On the opening day of the grouse season they were Harriet Beauchamp's guests on the moors of the family estate. The earl was a stickler for correct form, and the ladies were not invited to shoot on the opening day. They were, however, allowed to pick up or join the line of beaters. The earl wasn't very keen on foreigners, either, especially those who shot "under and over" rather than "side by side" and who favored Italian guns over English.

On the first drive, he placed Ramón out on the end of the line. Unexpectedly three coveys came through on the right, sliding low over the tops of the heather, going like furies on a thirty-mile-an-hour tailwind. Isabella was loading for Ramón. He killed four birds from each covey. He took a double out in front. Then, as the covey swept overhead, Isabella passed him the second gun. With it he took another double behind the line of butts. Twelve birds with twelve shots fired. Even the head keeper shook his grizzled old head. "In thirty-three seasons, I've no' seen the likes," he told the earl lugubriously. "He kills his bird like de

56

Grey or Walsingham—dead in the air with nary a flutter." It was high praise to be compared to the best shots in English history.

The earl promptly abrogated custom, and on the second drive, Ramón found himself in one of the favored butts in the center of the line. At the long dinner table that evening, he was elevated to within conversational range of the earl, who addressed most of his remarks to him over the heads of the bishop and the baronet between them. The weekend was off to a great start. Harriet had arranged for Ramón and Isabella to occupy adjoining rooms at the farthest end of the huge rambling old country house.

"Papa suffers from insomnia," she explained. "And you and Ramón in action sound like the Berlin Philharmonic performing Ravel's *Boléro*."

"You vulgar little slut," Isabella protested.

"Talking of sluts, lovey. Have you sprung your little surprise on Ramón yet?" Harriet asked sweetly.

"I'm waiting for the right moment." Isabella was immediately defensive.

"In my vast experience, there ain't no right moment for that sort of news."

Harriet was right for once. No opportunity presented itself that weekend. They were halfway back to London when Isabella abandoned any further attempt at subtlety. Fortunately, they had the first-class compartment to themselves.

"Darling, I went to see a doctor last Wednesday—not the embassy doctor, but a new one that Harriet recommended. He did a test, and we got the result on Friday . . ." She paused and watched his expression. There was no change; he regarded her with that remote green gaze, and she felt a sudden illogical dread. Surely nothing could tarnish their feelings for each other, nothing could spoil the perfection of their love, yet she sensed a wariness in him, a spiritual drawing away from her. She found herself blurting it out in a rush.

"I'm almost two months pregnant. It must have been in Spain, probably that day in Granada, after the bullfight . . ." She felt breathless and shaky, and she hurried on. "I just can't explain it. I mean, I've been taking the Pill religiously, I swear it, you've seen me . . ." She realized she was beginning to gabble out her explanations in an undignified and uncontrolled rush. "I know I've been an awful chump, darling, but you don't have to worry. It's all in hand. Harriet made a little slip last year. She went to see a doctor in Amsterdam; he took care of it with absolutely no muss and no fuss. She caught the evening flight on a Friday and was back in London on Sunday—as good as new. She's given me the address, and she's even offered to come with me to hold my hand—"

"Isabella!" he cut in sharply. "Stop it. Stop talking. Listen to me!" She broke off and stared at him fearfully.

"You don't know what you are saying." His voice cut her cruelly. "What you suggest is monstrous!"

"I'm sorry, Ramón." She was confused. "I shouldn't have bothered you with it. Harriet and I could have . . ."

"Harriet is a shallow, asinine little tramp. When you place the life of my child in her hands, then you make yourself every bit as culpable as she is."

Isabella stared at him. This was not what she had expected from him at all.

"This is a miracle, Isabella, the greatest miracle and mystery of the universe. You talk of destroying it. This is our child, Isabella. This is life, new beautiful life, that you and I have created in love. Don't you understand that?"

He leaned across and took her hands, and she saw the coldness of his eyes fade. "This is something that we have made together, our own wonderous creation. It belongs to both of us, to our love."

"You aren't angry?" she asked hesitantly. "I thought you would be angry."

"I am proud and humble," he whispered. "I love you. You are infinitely precious to me." He turned her hands, holding them by the wrists, and laid them on her stomach. "I love what you have here; it also is infinitely precious to me." He had said it at last. "I love you," he had said.

"Oh, Ramón." Her vision blurred, "You are so wonderful, so tender, so kind. The true miracle is that I was ever able to meet somebody like you."

"You will give birth to our child, my darling Bella."

"Oh, yes! Oh, a thousand times yes, my darling. You have made me so proud, so happy." All her uncertainty was gone, replaced by an excitement and anticipation that seemed to drive all else into insignificance.

This euphoria buoyed her up over the days that followed. It laid a new, rich texture on her love for Ramón; something that up until that time had been engrossing but random now had direction and purpose. A dozen times she had been on the point of telling Nanny, and had only succeeded in preventing herself when she realized that the old woman's excitement would be so uncontained that the entire embassy, including her father, would know of the coming event within twenty-four hours. This brought her at last to sober consideration of the prosaic details that had to be arranged. She was already over two months, and Nanny had an eagle eye and an earthy instinct. At home on the family estate of Weltevreden she called the shots on the maids and house servants and field girls with an uncanny accuracy. Nanny bathed her when she was at home, and the only surprise was that she hadn't already latched on to Isabella's change of condition.

That evening Ramón had tickets for the Festival of Flamenco at Drury Lane, but she rang him at his private number at the bank.

"Ramón darling, I don't feel like going out tonight. I just want to be alone with you. I'll cook dinner. I'll have it ready by the time you get back to the flat, and we can listen to the new von Karajan disc."

She could hear the reluctance in his voice. He had been looking forward to the flamenco dancing all week. He was so aggressively Spanish at times. He had even insisted that she begin learning the language and had given her a set of Linguaphone records. However, she wheedled him shamelessly, and finally he succumbed.

On the way from the embassy to the flat, Isabella double-parked the Mini and picked up a bottle of Pol Roger and another of Montrachet from her father's private bin at Berry Brothers, the wine merchants in St. James's Street. Then in the food hall at Harrods she selected two dozen Whitstable oysters and a pair of perfect veal cutlets.

She was watching from the front window as Ramón turned the corner and came striding down the pavement toward the front door. He looked so English in his three-piece suit. While in London, he even carried a rolled black umbrella and sported a bowler, the epitome of the young merchant banker. It was a peculiar gift he had of fitting perfectly into any environment, no matter how diverse, as though he were born to it.

She opened the champagne, and as soon as she heard his key in the front door she poured their glasses and placed them beside the silver tray of crushed ice on which she had arranged the open oysters. She restrained herself from rushing wildly into the tiny hall and instead met him as he came into the living room. Then her restraint faded and her kiss was long and melting.

"Special occasion?" he asked, his arm still around her waist, as he saw the tray of oysters and the two long-stemmed tulip glasses softly seething with the yellow wine. She went to fetch a glass and placed it in his hand. Then she looked at him over the rim of her own glass.

"Welcome home, Ramón. I wanted to give you just a little taste of what it's going to be like when you are married to me."

She saw his eyes flinch; it was more poignant in that she had never seen it happen before. His gaze was always level and steady.

He did not taste the wine but set his glass aside, and she felt an awful premonition of disaster.

"Ramón, what is it?" she asked.

Before she could drink, he took the champagne glass from her hand and placed it on the walnut table.

"Bella." He turned back to face her and took her hands in his. "Bella," he said again softly, with deep regret, and he turned her hands and kissed the open palms.

"What is it, Ramón?" She could barely draw breath, so tight was her chest with dread.

"I can't marry you, my darling." She stared at him and felt her legs tremble and go weak with the shock. "I can't marry you, at least not yet, my darling."

She drew her hands out of his grasp and turned away from him. She went slowly to the armchair and sank into it.

"Why?" she asked softly, without looking at him as he came and knelt in front of her. "You want me to bear your child. Then why can't you marry me?"

"Bella, there is nothing I want more in this life than to have you as my wife, and to be father of our child, but . . ."

"Then why?" she repeated almost listlessly.

"Please listen to me, my darling. Don't say anything more until you have heard me out."

Now she lifted her eyes and looked at his face, but she was very pale.

"Nine years ago I married a Cuban girl in Miami."

Isabella shuddered and closed her eyes.

"The marriage was a disaster from the very beginning. We spent only a few months together before we parted, but we are both Catholics . . ." He broke off and touched her pale cheek. She pulled back from his caress, and he sighed softly.

"I'm still married to her," he said simply.

"What is her name?" Isabella asked without opening her eyes.

"Why do you want to know that?"

"Tell me." Her voice firmed.

"Natalie." He shrugged.

"Children?" she asked. "How many children do you have?"

"None," he replied. "You will be the mother of my first-born." And he watched the petals of rose return to her cheeks. After a moment she opened her eyes again, but they were shadowed with such despair that the blue had turned to black.

"Oh, Ramón! What are we going to do?"

"I have already begun to do all I can," he told her. "When we returned from Spain, I knew then, even before you told me about the baby, I knew that above all else in my life I must have you as my wife."

"Oh, Ramón." She blinked hard and tightened her grip on his hands.

"Natalie is still living in Miami, with her family. I was able to contact her. We spoke on the telephone, more than once. She is very devout. There is nothing, she said, that would persuade her to divorce me."

Isabella was staring at him hard, and now she shook her head miserably.

"I called her again, on three consecutive evenings. At last we found something that was more important to her than her God and her confessor."

"What was that?"

"Money," he said, with a shade of contempt in his voice. "I still have most of the winnings from the pigeon shoot. For fifty thousand dollars, she finally agreed to move to Reno and file for divorce."

"Darling!" Isabella whispered, joy blooming in her eyes again. "Oh, thank God! When? When will she go?"

"That is the catch. It takes time. I can't push her too hard. I know Natalie. If she found out about you and guessed why I wanted the divorce, she would exploit her advantage to the utmost. She promised to leave for Reno at the beginning of next month. She says that she has her job and her family to consider. Her mother is not well."

"Yes, yes," Isabella cut in impatiently. "But how long will it take?"

"There is provision in the Nevada state laws for the period of residency in Reno. Three months before they will grant the divorce."

"I'll be six months gone by then." Isabella bit her knuckles, then her expression changed. "And Daddy and I are booked to leave for Cape Town. Oh, Ramón, what a mess!"

"You can't go back to Cape Town," Ramón told her flatly.

**61**

"I couldn't live without you, and besides, your pregnancy will be obvious to all your family and friends."

"What do you want me to do?"

"Stay with me until my divorce is final. I love you too much to let you go. I don't want to miss a day of my son's life."

She smiled at last. "So it's definitely a son, is it?"

"Of course." He nodded with mock gravity. "We must have an heir of the title, must we not? You will stay with me, won't you, Bella?"

"What will I tell my father, and my grandmother? Papa is a pushover, but my grandmother . . . !" Isabella rolled her eyes. "Centaine Courtney-Malcomess is the family dragon. She actually breathes fire and crunches up the bones of her victims."

"I will tame your dragon," he promised.

"I truly believe that you might." Isabella felt gay and light-headed with relief. "If anyone can charm Nana, it would be you, my darling."


The fact that Centaine Courtney-Malcomess was six thousand miles away did make the task a little easier. Isabella prepared the ground with great care. She worked on her father first. Over night she became once more the dutiful daughter and consummate hostess. She plunged headlong and with all her precious panache into organizing the final few weeks of social engagements that marked the end of Shasa Courtney's ambassadorial term.

"Welcome back from wherever it was you disappeared to," Shasa told her drily at the end of one of her more successful dinner parties. "I missed you, you know."

They were standing arm in arm on the front steps of Highveld, watching a limousine bearing the last departing guest pull away.

"One o'clock in the morning." Shasa glanced at his wristwatch, but Isabella forestalled him.

"Too early for bed." She squeezed his arm. "Let me fix a nightcap and a final cigar for you. We haven't had a chance to talk all evening."

That afternoon Davidoffs had delivered a dozen of his cigars from the stock they kept for him in their specially humidified storage in St. James's. She held one to her ear as she rolled it between her fingers.

"Perfect," she murmured.

Shasa lolled in the buttoned-leather armchair across the room. Earlier the company had done full justice to the claret and the port, but his single eye was still clear and bright. The black silk patch over the other eye was as pristine as the perfectly constructed bow at the throat of his snowy shiftfront.

He watched her with undiluted pleasure, as though she were a blood filly from his stables or the gem of his art collection. She was the most beautiful of all the Courtneys, he thought, arriving at a considered verdict.

In her youth his own mother had been a celebrated beauty. The years had dimmed Shasa's memory of her zenith, but there was a portrait of her in her prime by Annigoni in the drawing room of Weltevreden. Even allowing for the artist's kindly eye, she must have been an extraordinary woman. The force of her character shone out of the portrait's dark eyes. She was still, at sixty-nine years of age, a magnificent woman, handsome and vigorous, but at no time in her life could she have equaled her granddaughter, who now stood in the bright noonday of her youth.

Isabella cut the tip of the cigar with the gold cutter from her father's desk. She lit the cedarwood taper from the fire and held it for him until the cigar was drawing evenly. Then she extinguished the taper and went to dribble a little cognac into a crystal balloon glass.

"Professor Symmonds read the latest section of my thesis this morning."

"Ah, you are still gracing the university with your presence, are you?" Shasa studied his daughter's bare shoulders in the soft light of the fire. She had inherited that skin, as lustrous and unblemished as ivory, from her mother.

"He thinks it is good." Isabella ignored the jibe.

"If it is up to the same standard as the first hundred pages that you let me read, then Symmonds is probably correct."

"He wants me to stay on here to finish it." She was not looking at him. Shasa felt a sick little slide of dread in his chest.

"Here in London, on your own?" His response was instantaneous.

"On my own? With five hundred friends, the staff of Courtney Enterprises' London office, my mother . . . !" She took the brandy balloon to him. "Not really abandoned completely in a strange city, Papa."

Shasa made a noncommittal noise in his throat and tasted the cognac, searching desperately for some better reason why she should accompany him back to the Cape.

"Where would you stay?" he grumped.

"That wasn't even a good try." She laughed at him openly, taking the cigar from his hand. She drew on it with pursed red

63

lips, then blew a feather of smoke into his face. "In Cadogan Square there is a flat which cost you almost a million pounds. It is standing empty." She gave him back the cigar.

She was right, of course. Since the official ambassadorial residence went with the job, the family flat had been unused. He was silent, driven to the ropes, and Isabella gathered herself for the coup de grace.

"You are the one who was so frightfully keen on my doctorate, Pater. You won't deprive me of it now, will you?"

Shasa rallied gamely. "Since you have obviously thought this all out so carefully, you must already have spoken to your grandmother."

Isabella stooped over him as he sat in the armchair and kissed the top of his head.

"I was hoping that you would speak to Nana 't me, my darling daddy."

Shasa sighed. "Witch," he murmured. "You make me a party to my own undoing."

She could rely on her father to take care of Nana, but there was still Nanny to consider. However, Isabella softened her up for a day or two beforehand by reciting the names and virtues of all seventeen of the grandchildren who so eagerly awaited her return to Weltevreden. Nanny had been away from home for three years, and three long English winters.

"Just think of it, Nanny. It will be spring at the Cape when the boat docks, and Johannes will be waiting on the pier." Johannes was the head groom at Weltevreden and Nanny's favorite son. The old woman's eyes shone. So when Isabella finally broke her news Nanny threw her hands around and wailed about ingratitude and the decay of the modern generation's sense of duty. Then she sulked for two days, but without real venom.

Isabella went down to Southampton to see them all off. Shasa's new Aston Martin was hoisted on board the Union Castle liner by one of the giraffe-necked cranes, and then the servants lined up on the pier for their farewells. She embraced them all, from the Malay chef to Klonkie the chauffeur. Nanny burst into tears when Isabella kissed her.

"You'll probably never see this old woman again. You'll miss me when I've gone. Think of how I nursed you when you was a baby . . ."

"Go on with you, Nanny. You'll be there to nurse all my babies for me." It was a dangerous subject to broach, but Nanny's perceptions were dulled. The promise drove off the shadow of her imminent demise, and she cheered noticeably.

"You'll come home soon now, child, you hear, where old Nanny can keep an eye on you. All that hot Courtney blood—we'll find you a good clean South African boy."

When Isabella came to say good-bye to Shasa, she unexpectedly found herself also dissolving into a salty wash of tears. Shasa handed her the crisp white handkerchief from the pocket of his double-breasted blazer. When she had dried up and given it back to him, he blew his own nose loudly and then dabbed at his single eye.

"Damned wind!" he explained. "Got a bit of grit in it."

As the liner pulled away from the wharf and headed down-river, he was a tall and elegant figure at the ship's rail, high above her, but he stood alone, slightly separated from the other passengers. He had never remarried since the divorce. She knew that since then he had been seeing literally dozens of women, all elegant and talented and nubile, but he always walked on alone.

Doesn't he ever feel lonely? she wondered, and she waved until he was an indistinguishable speck on the ship's deck.

On the drive back to London, the road kept dissolving before her eyes in a glassy mirage of tears.

"It's the baby," she tried to excuse herself. "He's making me all gooey and sentimental." She clasped her belly and tried to find a lump, and was vaguely disappointed that her muscles were still flat and hard. "God, what if it's all just a false alarm!"

The possibility heightened her melancholy, and she reached for the packet of Kleenex in the cubbyhole of the Mini.

However, when she climbed the stairs to the flat, the door opened before she touched it and Ramón reached out and drew her into his arms. Her tears were forgotten.

# 6

The family flat in Cadogan Square occupied the first two floors of a listed red brick Victorian house. There were five double bedrooms, and the walls of the master suite were clad with powder blue and antique silver paneling that had reputedly graced the boudoir of Madame de Pompadour. The *plafond* was decorated with dancing circles of naked wood nymphs and leering satyrs. Much to Shasa's chagrin, Isabella referred to the decor as "Louis Quinze bordello."

She used it merely as an accommodation address, calling on Fridays to pick up her mail and have tea with the full-time housekeeper in the ground-floor pantry. The housekeeper was an ally and fielded all the long-distance telephone calls from Weltevreden and other parts afar.

Isabella made her true home in Ramón's tiny flat. When the wardrobe he allocated her proved to be inadequate, she rotated her clothes between it and the cavernous storage space at Cadogan Square. She found a dainty little lady's writing desk in an antique shop in Kensington Church Street that just fitted into the corner beside the bed, and made that her study.

Like a married couple, they settled into a routine. They were up before dawn for gym or riding; Isabella's gynecologist had forbidden jogging. "It's a fetus, not a milk shake, you are brewing, my dear." Then, when Ramón left for the bank, she settled down at her desk and worked steadily on her thesis until lunchtime, when they met at Justin de Blank or the health bar at Harrods, for Isabella had given up alcohol and put herself on a strict diet for the baby's sake.

"I refuse to let myself swell up like a toad. I don't want to revolt you."

"You are the most desirable woman in existence, and pregnancy has brought you to full bloom,'' he contradicted her, touching her bosom. It was magnificent.

"I asked the gyney, and he said it's quite okay; we don't have to hold back at all.'' She giggled. "I do hope the ambulance that takes me to the maternity home has a comfortable double stretcher so we can fit in a quickie on the way.''

After lunch she went on to visit her tutor or to spend the rest of the afternoon in the reading room of the British Museum. Finally there was a mad dash back to the flat in the Mini in time to start preparing Ramón's dinner. Fortunately, Shasa had arranged for her to retain her diplomatic plates, and she parked at the curb right outside the front door and smiled winningly at the hovering traffic warden.

In the evenings they went out less and less frequently, apart from an occasional play or an early dinner with Harriet and her latest beau. Usually they piled all the cushions on the floor and sprawled in front of the television, arguing and discussing and billing and cooing and ignoring the inane burble of *Coronation Street* and the game shows.

When at last the taut flat plain of her belly began to bulge, she opened the front of her silk dressing gown and exhibited it proudly. "Feel it!'' she urged Ramón. "Isn't it wonderful?''

He palpated it solemnly. "Yes,'' he nodded sagely. "Definitely a boy.''

"How do you know?''

"Here.'' He took her hand. "Can't you feel it?''

"Ah, it does stick out a bit. He must take after his papa. Funny how thinking about that makes me feel like bed.''

"Sleepy?'' he asked.

"Hardly,'' she replied.

Shasa had left her with her Harrods charge card, and she acquired most of her maternity clothes there, although Harriet kept discovering newly fashionable boutiques that specialized in clothes for the swinging young mother-to-be. Wearing one of her flowing new caftans, she enrolled in the antenatal classes her gynecologist recommended. Suddenly the company and conversation of her gravid classmates, which would once have bored her to distraction, was fun and fascinating.

At least once a month, Ramón had to fly out of town on bank business, and each time he was away for a week or more. However, he telephoned her whenever he had an opportunity. Although she missed him more painfully than she would admit even to herself, when he returned her joy was enhanced a hundredfold.

**67**

After one such trip, she met him at Heathrow and drove him directly back to the flat. He dropped his travel bag in the hall and threw his jacket over the back of the chair before going into the bathroom.

His Spanish passport slipped from the inner pocket of his jacket and plopped onto the carpet. She picked it up and riffled through it until she found his photograph. It wasn't bad, but no camera could do him full justice. She flipped the page and saw his date of birth. That reminded her that his birthday was just two weeks away. She had determined to make it a wonderful occasion. She had already seen a glass statuette in an antique shop in Mayfair, an exquisite little glass nude by René Lalique. She recognized the body as so similar to her own, even to the exaggerated length of leg and tight, boyish buttocks. But for the fact that it had been sculpted at the height of Lalique's popularity during the 1920s, Isabella could easily have been the model. However, the price daunted even her, and she was still plucking up sufficient courage to buy it for him.

She flipped over a few more pages of his passport, and a visa caught her eye. It had been stamped in Moscow that morning, and she blinked with surprise.

"Darling," she called through the bathroom door, "I thought you were in Rome. How did you end up in Moscow?" Everything she had ever learned, every facet of her South African upbringing, had always pointed to Russia as the great Antichrist. Even the hammer and sickle and the Cyrillic script stamped in his passport made the fine hairs on her forearms rise in repugnance.

There was silence beyond the locked door for a full minute. Then it was flung open abruptly, and Ramón strode out in his shirtsleeves and snatched the booklet from her hand. His expression was one of cold fury, and his eyes terrified her.

"Don't ever pry into my affairs again," he said softly.

Although he never mentioned the incident again, it was almost a week before she felt he had forgiven her. It had so intimidated her that thereafter she tried to put it completely out of her mind.

Then, in early November, when she called round at the Cadogan Square flat, the housekeeper handed her her mail. As always, there was a letter from her father, but under it was another envelope franked in Johannesburg, and with a lift of pleasure she recognized her brother Michael's handwriting.

Each of her three brothers was so distinctly different in looks, character and personality that it was impossible for her to have a favorite.

Sean, the eldest, was the flamboyant adventurer, a wild spirit, who, until she met Ramón, had been the most impossibly beautiful man she had ever known. Sean was the soldier and the hunter. He had already been decorated with the Silver Cross for valor in Rhodesia's grim little bush war. When he wasn't tracking down terrorists, he ran a vast hunting concession in the Zambezi Valley for Courtney Enterprises. Isabella adored him.

Garrick was her second brother, the ugly duckling, the myopic asthmatic who during his unhappy childhood had always been referred to as "poor Garry." However, although born deficient in most physical areas, he had inherited his full measure of the Courtney spirit and determination and shrewdness. He had worked on his puny body until it was almost grotesquely muscular with such a barrel of a chest and powerful arms that all his clothes had to be tailor-made for him. With nearsighted eyes behind thick horn-rimmed spectacles and no natural sporting ability, he had developed such powers of concentration that he had made himself into a four-goal polo player, a scratch golfer and an extraordinary shot with rifle and shotgun.

In addition, he had succeeded his father as chairman and chief executive officer of Courtney Enterprises. Not yet thirty years of age, he ran a multi-billion-dollar complex of companies with the same formidable application to detail and insatiable appetite for hard work that he brought to all his other endeavors. Yet he never forgot her birthday, and he responded instantly to any call Isabella made on him, no matter how onerous or how trivial. She called him "Teddy Bear" because he was so big and hairy and cuddly, and she loved him dearly.

Then there was Michael, the youngest—sweet, gentle Michael, the family peacemaker, the thoughtful, compassionate, poetic creature, the only Courtney who, despite the encouragement and example of his father and his two brothers, had never killed a wild bird or animal in his life. Instead, he had written and published three successful books, one a collection of poems and the other two on South African history and politics. The last two had both been banned by South Africa's industrious censors for their unseemly treatment of racial matters and their radical political flavor. He was also a highly regarded journalist and the deputy editor of the *Golden City Mail*, a large-circulation English-language newspaper that was stubbornly and outspokenly opposed to the National Afrikaner government of John

69

Vorster and its policy of apartheid. Of course, Courtney Enterprises owned 80 percent of the *Mail*'s stock; otherwise he might not have achieved such a responsible position at such a tender age.

During all of Isabella's childhood, Michael had been her protector and adviser and confident, and after Nana her favorite storyteller. She trusted Michael more than anybody else in her life, and if Sean hadn't been so wonderful and Garrick so lovable and cuddly, then Michael would definitely have been her favorite brother. It was a dead heat among the three of them for her affections, but she loved Michael as much as any of them, and now his handwriting on the envelope gave her a warm glow of pleasure and a prickle of guilt. She hadn't written to him since she had met Ramón, almost six months before.

The second paragraph of the first page caught her eye the instant she unfolded it, and she skipped the salutation and went straight to it.

Pater tells me that you are cozily ensconced in Cadogan Square and laboring mightily on your thesis. Good for you, Bella. However, I am sure that you are not presently occupying all five of the bedrooms, and I was hoping that you could fit me in somehow. I plan to be in London for three weeks from the fifteenth of the month. I will be out all day, every day. I have a full schedule of interviews and meetings, so I promise not to be a nuisance and interfere with your studies . . .

It was a complication, in that she would be forced to take up physical residence at Cadogan Square for the period of Michael's visit. However, most fortunately it coincided with one of Ramón's periodic travels abroad. She would have been alone anyway. Now at least she would have Michael's company.

She sent him a cable addressed to the *Mail*'s office in Johannesburg and set about making Cadogan Square look as though it were permanently lived in. She had a week to prepare for Michael's arrival.

"There will have to be some explanations," she told Ramón, clasping the neat little bulge of her tummy. "Luckily Michael is so understanding. I'm sure the two of you would get on well together. I wish you could meet him."

"I will try to complete my business ahead of time and get back to London while your brother is still here."

"Oh, Ramón darling, I would love that. Please do try."

She was waiting for Michael as he pushed his luggage trolley through the international arrivals barrier at Heathrow, and she let out a squeal of glee as she recognized him. He swung her off her feet, then his expression changed as he felt her stomach against him, and he set her down again with exaggerated gentleness.

As she drove him into town in the Mini, she kept darting glances at him. He was tanned—when you lived in London you noticed that immediately—and he had grown his hair fashionably long. It curled over the collar of his bottle green corduroy hacking jacket. However, his smile was still boyish and frank, and the blue Courtney eyes lacked the hard, acquisitive sparkle of all the other Courtneys', and were instead mild and thoughtful.

She pumped him for news of home, partly to satisfy her curiosity but mostly to keep the conversation away from her fecund belly. According to Michael, Pater had engrossed himself in his new duties as chairman of Armscor. Nana was growing more vigorous and more imperious every day, ruling Weltevreden with an iron fist. She had even taken up breeding retrievers and training them for gundog trials. Sean was still killing platoons of guerrillas and droves of buffalo. He had recently been promoted to a reserve captain in the Ballantyne Scouts, one of the crack Rhodesian regiments. Garry had just presented his shareholders with record company profits for the sixth year in succession. His wife, Holly, was about to produce another infant. They were all crossing their fingers for a girl this time.

As he said this, Michael glanced at her midriff significantly, but Isabella concentrated all her attention on the traffic to avoid an explanation and at last parked the Mini in the mews garage at the back of the square.

Michael was suffering from jet lag, so she ran him a foam bath and brought him a whisky and soda. While he was soaking, she sat on the closed lid of the toilet seat and chatted. She would never have contemplated sharing a bathroom with either Sean or Garry, but between Michael and herself nudity was natural and unremarked.

"Do you remember that silly little nonsense rhyme?" Michael asked at last. "How did it go again?"

> " 'Dum de dum-dum,
> And her father said, "Nelly,
> There is more in your belly
> Than ever went in through your mouth!' "

71

Isabella chuckled unashamedly. "Is that what they call 'the trained journalist eye?' You don't miss anything, do you, Mickey?"

"Miss it?" He laughed with her. "Your tummy damn near knocked out my trained journalistic eye!"

"Pretty, isn't it?" Isabella pushed it out as far as it would go and patted it proudly.

"Stunning!" Michael agreed. "And I am sure that Pater and Nana would agree if they could see it."

"You won't tell, will you, Mickey?"

"We don't tell each other's secrets, you and me. Never have, never will. But what are you going to do with the eventual, ah, result?"

"My son, your nephew—you call that a *result*? Shame on you, Mickey. Ramón calls it the greatest miracle and mystery of the universe."

"Ramón! So that is the culprit's name. I hope he's wearing bulletproof knickers when Nana catches up with him toting her trusty old shotgun loaded with buckshot."

"He's a marqués, Mickey. The Marqués de Santiago y Machado."

"Ah, that might make a difference. Nana is enough of a snob to be impressed. She will probably reduce the charge from buckshot to birdshot."

"By the time Nana finds out about it, I'll be a marquesa."

"So the nefarious Ramón intends making an honest woman out of you, does he? When?"

"Well, there is a little bit of a hitch," she admitted.

"You mean he's married already."

"How did you know that, Mickey?" She gaped at him.

"And his wife won't give him a divorce?"

"Mickey!"

"My love, that's the hoariest old chestnut in the packet," Michael stood up, cascading soapy bathwater, and reached for the towel.

"You don't know him, Mickey. He's not like that."

"May I take that as an impartial and totally unbiased opinion?" Michael stepped out of the bath and began to towel himself down.

"He loves me."

"So I see."

"Don't be flippant."

"Make me a promise, Bella. If anything goes wrong, come to me first. Will you promise me that?"

She nodded. "Yes, I promise. You are still my very best friend. I promise, but nothing is going to go wrong. You just wait and see."

She took him to dinner at Ma Cuisine in Walton Street. The restaurant was so popular they would never have gotten a table had not Isabella made the reservation the very day she'd heard Michael was coming to London.

"I like escorting a pregger," Michael remarked as they settled at the table. "Everybody smiles at me as though I am responsible."

"Nonsense. It's simply because you're so handsome." They talked about their work. Isabella made him promise to read her thesis and make suggestions. Then Michael explained that the main reason he was in London was to write a series of articles on the antiapartheid movement and the South African political exiles living in Britain.

"I have arranged interviews with some of the leading lights: Oliver Tambo, Denis Brutus . . ."

"Do you think our censors will let you publish the article?" Isabella asked. "They'll probably ban the entire edition again, and Garry will be furious. Anything that affects the profits makes Garry furious."

Michael chuckled. "Poor old Garry." The title was habitual but no longer appropriate. "Life is so simple for him—not the black and white of morality, but the black and red of the bank statement."

Over dessert Michael asked suddenly, "How is Mater? Have you seen her lately?"

"Not Mater, nor Mother, nor even Mummy," Isabella corrected him tartly. "You know that she thinks those terms terribly bourgeois. But to answer your question—no, I haven't seen Tara for some time."

"She is our mother, Bella."

"She might have thought of that when she deserted Pater and the rest of us and ran off with a black revolutionary and bore him a little brown bastard."

"And you might be a shade more charitable when it comes to bearing bastards," Michael said mildly. Then he saw the hurt in her eyes. "I'm sorry, Bella, but as in your case there are reasons for all things. We shouldn't judge her too harshly. Pater can't be the easiest man in the world to be married to, and not everybody can play the game to the rules Nana lays down. Some of us don't have the killer instinct developed finely

73

enough. I don't think Tara fitted into the family at all, not from the very beginning. She never was an elitist. Her sympathies were always with the underdog, and then Moses Gama came into her life . . ."

"Mickey darling"—Isabella leaned across the table and took his hand—"you are the most compassionate, understanding person in the world. You spend your life making excuses for us, protecting us from the Fates. I do love you so much. I don't even want to fight or argue with you."

"Good." He squeezed her hand. "Then you'll come along to see Tara with me. She writes to me regularly. She adores you, Isabella, and she misses you terribly. It hurts her when you avoid her."

"Oh, Mickey, you set a trap for me, you devil." She thought furiously for a second. "But what about my condition? I was hoping to be a little more discreet."

"Tara is your mother, she loves you, and they don't come any more broad-minded than our Tara. She's not going to do anything to hurt you, you know that."

"To please you," she sighed, capitulating. "Only to please you, Mickey."

So on the following Saturday morning they walked down Brompton Road. Michael had to stretch his long legs to match her flowing athletic stride.

"Are you training to have a bambino, or for the next Olympics?" he asked with a grin.

"You smoke too much," Isabella scoffed at him.

"My only vice."

Tara Courtney, or Tara Gama as she now called herself, was the manageress of a small residential hotel off Cromwell Road. Her clientele was composed almost exclusively of expatriates and new immigrants from Africa, India and the Caribbean.

It always amazed Isabella that an area like this existed only twenty minutes' walk from the grandeur of Cadogan Square. The Lord Kitchener Hotel was as shabby and run-down as its manageress. It also always amazed Isabella that her mother was the same person who had once presided over the great château of Weltevreden. Isabella's earliest memories were of her mother in a full-length ball gown, yellow diamonds from the Courtney mine at H'ani glittering at her smooth white throat and on her earlobes, her dark auburn hair piled high on her lovely head as she came down the sweep of the marble staircase. Isabella had never suspected the terrible dissatisfaction and misery that must have festered beneath that regal façade.

Now Tara's magnificent head of hair had greyed, and she had touched it up with a cheap home dye job that came up in variegated tones of ginger and brazen plum. Her skin, which Isabella had inherited in all its silken perfection, had withered and bagged and wrinkled with neglect. There were little blackheads lodged in the enlarged pores around the creases between her nose and mouth, and her false teeth were too large for her mouth, distorting the sweet line of her lips.

She rushed down the front steps of the hotel to embrace Isabella in a cloud of pungent cologne. Isabella returned her hug with the strength of a guilty conscience.

"Let me look at my darling daughter." She held Isabella at arm's length, and her eyes dropped immediately. "You have grown more beautiful, Bella, if that were possible, but the reason is pretty obvious. I see you are carrying a little bundle of fun and joy."

Isabella's smile crooked with annoyance, but she ignored the reference.

"You look well, Mummy—Tara, I mean." Tara wore the self-conscious uniform of the militant left-winger: a shapeless grey cardigan over a full-length granny-print shift and men's open brown sandals.

"It's been months," Tara complained, "almost a year, and you live just down the road. How can you neglect your old mum so?"

Michael intervened smoothly, deflecting Tara's self-pity, embracing her with unfeigned warmth and enthusiasm. She turned to him with theatrical mother love.

"Mickey, you were always the sweetest and most loving of all my children."

Isabella's smile began to hurt her lips. She wondered just how long she had to stay and when she could escape. She knew that it wasn't going to be easy, and that for once she could expect little support from Michael. Tara linked her arms through theirs. Michael on one side of her and Isabella on the other, she led them into the hotel.

"I've got tea and biscuits ready for you. I've been in an absolute tizz ever since Michael called to say you were coming."

On a Saturday morning the Lord Kitchener's public lounge was filled with Tara's guests. The air was thick with tobacco smoke and the cadences of Swahili and Gujarati and Xhosa. Tara introduced them to everybody in the room, even though Isabella had met many of them on her previous visits: "My son and daughter from Cape Town in South Africa.'' Isabella saw how some of the eyes flicked at the name of her country.

The hell with them, too, she decided defiantly. Funny how at home she thought of herself as a liberal, but when she was abroad and encountered that reaction she thought of herself as a patriot.

At last Tara seated them in a corner of the lounge, and while she poured the tea, she asked in a bright and cheery tone that carried clearly to everybody in the large room, ''So now, Bella, tell me about the baby. When are you expecting it, and who is the father?''

''This is hardly the time or the place, Tara.'' Isabella paled with irritation, but Tara laughed.

''Oh, we are all just one big family here at the Lordy. You can talk freely.''

This time Michael murmured gently, ''Bella really doesn't want all the world to know her private business. We'll talk about it later, Tara.''

''You funny old-fashioned thing.'' Tara reached across and tried to hug Isabella again but spilled some of her tea on her granny-print skirt and gave up the attempt. ''None of us here worries our head over bourgeois conventions.''

''That's enough, Tara,'' Michael said firmly, and then, to divert her, ''Where is Benjamin, and how is he doing?''

Tara took the bait. ''Oh, Ben is my pride and joy. He just popped out for a few minutes. He had to go down to the school to hand in an essay. He's such a clever boy, he's taking his A levels this year, only sixteen and his headmaster says he is the most brilliant, the cleverest child he has had in Ryham Grammar for the last ten years. All the girls adore him. He's so good-looking.'' Tara chattered on, and Isabella was relieved not to have to make conversation. Instead she listened to the recital of her half-brother's virtues.

Benjamin Gama was one of the many reasons Isabella felt uncomfortable in this other world in which her mother lived. So deep had been the disgrace and so poisonous the scandal Tara had brought on the Courtney family that her name was never mentioned at Weltevreden. Nana had forbidden it.

Only Michael had ever discussed it with her, and then in the most general terms. ''I'm sorry, Bella, I'm not going to repeat cruel rumor and hearsay. If you want that, you'll have to go elsewhere. I'll only tell you the facts, and those are that when Tara left South Africa after Moses Gama was arrested and imprisoned, no charges were ever brought against her and no proof was ever offered to implicate her in any criminal activity.''

"But didn't Pater arrange it that way to protect the family reputation?''

"Why don't you ask Pater himself?'' She had indeed tentatively broached the subject with her father, but Shasa, for once cold and aloof, had dismissed the inquiry. In an odd way Isabella had been relieved by his refusal to talk about it. She was honest enough to recognize her own cowardice. She didn't truly want to know the extent of her mother's guilt. Deep down, she didn't really want to know if her mother had indeed been a party to the notorious "Guy Fawkes" plot of her lover, Moses Gama, to blow up the South African Houses of Parliament, the attempt that had resulted in the death of Isabella's grandfather, Tara's own father. Perhaps her mother was a traitor and a murderess guilty of patricide. At the very least she was certainly a blatant adulteress and a miscegenist, which was a crime under South African law. Once again Isabella wondered just what she was doing here.

Suddenly Tara's features brightened, and for an instant she recaptured a faint glimmer of her lost beauty. "Ben!" she cried. "Look who have come to see us, Benjamin. Your brother and sister. Isn't that nice?''

Isabella swiveled in her chair, and her half brother stood in the doorway of the hotel lounge behind her. He had grown in the year since she had seen him, and obviously he had made the leap from puberty into manhood.

"Hello, Benjamin,'' she cried too enthusiastically, and although he smiled she sensed the reserve in him and saw the wariness in his dark eyes.

Tara had not been completely prejudiced by her maternal instincts. Benjamin was indeed a fine-looking lad. His natural African grace had combined well with his mother's more delicate features. His skin had a coppery tone, and his hair was a neat woolly cap of tight dark curls.

"Hello, Isabella.'' The south London accent on the tongue of this son of Africa startled her. She made no move to embrace him. From their very first meeting there had been a tacit agreement between them: no displays of simulated affection. They shook hands quickly, then both stepped back. Before Isabella could think of anything further to say, Benjamin had turned to Michael. Now his smile was a flash of perfect teeth and the sparkle of dark eyes.

"Mickey!" he said, and he took two quick light steps to meet his elder brother. They clasped each other around the shoulders.

Isabella envied Michael his exceptional ability to evoke trust and liking in everybody around him. Benjamin seemed truly to accept him as a brother and a friend without any of the reserve he showed toward Isabella. Soon all three of them, Tara, Ben, and Mickey, were chatting away with animation. Isabella felt excluded from their intimate little circle.

At last one of the black South African students crossed the lounge and spoke to Tara. She looked up in consternation, then glanced at her watch.

"My goodness, thank you for reminding me, Nelson." She smiled up at the student. "We were having such a good natter that we completely forgot about the time." Tara jumped to her feet. "Come on, everybody! If we are going to Trafalgar Square, we had better leave now."

There was a general exodus from the lounge, and Isabella edged across to Michael.

"What's this all about, Mickey? You seem to know what's going on. Fill me in."

"There is a rally in Trafalgar Square."

"Oh, God, no! Not another one of those antiapartheid jamborees. Why didn't you warn me?"

"It would have given you an excuse to duck out." Michael grinned at her. "Why don't you come along?"

"No, thanks. I've lived with that nonsense for the past three years, ever since Pater took over the embassy. What are you getting mixed up in that ridiculous business for?"

"It's my job, Bella my sweeting. That's what I came to London for, to write about this ridiculous business, as you call it. Come with us."

"Why should I bother?"

"To see the world from the other side of the fence for a change—you might find it refreshing—and to be with me. We could have fun together." She wavered uncertainly. Despite her disdain for the subject, she loved his company. They truly did have fun together, and with Ramón away she was lonely.

"Only if we ride on the top of a bus, not on the Tube. You know I can never resist a bus ride."

They were a party of twenty or so from the Lordy, including Nelson Litalongi, the South African student. Michael found a seat for her on the upper deck of the red bus, then he and Nelson squeezed in beside her. Tara and Benjamin were in the seat directly in front of them, but they faced around to join in the laughter and the joking. The mood was gay and carefree, and despite herself Isabella found she was indeed having fun. Michael was the center of everything, and he and Nelson began to sing. They both had fine voices, and the others joined in with the chorus of "This Is My Island in the Sun." Nelson could mimic Harry Belafonte to the life and resembled him except that the tone of his skin was lustrous charcoal. He and Michael had hit it off together from the beginning.

When they climbed off the bus in front of the National Gallery, the demonstrators were already assembling on the open square beneath the tall column, and Michael made a joke about Nelson and Horatio. Everybody laughed, and they trooped across the road into the square, and the pigeons rose in fluttering clouds from around their feet.

There was a temporary platform erected at the end of the square, directly in front of South Africa House, and an area had been roped off in which a few hundred demonstrators had already assembled. They joined the back ranks, and Tara produced a hand-lettered banner from her plastic shopping bag and held it aloft:

APARTHEID IS A CRIME AGAINST HUMANITY.

Isabella edged away from her and tried to pretend they were not related. "She really doesn't mind making a spectacle of herself, does she?" she whispered to Michael.

He laughed. "That's the whole object of the exercise."

Nevertheless, Isabella did find it interesting to be a part of this motley gathering. With distaste she had viewed many others like it from the high windows of the ambassador's office across the road, but this gave her a totally new perspective. The crowd was good-natured and well behaved. Four blue-uniformed bobbies stood by to see fair play and smiled in avuncular fashion when one of the speakers referred to London as a police state every bit as bad as Pretoria. To show her support and to dissociate herself from the remark, Isabella blew the nicest-looking copper a kiss, and his indulgent smile stretched into a delighted grin.

The speeches from the platform droned on against the rumble of the traffic and the passing scarlet buses. Isabella had heard it all before, and so had the others in the crowd, to judge by their phlegm and apathy. The best laugh of the day came when a pigeon wheeling high overhead ejected a spurt of whitewash that hit the speaker of the moment on his shiny bald pate and Isabella called out, "Fascist bird! Agent of the racist Pretoria regime!"

The meeting ended with a vote on the motion that John Vorster and his illegal regime should immediately resign and hand over power to the Democratic People's Government of South Africa. The motion was declared carried unanimously, and Michael remarked, "Which should make John Vorster tremble in his boots." The meeting broke up more peaceably than a crowd from a football match.

"Let's find a pub," Michael suggested. "All that toppling of fascist governments has made me thirsty."

"There is a good one in the Strand," Nelson Litalongi suggested.

"Lead the way," Michael encouraged him. When they bellied up to the bar, he bought the first round.

"Well," Isabella gave her judgment as she sipped her ginger beer, "that was a fair old waste of time. Two hundred little people spouting hot air aren't going to change anything."

"Don't be too sure of that." Michael wiped froth off his upper lip with the back of his hand. "Maybe it's the first little ripple lapping at the foot of the dam wall—soon that ripple could become a wavelet, and then a riptide and finally a tidal wave."

"Oh, nonsense, Mickey." Isabella dismissed the idea brusquely. "South Africa is too strong, too rich. America and Britain have too much invested in her. They won't let us down; they can't expect us to hand over our birthright to a pack of Marxist savages." She repeated the obvious truths that she had heard her father, the ambassador, voice so often over the last three years. She was discomfited by the acrimony and logic with which she was assailed by her mother and her half brother, and by Nelson Litalongi and the twenty other colored residents from the Lord Kitchener Hotel. It was not a happy experience. That evening when she and Michael returned to Cadogan Square, she was shaken and subdued.

"They are so bitter and angry, Mickey," she lamented.

"It's the new wave, Bella. If we are to survive it, we should try to understand and come to terms with it."

"It's not as though they are badly treated. Just think about Nanny and Klonkie and Gamiet and all our people at Weltevreden. I mean, Mickey, they are a damned sight better off than most of the whites living in this country."

"I know how you feel, Bella. You can drive yourself mad pondering on the rights and wrongs, but you've got to come back to one thing in the end. They are human beings, just like us, some of them a hell of a lot better and nicer. By what right,

80

divine or infernal, can we prevent them sharing all that the country of our birth has to offer?''

"That's very well in theory, but this afternoon they were talking about armed struggle. That means blowing women and children to pieces. That means blood and death, Mickey. Just like the Irish. How do you feel about that?''

"I don't know what I feel about that, Bella. Sometimes I feel—No! Killing and maiming and burning are never justified. Then at other times I feel—Sure, why not? Man has been killing his fellowmen for a million years to protect himself and his birthright. Pater, who rants and roars at the thought of an armed struggle in South Africa, is the same person who climbed into a Hurricane in 1940 and went off to machine-gun Ethiopians and Italians and Germans with gay old abandon in defense of what he saw as his freedom. Nana, that stalwart of the rule of law and the sanctity of private property, and defender of the free-market system, was the one who nodded happily and murmured, 'Quite right, too!' when she heard the news of the most appalling violence of all mankind's bloody and violent history, the bombs on Hiroshima and Nagasaki. So how immoral and bloodthirsty are Tara and Benjamin and Nelson Litalongi compared to us and our own family? Who is right and who is wrong, Bella?''

"You've given me a terrible headache." Isabella stood up. "I'm going to bed.''

The telephone woke her at six in the morning, and as she heard Ramón's voice the dark shadow over her life evaporated.

"Darling, where are you?''

"Athens.''

"Oh." Her spirits plunged. "I hoped you might be at Heathrow.''

"I've been delayed. I will be here for at least three more days. Why don't you come across and join me?''

"To Athens?" She was still half asleep.

"Yes, why not? You can still catch the ten o'clock flight on BEA. We could steal three days together. How about the Acropolis in the moonlight? We can get out to the islands, and there are some important people I would like you to meet.''

"Yes!" she cried. "Why not! Give me your telephone number. I'll ring you back as soon as I have a seat on the plane.'' But all the lines to British European Airways reservations were busy, and she was running out of time, so Michael drove her

81

out to Heathrow in the Mini and dropped her at the terminal entrance.

"I'll wait until you get a confirmed reservation," he suggested.

"No, Mickey, you're a darling, but I won't have any trouble at this time of year; the holiday season is over. You go off to your interview, and I'll call you at the flat when Ramón and I are on our way home."

As she walked into the terminal she realized she had been overoptimistic. Hordes of dejected and weary travelers blocked the aisles with their luggage. When she finally got to the head of the line at the information desk, she was told that a wildcat strike by the French air traffic controllers had delayed all flights by up to five hours, and that the Athens flight was fully booked. She would have to join the waiting list, even for a seat in first class.

She stood in another line to use a public telephone and finally got through to Ramón at the number he had given her in Athens. He sounded as disappointed as she felt.

"I was looking forward to your arrival. I have lauded you to the skies to the people I want you to meet here."

"I'm not going to give up," she declared. "Even if I have to sit here all day."

It was a day of discomfort and misery and frustration. When the flight was finally called at five o'clock that evening, she stood at the check-in counter praying for a seat. However, there were half a dozen other hopefuls ahead of her. In the end, the booking clerk shook her head regretfully.

"I'm so sorry, Miss Courtney."

The next flight to Athens was scheduled for ten the following morning, but there would certainly be delays and another waiting list. Finally Isabella gave up and went dejectedly to place another call to Athens. Ramón was not available, so she left a message for him with someone on the other end who spoke atrocious English. She hoped Ramón would understand that she was aborting the journey.

There were no taxis available: hundreds of other passengers like her had abandoned hope and were trying to get home. She lugged her bag down the pavement and stood in line for a bus to take her into town. It was after eight when she reached it and at last found a taxi to take her back to Cadogan Square.

Her back ached from the weight of the baby, and she was close to tears of frustration when at last she let herself into the flat. There was the delicious aroma of cooking, and she realized how hungry she was. She dumped her bag in the lobby, kicked off her shoes and went through to the kitchen. It was obvious Michael had made himself dinner. The used dishes on the table in the breakfast nook were still warm, and there were generous leftovers in the warmer. Like her, Michael was an excellent cook. She helped herself to the breasts of chicken Kiev and a slice of the cheesecake that remained. She noticed that there were two used wineglasses and an empty bottle of Pater's Nuits St. Georges 1961 on the draining board of the sink, but the significance of this did not really occur to her. She was too weary and dejected, and she wanted Michael to cheer her up.

She heard music coming from his bedroom suite upstairs, the sentimental strains of Mantovani, one of Michael's favorites. She climbed the stairs on stocking feet, went down the passage and pushed open the door to Michael's room.

For a long moment, she did not comprehend what she was seeing; it was too distant from her wildest expectations or imaginings.

Then she thought Michael was being attacked, and a scream rushed up her throat. She had to cover her mouth with both hands to contain it. At last understanding flooded over her.

Naked, Michael knelt on hands and knees in the center of the double bed. The satin eiderdown and bedsheets had spilled over onto the floor, and the bed was in disarray. She knew his body so well, lithe and elegantly muscled, tanned by the African sun to the color of ripe tobacco leaf except where his bathing trunks had left his skin pale and vulnerable-looking.

Also naked, Nelson Litalongi knelt beside him. In contrast, his torso shone with sweat like newly mined coal, so bright it seemed to have been freshly oiled.

Michael's dearly beloved features were contorted with a deep and particular anguish. His mouth was twisted into a savage rictus that struck her to the depth of her being. For a moment, he reminded her of a stricken animal on the very point of a dreadful death.

Then his vision cleared and focused and he saw her. Before her eyes, his face seemed to dissolve and run like molten wax, and re-form in an expression of terror and deadly shame. With a violent twist of his body, he broke the grip of the man who held him and rolled away from him, reaching for a crumpled pillow to cover his own groin.

Isabella whirled and rushed from the room.

Despite her exhaustion, she slept fitfully and with disjointed and confused dreams, in which she saw Michael struggling naked and terrified in the grip of some fearsome dark monster. Once she shouted out in her sleep so wildly that she woke herself.

Before dawn she abandoned all further attempts at resting and went down to the kitchen. She saw immediately that the dishes and cutlery of the previous evening's meal had been washed and packed away. The empty wineglasses and bottle had disappeared, and the kitchen was spotless.

She switched on the coffee percolator and went to check the letter box. It was too early for the newspaper to have been delivered, so she went back and poured a cup of coffee. She knew caffeine was bad for the baby, but this morning she needed fortification.

She had taken her first sip when she smelled cigarette smoke and looked up quickly. Michael stood in the doorway with the inevitable cigarette between his lips, slanting his eyes against the spiral of smoke.

"I say, the coffee smells good." He was dressed in a silk dressing gown. His eyes were underscored with leaden smudges, and there were shadows, sickly with guilt, in the blue of his eyes. Uncertainty and diffidence puckered at the corners of his mouth as he said, "I thought you were in Athens. I'm sorry."

They stared at each other across the kitchen for only a few seconds, but it seemed like an age. Then Isabella stood up and crossed to him. She reached up on tiptoe to embrace him, and kissed him full on the mouth. Then she held him close and pressed her cheek against his cheek, which was raspy with new beard.

"I love you, Mickey. You are the dearest, sweetest person in my life. I love you without reservation or qualification."

He sighed deeply. "Thank you, Bella. I should have known that you would be generous and understanding, but I was afraid. You'll never know how terrified I've been that you might reject me."

"No, Mickey. You had no reason to worry."

"I was going to tell you. I've been waiting for the right moment."

"You don't have to tell me, or anybody. It's your business alone."

"No, I wanted you to know. We've never had any secrets between us. I knew you would find out sooner or later. I wanted—oh God, I would have given anything for you not to have found out the way you did. It must have been a terrible shock for you."

84

She closed her eyes tightly and pressed her face harder to his, so that he could not see her expression. She tried to shut the image of what she had witnessed out of her mind. However, Michael's face in that contorted anguish of rapture still floated before her like a reel from a horror movie.

"It doesn't matter, Mickey. It makes no difference to us or to anything."

"Yes, it does, Bella," he contradicted her. Then he gently held her away from him so that he could study her face. What he saw there made him sadder. With an arm around her shoulders he led her back to her seat at the table in the breakfast nook and sat beside her on the banquette.

"Strange," he said. "In a way it's a relief that you know. I still hate the way you found out, but at last there is one person in the world with whom I can be my true self, somebody for whom I no longer have to lie and dissemble."

"Why hide it, Mickey? This is nineteen sixty-nine. If that's the way you are, why not be open? Nobody cares any more."

Michael fished a packet of Camels out of his dressing gown pocket and lit one. For a moment he studied the burning tip, then he said, "That might be true for others, but not for me." He shook his head. "Not for me. Like it or not, I'm a Courtney. There are Nana and Pater, Garry and Sean, the family, the name."

She wanted to deny it, but then she saw it was futile.

"Nana and Pater," Michael repeated. "It would destroy them. Don't think I haven't considered it—coming out of the closet." He grinned wryly. "God, what an awful expression."

She squeezed his hand hard, beginning at last to have some faint understanding of her brother's predicament. She knew he was right. He could never let Nana and Pater know. For them it would be as bad—no, it would be worse than Tara. Tara had been a foreigner; Michael was Courtney blood. They would not survive it. It would destroy part of them, and Michael was too kind, too unselfish, too loyal ever to let that happen. "How long have you known—about your nature?" she asked quietly.

"Since prep school," he answered frankly. "Since those first prepubescent gropings and explorations in the showers and the bog shop . . ." He broke off. "I've tried to deny myself. I've tried not to let it happen. Sometimes for months, a year even—but it's like a beast inside me, Bella, a raving beast over which I have no control."

She smiled softly, indulgently. "As Nanny would say, it's the hot Courtney blood, Mickey. We all have it; none of us can control it very well, not Pater and Garry and Sean—nor you and I.''

"You don't mind talking about it?" he asked diffidently. "I've kept it bottled up so long."

"You talk as much as you like. I'm here to listen."

"I've lived with it for fifteen years now and I suppose I'll have to live with it for another fifty. The strange thing—something that would make it even worse as far as the family is concerned—is that I am attracted by colored men. That would aggravate my guilt and degradation in the eyes of Nana and Pater, in the eyes of our courts at home. God, the scandal if I were discovered and charged under that Immorality Act of our enlightened government!'' He shuddered, stubbed out the cigarette and immediately lit another from the crumpled pack.

"I don't know why black men attract me so powerfully. I've thought about it a great deal. I suppose I'm like Tara, in a way. Perhaps it's a kind of racial guilt, a subconscious desire to appease and mollify their anger.'' He chuckled sardonically. "We've been screwing them for so long, why not give them a chance to get their own back?''

"Don't!'' Isabella said softly. "Don't degrade and belittle yourself by talking like that, Mickey. You are a fine and decent person. We are, none of us, responsible for our instincts.''

Isabella remembered Michael as the gentle, shy boy, self-effacing but with boundless affection and concern for every being around him, yet always with that wistful air of sadness about him. She understood now the source of that sadness. She realized what spiritual agony he must have been suffering, what he still suffered. Her heart went out to him as it never had before. The last vestiges of her physical repugnance faded. She knew she would never again hate what she had seen taking place in the room upstairs. She would think only of the agonies that still lay in wait for this dear person, and her instincts became fiercer and more protective.

"My poor darling Mickey,'' she whispered.

"Poor no longer,'' he denied. "Not with your love and understanding.''

# 7

Two days later, while Michael was out on one of his interviews and Isabella's desk was a jumble of open books and scattered papers, the telephone rang. She reached for it distractedly, and for a moment she did not recognize the husky voice or understand the words.

"Ramón? Is that you? Is something wrong? Where are you? Athens?"

"I'm at the flat . . ."

"Here in London?"

"Yes. Can you come quickly? I need you."

Isabella pushed the Mini through the lunch-hour traffic, and when she reached his flat she went up the stairs two at a time and arrived on the landing flushed and breathless. She fumbled with the key and at last threw the door open.

"Ramón!" There was no reply, and she ran through to the bedroom. His valise was open on the bed, and a crumpled shirt lay in the middle of the floor. It was stained with blood—patches of old dried blood, almost mulberry black in color, and also newer, brighter, blood.

"Ramón! Oh God! Ramón! Can you hear me?"

She ran to the bathroom door. It was locked from the inside. She stood back and kicked the lock with her heel. It was one of the karate kicks he had taught her, and the flimsy lock snapped and the door flew open.

Ramón lay on the tiled floor beside the toilet. He must have grabbed at the shelf above the washbasin as he fell, and her cosmetics had cascaded down into the basin and across the floor. He was naked from the waist up, but his chest was heavily strapped with bandages. She could tell at a glance that the bandages had been tied by a professional hand. Like his abandoned shirt, the white bandages were soaked with concentric rings of blood, some dark and old, some fresh and wet.

She dropped onto her knees beside him and turned his head. His skin was pale, almost opalescent, with a sheen of nauseous sweat upon it. She lifted his head into her lap. Then she snatched up the facecloth that hung over the edge of the bath. She could just reach the cold-water tap from where she sat. She soaked the cloth and wiped his face and neck.

His eyelids quivered and opened, and he looked up at her.

"Ramón."

His eyes focused. "I keeled over," he murmured.

"My darling, what happened to you? You've been badly hurt."

"Help me to the bed," he said.

Kneeling beside him, she propped him into a sitting position. She was almost as strong as a man, with arms and torso trained by riding and tennis. However, she knew that even she could not lift him unaided.

"Can you stand if I steady you?"

He grunted and made the effort, but halfway to his feet he winced and clutched at the bloodstained bandages as the pain knifed through him.

"Take it easy," she whispered.

For a minute he remained doubled over, then he straightened slowly. "All right." He gritted his teeth, and she led him through, taking most of his weight on her shoulder, and lowered him onto the bed.

"Did you come all the way from Athens in this condition?" she asked incredulously.

He nodded the lie. He had summoned Isabella to Athens to act as a courier. The need had risen urgently and unexpectedly. There had been no other agent available immediately, and it was time for her to be blooded in the field. She was ripe for it. By now she had been conditioned to accept his orders without question, and it was an easy first assignment that he had planned for her. She was the perfect innocent, an attractive and pregnant female who would instantly evoke sympathy. She was unmarked, unknown to any of the world's intelligence organizations, including the Mossad. In the jargon of the trade, she was a virgin. In addition, she carried a South African passport, and Israel had cordial, indeed intimate, relations with that country.

The plan was for her to catch the flight from Athens to Tel Aviv, make the pickup and leave by the same route. It would have been a day's work. The plan had foundered when she had not been able to make the flight to Athens. The pickup was crucial. It involved details of the cooperation between Israeli and South African scientists in the development of tactical nuclear weapons systems. Even though there was a high probability that he was marked by the Mossad, Ramón had been forced to make the pickup himself.

He had disguised his appearance as best he was able, and of course he had gone unarmed: it was madness to attempt to carry a weapon through an Israeli security check. He had used his Mexican passport in an assumed name. However, they must have gotten on to him at Ben Gurion Airport and tailed him to the pickup.

He had spotted the tail and taken emergency evasion procedure, but they had cornered him. He had broken the neck of one Mossad agent and in return had taken this hit. Even severely wounded, he had made it to the PLO safe house in Tel Aviv. Within twelve hours they had smuggled him out on their pipeline to Syria.

However, London was his safe ground. Despite the risks and his injuries, he had too much in play to remain in Damascus. The local KGB head of station had escorted him onto the Aeroflot flight to London. He had made the call to Isabella as he staggered into the flat. Then he had just managed to reach the bathroom before he collapsed.

"I must call a doctor," she said.

"No doctor!" Despite his weakness, his voice took on that cold, sibilant tone she was conditioned to obey.

"What must I do?" she asked.

"Get me the telephone," he ordered, and she hurried to bring the instrument through from its jack in the sitting room.

"Ramón, you look awful. At least let me get you something— a bowl of soup, darling?"

He nodded agreement but did not look up from the telephone as he dialed. She went through to the kitchen and heated up a can of thick vegetable soup. As she worked she could hear him speaking to somebody in Spanish on the telephone. However, her recent exercise with the Linguaphone course was insufficient to allow her to follow the conversation. She took the tray of soup and crackers through to him as he hung up.

"Darling, what has happened to you? Why won't you let me call the doctor?"

He grimaced. If a British doctor saw that injury, he would be bound to report it. If the Cuban embassy doctor came to the flat, it would almost certainly compromise this address and

89

Ramón's cover. So he had made alternative arrangements. However, he did not answer her question directly.

"I want you to go out immediately. Go to the westbound platform of Sloane Square Underground station and walk the full length of it slowly. Somebody will put an envelope in your hand . . ."

"Who? How will I recognize him?"

"You won't," he answered brusquely. "He will recognize you. You will not speak or acknowledge the messenger in any way. In the envelope will be a doctor's prescription and a detailed list of instructions to treat my injury. Take the prescription to the all-night chemist in Piccadilly Circus and bring the supplies back here."

"Yes, Ramón, but you haven't told me how you hurt yourself."

"You must learn to do as you are told—without all those tiresome questions. Now go!"

"Yes, Ramón." She picked up her jacket and scarf, then stooped over the bed to kiss him.

"I love you," she whispered. Halfway down the stairs, she stopped suddenly. Nobody, with the possible exception of Nana, had ever spoken to her in such forceful terms since childhood. Even her father made requests; he did not give her orders. Yet here she was scampering breathlessly as a schoolgirl to obey. She pulled a face and ran down into the street.

She had not reached the end of the Underground platform when, from behind, she felt a light touch on her wrist and an envelope was slipped into her hand. She glanced over her shoulder, but the messenger was already walking away. He wore a blue wool cap and dark overcoat, but she could not see his face.

At the chemist's the dispenser read the prescription and remarked, "You have somebody badly injured?" But she shook her head.

"I'm just Doctor Alves's receptionist. I don't know."

And he made up the package of medicines without further comment.

Ramón seemed to be sleeping, but he opened his eyes immediately when she entered the bedroom. All her previous fears for him returned in full force when she saw his face. His eyes seemed to have sunk into dark bruised cavities, and his skin had the pallor of a two-day-old corpse. However, she thrust aside her personal misgivings and steeled herself to act calmly.

While she was at university she had taken a course in first aid with the Red Cross. At Weltevreden she had often assisted the visiting doctor at his weekly clinic for the colored employees. She had seen enough missing fingers, crushed feet and other injuries inflicted by farm machinery to have overcome any squeamishness.

She laid out the supplies from the chemist and read swiftly through the simple typed instructions on the envelope. She washed in the bathroom basin, adding half a cup of Dettol to the water, then sat Ramón upright and began unwrapping the bandages.

The blood had dried, and the dressing stuck to the edges of the wound. He closed his eyes, and a light sweat dewed his forehead and chin as she worked it loose.

"I'm sorry," she whispered. "I'm trying not to hurt you."

The dressing came away at last, and she suppressed an exclamation as she saw the wounds. There was a deep puncture low down in the side of the chest and a second corresponding ragged aperture in the smooth muscles of his back that was clogged with a black plug of clotted blood. The skin around the wounds was hot and inflamed, and there was the faint, sickly smell of infection.

She knew instantly how those injuries had been inflicted. On her last visit to her brother Sean's hunting concession in the Zambezi valley, they had answered a call for assistance from a nearby Batonka village that had been attacked by terrorists. That was where she had first seen the distinctive entry puncture and enlarged exit of a through-and-through bullet wound. Ramón was watching her face, so she made no comment and tried to keep her expression neutral as she cleaned the area around the wounds with disinfectant, then strapped fresh dressings in place with crisp white bandages.

She knew she had done a proficient job, and as she eased him back on the pillows he murmured, "Good. You know what you are doing."

"Not finished yet. I have to give you a jab. Doctor's orders." And then, in an attempt at humor: "Show me your gorgeous bum, chum!"

She stood at the foot of the bed and removed his shoes and socks, then took a grip on the cuffs of his trousers and, while he arched his back and lifted himself slightly, pulled them off.

"Now your underpants." She drew them down and sighed with mock relief. "At least you didn't damage any of my special goodies. That would have made me really mad." This time he smiled, then rolled cautiously onto his side.

She filled the disposable syringe and injected an ampoule of broad-spectrum antibiotic into the smooth hard swell of his buttock. Then she covered him carefully with the down-filled duvet.

"Now," she said firmly, "two of these pills—and rest."

He did not protest, and when he had taken the sleeping pills she kissed him and switched out the bedside light.

"I'll be in the sitting room if you need me."

In the morning his color was much improved; obviously the antibiotic had done its work. His temperature was down, and his eyes were clear.

"How did you sleep?" she asked.

"Those pills are dynamite. It was like falling over a cliff. Now I could use a bath."

She ran the bath and helped him into it. Once he was seated waist deep, she used the sponge to clean around the edges of the bandage. Then her attentions moved lower and she plied the soapy sponge with cunning.

"Ah, you may be damaged on top, but down below things are all working very satisfactorily, I am glad to report."

"Merely as a matter of interest, Nurse, is what you are doing at the moment business or pleasure?"

"A little of one and considerably more of the other," she confessed.

Back on the bed, he protested halfheartedly when she filled the syringe with another measure of antibiotic, but she said sternly, "Why are men such cowards? Bottoms up!" And he rolled over obediently. "Good boy." She nodded as she withdrew the needle and swabbed the puncture mark with alcohol. "Now you've earned your breakfast, and I've got you a kipper as a reward."

She enjoyed nursing him. For once she was in a position to give him orders and have them obeyed. While she was busy in the kitchen, she heard him on the telephone, speaking Spanish that was too rapid and complicated for her to follow. She listened, trying, despite her limitations, to make sense of it, and the misgivings that had troubled her most of the night returned in full force. To fend them off she slipped down the stairs and ran to the flower and fruit stall on the corner opposite the entrance to the Tube station.

She chose a dark red Papa Meillon rosebud and a perfect golden peach, and ran all the way back. Ramón was still speaking on the telephone when she let herself in.

She arranged the rose and the peach on the breakfast tray. When she took them through to him he looked up from the

92

telephone and rewarded her with one of his rare and treasured smiles.

She sat on the edge of the bed and carefully forked the succulent flesh off the kipper bone and fed it to him, a mouthful at a time, while he continued his telephone conversation. When he had finished, she took the tray back to the kitchen, and while she was washing up she heard him hang up the telephone receiver.

Quickly she returned to the bedroom and settled down on her own side of the bed with her legs curled up sideways under her in that feminine double-jointed fashion that is impossible for a man to emulate.

"Ramón," she said quietly and seriously, "that is a bullet wound."

His eyes went cold and deadly green, and he stared back at her without expression.

"How did it happen?" she asked. He was silent, watching her, and she felt her resolution fade, but she steeled herself to continue.

"You are not a banker, are you?"

"I am a banker most of the time," he said softly.

"And at other times, what are you then?"

"I am a patriot. I serve my country."

She felt a hot rush of relief. During the night she had imagined a hundred horrid possibilities: that he was a drug smuggler, or a bank robber, or a member of some criminal syndicate involved in a gang war.

"Spain," she said. "You are a member of the Spanish secret service, is that it?"

He was silent again, watching her with careful calculation. He was a master of progressive revelation. She must be drawn in gradually, a little at a time, so that she was neither unwilling nor resistant, like an insect entrapped and slowly engulfed in a puddle of honey.

"You must realize, Bella, that if that were indeed the case I would not be able to tell you."

"Of course." She nodded happily. She had known another man from this dangerous and exciting world of espionage and intrigue. He was the only man before Ramón with whom she had believed herself to be in love. He had been a brigadier in the South African security police, another powerful, ruthless one who could match her spirit and control her wilder emotional excesses. She had lived as man and wife with Lothar De La Rey in the Johannesburg flat for six marvelously stormy months.

When he had ended it suddenly and without warning, she had been shattered. Now she realized that it had been shallow infatuation, nothing to compare even remotely with what she had found in Ramón Machado. "I understand completely, Ramón darling, and you can trust me. I won't ask any more silly questions."

"I have trusted you with my life already," he said. "You were the first person I called upon for help."

"I'm proud of that. Because you are Spanish and because you are my lover and the father of my baby, I feel myself to be in a large part Spanish as well. I want to help you any way I am able."

"Yes," he nodded. "I understand that. I have thought about the baby." He reached out and touched her stomach, and his hand felt cool and hard. "I want my son to be born in Spain, so that he, too, will be a Spaniard and his claim to the title will be secured."

She was startled. She had taken it for granted that she would have her baby here in London. The gynecologist had already made a tentative reservation at the maternity home.

"Will you do that for me, Bella? Will you make my son a full Spaniard?" he asked.

She hesitated not a moment longer. "Yes, of course, my darling. I will do whatever you wish." She leaned over him and kissed him. Then she snuggled down on the pillow beside him, careful not to jostle his injuries. "If that is what you want, then we will have to start making arrangements," she suggested.

"I have already done so," he confessed. "There is an excellent private clinic just outside Málaga. I have a friend at the bank's head office in Málaga who will find us a flat and a maid. I have arranged a transfer to the head office, so that I will be with you when the baby is born."

"It sounds so exciting," she agreed. "And if you get to choose where the baby is to be born, then I choose where we marry when we eventually can. That's fair, isn't it?"

He smiled. "Yes, that is fair."

"I want to be married at Weltevreden. There is an old slave church on the estate, built a hundred and fifty years ago. My grandmother, Nana, had it completely restored and renovated for my brother Garry's wedding. It's exquisite, and Nana filled it with flowers for Garry and Holly. I will have arum lilies. Some people believe they are unlucky, but they are my favorite flowers and I'm not superstitious, or not much anyway . . ."

Patiently he let her ramble on, occasionally murmuring encouragement, awaiting the precise moment for his next revelation. Finally she gave him the opening.

"But we are cutting things a little fine, Ramón darling. Nana will want at least six weeks to make all the arrangements, and by then I am going to be the size of a house. They'll play the 'Baby Elephant Walk' as I come down the aisle."

"No, Bella," he contradicted her. "At your wedding, you will be slim and beautiful—because you will no longer be pregnant."

She sat bolt upright on the bed. "What are you trying to tell me, Ramón? Something has happened, hasn't it?"

"Yes, you are right. There is bad news, I'm afraid. I have heard from Natalie. She's still in Florida. She is being obstinate, and there are legal delays."

"Oh, Ramón!"

"I am as unhappy as you are about it. If there was anything I could do, believe me, I would do it."

"I hate her," she whispered.

"Yes, sometimes I feel that way, too. But truly it is not a disaster, only an inconvenience at the most. We will still be married, and you will still have your little slave church and your arum lilies. It is just that our son will be born before that happens."

"Promise me, Ramón, swear it to me—that we will be married as soon as you are free."

"I swear it to you."

She settled down beside him, cradling her head on his good shoulder, hiding her face so he could not guess how disappointed she truly was.

"I hate her, but I love you," she said.

Ramón gave a grim little smile of satisfaction that she could not see.


He was confined to the flat by his wound for another week, and there was time to talk. She told Ramón about Michael and was flattered by the interest he showed in her brother.

She expanded on Michael's virtues, and on their special relationship. Ramón listened and drew her out gently. He was so easy to talk to. She looked upon him as an extension of herself. She found herself going on to tell him about the rest of her family, about what lay behind the public mask that they as a group presented to the world; about their secrets and their weaknesses and their scandals, about Shasa and Tara's divorce. She even told him about the dark suspicion that Nana had once given birth to a bastard son in the wild southern deserts of Africa.

"Of course, nobody has ever proved it. I don't think anybody would dare. Nana is a formidable force." She laughed. "And that is understating the fact. However, there was definitely some very fishy business back there in the nineteen-twenties."

In the end, Ramón brought the conversation back to Michael. "If he's here in London, why haven't you introduced us? Are you ashamed of me?"

"Oh, may I? May I bring him round here, Ramón? I've told him a little about you, about us. I know he'd love to meet you, and I'm sure you will like him. He's the only truly sweet and good Courtney. The rest of us—!" She rolled her eyes comically.

Michael arrived with a bottle of his father's burgundy under his arm. "I thought of bringing flowers," he explained, "but then I decided to get something useful instead."

He and Ramón scrutinized each other carefully as they shook hands. Isabella watched them anxiously, willing them to like each other.

"How are your ribs?" Michael asked. Isabella had told him that Ramón had taken a toss from his horse and broken three ribs.

"Your sister is holding me prisoner. There is nothing wrong with me—nothing a glass of that excellent burgundy won't cure." Ramón displayed that rare warmth and special charm of his that were irresistible. Isabella felt quite giddy with relief. Her two most favorite and important people were going to like each other.

She took the burgundy through to the kitchen to find a corkscrew. When she returned with the open bottle and two glasses, Michael was settled in the chair beside the bed and they were already engrossed in conversation. "We get the airmail edition of your paper, *The Golden City Mail*, at the bank," Ramón was telling him. "I particularly like your financial and economic coverage."

"Ah, you are in banking." Michael nodded. "Bella didn't tell me that."

"Merchant banking. We specialize in sub-Saharan Africa." And they were away at a conversational gallop. Bella kicked off her flat shoes, rolled up the bottoms of her blue jeans and perched on the bed beside Ramón. Although she took no part in the conversation, she listened avidly.

She had no idea that Ramón had such a grasp of African facts and realities, such a deep knowledge of the personalities and places and events that made up the rich and fascinating mosaic of her native land. Compared to this discussion, all her previous conversations with him had been shallow and trivial. Listening to the two of them, she learned new facts and heard ideas expressed that were totally fresh to her.

Michael was obviously as impressed as she was. His pleasure at finding a challenging and stimulating intellect on which to try out his own interpretations and beliefs was evident.

It was after midnight; the original bottle of wine and another that Isabella had dug out of her tiny stock in the kitchen was empty. The bedroom was thick with the smoke of Michael's Camels before she looked at her watch and exclaimed, "You were invited for one drink, Mickey, and Ramón is an invalid. Away with you, now." She went to fetch his overcoat.

While she helped him into it, Ramón said softly from the bed, "If you are doing a series on the political exiles, it wouldn't be complete without one on Raleigh Tabaka."

Mickey laughed ruefully. "I'd give my chance of salvation for a crack at Tabaka, the mystery man. It just ain't possible. As old Rudyard put it, 'If you know the track of the morning mist, then you know where his pickets are.' "

"I've met him in the line of duty at the bank. We keep tabs on all the players. I might be able to arrange for you to meet him," Ramón told him.

Michael froze and stared at him with one arm in the sleeve of his coat. "I've been trying to get hold of him for five years," he said. "If you could—"

"Call me tomorrow, around lunchtime," Ramón told him. "I'll see what I can do."

At the door Michael kissed Isabella. "I take it you are not coming home tonight?"

"This is home." She hugged him. "My temporary residence at Cadogan Square was just to impress you, but I don't have to do that any longer."

"He's a knockout, your Ramón," Michael said, and she felt a sudden shocking stab of jealousy, as though another woman had challenged her for Ramón's affection. She tried to suppress it, the only ugly feeling she had ever harbored toward Mickey. But the pain persisted as she went back to the bedroom and deepened again as Ramón said, "I like him. Your brother is one of the superior beings—they are rare enough."

She felt ashamed of her unkind feelings toward Mickey. How could she harbor the slightest doubt that Ramón was a man, a natural man? She knew he liked Michael only for his charm and fine intellect, and because he was her brother. And yet—and yet that dirty sneaking feeling persisted.

She stooped over the bed and kissed Ramón with a passion that surprised even her. After the first moment of shock, his mouth opened and their tongues slithered and rolled around each other, slippery as mating eels.

She broke away at last and looked up at him. "You swan around Europe for weeks on end, leaving me pining, and when you do come home you lie around in bed, hogging food and sleeping," she accused him in a husky voice, tight with her need of him. "And never a thought for the maid or the nurse. Well, Master Ramón, I'm here to tell you it's payday, and I've come to collect."

"I'll need some help," he warned her.

"You just lie still. Don't do a thing. Nurse's orders. We'll take care of the details."

She drew back the bed sheets and reached down under them. Her voice was a languorous coo. "We'll take care of things, he and I. You keep out of it."

She straddled him gently, taking care not to touch his bandaged chest. As she sank down on top of him, she saw her own deep need reflected in the green mirror of his eyes, and she felt all her doubts evaporate. He belonged to her and to her alone.

Afterward she lay at his good side, close and secure and happy, and they talked drowsily, hovering on the edge of sleep in the darkness. When he mentioned Michael again, she felt a twinge of remorse at her earlier doubts. She was so relaxed, so much off guard, and she trusted Ramón as she did herself. She wanted to explain and share it with him.

"Poor Mickey, I never suspected the agony he has had to endure all these years. I am closer to him than any person in the world, and yet even I did not know about it. A few days ago, I found out, quite by accident, that he is a practicing homosexual . . ."

The words were out before she could stop them, and suddenly she was appalled by what she had done. Mickey had trusted her, and she shivered, waiting for some reaction from Ramón. However, it was not what she had expected.

"Yes," he agreed calmly, "I knew that. There are some indications which are unmistakable. I knew it within the first half hour."

She felt a rush of relief. Ramón had known, so there was no betrayal on her part.

"You are not repelled by it?"

"No, not at all," Ramón answered. "Many of them are creative and intelligent and productive people."

"Yes, Mickey is like that," she agreed eagerly. "I was shocked at first, but now it means little to me. He is still my darling brother. However, I do worry about him being caught up in a criminal prosecution."

"I don't think there is much chance of that. Society has accepted—"

"You don't understand, Ramón. Michael likes black boys, and he lives in South Africa."

"Yes," Ramón agreed thoughtfully. "That could present some problems."

# 8

Michael phoned the flat from a pay phone in Fleet Street a little before noon. Ramón answered on the second ring. "The news is good," Ramón assured him. "Raleigh Tabaka is in London, and he knows of you. Did you write a series of newspaper articles back in nineteen-sixty under the title 'Rage'?"

"Yes, a series of six for the *Mail*; it got the paper banned by the security police."

"Tabaka read them and liked them. He has agreed to meet you."

"My God, Ramón. I can't tell you how grateful I am. This is the most marvelous break—"

Ramón cut short his thanks. "He'll meet you this evening, but he has laid down some conditions."

"Anything," Michael agreed quickly.

"You are to come to the meeting alone. No weapons, of course, and no tape recorder or camera. He does not want his voice or appearance on record. There is a pub in Shepherd's Bush." He gave Michael the address. "Be there at seven this evening. Carry a bunch of flowers—carnations. Someone will meet and take you to the rendezvous.''

"Right, I've got that."

"One other condition. Tabaka wants to read all your copy on the interview before you print it.''

Michael was silent for a slow count of five. The request contravened all his journalistic principles. It amounted to a form of censorship and cast a slur on his professional ethics. However, the price was an interview with one of the most wanted men in Africa.

"All right," he agreed heavily. "I'll give him first read." Then his tone brightened. "I owe you a favor, Ramón. I'll come around and tell you all about it tomorrow evening."

"Don't forget the bottle of wine."

Michael rushed back to Cadogan Square. As soon as he reached the telephone he canceled all the rest of the day's appointments, then settled down to plan his strategy for the interview. His questions had to be searching, but not so barbed as to cool Tabaka's cooperative mood. He had to be sincere and sympathetic, and yet, at the same time, severe, for he was dealing with a man who had deliberately chosen the path of violence and bloodshed. To achieve credibility his questions must be balanced and neutral, and at the same time designed to draw the man out. In particular he did not want a mere recital of all the radical slogans and revolutionary jargon.

"The term 'terrorist' is generally applied to a person who for reasons of political coercion commits an act of violence on a target of a nonmilitary nature during which there is a high probability of injury or death being inflicted on innocent bystanders. Do you accept that definition and, if so, does the label 'terrorist' apply to Umkhonto we Sizwe?''

He worked that out as his first question, and lit another Camel as he studied it.

"Good." That was what you called jumping straight in with both feet, but perhaps it needed a little honing and polishing. He worked on steadily, and by five-thirty he had prepared twenty questions that satisfied him. He made himself a smoked salmon sandwich and drank a bottle of Guinness while he reviewed and rehearsed his script.

Then he shrugged on his overcoat and armed himself with the bunch of carnations that he had bought at the corner stall. It was drizzling. He flagged down a taxi in Sloane Street.

The pub was steamy with body heat. The condensation ran down the stained-glass windows in rainbow rivulets. Michael displayed the carnations ostentatiously and peered through the soft blue mist of tobacco smoke. Almost immediately a neatly dressed Indian in a three-piece blue wool suit left the bar and made his way down the crowded room.

"Mr. Courtney, my name is Govan."

"From Natal." Michael recognized the accent.

"From Stanger." The man smiled. "But that was six years ago." He glanced at the shoulders of Michael's coat. "Has it stopped raining? Good, we can walk. It's not far."

His guide struck out down the main thoroughfare. Within a hundred yards he turned abruptly into a narrow alleyway and increased his pace. Michael had to trot to match him. He was wheezing when they reached the exit to the alley.

"Damned fags—I must cut down."

Govan turned out of the alley, and stopped abruptly around the corner. Michael was about to speak, but Govan gripped his arm to silence him. They waited for five minutes. Only when it was certain that they were not being followed did he relax his grip.

"You don't trust me." Michael smiled and dumped the carnations in the rubbish bin that bore a warning of the penalties for littering.

"We do not trust anybody." Govan led him away. "Especially not the Boers. They are learning new kinds of nastiness each day."

Ten minutes later they stopped again outside a modern block of flats in a broad well-lit street. There was a rank of Mercedeses and Jaguars parked at the curb. The lawn and small garden in front of the apartment block were carefully groomed. It was clearly an expensive residential enclave. "I will leave you here," said Govan. "Go in. There is a porter in the lobby. Tell him that you are a guest of Mr. Kendrick, Flat 505."

The lobby was in keeping with the façade of the building, Italian marble floor, wood-paneled walls and gilded doors to the lift. The uniformed porter saluted him. "Yes, Mr. Courtney, Mr. Kendrick is expecting you. Please go up to the fifth floor."

When the lift doors opened, there were two unsmiling young colored men waiting for him.

"Come this way, Mr. Courtney."

They led him down the carpeted passage to number 505 and let him into the flat.

As the door closed, they stepped in on each side of him and swiftly but thoroughly patted him down. Michael lifted his arms and spread his legs cooperatively. As they searched him, he

101

looked around him with a journalist's eye. The flat had been decorated with flair and taste—and money.

His escorts stepped back satisfied, and one of them opened the double doors ahead of him.

"Please," he said, and Michael went through into a spacious and beautifully decorated room. The sofas and easy chairs were covered with cream-colored Connolly leather. The thick pile of the wall-to-wall carpet was a soft cocoa. The tables and the cocktail bar were in crystal and chrome. On the walls hung four large Hockney paintings, from his swimming pool series.

Fifty thousand quid each, Michael estimated. Then his eyes flicked to the figure that stood in the center of the room.

There had been no recent photograph of this man, but Michael recognized him instantly from a blurred press picture in the *Mail*'s archives that dated back years to the Sharpeville era and the subsequent inquiries.

"Mr. Tabaka," he said. He was as tall as Michael, probably six foot one, but broader in the shoulder and narrower in the waist.

"Mr. Courtney." Raleigh Tabaka came forward to offer his hand. He moved like a boxer, fluidly in balance, poised and aggressive.

"You live in style?" Michael put a question in his voice.

Raleigh Tabaka frowned slightly. "This is the apartment of a sympathizer. I have no call for such frippery." His voice was firm and deep, melodious with the unmistakable echoes of Africa. Despite the denial, his suit was of pure new wool and draped elegantly over his warrior's frame. There were the tiny stirrups of the Gucci motif on his silk tie. He was an impressive man.

"I am grateful for this opportunity to meet you," Michael said.

"I read your 'Rage' series," Raleigh told him, studying Michael with those onyx eyes. "You understand my people. You examined their aspirations with a fair and impartial eye."

"Not everybody would agree with you—especially those in authority in South Africa."

Raleigh smiled. His teeth were even and white. "I have very little to tell you that will comfort them now. But first may I offer you a drink?"

"A gin and tonic."

"Ah, yes, the fuel on which the journalistic mind functions." Raleigh's tone was scornful. He went to the bar and poured a clear liquid from a crystal decanter, then squirted the tonic from a hand-held nozzle connected to the bar by a chrome-sheathed hose.

"You don't drink?" Michael asked.

Raleigh frowned again. "With so much work to be done, why should I cloud my mind?" He glanced at his wristwatch. "We have only an hour, then I must go."

"I mustn't waste a minute of it," Michael agreed. As they settled facing each other in the cream Connolly leather chairs, he said, "I have all the background I need: your place and date of birth, your education at Waterford School in Swaziland, your relationship to Moses Gama, your present position in the ANC. May I go on from there?" Raleigh inclined his head in assent.

"The term 'terrorist' is generally applied to . . ." Michael repeated his definition, and Raleigh's features tightened with anger as he listened.

"There are no innocent bystanders in South Africa," he cut in brusquely. "It is a war. Nobody can claim to be a neutral. We are all combatants."

"No matter how young, how old? No matter how sympathetic to your people's aspirations?"

"There are no bystanders," Raleigh repeated. "From the cradle to the grave, we are all in the battlefield. We all fall into one of two camps, either the oppressed or the oppressors."

"No man or woman has a choice?" Michael asked.

"Yes, there is a choice—to take one or the other side. Neutrality is not an option."

"If a bomb explodes in a crowded supermarket, some of your own people, your own sympathizers, may die or be maimed. Would you feel remorse?"

"Remorse is not a revolutionary emotion, just as it is not an emotion of the perpetrators of apartheid. Those who die are either enemy casualties or courageous and honorable sacrifices. In war both are unavoidable, even desirable."

Michael's pen dashed across the sheets of his notepad as he attempted to capture these frightful pronouncements. He felt shaken and aroused, both excited and terrified by what he was hearing. He had the feeling that, like a moth that circled the flame too closely, he would be scarred by the white heat of this man's rage. He knew he could faithfully record the words, but he could never reproduce the fierce spirit in which they were uttered.

The allotted hour sped away too fast, as Michael tried to use every second to the full, and when at last Raleigh glanced at his wristwatch and stood up he tried desperately to prolong it.

"You have spoken of your child warriors," he said. "What age, how young are they?"

"I will show you children of seven who will bear arms, and commanders of sections who are ten years old."

"You will show me?" Michael asked. "Is that possible—that you will show me?"

Raleigh studied him for a long moment. The intelligence Ramón Machado had passed on to him seemed to be valid. Here was a useful tool, one that could be fitted to his hand and his purpose. He might be well worth the effort that would be needed to develop him fully. He was one of Lenin's "useful idiots" who, to begin with, could be made to serve the cause unwittingly. Later, of course, it would be different. At first, he would be the spade and the plowshare; only later, when the time was ripe, would he be forged into the sword of war.

"Michael Courtney," he said softly, "I am disposed to trust you. I think that you are a decent and enlightened man. If you keep my trust, I will open doors for you into places you have never dreamed existed. I will take you into the streets and hovels of Soweto. Into the hearts of my people—and, yes, I will show you the children."

"When?" Michael demanded anxiously, aware that his time was running out.

"Soon," Raleigh promised. At that moment they heard the front door open.

"How will I find you?" Michael persisted.

"You won't. I will find you when I am ready."

The double doors to the sitting room swung open and a man stood at the threshold. Even in his preoccupation with Raleigh Tabaka's promise, Michael was struck, his attention was diverted. He recognized the newcomer instantly, even in his street clothes. The name Kendrick should have alerted him.

"This is our host who owns this apartment," Raleigh Tabaka introduced them. "Oliver Kendrick, this is Michael Courtney."

"I saw you dance Spartacus," Michael said, his voice subdued with awe. "Three times. Such virility and athleticism."

Oliver Kendrick smiled and crossed the room with the springing gait of the ballet dancer, and offered Michael his hand. It was surprisingly narrow and cool, and his bones felt light as those of a bird. It was appropriate, for they called him "the black swan." His neck was long and elegant as that of the bird, and his eyes were as luminous as a mountain pool reflected in the moonlight. His skin had the same dark luster.

Michael thought that close up he was more beautiful even than he had appeared in the romantic lighting of the stage set, and his breathing cramped. The dancer left his hand in Michael's grip as he turned his head to Raleigh. "Don't rush away, Raleigh," he pleaded in that musical West Indian lilt.

"I must go." Raleigh shook his head. "I'm afraid I have a plane to catch."

Oliver Kendrick turned back to Michael, still holding his hand. "I have had a beastly day. I swear I could simply curl up and die. Don't leave me alone, Michael. Do stay and distract me. You can be entertaining and distracting, can't you, Michael?"

Raleigh Tabaka left him and let himself out of the flat. One of his men was waiting for him outside the door, but they did not leave the building. Instead the man led Raleigh only a short distance down the passageway to a less ostentatious doorway that led into a second flat, much smaller and starkly furnished. Raleigh went through to the inner room, and the second of his men made to stand up from the chair beside the lit window in the side wall.

Raleigh gestured to him to remain seated and crossed to the window. It was of unusual shape, tall and narrow, like a full-length dressing mirror. The glass was shaded with that slight opacity that was characteristic of a two-way mirror viewed from the reverse side.

The room beyond was a bedroom, lavishly furnished like the rest of Oliver Kendrick's apartment. The color scheme was pale oyster and mushroom, and the satin bedspread matched exactly the shade of the deep pile of the carpet. Hidden lighting glimmered and glowed on the mirrored tiles of the ceiling. Set in an alcove facing the bed was an ancient phallic symbol carved from amber colored obsidian, a precious antique from a Hindu temple.

The room was empty, and Raleigh turned his attention to the camera equipment that stood ready, aimed through the two-way mirror.

The apartment and the camera equipment belonged to Oliver Kendrick. He had loaned it to Raleigh on previous occasions. It was odd that a man of Kendrick's talent and fame would consent to take part in an arranged tableau such as this. However, not only did he do so willingly, he had actually offered his equipment and his services to Raleigh. He participated with such unfeigned enthusiasm and inventive delight that it was obvious that this was very much to his particular taste. His only stipulation was that Raleigh hand over to him a copy of the videotapes and photographs to add to his huge private collection. The video equipment was of the very finest professional standard. Raleigh had been impressed by the quality of reproduction even in this low-light environment.

Raleigh glanced at his wristwatch again. He could safely leave the rest of it to his two bodyguards. They had done this before. However, a perverse curiosity made him linger. It was almost half an hour before the door to the bedroom opened and Kendrick and Michael Courtney entered. Raleigh's two assistants moved quickly to their positions, one to the video recorder, the other to the big black Hasselblad camera on its tripod. The still camera was loaded with monochrome theatrical film, rated at 3000 ASA, that rendered crisp prints in the poorest light conditions.

In the room beyond, the two men embraced, a long lingering kiss with open mouths, and the video recorder emitted a faint electric hum. The sound of the shutter of the Hasselblad was much louder, almost explosive, in the quiet dark room.

At one stage, as the white man lay expectantly in the center of the oyster satin bedspread, Kendrick crossed naked to stand in front of the two-way mirror. He pretended to examine his own body, in reality flaunting it before the men who, he knew, were watching on the far side of the glass. His musculature was extraordinarily developed by long hours at the practice barre. His calves and thighs were disproportionately massive.

He gazed arrogantly into the mirror, and the diamond earrings in his lobes glittered as he turned his head on its long swan's neck, striking a theatrical pose. He ran the tip of his tongue along the inside of his parted lips and stared through the darkling mirror into Raleigh Tabaka's eyes. It was the lewdest gesture Tabaka had ever witnessed, with a chill of evil to it that made him shiver briefly. Kendrick turned away and sauntered back toward the bed. His velvety black buttocks swayed in that stylized mincing gait, and the man on the bed raised both arms to greet him.

Raleigh turned away and left the apartment. He rode down in the lift and walked out into the chill of evening. He drew his overcoat tighter across his chest and took a slow breath of clean, cold air. Then he gathered himself and walked away with the long, determined stride of a man with important work to do.

# 9

When Michael left London he took with him a little of the special joy that had filled Isabella's life over these last weeks.

She drove him out to Heathrow. "We always seem to be saying goodbye, Mickey," she whispered. "I shall miss you so, as I always do."

"I'll see you at the wedding."

"There will probably be a christening before that," she answered, and he held her at arm's length.

"You didn't tell me," he accused.

"His wife," she explained. "We are moving to Spain at the end of January. Ramón wants the baby to be born there. He will adopt it under Spanish law."

"You must let me know where you are—at all times—and remember your promise."

She nodded. "You'll be the very first one I'll call on for help—if I need it."

At the doors to the departure hall, he looked back and blew her a kiss. When he disappeared she felt chilled with loneliness.

This was a feeling that evaporated swiftly in the Iberian sunlight.

The apartment that Ramón found was in a tiny fishing village a few miles down the coast from Málaga. It occupied the top two floors and had a wide paved terrace that looked out over the tops of the pines to the blue Mediterranean beyond. During the day, while Ramón was at the bank, Isabella in her tiniest bikini lay out on a protected corner of the terrace where the cold wind could not reach her and the sun tanned her face and body to the color of dark amber while she wrote the final section of her thesis. Born in Africa, she was a child of the sun, and she had missed it desperately during the London years.

Ramón was called upon by his bank to travel as frequently as when they had lived in London. She hated to see him go, but between his trips there were lyrical interludes spent together. While in Málaga his bank duties were light and he could slip away for the entire afternoon and take her to secret and unfrequented coves along the seashore, or to out-of-the-way restaurants that served the local seafood specialties and country wines.

His wound had healed cleanly. "It was the expert nurse I had," he told her. It left a pair of dimpled scars on his chest and back that were glossy with a pink cicatrice. The sun tanned the rest of his body to a much darker tone than hers, like oiled mahogany. In contrast to the tan, his eyes seemed a lighter, brighter green.

While Ramón was away she had Adra for company. Where Ramón had found her, Isabella was never able to ascertain. However, the choice was a masterstroke, for Adra Olivares was a marvelous substitute for Nanny. In some ways she surpassed the original, for she was not as garrulous and prying and domineering as the old woman.

Adra was a slim but physically robust woman in her early forties. She had jet black hair with just a few strands of dead white that she wore sleeked back into a bun the size of a cricket ball behind her head. Her face was dark and solemn, but at the same time kind and humorous. Her hands were brown and square and powerful when she performed the housework, but quick and light when she cooked or ironed Isabella's clothes to crisp crackling perfection, or gentle and infinitely comforting when she massaged Isabella's aching back or anointed her bulging sun-browned belly with olive oil to keep the muscles supple and the skin smooth and young and free of stretch marks.

She took over Isabella's tuition in the Spanish language, and their progress was so rapid that it surprised Ramón. Within a month Isabella was reading the local newspapers with ease, arguing fluently with the plumber and the television repair man, and supporting Adra as she haggled with the stall holders in the local marketplace.

Although she loved to question Isabella about her family and Africa, Adra was not forthcoming about her own origins. Isabella presumed that she was a local woman, until one morning she noticed among the mail in their postbox an envelope addressed to her that was stamped and franked in Havana, Cuba.

When she remarked, "Is it from your husband or family, Adra? Who is writing to you from Cuba?" the woman was brusque.

"It's only a friend, señora. My husband is dead." And for the rest of the day she was withdrawn and taciturn. It took until the end of the week for her to return to normal, and Isabella was careful not to mention the Cuban letter again.

As the weeks passed and the time of Isabella's parturition drew closer, so Adra's anticipation of the event increased. She took an intense interest in the layette Isabella was assembling. Michael had made the original contribution. An airmail parcel arrived from Johannesburg with a set of six cot sheets and pillow slips in finest cotton piped with blue silk ribbon, and an exquisite pair of woolen baby jackets. Each day Isabella added to the collection and Adra helped her with her selections. Together they scoured every possible source of babywear within a radius of an hour's drive in the Mini.

Whenever Ramón returned from his business trips, he always brought a further contribution. Although the clothing was often large enough to fit a teenager, Isabella was so touched by his concern that she could not bring herself to point out the discrepancy. On one occasion, he returned with a pram whose capacity, suspension and glistening paintwork were worthy of the Rolls-Royce workshops in Crewe. Adra presented Isabella with a silk christening robe that she had made herself with antique lace that she told Isabella came from her grandmother's wedding dress. Isabella was so touched that she broke down and wept. Her tears seemed to come closer to the surface as her pregnancy progressed, and she thought often of Weltevreden. When she telephoned her father and Nana, it was difficult to prevent herself blurting out something about Ramón or the baby. Her family believed she had merely gone into retreat in Spain to finish her thesis.

On several occasions before her pregnancy made it unwise for her to travel, Ramón asked her to undertake errands for him during his absence. In each case, she had merely to fly to a foreign destination in Europe, North Africa or the Middle East, there to make a rendezvous, receive an envelope or small packet and return home. When she flew to Tel Aviv, she used her South African passport, but in Benghazi and Cairo she showed them her British passport. All these trips lasted only a day and a night and were uneventful, but served to vary her lifestyle and give her a fine opportunity to shop for the baby. Only a week after her trip to Benghazi, the monarchy of Kin Idris I was overthrown by a military coup d'état led by Colonel Muammar al-Qaddafi, and Isabella was appalled when she realized how close she and her baby had come to being caught up in the revolution. Ramón shared her concern and promised not to ask her to undertake

109

another errand until after the baby was born. She never asked him if her journeys were in connection with bank business or the darker, clandestine side of his life.

Once a week, she went for a checkup at the clinic Ramón had selected for her. Adra always accompanied her. The gynecologist was a suave, cultured Spaniard with an austere aristocratic face and pale competent hands that felt cool against her skin as he examined her.

"Everything proceeds perfectly, señora. Nature is doing her work, and you are young and healthy and well formed for the task of childbirth."

"Will it be a boy?"

"Of course, señora. A beautiful healthy boy. I give you my personal guarantee."

The clinic was a former Moorish palace, restored, renovated and equipped with the most modern medical equipment. After the doctor had taken her on a tour of the facilities, Isabella realized the wisdom of Ramón's choice. She was sure that it was the finest available.

During one of her visits, when the doctor had finished his examination and Isabella was dressing in the curtained cubicle, she overheard him discussing her condition with Adra in the waiting room. By this time her Spanish was good enough for her to appreciate that the exchange was technical and specific, like that of two professionals. It surprised her.

On the drive home, she stopped at a seafront restaurant and, as was their established custom, ordered ice cream with chocolate sauce for both of them.

"I heard you talking to the doctor, Adra," Isabella said around a mouthful of ice cream. "You must once have been a nurse, you know so much about it—all those technical words."

Once again she encountered a strangely hostile reaction from the woman.

"I am too stupid for that. I am just a maid," Adra said harshly, and retreated into a sullen silence from which Isabella could not dislodge her.

The doctor anticipated that the baby would arrive during the first week in April, and Isabella made a spurt on her thesis to finish it before that time. She typed the final pages on the last day of March and sent it off to London. She was undecided whether it was arrant nonsense or sheer genius. After it had gone she agonized endlessly over fancied omissions and possible improvements she could have made to the text.

However, within a week she had a reply from the university

inviting her to defend her thesis during an oral examination with the examiners of the faculty.

"They like it," she exulted, "or they wouldn't bother."

Despite her advanced pregnancy she flew to London for three days to attend the exam. It went better than she could have hoped, but by the time she got back to Málaga she was exhausted.

"They promised to let me know as soon as possible!" she told Ramón. "But I think it's going to be all right—cross your fingers for me."

She made Ramón give his solemn promise not to leave her alone from now onward. Thus she was lying in his arms, both of them naked under the sheet in the moonlight, the doors to the terrace wide open to catch the faintest breeze off the sea, when the first pain woke her.

She lay quietly, not waking him, while she timed the intervals between contractions, feeling smug and accomplished as she entered the final stages of the long, fascinating process. When at last she shook Ramón awake, he was most gratifyingly solicitous. He hurried away in his pajamas to fetch Adra from the servant's room on the lower floor.

Isabella's suitcase was ready, and the three of them climbed into the Mini. With Isabella seated in splendid isolation on the tiny rear seat, Ramón drove them to the clinic.

As her doctor had predicted, it all went forward naturally and rapidly. Although the baby was large and Isabella's hips were relatively narrow, there were no complications. When the doctor called upon her from between her raised knees for a final effort, she thrust down with all her strength and then, as she felt the enormous slippery rushing release within her, she uttered a joyous and triumphant cry.

Anxiously she struggled up on one elbow and brushed the sweaty tangle of hair out of her eyes. "What is it?" she demanded. "Is it a boy?" The doctor held the skinny glistening red body high, and they all laughed at the petulant birth wail.

"There you are." Still holding him dangling by the ankles, the doctor turned the infant so that Isabella could see him better.

The child's face was scarlet and creased, the eyelids swollen tightly closed. His hair was dense and jet black, plastered wetly over the skull. His penis stuck out half as long as her forefinger in what seemed to be, to Isabella's partisan appraisal, a full and impressive erection.

"It's a boy!" she gasped, and then, with a chuckle of wonderment, "He's a boy and a Courtney!"

111

Isabella was unprepared for the overwhelming strength of her maternal instincts as they laid her firstborn son at her breast and he took her engorged nipple between his rubbery little gums and tugged at it with an animal strength that aroused sympathetic contractions in her distended womb and a deeper, more primeval pain in her heart.

He was the most beautiful creature she had ever touched, as beautiful as his father. In those first days she could not take her eyes off him, often rising in the night to bend over his cot and examine his tiny face in the moonlight or, while he suckled, opening his pink fists and studying each perfect little finger with an almost religious awe.

"He's mine. He belongs to me," she kept telling herself, not yet able to overcome the wonder of it.

Ramón spent most of those first three days with them in the big sunny private room of the clinic. He seemed to share her fascination with the child. They discussed, as they had during the previous months, what names they would christen him. In the end, by a slow and painful process of elimination, they struck out Shasa and Sean from her side of the family, and Huesca and Mahon from Ramón's side. They settled for Nicholas Miguel Ramón de Santiago y Machado. Miguel was a compromise for the Michael that Isabella had suggested.

On the fourth day, when Ramón came to her room in the clinic, he was accompanied by three sober-looking gentlemen in dark suits, all of them bearing important-looking briefcases. One was an attorney, another was an official from the state registrar's office and the third was the local magistrate.

The magistrate bore witness as Isabella signed the order of adoption, relinquishing her guardianship of Nicholas to the Marqués de Santiago y Machado, and he placed his official seal on the document. The birth certificate provided by the registrar showed Ramón to be the father.

After the officials had toasted the mother and child with a large glass of sherry and left, Ramón took Isabella tenderly in his arms.

"Your son's claim to the title is secure," he whispered.

"Our son," she whispered in reply, and kissed him. "My men, Nicky and Ramón."

When Ramón fetched them from the clinic and brought them back to the flat, Isabella insisted on carrying Nicholas up the stairs herself. Adra had filled bowls of flowers to welcome them.

She took the child out of Isabella's arms. "He is wet. I will change him." And Isabella felt like a lioness deprived of her cub.

Over the days that followed, an unspoken but nevertheless intense competition developed between the two women. Although Isabella acknowledged Adra's obvious expertise in dealing with the infant, she found herself resenting the intrusion. She wanted Nicholas all to herself, and she tried to anticipate his needs and to get to him ahead of Adra.

The florid birth tones of Nicky's face soon faded to a peachy perfection, and his thick dark hair curled. When he opened his eyes for the first time, they were the exact same shade of pale green as Ramón's. Isabella considered this one of the great miracles of the universe.

"You are as beautiful as your father," she told him as she suckled him. At least that was one service Adra could not render him.

In the months that they had lived in the village, Isabella had become a local favorite. Her loveliness and her easy, engaging manner, her pregnancy and her sincere efforts to master the language had delighted the tradespeople and the stall holders in the marketplace.

In response to their entreaties, when Nicky was barely ten days old, she laid him in the pram and paraded him through the village. It was a triumphal progress, and they returned to the flat laden with small gifts, their ears ringing with praises.

When she phoned home on Easter Day her grandmother asked severely, "What is so important in Spain that you cannot come home to Weltevreden?"

"Oh, Nana, I love you all, but it is just impossible. Please forgive me."

"If I know you, young lady, which I do, you are up to no good and it wears trousers."

"Nana, you are an absolute shocker. How can you believe that of me?"

"Twenty years of experience," Centaine Courtney-Malcomess told her drily. "Just don't get into any more trouble, child."

"I won't, I promise," Isabella told her sweetly, and hugged the infant at her bosom. Oh, if you only knew, she thought. He doesn't wear trousers; not yet, anyway.

"How is the thesis going?" her father asked, when he came on the line. She could not tell him that she had already submitted it, for that was her excuse for remaining in Spain.

"Almost done," she compromised. She hadn't thought about it since Nicholas had come along.

"Good luck with it." Shasa was silent for a moment. "Do you remember our talk, the promise you gave me?"

"Which one?" she procrastinated guiltily, knowing very well what he was referring to.

"You promised that if you were ever in any trouble, any trouble at all, you wouldn't try to go it alone, you would come to me."

"Yes, I remember."

"Are you all right, Bella baby?"

"I'm fine, wonderful, just marvelous, Daddy."

He heard the ring of it in her voice and sighed with relief.

"Happy Easter, my bright and beautiful daughter."

With Michael it was a relief to let it all out. They were on the telephone for forty-five minutes, Málaga to Johannesburg, and she tickled Nicholas to make him gurgle for his distant uncle.

"When are you coming home, Bella?" Michael asked at last.

"Ramón's divorce will be through by June, that's definite. We will have a civil marriage here in Spain and the church wedding at Weltevreden. I expect you to be at both functions."

"Try to stop me," he challenged her.

They celebrated Easter dinner at their favorite seaside restaurant with Nicholas's pram parked at the table. The patron's wife had knitted a jacket for the baby.

Adra was with them. She was part of their small family by now, and she wheeled the pram when they walked home to the flat. Isabella clung to Ramón's arm. She felt very married and maternal, and as happy as she had ever been in her entire life.

When they arrived at the flat, Adra took Nicholas away to change him. For once Isabella did not resent it.

In the front bedroom she lowered the shutters, and then came to Ramón.

"It's three weeks since Nicky was born. I'm not made of glass, you know. I won't break."

He was too gentle, too considerate for her mood. She had been without him for too long.

"I think you've forgotten how to do this," she said, and pushed him over on his back. "Let me refresh your memory, sir."

"Don't hurt yourself," he cautioned anxiously.

"If anybody gets hurt around here, it is more likely to be you, my friend. Now, fasten your seat belt. We are ready for takeoff."

114

Afterward, in the shuttered room, she lay against him in languorous exhaustion, their bodies sticking lightly together with the sweat of their loving. Suddenly he said, "I have to go away for four days next week."

She sat up quickly. "Oh, Ramón, so soon!" she protested, and then realized she was being possessive and unreasonable.

"You'll phone me every day, won't you?" she demanded.

"I'll do better than that. I'll be in Paris and I'll try to arrange for you to join me there. We will have dinner at Laserre."

"That would be lovely, but what about Nicky?"

"Nicky has got Adra to look after him," Ramón chuckled. "Nicky will be all right, and Adra will love the opportunity to have him all to herself."

"I don't know . . ." she said dubiously. The thought of being parted from her wondrous achievement for even an hour appalled her.

"It will be for one night only, and you have really earned a little reward. Besides, I need you, too, you know."

"Oh, my darling." His appeal touched her. Her flow of milk was copious. She could express enough to cover the feedings Nicky would need during such a short absence. "Of course I'd love to be with you. You are right. Nicky and Adra will survive a night without me. I'll come as soon as you call me."

# 10

"The woman gave birth to her brat almost a month ago," General Joseph Cicero whispered hoarsely. "What has been the delay? You should have terminated the operation immediately. The cost has been out of all proportion!"

"The general will recall that I am meeting the cost out of funds that I have provided, not out of the departmental budget," Ramón reminded him quietly.

Cicero coughed and rustled the copy of *France-Soir* that he held before his face. They sat side by side in a second-class coach of the Paris Métro. Cicero had entered the coach at the Concorde station and taken the seat beside Ramón. Neither of them had shown any sign of recognition. The rush of the train through the underground tunnel would foil any eavesdropper. Both of them used open newspapers to cover their face as they talked. This was one of their regular procedures for short meetings.

"I was not referring only to the cost in rubles," Cicero wheezed. "You have spent nearly a year on this project, an incalculable cost to the other work of the department."

Ramón was fascinated by the rapid course of the disease that was destroying his superior. It seemed that at every meeting Joe Cicero had deteriorated visibly. It would not be much longer, months rather than years.

"These few months of work will pay us back enormous dividends over the years and, yes, over the decades ahead."

"Work," snorted Cicero. "Stirring the honey pot with your spoon. If that is work, how do you define pleasure, Marqués? And why are you prolonging termination month after month?"

"If the woman is to be of the utmost value to us, it is absolutely necessary that she bond to the child before we proceed to the next step in the operation."

"When will that be?" Cicero demanded.

"It has happened already. The fruit is ripe for picking. Everything is in place. I need your cooperation in the final resolution. That is why I chose Paris for this meeting."

Cicero nodded. "Go on," he invited.

Ramón spoke quietly for another five minutes. Cicero listened without comment, but grudgingly he had to admit to himself that the plan was airtight. Once again he acceded privately that his successor seemed to have been well chosen, despite the original prejudice he had fostered toward him.

"Very well," he whispered at last. "You have approval to proceed. And as you request, I will monitor proceedings at this end." Cicero folded his newspaper and stood up as the coach slid into the Bastille Métro station on its silent rubber wheels.

As the doors opened, he stepped down onto the platform and walked away without looking back.

The notification from London University arrived the afternoon that Ramón left. It took the form of an express letter with the university's coat of arms embossed on the flap of the envelope.

"The chancellor and the faculty members of the University

of London take pleasure in informing Isabella Courtney that she has been awarded the degree of Doctor of Philosophy of the University.''

Isabella telephoned Weltevreden immediately. There was little time difference between Málaga and Cape Town, and Shasa had just returned from the polo field. He was still in boots and breeches, and he took the call in the downstairs study whose French windows overlooked the field.

"Son of a gun!" he let out a whoop when she told him. To her such an uncharacteristic display was proof of her father's deep delight. "When will they cap you, darling?"

"Not till June or July. I'll have to stay until then." It was the excuse she had been looking for.

"Of course," Shasa agreed immediately. "I'll come over."

"Oh, Daddy, it's such a long way."

"Nonsense, Dr. Courtney, I wouldn't miss it for the world. Your grandmother will probably want to come with me." Strangely, the prospect did not alarm her as it might have. She realized it was probably the ideal occasion for both her father and Nana to meet Ramón and Nicholas. Centaine Courtney-Malcomess off her home ground was not such a daunting prospect as she was when installed in all the splendor and tradition of Weltevreden.

At that moment, more than anything, Isabella wanted to share her joy in her achievement with Ramón, but he did not telephone that night, nor even the following day. By Thursday morning she was almost frantic with worry. It was so unlike Ramón; usually he telephoned every day they were apart.

When finally the telephone rang she was in the tiny kitchen having a heated argument with Adra as to how many cloves of garlic should go into the paella.

"You would inject the stuff into your veins if you were given the chance," she accused in her now fluent Spanish.

"We are making paella, not Irish stew," Adra retorted, holding her ground. Then the telephone rang. Isabella dropped the spoon with a clatter and knocked over the chair in the hall in her haste to reach it.

"Ramón darling, I was so worried. I missed your call."

"I'm sorry, Bella." The rich dark tones of his voice soothed her, so that her own voice became a purr.

"Do you still love me?"

"Come to Paris and I will prove it to you."

"When?"

"Now. I have made a reservation for you on the Air France

117

flight at eleven o'clock. They are holding your ticket at the airport. You'll be here by two o'clock.''

"Where will I meet you?''

"At the Plaza-Athénée. We have a suite.''

"You spoil me, Ramón darling.''

"No less than you deserve.''

She left the flat immediately. However, the Air France takeoff was delayed by forty minutes. In Paris the baggage handlers were working to rule, so she stood fuming and fretting at the baggage carousel for almost an hour before her overnight case made its leisurely appearance. It was after five in the evening before her taxi pulled up in the Avenue Montaigne before the elegant façade of the Plaza-Athénée with its scarlet awnings.

She half expected Ramón to be waiting for her in the marbled and mirrored foyer and looked about eagerly as she came in through the revolving glass doors. He was not there. She paid no heed to the gaunt figure who sat in one of the gilt and brocade armchairs opposite the reception desk. The man lifted his head of lank white hair and for a moment regarded her with strangely lifeless tar black eyes. Then he coughed harshly and returned his attention to the newspaper he was reading.

Isabella crossed quickly and expectantly to the concierge's counter.

"You have a guest, the Marqués de Santiago y Machado. I am his wife.''

"A moment, madame.'' The uniformed concierge consulted the guest list, then shook his head and frowned as he started again at the head of the list.

"I'm sorry, Marquesa. The Marqués is not staying with us at the moment.''

"Perhaps he has registered as Monsieur Machado.''

"I'm afraid not. We have nobody of that name.''

Isabella looked confused. "I don't understand. I spoke to him this morning.''

"I will make further inquiry.'' The concierge left her for a moment to consult the booking clerk and returned almost immediately. "Your husband is not with us, and there is no reservation for him.''

"He must have been delayed.'' Isabella tried to look unconcerned. "Do you have a room for me?''

"The hotel is fully booked.'' The concierge spread his hands apologetically. "It's spring, you understand. I am desolated, Marquesa. Paris is overflowing.''

"He must be coming." Isabella insisted brightly. "Do you mind if I wait for my husband in the gallery?"

"Of course not, Marquesa. The waiter will bring you coffee and whatever refreshment you wish. The porter will guard your baggage in his store."

As she moved toward the long gallery, which at the cocktail hour was the fashionable meeting place for *le tout Paris*, the white-haired gentleman rose from his armchair. He moved stiffly with the gait of a frail and sick old man, but Isabella in her consternation did not even glance in his direction. Joe Cicero went out into the street, and the doorman hailed a taxi for him. It dropped him in the rue Grenelle. He walked the last block to the Soviet embassy, and the guard at the night desk recognized him as he approached.

From the office of the military attaché on the second floor, Joe Cicero phoned a number in Málaga.

"The woman is waiting at the hotel," he whispered huskily. "She cannot return before noon tomorrow. You may proceed as planned."

A little before seven o'clock, the concierge came and found Isabella in the gallery.

"There has been a cancellation, Marquesa. We have a room for you now. I have already sent your baggage up."

She could have kissed him, but instead she tipped him a hundred francs.

From the room, she rang the flat in Málaga. She hoped Ramón might have left a message with Adra, now that the arrangements had so obviously gone awry. Although she let the telephone ring a hundred times, there was no reply. That truly alarmed her. Adra should have been there; the telephone was in the hallway just outside her bedroom door. Isabella telephoned again twice more during the night, each time without success.

"The telephone is out of order," she told herself with conviction, but she hardly slept at all.

As soon as the airline reservations office opened, she booked a flight back to Málaga. Despite her distress she managed to sleep for an hour during the journey. It was after midday when they landed at Málaga airport.

The taxi dropped her at the front door of the apartment block, and she dragged her bag to their front door. With fingers that shook with fatigue and agitation she finally got the key into the lock.

The apartment was strangely silent, and her voice rang through the open doorway.

119

"Adra, I'm back. Where are you?"

She glanced into the kitchen as she hurried to Adra's room. The room was empty. She started up the stairs at a run, then stopped abruptly at the door to her bedroom. It was wide open.

Nicholas's cot still stood in the alcove opposite the window. It was stripped of sheets and pillows and blankets, that exquisite layette that Michael had sent her from home. The table beside the cot, on which had stood Nicholas's platoon of soft toys, the teddies and bunnies and Disney creatures she had showered on him, was bare.

She stepped to the terrace door and glanced out. His pram was gone.

"Adra!" she cried, and heard the high thin tone of panic in her own voice. "Where are you?"

She raced through the other rooms. "Nicky! My baby! Oh, God, please! Where have you taken Nicky?"

She found herself back in the main bedroom beside his empty cot.

"I don't understand," she whispered. "What has happened?"

On a sudden impulse, she whirled and jerked open the drawers of Nicholas's bureau. They were all empty. The nappies and vests and jackets, all of them were gone.

"The hospital." Her voice was a sob. "Something has happened to my baby!"

She rushed down the stairs and seized the telephone. Then she froze as she saw the envelope taped to the cradle of the instrument. She dropped the telephone receiver and ripped open the envelope. Her hands shook so that she could barely read the words on the single sheet of notepaper.

However, she recognized Ramón's handwriting instantly and felt a treacherous rush of relief, which evaporated swiftly as she read the words:

Nicholas is with me. He is safe for the time being. If you wish to see him again, you must follow these instructions exactly. Do not speak to anybody in Málaga. I repeat, do not speak to anybody. Leave the flat immediately and return to London. You will be contacted at Cadogan Square. Tell nobody what has happened, not even your brother Michael. Follow these instructions implicitly. Your disobedience will have dire consequences for Nicky. You may never see him again. Destroy this note.

R

Her legs went soft and boneless under her, and she sank down against the wall and sat on the tiled floor with them sprawled out loosely in front of her as though they were disjointed at the hips. She read the note again, and then again, but it didn't make sense.

"My baby," she whispered. "My little Nicky." Then she read the terrible words aloud. " 'Your disobedience will have dire consequences for Nicky. You may never see him again.' "

She let the hand holding the note drop into her lap, and she stared at the wall opposite. She felt as though the world and her entire existence had been swept away. It left her as blank and meaningless as the empty expanse of brickwork in front of her.

She did not know how long she sat there. At last, with a supreme effort, she roused herself. Using the wall as a support, she regained her feet. Once more she climbed the stairs to their bedroom and went directly to Ramón's cupboard. She threw the doors open and found that it also was empty. Even the coat hangers were gone. She moved listlessly to his chest of drawers and opened each empty drawer. Ramón had left nothing.

She wandered back to Nicholas's alcove, moving like a survivor of a bomb blast, dazed and uncoordinated, and knelt beside the empty cot.

"My baby," she whispered. "What have they done with you?"

Then she saw that something had slipped down between the baby mattress and the wooden bars of the cot. She eased it free and held it in both hands. Kneeling at the cot as though it were a high altar, she held the sacrament in her hands. It was one of Nicholas's bootees, a scrap of soft knitted wool with a blue satin ribbon the drawstring for his chubby pink ankle. She lifted it to her face and inhaled the perfumed baby smell of her son.

Only then did she begin to weep. She wept with a bitter ferocity that drained her strength and left her exhausted. By that time the terrace and the bedroom were filled with the shades of evening and she had strength left only to crawl to the double bed and curl up on it. As she fell asleep she held the woolen bootee pressed to her cheek.

It was still dark when she awoke. She lay for long seconds with a dark sense of doom overpowering her, uncertain of its origin or cause. Then suddenly it all came back to her, and she struggled upright and looked about her with horror.

Ramón's note lay on the table beside the bed. She took it up and reread it, still trying to make sense of it.

"Ramón, my darling, why are you doing this to us?" she

whispered. Then, obedient to his instructions, she carried the note to the bathroom and, standing over the toilet bowl, tore it into tiny scraps. She dropped these into the bowl and flushed them away. She knew that every word would be graven on her mind forever; she had no need or wish to conserve that dreadful sheet of paper.

She showered and dressed and made herself a slice of toast and a pot of coffee. They were without taste. Her mouth felt numb, as though it had been scalded with boiling water.

Then she set herself to search the apartment thoroughly. She began in Adra's room. There was no trace left of Adra Olivares, not a shred of clothing, not a pot or a tube of ointment or cosmetics in her bathroom, not even a single hair from her head on the pillow of her bed.

Then she went over the living room and kitchen; again there was nothing except the hired furniture and crockery and the remains of food in the refrigerator.

She went up to the bedroom. There was a small wall safe in the back of Ramón's cupboard, but the steel door was ajar and all the documents were missing. Nicholas's birth certificate and adoption papers were gone with them.

She sat down on the bed and tried to think clearly, attempting desperately to find a reason for this madness. She went round and round, trying to examine it from every possible angle.

She was driven remorselessly to a single conclusion: Ramón must be in deep trouble. It was some horror from his clandestine life that had overtaken them. She knew he had been forced to leave with Nicholas under extreme duress. She understood that she must do everything in her power to help them, Ramón and Nicholas, the two most important elements in her life. She knew she must do as he ordered her. Their safety and possibly their lives depended upon it. Yet she could not leave it like that. She had to learn more; any morsel of knowledge might be of value.

She left the apartment and went downstairs. There was a small bakery shop across the street, and over the months Isabella had become friendly with the baker's wife. The woman was opening the shutters over the shop window as Isabella hurried across the road.

"Yes," the baker's wife told her, "after you left on Thursday, Adra went out with Nicholas in the pram. They went down toward the beach and returned just before I closed the shop. I saw them go up to your apartment, but I didn't see them again, not after that."

122

Isabella went up the street, stopping to question all the tradespeople whose businesses were within sight of the apartment block. Some of them had seen Adra and Nicky return on Thursday evening, but not one of them had seen them again since then. Her last resort was the shoeshine urchin at the corner of the park. Ramón always allowed the lad to polish his shoes and overtipped him exorbitantly. He was one of Isabella's favorites on the street.

"Sí, señora." He grinned at Isabella as he squatted over his box. "On Thursday night I work late, because of the cinema and the arcade. At ten o'clock I see the Marqués. He came in a big black car with two men. They park in the street and go upstairs."

"What did the other men look like, *chico*? Do you know them? Had you seen them before?"

"Never. They two tough *hombres*—policemen, I think. Much trouble. I don't like police. They all go upstairs, and then soon they come down. They all carry suitcases, big suitcases. Adra come with them. She carry baby Nico; they get into the car, all of them, and they drive away. That is all. I don't see them again."

The two tough *hombres* confirmed what Isabella had suspected: that Ramón was acting under coercion. She realized the only source of action open to her was to follow the instructions Ramón had given her in the note. She went back to the apartment and began to pack. Her redundant maternity clothes she left lying on the bedroom floor, and her good clothes filled only two cases.

When she came to the drawer that contained her cosmetics she found that the fat album of snapshots that she had accumulated since Nicholas's birth was missing, together with the envelopes of negatives. It came as a shock to realize that she had no record of her baby, no photograph or souvenir apart from the single woolen bootee she had retrieved from his cot.

She lugged her bulging cases downstairs and packed them into the back of the Mini. Then she crossed the street and spoke to the baker's wife.

"If my husband comes back and asks for me, tell him I have gone back to London."

"What about Nico? Are you all right, señora?" The woman was sympathetic, and Isabella smiled brightly.

"Nico is with my husband. I'll meet them in London soon. *Muchas gracias por su ayuda, señora. Adiós.*"

* * *

The drive northward seemed endless. Each episode of the last few days since she last had seen her son played over and over in her mind until she felt she was going slowly mad.

On the cross-Channel ferry, she forsook the loud bonhomie of the crowded saloon and went up on to the boat deck. It was a cold, grey day, with the north wind kicking the tops off the swells in dashing white spurts of spray. The wind and her despair chilled her through until she was shivering uncontrollably even in her padded anorak. However, in the end it was the ache in her swollen breasts that drove her below. In the woman's toilet she used the express pump to draw off the flow that should have been for her son.

"Oh, Nicky, Nicky!" she cried silently as she discharged the rich, creamy liquid into the toilet bowl, and she imagined once again his hot little mouth on her nipples and the smell and the feel of him against her breast.

She found herself weeping, and with a huge effort controlled herself. "You're losing your grip on reality," she warned herself. "You've got to be strong now. You can't let go. For Nicky's sake, you must be strong. No more crying and moping—no more."

It was raining when she drove into Cadogan Square, and the flat was chilly and uninviting. While she unpacked she thought about the promise she had made her father. Suddenly she threw down the dress that she held and ran through to the drawing room.

"International, I want to place a call to Cape Town, South Africa."

At this time of night the delay was less than ten minutes, and she heard the peals of the telephone at the other end. One of the servants answered it, and as she opened her mouth to ask for her father Ramón's strict injunction came back to her with all its force and threat. "Your disobedience will have dire consequences for Nicky."

She replaced the receiver on its cradle without speaking and resigned herself to waiting for the promised contact.

Nothing happened for six days. She never left the flat, not daring to put herself beyond the reach of the telephone. She rang nobody, spoke to nobody except the housekeeper, and tried to keep herself occupied by reading and watching television. The uncertainty aggravated her despair, and she found that although she stared at the pages of her book or at the small flickering screen of the television set, the printed words and the images were meaningless. Only her agony was real. Only her loss had poignant meaning. Only her pain abided.

She could barely bring herself to eat, and within three days her milk flow had dried up. She lost weight dramatically. Her hair, one of the high points of her beauty, turned dull and dry. Her face in the mirror was gaunt, her eyes sank into bruised-looking cavities and her golden amber Mediterranean tan became sallow and yellow like the skin of a malaria sufferer.

She waited, and the waiting was torture. Each hour was an insupportable eternity. Then, on the sixth day, the telephone rang. She snatched it up with desperate haste, before the second peal.

"I have a message from Ramón." It was a woman's voice with an elusive accent, probably middle European. "Leave now, immediately. Take a taxi to the junction of Royal Hospital Road and the Embankment. Walk down the Embankment toward Westminster. Somebody will greet you with the name Red Rose. Follow their orders," said the caller. "Repeat these instructions, please."

Breathlessly Isabella obeyed. "Good," said the woman, and broke the connection.

Isabella had not walked farther than a hundred yards along the Embankment above the Thames when a small unmarked van passed her, traveling slowly in the same direction. It pulled up to the curb ahead of her, and as she drew level with it the rear door opened to reveal a middle-aged woman in grey overalls sitting on the side bench of the body of the van.

"Red Rose," she said. Isabella recognized her voice from their telephone conversation. "Get in!"

Quickly Isabella slipped into the van and sat on the bench opposite the woman. She slammed the door, and immediately the van pulled away.

The body of the van was without windows or any opening except for the ventilator in the roof above Isabella's head. She could not see out and, though she tried to track their course by the turns and stops, she was soon totally confused and abandoned the attempt.

"Where are you taking me?" she asked the woman opposite her.

"Silence, please." And Isabella resigned herself. She pulled her collar up around her ears and thrust her hands deep into the pockets of her anorak. They drove for twenty-three minutes by her wristwatch. Then the van stopped again and the rear door was opened from outside.

They were in a parking garage. She judged from the unpainted concrete pillars that supported the low roof and from the steep

125

access ramp at the far end of the long, narrow chamber that it was an underground parking facility.

The woman in the grey overalls took her arm and helped her down from the van. The touch of her hand made Isabella aware of just how powerful she was. The hand felt like the paw of a gorilla, and she towered above Isabella with wide meaty shoulders under the grey cloth.

"This way," she ordered. Still holding Isabella's arm, she led her to the lift doors opposite the van. Despite the painful grip, Isabella glanced around her quickly. There were a dozen or so other vehicles parked in the bays alongside the van; at least two of them had diplomatic number plates.

The doors of the lift opened, and the woman pushed Isabella into it. A glance at the control panel showed Isabella that her assumption had been correct. The lighted stage indicator showed that they were at "Basement Level II." The woman pushed the button for the third floor and they rode up in silence. The lift stopped with the stage indicator at "Level III" and her escort urged her out into a bare corridor with cork flooring. They walked down it side by side, still in silence. The corridor was empty and the doors on each side were closed.

As they approached the end of the corridor, the facing door slid open. Another large female with flat Slavic features, also dressed in grey overalls, ushered them into what appeared to be a small lecture room or an intimate movie theater. A double row of easy chairs faced the raised dais and the screen that covered the far wall.

Isabella's escort led her to a chair in the front row center.

"Sit down," she said, and Isabella sank down on the smooth cold plastic padding. The two women moved around and took up positions behind Isabella. For several minutes there was silence. Then the small door to the right of the dais opened and a man came through.

He moved slowly, stiffly, like a frail, sick old man. His hair was dead white with a yellowish tinge, and hung over his forehead and ears. His features were very pale, lined and seamed with age and suffering, so that Isabella felt a twinge of sympathy for him—until the light caught his eyes.

With a small jolt of intense distaste she recognized those eyes. Once she had been with her father on a chartered fishing boat out of Black River. Shasa had been trolling a live bonito along the oceanic drop-off under the shadow of Le Morne Brabant on the island of Mauritius when he had hooked into a gigantic mako shark. After a battle that had lasted two hours, he had dragged the creature alongside. As its pointed snout broke through the surface, Isabella had been leaning over the rail, and she had looked into its eyes. They were black and pitiless, without definite iris or pupil, two holes that seemed to reach down into hell itself. Those were the same kind of eyes that were studying her now.

She held her breath under their implacable scrutiny until at last the man spoke. His voice came as a surprise. It was low and hoarse. She had to lean forward slightly to make sense of the words.

"Isabella Courtney, from now on we will never use that name again in any communication. You will be referred to and you will refer to yourself only as Red Rose. Do you understand?"

She nodded, not trusting her voice to reply. He lifted the cigarette that smoldered between his fingers and drew deeply on it. He spoke again through a cloud of exhaled smoke.

"I have a message for you, in the form of a videotape recording." He stepped down from the dais and took the chair at the end of the row farthest from her.

As he settled into it, the overhead lights dimmed. She heard the faint hum of electronic equipment, and then the screen lit up. The scene it displayed was a bare white-tiled room—a laboratory or an operating theater, she decided.

There was a table in the center of the room, and on it was a glass-sided tank much like an aquarium in which ornamental tropical fish are displayed in a pet shop. The tank was filled with water to within a few inches of the top. On the tabletop beside the tank stood some sort of electronic cabinet and an array of instruments and medical paraphernalia. She recognized a portable oxygen cylinder and an oxygen mask. The mask was a diminutive model suitable for infants and very small children.

A man was busy at the table. His back was toward the camera, and his features were hidden. He wore some type of white laboratory coat. He turned to face the camera, and Isabella saw that he wore a cloth theater cap and surgical mask.

His voice was dispassionate as he began to speak, and his accent was foreign, east European. He seemed to be addressing Isabella directly.

"Your orders were to speak to nobody, not in Málaga or elsewhere. You deliberately disobeyed those orders." He was staring at her from the screen with disembodied eyes.

"I'm sorry," she replied, as though he could hear her. "I was so worried. I couldn't—"

"Silence!" hissed one of the women behind her chair. A hand

**127**

fell on her shoulder, fingers dug into her flesh with a strength that made her wince.

On the screen, the man was still speaking. "You were warned that disobedience would have dire consequences for your son. You chose to ignore that warning. What you are about to witness is a first demonstration of the seriousness of those instructions."

He made a gesture to somebody off camera, and a figure entered from the side. It was impossible to tell whether it was male or female, for it also wore a cap and surgical mask that covered all of the face and head except for a narrow strip across the eyes. A full-length surgical gown fell to below the knees and was tucked into the tops of white rubber boots.

"This is a qualified doctor who will monitor all the proceedings," he explained.

The figure carried a bundle in its arms. Only when it deposited the bundle on the table beside the glass-side tank and a tiny bare leg kicked free of the swaddling cloth did Isabella realize it was a child. With quick, trained hands, the doctor unwrapped the infant, and the video camera zoomed in on Nicholas as he lay naked on the tabletop kicking his legs in the air. His gurgles sounded in the quiet room.

Isabella thrust the fingers of one hand into her mouth and bit down on them hard to prevent herself crying out again.

The doctor placed two small black suction cups on Nicky's bare chest. Thin wires dangled from them, and the doctor connected them to the electronic cabinet and switched it on. Dials in the panel were activated, and the narrator explained in a neutral voice: "The child's breathing and heartbeat will be recorded."

The doctor looked up and nodded. The narrator moved around behind the table and faced the camera.

"You are Red Rose," he said with peculiar emphasis on the name. "In future you will obey all orders given to you by that name."

He reached down and took both of Nicholas's ankles in one hand and lifted him. Nicholas let out a squawk of surprise as he hung head down like a small pink wingless bat.

"You are about to witness the consequences of disobedience."

He swung the child and held him head down over the glass-sided tank. Nicholas arched his back and tried to lift his head. He waved his arms and clenched and unclenched his fists, making small noises of uncertainty and alarm. Slowly the narrator lowered the child headfirst into the water, and the sounds of his

128

little voice were abruptly cut off. The video camera zoomed in through the glass side of the tank and focused on his face below the surface of the water. The color resolution of the film was true to life.

Isabella screamed wildly and tried to struggle out of her chair. The two women seized her from behind and forced her down again.

On the screen Nicholas struggled in the narrator's grip. His face was contorted, and silver bubbles streamed from his nostrils. His face seemed to swell and darken.

Isabella was still screaming and fighting when the masked doctor looked up quickly from the heart monitor and said sharply in Spanish, "Stop! That is enough, comrade!"

Immediately the man lifted the child clear of the tank. Water streamed from Nicholas's nostrils and open mouth. For long seconds he could not utter a sound except for tiny gasping breaths.

The narrator laid him down on the table, and the doctor clapped the oxygen mask over his swollen face and pressed down on his chest with the palm of his hand to induce regular breathing. Within a minute the dials on the cabinet had settled back to normal and Nicholas's movements were stronger. He howled into his mask with shock and outrage, his voice becoming louder and stronger with each cry.

The doctor removed the mask and stepped back from the table. He nodded at the narrator, who seized Nicholas's ankles once again and lifted him over the tank. Nicholas seemed to realize what was coming. His cries of protest reached a higher, terrified pitch, and he kicked and writhed in the man's grip.

"He's my son!" Isabella screamed. "You can't—you mustn't do this to my baby!"

Once again the narrator lowered Nicholas's head below the surface, and the child fought with all his strength. His frenzied exertions racked the tiny body, water splashed over the edge of the tank, and once again his face changed color swiftly.

Isabella screamed at him, "Stop it! I'll do anything you say, just stop torturing my baby! Please! Please!"

Once again the doctor intervened with a sharp warning. This time when Nicholas was lifted clear of the water his movements were weaker. He made little choking cawing sounds, and a mixture of water and vomit erupted from his open inverted mouth. Silver strings of mucus slid down from his flared nostrils.

The doctor worked swiftly, his alarm apparent, and said

**129**

something to the other man. The narrator looked up at the camera, seeming to stare directly at Isabella.

"We almost miscalculated that time. We exceeded the limit of safety." He and the doctor put their heads together and spoke so softly that Isabella could not catch the words. Then the narrator addressed her again. "That concludes our demonstration for the time being. I sincerely hope that it will not be necessary for you to witness another like it. It would be harrowing for you to have to watch the amputation of the child's limbs without anesthetic, or eventually his strangulation in front of the camera. Of course, it will depend on you, and on the degree of cooperation you are prepared to afford us."

The image faded, and the screen went blank. There was no sound in the darkened theater except for Isabella's sobs. These lasted for a long time. When they finally quieted, the lights were raised slowly and Joseph Cicero came to stand over Isabella.

"I assure you that none of us takes any particular pleasure in this sort of thing. We will try to avoid any repetition."

"How could he do it!" Isabella whispered brokenly. She was huddled down in the large chair. "How could any human being do that to a child?"

"I repeat, we do not enjoy the necessity. You must blame yourself, Red Rose. It was your disobedience that caused your son's discomfort."

"Discomfort! Is that what you call the torture of an innocent—?"

"Control yourself," Cicero warned her sharply. "For your child's sake, control your insolence."

"I'm sorry." Isabella dropped her voice. "It won't happen again. Just don't hurt Nicky again, please."

"If you cooperate, your son will not have to suffer further. He is in the care of a highly trained pediatric sister. He will receive the type of professional care that even you would not be able to give him. Later he will be given the best education that any boy or young man could hope for."

Isabella stared up at him, her face twisted with misery. "You speak as though he has been taken away from me forever, as though I will never see my baby again."

Cicero coughed and shook his head, struggled to regain his breath, then whispered hoarsely, "This is not the case, Red Rose. You will be allowed to earn the privilege of access to your son. To begin with you will receive regular reports of his progress. You will be shown video recordings of how he develops, when he first sits up unaided, when he begins to crawl, to walk."

130

"Oh, no!" she whispered. "You can't keep him from me that long. It will be months."

Cicero went on as though she had not spoken. "Later you will be allowed to spend some time with him each year. It is possible that some time in the future, if your conduct is satisfactory, you will be allowed to spend holidays together—days, even weeks in your son's company."

"No." Her voice was a pitiful sob. "You can't be so cruel as to keep us apart."

"Who knows, it is not beyond the bounds of possibility that one day we may remove all restrictions and allow you free access. For that to happen you would have to earn our complete trust and gratitude."

"Who are you?" Isabella asked in a small subdued voice. "Who is Ramón Machado? I thought I knew him so well, and yet I did not know him at all. Where is Ramón? Is he part of all this monstrous—" Isabella's voice broke, and she could not continue.

"You must put aside all thought of that nature. You must not seek to find the answer to the question of who we are," Cicero warned her. "Ramón Machado is under our control. Do not expect help from him. The child is his also. He is under the same constraint as you are."

"What must I do? What do you want of me?" Isabella asked.

Cicero nodded with satisfaction. There had been a remote chance that the woman might prove headstrong and uncontrollable. The psychiatrist's report on her had mentioned that possibility, but Cicero had never placed much credence in it. The hook on which they had hung her was sharp and fiercely barbed. Even if the child died, they would find a replacement to act in the video games and keep her dangling on the hook. No, he had expected her to be compliant, and those expectations had been vindicated.

"First, I must congratulate you, Red Rose, on your doctorate. It will make your work for us easier."

Isabella stared at him. It was difficult for her to make the mental leap from this terrifying world of torture and espionage back to the prosaic consideration of her studies and academic honors. She had to concentrate to keep up with what he was saying.

"You will return as soon as possible to Cape Town and your family, after making arrangements at the university to receive your doctorate in absentia, do you understand?"

Isabella nodded, not yet trusting herself to speak.

131

"On your return home, you will begin to take more interest in all the family activities. You will work to make yourself indispensable to your father. You will make yourself his assistant and confidante in all things, but especially in his new position as head of the armaments corporation. What is more, you will begin to take an active interest in South African politics."

"My father is a self-contained man. He does not need me."

"You are wrong, Red Rose. Your father is a very lonely and basically unhappy man. He is incapable of a lasting relationship with any woman, except your grandmother, his mother, Centaine Courtney-Malcomess, and you, his daughter. He needs that relationship very deeply—and you will give it to him."

"You want me to use my own father?" she whispered, horror blending with fresh horror in her eyes.

"For the survival of your son," Cicero agreed softly. "No harm will come to your father, but your son stands full in harm's way unless you cooperate."

Isabella took a handkerchief from her handbag and blew her nose. Her voice was soggy. "You want me to inveigle myself into my father's confidence to gain information on the national armaments program and pass it on to you?"

"You learn quickly, Red Rose. However, that is not all. You will use your father's political contacts within the South African Nationalist regime to foster your own political career within the party."

She shook her head. "I am not a political creature."

"You are now," Cicero contradicted her. "You have a doctorate in political theory. Your father will introduce you to the corridors of power."

Again she denied it. "My father is in political eclipse. He backed the wrong horse when John Vorster came to power in South Africa. That was why he was shunted into the ambassadorial post here, into political oblivion."

"Your father has exonerated himself by the way he performed his duties here in London. His appointment to such a responsible position as head of Armscor is indication of that. We anticipate that soon he will be totally reinstated within the party. We deem it highly probable that within two years he will be once more a member of the cabinet. You, Red Rose will ride upon his back. Twenty years from now you yourself could be a minister of the government."

"Twenty years!" Isabella echoed in disbelief. "Is that how long I must be your slave?"

"You still don't understand?" Cicero asked, shaking his head.

"Let me explain it to you. You belong to us, Red Rose, you, your lover Ramón Machado, and your son. Forever."

For many minutes Isabella stared sightlessly at the blank screen, contemplating the enormity of the vision he had conjured up for her.

Joe Cicero broke the silence. His voice was almost gentle. "You will be taken back now. They will leave you where they found you, on the Embankment. Follow your orders, Red Rose, and in the long run it will work out well for you and your son."

The women attendants helped Isabella to her feet and led her to the door.

When she had gone, the side door to the lecture theater opened, and Ramón Machado stepped through. "You were watching?" Joe Cicero asked. Ramón nodded. "I congratulate you," Cicero murmured reluctantly. "It has been well run. We may reap much of value from this operation. How is the child?"

"He suffered no ill effects. He and his nurse have arrived in Havana."

Joe Cicero lit another cigarette, coughed and sat down heavily on one of the plastic chairs.

Perhaps, he thought, just perhaps I will be able to leave the department in capable hands.

# 11

Amber Joy was about to "fail to find." They could all see it.

A palpable air of tension and expectation hung over the entire field of the trial.

The South African retriever championship trial was being conducted over the foothills of the Kabonkel Berg along the western end of the Weltevreden estate. The terrain was testing, and over the two days of the trials the field of dogs had been whittled down to these four.

The birds were mallard ducks, pen-reared on Weltevreden

and placed in the field under the supervision of the judges prior to each retrieve. This would probably be the last occasion on which they would be allowed to use mallards, Shasa Courtney reflected. The conservationists were kicking up such a terrible stink about unshot mallards escaping into the wild. There these exotic birds were highly attractive to the indigenous yellow-billed ducks. Avian Don Juans, he smiled.

The progeny of these illicit unions were hybrids, and the Department of Nature Conservation had proclaimed a ban on the release of mallards that would become effective at the end of the month. Thereafter they would be forced to use ring-necked doves or guinea fowl, which was a pity, they all agreed. These terrestrial birds did not float well on the water retrieves.

Shasa Courtney switched his full attention back to the retrieve in progress. Amber Joy was the main competition to Weltevreden's hopes of carrying off the cup for the first time. Amber Joy was a splendid yellow Labrador. His sire had been American field-trial champion for three years in a row. Up until now every single retrieve he had made during the last two days had been SOB, straight out and back. This time fortune had turned against him. The mallard had risen from its cage and flashed away along the edge of the dam. Garry Courtney and Shasa were the field guns, chosen for the task because both of them were renowned shots. The mallard was flying left, on Garry's side, and he had let it go to fifty yards before killing it so cleanly that it folded its wings and went in headfirst like a kamikaze. It fell close in to the reed beds, among the lily pads and "water blommetjies," the flowering aquatics that infested most dams in the Cape of Good Hope. The mallard's plunge had driven it deep, and it had not reemerged. Probably it was entangled with the plant stems below the surface of the muddy brown water.

The judge had called Amber Joy's number, and Bunty Charles, his owner and handler, had sent him away. While the spectators crowded the dam wall to watch, the dog had taken to the water and swum out toward the spot where the mallard had disappeared. However, he had deviated from the true line as he swam, going up above the bird, where any blood would drift away from him on the faint current set up by the inflowing river and the gusty southeaster that was sweeping across the open water.

Now Amber Joy was paddling around among the reeds in erratic circles, occasionally ducking his head below the surface but each time coming up with empty jaws, a little farther from the spot where the duck had plunged in.

His efforts were causing consternation on the bank. Bunty

Charles was dancing from one leg to the other in frustration. If he whistled and redirected Amber Joy to where the bird had fallen, he would lose points. There was still no guarantee that Amber Joy would find even with this assistance. On the other hand, time was running out. The three judges were already consulting their stopwatches. Amber Joy had been in the water for over three minutes.

Bunty Charles flashed an anxious glance at the next handler and dog in the line. Centaine Courtney-Malcomess and Dandy Lass of Weltevreden were his most bitter rivals. Up to now he and Amber Joy had managed to hold them off, but only by ten points. If they failed to find, they would certainly forfeit their hard-won lead.

Centaine Courtney-Malcomess was also under intense strain. She did not have Bunty's thirty years of field-trial experience. She had taken to the sport only recently. Yet she had brought all her immense energy and powers of concentration to it. Dandy Lass was the progeny of champions, a leggy golden retriever. She was bred for speed as a working gundog, strong and wiry, unlike the heavier show dogs with their classical points of breed but with their working instincts bred out of them. Dandy Lass had the heart and instinct to enter the heaviest cover or coldest water and work through it like a heroine. She had a fine nose to pick up the faintest scent of feather on the air, and her intelligence was uncanny. She and Centaine had developed an almost telepathic rapport.

Although she stood erect and utterly still, her face calm and imperturbable, inwardly Centaine was seething with agitation, and Dandy Lass picked it up from her. The judges would notice any word or gesture of restraint between them and mark them down immediately. However, Dandy Lass was sitting on the live coals of her eagerness. Her fluffy golden bottom barely came into contact with the ground, and she switched from haunch to haunch with tiny excited movements, not quite sufficient to incur the judges' wrath and penalty points. Whining or barking were grounds for instant elimination. With a huge effort, Dandy Lass prevented herself from giving tongue as she watched Amber Joy's frenzied efforts to find the bird. Yet her entire body shivered with eagerness, and the suppressed cries of excitement rumbled in her throat as she awaited her turn. Every few seconds she glanced up at Centaine with imploring eyes, begging for the command to go.

Shasa Courtney watched his mother from his place in the gun line. As always, she evoked in him the most profound sense of admiration. Centaine Courtney-Malcomess had turned seventy years old last New Year's Day. She had been named for her birth on the first day of the twentieth century, and yet she was as slim and straight as a teenage boy. The outline of her legs and buttocks under fine woolen cloth were aristocratic and elegant.

Who else would wear Chanel slacks to a field trial? He smiled. Her boots were of ostrich skin, handmade by Hermès of Paris.

Single-handed, she had raised Shasa from infancy when Shasa's father had been killed in action in France before his birth. Alone in the desert, she had discovered the first diamond that had led to the establishment of the fabulous H'ani mine. For thirty years she had run the mine and built up the sprawling financial empire that was to become Courtney Enterprises. Even though the chairmanship had passed to Shasa and then to her grandson Garry Courtney, Centaine still regularly took her seat on the board. Every word she uttered from that seat, every thought she expressed, was received with the utmost attention and respect. Every member of the family, from Shasa himself to Garry's brood of her great-grandchildren aged from four years to a few months, stood in total awe of Centaine Courtney-Malcomess. She was the only one who could give orders to Isabella Courtney and have them obeyed without argument or question.

She stood bareheaded in the bright sunshine of a golden Cape spring day with the pedigree bitch squatting beside her, and the sunlight sparkled on her hair. Her hair was one of her finer points, dense and thick and curling still, cut into a short cap the color of gunmetal touched with bright inlays of pure platinum. She held her chin high and the set of her head was alert.

The years had not eroded her beauty but had transformed it into a dignified serenity. Time might have withered that flawless skin but had been unable to affect the strong line of her jaw, the proud cheekbones and the high, intelligent forehead. Nor had it dimmed those dark eyes, eyes that could one moment reflect the ferocity of a cruel predator and the next moment shine with humor and wisdom.

One hell of a lady, Shasa thought. Just look at her, as hungry to win as she was fifty years ago.

One of the judges blew a single sharp blast on his whistle, and Bunty Charles's shoulders slumped with disappointment. Amber Joy had failed and was being recalled. Bunty Charles reinforced the recall with a blast on his own whistle and a brusque hand signal. Amber Joy came in obediently to the bank and lunged up out of the water. He shook himself, throwing a crystal curtain of water droplets into the sunlight. Then, to the horror of his owner and the amusement of the spectators, he lifted one leg and gave the nearest clump of reeds a contemptuous squirt, succinct expression of his opinion of the duck, the dam and the judges.

Such an unbridled display while under judges' orders was considered very poor form, and would certainly attract penalty points. However, Amber Joy was the picture of nonchalance as he trotted back to his owner, lolling his tongue and wagging his sodden tail.

By this stage Dandy Lass was in a turmoil of eagerness. She was shivering wildly, rolling her eyes like a berserker. She knew she would be called next, and the effort of keeping her backside pressed to the ground and maintaining her seat was destroying her from within.

Without looking down at her, Centaine exerted all her powers of telepathic communication to hold the bitch under control. The judges were sadistically relishing the delay, making a pretense of consulting each other and writing up their notes but in reality testing Dandy Lass to the outside limit of her endurance. If she broke now, she would be instantly eliminated; a whine or a bark would penalize her cruelly.

Bastards! Centaine thought bitterly. I hate every last man jack of you. Let my darling go. Let her go!

A faint choking whine escaped through Dandy's lips, a sound as though a bullfrog were being attacked by a swarm of bees under a blanket. Without seeming to move, Centaine extended her forefinger down the side seam of her Chanel slacks, and Dandy suppressed her next utterance.

The senior judge looked up from his notebook.

"Thank you. Number three," he called across the water. Centaine said sharply, "Fetch!" and Dandy Lass went away like a golden javelin launched from the sling.

As she came to the water, she folded her forelegs under her chest and went out from the bank in a stylish leap, like a thoroughbred steeplechaser. She hit the water three paces out, clear of the weeds, and came up swimming. Centaine's chest swelled with pride—only a true champion committed to water with such dash.

Dandy Lass swam like an otter, snaking through the water, leaving a broad V of ripples across the surface. Then the swelling in Centaine's chest turned to a cold weight of dread as she realized Dandy Lass was making the same mistake as Amber Joy had made. Perhaps the long delay had unsighted her, but she was veering slightly across the wind and the current, up into the blind spot where the scent would be carried away from her.

For an instant Centaine considered forfeiting points by redirecting her bitch. If Dandy found, even with assistance, she would still have wiped Amber Joy's eye, but they needed every single point if they were to win, and Centaine could already taste the sweetness of victory on the back of her tongue. She stood motionless, her whistle dangling on the loop around her neck.

Dandy Lass judged the length of the retrieve to within feet. She circled once on the edge of the far reed bank, but she was too high by three yards. Where Amber Joy had plowed on, getting ever farther from the bird, Dandy Lass stopped and, treading water, looked back to where Centaine stood on the far bank.

Deliberately Centaine thrust her left hand into the hip pocket of her slacks. Not even the strictest judge with the eyes of an eagle could have construed that tiny movement as a signal, but Shasa picked it up.

"The old girl hasn't changed." He shook his head, grinning. "Anything to win, any weapon in the arsenal, and the only sin is being caught out."

In the water Dandy Lass immediately turned left, downcurrent, paddling hard, and two seconds later her nose went up as she acknowledged scent. She made one more circle, the scent of blood rich and hot in her nostrils, as she placed the fallen mallard. Then she ducked her head into the cold brown water.

A roar of approval went up from the bank as she lifted her head again, streaming water, ears flat against her skull, the carcass of the mallard held in her jaws.

She left an arrowhead of ripples behind her as she headed back to the bank, the bird held neatly, wings folded, keeping it high to avoid dragging through the water. As her feet touched bottom, Dandy Lass flew up the bank. She did not even pause to shake herself. Not wasting a second, she went in to make her delivery.

As she dropped to sit in front of her mistress, Shasa felt a choke in his throat and his vision misted over. It was beautiful, he thought, to see that kind of rapport between a woman and a dog. Centaine took the carcass from Dandy Lass's mouth, and the iridescent patches in the wings burned like sapphires in the sunlight.

She handed it to the judge, and he examined it carefully, parting the feathers to check for teeth marks, for any sign of "hard mouthing." Centaine held her breath until the judge looked up again and nodded.

"Thank you, number three."

Not only had Centaine Courtney-Malcomess provided the venue for the trials, she was also the hostess for the prize-giving ceremony.

The candy-striped marquee tent, able to accommodate five hundred guests, was set up on the main polo field of the estate, and from Weltevreden's kitchens had come the gargantuan array of fine foods. The rock lobster had been caught by the fishing boats of Courtney Fishing and Canning company at Lambert's Bay; the turkey had been raised on Weltevreden; the succulent Karroo lamb came from Dragon's Fountain, the Courtney sheep station on the Camdeboo plains of the Karroo; and the wines were from the vineyards that began at the edge of the polo field outside the marquee tent.

The prime minister, John Vorster, had agreed to present the prizes. This was the fruit of Centaine's machinations over the years, a less-than-subtle hint to the world that the Courtneys were no longer a spent political force, that the days of their eclipse were ending.

Shasa Courtney had been a member of the faction within the Verwoerd cabinet that had opposed John Vorster's elevation to the premiership, and in consequence he had been sent into political exile. But over the years that he had been in London Centaine had labored within the party with all her finesse and skill to seek her son's rehabilitation. Of course, the fact that Shasa's term in London had been such an unequivocal triumph had reinforced her efforts. However, much of the credit for the Armscor appointment redounded directly to Centaine's tireless lobbying, her refusal to accept defeat and her blatant wielding of all her political and financial influence in her son's favor.

She would see to it that John Vorster's presence on the Weltevreden estate heralded a new golden era for the Courtneys. Vorster's round red face was the rising sun of their hopes and aspirations, Centaine thought comfortably as she looked around the crowded marquee. They were all gathered here at Weltevreden once again, all the power brokers and the power wielders. Although none of them had ever been so foolish or so reckless as to give Centaine Courtney-Malcomess direct offense or to write her off completely, there had been a period of cooling off while Shasa had been serving his term in London. Some had been cooler than others, Centaine reflected with a steely glint in her eye as she picked them out among the crowd, and she would remember them.

"Now is the winter of our discontent, made glorious summer," she thought with deep satisfaction. Almost as if to echo her sentiment the chairman of the South African Kennel Union rose to his feet and called for silence from the dais at the far end of the marquee. After welcoming the prime minster and spending a few minutes discussing the field-trial scene in general, the chairman began calling the prizewinners to the stand. The line of glistening silver trophies dwindled until only one remained in the center of the green baize-covered table, but it was the tallest and most ornate of them all with a statuette of a gundog on point surmounting the pinnacle.

"We come at last to the champion dog of trial." The chairman beamed round the tent until he picked out Centaine standing at the back of the tent surrounded by her family. "And it gives me much pleasure to call to the champion's berth for the first time a lady who in the few short years since she has taken to our sport has brought to it so much energy and enthusiasm that her contribution equals and in many cases surpasses those who have spent a lifetime working with gundogs. Ladies and gentlemen, I ask you to welcome Mrs. Centaine Courtney-Malcomess and Dandy Lass of Weltevreden."

Isabella had been waiting outside the tent with Dandy Lass on a leash. Now she came in with her, and while the crowd applauded Isabella handed the dog over to her grandmother.

Dandy Lass wore a fitted blanket in a daffodil yellow, Centaine's racing colors, with the Courtney insignia, a stylized silver diamond, embroidered in one corner. She fell in beside her mistress, heeling perfectly as Centaine started up toward the dais. The crowd laughed and applauded. Woman and dog made an elegant pair of thoroughbreds, and Dandy Lass grinned and lolled her tongue and wagged her tail at the fun of it.

On the dais, Dandy Lass curtsied politely in front of the prime minister, and at a word from Centaine offered him her right paw. The crowd loved it when John Vorster stooped to shake the proffered paw.

As he handed Centaine the enormous silver trophy, the prime minister smiled at her. For a man with such a formidable reputation for ruthless strength and granite resolve, his smile was boyishly infectious and his blue eyes twinkled.

As he shook Centaine's hand, he leaned a little closer, so that she alone could hear his words.

"Don't you and your family find that unbroken success in

everything you do becomes monotonous, Centaine?" he asked. They had come to first-name terms only in the last year or so.

"We try to be brave about enduring it, Uncle John," she assured him gravely.

The prime minster made a short and uncontroversial speech of congratulation, then circulated around the marquee with the alacrity of an adroit political gamesman. Smiling and shaking hands and passing on, he reached the end of the tent where Centaine was holding court.

"Once again my congratulations, Centaine. I wish I could stay longer to help you celebrate your famous victory." He glanced at his wristwatch.

"You have been generous with your time," Centaine agreed. "But before you leave, may I introduce the only one of my grandchildren whom you have not met?" She beckoned to Isabella, who was hovering close by. "Isabella has been in London serving as hostess for Shasa during his term at South Africa House."

As Isabella came forward, Centaine was watching the prime minister's craggy bulldog features attentively. She knew that Vorster was no philanderer; he could never have reached his position in the iron Calvinistic coils of his party if he had been. But despite the fact that for thirty years he had been happily and securely married he was still very much a man, and no man could remain unmoved when he looked at Isabella Courtney for the first time. Centaine saw the shift of his gaze, the way he hid his quick flare of attention behind that formidable frown.

Centaine and Isabella had planned for this meeting with care, ever since Isabella had amazed both Centaine and Shasa by her suddenly declared intention to enter the political arena.

"She'll get over it," Shasa predicted. But Centaine had shaken her head.

"Bella has changed. Something has happened to her since she went to London with you. She went as a flighty spoiled little bitch—"

"Oh, come, Mater." Predictably Shasa had risen to his precious daughter's defense, but Centaine went on without check.

"But she has returned a mature woman. However, there is more than that to it. She has steel now. She has a cutting edge, and there is something else." Centaine had hesitated as she tried to define it. "She has shed her romantic view of life; it is as though she has experienced a revelation, as though she has suffered and learned to hate, as though she has come through some portentous crisis and armed herself for whatever lies ahead."

141

"It's not like you to make these fanciful flights of imagination," Shasa had chaffed her. But Centaine had insisted.

"You mark my words, Bella has found her direction and she will prove herself as tough and ruthless as any of us."

"Surely not as tough and ruthless as you, Mater?"

"Have your little joke, Shasa Courtney, but time will prove me right." Centaine's eyes had gone out of focus and squinted slightly. Shasa knew that expression so well, when his mother indulged in furious concentration. He called them her scheming eyes. Then her eyes came back into focus. "She is going far, Shasa, probably farther than even you and I could dream—and I am going to help her."

And so Centaine had arranged this meeting, and now she watched her granddaughter acquit herself with all the aplomb she had expected of her.

Vorster asked Isabella, "So how did you enjoy the English winters?" It was clear that he expected a trivial response, but Isabella said, "It was worth putting up with them, if only to meet Harold Wilson and to have a firsthand account of the Labor government's attitude and intentions toward all of us who live in southern Africa."

Vorster's expression changed as he realized that there was a brain behind that lovely young face. He dropped his voice, and they talked quietly for a few minutes longer before Centaine intervened again.

"Isabella has just received her doctorate in political theory from London University." Artlessly she tossed out a little more bait.

"Oh so!" Vorster nodded. "Do we have a budding Helen Suzman in our midst?" He was referring to the only woman member of the South African parliament, the staunchest champion of human rights and the only really galling liberal thorn in the complacently thick hide of the Nationalist majority.

Isabella laughed, that husky sexual chuckle she knew could stir even the most hidebound misogynist. "Perhaps," she agreed. "A seat in the House might be my ultimate ambition, but that is still far ahead, and I don't think I would be as naïve as Mrs. Suzman, Prime Minister. My politics are very much in tune with that of my father and my grandmother," which of course made her a conservative. Now Vorster's regard was sharp blue and attentive as he studied her.

"The world is changing, Prime Minister," Centaine said, seizing the moment. "One day there may even be a place in your cabinet for a woman, don't you think?"

Vorster smiled and switched easily from English into Afrikaans.

"Even Dr. Courtney agrees that day is still far ahead. However, I do concede that such a pretty face would do much to lighten the deliberations of us ugly old men."

The change of language was, of course, a test. Nobody in South Africa with political aspirations could survive without fluency in Afrikaans, the language of the politically dominant group.

Isabella switched as easily as he had done. Her vocabulary was wide, her grammar perfect and her accent rang sweetly, even in the ear of a born Afrikaner.

Vorster smiled again, this time with pleasure, and continued the conversation for a few minutes more before glancing pointedly at his wristwatch and speaking to Centaine.

"I must go now. I have another function to attend." He turned back to Isabella. "*Totsiens*, Dr. Courtney, until we meet again. I will be watching your progress with interest."

Centaine and Shasa walked with him from the marquee to where his official car and driver waited on the edge of the polo ground.

"*Totsiens*, Centaine." Vorster shook her hand. "I congratulate you on the rearing of your granddaughter. I recognize many traits which she can only have inherited from you."

When Centaine returned to the marquee, she looked around quickly. Isabella was already the center of a circle of eager males.

"She has them panting like puppy dogs." Centaine suppressed a smile and caught her granddaughter's eye. Isabella left her admirers and came to her immediately, and Centaine took her arm in a comfortable proprietorial gesture.

"Well done, missy. You behaved like a veteran. Uncle John likes you. I rather think that we are on our way."

# 12

That evening, only the family sat down to dinner at the long table in Weltevreden's main dining room. However, Centaine had ordered the antique Limoges dinner service and the best silver. The table was resplendent in candlelight and a massed display of yellow roses.

As was usual on these family evenings, the women wore long dresses and the men were in black tie.

Only Sean was missing.

Sean had been invited—or, rather, Centaine had summoned him—but he was hunting with one of his most valuable clients on the Rhodesian concession and had sent his humble apologies. Centaine had accepted them reluctantly. She had wanted them all to celebrate her triumph with Dandy Lass, but she conceded that business came first.

The German industrialist Sean was guiding paid for sixty-three days of hunting each year at five hundred dollars a day. Of course, his vast business commitments in Germany would not allow him to spend that much time in the hunting veld. He was lucky if he could fit in two weeks in any one year. However, he paid for the additional days to secure the right to hunt three elephants instead of one. Sean had to be on call for him, even though he usually gave only a few day's notice of his intended arrival.

Centaine missed her eldest grandson. Sean was the handsomest and wildest of the three of them, and his presence was always stimulating. He seemed to charge the very air around him with the electricity of danger and excitement. It had cost her and the family tens of thousands of dollars to bail him out of the various scrapes his tempestuous nature led him into. Although she always expressed her outrage at these expenditures in the severest terms, secretly she did not grudge them. Her only fear was that one day **Sean** would go too far and get himself into real trouble from which even Centaine would be unable to extricate him. She dismissed that thought.

Tonight was not the night for morbid fancies.

The tall silver trophy glittered in the center of the long table. It stood on a pyramid of yellow roses. It was strange what satisfaction that bauble gave her. It had cost her countless hours of hard work in the field, but the winning had made it all worthwhile. It had always been like that for her. The burning need to excel was in her blood. She had passed on that divine contagion to those she loved.

At the far end of the table Shasa tapped the crystal glass in front of him with a silver spoon and in the ensuing silence rose to his feet. He was tall and elegant in his impeccable dinner jacket and black tie. He began one of those speeches for which he was renowned—easy and flowing, the wit and sentiment so cleverly timed and blended that he could at one moment raise a storm of laughter and at the next moisten every eye with a skillfully turned phrase.

Although he heaped her with praise and turned the attention of every person in the room full upon her, Centaine found her mind wandering to her other grandchildren. They were all hanging on their father's lips, so engrossed by his words that they were unaware of Centaine's appraisal.

Garry sat at her right hand, as befitted his importance in the family hierarchy. From the runt of the litter, myopic, weedy and asthmatic, he had transformed himself with little or no help from her or any of them into this bull of power and confidence. Now he was the helmsman of the family fortune, chairman of Courtney Enterprises. His bulk threatened the fragile legs of the genuine Chippendale chair, his thumbs were hooked into the pockets of his discreetly brocaded waistcoat. His dress shirt was a snowy expanse over the great chest, the starched wing collar too tight for a neck swollen not with fat but with muscle and sinew. His dense black hair stood up in a cockscomb at the crown, and his thick horn-rimmed spectacles glittered in the candlelight. His laughter rocked the room; full and unrestrained, it greeted each of Shasa's sallies, and it was so infectious that it transformed even his father's mildest remarks into wild hilarity.

Centaine switched her gaze to Garry's wife, Holly, who sat beside Shasa at the far end of the table. She was almost ten years Garry's senior. Centaine had opposed the union with all her power and cunning, but of course, she had not succeeded in preventing the marriage. She admitted to herself now that it had been a serious error of judgment to attempt to do so. She would now have had more control and influence over Holly had she not made the attempt. Instead she had raised barricades of mistrust in Holly's mind that she might never be able to pull down.

She had been wrong about Holly. She had proved the perfect wife for Garry. Holly had recognized qualities in him that none of them, not even Centaine, had fully perceived. She had brought them to full flower and carefully nurtured his self-confidence. In large measure she was responsible for Garry's success. She had given him strength and unflagging support. She had given him love and happiness, and she had given him three sons and a daughter. Centaine smiled as she thought of the little scamps asleep in the nursery wing upstairs, and then she sighed and frowned. The reserve Holly still felt toward her was a barrier between her and her great-grandchildren. Garry and Holly lived in Johannesburg, the nation's financial center, a thousand miles from Weltevreden.

The head office of Courtney Enterprises was in Johannesburg, as was the stock exchange. Garry was one of the main players; he had to be at the center of the arena. Thus there was every reason for him and Holly to have left Weltevreden, but Centaine felt that Holly was deliberately keeping the children from her. Although it was only a three-hour flight in the company jet, which Garry loved to pilot himself, these days Centaine very seldom saw them at Weltevreden. She wanted desperately to have the children close to her to guide and influence them, to protect and train them as she had their father, but Holly was the key. She would have to redouble her efforts to win her round. Now she deliberately caught her eye down the length of the long table, and smiled at her with all the warmth and affection she could convey. Holly smiled back, blonde and serene, her beauty given an extraordinary dimension by her particolored eyes, one blue, the other a startling violet.

"I'll make you like and trust me yet," Centaine promised silently. "You'll not be able to hold out forever, not against me. I'll have those children. This family is mine, those children are mine. You'll not keep them from me much longer."

Shasa had said something about her that she had missed in her preoccupation. Now every head at the table was turned toward Centaine, and they were all applauding with enthusiasm. She smiled and nodded her acknowledgement of whatever compliment Shasa had paid her, and as the applause faded Shasa continued.

"You may have thought to yourselves as you watched her

handling Dandy Lass today that it was a remarkable accomplishment. For any other woman, it might have been so, but here we have the lady who faced down a man-eating lion with me as an infant strapped upon her back . . .'' Shasa was reciting once again all the old stories about her that were the weft and the warp of the family legend. In itself this recitation at every important occasion had become tradition and, though they had all heard them a hundred times, their enjoyment was as fresh as ever.

Only one person at the table looked embarrassed by the extravagance of Shasa's eulogy.

Centaine felt a chill little breeze of annoyance ruffle the silken surface of her self-satisfaction. Of all her grandchildren, the one for whom she felt the least warmth and concern was Michael He sat near the center of the long table at the lowliest position, not simply because he was the youngest of her grandsons. Michael did not fit into Centaine's scheme of things. There were secret depths and hidden places in his nature that she had not yet fathomed, and that therefore annoyed her.

She had never been able to wean Michael away from his natural mother. Even the thought of Tara Courtney sent a scalding acidic rush of hatred through Centaine's bowels. Tara had outraged every principle and concept of decency and morality that Centaine held sacrosanct. She was a Marxist and a miscegenist, a traitor and a patricide. A portion of Centaine's feelings toward Tara were passed on to this one of her sons.

The force of her gaze must have been fierce enough for Michael to sense it. He glanced up at her suddenly and paled under Centaine's dark eyes, then looked away again hurriedly, almost guiltily.

At Shasa's insistence, and over her objections, the family had acquired a controlling interest in the media company that counted among its assets *The Golden City Mail*. Shasa's motive had been to secure a place for Michael at the top of his chosen profession. His idea had been to build up the *Mail* as a powerful and conservative voice of reason, and for Michael, once he had earned his spurs, to take over as publisher and editor. That day had not yet dawned, and Michael was still only a deputy editor. If it had been left to Shasa, he would have pushed Michael earlier. However, both Garry and Centaine had kept his paternal indulgence in check. The two of them had reasoned that Michael was not yet ready for the job. His financial and administrative instincts were underdeveloped and his political judgement was naïve, perhaps irreparably flawed. It was Michael's influence on editorial policy that continually nudged the *Mail* off the center of the road, slanting it dangerously to the left, so that the newspaper had become distrusted not only by government but also by the establishment of finance and mining and industry, those who paid for advertising space.

On three previous occasions the *Mail* had been banned by government decree, each time at a financial cost that infuriated Garry and with a loss of prestige and influence that made Centaine uneasy.

He's not a true Courtney, Centaine thought, as she studied Michael's pretty features. Even Bella has more steel in one of her little fingers than he has in his entire body. Michael is a waverer and a bleeder. His concern is for strangers and for the losers, not for the family. For Centaine that was the most heinous form of treachery. He doesn't take after any of us, she thought, he takes after his mother. And that was her most damning judgment. He has even tried to corrupt Bella.

Centaine knew about the presence of her two grandchildren at the antiapartheid rally in Trafalgar Square. They had been photographed by South African intelligence from the windows of South Africa House, and Centaine had received a warning call from one of her important contacts in the government. Fortunately, Centaine had been able to smooth things over. Isabella had done some undercover work for South African intelligence during her passionate love affair with Lothar De La Rey. Lothar had been a colonel in the police at the time, and he was now a member of parliament and a deputy minister in the Ministry of Law and Order.

Centaine had called on Lothar personally. She had enormous influence over him; there were secrets that involved Lothar's father and other mysteries Lothar could only guess at. In addition, Lothar had been Bella's lover and, Centaine suspected, was still more than a little in love with her.

"I will include a full explanation of her presence at the rally in Isabella's file," Lothar assured her. "We know that she is a patriot, she has worked for us before, but I can't promise anything for Michael, Tantie." Lothar used the respectful term of address which meant more than simply "Aunt." "Michael has too many black marks on his file already, I'm afraid."

Yes, thought Centaine grimly, Michael has accumulated black marks like a dog picks up fleas, and some of them hop off on to all of us.

At that moment Shasa finished his speech and all of them turned toward Centaine's end of the table expectantly. As a speaker she was every bit as good as her son, but there was often a little more of a sting in her words, and a little more directness in her views. They waited with anticipation for the customary fireworks as she began her reply, but tonight they were disappointed.

Centaine seemed in an unusually mild and benevolent mood. Rather than censure, she had praise and appreciation for all of them. Garry's financial results, Isabella's academic achievements, Holly's architectural plans for the new Courtney luxury hotel on the Zululand coast and her forthcoming birthday.

"So sorry you won't be able to stay over with us for the big day, Holly darling."

Even Michael came in for praise, albeit much fainter praise, with the publication of his most recent book. "One doesn't have to agree with your conclusions or with the solutions you suggest, Mickey dear, to appreciate just how much thought and hard work went into the writing of it."

When she asked them to rise and drink a toast to "our family and every single person in it," they responded with gusto. Then Shasa came to the head of the table to take her arm and lead her into the blue drawing room where coffee, liqueurs and cigars were waiting. Centaine would never accede to the barbarous custom of leaving the men alone with their cigars after dinner. If there were anything worth talking about, she wanted to be part of those discussions.

Quickly Michael crossed to Isabella as she rose from her seat at the table and took her arm.

"I've missed you, Bella. Why didn't you answer my letters? There is so much I want to know. Ramón and Nicky—" He saw her expression change, and his alarm was quick.

"Is something wrong, Bella?"

"Not now, Mickey," she warned him quickly. This was the first time they had spoken in almost six months, since Nicky had gone. She had not telephoned him or answered his letters. Moreover, she had avoided being alone with him ever since he had arrived at Weltevreden that morning.

"There is something wrong," Michael insisted.

"Smile!" she ordered him, smiling herself. "Don't make a fuss. I'll come to your room later. No questions now." She squeezed his arm and laughed gaily as they all trooped through to the blue drawing room and clustered round attentively while Centaine settled herself in her customary place on the long sofa facing the roaring log fire in the Adam fireplace.

"Let me have my girls with me tonight," she decided, and picked out Holly. "Come and sit this side, my dear." She patted the sofa beside her. "Bella, you on this side of me, please."

Centaine seldom did anything without good reason, and as soon as the servants had given them coffee and Shasa had poured cognac for the men she played her high card.

"I've been waiting for a chance to do this, Holly," she said in a voice that commanded all their attention. "And I suppose your birthday is the best excuse I'll ever have. You are my eldest granddaughter, so I'm going to establish a little family tradition tonight."

Centaine reached up behind her own neck and unclasped the necklace she wore. She held it in her hands, a glittering treasure, more than a thousand carats of perfect yellow diamonds. She had personally selected each stone from the production of her fabulous H'ani mine in the far north. It has taken ten years for her to accumulate them, and Garrards of London had designed and manufactured the setting in pure platinum.

"Something so lovely should be worn only by a beautiful woman," Centaine whispered regretfully, and the tears that sparkled in her dark eyes were genuine. "Alas, I no longer fulfil that requirement, so it is time for me to pass them on to somebody who does."

She turned to Holly. "Wear these with joy," she said and hung them at her throat.

Holly sat as though stunned, and everybody in the room was silent with awe. They all knew what that necklace meant to Centaine; they knew she placed a far higher value on it than the mere two million sterling the Lloyd's assessors had recently decided was its intrinsic worth.

Holly lifted her right hand and stroked the bright stars at her throat with a look of total disbelief on her delicate features. Then she choked and sobbed and turned to Centaine and embraced her. The two women clung together for a moment before Holly could find her voice. It was muffled and small, but all of them heard it clearly.

"Thank you, Nana." Only close members of the family called Centaine that, and Holly had never done so before.

Centaine held her tightly, closing her eyes and pressing her face against Holly's golden head so that none of them would see the little smile of triumph on her lips and the satisfied gleam through the tears in her eyes.

* * *

Nanny was waiting in Isabella's suite.

"It's after one o'clock," Isabella exclaimed. "I've told you not to wait up for me, you silly old woman."

"I've been waiting up for you twenty-five years." Nanny came to unhook the back of her dress.

"It makes me feel terrible," Isabella protested.

"It makes me feel good," Nanny grunted. "I don't feel happy 'less I know what you been up to, missy. I'll run your bath— didn't do it before, didn't want it to turn cold."

"A bath at one o'clock in the morning!" Isabella dismissed the idea strenuously. She had not allowed Nanny to see her naked since her return. The old woman's eyes were much too sharp. She would pick up the tiny changes that childbirth had wrought on Isabella's body; the darkening and enlarging of her nipples, the faint stria where the skin had stretched across her hips and lower belly.

She sensed that Nanny was becoming suspicious at this change of behavior, and to divert her she said: "Off with you now, Nanny. Go and warm Bossie's bed for him."

Nanny looked shocked. "Who's been telling you scandal stories?" she demanded.

"You're not the only one who knows what's going on at Weltevreden," Isabella informed her gleefully. "Old Bossie has been after you for years. About time you took pity on him. He's a good man." Bossie was the estate blacksmith who had come to work for Centaine as an apprentice thirty-five years ago. "You go off and hammer his anvil for him."

"That's dirty talk," Nanny sniffed. "A real lady don't talk dirty." Nanny tried to hide her confusion behind a prim expression, but she backed off toward the door. Isabella sighed with relief as it closed behind her.

She went through to her bathroom and swiftly removed her makeup, tossed her evening dress over the back of the sofa for Nanny to deal with in the morning and slipped into a silk bathrobe. As she belted the robe, she crossed her bedroom and then paused with her fingers on the door handle.

"What am I going to tell Mickey?" If she had asked herself that question only three days ago, the answer would have been obvious, but since then circumstances had changed. A packet had arrived.

The last communication she had received from Joe Cicero had been on the day before she left London to return to the Cape of Good Hope. He had telephoned her at Cadogan Square while she was in the process of packing.

"Red Rose." She had recognized the husky wheeze of his voice instantly, and as always it had frozen her with dread and loathing. "I am going to give you your contact address. Use it only in an emergency. It is an answering service, so do not waste time and energy checking it. A telegram or letter addressed to Hoffman, care of Mason's Agency, 10 Blushing Lane, Soho, will find me. Memorize that address. Do not write it down."

"I have it," Isabella whispered.

"On your return home, you will hire a post office box at a location not associated with Weltevreden. Use a fictitious name and inform me at the Blushing Lane address when it is established. Is that clear?"

Within days of arriving back at Weltevreden, Isabella had driven over the Constantiaberg Pass to the sprawling suburb of Camps Bay on the Atlantic seaboard of the Cape peninsula. The post office there was far enough removed from Weltevreden for none of the postal staff to recognize her. She hired the box in the name of Mrs. Rose Cohen and sent a registered letter to Blushing Lane with this box number.

She checked the box for a letter each evening as she returned from her office in Centaine House in central Cape Town, driving the Mini over the neck between Signal Hill and the mountain, the more circuitous route around the back of Table Mountain, to reach Weltevreden. Even though the box remained empty day after day and week after week, she never varied her routine.

The lack of news of Nicholas ate away at the fabric of her soul. The day-to-day events of her life seemed all a sham and a pretense. Although she channeled all her energy into her work as Shasa's assistant, the effort was not the opiate for her pain that she had hoped it might be.

She smiled and laughed, she rode with Nana and on weekends played tennis or sailed with her old friends. She worked and played as though everything were the same, but it was all acting.

The nights were long and lonely. In the midnight hours, she would resolve to go to Shasa and describe in detail the web in which she was enmeshed, but then in daylight she would ask herself, "What can Pater do? What can anybody do to help me?" And she remembered Nicholas's swollen face and the silver bubbles streaming from his nose as he almost drowned, and she knew she could not risk that ever happening again. Strangely, the passage of time did not reduce the pain of her loss; instead it seemed to inflame her wounds, and the lack of news of Nicholas irritated them still further. Each day her suffering was harder to bear alone.

Then she heard that Michael was coming down from Johannesburg to Weltevreden for the trials, and it seemed fortuitous. Michael was the perfect confidant. She would not expect him to do anything except share her suffering and lighten the terrible load which up until now she had carried alone.

On the Friday before Michael's arrival, she had driven over the neck to Camps Bay and parked the Mini in the street beyond the post office. She walked back slowly and glanced into the side hall that housed the tiers of tiny steel postboxes. It was almost six in the evening, and the main post office had long ago closed. There were a couple of teenagers necking in the corner of postal hall, but they scurried away guiltily as she glared at them. Isabella took the precaution of never approaching or opening her box while a stranger was in the hall.

She glanced back at the entrance to make sure she was alone, then inserted her key into the lock of the tiny steel door in the fifth row of tiered boxes. The shock was greater for the fact that she was expecting the box to be empty. Adrenaline squirted into her bloodstream, and she felt her cheeks burn and her breathing choke.

She snatched up the thick brown envelope and crammed it into her sling bag. Then, guilty as a thief, she slammed and locked the box and ran back to where the Mini was parked. She was trembling so hard that she had difficulty fitting the key into the door lock. She was breathing as hard as though she had played a long rally on the tennis court as she started the Mini and U-turned back across the road.

She parked above the beach under the palms that lined the drive. At this hour the beach was almost deserted. An elderly couple exercised an Irish setter at the edge of the water, and a single bather braved the southeaster and the icy green waters of the Benguela current. She rolled up the windows and locked both doors of the Mini before she took the envelope out of her bag and held it in her lap.

The address was typed, Mrs. Rose Cohen, and the Queen's-head postage stamps had been franked at Trafalgar Square post office. She turned the envelope over, reluctant to open it, terrified of what it might contain. There was no return address on the reverse. Still delaying the moment, she searched for the gold lady's penknife in her bag and carefully slit the flap of the envelope with its razor-edged blade.

A colored photograph slid out, and every nerve in her body tingled as she turned it face up and recognized her son.

Nicky sat on a blue blanket on a garden lawn. He wore only a diaper. He was sitting up unsupported, and she reminded herself that he was nearly seven months old. He had grown, his cheeks were not so chubby, his limbs were longer and sleeker. His hair was thicker and longer, curling darkly onto his forehead. His expression was quizzical, but there was a smile hovering at the corners of his mouth, and his eyes were bright and green as emeralds.

"Oh, God. He's more beautiful!" she gasped, holding the photograph up to the light to study every tiny detail of his face. "He's grown so big already, and sitting up on his own. My clever little manikin." She touched the image and then saw with consternation that she had left a fingerprint on the glossy surface of the photograph. She wiped it off carefully with a Kleenex.

"My baby," she whispered, and felt her loss tear at her heart with renewed ferocity. "Oh, my baby!"

The sun had sunk to touch the line of the horizon far out on the Atlantic before she could rouse herself. Only then, as she returned the photograph to the envelope, did she realize she had overlooked the other items it contained.

First, there was a photostat copy of a page from what was obviously a medical register at some children's clinic, but the name and address of the clinic had been obliterated. It was written in Spanish.

His name was at the head of the sheet: "Nicholas Miguel Ramón de Machado," followed by his date of birth and a record of weekly visits to the clinic. Each dated entry was in a variety of handwritings and signed by the clinic's doctors or sisters.

It showed his weight and diet and dental records. She saw that on July 15 he had been treated for a rash the doctor diagnosed as prickly heat and two weeks later for mild oral thrush. Otherwise he was healthy and normal. With a rush of maternal pride, she read that his first two teeth had erupted at four months, and he weighed almost sixteen kilos.

Isabella turned to the last folded sheet of paper the envelope contained and immediately recognized the handwriting. It was in Spanish, in Adra's firm, restrained hand.

Señorita Bella,
Nicky grows every day stronger and cleverer. He has a temper like one of the bulls of the *corrida*. He can crawl on hands and knees almost as fast as I can run, and I expect that any day now he will rise up on his back legs and walk.

The first word he spoke was "Mamma," and I tell him each day how beautiful you are and how one day you will come to him. He does not yet understand, but one day he will.

I think of you often, señorita. You must believe that I will care for Nicky with my own life. Please do not do anything to endanger him.

Respectfully,
ADRA OLIVARES

The warning contained in the last line twisted like a knife between her ribs, and was more urgent and poignant for being so mildly expressed. She knew then that she could never risk telling anyone, not Pater or Nana or even Michael.

She hesitated now with her hand on the handle of her bedroom door. "I have to lie to you, Mickey. I'm sorry. Perhaps one day I will tell you the truth." She listened for a moment, but the great house was silent, and she turned the handle and quietly swung the door open.

The long gallery was deserted with only the night-lights burning in their brackets on the wood-paneled walls. On bare feet, Isabella slipped silently over the Persian carpets scattered on the parquet floor. Since he was so seldom at Weltevreden, Michael had kept his old room in the nursery wing.

He was sitting up in bed reading. As soon as she pushed the door open, he dropped the book on the bedside table and lifted the bedclothes for her.

As she climbed in beside him, he tucked the eiderdown around her shoulders and she clung to him, shivering with misery. They held each other for a long time in silence before Michael invited her gently:

"Tell me, Bella."

Even then she could not say it immediately. Her good intentions wavered, and she felt a desperate temptation to ignore Adra's warning. Mickey was the only one of the family who knew Ramón and Nicholas even existed. She wanted desperately to blurt it all out to him and have his gentle warming comfort help fill the terrible void in her soul.

Then the image of Nicholas that she had watched on the videotape flashed before her eyes once more. She drew a deep breath and pressed her face to Michael's chest. "Nicky is dead," she whispered, and she felt him flinch in her embrace. He did not reply at once.

"It's true," she consoled herself silently. "Nicky is dead to all of us now." And yet the words seemed a dreadful betrayal of both Michael and Nicholas. She did not, dared not, trust him. She had denied the existence of her own son to him, and the

155

falsehood seemed to increase her own misery and isolation, if that were possible.

"How?" Michael asked at last.

She had anticipated the question. "Cot death," she whispered. "I went to wake him for his feed, and he was cold and dead."

She felt Michael shiver against her. "Oh, God! My poor Bella! How horrible! How cruel!"

The reality was crueler and more horrible than he could imagine, but she could not share it with him.

After a long minute, he asked: "Ramón? Where is Ramón? He should be here to comfort you."

"Ramón," she repeated his name, trying to keep fear out of her voice. "When Nicky was gone, Ramón changed completely. I think he blamed me. His love for me died with Nicky." She found herself weeping now, hard tearing sobs that expressed all the grief and terror and loneliness that had haunted her for so long. "Nicky is gone. Ramón is gone. I will never see either of them again, not as long as I live."

Michael hugged her tightly. His body was hard and warm and strong. Masculine strength that was completely devoid of sexuality was what she needed most. She felt it flowing into her like water filling the depleted dam of her courage and fortitude, and she clung to him silently.

After a while he began to talk. She lay and listened, her ear pressed to his chest so that his voice was a reverberating murmur. He talked of love and suffering, of loneliness and of hope, and at last of death.

"The true terror of death is its finality. The ending so abrupt, the void beyond so irrevocable. You cannot challenge death or appeal against it. You only break your heart if you try."

Platitudes, she thought, old clichés, the same ones with which man has tried to console himself for tens of thousands of years. Yet, like most clichés, they were true, and they were the only comfort she had available to her. More important than the sense of the words, was the soft lulling music of Michael's voice, the warmth and strength of his body, and his love for her.

At last she fell asleep.

She awoke before dawn, immediately aware that he had lain all night without moving so as not to disturb her, and that he was awake also.

"Thank you, Mickey," she whispered. "You'll never know how alone I have been. I needed that badly."

"I do know, Bella. I know what loneliness is." And she felt

her heart go out to him, her own pain temporarily assuaged. She wanted to be there for him now. It was his turn.

"Tell me about your new book, Mickey. I haven't read it yet—I'm sorry." He had sent her a prepublication copy, lovingly inscribed, but she had been totally engrossed with her own suffering. There had been no time for anybody else, not even Michael. So this time, while she listened, he talked about the book and then about himself and his view of the world around them.

"I have spoken to Raleigh Tabaka again," he said suddenly. She was startled. She had not thought of that name since she left London.

"Where? Where did you meet him?"

Michael shook his head. "I did not meet him. We spoke on the telephone, very briefly. I think he was calling from another country, but he will be here soon. He is a will-o'-the-wisp, a Black Pimpernel. He comes and goes across borders like a shadow."

"You have arranged to meet him?" she asked.

"Yes. He is as good as his word."

"Be careful, Mickey. Please promise me you will be careful. He is a dangerous man."

"There is nothing for you to worry about," he assured her. "I'm no hero. I'm not like Sean or Garry. I'll be careful, very careful. I promise you."

# 13

Michael Courtney parked his battered Valiant in the carpark of a drive-in restaurant on an off ramp of the main Johannesburg-to-Durban highway.

He switched off the ignition, but the engine continued running on preignition for a few unsteady beats. It had been missing badly all the way down from the offices of *The Golden City Mail* in central Johannesburg. The car had clocked over seventy thousand miles and should have been sold two years previously.

His contract stipulated that as deputy editor he was entitled to a new "luxury" vehicle every twelve months. However, Michael had developed an affection for the old Valiant. All its scars and scrapes had been honorably acquired, while over the years the driver's seat had taken on the contours of his body.

He studied the other vehicles in the carpark, but none of them answered the description he had been given. He glanced at his wristwatch, a Japanese digital for which he had paid five dollars on a trip to Tokyo for the newspaper the previous year. He was twenty minutes early, so he lit a cigarette and slumped down in the comfortable, shabby old seat.

Thinking about the car and the watch made him smile. He really was the odd man out in his family. From Nana down to Isabella, they were all obsessed with material possessions. Nana had her daffodil-colored Daimlers; the color was always the same, although the model changed each year. Pater kept a garage filled with classic cars, mostly British sports cars like the SS Jaguar and the big six-liter touring Bentley in racing green. Garry had his fancy Italian Maseratis and Ferraris. Sean bolstered his tough-guy image with elaborately outfitted four-wheel-drive hunting vehicles, and even Isabella drove a souped-up little thing that cost twice as much as a new Valiant.

Not one of them would have worn a digital wristwatch, not Nana with her diamond Piaget nor Sean with his macho gold Rolex. "Things." Michael's smile turned down at the corners of his mouth. "All they see are things, not people. It's the sickness of our country."

There was a tap on the side window of the Valiant and Michael started and looked round, expecting his contact.

There was nobody there.

He was startled. Then a small black hand with a pink palm came into view and diffidently tapped on the glass with one finger.

Michael rolled down the window and stuck his head out. A black urchin grinned up at him. He could not have been more than five or six years of age. He was barefoot, and his singlet and shorts were ragged. Although his nostrils were crusted with white flakes of dried snot, his smile was radiant.

"Please, *Baas*," he piped, and cupped his hands in a beggar's gesture. "Me hungry. Please give one cent, *Baas!*"

Michael opened the door, and the child backed away uncertainly. Michael picked up his cardigan, which he had thrown on the seat beside him, and slipped it over the child's head. It hung down almost to his ankles, and the sleeves drooped a foot beyond his fingertips. Michael rolled them up for him and said in fluent Xhosa, "Where do you live, little one?"

The boy was obviously flabbergasted, not only by this attention but also to hear a white man speak Xhosa. Six years before, Michael had realized that it was impossible to understand a man unless you spoke his language. He had been studying and practicing since then. Not one white in a thousand went to those lengths. All blacks were expected to learn either English or Afrikaans; otherwise they were virtually unemployable. Now Michael spoke both Xhosa and Zulu. These languages were closely related and between them covered the vast majority of the black population of southern Africa.

"I live at Drake's Farm, Nkosi."

Drake's Farm was the sprawling black township almost a million souls called home. From here it was out of view to the east of the highway, but the smoke from the thousands of cooking-fires hazed the sky to a dirty leaden grey. The wage earners of Drake's Farm commuted daily by train or bus to their workplaces in the homes and factories and businesses of the white areas of the Witwatersrand.

The huge commercial and mining complex of greater Johannesburg was surrounded by these dormitory townships, Drake's Farm and Soweto and Alexandria. Under the bizarre conditions of the Group Areas Act, the entire country was divided up into areas reserved for each of the racial groups.

"When did you last eat?" Michael asked the child gently.

"I ate yesterday, in the morning, great chief."

Michael took a five-rand banknote from his wallet. The child's eyes seemed to expand into a pair of luminous pools as he stared at it. He had almost certainly never possessed so much money at one time in his short life.

Michael proffered the note. The child snatched it and turned and ran, tripping over the skirts of the dangling cardigan. He gave no thanks, and his expression was one of desperate terror lest the gift be taken back from him before he could escape.

Michael laughed with delight at his antics. Suddenly his amusement turned to outrage. Was there another country in the modern First World, he wondered, where little children were still forced to beg on the streets? Then mingled with his anger was a sense of utter hopelessness.

Was there any other country that embraced both the members of the First World, like his own family with its vast estates and stunning collection of treasures, and the desperate poverty of the Third World epitomized here in the townships? The contrast was all the crueler for being so closely juxtaposed.

"If only there was something I could do," he lamented, and drew so hard on his cigarette that a full inch of ash glowed and a spark fell unnoticed onto his tie and scorched a spot the size of a pinhead. It did not make much difference to the general appearance of his attire.

A small blue delivery van turned off the main highway into the carpark. It was driven by a young black man in a peaked cap. The sign on the body read: "Phuza Muhle Butchery. 12th Avenue, Drake's Farm." The name promised "good eating."

Michael flashed his lights as he had been instructed to do. The van pulled into the parking bay directly in front of him. Michael climbed out and locked the Valiant before he crossed to the blue van. The rear doors were unlocked. Michael climbed in and slammed them behind him. The body of the van was more than half filled with baskets containing packages of raw meat, and the skinned carcasses of a number of sheep hung from hooks in the roof.

"Come this way," the driver called to him in Zulu, and Michael crawled down the length of the body. The hanging carcasses brushed against him, and the drippings stained the knees of his corduroy trousers. The driver had prepared a niche for him between two of the meat baskets where he would be hidden from casual inspection.

"There will be no trouble," the driver assured him in cheerful Zulu. "Nobody ever stops this van."

He pulled away, and Michael settled down on the grubby floor. These theatrical precautions were annoying but necessary. No white was allowed into the township without a permit issued by the local police station in consultation with the township management council. In the ordinary course of events this permit was not difficult to obtain. However, Michael Courtney was a marked man. He had three previous convictions for contravention of the Publications Control Act, for which he and his newspaper had been heavily fined.

Under the act, the government censors had been given almost unlimited powers of banning and suppression of any material or publication, and they were encouraged by the full caucus of the ruling National Party not to flinch from exercising those powers to uphold the Calvinistic moral views of the Dutch Reformed Church and to protect the political status quo.

What chance, then, did Michael's writings have against their vigilance? Michael's application for a permit to enter Drake's Farm township had been summarily rejected.

The blue van entered the main gates of the township without a check. The indolent uniformed black guards did not even glance up from their game of African Ludo, played with Coca-Cola crown tops on a carved wooden board.

"You can come up front now," the driver called, and Michael clambered over the meat baskets to reach the passenger seat in the cab.

The township always fascinated him. It was almost like visiting an alien planet.

It was back in 1960, almost eleven years ago, that he had last visited Drake's Farm. At that time, he had been a cub reporter for the *Mail*. That was the year in which he had written the "Rage" series of articles that were the foundation on which his journalistic reputation had been built, and incidentally the grounds for his first conviction under the Publications Control Act.

He smiled at the memory and looked around him with interest as they drove through the old section of the township. This dated from the previous century, the Victorian era, during which the fabulous golden reefs of the Witwatersrand had first been discovered close by.

The old section was a maze of lanes and alleys and higgledy-piggledy buildings, shacks and shanties of unburnt brick and cracked plaster, of corrugated iron roofs painted all the shades of an artist's palette. Most of the original colors had faded and were running with the red leprosy of rust.

The narrow streets were rutted and studded with potholes and puddles of indeterminate liquid. Scrawny chickens scurried and scratched in the litter of rubbish. A huge sow with a pink hide that looked as though it had been parboiled wallowed in one of the puddles and grunted irritably as the van passed. The stink was wondrous. The sour stench of ripening garbage mingled with that of the open drains and the earthen toilets that stood like sentry boxes behind the hovels.

The government health inspector had long ago abandoned all hope of ever regulating the old section of Drake's Farm. One day the bulldozers would arrive and the *Mail* would run front-page photographs of the distraught black families crouching on the pathetic piles of their worldly possessions, watching the brutal machines demolishing their homes. A white civil servant in a dark suit would make a statement on the state television network about "this festering health hazard making way for comfortable modern bungalows." The anticipation of that day made Michael angry all over again.

The blue van bumped and weaved over the rutted lanes, passing the dismal shebeens and whorehouses, and then crossed the invisible line from the old section into the new one, which the same civil servant would describe as comfortable modern bungalows. Thousands of identical brick boxes with grey corrugated-asbestos roofs stood in endless lines upon the treeless veld. They reminded Michael of the rows of white wooden crosses he had seen in the military cemeteries of France.

Yet somehow the black residents had managed to imprint their character and individuality on this forbidding townscape. Here and there a house had been repainted a startling color in the monotonous grubby white lines. Pink or sky blue or vivid orange, they bore witness to the African love of bright color. Michael noticed one that had been beautifully decorated in the traditional geometric designs of the Ndebele tribe from the north.

The tiny front gardens were a mirror of the personal style of the occupants. One was a square of dusty bare earth; another was planted with rows of maize plants and had a milking goat tethered at the front door; yet another boasted a garden of straggly geranium plants in old five-gallon paint tins; still another was fenced with high barbed wire and the weed-clogged yard was patrolled by a bony but ferocious mongrel guard dog.

Some of the plots were separated from each other by ornamental walls of concrete breeze blocks or old truck tires painted gaudy colors and half buried in the brick-hard earth. Most of the cottages had extraneous additions tacked on to them, usually a lean-to of salvaged lumber and rusty corrugated iron into which a family of the owners' relatives had overflowed. There were abandoned motor vehicles, sans engine or wheels, parked at the curbs. Hillocks of old mattresses, disintegrating cardboard boxes and other discarded rubbish the refuse removal service had overlooked stood on the street corners.

Across this stage moved the people of the townships. These were the people whom Michael loved more than his own race or class, the people with whom he empathized and for whom he agonized. They delighted and amazed him endlessly with their strength and fortitude and will to survive.

The children were everywhere he looked, the crawlers and totterers and squawkers who rolled and roistered in the streets like litters of glossy black Labrador puppies or rode high, strapped to their mother's backs in the traditional style. The older children played their simple games with wire and empty beer cans they had fashioned into toy automobiles. The little girls played with skipping ropes in the middle of the road or imitated the games of hopscotch and catch they had seen the white children play. They were tardy and reluctant to clear the roadway when the driver of the blue van hooted at them.

When they saw Michael's white face they danced beside the slow-moving van with cries of "Sweetie! Sweetie!" Michael had come prepared, and he tossed them the hard sugar candies with which he had stuffed his pockets.

Though most of the adult population had made the long daily journey to their workplaces in the city, the mothers, the old people and the unemployed had been left behind.

Gangs of street youths stared at him expressionlessly as he passed, gathered in idle groups on the littered street corners. Though he knew these teenagers were the jackals of the townships who preyed on their own kind, Michael's sympathy went out to them. He understood their despair. He knew that even before they had fairly embarked on life's journey they were aware it held nothing for them, no expectation or hope of better things or kinder times.

Then there were the women at their chores, hanging the long lines of laundry to dry like prayer flags on the breeze or stooped over the black three-legged pots in the backyards, cooking the staple maize porridge of their diet over open fires in the traditional way, preferring that to the iron stoves in the tiny cottage kitchens. The smoke of the fires mingled with the blown dust to form the cloud that perpetually hung over the township.

The illegal hawkers, or *spouzas*, who had eluded the Afrikaner government's passion for regulations and licensing, wheeled their barrows and shouted their wares in the busy streets. Housewives bartered with them for a single potato or cigarette or orange or slice of white bread, depending on their circumstances.

Despite these dreary surroundings and the evidence of poverty and neglect, Michael heard in every street and at every corner they turned the sound of laughter and music. The laughter was spontaneous and merry. Their shouted greetings and repartee were carefree. Wherever he looked were those lovely African smiles that filled his heart and squeezed it to the point of pain.

The music rang and echoed from the bleak little cottages and, in the streets, from the transistor radios that men and women carried in hand or balanced on their heads as they walked. The children played their penny whistles and banjos made from paraffin tins and wood and pieces of wire. They danced and they

163

sang in a spontaneous expression of the sheer joy of living, even in these most insalubrious circumstances.

For Michael the laughter and the music depicted the indomitable spirit of the black African in the face of all hardship. For him there could not be another race on earth quite like them. Michael loved them, every one of them, no matter what age or sex or tribe or condition. He was of Africa, and these were his people.

"What can I do for you, my brothers?" he whispered. "What can I do to help you? I wish I knew. Everything I have attempted so far has failed. All my efforts have died like a hopeless shout upon the desert air. If only I could find the way."

Then abruptly he was distracted. They topped a rise in the gently undulating veld, and Michael straightened in his seat.

Eleven years ago, when last he had passed this way, there had been nothing but open grassland here, with a few scrawny goats grazing amongst the red wounds which erosion and neglect had raked into the earth.

"Nobs Hill." The driver of the van chuckled at his surprise. "Beautiful, hey?"

Such is the determination and fortitude of men that even in the face of the most adverse circumstances there are those few who will not only survive, but who with courage and ingenuity far beyond the average will flourish and rise high above the obstacles and pitfalls with which their path is strewn. Along the low ridge of ground, standing above the huddled shacks and cottages of Drake's Farm, were the homes of the black elite. There were a hundred or so of these successful men set apart from all the million inhabitants of Drake's Farm. Through business acumen, natural ability and hard work they had wrested material success from the hands of their white political masters, from those who had attempted to dictate their fate through the monumental framework of interlocking laws and regulations that was the Verwoerd-inspired policy of apartheid in action.

Yet their victory over circumstances was hollow. No matter that they could afford to make their homes in any part of this land, they were constrained by the Group Areas Act to live only in the areas the architects of apartheid had set aside for them. The homes these black businessmen and doctors and lawyers and successful criminals had built for themselves would have graced the elegant suburbs of Sandton or La Lucia or Constantia, where their white counterparts lived.

"See!" The driver of the van pointed proudly. "The pink house with big windows. It is the home of Josia Nrubu, the famous witch doctor. He sells his charms and potions and spells by mail order all over Africa, even to Nigeria and Kenya. He sells a charm to make all men and women love you, and lion bones to give you success in business and money matters. He can give you the fat of vultures for your eyesight and another potion made from the hymen of a virgin that will make your meat plow hard as granite and tireless as a war *assegai*. He has four new Cadillac motorcars and his sons go to university in America.''

"I'll take the lion bones," Michael chuckled. *The Golden City Mail* had run at a loss for the last four years, much to the chagrin of Nana and Garry.

"See! The house with the green roof and the high wall. There lives Peter Ngonyama. His tribe grows the weed that we call dagga or boom and which you whites call cannabis. They harvest the dagga in the secret places in the hills and send it by the truckload to Cape Town and Johannesburg and Durban. He has twenty-five wives and is very rich."

They left the crumbling surface of the old road for the smooth blue asphalt expanse of the newly laid boulevard. The driver accelerated down between the green lawns and high brick walls of Nobs Hill, officially designated Drake's Farm Extension IV.

Suddenly he braked and turned off to pause before the steel gates of one of the more luxurious mansions. The electric gates slid aside silently, then closed again behind them as they drove into a garden of planted shrubs and green lawns. There was a free-form swimming pool below the terrace with a rock fountain at the center. Sprinklers played on the lawns, and Michael noticed two black gardeners in overalls working among the flowering plants.

The building was of ultramodern design with plate glass picture windows and exposed woodwork. The roof was split into various levels and planes. The driver parked below the main terrace, and a tall figure came down the steps to welcome Michael as he stepped out of the van.

"Michael!" Raleigh Tabaka's greeting took him unprepared, as did the friendly smile and handclasp. It was so different from the spirit of their last meeting in London.

Raleigh wore casual slacks and a white open-necked shirt that emphasized his fine unblemished skin and his romantic African features. Michael felt a charge of sexual electricity ripple across his fingertips as they shook hands. Raleigh was still one of the most impressive and attractive men he had ever met.

"You are welcome," he said.

**165**

Michael looked around him and lifted an eyebrow. "Not bad, Raleigh. You are still keeping fine style."

Raleigh shook his head. "This does not belong to me. I own nothing other than the clothes on my back."

"Who does all this belong to, then?"

"Questions, always questions," Raleigh chided him with an edge to his voice.

"I am a journalist," Michael pointed out. "Questions are my meat and drink."

"Of course. This house was built by the Trans Africa Foundation of America for the lady you are about to meet."

"Trans Africa—that's an American civil rights group?" Michael asked. "Isn't it run by the colored evangelist preacher from Chicago, Dr. Rondall?"

"You are well informed." Raleigh took his arm and led him up on to the wide terrace.

"It must have cost half a million dollars," Michael persisted.

Raleigh shrugged and changed the subject. "I promised to show you the children of apartheid, Michael, but first I want you to meet their mother, the mother of the nation."

He led Michael across the terrace. There were beach umbrellas spread in the sunshine like a field of brightly colored mushrooms. A dozen black children sat at the white plastic tables drinking Coca-Cola from the cans and listening to one of the ubiquitous portable transistor radios from which blared the driving rhythms of African jazz.

They were boys ranging in age from eight or nine years to the late teens. All of them wore canary yellow T-shirts with the legend "Gama Athletics Club" printed across the chest. None of them stood up as Michael passed, but they watched him with flat incurious stares.

The glass doors of the main building stood open to the terrace, and Raleigh led the way into a split-level living room whose walls were decorated with carved wooden masks and fetish statuettes. The stone floor was covered with animal-skin rugs.

"Something to drink, Michael?" Raleigh asked. "Coffee or tea?"

Michael shook his head. "Nothing, but do you mind if I smoke?"

"I remember your habit." Raleigh smiled. "Go ahead. I'm sorry I can't offer you a match."

Michael paused with the lighter in his hand and glanced toward the upper level of the spacious room.

A woman was coming down the steps toward them. Michael

took the unlit cigarette from his lips and stared at her. He knew who she was, of course. They called her the black Evita, the mother of the nation. However, none of the photographs had been able to capture her particular dark beauty and regal presence.

"Victoria Gama," Raleigh introduced them. "This is Michael Courtney, the newspaperman I told you about."

"Yes," Victoria Gama said. "I know who Michael Courtney is."

She swept toward him with a stately dignity. She wore a full ankle-length caftan in striking green, yellow and black, the colors of the banned African National Congress. Around her head was an emerald-green turban; the caftan and the turban were her trademarks.

She held out her hand to Michael. It was fine-boned, but the grip of her long tapered fingers was firm and cool, almost cold. Her skin was velvety smooth and the color of dark amber.

"Your mother was my husband's second wife," she told Michael softly. "She bore Moses Gama a son, as I did. Your mother is a fine woman, one of us."

Michael was always astounded by the total lack of jealousy among the wives of an African man. The wives regarded each other not as rivals, but rather as sisters with family ties and loyalties.

"How is Tara?" Victoria persisted as she led Michael to one of the sofas and seated him comfortably. "I have not seen her for many years. Is she still living in England? And how is Moses's son Benjamin?"

"Yes, they are living in England," Michael told her. "I saw them both in London recently. Benjamin is a big lad now. He is doing very well. He is studying chemical engineering at Leeds University."

"I wonder if he will ever return to Africa." Victoria sat down beside him. They chatted easily for a while, and Michael found himself coming under the spell of her charming personality.

At last she asked, "So you want to meet some of my children, the children of apartheid?"

It struck Michael that this was the only title for his article or perhaps series of articles that he would write.

"The children of apartheid," he repeated. "Yes, Mrs. Gama, I would like to meet your children."

"Please call me Vicky. We are of the same family, Michael. Dare I also hope that our dreams and hopes are the same?"

"Yes, I think we have a great deal in common, Vicky."

**167**

She led him back to the terrace, where she called the children and youths around her and introduced them to Michael.

"He is our friend," she told them. "You may speak freely to him. Answer his questions. Tell him whatever he wants to know."

Michael threw off his jacket and tie and sat under one of the umbrellas. The boys crowded around him. With Victoria Gama's endorsement and assurance they seemed to accept him immediately and were delighted that Michael spoke their language. Michael knew how to draw them out. Soon they were competing for his attention. He did not use his notepad to write down what they told him, for he knew that would inhibit them. He valued their spontaneity and frankness. Besides which, he did not need notes. He would not forget their words, and the sound of their young voices.

They told him some stories that were funny and others that were harrowing. One of the boys had been at Sharpeville on that fateful day, an infant strapped to his mother's back. The same police bullet that had killed her had shattered one of his legs. The bone had set crookedly, and the other children called him "Cripple Pete." Michael wanted to weep as he listened to his story.

The afternoon passed too swiftly. Some of the boys left the group to swim in the pool. They stripped naked and plunged into the clear bright waters. They shrieked with laughter and splashed each other as they played.

Raleigh sat aside with Victoria Gama and watched the scene. He saw the way Michael looked at the naked children, and he said to Vicky, "I want you to keep him here tonight." She nodded, and he went on, "He likes boys. Do you have one for him?"

She laughed softly. "He can take his pick. My boys will do whatever I tell them to do."

She stood up and walked across to where Michael sat and placed her hand on his shoulder.

"Why don't you write your articles here? Stay with us tonight. I have a typewriter upstairs that you can use. Spend tomorrow with us also. The boys like you, and there are so many stories to hear . . ."

Michael's fingers flew over the typewriter keys in an exuberant allegro, and the words appeared on the blank white page in serried ranks like warriors of the mind, ready to charge into battle. The story wrote itself. It was not the smoke that spiraled up from the cigarette between his lips that made Michael's eye-

168

lids prickle as he read what he was writing. Very seldom did he have this conviction of the vital worth and weight of his own composition. He knew, deep in his guts, that this was good, really good. This was the story of the "children" as the world should hear it.

He finished the article, which he now knew was only the first of a triumphant series, and found he was trembling with excitement. He glanced at his watch and saw it was a few minutes before midnight, but he knew he could not sleep. The story still fizzed in his blood and seethed in his brain like some heady champagne.

There was a demure tap on the door that startled him. He called softly in Xhosa, "It is open. Enter!" One of the boys slipped into the bedroom. He was dressed only in a pair of blue soccer shorts.

"I heard you typing," he said. "I thought that you might like me to bring you some tea."

He was the youth Michael had most admired in the swimming pool. He had told Michael that he was sixteen years old. His body was sleek and inviting to stroke as a black cat's.

"Thank you." Michael found that his voice was husky. "I would like that very much."

"What are you writing?" The youth came to stand behind his chair and leaned over him to read the page. "Is this what I told you today?"

"Yes," Michael whispered. The boy placed his hand on Michael's shoulder and turned his head to smile shyly into Michael's eyes. His breath was warm on Michael's face. "I like you," he said.

Raleigh Tabaka read the article as they sat together beside the pool in the early-morning sunlight. When he finished he held the sheaf of pages in both hands and was silent for a long while.

"You have a special genius," he said at last. "I have never read anything so powerful. But it is too powerful. You dare not publish this."

"Not in this country," Michael agreed. "*The Guardian* in London has invited me to submit it to them."

"It would have the greatest effect there," Raleigh agreed. "I congratulate you. Something like this turns the bullets of the oppressor to water. You must finish the series as soon as possible. Stay here another night at least. You seem to work so well when you are close to your subjects."

* * *

169

As Michael came awake he was not certain what had disturbed him. He reached out and touched the warm smooth body of the boy who lay beside him. The boy muttered and rolled over in his sleep. One of his arms was flung out across Michael's chest.

Then the sound that had woken Michael came again. It was faint, from the floor below in the far reaches of the house. It sounded like a cry of terrible pain.

Michael lifted the arm of the sleeping boy from his chest and slipped out from under it. There was a glimmer of moonlight through the open window, sufficient for him to find his underpants. He moved quietly across the bedroom and let himself out into the passageway. He crept toward the head of the stairs and stood there listening. The sound came up to him again much louder, another wild cry like the voice of a seabird, and it was punctuated by a sharp snapping sound he could not place.

He stared down the stairs but had not reached the bottom before a voice arrested him.

"Michael. What are you doing?" Raleigh Tabaka's voice was sharp and accusing, and Michael started guiltily and looked back up the stairs. Raleigh stood on the landing in his dressing gown.

"I heard something," Michael said. "It sounded like—"

"It is nothing. Go to your room, Michael."

"But I thought that I heard—"

"Go to your room!" Raleigh spoke softly, but it was not an order Michael could disobey. He turned and went back up the stairs. Raleigh reached out to touch his arm as he passed.

"Sometimes one's hearing plays strange tricks in the night. You heard nothing, Michael. It was a cat, perhaps—or the wind. Go to sleep now. We will talk in the morning."

Raleigh waited until Michael had returned to his bedroom and closed the door before he ran down the stairs. He went directly to the kitchen door and threw it open.

Victoria Gama, the black Evita, the mother of the nation, stood in the center of the tiled floor. She was naked to the waist. Her breasts were beautifully shaped, smooth as velvet, black as sable fur, large as the ripe tsama melons of the Kalahari Desert.

In her right hand she held a supple whip made of cured hippo hide, the terrible African *sjambok*. It was slim as one of her elegant fingers and as long as her arm. In her other hand she held a glass. She was drinking from it as Raleigh burst into the room. A gin bottle stood on the sink behind her.

There were two members of the Gama Athletics Club in the kitchen with her. They were the eldest and biggest of all her bodyguards. Both of them were in their late teens. They were also bare to the waist. They stood at either end of the long kitchen table and held a naked body pinioned down on the table.

The flogging must have been in progress for some considerable time, for the whip weals were latticed closely across the shiny black skin, raised and purple. Some of them had cut through into the flesh and were bleeding. Blood formed a puddle under the body and spilled over to drip onto the tiled kitchen floor.

"Are you mad?" Raleigh hissed at her. "With the journalist in the house?"

"He is a police spy," Victoria snarled at him. "He is a traitor. I have to teach him a lesson."

"You are drunk again." Raleigh struck the glass from her hand, and it spun into the corner and shattered against the wall. "Can't you enjoy your little boys without having to warm yourself up to it?"

Her eyes blazed with fury, and she lifted the whip to slash at his face. He caught her wrist and held it easily. He twisted the whip out of her fingers and flung it into the sink. Still holding her wrist, he spoke to her young bodyguards.

"Get rid of this." He indicated the bleeding figure on the table. "Then clean the place up. No more of this sort of thing while the white man is in the house. Do you understand?"

They lifted the boy off the table, and he moaned and blubbered as they half carried him to the door.

As soon as they were alone, Raleigh turned back to Victoria. "You bear an illustrious name. If you bring dishonor upon it, I will kill you myself. Now go to your room."

She marched from the room. Despite the gin, her step was regal. She carried her liquor well. If only she could carry her fame and the adulation of the media as well, he thought grimly.

He had watched her change over a few short years. When Moses Gama had married her, she had been a bright, pure flame, committed to her husband and the struggle. Then the American left had discovered her, and the media had showered praise and money on her to the point where she believed all they said about her.

From there the disintegration had been swift. Of course the struggle was fierce. Of course freedom must be won through rivers of blood. However, for Victoria Gama the spilling of blood had become a pleasure and not a duty, and her search for personal glory had eclipsed the call of freedom. It was time to consider carefully what must be done about her.

They took Michael back to the carpark where he had left his old Valiant. Raleigh Tabaka sat up beside the driver in the front seat of the butchery van while Michael crouched in the back. Michael was surprised to see that his car was still standing where he had left it.

"Nobody took the trouble to steal it," he remarked.

"No," Raleigh agreed. "It was guarded by our people. We look after our own."

They shook hands, and Michael began to turn away, but Raleigh was not yet ready to let him go.

"I believe you own an aircraft, Michael?" he asked.

"Of a sort." Michael laughed. "It's an old Centurion that has already flown over three thousand hours."

"I have a favor to ask of you."

"I owe you one," Michael agreed. "What do you want me to do?"

"Will you fly to Botswana for me?" Raleigh asked.

"With a passenger?"

"No. Fly there on your own—and return on your own."

Michael hesitated a moment longer. "Is it to do with your struggle?"

"Of course." Raleigh replied frankly. "Everything in my life is to do with the struggle."

"When do you want me to go?" Michael asked.

Raleigh did not let his relief show in his expression. Perhaps, after all, it might not be necessary to use the material they had filmed in the ballet dancer's flat in London.

"When can you get away for a few days?" he asked.

Unlike his father and brothers, Michael had not taken to flying early in life. Looking back on it, he realized it was because of their passionate love of aircraft that he had shied away from them. Instinctively he had resented his father's efforts to interest and to instruct him. He didn't want to be like them. He refused to be forced into the mold his father had prepared for him.

Later, when he moved outside the cloying family influence, he discovered the fascination of flight all by himself. He had bought the Centurion out of his own savings. Despite its age, the aircraft was fast and comfortable. It cruised at 210 knots and took him up to Maun in northern Botswana in a little over three hours.

He loved Botswana. It was the only truly democratic country in all of Africa. It had never been colonized by any of the European powers, although Britain had been its protector from the 1880s, when the Boer Republic had threatened to muscle in and take the land from the Tswana tribe.

After Britain had relinquished its status as protector and handed the country back to the people, it had swiftly transformed itself into a model for the rest of the continent. It was a multiparty democracy with universal suffrage and regular elections. The government was truly responsible to the electorate. There were no tyrants or dictators. By African standards, very little corruption existed. The minority white population was accepted as a useful and productive section of the population. There was little inverse racism or tribalism. After South Africa, it was the most prosperous state in all of Africa. In fact, it had achieved almost effortlessly the condition Michael prayed his own country would someday be able to arrive at, after all the suffering and strife. Michael loved Botswana and was happy to be going back there.

At Maun he cleared the formalities in the small single-roomed building that housed both Customs and Immigration, then took off again for a short northern leg into the Okavango delta.

The delta was an extraordinary wetland area where the mighty Okavango River debouched into the northern Kalahari Desert and formed a vast swamp. It was not a swamp of reeking black mud and dreary wastes. The waters were clear as a trout stream. The sandbanks and bottoms of the maze of waterways were sugary white sand. The islands were decked with palms and luxuriant growth. The wild fig trees were loaded with yellow fruit, and fat green pigeons swarmed in their branches. Strange and rare fishing owls, seeming more like apes than like birds, nested in the tall ebony trees.

The fabled lions of the Okavango, with manes like russet haystacks, moved quick as otters in the lambent waters. Great herds of buffalo grazed in the reed beds with a canopy of snowy egrets hovering over them. Weird sitatunga antelope with elongated hoofs, corkscrew horns and shaggy coats spent their entire amphibian lives in the tall papyrus, and clouds of duck and geese and waterfowl shaded the blazing orange sunsets.

Michael landed the Centurion on an airstrip on one of the larger islands. There were two river bushmen in a dugout canoe to ferry him to the camp across a lagoon perfumed with water lilies.

The camp was called the Gay Goose Lodge, and it catered for up to forty guests who lived in picturesque little reed huts. The ostensible reason for their visit was to study and photograph the animals and bird life of the delta or to troll for the glittering striped tigerfish that shoaled in the waterways. Each morning and evening expeditions of guests ventured out in the primitive canoes, to be poled silently through the reed beds and channels by the black boatmen.

However, the guests were almost exclusively male, and the name Gay Goose had been chosen with good reason. All of the staff were good-looking young Tswana lads who were also chosen with good reason. The camp was run by a political refugee from South Africa, Brian Susskind, a striking fellow in his mid-thirties. He had long blond hair, bleached almost white by the sun. He wore earrings in his pierced earlobes, gold chains around his neck that tinkled on his bare muscular chest, and bangles of ivory and plaited elephant hair at his wrists.

"God, darling," he greeted Michael, "it's just so lovely to meet you. Raleigh has told me all about you. You are going to absolutely love it here. We've got such fun people with us. They are in an absolute tizz to meet you, too."

Michael spent a long and exciting weekend at Gay Goose camp, and when it was time to leave Brian Susskind came across the lagoon in the Makorro canoe to see him off.

"It's been such fun, Mickey." He squeezed Michael's hand. "I think we'll be seeing a lot more of each other. Don't forget to trim your plane. You may be a touch tail-heavy on takeoff."

Michael took off without looking in the hidden compartment below the passenger seats, but he noticed the small alteration in trim that Brian had warned him of. The cargo Brian had loaded must be very heavy for its bulk. He had been told not to touch it or try to examine it. He followed his instructions strictly.

As he cleared Customs on his arrival at Lanseria Airport his nerves were stretched tight and he puffed on his cigarette. He need not have worried. The Customs officer recognized him from many previous occasions and did not even bother to examine his luggage, let alone traipse out onto the tarmac to inspect the Centurion.

That night one of the black night watchmen in the Lanseria hangar unloaded a heavy box from under the Centurion's backseat and passed it through the fence to the driver of a small blue butcher's delivery van.

In the kitchen at Nobs Hill in Drake's Farm township, Raleigh Tabaka inspected the seals on the crate. They were all intact. Nobody had tampered with the cargo. Raleigh nodded with satisfaction and unscrewed the lid. The crate contained seventy copies of the Holy Bible. Michael Courtney had passed another test.

Michael flew up to Gay Goose camp again five weeks later. This time, on his return the crate contained twenty mini-limpet mines of Russian manufacture. He would pay another nine visits to Gay Goose over the following year, and each time the entry through South African Customs at Lanseria would be easier on his nerves.

Two years after he had first met Raleigh Tabaka, Michael would be invited to join the African National Congress as a member of its military wing, Umkhonto we Sizwe, the "Spear of the Nation."

"I've been thinking about this a lot recently," he would answer Raleigh, "and reluctantly I've reached the conclusion that sometimes the pen alone is not enough. At last I've come to realize that, even though it goes against my deeply ingrained feelings, there comes a time when a man must take up the sword. Even a year ago I would have refused what you are offering me, but now I accept the dictates of my conscience. I am ready to join the armed struggle."

# 14

"All right, Bella." Centaine Courtney-Malcomess nodded firmly. "You will begin at the far end of the street—and I'll take this end." Then she transferred her attention to the back of the chauffeur's head. "Klonkie, drop us round the corner, then you can pick us up again at lunchtime."

Obediently Klonkie slowed the yellow Daimler, eased it around the corner and pulled it to the pavement.

The two women climbed out and watched the limousine pull away. "You don't want the voters to see you in a great luxury wagon with a chauffeur," Centaine explained. "Envy is a corrosive emotion, and you'll find it at every level of society." She turned her full attention on her granddaughter and inspected her carefully from head to foot.

Isabella's hair was freshly shampooed and gleaming with ruby highlights in the sunshine. However, Centaine had insisted that she pull it back into a severe bun behind the head. Her makeup was limited to a moisturizing cream that gave her a scrubbed schoolgirl complexion. She wore no lipstick, but her lips were a natural youthful pink.

Centaine nodded and ran her eyes downwards. Isabella wore a classic cashmere outfit with low-heeled sensible shoes. Centaine nodded again with complete satisfaction. She smoothed her own tweed skirt over her hips.

"All right, Bella. Remember we are aiming at the ladies this morning." They had timed their visit for midmorning, when the men were out of the house, the children were at school, and the main chores were behind the lower-middle-class housewives who lived in this area below the slopes of Signal Hill, overlooking the city and the harbor of Cape Town.

The previous evening Isabella had addressed a predominantly male audience in the Sea Point Masonic Hall. Most of them had come out of curiosity to listen to the first ever female National Party candidate in their constituency.

On that occasion Bella's dress and makeup had evoked a chorus of wolf whistles from the body of the hall when she stood up to speak. They had heckled her good-naturedly for the first few minutes while she struggled to overcome her nervousness. However, the horseplay had roused her anger, and she had flushed and snapped at them.

"Gentlemen, your behavior does none of us credit. If you have any sense of fair play, you'll give me a sporting chance."

They grinned shamefacedly, shuffled their feet and relapsed into a silence that grew more attentive as she spoke. She and Centaine had studied the issues that concerned them most, and they listened as she addressed herself to them.

It had been a good baptism of fire, and, without making it too obvious, Centaine was proud of her.

"All right," she said now. "You'll do, missy. Here we go for Saint George, for Harry, and for England."

The war cry was entirely inappropriate to the occasion, Isabella smiled wryly, and misquoted to boot, but who would dare tell **Nana** that? They separated and went to their respective ends of the street.

Number twelve was a semidetached cottage with a bull-nosed corrugated iron roof and a Victorian fretwork cast iron trellis beneath the eaves. The front garden was only five paces deep, but the dahlias were in full bloom. Isabella went up the path and quieted the yapping fox terrier on the step with a sharp word. She had always been good with dogs and horses.

A housewife came to the door and peered suspiciously at Isabella through the fly screen. Her hair was in yellow plastic curlers.

"Yes? What do you want?"

"My name is Isabella Courtney, and I am your National Party candidate for next month's by-election. May I talk to you for a few minutes?"

"Hold on." The woman disappeared and came back a minute later with a headscarf over her curlers.

"We are United Party supporters," she said, declaring her allegiance, but Isabella distracted her.

"What beautiful dahlias!"

This was an opposition party stronghold. Isabella was a political fledgling. Her own party would never have allowed her to contest a safe Nationalist seat. Those were reserved for others who had already proven their worth. As it was, it had taken all Nana's influence and persuasive ability, together with Isabella's own personality and presentability, to persuade the party machine to let her make this foredoomed attempt. The very best Isabella could hope for was a good showing and a gallant defeat. Nana had set their objective. In the last general election the United Party had taken this seat with a five thousand majority.

"If we can cut the majority to three thousand, then in the next election we can force them to give you a better constituency to contest."

Now the housewife softened with gratification as Isabella looked at her prizewinning dahlias and wavered.

"May I come in?" Isabella smiled her sweetest and most winning smile, and the woman stood aside reluctantly.

"Well, just for a few minutes."

"What work does your husband do?"

"He's a motor mechanic."

"What does he think about trade fragmentation and black trade unions?" Isabella struck hard, and the woman looked grave. Isabella was talking about family survival and the bread in her children's mouths.

"May I get you a cup of coffee, Mrs. Courtney?" she asked. Isabella did not correct her form of address.

Fifteen minutes later she shook the housewife's hand and went

177

back down the short garden path. She had followed Nana's maxim: "Be forceful, but be brief."

She felt a flush of achievement. Her victim had begun as a definite "No" and gradually mellowed under Isabella's persuasive logic to a tentative "Maybe." Isabella marked her so on her copy of the voters' roll.

"One down," she whispered. "Two thousand more to go."

She marched across the street to the door of number eleven, and a child opened the door.

"Is your mummy at home?"

The child was a freckle-faced little boy with curly blond hair and sticky lips. He held a half-devoured slice of bread and jam in one hand and smiled at her shyly. He was at least five years old, but she thought of Nicholas, and her resolve hardened.

"I am Isabella Courtney," she said, as the mother came to the door, "and I am your National Party candidate in next month's by-election."

After the third call she found to her astonishment that she was starting to enjoy herself. She was seeing a side of life she had never imagined existed. She found herself warming to these ordinary simple folk and developing an understanding and concern for their problems, their fears and their way of life, which was so alien from her own existence.

"Privilege carries responsibilities." She had heard her father say it so often. "Noblesse oblige." She had not thought deeply about it but had believed she understood the concept; not that she had ever intended doing anything about it, of course. Up until now, life had been too busy. Her own needs and desires had been too pressing to care or worry about other, insignificant people such as these.

Now she felt herself drawn to them. She felt a genuine warmth for them, a sympathy and a desire to understand and protect them.

Perhaps motherhood has mellowed me a little, she thought, and the ache of her loss immediately followed the thought. Was this some displacement emotion, a diversion of her frustrated maternal instincts? She did not know, and she did not really care. All that was important was that she wanted to do this, she truly wanted to help these people. She wanted very strongly to win a seat in Parliament and to put her time and her talents to good, unselfish use.

She felt a genuine regret when after the eighth call she checked her wristwatch and found it was time to meet Nana and call it a day.

Centaine was waiting for her at the rendezvous at the street corner. She looked fresh and alert, bubbling with the energy of a much younger woman.

"How did you go, Bella?" she demanded briskly. "How many calls?"

"Eight," Bella told her with satisfaction. "Two 'yesses' and a 'maybe.' How about you, Nana?"

"Fourteen calls and five 'yesses.' I don't count 'maybes' or 'might have beens.' Never have."

She took Isabella's arm as the yellow Daimler came into view and slowed to pick them up.

"Now, as soon as we get home you will send them each a personal handwritten note—I hope you noted their children's names and ages and some personal details about each of them."

"Do I have to write to all of them?"

"All of them," Centaine confirmed. " 'Yesses,' 'noes,' and 'maybes.' Then we will follow it up with another note a few days before polling, just to remind them."

"You make it such hard work, Nana," Isabella protested mildly.

"Nothing of value is ever achieved without hard work, missy." She stepped into the Daimler and settled onto the cream leather seat. "And don't forget the meeting this evening. Have you got your speech written yet? We'll go over it together."

"Nana, I've still got a pile of work to do for Pater."

"Keep you out of mischief," Centaine agreed complacently. "Home to Weltevreden, Klonkie," she told the chauffeur.

Isabella cheated a little. She had her secretary type a standard letter to all of the constituents she and Nana had visited, but she checked and signed each of these personally. By exercising these little economies of time she was able to discharge her political aspirations and also keep abreast of the work her father piled on her desk.

Shasa had given her a corner suite of offices in Centaine House. Her new secretary was one of the stalwarts who had worked for Courtney Enterprises for twenty years. She occupied the outer office of the suite. Isabella's inner office was paneled in indigenous yellow wood that Shasa had salvaged from a two-hundred-year-old building that had been demolished to make way for a block of modern apartments in Sea Point. The wood had a glorious buttery glow. Shasa had loaned her four paintings from his collection, two Pierneefs and a pair of landscapes by Hugo Naudé. Their colors stood out very well on the light-toned pan-

179

els. All the books on the shelves were fully bound in royal blue calf leather, though Isabella doubted she would have much call for thirty years' worth of Hansard's parliamentary reports.

The windows of her suite looked out onto the park and St. George's Cathedral, with a backdrop of Table Mountain beyond. There was a saying that you hadn't arrived in Cape Town unless you had a view of the mountain from your window.

She signed the last of her form letters to her prospective constituents and carried the batch through to her secretary's office. The secretary's office was empty, and the cover was on the Underwood typewriter. Isabella checked her wristwatch.

"Good grief—it's after five already."

She felt a quick relief in the fact that time had passed so swiftly and painlessly. It hadn't always been like that since she had lost Nicholas. She had come to rely on hard work and long hours as an opiate for the deep gnawing pain of her bereavement.

Dinner at Weltevreden was at eight-thirty sharp, cocktails thirty minutes before. She had time to fill, so she went back to her own desk. Shasa had left a draft copy of his report on her desk with a note: "I need it back tomorrow A.M. Love you, Pater."

During their time together at the embassy they had fallen into this routine in which she checked his speeches and written reports for style and syntax. Shasa did not truly need such assistance. He could craft a telling phrase with the best of them. However, the custom gave them both pleasure, and Shasa occasionally went over the top with a metaphor or let an unseemly cliché creep into his compositions. At the very least, he enjoyed her praises.

She read the twelve-page report through carefully and suggested one change. Then she wrote "What a clever father I chose!" on the foot of it and took it down to his office at the end of the long carpeted corridor.

His office was locked. She had a key and let herself in.

Shasa's office was four times larger and grander than hers was. His desk was reputed to have come from the Dauphin's apartments at Versailles. He had an original auctioneer's receipt dated 1791 that showed that provenance.

Isabella placed the corrected report in the center of the delicate marquetry desk top, then changed her mind. The report was destined to be read only by the prime minister and members of his cabinet. Some of the facts and figures that it contained were highly confidential, and crucial to the nation's security.

Shasa should not have left it unprotected on her desk, but then he was often careless with important documents.

She retrieved the report and took it to his personal safe. The safe was concealed behind a false bookcase. The mechanism was incorporated into the lamp on its wall bracket above the bookcase. The release was in the shape of an art deco bronze nymph holding the light bulb above her head like a torch.

Isabella rotated the bracket on its hinge, and the false bookcase slid noiselessly aside, revealing the massive green-painted steel Chubb door.

Shasa's choice of numerals for the combination lacked both subtlety and originality. It was simply his own birthdate in inverted sequence. Apart from Shasa himself, Isabella, in her capacity as his personal assistant, was the only one who had the combination. He had not even given it to Nana or Garry.

She set the combination, swung the heavy steel door open and walked into the cavernous strong room. She often had to nag her father to keep the room tidy, and now she clucked her tongue with disapproval as she saw two green Armscor files piled haphazardly on the central table. She tidied up quickly, locked the strong room and then stopped in the ladies' washroom on her way back to her own office.

As she settled into the driving seat of the Mini, she sighed. It had been a long day, and she still had the election meeting after dinner. She wouldn't be in bed until long after midnight.

For a moment she considered taking the shortest route back to Weltevreden. However, the Mini took the road up the slope of the mountain almost of its own volition, and fifteen minutes later she parked in the side street around the corner from the Camps Bay post office.

She felt that familiar heavy rock of dread in the pit of her stomach as she approached her postbox. Would it be empty, as it had been for so many weeks? Would she never have word of Nicholas again?

She opened the box, and her heart seemed to bounce against her ribs with a single wild lunge. Like a thief she snatched out the slim envelope and thrust it deep into her jacket pocket.

As was her habit, she parked above the beach, under the palms, and read the four lines of typewritten instructions with a mixture of dread and anticipation.

This was something new.

In strict accordance with her standing instructions she memorized the contents of the letter, then burned it and crushed the ashes to dust.

181

On Friday morning, three days after receiving the Red Rose letter, Isabella left the Mini in the carpark of the new Pick 'n' Pay supermarket in the suburb of Claremont.

She locked the driver's door but left the side window open an inch at the top as she had been instructed. She entered the back door of the bustling supermarket. It was the last Friday of the month, and payday for tens of thousands of office workers and civil servants. The lines at the checkout tills were scores long.

Isabella passed quickly out through the front entrance into the main street of the suburb and turned left. She pushed her way along the crowded pavements until she reached the new post office building. There was a pair of teenage girls in the glass cubicle of the first public telephone booth from the left. They giggled into the receiver and jangled their fake gold earrings and rolled their eyes at each other as they listened to the boy on the other end of the line, sharing the earpiece of the telephone.

Isabella checked her watch. It was five minutes short of the hour, and she felt a stab of anxiety. She tapped imperiously on the glass door, and one of the girls pushed out her tongue at her and went on speaking.

A minute later Isabella tapped again. With ill grace the pair hung up the receiver and flounced away angrily. Isabella darted into the booth and closed the door. She did not lift the receiver, but made a show of searching for small change in her purse. She was watching the minute hand of her wristwatch. As it touched the pip at the top of the dial the telephone rang and she snatched it up.

"Red Rose," she whispered breathlessly, and a voice said, "Return immediately to your vehicle." The connection was broken and the burr of the dial tone echoed in her ears. Even in her perplexity, Isabella thought she had recognized the heavy accent of the large, powerful woman who had picked her up in the closed van on the Thames Embankment almost three years previously.

Isabella dropped the receiver back onto its cradle and fled from the booth. It took her three minutes to reach the Mini in the Pick 'n' Pay carpark. As she inserted the key in the door lock she saw the envelope lying on the driver's seat, and she understood. She had read the books of Le Carré and Len Deighton, and she realized that this was a dead-letter drop.

She knew that she was almost certainly under observation at that moment. She glanced around the carpark furtively. It was almost two acres in extent, and there were several hundred other vehicles parked around her. Dozens of shoppers pushed their laden shopping trolleys to the waiting motorcars, and beggars and off-duty schoolchildren loitered and idled about the carpark. Cars pulled in and out of the gates in a steady two-way stream. It would be impossible to pick out the watcher from this crowd.

She slipped behind the wheel and drove carefully back to Weltevreden. The letter was obviously too important to be entrusted to the postal service. This was an ingenious form of hand delivery. Locked in the safety of her own private bedroom suite, she at last opened the envelope.

First, there was a recent color photograph of Nicholas. He was dressed in bathing trunks. He had developed into a sturdy and beautiful child of nearly three years of age. He stood on a beach of white coral sand with the blue ocean behind him.

The letter that accompanied the photograph was terse and unequivocal:

As soon as possible, you will acquire full technical specifications of the new Siemens computer-linked coastal radar network presently being installed by Armscor at Silver Mine naval headquarters on the Cape peninsula.

Inform us in the usual way once these plans are in your possession. After you have delivered, arrangements will be made for your first meeting with your son.

There was no signature.

Standing over the toilet bowl in her bathroom, Isabella burned the letter and, as the flames scorched her fingertips, dropped it into the bowl and flushed the ashes away. She closed the toilet cover and sat upon it, staring at the tiled wall opposite.

So it had come at last—as she had known it must. For three years she had waited for the order to commit an act that would finally put her beyond the pale.

Up until now she had been instructed merely to inveigle herself into her father's complete confidence. She had been told to make herself indispensable to him, and she had done so. She had been ordered to join the National Party and seek election to parliamentary office. With Nana's help and guidance, she had done so.

However, this was different. She recognized that she had at last reached the point of no return. She could turn back from treason—and abandon her son; or she could go forward into the dangerous unknown.

"Oh, God, help me," she whispered aloud. "What can I do—what must I do?"

She felt great serpentine coils of dread and guilt tighten about her. She knew what the answer to her question must be.

A copy of the Siemens radar installation report was in her father's strongroom in Centaine House at this moment. On Monday the file would be returned by special courier to naval headquarters in the nuclear-proof bunker complex built into Silver Mine mountain.

However, her father was flying up to the sheep ranch at Camdeboo over the weekend. She had already refused his invitation to accompany him on the excuse that she had so much work to catch up on. On Saturday and Sunday, Nana was judging the Cape gundog trials. Garry was in Europe with Holly and the children. Isabella would have the top floor of Centaine House to herself for the entire weekend. She had full security clearance, and the guards at the front door knew her well.

# 15

The wind was out of the north. The first snowflakes eddied down, silver bright against the grey sow's belly of the sky. There were a dozen men at the graveside, no women. Just as there had been no women in Joe Cicero's life, now there was none at his death. All the mourners were officers from the department. They had been delegated to this duty. They stood stolidly to attention in a single rank. All of them wore uniform greatcoats and scarlet-piped dress caps. Their noses were red, with cold rather than with grief. Joe Cicero had no friends. He had seldom evoked any emotion in his peers other than envious admiration or fear.

The honor guard stepped smartly forward and, at the order, raised their rifles and pointed them to the sky. Volleys rang out, punctuated by the rattle of the bolts. At the next order they shouldered their weapons and marched away, boots slamming into the gravel path, clenched fists swinging high across the chest.

The official mourners broke their ranks, shook hands briefly and expressionlessly, then hurried to the waiting vehicles.

Ramón Machado was the only one left at the graveside. He also wore the full-dress uniform of a KGB colonel, and beneath his greatcoat the gaudy lines of his decorations reached below his ribcage.

"And so, you old bastard, for you the game is over at last— but it took you long enough to clear the stage." Although Ramón had been head of section for two years now, he had never truly felt he had succeeded to the title as long as Joe Cicero was still alive.

The old man had died grudgingly. He had held the cancer in remission for long, agonizing months. He had even kept his office in the Lubyanka right up to the last day. His gaunt spectral presence had presided at every meeting of section heads, his will and his enmity had inhibited Ramón at every turn, right to the last.

"Good-bye, Joe Cicero. The devil can have you know." Ramón smiled, and his lips felt as though they might tear in the cold.

He turned away from the grave. His car was the last one remaining under the row of tall dark yews. With his rank, Ramón now rated a black Chaika and a corporal driver. The driver opened the door for him. As Ramón settled into the backseat he brushed the snowflakes from his shoulders with his gloves.

"Back to the office," he said.

The corporal drove fast but skillfully, and Ramón relaxed and watched the streets of Moscow unfold ahead of the departmental pennant on the shining black bonnet of the Chaika.

Ramón loved Moscow. He loved the broad boulevards Joseph Stalin had built after the Great Patriotic War. He loved the pure classical lines of some of the buildings and the brilliant contrast they struck with those in the rococo style alongside the skyscrapers Stalin had built and topped with their red stars. The concept of Soviet giantism excited him. They drove past the massive bronze statues of the heroes of the people, the monstrous figures of men and women marching forward together brandishing submachine guns and sickles and hammers, raising high the socialist banner and the red star.

There were no commercial advertisements, no exhortations to drink Coca-Cola or smoke Marlboros or invest with Prudential Insurance or read the *Sun*. That was the most striking difference between the cities of Mother Russia and those of the crass and avaricious capitalistic West. It offended Ramón's instinct that the appetites of the people should be stimulated for such shoddy and indulgent goods, that a nation's productive capacity should be diverted from the essential to the trivial.

From the backseat of the Chaika he looked on the Russian people, and he felt a glow of righteous approval. Here was a people organized and committed to the good of the state, to the betterment of the whole, not the individual parts. He observed them, patient and obedient, standing at the bus stops, standing in the food lines, orderly and regimented.

In his mind he compared them to the American people. America, that fractious childlike nation, where each man pulled against the other; where avarice was considered the greatest virtue; where patience and subtlety were considered the greatest vice. Was there any other nation in history that had perverted the ideal of democracy to the point where individual freedom and rights had become a tyranny on the rest of society? Was there any other nation that so glorified its criminals—Bonnie and Clyde, Al Capone, Billy the Kid, the Mafia, the black drug lords? Would Russia or any other sensate government emasculate and shackle its armed forces with such rules of disclosure and publicly debated budget allocations?

The Chaika stopped at a set of traffic lights. Apart from two public buses it was the only vehicle on the broad thoroughfare. Whereas every American had his own automobile, there was no such wasteful ownership in Russian society. Ramón watched the pedestrians cross the street in an orderly stream in front of his vehicle. The faces were handsome and intelligent, the expressions patient and reserved. Their dress had none of the wild eccentricity that would be evident in any American street. Apart from the predominance of military uniforms, the clothing of both men and women was sober and conservative.

Compared to this educated and scholarly people, the Americans were illiterate oafs. Even the workers in the Russian fields could quote Pushkin. The classic books were among the most sought-after items on the black market. Any day one visited the cemetery at the monastery of Alexander Nevsky in Leningrad one would find the graves of Dostoevsky and Tchaikovsky piled with fresh flowers, daily tributes from ordinary people. By contrast, half the American high school graduates, especially the blacks, had reading skills barely adequate to follow the captions in a Batman comic book.

Here, then, was the reward for almost sixty years of the socialist revolution. A structured and delicately layered society, secretive and protected in depth. Ramón often compared it to the Matryoshka dolls in the Beriozka tourist stores, those cunningly carved nests of human figures that fitted one within the other, the outer layers protecting and hiding the precious center.

Even the Russian economy was deceptive to the Western eye. The Americans looked at the food lines and the lack of consumer goods in the gigantic GUM department stores, and in their naïve and simple-minded way they saw this as the sign of a failed or at least an ailing system. Hidden from them was the internal economy of the military productive machine, a vast, highly efficient and powerful structure that not only matched but far outstripped its American capitalistic counterpart.

Ramón smiled at the story of the American astronaut perched in the nose capsule of his rocket waiting for blast-off who, when asked by ground control if he was nervous, answered, "How would you like to be sitting on top of the efforts of a thousand low bidders?" There were no low bidders in the Russian armaments industry. There was only the best.

In much the same way, there were no siftings from the "equal opportunity" school of employment, or rejects from IBM and GM, in the upper echelons of the Russian military. There were only the best. Ramón was aware that he was one of them, one of the very best.

He straightened up in his seat as the Chaika entered Dzerzhinsky Square, passed the heroic statue of the founder of the organization of state security on its raised plinth and moved up the hill toward the elegant but substantial edifice of the Lubyanka.

The driver pulled into the narrower street that ran behind the headquarters and parked with the rows of other official KGB vehicles in the rank reserved for them. Ramón waited for him to open the door. Then he crossed the road to the rear entrance and entered the building through the massive cast iron grille doors.

There were two other KGB officers ahead of him at the security desk. He waited his turn for clearance. The captain of the security guard was thorough and painstaking. He compared Ramón's features to those of the photograph on his identity document the regulation three times before allowing him to sign the register.

Ramón mounted to the second floor in the antique lift of etched glass and polished bronze. The lift and the chandeliers were relics from prerevolutionary times, when the building had been a foreign embassy.

His secretary stood to attention beside her desk when he entered his office and greeted him as he hung his greatcoat at the door.

"Good morning, Comrade Colonel." He saw that overnight she had set her hair with hot curling tongs into crisp, tight curls. He preferred it loose and soft. Katrina's eyes were almond-shaped and hooded, a legacy from some distant Tartar ancestor. She was twenty-four years old, the widow of an air force test pilot who had died flying a prototype of the new MiG-27 series.

Katrina indicated the cardboard box on the corner of her desk. "What should I do with these, Comrade Colonel?"

She opened the lid, and Ramón glanced at the contents. They were all that remained of General Cicero's presence. She had cleared the drawers of the desk that now, at last, belonged to Ramón alone.

Apart from a gold-plated Parker ballpoint pen and a leather wallet, there were no personal items in the box. Ramón picked up the wallet and opened it. There were half a dozen photographs in the compartments. In each of them Joe Cicero posed with a prominent African leader: Nyerere, Kaunda, Nkrumah.

He dropped the wallet back into the box, and his hand brushed against Katrina's soft, pale fingers. She trembled slightly, and he heard her catch her breath.

"Take it all down to Archives. Get a receipt from them," he ordered.

"Immediately, Comrade Colonel."

She was an attractive, placid woman with a narrow waist and wide, comfortable hips. Of course, she had the highest security clearance, and Ramón had meticulously recorded their relationship in his daybook. Their relationship had the tacit sanction of the head of department. Her flat was a convenient base for him while he was in Moscow, even though she shared the two rooms with her elderly parents and her three-year-old son.

"There is a green-flash dispatch on your desk, Comrade Colonel," Katrina said huskily as she picked up the cardboard box. Her cheeks were still lightly flushed from the brief physical contact. Ramón felt a shaded regret that he would be leaving Moscow at midnight. On average he spent only a few days in the mother city in any one month. He saw so little of Katrina that her appeal was still fresh, even after two years.

She must have read his mind, for she dropped her voice to a

whisper. "Will you dine at the flat tonight, before you leave? Mamma has found an excellent sausage and a bottle of vodka."

"Very well, little one," he agreed, and then went through to his own office.

The green-flash box was on his desk, and he unbuttoned his tunic and split the security seal the cipher department had affixed.

As he read the code "Red Rose" he felt a sharp elevation of his pulse rate. That annoyed him.

Red Rose was merely an agent like a hundred others under his control. If he allowed personalities to intrude, his own efficiency would be diminished. Even so, as he lifted the Red Rose folder from the box he was struck suddenly by a mental image of a naked woman perched on a black boulder in a Spanish mountain stream. The picture was extraordinarily vivid, even down to the deep indigo blue of her eyes.

He opened the file and saw at a glance that it was the report on the South African naval radar chain that he had called for. It had come in via the London embassy bag. He nodded with satisfaction and then consulted his daybook. With the log open before him he lifted the handset of his departmental intercom and dialed Records.

"A printout. Reference 'Protea,' item number 1178. Urgent, please."

While he waited for the printout to be delivered, he rose from his desk and crossed to the windows. The view was novel enough to engage his interest. Over the statue of the founder he looked across the stately forest of buildings to the colorful onion-shaped domes of the Cathedral of St. Basil the Blessed and the walls of the Kremlin.

He was still disturbed by the memories the Red Rose dispatch had evoked. On a logical train of thought his mind went on to the journey that would begin for him at midnight from Sheremetyevo Airport and the child who would be waiting for him at the journey's end.

He had not seen Nicholas for over two months. He would have grown again, and he would be speaking even more fluently. His vocabulary was quite unusual for his age. Paternal pride was a bourgeois emotion, and Ramón sought to suppress it. He should not be standing dreaming out of the window while there was so much work to be done. He checked his wristwatch. In forty-eight minutes there was a meeting scheduled, the result of which would vitally affect his career over the next decade.

He returned to his desk and took his notes for the meeting

from the top drawer. Katrina had typed them out in double spacing. He flipped through the pages and found he still knew every word by heart. His presentation was memorized word-perfect. Further study would only affect the spontaneity of his delivery. He set the report aside.

At that moment there was a knock on the door and Katrina ushered the records clerk into his office. Ramón signed for the computer printout in the records book, and after Katrina and the clerk had left he slit open the envelope and spread the printout on his desk.

Protea was the code name of another of his South African agents. His real name was Dieter Reinhardt, a German national, born in Dresden in 1930. His father had commanded one of Admiral Doenitz's U-boats with distinction. After the partition of Germany, Reinhardt had enrolled as a cadet officer in the fledgling navy of the German Democratic Republic, and two years later he had been recruited by the KGB.

His subsequent "escape" over the Berlin Wall to the West had been carefully stage-managed by Joe Cicero personally. Reinhardt and his wife had emigrated to South Africa in 1960, and after he had become a naturalized South African citizen he had joined the South African navy and worked his way up to the rank of commandant. He was presently chief of signals on headquarters staff at Silver Mine command bunker.

The printout was a copy of the report he had filed three weeks previously concerning the Siemens radar chain at Silver Mine.

Ramón laid the Red Rose report of the same installation alongside Protea's and began comparing them item by item, paragraph by paragraph. Within ten minutes he was satisfied that they were in total agreement, in general and in detail.

The integrity of Protea was of the highest order. It had been tested repeatedly over a decade and long ago rated Class I, the highest-category source.

Red Rose had just survived her first security check. She could now be considered as active and given a Class III rating. After almost four years of carefully executed preparation, Ramón considered the price acceptable. He smiled at the portrait of Leonid Brezhnev on the opposite wall, and the general secretary stared back at him solemnly from under beetling brows.

Katrina rang through on his private line. "Comrade Colonel, you are expected on the top floor in six minutes."

"Thank you, comrade. Please come through to witness destruction of documents."

She stood at his side while he fed the printout of the Protea report into the paper shredder, and then she countersigned the entry in his daybook to attest to the destruction.

She watched him button his tunic and adjust the block of medal ribbons on his chest in the small wall mirror. Then she handed him the sheaf of notes for the meeting.

"Good luck, Comrade Colonel." She stood close to him with her face upturned.

"Thank you." He turned away without touching her: never in the office.

Ramón waited alone in the secure conference room on the top floor. They kept him waiting for ten minutes. The walls of the room were bare plaster, painted white. There was no paneling that might conceal a microphone. Apart from the obligatory portraits of Lenin and Brezhnev, there was no decoration. There were a dozen chairs at the long conference table, and Ramón stood at the lower end for the full ten minutes.

At last the door from the director's suite opened.

General Yuri Borodin was head of the Fourth Directorate. In his new capacity Ramón reported directly to him. He was a chunky grey-haired septuagenarian, a cautious, devious man in a shiny striped suit. Ramón admired him and held him in awe.

The man that followed him into the conference room deserved even greater respect. He was younger than Borodin, not much over fifty, yet he was already a member of the Presidium of the Supreme Soviet and a deputy minister at the Department of Foreign Affairs.

Ramón's report had drawn a much heavier reaction than he had anticipated. He was being invited to defend his thesis in front of one of the hundred most influential men in Russia.

Aleksei Yudenich was short and slight in stature, but he had the fierce penetrating gaze of a mystic. He shook Ramón's hand briefly and stared into his eyes while Borodin introduced them. Then he took the seat at the head of the table with his aides on each side of him.

"You have novel ideas, young man," he began abruptly. Ramón knew his choice of adjectives was not necessarily complimentary. Youth was not a commodity by which the Department of Foreign Affairs set as much store as they did by traditional and well-tried policies. "You wish to abandon our long-standing support for the liberation movements in southern Africa—the African National Congress and the South African Communist Party—and for the armed struggle in southern Africa in general."

191

"With respect, Comrade Director," Ramón replied carefully, "that is not my intention."

"Then I have misread your paper. Have you not stated that the ANC has proved to be the most inept and unproductive guerrilla organization in modern history?"

"I have pointed out the reasons for this, and the manner in which previous mistakes may be rectified."

Yudenich grunted and turned a sheet of his copy of the report. "Continue. Explain to me why the armed struggle should not succeed in South Africa as it did in, for instance, Algeria."

"There are basic differences, Minister. The settlers in Algeria, the *pieds noirs*, were Frenchmen, and France was a short boat ride away across the Mediterranean. The white Afrikaner has no such escape route. He stands with his back to the Atlantic Ocean. He must fight. Africa is his motherland."

"Yes," Yudenich nodded. "Continue."

"The FLN guerrillas in Algeria were united by the Muslim religion and a common language. They were waging a holy war, a *jihad*. On the other hand, the black Africans are not so inspired. They are splintered by language and tribal enmities. The ANC, as an example, is an almost exclusively Xhosa tribal organization which excludes the most numerous and powerful tribe, the Zulu nation, from its ranks."

Yudenich listened for fifteen minutes without interruption. His gaze never left Ramón's face. When at last Ramón finished speaking he asked softly, "So what is the alternative you propose?"

"Not an alternative." Ramón shook his head. "The armed struggle must, of course, continue. There are younger, brighter and more committed men coming forward in its ranks, men like Raleigh Tabaka. From them we may see greater success in future. What I propose is an adjunct to the struggle, an economic onslaught, a series of boycotts and mandatory sanctions . . ."

"We do not have economic contacts with South Africa," Yudenich pointed out brusquely.

"I propose that we let our archenemy do the job for us. I propose that we orchestrate in America and Western Europe a campaign to destroy the South African economy. Let our enemies prepare the ground for us and plant the seeds of revolution. We will harvest the fruits."

"How do you suggest we go about this?"

"You know that we have excellent penetration of the American Democratic Party. We have access to the American media at the highest possible levels. Our influence in such organizations as the NAACP and the Trans Africa Foundation is pervasive. I propose that we make South Africa and apartheid a rallying cry for the American left. They are looking for a cause to unite them. We will give them that cause. We will make South Africa a domestic political issue in the United States of America. The black Americans will flock to the standard and, to secure their votes, the Democratic Party will follow them. We will orchestrate a campaign in the ghettos and on the campuses of America for comprehensive mandatory sanctions that will destroy the South African economy and bring its government crashing down in ruins, unable any longer to protect itself or to keep its security forces in the field. When that happens we will step in and place our own surrogate government in power."

The others were silent a while, contemplating this startling vision. Aleksei Yudenich coughed and asked quietly, "How much will this cost—in financial terms?"

"Billions of dollars," Ramón admitted. When Yudenich's expression tightened, he went on, "Billions of *American* dollars, Comrade Minister. We will let the Democratic Party call the tune for us and the American people pay the piper."

Minister Yudenich smiled for the first time that afternoon. The discussions lasted another two hours before Yuri Borodin rang the bell to summon his aide.

"Vodka," he said.

It came on a silver tray, the bottle thickly crusted with frost from the freezer.

Aleksei Yudenich gave them the first of many toasts.

"The Democratic Party of America!" And they laughed and drained their glasses and shook hands and clapped one another's backs.

Director Borodin moved slightly, until he and Ramón Machado were standing shoulder to shoulder. It was a gesture that was not lost on any of them. He was aligning himself with his brilliant young subordinate.

# 16

Katrina's flat was in one of the more pleasant sections of the city. From her bedroom window there was a view of Gorky Park and the amusement ground. On the skyline the big Ferris wheel, lit with myriad fairy lights, revolved slowly against the cold grey clouds as Ramón stepped out of the Chaika and went in through the front entrance of the apartment building.

It was a relic from Tsarist Russia, a wedding cake of a building in rococo style. There was no lift, and Ramón climbed the stairs to the sixth floor. The exercise helped clear the vodka fumes from his brain.

Katrina's mother had lovingly prepared the thick pork sausage with a side dish of cabbage—always cabbage. The entire apartment block smelled of boiled cabbage.

Katrina's parents treated Ramón with servile and fawning respect. Her mother served Ramón the greater portion of the sausage, while Katrina poured pepper vodka into his tumbler. When they had eaten, Katrina's parents took the child with them and went to watch television in a neighbor's apartment, discreetly leaving Ramón and Katrina to say their farewells.

"I shall miss you," Katrina whispered as she led him to the single bed in her tiny room and let the skirt of her tunic fall around her ankles. "Please return soon."

They had an hour before Ramón had to leave for the airport. Her skin was velvety smooth and warm to his touch. There were tiny blue veins radiating out from around her large rosy brown nipples. There was plenty of time for Ramón to make it really good for her.

He left her with barely enough strength to totter to the door. Her threadbare dressing gown was clutched around her flawless shoulders, and her crisp curls were in tangled disarray.

At the door, she leaned heavily against him and kissed him deeply. "Come back to me soon, please. Oh, please!"

At this time of night there was very little traffic on the airport road, only a few rumbling military trucks. The journey took less than half an hour.

Ramón traveled so often that he had his own regime for minimizing the adverse effects of jet lag. He neither ate nor touched alcohol during the flight, and he had trained himself to sleep in any circumstance. A man who could fall asleep on a bed of jagged Ethiopian rock in a temperature of forty-two degrees, or in the hothouse of a dripping Central American rain forest with centipedes crawling over his skin, could do so even in the torturous seat of an Ilyushin passenger jet.

Although the sun burned down with a peculiar brilliance and dampened his open sports shirt along the spine and at the armpits, it was by his reckoning a Moscow winter midnight and not a balmy Caribbean noon when he stepped off the plane at Havana's José Marti Airport. He made the local connection on a scheduled flight, an old prop-driven Dakota that flew him down to Cienfuegos.

Lugging his own valise from the airport building, he bargained with the driver of one of the vintage Detroit model taxis standing at the "Piqueras" rank and rode out to the military cantonment of Buenaventura.

On the way they skirted the sparkling water of the Bahia de Cochinos and passed the museum dedicated to the battle of the Bay of Pigs. It always gave him a satisfied glow of achievement when he recalled his own role in that salutary humiliation of the American barbarians.

It was late afternoon when the taxi dropped him at the gates of the Buenaventura camp. The day's activity was coming to an end, and columns of the Che Guevara paratrooper regiment were marching back to barracks. These were crack troops in brown fatigues, especially trained for an assault role in any theater of the world, but since the last meeting of the Politburo in Havana they had been exercising and training for deployment in Africa.

Ramón paused to watch a unit of them pass by. Young men and women, they were singing one of the revolutionary songs he remembered so well from the bitter days in the Sierra Maestra. "Land of the Landless" was the title, and the lyric made his skin prickle even though it was all so long ago. He showed his pass at the gate to the married officers' quarters.

Even though Ramón was dressed in sports shirt and light cotton slacks with open sandals on his feet, the sergeant of the guard saluted him deferentially when he recognized his name and rank. Ramón was one of the eighty-two heroes whose names were recited in the schoolrooms and sung in the *bodegas*.

His cottage was one in a row of identical two-bedroomed flat-roofed adobe-walled dwellings set among the palms above the beach. The calm waters of the Bay of Pigs sparkled between the long curved trunks of the palms.

Adra Olivares was sweeping the narrow front veranda, but when he was still a hundred paces distant she looked up and saw him and her expression smoothed into neutrality.

"Welcome, Comrade Colonel," she said quietly as he stepped up onto the veranda, and although she cast down her gaze she could not conceal the fear in her eyes.

"Where is Nicholas?" he asked as he dropped his valise on the concrete floor. In reply she looked away down toward the beach.

There was a group of children frolicking at the edge of the water. Their shrill, excited cries carried above the clatter of the trade wind in the palm fronds. The children were all wearing bathing suits, and their bodies were brown and sleek with sun and water.

Nicholas stood a little apart from the other children, and Ramón felt his heart turn over as he recognized his son. It was only within the last year that he had begun to think of him that way. Before that he had always been "the child" and in his departmental reports he had been "the child of Red Rose." Insidiously he had become "my son," but only in his mind. The words were never spoken or written down.

Ramón left the veranda of the cottage and drifted down through the palms to the beach. At the high-water mark he sat on the low seawall and watched his son.

Nicholas was just three years old. He was precocious and physically well developed for his age. He would grow to be tall; already his limbs were long and coltish without any trace of baby fat. He stood with one hip thrust out, his weight all on one leg, his hand on one hip in a pose that called to mind Michelangelo's "David."

Ramón's interest in the child had been awakened only after it became clear that he was exceptionally intelligent. The reports from his teacher at the camp nursery school had been euphoric. His drawings and speech were those of a child many years older. Until that time Ramón had taken no active part in the child's upbringing. He had arranged this accommodation for Adra Olivares and Nicholas through the DGA in Havana. Adra was now a lieutenant in the organization of state security.

Ramón had arranged that also. It was necessary for her to have officer's rank in order to qualify for one of the Buenaventura cottages, and to enable Nicholas to attend the military crèche and nursery school.

For the first two years Ramón had not seen the child, although the various reports from the military clinic and the education department had passed over his desk when he prepared dispatches for Red Rose. Eventually these reports and the accompanying photographs had piqued his interest, and he had made the journey from the capital down to Buenaventura.

It seemed the child had recognized him immediately. He had hidden behind Adra's legs and peered out at Ramón fearfully. The last time he had seen his father was in that white-tiled operating theater in the Buenaventura military clinic, when Ramón had staged his partial drowning in front of the camera to coerce Red Rose into accepting his authority. Nicholas had been only a few weeks old at the time. It was impossible that he could remember the incident—and yet his reaction to Ramón had been too intense to be merely coincidental.

Ramón had been taken unawares by his response to the child's terror. He was accustomed to other people's trepidation in his presence, seldom needing one of his ruthless demonstrations to instill fear in those around him, but this had been different.

Apart from his own mother and his cousin Fidel, he had felt no deep sympathetic response to any of his fellow human beings. He had always deemed this to be one of his great strengths. He was almost impervious to sentimental or emotional considerations. This allowed him to make his decisions and base his actions entirely on logic and intellectual judgment. When necessary he was able to sacrifice a comrade of many years' standing without flinching and with no futile and debilitating regrets later. He could make tender and unselfish love to a beautiful woman and only hours later, without a moment's hesitation, order her execution. He had trained himself to be above all feeble, mundane considerations. He had forged and tempered himself into one of Lenin's steely men and honed the edges of his strength and resolve into a terrible shining weapon. Then, unexpectedly, he had found this flaw in the metal of his soul.

"A tiny flaw," he consoled himself as he sat on the seawall in the bright Caribbean sunshine and watched the child. "Only a hairline crack in the blade, and then only because this is part

197

of me. Blood of my blood, flesh of my flesh, and my hope for immortality.''

He cast his mind back to that episode in the military clinic. In his imagination he saw once again the infant squirming in the doctor's grip and heard the outraged terrified squeals and the painful choking breath as he lifted the sodden little head from the waters of the tank. He did not flinch from the memory.

At the time it was necessary, he thought. Never regret the strong, necessary action, the deed of steel.

The child stooped and picked a shell from the sand at his feet. He turned it in his hands and bowed his head to examine the iridescent pearly fragment.

Nicholas's curls were dark and dense, and although damp with sea salt, showed little reddish sunstruck sparks. He had inherited many features from his mother. Even Ramón recognized that chiseled classical nose and the clean sweet line of his jaw. However, the green eyes were Ramón's.

Suddenly the child threw back his arm and sent the shell skimming out across the still water, leaving a series of tiny dimples where it touched the surface. Then he turned away and began to walk alone along the edge of the water. But at that moment there came an anguished squeal from the group of children farther up the beach. One of the little girls had been knocked over in the rough-and-tumble, and she sprawled on the white sand and howled.

"Nicholas!"

With a patient sigh Nicholas turned back to her and lifted her to her feet. She was a pretty little imp with sand on one cheek and tears welling from her huge dark eyes. Her costume had slid halfway down to her knees, revealing the cleft between her chubby pink little buttocks.

Nicholas hauled up her costume for her, restoring her modesty but almost lifting her off her feet in the process. Then he led her by the hand to the water. He washed the sand off her cheek and wiped the tears from her eyes. The girl gave one last convulsive sniff and stopped howling.

She took Nicholas's hand and trotted beside him as he led her up the beach.

"I will take you back to your mamma," Nicholas seemed to be telling her. Then he looked up and saw his father. He stopped abruptly and stared at him.

Ramón saw the flare of terror in his eyes that was instantly hidden. Then Nicholas lifted his chin in a defiant gesture, and his expression went dead.

**198**

Ramón liked what he saw. It was good that the boy felt fear, for fear was the basis of respect and obedience. It was good also that he could control and hide that fear. The ability to conceal fear was one of the qualities of leadership. Already he showed a strength and resolve far beyond his tender years.

He is my son, Ramón thought, and he raised one hand in a gesture of command.

"Come here, boy," he called.

The little girl shrank away from him. Then she released Nicholas's hand and fled up the beach, bawling once again, but this time for her mother. Ramón did not even glance in her direction. He often had that effect on children.

Nicholas steeled himself visibly, then came to his father's bidding. "Good day, Padre." He held out his hand solemnly.

"Good day, Nicholas." Ramón took the proffered hand. He had schooled the child to shake hands like a man, but Adra had taught him the term of address "padre." He should not have allowed it, but he was pleased that in the end he had done so. It gave him another little twinge of sentimentality to be addressed as "father," but that was an indulgence he could afford. There were few enough he allowed himself.

"Sit here." Ramón indicated the wall beside him, and Nicholas scrambled up and sat with his little legs dangling.

They were silent for a while. Ramón did not approve of childish chatter. When he finally asked, "What have you been doing?" Nicholas considered the question gravely.

"I have been to school every day."

"What do they teach you at school?"

"We learn the drills and the songs of the revolution," Nicholas thought about it a little longer. "And we paint."

They were silent again until Nicholas added helpfully. "In the afternoons we swim and play soccer, and in the evenings I help Adra with the housework. Then we watch the TV together."

He was three years old, Ramón reminded himself. A Western child who was asked the same question might have replied "Nothing" or "Just stuff." Nicholas had spoken like a man, a little old man.

"I have brought you a present," Ramón told him.

"Thank you, Padre."

"Don't you want to know what it is?"

"You will show it to me," Nicholas pointed out. "And then I will know what it is."

It was a plastic model of an AK-47 assault rifle. Although it was a miniature, it was perfect in detail and had a removable magazine loaded with metallic painted bullets. Ramón had bought it at a toy shop on his last visit to London.

Nicholas's eyes shone as he raised it to his shoulder and aimed it down toward the beach. Apart from the first flash of fear, it was the only real emotion he had displayed since Ramón's arrival. When he pulled the trigger the toy rifle made a satisfying warlike clatter.

"It is very beautiful," Nicholas said. "Thank you, Padre."

"It is a good toy for a brave son of the revolution," Ramón told him.

"Am I a brave son of the revolution?"

"One day you will be," Ramón told him.

"Comrade Colonel, it is time for the child's bath," Adra intervened diffidently.

She took Nicholas and led him from the veranda into the cottage. Ramón put aside the temptation to follow them. It was unseemly for him to participate in such a bourgeois domestic ritual. Instead he went to the small table at the end of the veranda where Adra had set out a jug of lime juice and a bottle of Havana Club rum, indisputably the finest rum in the world.

Ramón mixed himself a *mojito* and then selected a cigar from the box on the table. He smoked only when he was at home in Cuba and then only the premium cigars of Miguel Fernandez Roig, and Adra knew this. Like the Havana Club, they were the finest in the world. He took the tall sugared glass and the cigar back to his seat and watched the sunset turn the waters of the bay to bloodied gold.

From the bathroom, he heard the splashing and the happy cries of his son, and Adra's soft replies.

Ramón was a warrior and a wanderer on the face of the earth. This was the closest he would ever come to a home of his own; perhaps the child had made it so for him.

Adra served a meal of chicken and *Moros y Cristianos*, or "Moors and Christians," a mixture of black beans and white rice. Through the DGA, Ramón had arranged a preferential ration book for the little household. He wanted the boy to grow up strong and well nourished.

"Soon you are going on a journey with me," he told Nicholas as they ate. "Across the sea. Would you like that, Nicholas?"

"Will Adra come with us?"

The question irritated Ramón. He did not recognize his annoyance as jealousy. He answered shortly, *"Sí."*

"Then I will like that," Nicholas nodded. "Where will we go?"

"To Spain," Ramón told him. "To the land of your ancestors and the land of your birth."

After dinner, Nicholas was allowed to watch the television for one hour. When his eyelids drooped, Adra took him to his bedroom.

When she returned to the small, starkly furnished living room she asked Ramón, "Do you want me tonight?"

Ramón nodded. She was over forty years of age. However, her belly was flat, and her thighs were firm and powerful. She had never given birth, and she had extraordinary muscular control. At his request she often excited him with a little trick. He would hold one end of a lead pencil while she snapped it in half with a spasmodic constriction of her vaginal sphincter.

She was an adept, one of the most natural, intuitive lovers he had ever known. Furthermore, she was terrified of him, which enhanced both her pleasure and his.

At dawn Ramón swam down to the head of the bay and then made the hard two-mile return against the tide, plowing through the choppy water in a crawl.

When he came up from the beach, Nicholas was ready for school and there was an army jeep and driver waiting at the back door of the cottage. Ramón was dressed in plain brown paratrooper fatigues and soft cap. This was revolutionary uniform, so different from the flamboyant Russian braid and scarlet piping and tiers of medal ribbons. Nicholas sat proudly beside him in the jeep for the short ride until they dropped him off at the nursery school near the main gate.

The drive up to Havana took a little over two hours, for the sugar harvest was in progress. The sky over the hills was smudged with smoke from the cane fires, and the road was congested with behemoth trucks piled high with cargoes of cut cane en route to the mills.

When they reached the city, the driver dropped Ramón at the far end of the vast Plaza de la Revolución, with its 350-foot obelisk to the memory of José Martí, hero of the people, who had founded the Cuban Revolutionary Party way back in 1892.

The square was the scene of many of the moving rallies of the party, where a million and more of the Cuban people gathered to listen to Fidel Castro's speeches. The president's office was in the building of the Central Committee of the Communist Party of Cuba, of which El Jefe was the first secretary.

The office in which he welcomed Ramón was as austere as revolutionary principles dictated. Under the revolving ceiling

201

fan, the massive desk was piled with working documents and reports. However, the white walls were bare of all ornament, except for the portrait of Lenin on the wall behind his desk. Fidel Castro came to embrace Ramón.

*"Mi Zorro Dorado,"* he chuckled with pleasure. "My Golden Fox. It is good to see you. You have been away too long, old comrade. Much too long."

"It is good to be back, El Jefe." Ramón truly meant it. Here was one man he respected and loved above all others. He was always startled by the size of the man he called the Leader. Castro towered over him and smothered Ramón in his embrace. Then he held him at arm's length and studied his face.

"You look tired, comrade. You have been working hard."

"With excellent results," Ramón assured him.

"Come, sit down by the window," Castro invited him. "Tell me about it."

He selected two Roig cigars from the box on the corner of his desk and gave one to Ramón. He held the burning taper for him, then lit his own before he settled into the straight-backed chair and leaned forward with the cigar stuck out of the corner of his mouth, puffing smoke around it.

"So tell me, what is the news from Moscow? You saw Yudenich?"

"I saw him, El Jefe, and the meeting went well . . ." Ramón launched into his report. It was typical of them that there was no small talk, no preamble to serious discussion. Neither of them had to maneuver for position or advantage. Ramón could speak with total honesty, without worrying about giving offense or trying to improve his own position. His position was unassailable. They were brothers of the blood and of the soul.

Of course, Castro could be changeable. His affections could shift. It had been that way with Che Guevara, another of the eighty-two heroes who had come ashore from *Granma*. Che had fallen from grace after he had disagreed with Castro's economic policies, and he had been driven out to become a wandering knight of the revolution, a Walt Whitman with grenade and AK-47. Yes, it had happened to Che, but it could never happen to Ramón.

"Yudenich has agreed to back our new export drive," Ramón said, and Castro chuckled. It was a little joke between them. Castro was an inspired political genius with that rare gift of being able to communicate his passionate vision to the masses. However, although he was an educated man, a qualified lawyer who had practiced his profession before the revolution had swept him up, he was no economist.

His grasp of the arcane science of economics was weak. He could not bother himself with the balance of payments and employment and productivity. His vision was sweeping and transcended those petty aspects of the body politic. He liked the bold and the big. Ramón had conceived the entire plan to appeal to El Jefe. It was bold and it was direct.

The problem was that Cuba's wealth was based on three staples: sugar, tobacco and coffee. These were insufficient to provide the hard currency to fuel Castro's ambitious plans for urban renewal and social welfare, let alone to provide full employment for an exploding population.

Since the revolution the population had doubled. According to the forecasts it would double again in the next ten years. Ramón's plan had been devised to counter these problems. It would provide hard cash and go far to ending unemployment on the island.

The "new export drive" was simply the export of men, of fighting men and women. They would be sent out in tens of thousands as mercenaries to pursue the revolution at the ends of the earth. Perhaps as many as a hundred thousand, nearly 10 percent of the island's total work force, could be exported. At one stroke they would end unemployment and swell the public coffer with the fees of a mercenary army.

Castro had liked the plan from the first day Ramón had propounded it to him. It was the kind of economics he could understand and applaud.

"Yudenich will recommend it to Brezhnev," Ramón assured him, and Castro stroked his beard as though it were a shaggy black cat.

"If Yudenich recommends it, then we have no worries." He leaned forward with his hands on his knees. "And we both know where you want them sent."

"I have meetings this afternoon at the Tanzanian embassy," Ramón said.

There were seventeen African embassies in Havana, all of them representatives of socialist governments newly liberated from colonial oppression.

Tanzania, under Julius Nyerere, was among the most Marxist of them all. Already Nyerere had declared that any person who owned more than one acre of property was a "capitalist and enemy of the people" and would be punished by having all property confiscated by the state. The Tanzanians were active in their support for the others struggling for liberation in the colonial slave states in the rest of Africa. They provided shelter for freedom fighters from Portuguese Angola and Mozambique, from that racist pariah South Africa, and from the medieval serfdom of the ancient tyrant Emperor Haile Selassie of Ethiopia. In all those countries there would be work for the army of Cuban mercenaries.

"I am meeting officers of the Ethiopian army who are dedicated to the cause of Marxist socialism, and who are prepared to risk their lives to break the yoke of the oppressor."

"Yes," Castro nodded, "Ethiopia is ripe for us."

Ramón considered the ash of his cigar; it was firm and crisp, almost two inches long.

"We both know that destiny has dictated that you play a role beyond the shores of this lovely island. Africa awaits you."

Castro leaned back with satisfaction and placed his huge, powerful hands on his knees as Ramón went on, "The Africans have a natural distrust of Mother Russia. The Russians in the Kremlin are all Caucasians—the word originates in that country. It is an unfortunate fact that despite all their other virtues most Russians are racists. We cannot escape that fact. Many of the African leaders, especially the young ones, have studied in Russia. They have heard the name *obezyana*, 'monkey,' whispered as they pass in the corridors of Patrice Lumumba University. The Russians are white men and racists—deep in his heart the African does not trust them."

Ramón drew evenly on his cigar, and they were silent a while. Castro broke the silence.

"Go on."

"On the other hand, you, El Jefe, are a great-grandson of Africa . . ." But Castro shook his head.

"I am Spanish," he contradicted.

Ramón smiled and went on. "If you were to claim that your forefathers were sold on the slave block in Havana—who would doubt it?" he suggested delicately. "And how vast might your influence in Africa become?"

Castro was silent, contemplating that vision, and Ramón went on softly, "We must arrange a tour for you. A triumphant cavalcade beginning in Egypt and going southward through twenty nations in which you could declare your concern, your commitment to the African people. If you could demonstrate your Africanism to two hundred million Africans, how great might your influence become?" Ramón leaned forward and touched his wrist. "No longer the president of a tiny beleaguered island, no longer the plaything of America, but a statesman of world influence and power."

"My Golden Fox," Castro said softly. "No wonder I love you."

The Tanzanian embassy was temporarily accommodated in one of the Spanish colonial buildings in the old city.

There the Ethiopians were waiting for Ramón. There were three of them, all young officers in the imperial army of Emperor Haile Selassie. Only one of the three interested Ramón Machado. He had met Captain Getachew Abebe on several previous visits to Addis Ababa.

In Ethiopia ethnic lines cannot be distinguished. A thousand years of invasion and interbreeding between Caucasian tribes from across the Red Sea and those from the heartland of the African continent have resulted in a mélange that cannot be separated. Definitions such as Galla and Amharic refer to linguistic and cultural groupings rather than to bloodlines.

However, in Captain Getachew Abebe the pure African ancestral influence dominated. He was very dark-skinned with full lips and pock-marked skin. He was a product of the University of Addis Ababa. Joe Cicero had succeeded in infiltrating a strong cadre of American and British Marxists into the university in the roles of professors and lecturers. One of their star students, Getachew Abebe had been transformed into a dedicated Marxist-Leninist.

Ramón had studied and courted him over the years until now he judged that he was the right man. At the very least, he was intelligent, hard and ruthless—and totally committed to the cause. Although he was only in his middle thirties, he was Ramón's provisional choice for the next leader of Ethiopia.

As they shook hands in the shuttered sitting room at the back of the Tanzanian embassy, Ramón cautioned him with a glance and a small gesture toward the collection of African tribal masks that covered the walls. Any one of these could conceal a microphone.

The conversation that followed was trivial and inconclusive and lasted less than half an hour. As they shook hands, Ramón leaned close to Abebe and whispered four words—a place and a time.

The two of them met again an hour later in the Bodeguita del Medio. It was the most famous bar in the old city. There was sawdust on the floor, and the tables and chairs were scarred and battered. The walls were pitted and scratched with graffiti and signatures of the famous and the ordinary: from Hemingway to Spencer Tracy and Edward, Duke of Windsor, they had all drunk here. Their faded, yellowed photographs were tacked into plain wooden frames that hung, fly-spotted and askew, on the grubby walls. The long, narrow room was thick with smoke. The cacophony of a portable radio blaring "Bembé" folk music and the shouted tiddly conversation of the customers covered their own quiet discussion.

They sat in the farthest corner, a *mojito* on the table in front of each of them. Condensation ran down the glasses and formed wet rings on the wood, but neither of them touched the drinks.

"Comrade, the time is almost ripe," Ramón said.

Abebe nodded. "The lion of Amhara has grown old and toothless; his son is a weak indulgent idiot. The nation groans under his tyranny and hungers in the worst famine and drought for a hundred years. The time is ripe."

"There are two things we must avoid," Ramón cautioned. "The first is an armed revolution. If the army rises and executes the emperor immediately, you will be passed over. You are still too junior in rank. One of the generals will seize power."

"So?" Abebe asked. "What is the solution?"

"A creeping revolution," Ramón told him. It was the first time Abebe had ever heard the term used, though he would not admit it.

"I see," he murmured, and Ramón went on to enlighten him.

"The Derg must call Haile Selassie to account and demand his abdication. As you say, the old lion has lost his teeth. He is isolated and out of touch. He must comply. You will use all your influence in the Derg, and I will exert all of mine."

The Derg was the Ethiopian parliament, an assembly of all the tribal and army chiefs, the heads of government departments and the religious elders. The entire body had been infiltrated by the Marxist products of the University of Addis Ababa. Most of them were under the direct influence of Ramón's Fourth Directorate. All of them had accepted Getachew Abebe as their leader.

"Then we will put in place a provisional military-based junta and I will arrange to move in a considerable Cuban force. With this we will consolidate your position. When it is secure we will be ready for the next step."

"What will that be?" Abebe asked.

"The emperor must be eliminated," Ramón told him, "to prevent a royalist backlash."

"Execution?"

"Executions are too public and too emotional." Ramón shook

his head. "He is a sick old man. He will simply die, and then . . ."

"And then an election?" Abebe interjected. Ramón looked at him sharply. Only when he saw the cynical smile on the Ethiopian's thick purple lips did he smile thinly.

"You startled me, comrade," Ramón admitted. "For a moment I thought you were serious. The very last thing we want is an election before we have chosen the new president and the form of government. Nowhere have the masses ever been capable of governing themselves; even less have they been able to choose the persons who should govern them. It is our duty to make that choice for them. Later, much later, after you are declared president of a Marxist socialist government, we will hold a controlled and orderly election to confirm our choice."

"I will need you in Addis, comrade," Abebe told him. "I will need your guidance and the strong right hand of Cuba to see the struggle through the dangerous and exciting days ahead."

"I will be there, comrade," Ramón promised him. "Together, you and I will show the world how a revolution should be conducted."

# 17

There were always risks, Ramón thought, but they had to be weighed carefully against the possible rewards. Then all possible precautions must be taken to minimize those risks. It was time for Red Rose to be given access to the child, just as she had been given time to make the initial bonding after Nicholas's birth. She had been allowed then to feel the child feeding at her breast, and to come to know every exquisite detail of the tiny body, but that had been three years ago, and the bond would be weakening. Ramón had used the threat video, the photographs and the clinic and nursery school reports to reinforce her maternal instincts. However, three years was a long time, and he sensed his control over Red Rose was weakening.

She must be rewarded for delivering the authentic Siemens radar report and taught that cooperation was the only possible avenue open to her. On the other hand, she must not be stimulated to attempt some wild endeavor. She was a strong and willful personality. She possessed a dangerous spirit, a core of strength Ramón sensed would be difficult to shatter. She could be cowed, but could she ever be completely subjugated? He was not yet certain. She had to be played with extreme delicacy.

She must not be tempted to believe that this meeting with Nicholas was an indication of leniency. She must be taught that she was held in the trap by bands of steel.

Ramón had considered all the possible adverse reactions the visit might generate. The most likely was that Red Rose might conceive some foolhardy idea of escaping with the child or planning a rescue.

He had taken precautions against this. The hacienda was remote. It was the property of a member of the Spanish Communist Party who was on a visit to New York with all his family. Ramón had moved a section of KGB staff in to cover the meeting.

There were twelve guards strategically placed in and around the hacienda. All of them were armed. The weapons had come in the diplomatic bag to Madrid, along with the two-way radios and the drugs that might be needed if Red Rose became dangerously hysterical on seeing her son.

He had chosen Spain for the meeting for a good reason. Red Rose must never be allowed to know where Nicholas was being kept. Ramón was fully aware of the power and influence of the Courtney family. If Red Rose went to her father and they knew where the child was being held, then they might hire mercenaries or prevail on the South African security services to mount some kind of kidnap attempt.

She must be led to believe that Nicholas was being held in Spain.

It was quite logical, of course. Nicholas had been born there. She knew Ramón was Spanish. The last time she had seen the boy was in Spain. She had no reason to think he had been transferred to another country, especially not across the Altantic Ocean.

They had come in on the Aeroflot flight from Havana to London and transferred to Iberian Airways from Heathrow. After the meeting, Adra and the child would return the same way with two KGB bodyguards, while Ramón flew south to Ethiopia.

Ramón stood at the shuttered window in the bell tower of the hacienda. Through the slats he looked down at the red-tiled roof that was mellowed and spotted with a century's accumulation of lichen and mosses. The building was of traditional design. Its thick white plastered walls were built around a central courtyard. In the center of the lawned courtyard was a swimming pool. An ornamental date palm stood at each corner of the pool. Below the long graceful fronds of each palm hung bunches of ripening yellow fruit.

From his position in the tower Ramón could survey not only the courtyard, but also the fields and vineyards surrounding the hacienda. However, he was concealed by the wooden shutters. There were vehicles concealed in the walled lanes that divided the vineyards. They were ready to react to his radio command and cut off any escape route. Ramón had placed eight guards around the estate and at windows overlooking the courtyard. One of these was armed with a sniper's rifle, another with a dart gun, but he did not really believe there would be a call for them.

What with airfares and the personnel involved, the entire operation had been extremely costly. However, he had been able to use guards and vehicles from the Russian embassy in Madrid, and the owner of the hacienda had not required any payment. Thinking about the parsimony of the finance section and the time he had to spend filling in expense sheets and justifying each item to one of the accountants, Ramón again felt a sour burn in his stomach. How could an accountant ever understand the necessities and priorities of field operations? How much more could be achieved without this continuous audit to which he was subjected? What price could they place on a nation brought into the fold of Soviet socialism?

The soft crackle of the radio interrupted these unpleasant speculations.

"*Da?* Yes?" He spoke Russian into the microphone.

"This is number three." That was the guard at the far end of the lane on the south side of the estate. "The vehicle is visual."

Ramón crossed to the southern window of the tower. He could see the pale yellow dust of the approaching car spreading over the vineyards.

"Very well." He went back to his original position and nodded to the female signals clerk from the embassy. She sat at the electronic console with the directional microphone trained down into the courtyard. Every word or sound uttered in the courtyard would be recorded, and the meeting would be filmed on videotape.

There were, of course, voice-activated microphones and concealed cameras in every room of the hacienda that Red Rose might enter, including the toilets and bathroom. Ramón had requisitioned this equipment from the embassy in Madrid. The voiceprints and up-to-date photographs would be a nice little spin-off from the main object of the operation.

The car, a blue Cortina with diplomatic plates, came into view. It turned into the gates of the estate and drew up at the front door of the hacienda.

Isabella Courtney was the first to alight, followed by the female embassy guard who had escorted her from the airport. Isabella paused on the paved driveway and looked up at the shuttered windows of the tower, almost as though she sensed his gaze upon her. Ramón picked up his binoculars and studied her upturned face.

She had changed dramatically in the years since he had last seen her. Few vestiges of the silly, flighty girl remained. She was a mature woman now. There was poise and determination in the way she carried herself. Her features seemed to have firmed. She was thin, too thin, and there were dark smudges below her eyes. Even from this distance he could make out the first faint chiseling by life's hardship and care at the corners of her mouth, and a new hard line to her jaw. There was a tragic air about her, a sense of suffering that appealed to him. She was not as pretty, but considerably more attractive and interesting, than he remembered her.

Quite unexpectedly the thought that this was Nicholas's mother occurred to him, and in the next instant he felt a stab of pity for her. The treachery of his emotion made him angry, and he crushed down the sense of pity. He could not remember ever having such a soft and enervating feeling toward a subject before, not even when they were in the interrogation cells below the Lubyanka or on the torture racks in the Congo jungle. His anger turned on himself, then on her. She was responsible for inducing that momentary weakness. He shielded his anger, the way he might cup his hands around a match flame on a windy night.

Isabella thought she had glimpsed an obscure movement beyond the shuttered window in the high tower, but it must have been her imagination.

The woman who had escorted her touched her arm and said in only slightly accented English, "Come. We will go in."

Isabella lowered her gaze from the belltower to the carved teak front door just as it swung open. There was another female waiting for them. Isabella buttoned the jacket of her grey business suit as though it might protect her like a coat of mail. She drew back her shoulders and went in through the doorway.

The interior was gloomy and cool. There were worn, somber-colored rugs on the flagstone floor and dark heavy furniture. The doors were black oak studded with iron. The windows were shuttered and barred. The house had a brooding, forbidding atmosphere that made her pause in the entrance hall.

"This way!" The woman led her into a small antechamber off the main hall. Her escort followed her, carrying the single suitcase and the large parcel Isabella had brought with her. She placed the suitcase and parcel on a heavy oak table, then locked the door.

"Keys." She held out her hand, and Isabella searched in her handbag and gave them to her.

Methodically the two women went through the contents of the suitcase. It was obvious they had been trained for the task. They unfolded each item of clothing and examined the seams and linings. They opened each jar of cosmetics and probed the creams and ointments they contained with a knitting needle. They palpated every tube and removed the batteries from the electric shaver Isabella used on her underarm hair. They tested the heels of her spare pair of shoes and the lining of the case. Then they turned their attention to the wrapped parcel. It contained the gift she had brought for Nicholas. One of them reached for her handbag, and Isabella handed it over. They went through it with as much care.

"Please to remove clothes." Isabella shrugged and began to undress. They took each item as she removed it and examined it minutely. They removed the shoulder pads from her jacket and examined the lining of her bra.

When she was entirely naked one of the women ordered, "Lift the arms."

She obeyed, and then to her horror one of the women slipped a surgical rubber glove on to her right hand and dipped two fingers into a pot of Vaseline.

"Turn around," she ordered.

"No." Isabella shook her head.

"Do you want to see the boy?" the woman asked heavily, holding up her two gloved fingers glistening with Vaseline. "Turn around."

Isabella shivered and felt goose pimples rise on her arms.

**211**

"Please," she whispered. "I give you my word. I'm not hiding anything. This isn't necessary."

"Turn around." The woman's voice did not change. Slowly Isabella turned.

"Bend over," the woman said. "Put your hands on the table."

She leaned forward and gripped the edge of the table hard.

"Move your feet apart."

Isabella realized she was deliberately being humiliated. She knew it was all part of the process. She tried to close her mind to it, but she gasped as she felt the woman's fingers slide into her, and she started to pull away.

"Stay still."

She bit down on her lip and closed her eyes. The examination was leisurely and thorough.

"All right." The woman stepped back. "Get dressed."

Isabella found that there were tears on her cheeks. She took a Kleenex from her jacket pocket and wiped them away. They were tears of fury.

"Wait here." The woman stripped the glove from her hand and threw it into the wastepaper bin.

The two of them left the room and locked the door.

Isabella dressed quickly and sat down on the bench. Her hands were shaking. She clenched them into fists and thrust them into the pockets of her jacket.

They kept her waiting almost an hour.

Ramón had watched the search and the physical examination on the small screen of the remote video camera.

The camera had been carefully positioned to give him a full view of Isabella's face during the entire process. What he could see of her expression gave him cause for disquiet. He had hoped, but not truly expected, to cow her completely. Instead he saw that cold fury in her eyes, the stubborn reckless line of her clenched jaw. He studied her carefully, leaning closer to the screen. Was that fury murderous or suicidal? He could not be certain.

At that moment Isabella glanced up and looked directly at the lens of the concealed camera. She recognized the camera for what it was, and he saw her take control of herself. A veil fell over those glittering dark blue eyes, and her expression smoothed into blank neutrality.

Ramón straightened up. He sighed. As he had suspected all along, this subject could not be pushed beyond a certain point.

He sensed that the point was very close now. She was on the edge of rebellion. It called for a change of tactics. Very well; he was prepared for that. A change was often good procedure; it confused and unsettled the subject. Ramón was always flexible and versatile.

He turned away from the screen and called softly, "Bring the child."

Adra came through from the next room, leading Nicholas by the hand.

Ramón studied him as carefully as he had the boy's mother. Adra had washed his hair for him that morning. His curls, shiny and springing, tumbled onto his forehead. She had dressed him in a plain short-sleeved shirt and short cotton trousers. His limbs were slim and smoothly tanned, his lips were a sensitive pink and his brows were darkly curved over his huge solemn eyes. He would break any mother's heart.

"Do you remember what I told you, Nicholas?"

"Sí, Padre."

"You will meet a very kind lady. She likes you very much. She has a present for you. You will be nice to her and you will call her 'Mamma.' "

"Is she going to take me away from Adra?"

"No, Nicholas. She has come only to talk to you for a while and give you a present. Then she will go away. Will you be nice to her? If you are, Adra will let you watch a Woody Woodpecker video this evening. Would you like that?"

"Yes, Padre." Nicholas smiled happily at the promise.

"Off you go now."

Ramón turned back to the shuttered window and looked through the slats. In the courtyard below one of the KGB women was leading Isabella out into the sunlight. She pointed to the bench beside the swimming pool, and her voice was amplified through the directional microphone the signals clerk trained on her.

"Please to wait here. The child will come to you."

The woman turned away, and Isabella went to the bench. She sat down, took a pair of sunglasses from her handbag and placed them over her eyes. From behind the dark lenses she studied her surroundings covertly.

Ramón depressed the "transmit" button on his two-way radio. "All stations, this is number one. Full alert. The contact is in progress."

Apart from the electronic surveillance equipment, Isabella now had a 7.62-millimeter Dragunov sniper's rifle and a dart gun aimed at her. The dart gun was loaded with Tentanyl and would immobilize a human victim within two minutes. Ramón had two 10-milligram phials of Nalorphine on hand as an antidote. Even as a last resort, he did not want to risk losing such a potentially valuable operative as Red Rose.

Abruptly Isabella leaped to her feet and stared across the courtyard. Ramón glanced down. Directly below the tower Adra and Nicholas had appeared. He could see the tops of their heads.

With a supreme effort Isabella prevented herself from rushing across the lawn and sweeping her son into her arms. She knew intuitively that such an action on her part would confuse and distress the child. He was at the age when any boy hated to be treated like a baby. Isabella had studied her copy of Dr. Spock until it was tired and dog-eared.

Slowly she removed her sunglasses and remained still. Nicholas hung on to Adra's hand and studied his mother with great interest.

Isabella had thought she was prepared for his physical appearance. The last photograph she had of him was only two months old, but it was nothing like the reality. It could not capture his coloring, nor the texture of his skin, nor those curls—and those eyes. Oh, those eyes!

"Oh God," she whispered. "He's the loveliest child. There could never be another like this. Please, God, help him to like me."

Adra tugged gently at Nicholas's hand, urging him forward, and they skirted the swimming pool and stopped in front of Isabella.

"*Buenos días*, Señorita Bella," Adra said softly in Spanish. "Nicholas likes to swim. There is a costume for both you and Nicholas if you want to swim with him. They are in the cabana." She pointed to the shuttered door of the bathhouse. "You may change in there."

Then she looked down at Nicholas. "Greet the lady, your mother," she instructed him gently, and released his hand. She turned and hurried from the courtyard, leaving them alone together.

Nicholas had not smiled or taken his eyes from Isabella's face. Now he stepped forward dutifully and held out his right hand.

"Good day, Mamma. My name is Nicholas Machado and I am pleased to meet you."

Isabella wanted to drop onto her knees and hug him with all her strength. The word "Mamma" had stabbed through her heart like a bayonet. Instead she took his hand and shook it carefully.

"You are a fine young man, Nicholas. I hear that you are doing very well at nursery school."

"Yes," Nicholas agreed. "And next year I am to join the young pioneers."

"That will be nice for you," Isabella nodded. "Who are the young pioneers, Nicholas?"

"Everybody knows." He was obviously amused by her ignorance. "They are the sons and daughters of the revolution."

"That's wonderful," Isabella went on hastily. "I have brought a present for you."

"Thank you, Mamma." Uncontrollably Nicholas's eyes slid toward the package.

Isabella sat on the bench and handed him the gift. Nicholas squatted in front of her and unwrapped it carefully. Then he was silent.

"Do you like it?" Isabella asked nervously.

"It's a soccer ball," Nicholas pronounced.

"Yes. Do you like it?"

"It's the best gift anybody has ever given me," he said.

He looked up at her, and she saw in his eyes that despite his formal, stilted speech he truly meant it. What a reserved, self-possessed little old man he is, she thought. What terrible events and nightmares have made him like this?

"I have never played soccer," Isabella told him. "Will you teach me?"

"You're a girl." Nicholas looked doubtful.

"Still, I'd like to try."

"All right." He stood up with the ball under one arm. "But you'll have to take your shoes off."

Within minutes all the child's reserves evaporated. He shrieked with excitement as he dribbled and darted after the ball. He was nimble as a field mouse, and Isabella raced after him, laughing with him, obeying his instructions and allowing him to score five goals between the legs of the bench.

When at last they both collapsed on the lawn, Nicholas informed her between gasps, "You are quite good—for a girl."

They changed into swimming costumes, and Nicholas gave her an exhibition of his prowess. First he swam a length dog-paddle, and her praises were so fulsome that he declared, "I can do a width underwater. Watch me." He almost made it across and surfaced just short of the bar, blowing and huffing and red-faced.

Sitting waist-deep on the shallow-end steps, Isabella felt a moment of physical revulsion as she remembered the last time she had seen her son immersed, but she managed to smile and sound enthusiastic.

"Oh, well done, Nicholas."

He came to her, still puffing for breath, and without warning he climbed into her lap.

"You are pretty," he said. "I like you."

Carefully, as though he might shatter like a precious crystal, she wrapped her arms around him and held him. Through the cool water his body was warm and slippery and she could feel her heart twist and tear within her.

"Nicholas," she mumbled. "Oh, my baby. How I love you. How I miss you."

The afternoon passed like a flash of sheet lightning in a summer sky, and then Adra came to fetch him. "It is time for Nicholas's dinner. Do you wish to eat with him, señorita?"

They ate al fresco, at a table Adra set for them in the courtyard. They shared a baked *besugo*, a sea bream from the Atlantic, and salads. There was a glass of fresh orange juice for Nicholas and a sherry for her. Isabella shredded the flesh of the bream to remove any bones, but Nicholas fed himself.

As Nicholas was finishing his ice cream, Isabella's vision began to swim. She heard a rushing in her ears, and Nicholas's face seemed to expand and blur.

Adra caught her before she slipped from the chair, and Ramón stepped into the courtyard from the doorway behind her. The two KGB women followed him.

"You have been a good boy, Nicholas," Ramón said. "Now, go off to bed with Adra."

"What is wrong with the nice lady?"

"There is nothing wrong," Ramón told him. "She is just very sleepy. You are sleepy, too, Nicholas."

"Yes, Padre." At the suggestion he yawned and rubbed his eyes with the backs of his fists. Adra led him away, and Ramón nodded at the waiting women.

"Take her to the room."

While they lifted Isabella out of her chair, Ramón picked up the empty sherry glass from the dinner table and wiped out the last traces of the drug with his handkerchief.

Isabella woke in a strange bedroom. She felt rested and at peace. The early sun streamed in through the slats of the shuttered window. She blinked drowsily and pulled the single sheet up around her naked shoulders. She wondered without any real urgency where she was, but her memory was fuzzy.

She was suddenly aware that she was totally nude under the sheet. She lifted her head. Her clothing was neatly folded on the chair beside the open bathroom door. Her suitcase was on the luggage rack.

Then out of the corner of her eye she caught a movement and she stiffened and came fully awake. There was a man in the bedroom with her. She opened her mouth to scream, but he signaled her urgently to silence.

"Ra—" She started to say his name, but with two rapid paces he reached the bedside and laid his open hand on her lips to keep her from speaking.

She stared at him, stunned and completely bemused. Ramón! Joy rose in her like a spring tide.

He left her and crossed quickly to the nearest wall of the bedroom. On it hung a dark oil painting in the style of Goya. Ramón swiveled the painting to one side to reveal a hidden microphone the size of a silver dollar attached to the wall.

Once again he made a gesture to silence her and came back. He lifted the shade off the lamp on the bedside table and showed her the second microphone taped to the stand below the bulb.

Then he leaned so close to her that his warm breath fanned her cheek.

"Come." He touched her bare shoulder through the sheet. It had been so long that despite her happiness she felt strange and shy in his presence.

"I will explain—come." His eyes were so full of pain and suffering that she felt her joy waver.

He took her hand, which held the sheet to her chin, and drew her, suddenly unresisting, from the bed. Still holding her hand, he led her, stark naked, to the bathroom. She was oblivious of her nudity, and she staggered a little from the aftereffects of the drug.

In the bathroom Ramón flushed the toilet, opened the taps in the handbasin and in the bath, and switched on the shower in the glass-walled cabinet.

Then he came back to her. She drew away from him, afraid to touch him. Her naked back was pressed to the cold tiles.

"What is happening to us? Are you one of them, Ramón? I am so confused. Please tell me what is happening."

His marvelous features contorted with agony. "I am like you. I have to cooperate, for Nicky's sake. I can't explain now—forces greater than we are. We have been caught up, all three of

**217**

us. Oh, my darling, how I have wanted to hold you and explain it all to you, but I have so little time."

"Ramón, tell me you still love me," she whispered timidly.

"Yes, my darling. More than I ever did. I know what hell you must have lived through. I have shared it with you, every moment of it. I know what you must have thought of me. One day you will understand that everything I have done has been for Nicky and for you."

She wanted to believe him. Desperately, wildly, she wanted it to be true.

"Soon," he whispered, taking her face between his cupped hands. "Soon we'll be together, just the three of us—you and Nicky and me. You must trust me."

"Ramón!" It came out as a choking sob, and she wound both arms around his neck and clung to him with all her strength. Against all reason or logic she believed him completely.

"We have only a few minutes together. We dare not risk more. It is so dangerous. You can never know what terrible danger Nicky is in."

"And you also," her voice quavered.

"My life does not matter. It's Nicky . . ."

"Both of you," she denied. "You are both so precious."

"Promise me that you will do nothing to harm Nicky." He kissed her mouth. "Please do whatever they say. It will not be for much longer. I will get us free of this thing, if you will help me. But you must trust me."

"Oh, my love. Oh, my darling. I knew deep down. I knew there must be a reason. Of course I trust you, my heart."

"Be strong for all of us."

"I swear it to you." She nodded violently, her face smeared with tears. "Oh, God, how I love you. I have suppressed it so long."

"I know, my darling. I know."

"Please, please, make love to me, Ramón. I've been without you for so long. I've been withering away. Make love to me before you have to go."

He took her quickly, yet it crashed over her like the winds of a hurricane and left her shattered.

When he was gone, breaking away with a last long lingering kiss, her legs could no longer support her. She sank slowly down the tiled wall and sat on the floor with her legs sprawled jointlessly under her. The taps roared and billows of steam filled the room. She didn't understand it all. She didn't have to, and she didn't care anymore. All that mattered was Nicky and Ramón.

"Oh, thank God," she whispered. "It wasn't true. None of the horrors was true. Ramón loves me still. We will be all right, the three of us. We'll come through this together. Somehow. Sometime."

She dragged herself to her feet. "Now I must pull myself together. They mustn't suspect . . ." She staggered to the shower.

She was still in bra and panties when, without a knock, the door opened and the large heavy-featured woman who had escorted her from the airport and had conducted that dreadful body search entered the room. She looked at Isabella's body in a way that made Isabella's flesh crawl. Isabella stepped hurriedly into the skirt of her grey suit.

"What do you want?"

"You leave in twenty minutes to airport."

"Where is Nicky? Where is my son?"

"Child has gone."

"I want to see him, please."

"Is not possible. Child has gone."

Isabella felt the ebullient mood of hope, which her brief interlude with Ramón had raised, begin to evaporate.

The nightmare begins again, she thought, and tried to steel herself against the creeping sense of despair.

"I must trust Ramón. I must be strong."

The woman sat beside Isabella in the backseat of the Cortina on the drive back to the airport. It was a hot morning, and the car was not air-conditioned. The woman's body odor was rank as a man's. Isabella felt she was going to be ill, and she opened the side window and let the wind blow in her face.

The driver of the Cortina stopped outside the international departures terminal and, while he went to unlock the boot and lift out Isabella's suitcase, the woman spoke for the first time since leaving the hacienda.

"Is for you," she said, and handed over a sealed unaddressed envelope.

Isabella opened her handbag and secreted the envelope. The woman was staring straight ahead through the windscreen. She offered no word of farewell. Isabella stepped out of the Cortina and picked up her suitcase. The driver slammed the door and drove away.

Standing on the pavement, in the midst of the throng of package-tour travelers, Isabella felt alone, more alone and frightened than she had been before she had seen Nicky and Ramón again.

"I must trust him," she repeated to herself as a litany of faith, and went to the Iberia check-in desk.

After checking in, she went to the women's washroom in the first-class lounge and locked herself in one of the cubicles. She sat on the closed lid of the toilet and tore open the envelope.

Red Rose,
You will ascertain precisely what stage the development of a nuclear explosive device by Armscor and the nuclear research institute at Pelindaba has reached. You will report on the test site that has been selected and the date for the preliminary testing of the device.

On receipt of this data a further meeting with your son will be arranged. The duration of this meeting will depend on the depth and scope of information that you deliver.

There was, as usual, no signature, and the message was typed on a sheet of plain paper. She stared at it sightlessly.

"Deeper and deeper," she whispered. "First the radar report." That had not seemed so bad. Radar was a defensive weapon—but this? An atomic bomb? Would there ever be an end to it?

She shook her head. "I can't—I'll tell them, I can't."

Her father had never even hinted at any interest in the Pelindaba Institute. She had never seen a file or even a single letter that addressed the subject of a nuclear explosive device. She had read in the press that the research at Pelindaba was directed toward refinement and processing of the country's huge uranium production, and toward the development of a reactor for industrial and urban electrical power. The prime minister had given repeated assurances that South Africa was not developing an atomic bomb.

Despite that, her instructions were not to ascertain if production were in progress. That was taken as a fact. She had been ordered to find out where and when the first device would be tested.

She began to shred the message between nervous fingers.

"I can't," she whispered. She stood up and raised the toilet seat. She dropped each tiny scrap of paper into the bowl separately and flushed them away.

"I'll tell them I can't." But already her mind was busy.

I'll have to work on Pater, she thought, and immediately she began to plan it.

* * *

Isabella had been out of the country on her visit to Spain for only five days. Nevertheless, Nana was angry, and sniffed at her weak excuse for leaving in the middle of her election campaign. The Friday before polling day, the prime minister, John Vorster, was to address a meeting in the Sea Point town hall in support of the National Party candidate.

It had taken all Centaine Courtney-Malcomess's wiles and wit to get him to cancel two other important engagements to make the speech. The party machine realized Sea Point was a safe opposition seat and that they were simply going through the motions. They were reluctant to wheel out their big gun, but Centaine prevailed, as she usually did.

With the promise of hearing the prime minister speak, the town hall was jam-packed. The meeting began with the usual heckling from the body of the hall, but it was fairly good-natured.

Isabella spoke first. She kept it short, ten minutes. It was her best speech of the entire campaign. She had gathered valuable experience and confidence over the preceding weeks, and her jaunt to Spain seemed to have revitalized her. Both Nana and Shasa had gone over the text with her, and she had rehearsed her delivery in front of them. These two shrewd old political war-horses had given her valuable tips and suggestions.

Standing on the platform in front of the crowded hall, Isabella cut a slim, determined figure, and the heart of the audience seemed to go out to her youth and loveliness. They gave her a standing ovation at the end, while John Vorster stood beside her, red-faced and benign, nodding and clapping his approval.

The following Wednesday evening Shasa and Nana were standing on either side of Isabella, wearing huge party rosettes and straw boaters with the party colors, when the results of the polling were read out.

There were no upsets. The Progressive Party regained the seat, but Isabella had cut their majority to a mere twelve hundred votes. Her supporters chaired her shoulder-high from the hall as though she were the victor and not the vanquished.

A week later John Vorster invited her to a meeting in his office in the parliament building. Isabella knew the building intimately. When her father had been a cabinet minister in Hendrik Verwoerd's government, his office had been on the same floor, only a few doors down the corridor from the prime minister's office.

During his tenure Shasa had given her the run of his office, and she had used it as a club whenever she was in central Cape Town. It brought back so many memories to walk down the wide

221

corridor once again. As a teenager she had not in any way appreciated the aura of history with which the magnificent old building was imbued.

Now, with political aspirations thrust upon her against her will, she was entranced by the portraits of great men, both good and evil, that decorated the paneled walls.

The prime minister kept her waiting only a few minutes. When she went into his office he came around his desk to greet her.

"It's so good of you to want to see me, Oom John," Isabella said in flawless Afrikaans. It was naughty of her to use such familiar address without being invited to do so. However, the term, "Oom," or "Uncle," was one of great respect, and the gamble paid off. Vorster's blue eyes twinkled in acknowledgment of her nerve.

"I wanted to congratulate you on your showing at Sea Point, Bella," he replied, and she felt a thrill of acceptance. Use of her pet name was an unusual accolade.

"I'm having a coffee break." Vorster waved at the silver and porcelain service on a side table. "Will you pour a cup for both of us?

"Now, young lady," he addressed her sternly over the rim of his cup. "What are you going to do with yourself? Since you aren't going to be an MP."

"Well, Oom John, I am working for my father—"

"Of course, I know that," he interrupted her. "But we can't let all that fresh young political talent go begging. Have you considered a seat in the Senate?"

"The Senate?" Isabella gulped, and the coffee scalded her tongue. "No, Prime Minister, I haven't. Nobody ever suggested—"

"Well, somebody is suggesting it now. Old Kleinhans is retiring next month. I have to nominate somebody to take his seat. It will do until we can find a safe seat in the lower house for you."

The Senate was the upper of the two legislative houses of the Republic of South Africa. Its duties were similar to those of the House of Lords in England, and it had the power to hold up dubious legislation and refer it back to the lower house. It had been considerably expanded back in the 1950s when the then prime minister, Malan, had set out to disfranchise those colored voters who had the vote. He had packed the upper house with senators nominated by himself in order to force through the distasteful act that had stripped the coloreds of their vote. Some of the seats in the upper house were still in the prime minister's gift, and Vorster was offering her one of these.

Isabella set down her coffee cup and stared speechlessly at him. Her mind was racing to keep up with this new development.

"Will you accept the nomination?" Vorster asked.

It was a marvelous shortcut, one that none of them—not Shasa nor even Nana—had dreamed of.

Hendrik Verwoerd himself had started his political career in the Senate. At twenty-eight years of age, she would almost certainly be the youngest, the brightest and certainly the most attractive senator in the upper house.

Appointments to various commissions and house committees would certainly follow her nomination. If she were only half as good as she knew she was, the National Party would turn her into their prime feminist political figure. Her entry to the innermost circles of power, to the innermost state secrets, would come very swiftly.

"You do me great honor, Prime Minister." Her voice was a whisper.

"I know you will serve your country with even greater honor." Vorster held out his hand. "Congratulations, Senator."

As Isabella took his hand, she felt an icy finger of guilt trace down her spine, the chill of treason and treachery. She forced it back. The reaction followed swiftly—with a great surge of her spirits she realized that Red Rose was now invaluable to her masters. Soon she could set her own terms and demand her own rewards from them.

Nicky and Ramón, she thought. Ramón and Nicky—it will be soon now. Much sooner than we could ever have believed. We will be together again.

# 18

Isabella had come to love the austere grandeur of the Karroo.

Shasa had purchased the vast sheep ranch while she was still a child. On her first visit she had hated the grim stony kopjes and forbidding plains that spread aimlessly to a distant horizon blurred by sun and dust until the juncture of earth and a milky luminous sky was obscured. Then as a teenager she had read Eve Palmer's *The Plains of Camdeboo*, and she had begun to understand just what a wondrous world the Karroo really was.

With her father she had hunted for fossils in the upthrust sedimentary beds that had been a vast antediluvian swamp in the age of the great reptiles, and she had stood amazed and filled with awe by their petrified bones and fangs.

.The homestead was named Dragon's Fountain in memory of those terrible creatures, and for the spring of clear sweet water that gushed ceaselessly from a grotto at the base of one of the tabletop mountains. The sheer wall of red rock towered above the sprawling mansion with its green lawns and lush gardens nurtured by the spring. Vultures and eagles nested in the crags, and their droppings whitewashed the weathered precipice.

The sheep ranch spread over sixty thousand acres of this fascinating wilderness. Mingled with the flocks of merino sheep were vast herds of springbok. These graceful little antelopes danced on the plains like puffs of wind-driven dust. Their delicate bodies were pale cinnamon slashed with bars of chocolate and blazing white. Their lovely patterned heads and lyre-shaped horns made them Isabella's favorites among all the multitudinous life-forms that inhabited the plains of Camdeboo. Both sheep and antelope flourished on the low wiry desert bush, and the diet flavored their flesh with the taste of sage and wild herbs.

Each winter, at the commencement of the hunting season, Shasa invited a party to Dragon's Fountain to join the annual springbok cull. Anything over four inches of rainfall in the Karroo was considered a good year, and in such a season the springbok ewes lambed twice. The resulting explosion of the herds had to be controlled. In a year such as this it was necessary to cull a thousand head of springbok to protect the fragile desert growth from their ravages.

Garry brought a party of his friends and their families down from Johannesburg. The landing strip at Dragon's Fountain had been extended and macadamized to accommodate the new Lear jet. Shasa brought the rest of the guests up from Cape Town in the twin-engined Queen Air.

Isabella had not been able to leave Cape Town until the Senate went into recess. Then she drove up with Nana in the silver-grey Porsche her father had given her on her twenty-ninth birthday to replace the aged Mini. She enjoyed having Nana as a passenger, for the old lady's stories whiled away the hours of the long drive, and unlike Shasa, Nana did not watch the speed-ometer. At one stage on the arrow-straight stretch of road between Beaufort West and the ranch, Isabella wound the Porsche up to almost 160 miles per hour without a word of protest from Nana.

It was midafternoon when they pulled into the kitchen yard at Dragon's Fountain. Servants and dogs came pouring out of the kitchen and outbuildings to give them a riotous welcome. When at last Isabella escaped to her own room, Nanny was already running her bath and unpacking her three suitcases.

"God, I'm bushed, Nanny. I'm going to sleep for a week."

"Thou shall not take the name of the Lord thy God in vain," Nanny warned her darkly.

"Don't come that with me, Nanny. You're a Muslim."

"We got the same rules." Nanny sniffed haughtily.

"Where are all the men?" Isabella flopped on to the bed.

"Out hunting, of course."

"Are there any nice ones, Nanny?"

"Yes, but they are all married. You shoulda brought your own, Miss Bella." Nanny paused. "Come to think of it, there is a new one that got no wife." Then she shook her head. "You won't like him."

"Why not?"

"He got no hair on his head," Nanny cackled merrily. "What you'd call an eggshell blond."

Nanny was correct. He didn't tickle Isabella's fancy, although he had a kind and rather sensitive face and beautiful Jewish sloe eyes. His bald head was a damper. It was tanned and freckled like a plover's egg with a thick fringe of dark curls around the back in the style of Friar Tuck. He was talking to Garry on the wide front stoep.

Isabella felt good when she came down for predinner cocktails. She had managed an hour's sleep after the hot bath. She was wearing a deceptively simple blue silk sheath with a risqué décolletage whose cunning cut and drape caught the eye of every man present, married or not.

She went to Garry immediately. She hadn't seen him for months. "My big teddy bear." She hugged him.

With his arm still around her waist, Garry introduced them. "Bella, this is Professor Aaron Friedman. Aaron, this is my baby sister, Senator Doctor Isabella Courtney."

"Oh, come on, Garry!" she protested modestly at his use of all her titles, and took Aaron Friedman's hand. It was fine-boned but strong, the hands of a pianist or a surgeon.

"Aaron is on a sabbatical from the University of Jerusalem."

"Oh, I love Jerusalem," Isabella told him politely. "In fact, I love Israel. It's such an exciting, vibrant country, so steeped in history and religion."

She gave him another minute of her attention, then moved down the veranda to find her father. He had three of the prettiest wives grouped around him, giggling at his wit.

"My beautiful daddy." She kissed him and took her place beside him with her arm linked through his in proprietorial fashion. She knew just how good they looked together. As usual, the two of them swiftly became the center of the elegant little gathering.

They sipped their champagne and laughed and chatted and flirted while a flamboyant Karroo sunset lit the gaunt kopjes with a ruddy glow and set the clouds on fire.

One of the men mentioned casually, "I was listening to the radio while I dressed. It seems the Ethiopians have forced Haile Selassie to abdicate."

"Damned fuzzy-wuzzies, bunch of bandits and Shufta," said another. "I was there with the Sixth Division during the war—we went the hard way, on foot, while Shasa was swanning around in his Hurricane."

Shasa touched the black eye patch. "We called it Abyssinia then. We went to keep an eye on them, and dashed if I didn't leave one of mine behind."

They laughed, and somebody else remarked, "Haile Selassie was a marvelous old fellow, really. Wonder what will happen now."

"The same as the rest of black Africa—chaos and confusion and communism, murder and mayhem and Marxism."

There was a general murmur of agreement. Then they dismissed the subject and turned their attention to the splendor of the final moments of the sunset.

Night fell with the suddenness of a stage curtain, and immediately the evening chill struck through their light clothing. With perfect timing, the dinner gong chimed. Centaine rose from her seat at the end of the veranda to lead the entire party through the French windows into the long dining room, where candlelight glinted on silver and crystal and polished walnut glowed with a precious antique luster.

Isabella found her place card and checked those on either side of her: Garry and Aaron Friedman.

Damn, she thought. She had noticed him mooning after her ever since Garry had introduced them. It was natural Nana would pair her with the only single male in the company.

Aaron hurried across to hold her chair for her. As he seated her, she set herself the task of being pleasant. She soon discovered that he was a delightful conversationalist with a droll sense of humor that amused her. She no longer noticed his bald head.

Garry had been occupied with his dinner partner, but now he turned and leaned forward to speak to Aaron across Isabella.

"By the way, Aaron, if you really have got to be back at Pelindaba by Monday afternoon, I'll fly you up in the Lear."

As the significance of the casual mention of that name struck her, Isabella felt her cheeks chill.

"Are you all right, Bella?" Garry was watching her with concern.

"Of course I am."

"For a moment you looked quite strange."

"Nonsense, Garry, you're imagining things." But she was thinking furiously as Garry and Aaron made their arrangements. By the time Garry turned his attention back to his own partner, she had gathered herself.

"I have neglected to ask you what discipline you teach, Professor."

"Won't you call me Aaron, Doctor?"

She smiled. "Only if you call me Isabella, Professor."

"I am a physicist, Isabella, a nuclear physicist. Very boring, I'm afraid."

"That's not fair on yourself, Aaron." She touched his wrist lightly. "It's the science of the future, in war and in peace."

Still touching him, she turned one shoulder and leaned toward

227

him so that the sheer silk of her décolletage fell away from her bosom. She wore no bra. When his eyes changed their direction of gaze and opened very wide, she knew that he was staring at her nipple. She gave him two seconds more before she straightened up, ending the show, and she lifted her fingers from his wrist.

In those two seconds Aaron Friedman had undergone a profound change. He was now a man bewitched.

"Where is your wife, Aaron?" she asked.

"My wife and I were divorced almost five years ago."

"Oh, I'm so sorry." She lowered her voice to a husky murmur and let her sympathy show in her eyes, gazing deeply into his.

Later that evening, while preparing for bed, Isabella sat in front of her dressing table and regarded herself in the mirror as she creamed away the last traces of her makeup.

"Israel, Pelindaba, nuclear physics . . ." she murmured. "It just has to add up to one big bang."

Not a month had passed during the past two years that she had not been able to send some intelligence to her masters. Most of it was routine reports and minutes of meetings. But this could at last hasten her next meeting with Nicholas.

During dinner Aaron had professed a great love of horses and riding—but, then, he would probably have declared a fascination with polar exploration and munching razor blades if he thought that was what she wanted to hear. She would soon see how well he sat a horse. They had a date to ride out at dawn tomorrow morning.

"How far will you go?" Isabella asked herself in the mirror. She thought about it carefully before she answered. "Well, he is terribly amusing and quite sweet, and they do say that men with bald heads have a tremendous libido." She pulled a face at herself in the mirror. "You are a terrible little tart, aren't you? A regular Mata Hari."

When she was fourteen years old her brother Sean had taught her a smutty rhyme about Mata Hari. How did it go? She cast her mind back.

> *"She learnt the location*
> *Of a very secret station*
> *On the point of emission.*
> *In the twenty-third position."*

When she had asked him what "emission" meant, Sean had sniggered dirtily and darkly. She had been obliged to look it up in the dictionary, which didn't do much to clarify the issue. She smiled at her unintended pun.

"Would you actually go that far?" she demanded of herself and grinned again. "Well, perhaps not as far as the twenty-third. The second or third position should do the trick quite nicely." Beneath the flippancy she knew she would do anything for Nicky and Ramón.

Dawn was still only a pale promise in the east when she went down to the stables the following morning, but already Aaron was waiting for her. He wore jodhpurs and riding boots. That he had his own riding gear was encouraging.

The syce was already walking the saddled horses. The animals at Dragon's Fountain were seldom exercised sufficiently, and there were always fields full of lucerne and oats irrigated from the spring. The horses were thus usually full of pep. However, she had ordered the quietest old gelding in the stables for Aaron. She hoped he could manage him, and she watched uneasily as he approached his mount. She need not have worried. Aaron went up into the saddle, and she saw immediately that he had a good solid seat and gentle hands.

They skirted the kopje as the sun burst over the horizon. It was cool enough to make her grateful for the waxed cotton Barbour hacking jacket she wore. The still air had that peculiar desert lambency that made her believe she could see to the very ends of the earth.

The vultures left their shaggy nests in the rock cliff above them and soared on wide graceful wings overhead. Out on the plain the springbok herds were still nervous and jittery from the previous day's hunting. In their alarm they erected snowy plumes of mane from the pouches of skin along their spines and flashed them in the bright morning sunlight as they blew away, light as smoke, into the purple blossoming sage. The sweet clean air seemed to fizz like champagne in Isabella's head, and she felt gay and reckless.

Once the horses had warmed up, Isabella urged her mare into a gallop and led them on a wildly exhilarating charge along the old dry riverbed and down to the dam. Huge flocks of Egyptian geese rose honking from the muddy brown water as they reined up on the bank.

Isabella slid from the saddle and dabbed theatrically at her eye with the end of her silk scarf. Aaron tumbled from the saddle with gratifying concern.

"Are you all right, Isabella?"

"I seem to have something in my eye."

"May I look?"

She turned her face up to him. He cupped it gently in his hands and stared into her eye.

"I don't see anything."

She blinked her long dark lashes, and the early sunlight splintered into myriad pinpoints of pure sapphire in the depths of her iris.

"Are you sure?" she asked. His breath was sweet, and his body odor was clean and manly. She stared back into his eyes. They were dark and shining as burnt wild honey.

He touched her lower lid, gently massaging the eyeball through the skin.

"How does that feel?" he asked, and she blinked again.

"You have a magic touch. That's much better, thank you." And she kissed him with wet and open lips.

Aaron shuddered with shock, then recovered swiftly and seized her round the waist. She pressed her hips forward and let him explore the inside of her mouth with his tongue for a few seconds. The moment she felt his loins flare she broke away.

"I'll race you back to the stables." She laughed her husky sexy laugh at him and went up into the saddle with a lithe bound. The gelding was no match for her chestnut mare, and besides, she had two hundred yards' start.

Over the next three days she made Aaron Friedman's life an exquisite torment. She touched his thigh under the dinner table. She let him have a good grope while they were playing water polo in the swimming pool that was fed directly from the spring. Innocently she adjusted her bikini top in front of him while they lay on the lawn and he read Shelley to her. When he helped her up into the back of the hunting Land-Rover she gave him a glimpse of the transparent Janet Reger panties she had donned for the occasion. When they danced on the veranda, she rotated and oscillated her hips in lewd and lazy circles. Trapped between them was something that felt like the handle of a cricket bat.

On the night before he left Dragon's Fountain to fly back to the Transvaal with Garry, she allowed Aaron to see her up to her room and say good night to her in the corridor outside the door of her suite. Without breaking the kiss he maneuvered her until her back was pressed firmly against the wall and her skirt was up around her waist. Once he hit his stride he was really rather masterful.

Isabella liked that and soon found she was almost as breath-

**230**

less as he was. She didn't really want him to stop. Her first impression had been intuitive; with those fingers he should have been a concert pianist, his touch was light and artistic. Unwittingly she found herself on the very threshold.

"Won't you leave your door unlocked tonight?" he whispered into her ear. With an effort she roused herself from a trance of lust and pushed him away.

"Are you crazy?" she whispered back, smoothing down her skirt with trembling fingers. "The house is crawling with my family—my father, my brother, my grandmother, my nanny."

"Yes, I'm crazy—you're driving me mad. I love you. I want you. It's torture, Bella. I can't go on like this."

"I know," she said. "Me, too. I'll come up to Johannesburg."

"When? Oh, tell me when, my darling."

"I'll telephone you. Leave me your number."

# 19

Isabella was serving on the Senate committee of inquiry into civil service pensions. She and the two other members of the committee were taking evidence in the Transvaal the following months. She drove up to Johannesburg in the Porsche. She stayed with Garry and Holly in their lovely new home in Sandton and telephoned Aaron at the Pelindaba Institute the morning she arrived.

She drove out to fetch him, and they dined at a chic little restaurant. Over the crayfish cocktails she sounded him out discreetly about his work at the nuclear research institute.

"Oh, it's all terribly boring really. Antiparticles and quarks." He was genially evasive. "Did you know that the name originated from a James Joyce quotation, 'Three Quarks for Muster Mark,' and should be pronounced 'Quart'?"

"How fascinating." She touched his thigh under the table,

231

and he seized her hand. "What you do must be very hard," she said.

"Yes." He moved her fingers a few inches higher. "It is, rather."

"I see what you mean." She widened her eyes. "Do you really want to go dancing after dinner?"

"We could go back to my place for coffee."

"I'm not all that hungry. The crayfish was very filling. Let's skip the second course," she suggested.

"Waiter. The bill, please."

Aaron had a flat in the apartment block in the residential compound of the institute. Although the security was not nearly so strict as in the main research and reactor area of the facility, Aaron was obliged to show his pass at the gate and Isabella had to go with him into the security office to sign the visitors' book and fill in all her particulars, including telephone number and residential address. The guard looked knowing and smug as he issued her a visitor's pass.

She had been much too long without love, and Aaron was an immensely satisfying lover. At first he was gentle and patient. Then as her passion mounted under his lips and cunning fingers, he became forceful and demanding. He pushed her to the edge half a dozen times, then held her back at the very brink until she screamed with exquisite frustration.

When at last she plunged over the top he went with her, and let her down softly on the other side. He held her and caressed her and murmured flatteries until she glowed with contentment and asked with a happy little sigh, "What is your birth sign?"

"Scorpio."

"Ah, yes—Scorpios are always wonderful lovers. What date?"

"November the seventh."

In the morning they made breakfast together, scrambled eggs and laughter. When she saw him off to work at the door of the flat, she was dressed in one of his pajama tops with the sleeves rolled up and the shirt trailing to her knees.

"I'll sort things out with the guard at the main gate—you don't have to leave until you are ready." He kissed her. "In fact, if you were still here at lunchtime, I wouldn't mind a bit."

"No chance." She shook her head. "I've got work to do today."

As soon as he was gone she double-latched the door. The safe was in his study. She had looked for it as soon as she entered the flat the previous evening. There had been no attempt to conceal it behind paneling. It stood foursquare beside his desk. It was a heavy expensive jeweler's-quality Chubb with a six-numeral combination lock.

She sat cross-legged in front of it.

"November the seventh," she mumbled, "and he's about forty-two or forty-three years old. That makes it 1931 or 1932."

She got it on the fourth try. Aaron hadn't even been as cunning as Shasa, who had at least inverted his birthdate.

"Why are so many truly brilliant men such naïve idiots?" she wondered. Before she swung the thick steel door open, she ran her fingers around the door seal. There was a tiny scrap of Sellotape across one hinge. "Not such an idiot."

Aaron obviously liked working at home. The safe was neatly packed with files, most of them the familiar Armscor green.

From the day Red Rose had been given this assignment at Madrid Airport, Isabella had begun a study of nuclear weapons and their development.

She had stopped over for two extra days in London and spent them in the reading room at the British Museum. She still had her card from her student days. She had requested and read every book that was listed under the subject in the library catalogue and filled two notebooks with her scribbles. For a layperson, she was now exceptionally well versed in the mysteries of the most dreadful process man's infernal intelligence had yet devised.

The green Armscor file on top of the pile was stamped with the highest security clearance. The copies were limited to eight, of which this was number four. The eight names with clearance to the files were listed on the cover and included the Minister of Defense and the commander in chief of the defense forces, her father as chairman of Armscor, Professor A. Friedman and four others who, judging by their scientific qualifications, were all scientists. One of the names she recognized as the head electrical engineer at Armscor, who was often a guest at Weltevreden. No wonder her father had never allowed her to see one of these files.

The code name on the green cover was "Project Skylight." She lifted it out, careful not to disturb anything else in the safe. She opened the file and began to scan the contents. While she had been assembling material for her thesis, she had taught herself the technique of speed reading, and now she turned the pages at a steady tempo.

The vast bulk of the material was so technical as to be utterly meaningless to her, even with the benefit of all her study. But she understood sufficient of it to realize that this was a series of reports on the progress being made at Pelindaba in the process of separating massive amounts of highly fissionable uranium 235 out of the common uranium isotope, uranium 238. She knew that this was the basic step in the production of nuclear-fission weapons.

The reports were filed in chronological order, and before she reached the last page she realized that success had been achieved almost three years previously and that sufficient uranium 235 had already been manufactured for the production of approximately two hundred fissionable explosive devices with a yield of up to fifty kilotons. Much of this seemed to have been exported to Israel in return for technical assistance with the manufacture of the uranium. She blinked as she digested that information. At twenty kilotons the Hiroshima bomb had been less than half as powerful as one of these weapons.

She laid the file aside and reached for the next. She took pains to note the exact order and position of each file in the safe, so that she could replace them without arousing suspicion that they had been tampered with. She read on. The main object of Project Skylight was the development of a series of tactical nuclear warheads of varying power and application, suitable for delivery not only by aircraft but also by ground artillery.

She knew that Armscor was already building a 155-millimeter howitzer designated G5, which would be capable of firing a forty-seven-kilo shell with an eleven-kilo payload and a maximum sea-level range of thirty-nine kilometers. This would, she realized, make an ideal delivery system for a nuclear warhead. The report gave high priority to developing a nuclear artillery round for the G5.

The basic principles of the nuclear weapon were common knowledge. They consisted of assembling two subcritical masses of fissionable enriched uranium. One was a female charge with a vaginal recess. The second, or male, charge was propelled by a conventional explosive to implode into the female recess with such velocity as instantly to render the entire mass supercritical and set off the fission reaction.

However, there were many technical pitfalls and obstacles to the actual manufacture of a viable device, particularly in the making of a warhead that weighed less than eleven kilos and was able to be contained in the casing of a 155-millimeter artillery round.

Isabella raced through the series of reports and working papers with a sense of rising excitement. She felt a strange proprietorial pride in the ingenuity and dedication of the development team. A dozen times she recognized her father's touch and influence as she read how each pitfall had been circumvented and the whole massive project had gathered momentum and rolled toward its climax.

The last report in the file was dated only five days previously. She read it quickly, then read it again.

The first South African atomic bomb would be tested in a little less than two months from today.

"But where?" she whispered desperately. The next file she opened gave her the answer to that question.

She replaced the files in their exact order and remembered to stick the scrap of Sellotape over the hinge and to reset the combination of the lock in the same sequence she had found it.

Two years' study and deliberation had gone into choosing the site for the test. The prime consideration had been that of contamination by radioactive fallout.

South Africa maintained a weather station at Gough Island in the Antarctic. They had considered an Antarctic site, but had swiftly rejected that idea. Not only would contamination be difficult to control, but detection before or after the test would be a foregone conclusion. There were too many others, notably the Australians, who were interested in that bleak and beautiful continent at the foot of the world.

For security reasons, then, the test had to be conducted on national soil or within South African airspace. The idea of an aerial test was soon abandoned. Again, detection would be a serious threat and the risk of contamination from fallout would be suicidal.

At the end it had come down to an underground test. The South African gold mines are the deepest underground workings in the world. For sixty years the South Africans have been the leaders in deep-mining techniques, and associated with the mines are the art and science of deep drilling.

Courtney Enterprises owned Orion Explorations, a specialist drilling company. The gnarled old magicians at Orion were able to sink a borehole two miles below the surface of the earth and bring up cores of rock from that depth. They could drive a straight hole or incline it at any angle they chose, or they could go straight down a mile and a half and then kick the bit off at an angle of forty-five degrees.

It was this incredible skill that filled Shasa Courtney with a sense of awe and deep respect as he stood at the test site on a bright sunlit day and looked around him at the gargantuan machines that made up the drilling rig.

The entire rig was self-propelled. One truck the size of a modern fire engine carried the power plant. It was a diesel engine that could have driven an ocean liner. Another truck housed the control room and electronic monitoring equipment. A third incorporated the actual drill and base plate for the shot hole. A fourth was the hydraulic lift and crane for the steel boring rods.

The drill site was surrounded by a community of residential caravans and supply trucks. The steel drilling rods were piled into a storage area many acres in extent. At night the entire area was lit by the brutal blue-white glare of arc lamps, for the work continued around the clock. When completed, the hole would have cost almost three hundred thousand U.S. dollars to sink.

Shasa lifted his hat and wiped his brow with his forearm. It was hot.

This was the fringe of the Kalahari Desert, which the little yellow Bushmen call "The Great Dry Place."

The low, undulating red dunes rolled like the waves of a turbulent ocean into the monotonous distance. The desert grasses were sparse and silver dry. In the troughs between the dunes stood isolated desert camelthorn trees. The foliage was dark green, and the bark was rough as a crocodile's back. In the nearest tree a colony of social weavers had built their communal nest. Hundreds of pairs of the drab little brown birds had combined their labors. The result was a shapeless edifice the size of a haystack that dwarfed the tall thorn tree that supported it. Each pair of birds occupied a separate chamber in the nest and helped to keep the whole structure in good repair the year round. One nest near Upington on the Orange River had been continuously occupied by successive generations of weavers for over a hundred years.

This district was a vast, sparsely populated wilderness. Courtney Mineral Exploration Company owned the 150,000-acre concession on which the drilling rig now stood. The entire property was posted and fenced. There were guards at every access point and gate. Nobody outside the company would ever see this encampment—and if they did . . . well, it was simply another mineral exploration drill in progress.

Shasa glanced up at the sky. There was not a single cloud to sully the high, achingly blue bowl. This section of the Kalahari was a restricted military zone, and overflight by either commercial or private aircraft was forbidden. It was often used for military exercises by the artillery and tank school based at Kimberley, only a few hundred miles to the south.

Still Shasa worried. They were at D minus eight. The hole should be completed by the weekend. On Saturday evening the heavily guarded convoy would leave Pelindaba to arrive on Sunday at noon. It would bring the team of scientists and the bomb.

The test bomb would be positioned in the hole by Monday evening. The Minister of Defense and General Malan would fly up from Cape Town on D minus one.

He shook his head. "It's all going just beautifully," he assured himself, and climbed the steel steps into the mobile control room.

The chief drilling engineer had worked for Orion for twelve years. He rose from his seat and offered Shasa a broad, callused hand.

"How is it going, Mick?"

"*Bak gat*, Mr. Courtney!" The driller used a coarse Afrikaans expression of ultimate approbation. "We hit the three-thousand-meter mark at nine this morning."

He indicated the plot on the display screen. It graphically illustrated the dogleg in the line of the hole that would help to contain the blast.

"Don't let me bother you." Shasa took the seat beside the engineer. "Get on with it, man."

Mick turned his full attention back to the control console.

Shasa lit a cheroot and imagined that flexible steel worm gnawing its way into the earth below where he sat, down to the edge of the earth's crust, far below the subterranean water table, down to the very edge of the magma where the earth's temperature would approximate that of a domestic oven.

A telephone rang in the control room, but Shasa was wrapped up in his imagination. The junior technician who answered the phone had to call him twice.

"Mr. Courtney, it's for you."

"Ask who it is," Shasa snapped irritably. "Take a message."

"It's Mr. Vorster, sir."

"Which Mr. Vorster?"

"The prime minister, sir. In person."

Shasa snatched the receiver out of his hand. He had a sudden sickening premonition of disaster.

"*Ja*, Oom John?" he asked.

"Shasa, within the last hour the ambassadors of Britain, America and France have all presented notes of protest from their respective governments."

"What about?"

"At nine o'clock this morning an American satellite photographed the drill site. *Ons is in die kak*—we are in deep shit. They have somehow tumbled to Skylight, and they are demanding that we abandon the test immediately. How long will it take you to get back to Cape Town?"

"My jet is standing on the strip. I'll be in your office in four hours."

"I've called a full cabinet meeting. I want you to brief them."

"I'll be there."

Shasa had never seen John Vorster so worried and angry. As they shook hands he growled, "Since I spoke to you the Russians have called an emergency meeting of the U.N. Security Council. They are threatening immediate mandatory sanctions if we proceed with the test."

Shasa realized they all had very good reason to be worried.

"The Americans and the Brits have warned that they won't use their veto to save us if we test."

"You haven't admitted anything, Prime Minister?"

"Of course not," Vorster snarled at him. "But they want to inspect the drill site. They have aerial photographs—and they know the code name Skylight."

"They have our code?" Shasa stared at him.

Vorster nodded heavily. "*Ja*, man, they have the code name."

"You know what that means, Prime Minister? We have a traitor—and at a very high level. At the very top."

In the United Nations the representatives of Third World and nonaligned nations rose one after the other in the General Assembly to castigate and condemn South Africa and her attempt to join the nuclear club. She was judged guilty as soon as the accusation was leveled. Both India and China had tested nuclear bombs in the previous year or two, but that was different. Despite assurances from the South African prime minister that no test had been conducted, the ambassadors of Great Britain and the United States insisted on a personal inspection of the site. They were flown up into the Kalahari in an air force Puma helicopter. By the time they had arrived, the drilling rig and every other vehicle had been removed. There was only a borehole casing capped with fresh concrete left standing forlornly in an area of rutted and trampled earth.

"What was the purpose of the drilling?" the British ambassador asked Shasa, not for the first time. Sir Percy was an old friend who had dined at Weltevreden and hunted at Dragon's Fountain.

"Oil prospecting," Shasa answered him with a straight face. The ambassador lifted an eyebrow and made no further comment. However, three days later Great Britain vetoed the sanctions proposed in the Security Council, and the storm began to blow over.

Aaron Friedman telephoned Isabella to tell her of his immediate departure for Israel. He wanted her to go with him. He didn't however, mention to her that the United States had put enormous pressure on the Israeli government for him to be recalled to Jerusalem.

"You are a darling, Aaron," she told him, "and I wouldn't have missed it for the world, but you have your life and I have mine. Perhaps we'll meet again someday."

"I'll never forget you, Bella."

The South African Bureau for State Security began a witch-hunt for the traitor that dragged on for months without any conclusive results. In the end it was accepted that one of the four Israeli scientists, who had by that stage all left the country, must have been responsible.

When Shasa read the secret report of the investigation he was embarrassed to learn that his darling daughter had signed into the Pelindaba residential compound and had apparently stayed overnight as a guest of the good professor.

"Well, you didn't think she was a virgin?" Centaine asked, when he mentioned it to her. "Did you?"

"Hardly," Shasa admitted. "But still, one doesn't like having one's nose rubbed in it, does one?"

"One has not had one's nose rubbed in it," she corrected him. "Bella seems to have been uncharacteristically discreet, for a change."

"Still, it's a good thing he's gone."

"He might have been quite a catch," Centaine teased him.

He looked shocked. "Good Lord, he was old enough to be her father."

"Bella is thirty," Centaine pointed out. "Almost an old maid."

"Is she that old?" Shasa looked startled. "I often forget how the years go by."

"We must seriously do something about finding her a husband."

"There is no desperate hurry." Shasa did not relish the prospect of losing her. He had become accustomed to things just the way they were.

Isabella's reward came swiftly. Within months she was promised a holiday with Nicholas and instructed to make arrangements to be absent from the country for two weeks.

"Two weeks!" she exulted. "With my baby! I can hardly believe it's happening at last."

Her euphoria was enough to banish the crippling sense of guilt that she had lived with since the Skylight furor had made world headlines. She tried to appease her conscience by assuring herself that she had helped to avert an escalation of the nuclear menace and that her treachery would, in the long run, yield beneficial results for all mankind.

Naturally, she registered a patriotic sense of outrage when she discussed the subject with her family or with other senators in the halls of the parliament building, but the truth haunted her in the night. She was a traitor—and the penalty was death.

She told Nana and Shasa that she was meeting Harriet Beauchamp in Zurich. They planned to hire a kombi and cruise around Switzerland for two weeks, going wherever the snow was good, eating fondue and trying all the most famous runs.

"Don't expect to hear from me until I get back," she warned them.

"Have you got enough money, Bella?" Shasa wanted to know.

"That's a silly question, Pater." She kissed him. "Wasn't it you who set up my trust fund—who gives me a ridiculous salary each month, twice as much as my pay from the Senate?"

"Well, I'll give you the name of somebody at Crédit Suisse in Lausanne, just in case you run short."

"You are sweet, but I'm not sixteen any more."

"Sometimes I wish you were, my love."

Isabella caught the Swissair flight for Zurich but left the aircraft at Nairobi. She checked in at the Norfolk Hotel and the following morning telephoned Weltevreden and spoke to Nana, pretending she was calling from Zurich.

"Have fun and keep your eyes open for a nice millionaire," Nana told her.

"For you or for me, Nana?"

"That's enough of your sauce, missy."

As she had been instructed, Isabella caught the Air Kenya flight to Lusaka in Zambia and the airline bus from the airport to the Ridgeway Hotel. She found that a single room had been reserved for her. This was as far as her instructions took her.

Before dinner she sat on the swimming pool terrace and ordered a gin and tonic. A few minutes later, a tall, good-looking black man sitting at the bar sauntered across to her table.

"Red Rose," he said.

"Sit down." She nodded, her heart pounding and her palms damp.

"My name is Paul." He refused the drink she offered him. "I will not trouble you any longer than necessary. Will you please be ready at nine o'clock tomorrow morning? I will meet you with transport at the front entrance of the hotel."

"Where are you taking me?"

"I don't know," he said as he stood up. "And you shouldn't ask."

She was waiting for him as he had instructed. He drove her back to the airport in a battered Volkswagen, but bypassed the commercial terminal and drove on to the gates of the restricted military area.

The remains of Zambia's squadron of MiG fighters stood on the apron in the sunlight. There had been four crashes in the last month alone. Not only had Zambian pilots been inadequately trained in East Germany, they had also not adjusted well to the complexity of supersonic flight. In addition, the MiGs had done almost twenty years of service in Eastern Europe before being sold to Zambia. Zambia's copper-based economy had been sent reeling by the fall in the price of the metal, and by two decades of gross mismanagement. Costs had been pruned in the maintenance of the fighter squadron, and they were familiarly known as "The Flying Bombs."

Beyond the fighters was parked an enormous unmarked aircraft with four turbofan engines and a tail fin taller than a two-story house. Although Isabella did not recognize it as such, it was an Ilyushin Il 76 with the NATO reporting name "Candid." It was the standard Russian military heavy freight-carrying transport.

Paul, her escort, spoke to the guards at the gate and showed them a document from his briefcase. The guard commander studied the paper and then went into his kiosk. He spoke on the telephone to a superior. Then he handed Paul back his papers, opened the gates and saluted as they drove through.

Two pilots in flying overalls were supervising the refueling of the huge Candid. Paul parked the Volkswagen alongside the main hangar and walked across to the aircraft. He spoke to one of the pilots, then beckoned to Isabella to follow. They watched her struggling with her suitcase, but none of them offered to help her.

"You will go with the aircraft." Paul told her.

"What about my luggage?" she asked. The chief pilot shrugged and answered in a heavy accent, "Leave here. Me fix. Come."

Isabella looked round, but Paul was already halfway back to the Volkswagen. She followed the pilot up the loading ramp of the Candid.

The hold was filled with cargo packed on wooden pallets under heavy nylon netting. There were literally hundreds of wooden cases of various sizes. Most of them were stenciled in black paint with letters and numerals in Cyrillic script. The pilot led her down the side aisle of the cavernous compartment and up the ladder to the flight deck.

"Sit." He pointed at one of the folding jump seats in the rear bulkhead of the flight deck.

There were no formalities when the Candid took off an hour later.

From her seat in the rear of the compartment Isabella had a clear view of the instrument panel over the pilot's shoulder. The Candid leveled out into a cruise altitude of thirty thousand feet and settled on a course of 300 degrees magnetic.

Surreptitiously she checked the time on her wristwatch. She wanted to know how long they would fly on this northwesterly heading. She conjured up a map of the continent in her mind. Although she had no idea of the aircraft's ground speed, the needle on the air-speed indicator quivered at around 475 knots.

After an hour's flight she guessed they had crossed from Zambia into Angola, and she shivered slightly. Angola was not her number-one choice for a holiday. She had recently been nominated to the African Affairs Committee of the Senate, and she had attended all the special briefings on the subject of Angola. She had also read the confidential reports assembled by military intelligence on that country.

She looked down at the mosaic of savannah and mountains and jungle that passed slowly beneath the Candid and tried to recall every detail she had read about this troubled land.

Angola had long been the pearl of the Portugese empire. After South Africa itself, Angola was the richest and most beautiful of all African countries.

This thousand-mile stretch of the West African Atlantic seaboard was rich with marine resources. Vast shoals of pelagic fish swarmed within easy reach of secure natural harbors. Off-shore drilling by American companies had recently shown huge reserves of oil and natural gas. Inland lay rich, fertile plains and valleys, marvelous forests of hardwoods and pleasant, well-watered highlands from which flowed numerous great rivers—in Africa water was a natural resource almost as precious as oil. Apart from her oil, Angola produced gold, diamonds and iron ore. Her climate was temperate and benign.

Despite all these blessings, Angola had for a decade been racked by a savage, bitter civil war. Her indigenous African peoples had been struggling to throw off the five-hundred-year colonial rule of Lisbon.

The liberation struggle had not been united. Many armies under all the usual flamboyant warlike names had fought not only the Portuguese but one another as well. There was the MPLA, the People's Movement for the Liberation of Angola; the FNLA, the National Front for the Liberation of Angola; UNITA, the National Union for the Total Independence of Angola; and a rash of other private armies and guerrilla movements.

· The Portuguese had held on to their colony grimly. Tens of thousands of young Portuguese conscripts had come out to Africa, many of them to bleed and die by bullet and mine and tropical disease far from their native land. Then suddenly had come the left-wing coup d'état by the military junta in Mother Portugal, and shortly thereafter the declaration that Portugal was to give Angola its independence and hold popular elections to select a new government and write a constitution.

Now, in the months leading up to the proposed elections, the country was in even greater turmoil than it had been during the civil war, as the various factions jockeyed for power and the great powers and other African governments played their favorites while the guerrilla leaders themselves indulged in an orgy of intrigue, torture and intimidation of a population already cowed by years of war. Reading between the lines of the intelligence reports, Isabella sensed that nobody really knew what was happening in Luanda, the capital, let alone in the remote jungles and mountains.

Admiral Rosa Coutinho, the Red Admiral, appointed as governor-general by the armed forces movement after the coup d'état, seemed to favor Agostinho Neto and his "purified" MPLA. The "purification" process consisted of torturing all other factions of the party to death. This was done by gradually tightening a wooden frame around a prisoner's heads until the skull collapsed.

The American CIA, out of touch as always, appeared to be supporting the FNLA, which was the weakest, most tribally based and corrupt of the three. It was slipping them niggardly amounts of financial aid the United States Senate would not have approved had it been aware of them. The Chinese were also betting on the FNLA, as were the North Koreans.

# 20

The motorcade of black Chaikas crossed the moat bridge and entered the fortress of the Kremlin through the gate below the Borovitskaya Tower.

The two Cuban generals rode in the leading limousine. Senen Casas Requerión was chief of staff of the Cuban army, and with him was his army logistics chief. Colonel-General Ramón Machado was in the second vehicle with President Fidel Castro, acting as host and interpreter for the visiting head of state.

Ramón's promotion had been announced within weeks of his return from Ethiopia, where he had masterminded the abdication of the Emperor Haile Selassie, the abolition of the monarchy and the formal declaration by the Ethiopian Derg of a Marxist socialist state.

He was now the second-youngest general in the entire Russian military service, and by far the youngest in the KGB. His immediate senior in the secret service was fifty-three years of age. His predecessor, Joe Cicero, had been elevated to general officer rank only just before his retirement. The promotion was all the more extraordinary in that Ramón was not a Russian national by birth. His naturalization papers had been served only eight years before.

Ethiopia had been a triumph for him. He had steered the first stage of the revolution through without any visible Russian presence in the country and, more important, with the expenditure of a paltry few million rubles.

Immediately following had been his clandestine but equally successful visit to Luanda in Angola, where Ramón had met the Red Admiral, Rosa Coutinho. Coutinho was a member of the Portuguese Communist Party. He had been appointed governor-general of Angola by the left-wing military forces committee that now governed Portugal. He had been charged with organizing the popular elections to select an African government to bring the former Portuguese colony of Angola to independence. However, during his meeting with Ramón he had proven to be a political soulmate.

"We must ensure that under no circumstances will popular elections take place," he had told Ramón. "If we allow that to happen, Jonas Savimbi will be the first president of Angola, if only because his Ovimbundu tribe is the largest in the country."

"We cannot allow it," Ramón agreed. He did not have to elaborate. Jonas Savimbi was the boldest and most successful of all the Angolan guerrilla leaders. His UNITA army had fought the Portuguese with skill and dogged determination for a decade. He was intelligent, well educated and strong-willed. Although he had never declared his political allegiances, he was certainly not a Marxist, probably not even a socialist, and they could not take a chance on his coming to power.

"The only possible solution," Ramón went on, "is for you to declare that owing to the state of chaos in the country, it will be impractical to hold elections. You should then declare that the solution is to recognize the MPLA as the only party capable of assuming the reins of government, and to persuade Lisbon to transfer power to Agostinho Neto and the MPLA as soon as possible."

Neto was the Soviet choice. He was devious, weak, cruel and malleable. He could be controlled, whereas Savimbi could not.

"I agree." Coutinho nodded. "But can I count on full support from Russia and Cuba?"

"If I am able to promise you that support, will you be prepared to hand over strategic military bases and airfields to us to allow us to rush in troops and military supplies?" Ramón countered.

"You have my hand on it." The Red Admiral stretched across his desk, and Ramón took his hand with a soaring sense of triumph.

He was about to deliver two nations into Soviet sovereignty. Surely no single man had achieved more in Africa.

"I am flying directly from here to Havana," he assured Coutinho. "I anticipate that within a matter of days talks between

245

Cuba and Moscow will be under way at the highest possible level. I will have your answer for you by the end of the month."

Coutinho rose to his feet. "You are an extraordinary man, Comrade Colonel-General. Seldom have I been privileged to work with one who sees so clearly to the very heart of a problem, and who is prepared to deliver the bold, expert cut of a surgeon to excise it."

Now Ramón sat in the rear seat of the Chaika with President Fidel Castro beside him as they entered the citadel of Soviet socialism. The cavalcade led by the motorcycle escort moved swiftly up the broad cobbled avenue. They passed the famous armory, the great treasure house of imperial Russia, which still housed a stunning wealth of ambassadorial gifts and Tsarist regalia from the crown of Ivan the Terrible to the jewel-encrusted court robes of Catherine the Great.

A line of foreign tourists at the doors to the museum watched them pass, their expressions lighting with curiosity as they recognized the great bearded figure of Castro in the second car.

Swiftly they moved on, passing on their left the square around which were clustered the cathedrals of the Archangel, of the Annunciation and of the Assumption. The immense spires and towers and golden domes burned in the pale spring sunshine. The peach and cherry trees in the gardens were in full blossom. They swung into the square, passed the palace of the Presidium of the Supreme Soviet and drew up at the front entrance of the Council of Ministers building.

An honor guard paraded to welcome them, and a dozen political and military dignitaries were present.

Deputy Minister Aleksei Yudenich stepped forward to embrace Castro and lead him into the Council of Ministers. In the Hall of Mirrors, Castro began to speak from his seat at the head of the long table.

He spoke clearly, pausing at the end of each sentence to allow the Russian translator to catch up with him. Even Ramón, an old and intimate comrade-in-arms, was fascinated by his grasp of the African situation and his calculated assessment of the risks and options open to them. He had absorbed every word of Ramón's briefing.

"The Western Europeans are divided and spineless. NATO depends militarily on America. They would never be able to muster any organized response to our determined entrance into the Angolan arena. We need not waste serious thought on them."

"What about America?" Yudenich asked soberly.

"America is still bleeding from the humiliation of Vietnam.

Their Senate will never allow American troops to operate in Africa. The Americans have been whipped. They are still sniveling with their tails between their legs. The only threat they pose is that they might choose a surrogate army to fight for them.''

"South Africa," Yudenich forestalled him.

"Yes. South Africa has the most dangerous army in Africa. Kissinger may recruit them and send them across the Angolan border.''

"Can we afford to fight the South Africans? Their lines of supply are shorter than ours by ten thousand miles, and their troops are reputed to be the finest bush fighters in Africa. If they are equipped and supplied by America . . .''

"We won't have to fight them," Castro promised. "As they cross the border, America and South Africa will be immediately defeated, not by Soviet or Cuban might, but by the practice of white minority government and the policy of apartheid.''

"Explain this to us, Mr. President," Yudenich invited.

"In the West there is such a desire by American liberals and the European antiapartheid movement to destroy the white regime in South Africa that they will make any sacrifice to that end. They will sacrifice Angola rather than let South Africans defend it. The moment the first South African crosses the border, our war will be won. There will be such an outcry from the American Democratic Party, and from the European champions of so-called democracy, that the South Africans will never get to do any fighting. In the face of hysterical worldwide condemnation they will be forced to retire. Their attempted intervention will settle the matter firmly in our favor. Once the South Africans have tarnished the shield, no Western politician will dare to take it up again. Angola will be ours.''

They were all nodding agreement, all the generals and ministers. Once again Castro had amazed Ramón with his powers of rhetoric and persuasion. It was the main reason Ramón had prevailed on him to come to Moscow in person. None of Castro's generals or ministers would have been able to swing the issue as he had just done. His shrewd, devious view would appeal irresistibly to the Russian mind.

"He calls me the Golden Fox," Ramón smiled to himself. "But he is the king of all the foxes.''

However, Castro was not yet finished. His timing was consummate. He smiled genially down the long table, stroking the curling bush of his beard. "Angola will be ours, but that will be only a beginning. After Angola the ultimate prize is South

Africa itself." They all leaned forward eagerly, their eyes shining like those of a pack of wolves scenting blood.

"Once we have Angola, we will have South Africa surrounded, with bases on her very borders from which our black freedom fighters can strike with impunity. South Africa is the treasury and economic powerhouse of the whole of Africa. Once we have it, the rest of the continent will fall into our laps."

He placed his huge hands palm down on the tabletop and leaned forward over them.

"I pledge you all the fighting men we need to do the job, a hundred thousand if necessary. If you provide the weapons and equipment and transport, there is a fruit ripe for the plucking. Shall we do it, comrades? Shall we make the bold and courageous stroke together?"

Only a month later a group of Portuguese military officers loyal to the Red Admiral Coutinho handed over the strategic military air base at Saurimo to Colonel Angel Botello, who was chief of logistics in the Cuban air force. Saurimo was five hundred miles inland from the capital of Luanda, and therefore comparatively secure from surveillance by the CIA and other Western agencies.

The first Ilyushin Candid transport landed at Saurimo twenty-four hours later. On board were a full cargo of military equipment and fifty Cuban "advisers." The Russian military observer on the same aircraft was Colonel-General Ramón Machado.

It was an exhausting but exciting period for Ramón. His reputation and his nickname were swiftly spreading the length and breadth of the continent. The Cuban contingent had brought the name with them from Havana.

"El Zorro," they whispered it abroad, "El Zorro has arrived. Now things will begin to happen."

Like the fox, his namesake, he was constantly on the move. He seldom slept two consecutive nights in the same bed. Often there was no bed at all but the mud floor of a grass hut, the cramped seat of a light aircraft or the dirty wooden deck of a small launch threading its way through the swamps and sandbars of a remote African river.

El Jefe had been right as usual. There was no concerted Western response to the Cuban buildup. Admiral Coutinho was able to head off the few timid inquiries, while Western journalists were successfully prevented from collecting hard evidence in the field. The arms and troops were flown in to Saurimo or shipped to Brazzaville in the Congo and distributed from there by light aircraft and river launch to the MPLA cadres in their camps deep in the bush.

Angola was only one of many operations Ramón was running simultaneously. There were Ethiopia and Mozambique to deal with, as well as his network of agents and the coordination of the activities of the South African freedom fighters. Angola was a marvelous new springboard for the liberation movements. Ramón set up training camps for both SWAPO, the South-West African People's Organization, and the ANC, the African National Congress.

The headquarters of the two organizations were sited in separate areas of the country. The SWAPO troops were in the south, where they were able to cross the border into South West Africa, or Namibia, readily and to operate among their own tribes, the Ovahimbo and Ovambo.

However, Ramón maintained a particular interest in the ANC. He never lost sight for a moment of the facts that South Africa was the gateway to the entire continent and that the ANC were the freedom fighters of South Africa. Raleigh Tabaka, his old comrade from London, was promoted to ANC chief of logistics in Angola. Between them they chose the site for the main ANC base in northern Angola.

They flew hundreds of hours together in an Antonov military biplane. They scoured the northern seaside province of Kungo before they found a site suitable for their base.

It was a small fishing village situated on a lagoon and estuary of the Chicamba River. The mouth of the lagoon was open to the Atlantic, and at high tide vessels of two hundred or so tons could cross the bar and enter the river. In addition, there were extensive fields of peasant cultivation a few miles upstream. Although these had been neglected during the savage decade of civil war, it would require very little effort to open a landing strip over the level, deforested fields. The fishing village had likewise been abandoned during the war and there was no local population that otherwise would have had to be evacuated or eliminated.

However, the main recommendation for the site was its distance from any South African border or base. The South Africans were formidable opponents. Like the Israelis, they would not hesitate to violate any international border in hot pursuit of a guerrilla unit. Chicamba was out of range of the South African Alouette helicopters, and thousands of kilometers of mountain had jungle isolating it from any overland hostile expedition by the Boers. They named the base Tercio.

Raleigh Tabaka took the first cadre of five hundred ANC recruits up to Tercio base in a fishing trawler requisitioned by Admiral Coutinho from the Portuguese canning factory in Luanda.

They began construction work on the airstrip and training camp immediately. When Ramón flew in ten days later the airstrip had been cleared and leveled and was in the process of being surfaced in red clay and gravel that would set like concrete and ensure a good all-weather runway.

On his second inspection, Ramón was so impressed by the remoteness and security of the area that he decided to set up a separate compound near the mouth of the river, overlooking the beach.

He planned this to be his own private headquarters. He always needed a secure base for communications where sensitive KGB training and planning could be undertaken, and where intense interrogation and elimination of captives could be undertaken without risk of discovery or interference.

He ordered Raleigh Tabaka's men to give construction of his own beach compound the utmost priority. On his next visit he found that the fencing and defenses had already been laid out and that work on the interrogation block and the officers' quarters was far advanced.

On his return to Havana, he requisitioned the necessary radio and electronic equipment and had it flown out to Tercio base on the next available transport.

On his frequent visits to Havana and Moscow, Ramón kept well abreast of all the dozens of projects he had in progress down the length of the African continent, in particular his own personal case, the operation and control of Red Rose.

Looking back down the years to her recruitment in London and Spain, he realized he had underestimated just how valuable Red Rose would one day become.

Since she had entered the South African Senate she had served on five house bodies. From all of these she had delivered extraordinary intelligence in the form of reports and recommendations on all the various subjects covered by those committees.

Then in February 1975 she was made a member of the Senate Advisory Board on African Affairs. Through her Ramón received the information, only hours old, that President Ford and Henry Kissinger, through the CIA, had signaled Pretoria that they would not oppose a military adventure by the South African army into southern Angola. He learned from Red Rose that the CIA had promised South Africa diplomatic support and military equipment to support their thrust toward Luanda.

After alerting his superiors in the Lubyanka, Ramón flew to Havana to consult Castro.

"You were right all the way, El Jefe," he told him admiringly. "The Yankees are sending in the Boers to do their dirty work for them."

"We must let them stick their head into the trap." Castro smiled. "I want you to return to Angola immediately. Take my personal orders. Pull back our forces and hold them on a defensive line on the rivers south of the capital. Let them come in before we tweak Uncle Sam's beard and kick the Boers in the *cojones*."

In October the South African cavalry crossed the Cunene River and made a spectacular dash northward in their fast Panhard armored cars. In a matter of days they had swept to within a hundred and fifty miles of the capital. They were superbly trained and well-led young fighting men, and their morale was high, but they lacked bridging equipment to cross the rivers and artillery to engage heavy armor.

When they reached the river, Ramón sent a signal to Havana.

"Now," said Castro grimly. "we pull out the rug. Let the armor loose."

The South Africans were held on the rivers by the Russian T-54 tanks and assault helicopters. Ramón released the news of the South African presence to the Western media, and the diplomatic storm broke just as Castro had predicted.

Nigeria, after South Africa the most powerful nation in Africa, switched its support within days of the South African presence being disclosed to the world by Russian and Cuban intelligence. It abandoned Savimbi and his UNITA movement and formally recognized the Soviet-supported MPLA government. To emphasize its position, Nigeria sent thirty million dollars in aid to Agostinho Neto in Luanda.

In the United States Senate, Dick Clark, the Democratic representative from Iowa, began the process of making certain that the South African expeditionary force in Angola was isolated and deprived of support. He accused the CIA of cooperating illegally with South Africa, and Kissinger and the CIA took evasive action. Members of the joint chiefs threatened to resign unless American support was withdrawn immediately. In December the Clark amendment was rushed through the Senate and all American military aid to Angola was cut off. It had all worked exactly as Castro had planned it.

Another African nation was delivered, trussed and tied, to Soviet sovereignty, and millions of black Angolans were condemned to another decade of brutal civil war.

In Moscow Colonel-General Ramón Machado was awarded the Order of Lenin, first class. The medal was pinned on his chest by General Secretary Brezhnev personally.

Then Ramón was called urgently to Ethiopia. The creeping revolution there had reached a crucial stage.

# 21

As the Ilyushin began its descent into Addis Ababa, Ramón sat behind the Russian pilot on the flight deck so he had an uninterrupted view of the savage, mountainous country ahead.

Over the centuries all the trees around the capital had been cut down for firewood, so the hills were bare and desolate. In the misty blue distance rose the peculiar flat-topped mountains known as the Ambas that were so characteristic of this mysterious corner of eastern Africa below the great horn. The sheer sides of the Ambas dropped many thousands of feet into the rocky valleys, in the depths of which great torrents gouged ever deeper into the red earth.

It was an ancient land into which the Egyptian pharaohs had first sent their armies marauding for slaves and ivory and other exotic treasures.

The Ethiopians were a fiercely proud and warlike people, most of them Christians, but members of the Coptic Church, an ancient branch of the Catholic Church that had its origins in Alexandria in Egypt.

Since 1930 the country had been ruled by the Negus Negusti, the Supreme Emperor, Haile Selassie. He was the last absolute monarch of history who ruled by decree. All his decrees were formally ratified by his Derg, a council made up of nobles and great *rases* and chieftains. So complete was his power that he personally ordered every facet of his country's government from the most momentous decisions of state down to the appointment of middle-ranking provincial civil servants.

Despite these absolute powers and the feudal organization of his government, he was a benevolent dictator much loved by the common people for his almost saintly virtues and his total incorruptibility. In stature he was small and delicately boned, with tiny, feminine feet and hands and delicate facial features.

In his personal habits he was austere and abstemious. Except on occasions of state, he dressed in unadorned clothing and ate frugally and simply. Unlike other African rulers, he accumulated no great personal wealth. His main, perhaps his only, concern was for the welfare of his people.

In the forty-five years since he had been crowned emperor he had steered Ethiopia through rebellion and foreign invasion and turbulent times with a quiet wisdom and tenacity to duty.

Only five years after his coronation, his mountainous kingdom had been invaded by Mussolini's generals and he had been driven into exile in England. His nation has resisted the invader, fighting tanks and modern aircraft and poison gas with muzzle-loading rifles and swords and often with their bare hands.

After the defeat of the axis powers Haile Selassie returned to his Ethiopian throne and ruled in his old benign fashion. However, there were new forces let loose in the world. In his cautious efforts to modernize his country and bring its largely pastoral and agrarian society into the mainstream of the twentieth century, Haile Selassie allowed a virus to enter his little kingdom.

The infection began in the new university he endowed in Addis Ababa. Long-haired wild-eyed Europeans began to preach to his young students a strange and heady philosophy that all men were equal, and that kings and nobles had no divine rights. As the ageing emperor's physical strength waned, so the very elements seemed to conspire against him. Africa is a land of savage extremes where heat follows icy cold, and drought succeeds flood, and the earth turns bountiful or hostile with neither rhythm nor reason.

A terrible drought fell upon Ethiopia, and with it rode another ghostly horseman, famine. The crops failed, the rivers and wells dried up, and the soil turned to dust and blew away on the desert winds. Flocks and herds died, and at their mothers' withered dugs human infants were tiny skeletal figures with huge haunted eyes in skull-like heads too large for their wasted bodies.

The land cried out in agony.

African famine was an old story of no particular interest, and Africa was far away. The world took no notice until the BBC sent Richard Dimbleby to Ethiopia with a television crew. Dimbleby filmed the dreadful suffering in the villages. He also attended a state banquet in Addis Ababa.

With calculated malevolence he intercut scenes of famine and lingering death with those of feasting nobles dressed in scarlet and gold lace and flowing white robes and the emperor seated at a board that groaned with rich food.

Dimbleby had an enormous following. The world took notice. The young students from Addis Ababa University, trained by their carefully selected mentors, began to march and agitate. The Church and the missionaries preached against total power vested in one man and dreamed of that elusive Utopia where man would love his fellowman and the lion would lie down with the lamb.

Many of the members of the Derg saw an opportunity to settle old scores and gain personal advancement. In a totally unrelated but significant development, the Arab oil producers doubled the price of oil and held the world to ransom. In Ethiopia the cost of living soared, placing unbearable hardships on a populace already hard hit by famine. There was runaway inflation. Those who were able hoarded food, and those who could not went on strike or rioted and looted the food shops.

Many of the young army officers were products of Addis Ababa University, and they led an army mutiny. These rebels formed a revolutionary committee and seized control of the Derg.

They arrested the prime minister and the members of the royal family and isolated the emperor in his palace. They spread rumors that Haile Selassie had stolen huge sums of public money and transferred them to a Swiss bank account. They organized demonstrations of students and malcontents outside the palace. The mob clamored for his abdication. The priests of the Coptic Church and the Muslim leaders joined in the chorus of accusation and demands for his abdication and the installation of a people's democracy.

The military council now felt strong enough to take the next significant step. Through the Derg they issued a formal declaration deposing the emperor and they sent a deputation of young army officers to arrest him and remove him from the palace.

As the officers led him down the palace steps the frail old man remarked quietly, "If what you do is for the good of my people, then I go gladly, and I pray for the success of your revolution."

To humiliate him they confined him in a sordid little hut on the outskirts of the city, but the common people gathered in their thousands outside the single room to offer their condolences and pledge their loyalty. At the order of the military council the guards drove them away at bayonet point.

The country was ripe, but it was all teetering in the balance when the Ilyushin touched down at Addis Ababa airport and taxied to the far end of the field, where twenty jeeps and troop trucks of the Ethiopian army were drawn up to welcome it.

Ramón was the first man out of the aircraft as the loading ramp touched the ground.

"Welcome, Colonel-General." Colonel Gotachow Abobo jumped down from his command jeep and strode forward to meet him.

They shook hands briefly. "Your arrival is timely," Abebe told him, and they both turned and shaded their eyes as they looked into the sun.

A second Ilyushin made its final approach and touched down. As it taxied toward them, a third and then a fourth gigantic aircraft turned across the sun and one after the other landed.

As they pulled up in a staggered row and switched off their engines, men poured out of the cavernous bellies. They were paratroopers of the crack Che Guevara Regiment.

"What is the latest position?" Ramón demanded brusquely.

"The Derg has voted for Andom," Abebe told him. Ramón's expression became serious. General Aman Andom was the head of the army. He was a man of high integrity and superior intelligence, popular with both the army and the civilian populace. His election as the new leader of the nation came as no surprise.

"Where is he now?"

"He is in his palace—about five miles from here."

"How many men?"

"A bodyguard of fifty or sixty . . ."

Ramón turned to watch his paratroopers disembarking.

"How many members of the Derg stand for you?"

Abebe reeled off a dozen names, all young left-wing army officers.

"Tafu?" Ramón demanded. Abebe nodded. Colonel Tafu commanded a squadron of Russian T-53 tanks, the most modern unit in the army.

"All right," Ramón said softly. "We can do it—but we must move swiftly now."

255

He gave the order to the commander of the Cuban paratroopers. Carrying their weapons at the trail, the long ranks of camouflage-clad assault troops trotted forward and began to board the waiting trucks.

Ramón seated himself beside Abebe in the command jeep, and the long column rolled away toward the city. Parched to talcum by drought and fierce sunlight, red dust rose in a dense cloud behind the column and rolled away on the wind that came down hot from the deserts to the north.

On the outskirts of the city they met caravans of camels and mules. The men with them watched the column pass without showing any emotion. In these dangerous days since the emperor had been deposed they had become accustomed to the movement of armed men on the roads. They were men from the Danakil Desert and the mountains, turbaned Muslims in flowing robes or bearded Copts with bushy hair and broad-swords on their belts and round steel shields on their shoulders.

At an order from Colonel Abebe, the jeep swung on to a side road and skirted the city, speeding down rutted roads between the crowded flat-roofed hovels. Abebe used the radio, speaking swiftly in Amharic and then translating for Ramón.

"I have men watching Andom's palace," he explained. "He seems to have called a meeting of all the officers in the Derg who support him. They are assembling now."

"Good. All the chickens will be in one nest."

The column turned away from the city and sped through open fields. They were bare and desiccated. The drought had left no blade of grass or green leaf. The chalky rocks that littered the earth were white as skulls.

"There." Abebe pointed ahead.

The general was a member of the nobility, and his residence stood a few miles outside the city on the first of a series of low hills. The hills were bare except for the grove of Australian eucalyptus trees that surrounded the palace. Even these were drooping in the heat and the drought. The palace was surrounded by a thick wall of red terra-cotta. At a glance Ramón saw that it was a formidable fortification. It would require artillery to breach it.

Abebe had read his thoughts. "We have surprise on our side," he pointed out. "There is a good chance that we will be able to drive in through the gate . . ."

"No," Ramón contradicted him. "They will have seen the aircraft arriving. That is probably why Andom has called his council."

Out on a rocky plain between them and the palace, a staff car was speeding toward the open gate.

"Pull in here," Ramón ordered, and the column halted in a fold of ground. Ramón stood on the rear seat of the open jeep and focused his binoculars on the gateway in the palace wall. He watched the staff car drive through it, and then the massive wooden gate swung ponderously closed.

"Where is Tafu with his tanks?"

"He is still in barracks, on the other side of the city."

"How long to get them here?"

"Two hours."

"Every minute is vital." Ramón spoke without lowering his binoculars. "Order Tafu to bring his armor in as quickly as possible—but we cannot wait until he arrives."

Abebe turned to the radio, and Ramón dropped the binoculars onto his chest and jumped down from the jeep. The commander of the paratroopers and his company leaders gathered around him, and he gave his orders quietly, pointing out the features of the terrain as he spoke.

Abebe hung up the microphone of the radio and came to join them. "Colonel Tafu has one T-53 in the city, guarding the emperor's palace. He is sending it to us. It will be here in an hour. The rest of the squadron will follow."

"Very good." Ramón nodded. "Now describe the layout of the interior of Andom's palace over there. Where will we find Andom himself?"

They squatted in a circle while Abebe sketched in the dust. Then Ramón gave his final orders.

Once again the column moved forward, but now there was a large white flag on the bonnet of the command jeep, a bed sheet that fluttered on its makeshift flagpole. The trucks kept in tight formation. The paratroopers were concealed beneath the hoods of the troop carriers, and all weapons were kept out of sight.

As they approached the palace a line of heads appeared over the wall above the gate, but the flag of truce had an inhibiting effect and no shot was fired.

The lead jeep drew up in front of the gate, and Ramón assessed its strength. The gate was of weathered teak, almost a foot thick, reinforced with bands of wrought iron. The hinges were rebated into the columns on each side of the gateway. He abandoned any idea of driving a truck through it.

From the top of the wall twenty feet above them the captain of the guard challenged them in Amharic. Abebe stood up to reply. They haggled for a few minutes, Abebe repeating that he had an urgent despatch for General Andom and demanding entrance. The guard shouted back his refusal, and the exchange became heated.

As soon as Ramón was certain that all the guard's attention was on the jeep he spoke softly into the two-way radio. The trucks behind the jeep roared forward and then peeled off left and right. They bumped over the rocky ground on each side of the roadway and drew up below the walls. From under the canvas hoods, paratroopers clambered onto the roofs of the vehicles. Ten of them were armed with grappling hooks that they swung around their heads and then heaved up over the top of the wall. The nylon ropes streamed out behind the hooks and dangled down.

"Open fire!" Ramón snapped into the radio, and a storm of automatic fire swept the top of the wall, kicking lumps of clay and brick from the rim. The ricochets whined away into the branches of the blue gum trees. The heads of guards disappeared silently, some of them ducking away but at least one of them hit by a bullet. Ramón saw his helmet spin into the air and the top of his skull lift off. A pink mist of blood and brain hung in the air for an instant after he was snatched away.

Now the paratroopers were swarming up the wall, three or four of them on each dangling rope at the same time. They were as agile as monkeys, and within seconds thirty of them were over and into the palace grounds. There were bursts of automatic fire and the thump of a single grenade. Seconds later the great wooden gate swung open and Ramón urged the jeep driver forward.

The bodies of the palace guards lay in the courtyard where they had been shot down. Ramón saw one of his paras huddled beside the gateway clutching his belly with blood oozing through his fingers. The other paras grabbed on to the jeep as it roared forward.

Ramón was standing behind the .50-caliber Browning heavy machine gun that was mounted above the driver's seat. He fired a long raking burst at the remaining guards as they fled like rabbits into the maze of adobe buildings on the far side of the courtyard.

One of the guards whirled and dropped onto one knee. He raised the launcher of the RPG 7 rocket he carried to his shoulder and aimed at the approaching jeep. Ramón swiveled the Browning onto him, but at that moment the front wheels struck one of the corpses and the jeep bounced wildly, throwing his aim high.

The guard fired the rocket. It whooshed across the open court-yard and hit the jeep full in the center of the radiator. There was a flash and a roar as the rocket exploded. Although the engine block smothered most of the blast, the front suspension collapsed and the vehicle cartwheeled end over end.

They were all thrown clear, but the shattered body of the jeep blocked the entrance and the troop trucks were backed up beyond the open gateway.

The attack was stalling already, and the defense was rallying. Automatic fire was stuttering from the windows and doorways of the palace building.

The Cuban paras sprang out of the stationary trucks and rushed forward, but another rocket hissed down the alley facing them. It flashed inches over Ramón's head, blinding him with smoke and struck the leading truck, ripping the bonnet open and shattering the windscreen. Diesel fuel spilled from the ruptured tank and ignited with a sullen roar. Black smoke billowed out over the courtyard.

There was shouting and more firing in front of them. Beside Ramón another para was hit and went sprawling.

Ramón snatched up his machine pistol and waved the attack forward, just as a heavy machine gun opened up on them from one of the windows. Ramón rolled under the blast of shot and came up against the mud wall directly below the window. The machine gun was firing over his head, and the muzzle blast drove in his eardrums.

Ramón snatched a grenade from his webbing pocket, pulled the pin and went up on one knee to post it through the window. He ducked and covered his ears.

There was a wild shout, and the machine gun fell silent. Moments later the grenade exhaled in a fiery breath above his head.

"Come on!" Ramón yelled again, and led half a dozen paras through the shattered window. The gun had been knocked off its mounting and the floor was wet and slippery with blood.

It was room to room and hand to hand now. The advantage passed to the defenders as they retreated through the maze of rooms and alleys and courtyards, doggedly holding each strong point until they were driven from it.

Slowly the attack lost impetus and, although Ramón threatened and swore and tried to inspire them with his example, they bogged down in the twisting alleys and interconnecting passageways and rooms. He realized that Andom was certainly radioing for reinforcements of loyal troops, and that minutes lost now could mean the defeat and failure of the revolution.

He heard Abebe's voice raised angrily, urging his men on in a fog of smoke and dust. Ramón crawled across to him and seized his shoulder. Face to dusty smoke-grimed face, they shouted at each other to make themselves heard above the cacophony of guns.

"Where is that bloody tank?"

"How long since I called?"

"It's over an hour." Was it that long? It seemed that only minutes had passed since the attack began.

"Get back to the radio." Ramón yelled. "Tell them—"

At that moment they both heard it, a shrill metallic squeal and a rumble of tracks.

"Come on!" Ramón lunged to his feet, and they ran together, doubled over, with bullets fluttering in the air around their heads, back through the blood-smeared rooms with walls pocked by bullets and shrapnel.

As they reached the entrance courtyard the tank butted its way in through the blocked gateway. The turret was reversed, the long 55-millimeter gun barrel pointed backward. The carcass of the rocket-shattered jeep was forced forward by the mass of armor, and it rolled clear of the gateway. The T-53 burst into the courtyard with its diesels bellowing. The turret was open, and the commander's helmeted head protruded from the hatch.

Ramón windmilled his right arm in the cavalry signal to advance and pointed into the tangle of alleys and buildings.

The tank pivoted on its churning steel tracks and crashed into the nearest wall. The mud bricks collapsed before it, and the roof tilted and sagged and buried the T-53 beneath it.

The tank shook itself free and roared forward. Ramón and his paras poured into the breach it had opened. Walls toppled and timbers crackled as the steel monster crawled forward, tilting and rocking over piles of rubble and human bodies.

The screams of the defenders rose higher than the uproar, and their firing died away. They came stumbling out of the ruined buildings, throwing down their weapons and raising their arms in surrender.

"Where is Andom?" Ramón's throat was rough and sore with the dust and the shouting. "We must get him. Don't let him escape."

The general was among the last to surrender. Only when the T-53 flattened the thick mud walls of the main hall did he come out with four of his senior officers. There was a blood-soaked bandage around his forehead and over his left eye. His beard was thick with dust and blood, and one of the scarlet tabs was torn from his collar.

His good eye was fierce. Despite his wound, his voice was firm and his bearing dignified. "Colonel Abebe," he challenged. "This is mutiny and treachery. I am the president of Ethiopia—my appointment was confirmed by the Derg this morning."

Ramón nodded to his paratroopers. They seized the general's arms and forced him to his knees. Ramón opened the flap of his holster and handed his Tokarev pistol to Abebe.

The colonel placed the muzzle between the captive's eyes and said quietly, "President Aman Andom, in the name of the people's revolution, I call upon you to resign." And he blew the top off the general's skull.

The corpse fell face forward, splattering custard yellow brains onto Abebe's boots.

Abebe clicked the safety on the Tokarev, reversed it and handed it buttfirst to Ramón.

"Thank you, Colonel-General," he said.

"I am honored to have been of service." Ramón bowed formally as he accepted the weapon back.

"How many members of the Derg voted for Andom?" he asked as the column sped back towards Addis Ababa.

"Sixty-three."

"Then we still have much work to do before the revolution is secure."

Abebe radioed ahead to Colonel Tafu's squadron of T-53 tanks. They were entering from the eastern side of the city, and he ordered them to surround the building that housed the Derg and to train their guns upon it. Elements of the army were ordered to seal off all foreign embassies and consulates. No legation staff were allowed to leave the premises, for their own safety.

All foreigners in the country, especially journalists and television personnel, were rounded up and escorted to the airport for immediate evacuation. There were to be no witnesses of what followed.

Small units of Abebe's most loyal troops, backed up by Cuban paratroopers, were rushed to the homes of members of the military council and the Derg who had declared for Andom. They were stripped of their weapons and badges of rank, dragged out and thrown into the waiting trucks and driven back to the Derg, where a revolutionary court awaited them in the main assembly chamber.

The court consisted of Colonel Abebe and two of his junior officers. "You are accused of counterrevolutionary criminal acts against the people's democratic government. Have you anything to say before sentence of death is passed upon you?"

They were taken directly out from the trial into the courtyard of the building, placed against the north wall of the chamber and executed by firing squad. The executions were carried out in full view of the revolutionary judges and the prisoners still awaiting trial. The volleys of rifle fire periodically interrupted the proceedings of the court.

The corpses were tied by the heels in bunches and dragged behind a truck through the streets to the main rubbish dump outside the city limits.

"The populace must witness the course of revolutionary justice and the price of disobedience," Ramón said to explain the necessity of these exhibitions.

The court ruled that the corpses should not be removed from the rubbish dump, and their families were forbidden to indulge in the ritual of mourning or to exhibit any public signs of grief. The grim work went on until after midnight, the last batch executed by the headlight beams of the trucks awaiting to drag them to the rubbish tip.

Although they were both exhausted, neither Ramón nor the future president could afford to sleep until the revolution was secure. Ramón had a bottle of vodka in his pack. He and Abebe shared it as they sat beside the radio and listened to the reports coming in.

One after the other, Abebe's loyal officers, with Cuban support, took over command of the various units of the army and seized all the important points in the city and its surroundings.

As the sun rose, they had control of the airport and railway station, the radio and television broadcasting studios, and all the military forts and barracks. Only then could Ramón and Abebe snatch a few hours' sleep. Guarded by Ramón's paras, they stretched out on mattresses on the chamber floor, but at noon they were in fresh uniforms for the meeting of the purified Derg. There were armed paras at the door of the chamber and T-53 tanks drawn up in the street outside.

As Colonel-General Machado congratulated Abebe, he said quietly, "If you kill Brutus, then you must kill all the sons of Brutus. Niccolò Machiavelli said that in 1510, Mr. President, and it is still the best possible advice."

"So we must begin at once."

262

"Yes," agreed Ramón. "The Red Terror must be allowed to run its course."

"The Red Terror shall flourish." The hastily printed posters in four languages were pasted on every street corner, and the hourly radio and television broadcasts proclaimed the new president and exhorted the populace to denouce all traitors and counter-revolutionaries.

There was so much work to do that Abebe divided the city into forty cells and appointed a separate revolutionary court for each cell. The presidents of these courts were loyal junior officers who were given full power to "undertake revolutionary action." Each had a team of executioners working under him. They began with the members of the nobility, the *rases* and the chieftains along with their families.

"The Red Terror is a proven tool of the revolution," Ramón Machado explained. "We know those who will prove awkward later. We know those who will oppose the pure doctrine of Marxism. It is more expedient to eliminate them now, in the first wild flush of victory, rather than undertake the tedious business of dealing with them piecemeal at a later date." He lifted his cap and raked his fingers through his thick dark curls. He was tired, his marvelous classical features strained and drawn. Dark smudges underlined his eyes, but there was no uncertainty in them. Abebe was at once grateful for his strength and awed by his iron resolution.

"We must root out every rotten apple from the barrel. We must eliminate not only the opposition, but also the thought of opposition. We must break the nation's will to resist. It must be cowed and deprived of any sense of self or self-determination. The board must be swept entirely clean. Only then will we be in a position to rebuild the nation in a new and shining image." The corpses of nobles and petty chieftains and their entire families were piled on street corners like garbage. The revolutionary patrols drove through the city and picked up children they found playing in the streets at random.

"Where do you live? Take us to your parents' home."

The parents were dragged out of their houses and forced to watch as their children were shot in the head at point-blank range. The little corpses were left at the front door, swelling and stinking in the heat. The parents were forbidden to remove them or to mourn them.

"The Red Terror will flourish," decreed the posters. But in

the mountains some of the old warriors and their families resisted the death squads.

Tanks surrounded the villages, and the women and children and old men were driven into their huts. The huts were set on fire, and screams mingled with the crackle of flames. The men were marched to the fields and forced to lie facedown in rows. The tanks drove over them, locking their tracks to pivot on the piles of bodies and grind them into a paste with the drought-stricken earth.

"Now for the priests," Ramón said.

"The priests were instrumental in the overthrow of the monarchy," Abebe pointed out.

"Yes, the church and the mosque, the bishops and priests and the imams and the ayatollahs are always useful in the beginning. The revolution can be nurtured in the pulpit, for the priests are by their training unwordly and idealistic creatures who respond to a vision of freedom and equality and brotherly love. They can be easily persuaded, but always remember that they are also in competition with us for the souls of men. When they witness the revolution in action they will challenge us. We cannot brook that competition. The priests must be disciplined and controlled—just as all other men must be."

They entered the great mosque and arrested the imam's fourteen-year-old daughter. They put out her eyes and cut out her tongue. Then they placed two ounces of raw chili pepper in her vagina and took her back to her father's house. They locked her in a room of the house with guards at the door. Her parents were forced to squat outside the door and listen to their daughter's death agonies.

The sons of the *abuna*, the archbishop of the Coptic Church, were taken to one of the revolutionary courts and tortured. Their hands and feet were crushed in steel vises and their bodies were burned with electricity. Their eyes were gouged out and left dangling onto their cheeks by the optic nerves. Their genitalia were cut off and forced into their mouths. Then they were taken home and placed outside the front door. Once again the parents were forbidden to remove their bodies for Christian burial.

Radio and television broadcasts harangued against the decadence and revisionism of the church, and death squads waited at the doors of the mosque when the muezzin began his chant. The faithful stayed at home.

"All the sons of Brutus are dead," Abebe told Ramón as they toured the quiescent city.

264

"Not all of them," Ramón disagreed. Abebe turned to stare at him. He knew what Ramón meant.

"It must be done," Ramón insisted. "Then there can be no turning back. The ancient bourgeois taboo will be shattered forever, as it was on the guillotine in the Place de la Concorde and in the Russian cellar when Tsar Nicholas and his family died. Once it is done, there will be no return and the revolution will be secure."

"Who will do it?" Abebe asked.

Ramón answered without hesitation. "I will."

"It would be best that way," Abebe agreed, looking away to conceal the relief he felt. "Do it as soon as possible."

Ramón drove down through the old quarter of the city. He was alone at the wheel of the open jeep. The streets were deserted, except for revolutionary patrols. The windows of the houses were shuttered and curtained. No face peered out at him, no children romped in the yards, no voices or sounds of laughter came from behind the closed doors of the mud-brick hovels.

Revolutionary posters were pasted to the cracked and chipped plaster of the walls: "The Red Terror shall flourish."

There had been no hygienic services since the Red Terror had begun. Rubbish clogged the streets, and sewage buckets overflowed and puddled in the gutters. The bodies of the victims of the Terror were heaped at the street corners like cords of firewood. They were so bloated and bullet-riddled that they were no longer recognizable as human. Their gas-filled bellies had stretched their clothing until it burst at the seams, and their flesh was empurpled and blackened by the sun. The only living things were the crows and kites and vultures that hopped and picked at the piles of the dead, and the fat, gorged rats that scuttled away in front of the jeep.

Ramón wrapped his silk scarf across his mouth and nose to protect them from the stench, but apart from that he was unmoved by what he saw around him, as a victorious general is unaffected by the carnage of the battlefield.

The hut was at the end of the noisome alleyway, and there were two guards at the front door. They recognized Ramón as he parked the jeep and picked his way through the accumulated filth. They saluted him respectfully.

"You are relieved of your duties. You may go," Ramón ordered.

He watched them hurry to the end of the alley before he opened the door and stooped under the lintel.

It was semidark in the room, and he removed his sunglasses.

The walls were limed but bare except for a silver Coptic cross suspended above the bed. There were rush mats on the stone floor. The room smelled of sickness and old age. An old woman sat on the floor at the foot of the bed. She wailed and pulled the hood of her robe over her head when she saw Ramón.

"Go." He gestured at the door, and she crawled across the floor, her head still covered, making obeisance and wailing and drooling with terror.

With the heel of his combat boot Ramón pushed the door closed behind her and studied the figure that lay on the bed.

"Negus Negusti, King of Kings," he said with a dry irony.

The old man stirred and looked up at him. He was dressed in a spotless white robe, but his head was bare. He was thin, impossibly thin. Ramón knew he suffered from the ailments of great age, his prostate and digestion were diseased, but his mind was clear. His feet and hands protruding from the folds of the white robe were childlike and emaciated. Each tiny bone showed clearly through the waxen amber skin. His beard and hair were untrimmed and bleached to the luster of platinum. The flesh had melted from his face, so the nose was thin and aquiline. His lips had shrunk and drawn back. His teeth were yellow and too large for the delicate bones of his cheeks and brow. His eyes were enormous, black as pools of tar, bright as those of a biblical prophet.

"I recognize you," he said softly.

"We have never met," Ramón corrected him.

"Still, I know you well. I recognize the smell of you. I know every line of your face and the inflection and timbre of your voice."

"Who am I, then?" Ramón challenged him softly.

"You are the first of a legion—and your name is Death."

"You are wise and perceptive, old man," Ramón told him, and he advanced to the bed.

"I forgive you for what you do to me," said Haile Selassie, Negus Negusti, Emperor of Ethiopia. "But I cannot forgive you for what you have done to my people."

"Commend yourself to your God, old man," said Ramón as he picked up the pillow from the bed. "This world is no longer for you."

He pressed the pillow down over the old man's face and leaned his weight upon it.

Haile Selassie's struggles were like those of a trapped bird. His thin fingers clutched tightly at Ramón's wrists and plucked softly at his sleeves. He kicked and danced, and his robe rode

266

up above his knees. His legs were thin and dark as sticks of dried tobacco, and his knees were knots enlarged out of all proportion to his skinny shanks.

Gradually his struggles grew weaker, and there was a soft spluttering under his robes as his sphincter relaxed and his bowels voided. Ramón leaned on the pillow for five minutes after the old man was completely still. He felt an almost religious ecstasy come over him. Nothing he had done before had ever given him this sense of gratification. It was physical and emotional, it was spiritual and at the same time deeply sexual.

He had killed a king.

He straightened up and removed the pillow. He plumped it up, then lifted the old man's head and set the pillow beneath it. He pulled the hem of the robe down to Haile Selassie's ankles and folded the little childlike hands on his breast. Then with thumb and forefinger he drew down his eyelids.

He stood for a long time studying the emperor's death face. He wanted to fix the image in his mind forever. He was unaware of the heat and the stench in the closed room. He sensed that this was one of the high points in his life. The frail body before him epitomized all that he had pledged to destroy in this world.

He wanted the memory of that destruction to be strong and vivid enough to last a lifetime.

# 22

All possible opposition had been eliminated. The voice of dissent was silenced. The sons of Brutus were all of them dead, and the revolution was secure.

There were many other important issues needing Ramón's attention elsewhere in Africa. With a clear conscience he could hand over his position as security adviser to the People's Democratic Government of Ethiopia. His successor in office was a general in the security police of the German Democratic Republic. He was almost as skilled as Ramón Machado in the enforcement of pragmatic democracy on a recalcitrant population.

Ramón embraced Abebe and boarded one of the Ilyushin transports that now flew regularly in and out of Addis. It was a most convenient port of entry to the entire continent.

They refueled in Brazzaville and then flew south and west to land on the new airstrip at Tercio base on the Chicamba River just as the sun set into the blue Atlantic Ocean.

Raleigh Tabaka met him. During the drive from the airstrip to Ramón's new headquarters compound in the palm grove above the white coral beach, Raleigh brought him fully up to date with developments during his absence.

Ramón's private quarters were austere. A thatched roof and large unglazed windows with roll-up blinds of split bamboo; bare uncarpeted floors and chunky but comfortable furniture made by a local carpenter from hand-sawn indigenous timber. Only the electronic communications equipment was modern. He had direct satellite links to Moscow, Luanda, Havana and Lisbon.

As Ramón entered this simple dwelling he was reminded forcefully of the cottage at Buenaventura in Cuba. Immediately he felt at home here, with the trade winds in the palms and the ocean breathing heavily on the white beach below his window.

He was exhausted. This deep bone-weariness had accumulated over the weeks and months. As soon as Raleigh Tabaka left him, he dropped his combat uniform in a heap on the mud floor and crawled under the mosquito net. The gentle warm gusts of the trade winds through the open window billowed the mosquito net and caressed his naked body.

He felt replete. He had performed a difficult but infinitely worthwhile task with skill and success. He knew that he had earned new honors and rewards, but none would be as satisfying as this deep sense of achievement that buoyed his weary spirit.

His creation surpassed that of a Mozart or a Michelangelo. He had used as his raw materials a land and a people, mountains and valleys and lakes and rivers and plains and millions of human beings. He had mixed them on his palette and then, in blood and flames and gunfire, he had fashioned and worked them into a masterpiece. His creation surpassed that of any artist who had lived before him. He knew there was no God—at least, not as the bishops and imams whom he had so recently disciplined and humiliated imagined God to be. The god Ramón knew was of this world. He was the twin god of power and political mastery—and Ramón was his prophet. The work had only just begun. First a single nation, he thought, then another and another, until finally an entire continent. His elation staved off sleep for a few minutes longer, but as he succumbed his mind took another turn.

Maybe it was the hut and the wind and the sound of the sea—whatever the association of ideas, he thought of Nicholas. In the night he dreamed of his son. He saw again his shy, reluctant smile, heard his voice and laughter in his head, felt the small warm hand curled in his hand like the timorous body of a tiny creature.

When he awoke the longing was even more intense. While he worked at his desk the image of his son's face receded and he could concentrate on the coded messages from Havana and Moscow that flashed down from the orbiting satellite. However, when he stood up from his desk and looked down through the open window to the beach, he imagined he saw a slim tanned little body splashing in the green surf and heard the sweet treble cries of the child.

Perhaps it was merely a reaction to the slaughter in the streets of Addis Ababa, or the memory of the corpses of the sons of the *abuna* with their eyeballs hanging onto their cheeks and their immature genitals stuffed into their mouths, but over the next few days the desire to see his son became an obsession.

He could not leave Tercio base now, not with so much in play, so many prizes at stake on the great gaming board of Africa. Instead he sent a satellite message to Havana and within an hour had his reply.

After Ethiopia they would deny him nothing. Nicholas and Adra were on the next transport flight from Cuba. Ramón was waiting at the airstrip when the Ilyushin landed at Tercio base.

He watched his son come down the ramp. Nicholas walked ahead of Adra, no longer clinging to her hand like a baby. There was alertness in the way he carried his head, a spring to his step and a sparkle of curiosity and intelligence in his eyes as he paused at the bottom of the ramp and looked about him keenly.

Ramón felt an extraordinary emotion, an intensification of the longing and pride with which he had anticipated the boy's arrival. No other human being had ever moved him in this way. For long aching moments he watched his son in secret, concealed in the throng of disembarking troops and swarming porters, his eyes hidden behind sunglasses. He was reluctant to give a name to this emotion he felt. He would never have entertained the word "love."

Then Nicholas picked him out. He saw the boy's entire atti-

269

tude change. He started forward at a run, but within a dozen paces he took control of himself. The look of extreme pleasure on his lovely face was swiftly masked. He was expressionless as he walked calmly to the side of the jeep in which Ramón sat and held out his hand.

"Good day, Padre," he said softly. "How does it go with you?"

Ramón felt an almost irresistible compulsion to embrace him. He sat very still while he overcame it. Then he took Nicholas's hand and returned his formal greeting.

Nicholas rode in the front of the jeep beside his father. Adra sat in the back. They skirted the guerrilla camp on the way from the airstrip to the beach compound, and Nicholas could not contain his curiosity. He asked the first question hesitantly, in a subdued voice.

"Why are all these men here? Are they sons of the revolution like we are, Padre?"

When Ramón replied without any sign of irritability, his next question was bolder. When the reply to that was also friendly, he relaxed further and took a lively interest in everything around them.

The men at the roadside saluted Ramón as the jeep passed. From the corner of his eye he saw Nicholas stiffen in the front seat and return the salute with all the aplomb of a veteran. Ramón had to turn his face away to hide his smile. The men had noticed it also and grinned after the departing vehicle.

When they arrived at the compound, Ramón's orderly had a batch of satellite messages for his attention. However, there was little of importance among them, and Ramón dealt with them swiftly. He went to the hut alongside his own that he had allocated to Nicholas and Adra. He heard the boy's excited chatter as he stepped up on to the stoep, but it was cut off abruptly as he appeared in the doorway. Again Nicholas was strange and withdrawn, watching his father warily.

"Did you bring your bathing suit?" Ramón asked him.

"Yes, Padre."

"Good. Put it on. We will swim together."

The water inside the reef was calm and warm.

"Look, Padre, I can swim the crawl now—no more baby paddle," Nicholas boasted.

With Ramón swimming beside him, he made it out to the reef with only a half-dozen pauses to tread water while he regained his breath. They sat side by side on a coral head, and while they discussed seriously how the reef had been formed by millions of tiny living creatures Ramón studied the boy carefully. He was well favored, tall and strong for his age. His vocabulary had expanded again since last they had been together. At times it was almost like talking to a grown man.

They ate dinner together on the veranda. Ramón discovered how much he had missed Adra's cooking. Every minute Nicholas seemed more relaxed. His appetite was good. He asked for more of the baked mullet. Ramón allowed him half a glass of well-watered wine. Nicholas sipped it like a connoisseur, swelling with pride at being treated as an adult.

When Adra came to fetch him to bed, he slipped off his chair without argument but pulled away from her hand and came around the table to his father.

"I am very happy to be here, Padre," he said formally, and took his hand.

As Ramón shook his hand he experienced an actual physical constriction of his chest.

Within a week Nicholas had become a favorite at Tercio camp. Some of the ANC instructors and recruits had their families with them. One of the wives was a trained primary school teacher from the University of the Western Cape in South Africa. She had set up a school for the children in the camp. Ramón sent Nicholas to take part in the classes. The schoolroom was a thatched building with open sides and rows of benches made of roughly planed native timber.

Almost immediately it was clear that Nicholas was as bright and advanced as children three and four years older than he was. English was the language of instruction, and he made swift progress in it. He had a clear, sweet voice and led the singing. He taught them "Land of the Landless" and other revolutionary songs, which the teacher translated into English. He had brought his soccer ball with him, and this gave him tremendous social prestige among his peers. A work detail from the camp under orders from Colonel-General Machado leveled a soccer pitch for the school, laid out the markings in lime and set up goalposts. Such was Nicholas's prowess on the field that they nick named him Pele, and the daily matches became a popular feature of camp life.

As the general's son, Nicholas had special standing and privilege. He had the run of the camp, including the induction classes for new recruits. The instructors allowed him to handle the weapons.

Ramón watched with carefully concealed pride as his son stood up before a class of adult recruits and demonstrated the

271

stripping and reassembling of an AK-47 assault rifle. Then he took his place on the range and fired a magazine of live ammunition. Twelve of the twenty rounds struck the man-sized target at which he was aiming.

Without Ramón's knowledge, José, the Cuban driver, taught Nicholas to drive the jeep. The first Ramón knew of his son's latest accomplishment was when Nicholas, sitting on a cushion, proudly drove him down to the airstrip to meet the incoming Ilyushin transport flight.

The men along the road cheered them as they passed with cries of "Viva Pele!"

The camp tailor made Nicholas his own set of camouflage combat fatigues and a soft Cuban-style cap. He wore the cap cocked at an angle over one-eye, just as his father did, and imitated Ramón's mannerisms, lifting his cap to rake his fingers through his hair or hooking his thumbs in his belt as he stood at rest. He became Ramón's unofficial driver, and wherever they went huge grins of delight followed the jeep.

On some afternoons Ramón and Nicholas took one of the boats powered by a fifty-horsepower outboard motor and raced out through the pass in the coral reef into the blue Atlantic waters. They anchored the boat over one of the deep reefs and fished with hand lines. The coral teemed with fish of every possible shape, size and color. Ramón taught Nicholas how to chop the carcass of a large fish, preserved from their previous expedition, into a fine mince. They mixed this with beach sand to make it sink swiftly and ground-baited the reef below the anchored boat.

Soon they could make out the shadowy shapes of large fish darting and swirling in the blue depths sixty feet below their hull. The scent of the ground bait had goaded them into a feeding frenzy. As they dropped their baited hooks among them the thick line was jerked through their fingers and Nicholas squealed with glee.

The reef fish glittered and glowed with peacock blue and iridescent green; with clear daffodil yellow and startling scarlet. They were spotted with jade and sapphire, striped like zebra and splashed with flaming ruby and opal. They were shaped like bullets and butterflies, and winged like exotic birds. They were armed with daggers and barbed spines and rows of porcelain-white fangs. They squeaked and grunted like pigs as they were hauled flapping and squirming over the gunwale of the assault boat. Some were so large that Ramón had to give Nicholas a hand to drag them from the water. He hated anybody, even his father, to help him. He hated even more to stop fishing at the close of the day.

"One more, Padre—just one more," he cried eagerly, and in the end Ramón had to take the line out of his hands.

One evening they stayed later than usual. Darkness was falling as they hauled the anchor and started the outboard. The trade wind had turned chilly, and the wind of their passage blew over them as they bounced over the tops of the swells on their way back to the river mouth. Gooseflesh pimpled Nicholas's arms as he hugged himself. He shivered with cold and exhaustion and the reaction from so much excitement.

Steering the boat with one hand, Ramón put his other arm around Nicholas's shoulders. For a moment the child froze with shock at his unfamiliar touch, and then his body relaxed and he crept closer to his father and cuddled against his chest.

As he steered through the darkness with the small shivering body pressed to his, Ramón was assailed once again by the memory of the *abuna* of Addis Ababa's sons propped against the front wall of their father's home with empty eye sockets, each with his tiny dark penis protruding like a finger from between his dead lips. Ramón was not touched by either guilt or regret. It had been necessary, just as once it had been necessary to half drown the child who now cuddled against his chest. Duty was often hard and cruel, but he had never flinched from its call. Still, he had never before felt the way he did now.

They beached the boat and handed it over to José, the Cuban driver, to care for. Then they made their way by lantern light through the palm grove toward the stockade of the compound.

Nicholas stumbled against him in the darkness, and Ramón took his hand to steady him. The child made no effort to pull his hand away.

They walked on without speaking until they reached the gate of the compound. Then Nicholas whispered softly, "I wish I could stay here at Tercio with you always."

Ramón pretended he had not heard him, but he found it difficult to draw his next breath.

The signals clerk woke him at ten minutes after midnight. It needed only a light tap on the door of the hut for Ramón to come fully awake with the Tokarev pistol in his hand.

"What is it?"

"A Red Rose relay from Moscow," the clerk answered him. They had strict instructions to call him at any time of day or night for a Red Rose communication.

"I will come immediately."

The message was in code, and Ramón fetched his copy of the code pad from the steel safe. They used a "one-time" pad, a separate code randomly generated by computer for each sheet. He and Red Rose had the only existing copies of the pad, and they used a single sheet for each message.

He matched her sheet and began to decode the message.

"Project is code-named Skylight," the message read. "First subterranean test of 30-megaton fission device scheduled October 26. Test site located 27°35'S 24°25'E. Full specifications of device on hand."

Ramón sent his driver to the main ANC camp upriver, and Raleigh Tabaka was in his office within forty minutes.

"We must leave for London immediately," Ramón told him as Raleigh read the message. "This is too important to coordinate from here. We will orchestrate through the London embassy and the ANC office in the U.K."

Ramón smiled with quiet satisfaction. "We will have the Boers on the mat in front of the Security Council before the week is out. Once again, they have played right into our hands."

He woke Nicholas to say good-bye to him.

"When will you come back, Padre?" the child asked bravely, hiding any sign of distress.

"I don't know, Nicky." Ramón used the diminutive of his name for the first time, and it sat awkwardly on his tongue.

"You will come back, won't you, Padre?"

"Yes, I will come back. I promise you that."

"And you will let me and Adra stay here at Tercio? You won't send us away?"

"Yes, Nicky. You and Adra will stay here."

"Thank you. I am glad," said Nicholas. "Good-bye, Padre."

They shook hands solemnly. Then Ramón turned away quickly and ran down the steps to the waiting jeep.

Preventing the Skylight test was of secondary importance. It was almost three years since they had first learned of the South African plans to build a nuclear bomb, and Ramón knew that by now they had a viable weapon. However, a nuclear weapon had very little practical application in the type of bush war that was typically African.

What was of primary importance was to isolate South Africa even further from its last remaining support in the Western world. It was already a political pariah, and this was an opportunity he had waited for, to brand it a nuclear rogue into the bargain.

They met in the ambassador's safe room in the cellar of the

Soviet embassy. The embassy was set in the intimate diplomatic enclave behind Kensington Palace.

Both General Borodin and Aleksei Yudenich had flown in from Moscow. Their presence gave weight to the deliberations. It underlined both the foreign ministry's and the KGB's renewed interest in the African section and gave Colonel-General Machado tremendous personal prestige.

The Africans were represented by Raleigh Tabaka and the secretary-general of the ANC. Oliver Tambo, the president of the ANC, was on an unofficial visit to East Germany and could not return to London in time for the meeting.

There was a great deal of urgency, for the South Africans were due to test Skylight within the coming week. Red Rose had reinforced her initial dispatch with quite extensive information concerning the enriching of the uranium, the specifications of the bomb, its projected delivery in the new G5 artillery round, the position and depth of the test hole and the ignition system that would be used to detonate the bomb.

"What we have to decide today," Yudenich said, opening the discussion, "is how best to use this information."

"I think, comrade," the secretary-general of the ANC cut in eagerly, "that you should allow us to call a press conference here in London."

Ramón's lips curled into a small cynical smile. Of course they wanted it. What a blaze of publicity the ANC would bring down upon itself.

"Comrade Secretary-General." Yudenich smiled broadly. "I think the announcement would carry a little more weight if it were to be made by the president of the USSR, rather than the president of the ANC." His tone was heavy with sarcasm. Yudenich didn't like blacks.

In private, before this meeting, he had remarked to Ramón that it was a pity they had been obliged to invite the "monkeys" rather than deciding the issue between civilized human beings. "It is difficult to bring one's mind down to their level," he had chuckled. "But, then, you have had much experience with them, Comrade. Should I have brought a packet of nuts for them, do you think?"

Ramón sat aloof from the discussion for nearly twenty minutes. The voices of both Yudenich and the secretary-general were becoming louder and more strained. It was Borodin who at last suggested mildly, "Should we perhaps ask Comrade General Machado's views? His source provided the information—perhaps he has ideas how best to take advantage of it."

They all looked down the table at him. Ramón had his reply prepared.

"Comrades, all that you have said has good sense and reason. However, if either the ANC or the president of the USSR breaks the news it will be a one-day sensation. I believe that to extract the most benefit we should draw out the process. We should release a few scraps of information at a time and allow interest to build up over a protracted period."

They looked thoughtful, and Ramón went on, "I also believe that if we break it ourselves, either through Moscow or through the ANC, it will be looked upon as biased or at least highly prejudiced information. I think we should give the news to the most powerful voice in America to spread for us. The voice that governs the United States—and, through it, the Western world."

Yudenich looked confused. "Gerald Ford? The president of the United States?"

"No, Comrade Minister. The news media. The true government of America. In their single-minded obsession with freedom of speech, the Americans have created a dictatorship more powerful than anything we can devise. Let us give this to the American television networks. We make no announcements, we hold no press conferences. We simply give them a mere whiff of the scent, show them the tracks of the hare, and let them hunt it down and tear the animal to pieces themselves. You know well how it works; like a pack of hounds, their excitement and their blood lust will be more thoroughly aroused if they believe the prey is theirs alone. They call it 'investigative journalism' and give prizes to the ones who do most damage to their government, their allies and the capitalist system that supports them."

Yudenich stared at him a little longer before he began to chuckle. "I hear that in Africa they call you the Fox, Comrade General."

"Golden Fox," Borodin corrected him. Yudenich burst into full-throated laughter.

"I see you merit your name, Comrade General. Let the Americans and the British do our work for us once again."

The total success of the Skylight operation reaffirmed Red Rose's worth a hundredfold, but it brought with it its own problems.

The more valuable Red Rose became, the more skillfully and carefully she must be controlled. Every possible precaution had to be taken to protect and guard her in the field, and to give her incentives to continue. She must be rewarded immediately for Skylight and given access to Nicholas as soon as reasonably possible. However, this again was complicated by Ramón's changing attitude toward his son.

He was determined that these sickly bourgeois sentiments that recently had intruded on his sense of purpose must never be allowed to interfere with his duty. He knew that, if necessary, given the right circumstances, he must be ready to sacrifice Nicholas, just as he was completely resigned to laying down his own life if duty dictated it.

Until that day, however, Nicholas must never be placed in any possibility of danger. Especially there must never be the least possibility of Red Rose or any other person laying hands on the boy and removing him from Ramón's custody.

He considered once again arranging the next access at the hacienda in Spain. This would mean moving from Tercio; that involved a degree of risk, a very small degree, but a certain risk nonetheless. It was just possible that Red Rose—say, with the assistance of South African agents—might succeed in spiriting the child to the British embassy in Madrid. He knew that Red Rose possessed a British passport and dual nationality. Spain was no longer secure enough to satisfy Ramón.

Of course, he could arrange the meeting in either Havana or Moscow. This entailed considerable logistical problems in getting Red Rose to those locations. It would also reveal to her beyond any doubt who were her ultimate masters. He wanted to avoid that if at all possible.

The most secure location outside Cuba or Russia was Tercio base on the Chicamba River. It was remote and heavily guarded. There was no foreign embassy within a thousand miles. Nicholas was already installed there. Red Rose could be brought in with very little inconvenience. Once she was at Tercio she would be more completely under his control than in any other place on this earth.

Tercio it would have to be.

# 23

Isabella came fully awake with a guilty start. For a moment she did not know where she was or what had woken her. Then she remembered, and realized that it was the change in the sound of Ilyushin's engines and the canting of the deck beneath her that had awakened her. Despite her best intentions, she had fallen asleep in the uncomfortable jump seat.

She glanced quickly at her wristwatch. Two hours, fifty minutes since takeoff from Lusaka.

She lifted herself slightly in her seat and checked the instrument panel over the pilot's shoulder. They were still on the same heading, but they were beginning their descent. The altimeter began to unwind steadily.

She looked ahead through the windscreen of the cockpit. It was late afternoon and hazy, but suddenly the low sun flashed on a large body of water ahead.

Lake? she thought, searching her memory for one that large. The African lakes all lay along the Great Rift Valley, thousands of miles in the opposite direction. Then suddenly it occurred to her.

"The Atlantic! We have reached the west coast." She reassembled the map of Africa in her mind. "Angola or Zaïre, or the Angolan enclave."

The Candid banked onto an approach heading. The undercarriage whined and vibrated as it was lowered. Ahead she saw white coral beaches and the shape of the reefs beneath the blue Atlantic waters.

There was a river mouth, with low surf breaking on the bar and a deeper serpentine channel crawling into the lagoon. The river was broad and brown, but not large enough to be one of the major African drainages, neither the Congo nor the Luanda River. She tried to memorize every detail. A few miles above the lagoon the river formed a distinctive oxbow, a double *S*. Dead ahead was a long red clay landing strip, and she made out the thatched roofs of a large settlement in the bend of the river beyond it.

The Candid touched down and taxied to the far end of the strip. As the pilot shut down the engines, a convoy of trucks trundled out to surround it. She saw many armed men in camouflage and combat fatigues.

"Wait," the pilot told her. "Men come fetch."

Two officers entered the flight deck. One was a major. They were both swarthy and wore mustaches. They were dressed in camouflage with no insignia apart from their badges of rank.

South Americans, she thought. Or Mexicans. This was confirmed when the major addressed her in Spanish.

"Welcome, señora. You will please come with us."

"My suitcase." She indicated her luggage with all the hauteur she could muster, and the major snapped an order at his junior. The lieutenant carried her baggage down the ramp and loaded it into a waiting truck.

They drove her in silence for twenty minutes, passing the barbed-wire stockade beyond which stood the thatched buildings she had first seen from the air. There were armed guards at the gate. They followed a single track, and she caught glimpses of the river through the trees. The track became progressively softer and sandier, and she guessed they were headed toward the river mouth and the sea.

They reached another, smaller stockade. The gate was guarded, but they were allowed to pass straight through. The huts were thatched, but seemed smaller and neater than the others she had seen. There were nine of them along the edge of the beach.

As she stepped down from the truck she looked around her. It was a pretty spot. It reminded her of a brochure for a Club Méditerranée holiday—sea, sand, palms and thatched huts.

The major escorted her politely into the largest hut, and as soon as Isabella saw the two uniformed females who were waiting to meet her she felt her flesh crawl. She remembered the degrading deep body search that had been inflicted on her on the previous occasion.

Her fears were without substance. The two young women were almost apologetic as they searched her suitcase and handbag. They patted her down but did not force her to undress for a body search.

There was minor consternation when they discovered her

279

camera. It was a small "Swinger" type Kodak. They discussed it with obvious alarm, and Isabella resigned herself to losing it.

"It is of no value," she told them in Spanish. "You may take it if you wish."

In the end one of the women took the camera and the two spare rolls of film and disappeared with them through the door at the back of the room.

Ramón was watching through the peephole in the wall as the two women signalers conducted the search. He had ordered them to behave with circumspection and not to give unnecessary offense, so he nodded with approval when one of them came through and handed him the camera and film.

He examined them quickly but thoroughly. He exposed a single frame to ensure that the trigger mechanism functioned and that the film wound on properly. Then he nodded and handed the camera back to the woman.

Isabella was surprised and obviously pleased when it was returned to her. Through the peephole, Ramón studied her expression with interest. She had grown her hair longer, and her features had matured and become stronger. She was even more poised and self-possessed than she had been when last he had seen her in Spain. She carried authority and success well, and he reminded himself of her considerable achievements and the high place she had carved out for herself in a few short years.

She had obviously kept herself in top physical condition. She was slim and fit-looking. Her legs and arms under the short cotton blouse and Bermuda shorts were tanned and shapely. Her muscle tone was as taut as that of a professional athlete. He considered her objectively and thought that she was probably one of the three or four most physically attractive women of the hundreds he had known. He was highly pleased with her. She was in large measure responsible for his own career success.

The two women finished the search and repacked and closed Isabella's suitcase. One of them picked it up and asked Isabella to follow her. She took her to the end of the compound to a gate in a screen fence made of dried palm fronds. Isabella found herself in a small enclosure that contained only two huts.

The woman led her to the nearest of these and ushered her into a single large room that had a mosquito-netted bed in a side alcove. She deposited the suitcase on the bed and left Isabella alone.

Isabella explored quickly. There was a shower room and earth toilet at the rear, all very bucolic but more than adequate for her needs. It reminded her of one of Sean's hunting camps in the Chiwewe concession.

She began unpacking her suitcase. There were a hanging space and shelves behind a curtain, but before she could finish the chore a sound carried to her through the open window overlooking the beach.

It was a sound that pierced her soul, the high joyous shout of a child she would have recognized wherever or whenever she heard it.

She rushed to the window.

Nicholas was on the beach. He wore only bathing trunks, and at first glance she saw that he had grown several inches since their last meeting in Spain.

He had a puppy with him, a black and white spotted mongrel with a thin muzzle and a long whippy tail. Nicholas was holding a stick out of reach as he raced along the water's edge, and the puppy gamboled and leaped beside him, trying to reach the stick. Nicholas was shrieking with laughter, and the puppy yapped hysterically.

Nicholas hurled the stick out into the sea and shouted, "Fetch!" The puppy plunged in gamely and swam out to the floating stick, picked it up in its jaws and turned back.

"Good boy! Come on!" Nicholas encouraged him. As the puppy came ashore it shook a gale of water drops over him, and Nicholas howled in protest and seized one end of the stick. Boy and dog began a laughing growling tug-of-war.

Isabella found her vision misting over, and she had to blink rapidly to clear her eyes. She left the hut and went down softly to the high-water mark. Nicholas was so absorbed with his pet that she was able to sit still and observe him for almost ten minutes before he noticed her.

Immediately his manner altered. He pushed the puppy away. "Down!" he commanded sternly, and it obeyed. "Sit!" he said. "Stay!"

He left it at the water's edge and came to Isabella.

"Good day, Mamma." He held out his hand solemnly. "How goes it with you today?"

"Did you know I was coming?"

"Yes. I am to be good and kind to you," he replied frankly. "But I will not be allowed to go to school while you are here."

"Do you like school, Nicholas?"

"Yes, Mamma, very much. I can read now. And we are learning in English," he replied in that language.

"Your English is very good, Nicky. Luckily I have brought

281

you some English books.'' She tried to make up for denied pleasure. "I think you will like them."

"Thank you."

She felt rejected, an interloper in his compact little world.

"What is your puppy's name?"

"July Twenty-six."

"That is an odd name for a puppy. Why do you call him that?"

He looked astonished at her ignorance. "July Twenty-six is the date of the beginning of the revolution. Everybody knows that."

"Of course. How foolish of me."

He took pity on her. "I call him just plain Twenty-six." He whistled to the puppy, and it came bounding up the beach. "Sit!" he ordered. "Shake hands."

The puppy offered her its paw.

"Twenty-six is very clever. You have trained him well."

"Yes," he agreed calmly. "He is the cleverest dog in the world."

"My baby," she lamented silently, "what are they doing to you? What tricks are they playing on your susceptible young mind that you call your puppy after some violent political event?" She did not know what revolution Nicholas was referring to, but the anguish must have twisted her features, for he asked, "Are you all right, Mamma?"

"Oh, yes."

"I will take you to meet Adra," he invited. As they walked back through the palms she casually tried to take his hand, but he firmly and politely disengaged her fingers.

"I still have the soccer ball you gave me," he said to mollify her. She knew she would have to win his confidence and liking all over again, and the knowledge made her eyes sting once more.

"I must take it very easy," she cautioned herself. "I mustn't press him too hard."

She was totally unprepared for the shock of seeing Nicholas in his combat fatigues. With his cap cocked over one eye and his thumbs hooked in his belt, he swaggered like a legionnaire and strutted for her approval. She covered up her distress and made suitable noises of admiration.

She had brought with her a selection of books she hoped might appeal to a boy of Nicholas's age. By a fortunate chance one of these was the African classic *Jock of the Bushveld*, a story of a man and his dog.

The illustrations intrigued Nicholas immediately, and he professed to see in Jock a resemblance to his own Twenty-six. They discussed this at great length, and then Nicholas wanted to read the text. It was a simple story, but beautifully written. He read aloud. Despite herself she was impressed by his ability, although once or twice he appealed to her for help with a difficult word or the name of an African animal with which he was unfamiliar.

By the time Adra came to fetch him to bed, they had made up most of the lost time and ground, and were once again on the slippery footing of tentative friendship.

"Don't push too hard," she had to keep warning herself.

As he said good night and shook her hand formally, he suddenly blurted out, "It is a good story. I like Jock the dog, and I am glad you have come to see me again. I don't really mind not going to school." His outburst had clearly embarrassed him, and he hurried from the room.

Isabella waited until she saw the light go out in his bedroom, then went to find Adra. She wanted to speak to her alone and try to estimate just what part she had played in Nicholas's abduction and where her sympathies now lay. She also wanted news of Ramón, and to find out from Adra when she would see him again.

Adra was in the kitchen, washing the dinner dishes, but as Isabella entered her expression went dead and she withdrew behind an iron-cold reserve. She replied to Isabella in monosyllables and would not meet her eyes. Very shortly Isabella gave up the effort and went back to her own hut.

Despite the fatigue of travel she slept fitfully and woke in the dawn light, eager for her first full day with her son.

They spent the entire day with Twenty-six on the beach. In the bag of gifts that Isabella had brought with her was a tennis ball. This kept boy and dog amused for hours on end.

Then they swam out to the reef. Nicholas showed her how to hook the sea cats out of their holes in the coral. He was delighted at her horror of the writhing slimy legs of the miniature octopuses and the huge luminous eyes that gave them their name.

"Adra will cook them for dinner," he promised.

"You love Adra, don't you?" she asked.

"Of course," he replied. "Adra is my mother." He caught himself as he realized his gaffe. "I mean, you are my mamma, but Adra is my real mother."

The hurt made her want to weep.

On the second morning Nicholas came to her hut and woke

283

her while it was still dark. "We are going fishing," he exulted. "José is going to take us out in the boat."

José was one of the camp guards she had noticed on her arrival. He was a dark-skinned young man with crooked teeth and pockmarked face. He was obviously one of Nicholas's favorites. The two of them chatted easily while they readied the boat and the fishing lines.

"Why do you call him Pele?" she asked José in Spanish.

Nicholas answered for him. "Because I am the champion soccer player in the school—not so, José?"

Nicholas showed her how to bait her line and was patronizingly indulgent of her inability to remove the hook from the mouth of a leaping, quivering fish.

That evening they read another chapter of *Jock* together. When Nicholas was in bed, Isabella tried once again to engage Adra in friendly conversation. She received the same taciturn, hostile response. However, when she gave up and left the kitchen, Adra followed her out into the darkness and gripped her arm. With her lips almost touching Isabella's ear she hissed, "I cannot talk to you. They are watching us every minute."

Before Isabella could recover, Adra had disappeared back into the kitchen.

In the morning Nicholas had another surprise for her. He took her down to the beach where José waited for them. At a word from Nicholas he handed over his weapon and stood by grinning with crooked teeth while the boy stripped the AKM. Nicholas's fingers were nimble and fast. He called out the name of each separate part of the weapon as he detached it.

"How long?" he demanded of José as he finished.

"Twenty-five seconds, Pele." The guard laughed with admiration. "Very good. We will make you a para, yet."

"Twenty-five seconds, Mamma," he repeated to Isabella proudly, and although she was appalled by the demonstration she tried to make her congratulations sound sincere.

"Now, José, you must time me again when I reassemble," Nicholas ordered. "And you must take my photograph, Mamma."

The camera was a great attraction, and she obeyed. Then Nicholas posed with the rifle and demanded another photograph. Watching him through the lens, she was reminded strongly of the photographs she had seen of the child warriors trained by the Vietcong. They were children dwarfed by the weapons they carried, little boys and girls with faces like cherubs and big innocent eyes. She had also read about the atrocities committed by these aberrant little monsters. Was Nicholas being turned into one of these? The thought made her feel physically sick.

"Can I shoot, José?" Nicholas wheedled him, and they argued playfully until at last José allowed himself to be won over.

He threw an empty bottle out into the lagoon, and Nicholas stood at the edge of the water and fired with the selector of the rifle on single shot. The sound of gunfire brought half a dozen paratroopers and the women signalers from the compound. They stood at the high-water mark and cheered him on. On the fifth shot the bottle exploded and there were shouts of "Viva, Pele!" and "Courage, Pele!" from the onlookers.

"Take my picture again, Mamma," Nicholas pleaded, and he posed with his admirers on either side of him and the rifle held at high port across his chest.

Adra gave them a picnic lunch of fruit and cold smoked fish to eat on the beach. As they sat together Nicholas remarked suddenly through a mouthful of food, "José has fought in many battles. He has killed five men with his rifle. One day I will be a true son of the revolution—just as he is."

That night she lay under her mosquito net and tried to fight off the dark waves of despair and helplessness that flooded over her.

"They are turning my baby into a monster. How can I stop them? How can I get him away from them?"

She did not even know who "they" were, and her sense of helplessness was overwhelming.

"Oh, where is Ramón? If only he would come to me. With his help, I know I can be strong. With him beside me, we can see this dreadful thing through."

She tried to approach Adra again, but the woman was cold and intractable.

Nicholas was becoming restless. Although he was still polite and friendly, she could tell he was becoming bored with her company alone. He spoke of school and soccer matches and his friends and what they would do when he was allowed to return to them. She tried desperately to distract him, but there was a limit to the games she could devise, to the fascination of the books and stories she provided for him.

A kind of wild desperation came over her. She dreamed of escaping with him to the safe and sane world of Weltevreden. She imagined him dressed in the uniform of a first-class public school, rather than in military camouflage. She fantasized about making some bargain with the mysterious powers that controlled their destinies so completely.

"I would do anything—if only they would give my baby back to me." Yet even as she thought it, she knew it was in vain.

Then in the dark and hopeless watches of the night her imagination became morbid. She thought of ending it, ending the torment for both herself and her son.

"It would be the only way to save him, the only way out for both of us."

She could use José's rifle. She would ask Nicholas to show it to her, and once she had it in her hands . . . She shuddered at the thought and could take it no further.

Colonel-General Ramón Machado recognized the change in her. He had been anticipating it.

For ten days he had been observing her closely. There were cameras and microphones in the huts that Isabella had not discovered. While she and the child had been together on the beach or in the boat they had been filmed with a high-powered telescopic lens. For hours at a time Ramón studied her through binoculars from carefully prepared vantage points above the beach.

He had watched her first wild elation slowly change to simple single-minded enjoyment of her son, then slowly sour into despair and corroding discontent as she came to appreciate fully the invidious circumstances in which she was trapped.

He guessed that she had probably reached the stage when she might try something desperate that would destroy all the beneficial results that had been achieved by the visit so far.

He gave Adra new orders.

As she served dinner that evening, Adra abruptly sent Nicholas on an errand that got him out of the hut for a few minutes. Then, as she spooned thick fish soup into Isabella's bowl, she leaned so close to her that a loose strand of her hair brushed her cheek.

"Do not speak or look at me," she whispered. "I have a message from the marqués." Isabella dropped her spoon with a clatter. "Careful. Give no sign. He says he will try to come to you, but it is difficult and dangerous. He says he loves you. He says to be brave."

All thought of suicide was driven from her mind. Ramón was close. Ramón loved her. She knew deep in her heart that it would be all right as long as she had the fortitude to brave it through, and Ramón's help.

The knowledge kept her going through the next two days.

There was a new sparkle and zest in her that she was able to share with Nicholas. The restlessness and creeping ennui that had begun to affect their relationship evaporated. Once again they were happy together.

At night she lay awake in her hut, no longer devoured by doubt and brooding fears, waiting for Ramón.

"He will come. I know he will."

Then one of the women who had met her and searched her luggage on arrival came to her with a message.

"There is an aircraft departing at nine o'clock tomorrow. You will leave with it."

"The child!" she demanded. "Nicholas—Pele?"

The woman shook her head. "The child remains. Your visit is terminated. They will fetch you at eight o'clock tomorrow morning. You must be ready. Those are my orders."

She wanted to take some memento of her son with her. After she had showered and changed for dinner she took a pair of nail scissors from her toilet bag and hid them in the pocket of her Bermudas. When Nicholas was seated at the dinner table she came up behind him, and before he could pull away she snipped a thick dark curl from the back of his head.

"Hey," he protested halfheartedly. "Why do you do that?"

"I want something to remember you by when I am gone."

He thought about that for a while and then asked shyly, "Can I have some of your hair as well—to remember you?"

Without a word she handed him the scissors. He stood in front of her and streamed one of her tresses between his fingers.

"Not too much," she warned him. He laughed and cut a lock and curled it around his finger.

"Your hair is soft—and pretty," he whispered. "Do you really have to go, Mamma?"

"I am afraid so, Nicky."

"Will you come and visit me again?"

"Yes, I will. I promise you that."

"I will keep this piece of your hair in my *Jock* book." He fetched the book and pressed the curl between the pages. "Every time I read the book I will think of you."

The moon was almost full. The silver radiance sifted in through the open sides of her hut and cast stark shadows that moved softly across the floor to mark the passage of the hours.

"He *must* come," she told herself, lying rigid with fearful hope on the hard mattress. "Please let him come."

Suddenly she sat bolt upright. She had heard nothing, seen nothing, but she knew with utter certainty that he was close.

She had to force herself not to call his name aloud. She waited with every sense alert, and then suddenly without sound he was there.

He appeared like a wraith in the silver moonlight, and she gagged the cry that rose in her throat. She threw back the mosquito net and with three quick steps had crossed the hut and was in his arms. Their kiss seemed to last a moment and all of infinity. Then, still without a word, he drew her down the front steps of the hut and into the sanctuary of the palm grove.

"We do not have long," he warned her softly, and she choked back a sob and clung to him.

"What is happening to us, darling?" she pleaded. "I don't understand any of it. Why are you doing this to us?"

"For the same reason that you are forced to obey. For Nicholas, and for you."

"I don't understand. I cannot go on, Ramón. I have reached the end of my strength."

"Not much longer, my darling. I promise you that. Soon it will be over, and we will be together."

"You said that last time, darling. I have done all I can . . ."

"I know, Bella. What you have done has saved us. Both of us, Nicholas and me. Without you we would have long since been destroyed. You have brought time and life for us."

"They have made me do terrible, terrible things, Ramón. They have made me betray my family and my country."

"They are pleased with you, Bella. This visit is proof of that. They have given you two weeks with Nicholas. If only you can last a little longer—give them just a little more of what they want."

"They will never let me go, Ramón. I know that. They will hold me forever, and bleed the last drop."

"Bella, darling." He stroked her body through the thin silk of her nightgown. "I have a plan. If you can keep them happy just a little longer, next time they will be more lenient. They will trust you a little more. They will start to become careless—and then, I promise, I will bring Nicky to you."

"Who are 'they'?" she whispered, but he was beginning to make love to her and the question faltered.

"Quiet, my love. Don't ask. It is best you don't know."

"At first I thought it was the Russians, but the Americans acted on my Skylight message. The Americans used my information on the Angola raid. Is it the American CIA, Ramón?"

"You may be right, my love, but for Nicky's sake don't provoke them."

"Oh, God, Ramón. I am so unhappy. I didn't believe that any civilized people could treat others in this way."

"Not much longer," he whispered. "Be strong. Give them what they want for just a little longer, and then Nicky and I will be with you."

"Make love to me, Ramón. It's the only thing in the world that can keep me from going mad."

Nicholas drove her to the airstrip the following morning. He was tremendously proud of his driving skill, and she was effusive in her praise. José and the regular driver were in the back of the jeep, and she overheard a remark that one made to the other that at the time made little sense but stuck in her memory like a burr.

"Pele is the true cub of the fox, El Zorro."

At the ramp of the Ilyushin they said good-bye to each other.

"You promise to come to see me again, Mamma," Nicholas reminded her.

"Of course, Nicky. What present should I bring you?"

"My soccer ball is worn and leaking. We have to pump it many times during the matches."

"I will bring you another."

"Thank you, Mamma." He offered her his hand, but she could not restrain herself. She dropped to her knees and hugged him to her breast.

For a shocked moment he stood very still in her arms. Then he tore himself violently from her embrace. His face was scarlet with humiliation. He glared at her, then whirled and ran for the jeep.

From the small side window in the flight deck of the Ilyushin she peered down, but Nicholas was gone. She saw the fine pall of dust still hanging over the road to the beach. His going left a great emptiness in her soul.

She disembarked from the Ilyushin in Libya, where it landed to refuel, and caught a Swissair flight to Zurich. She airmailed postcards to everybody in the family including Nanny and used her credit cards to establish her presence in Switzerland. She even called on Shasa's bankers in Lausanne to withdraw ten thousand francs and thus allay any suspicions her father might have about her holiday.

The photographs she had taken of Nicholas were beautiful. She had captured his typical expressions and moods and characteristic poses. Even the ones of him in his camouflage fatigues handling that dreadful assault rifle gave her more pleasure than distress.

She was keeping a journal for Nicholas. It was a thick bound book with pockets inside the covers, and it contained every memento of Nicholas that she had accumulated over the years.

There was a copy of his official Spanish birth certificate and adoption papers. She had hired a London firm that specialized in this type of work to trace the Machado family back three centuries. A copy of the family tree and the Machado heraldic arms were in the front pockets of the journal.

There was also the baby bootee she had retrieved from under his cot in the flat in Málaga. She had pasted in the copies of the reports from his nursery school and the pediatric clinic, together with every photograph they had ever sent her. On the alternate pages she wrote her own comments and descriptions of her feelings of love and hope and despair.

When she returned to Weltevreden she added the lock of his hair and the photographs she had taken of him to her hoard, and included a description of their interlude together. She even recorded their conversations and every amusing or poignant comment he had made.

Whenever she felt deeply depressed and unhappy she would lock herself in her suite, retrieve the journal from her personal safe and gloat over every item in it.

It gave her the strength to go on.

# 24

The Beechcraft banked into a steep descending turn, and the release of gravity made Isabella feel light in the near seat.

"There." Garry shouted from the pilot's left front seat. "See them? At the foot of the hill. Three of them."

Isabella stared down at the forest top and the broken ground along the rim of the escarpment. The rock was fractured into battlements and turrets, wild cliffs and tumbled towers like the ruins of some fabulous fairy castle.

The forest filled the valleys and the ravines between the rocky castles with splendid chaos; great tree trunks towered up a hundred feet or more, their widespread branches clothed in autumn livery, gilded with all the amalgams of gold and copper and bronze. Others of the great trees were already bare of leaf; the bloated baobabs with their reptilian bark squatted grotesque as creatures from the age of the dinosaurs. At the very wing tip of the Beechcraft a giant African ebony flashed by, its leaves still a dark shining green, its top branches studded with ripe yellow fruit.

A flock of green pigeons hurled themselves into the air in wild alarm, darting by so close that she could see their bright yellow beaks and the beady shine of their eyes. Then abruptly the forest ended and a glade of pale winter grass stretched below them. The Beechcraft roared straight at the tall cliff of rock on the far side.

"There! Can you see them, Bella?" Garry called again.

"Yes! Yes! Aren't they magnificent?" she shouted back.

At the far end of the clearing, three bull elephants were running in single file. Their ears were spread wide as the lateen sail on an Arab dhow. Their backs were humped so that she could see the curved and crested ridge of the spine beneath the grey hide and the gleam of long curved ivory carried high.

As they flashed twenty feet over the lead bull, it turned to confront them, reaching up with a long serpentine trunk as though to pluck them from the sky. Garry pulled back on the control column, gravity sucked at Isabella's bowels, and the aircraft hurtled up to skim the raw blue granite, then bore up high into the cloudless African sky.

"That big one would go all of seventy pounds." Garry judged the weight of the bull's tusks as he twisted in his seat, looking back over his shoulder, flying by instinct alone, even in this critical angle of climb.

"Are they in our area, Pater?" he asked as he rotated the nose down and eased back on the throttle and pitch to resume level flight.

"On the edge of it." Shasa, in the right-hand seat beside him, was relaxed. He had taught Garry to fly and knew his capabilities. "That's the national park over there—you can see the cutline through the forest that marks the boundary."

"Those old jumbo are heading straight for it." Isabella leaned on the back of her father's seat, and he turned and grinned at her.

"You bet your sweet life they are," he agreed.

"You mean they know which is hunting concession and which is the sanctuary?"

"Like you know the way to your own bathroom. At the very first hint of trouble they head for home and mother."

"Can you see the camp?" Garry asked.

"Just south of that kopje." Shasa pointed ahead through the windscreen. "There, now you can see the smoke. The landing strip runs parallel to that dark patch of Jesse bush."

Garry eased the power again, sinking back toward the wilderness, winging low over the rough bush strip to check that it was clear.

A small herd of zebra that had been grazing on the grass strip scattered at their approach and plunged away at full gallop. Each of them towed a pale feather of dust behind it.

"Damned donkeys," Garry muttered. "Hit one of those and he'll take your wing off."

Below her Isabella saw an open truck parked near the crude windsock. She looked for her elder brother at the wheel, but it was one of his black drivers. She felt a tingle of disappointment. She hadn't seen Sean in over two years, and she missed him.

Garry turned the twin-engined Beechcraft onto final approach and lined up with the strip. He lowered the undercarriage, and three green lights lit up on the dashboard. His hands were powerful and sure on the controls as he completed his landing checks and brought her in at a steep angle to avoid the treetops that crowded the strip.

"He is a marvelous pilot," Isabella said, admiring his technique. "Almost as good as Pater."

Garry had flown them up from Johannesburg in the company jet. They had stayed over in Salisbury at the Monomatapa Hotel. Shasa and Garry had had a meeting with Ian Smith, the Rhodesian prime minister. Then they had flown this last leg in the smaller Beechcraft. The jet needed a thousand meters of metaled runway to make a safe landing, whereas the twin-engined Beechcraft could sneak into the short grass strip at Chiwewe with a skillful pilot at the controls.

It was a full-flap landing, and Garry set the plane down firmly with no float or bounce. The machine jolted and pitched on the rough surface. He thrust on maximum safe braking as the wall of trees at the far end of the strip rushed toward them. Then he wheeled the plane with another burst of engine and taxied in a blown dust devil to where a truck waited for them.

The camp staff swarmed around the Beechcraft the moment Garry cut the engines. Shasa opened the hatch and jumped down off the wing to shake their hands and greet each one of them in strict order of seniority. Most of the safari staff had been with the company from the beginning, so Shasa knew each of them by name.

The pleasure of the camp staff was even greater when Isabella jumped down off the wing, and those marvelous white African smiles stretched to the limit. Although her visits to Chiwewe were intermittent, she was a firm favorite amongst them. They called her Kwezi, the Morning Star.

"I have fresh tomatoes and lettuce for you, Kwezi," Lot, the head gardener, assured her. The garden at Chiwewe camp was fertilized with buffalo and elephant dung and yielded fruit and vegetables that would have won prizes at any agricultural show. They all knew Kwezi's weakness for salads.

"I put your tent at the end, Kwezi," Isaac, the camp butler, told her. "So you can listen to the birds in the morning. Chef has got your special *rooibos* tea for you." The herbal tea from the Cape mountains was another of Isabella's weaknesses.

Garry ran the Beechcraft into its jackal-wire hangar to prevent the lions and hyenas gnawing on the tires during the night. The staff loaded their baggage onto the back of the open truck. Then with Garry at the Toyota's wheel they bumped along the rough track through the combretum forest.

It had been a good rainy season, and game was plentiful. The sandy track was dimpled with their spoor. When they came out into the wide glade in front of the camp, there were herds of zebra and sleek red-brown impala standing out unafraid on the silvery winter-grass pasture. It was one of Sean's strict rules that no shot was ever fired within two miles of the camp. This was no inhibiting restriction, for the Chiwewe concession spread over ten thousand square kilometers.

The camp overlooked the glade and the muddy water hole at its center. Later in the season, when the water dried up, the game would migrate. Then Sean would be obliged to pack up this entire camp and follow them down the escarpment to his other campsite on the shore of Lake Kariba.

The row of green tents was set back discreetly within the forest, each with its own shower and earthen toilet standing behind it. The dining tent was surrounded by a thatch-walled *boma* that was open to the sky. The canvas camp chairs were set around the campfire, great logs of leadwood and mopane that were kept burning day and night. The camp servants all wore crisply starched uniforms, and Isaac, as camp butler, sported a crimson sash over one shoulder.

A portable generator provided lighting and power for the bank of refrigerators and deep freezers in the mud-walled pantry. From his thatched kitchen the chef conjured up a sequence of gourmet dishes. There were all the refinements of what was known as a "Hemingway camp." Chief among these were the tubs of ice on the bar table and the regiments of liquor bottles drawn up in ranks. There were five different brands of premium whisky and three of single malt. A grand cru Chablis Vaudésir reposed in a silver ice bucket. There were also the ingredients for Pimm's No. 1 and Bloody Marys, to cater to those with more mundane tastes. All the glasses were Stuart crystal. The types of clients who could afford the safari fees expected and made damn sure they got these basic necessities of life.

The uniformed attendants had filled the tanks of the individual showers with piping hot water. While the guests washed off the dust and grime of their travels, they unpacked and laid out their safari clothes in each tent.

Bathed and refreshed, the family gathered at the campfire, and Shasa glanced at his wristwatch.

"Bit early for a peg?"

"Nonsense," said Garry. "We are on holiday." He called the barman to take their orders.

Isabella sipped her cold white wine. For the first time in almost two years she felt safe and at peace, and incongruously she thought of Michael. He was the only thing missing. She watched the procession of beautiful wild animals coming down to drink at the water hole and listened to her father and Garry with only half her attention.

They were discussing Sean's client. He was a German industrialist named Otto Heider.

"He's twenty years older than Sean, but they are soulmates. Both of them are thrusters. God, they take some chances together," Shasa told them. "The more hairy and dangerous the action, the more old Otto loves it. He won't hunt with anybody except Sean."

"I had Special Services run a full report on him," Garry nodded. Special Services was a closed section of Courtney Enterprises whose director reported directly to Garry. It was his private intelligence system. It dealt with everything from company security to industrial espionage. "Otto Heider is a player, all right. The list of his assets runs to four typed pages, but he is a wild player. I don't think we should get financially involved with him. He takes too many chances. According to my calculations, he is undercapitalized by at least three billion Deutschmarks.''

"I agree." Shasa inclined his head. "He's an interesting character, but not for us. Do you know he brings his own blood bank on safari, just in case he gets stamped on by an elephant or hooked by a buffalo?''

"No, I didn't know that." Garry sat forward in his camp chair.

"Fresh, sweet blood." Shasa smiled. "On the hoof, so to speak. Self-administering transfusions.''

"What does that mean?" Even Isabella was interested.

"He brings two qualified nurses with him. Both blond, both beautiful and under twenty-five years old, both blood type AB positive. If he needs blood, he can tap it straight off one of them and at the same time have expert nursing care.''

Garry let out an admiring snort of laughter. "And even if he does not need blood, they are still extremely useful items to have on a safari. The transfusions simply flow in the opposite direction.''

"You're disgusting, Garry." Isabella smiled.

"Not me! Old Otto is the disgusting one. I think I'm changing my opinion of him. We might still do business together. Such forethought is most commendable.''

"Forget it. Otto is flying out first thing in the morning with his two nurses. The client we are really interested in arrives tomorrow afternoon. Sean will drop Otto in Salisbury and bring the other one back—'' Shasa broke off and shaded his eyes, staring out across the wide glade in front of the camp.

"I hear Sean's truck. Yes, there he comes.''

The tiny shape of a hunting vehicle darted out of the forest edge a mile away across the open grassland.

"Master Sean is in a real hurry.''

The sound of the truck engine mounted to a roar. A tall column of dust rose into the still evening sky. The animals at the water hole panicked and galloped for the trees.

As the distance closed rapidly, they could make out the occupants of the open Toyota. The cab and the bodywork had been removed and the windscreen lay flat over the engine bonnet. On a high rear seat were four figures, Sean's two black trackers in khaki fatigues and two white women. These, Isabella presumed, were the German nurses, for they fitted the description, young and blond and pretty.

In the front of the passenger seat was a middle-aged man dressed in custom-tailored safari clothing. He wore gold-rimmed spectacles and a leopard-skin band around his Stetson. He exuded an air of jaunty self-confidence that marked him as Otto Heider, the client they had been discussing.

Sean was at the wheel of the speeding Toyota, and Isabella could not restrain herself. She jumped up from the camp chair and ran to the gate of the *boma*.

Sean wore a bush shirt with two heavy-caliber brass cartridges in the loops on his breast. His shirtsleeves had been cut away at the shoulders, so that his arms were bare. His muscles were tanned and glowing with abundant health as though they had been oiled. His shoulder-length hair was cut in a Prince Valiant bob. The Comanche-style leather thong around his forehead could not restrain the shimmering jet black locks that danced and fluttered like a flag around his head as he drove the truck at high speed up to the entrance of the *boma*.

He hit the brakes so hard that the heavy vehicle spun into a broadside and came to a halt in a billowing cloud of dust. Sean leapt out and strode toward them. His khaki shorts were cut away high on the thighs, and his sockless feet were thrust into kudu-skin *velskoen*.

"Sean!" Isabella let out a happy cry, but he brushed past her with an expression of dark fury on his face. She stared after him in bewilderment.

Sean ignored his father as he had his sister and stopped in front of his younger brother.

"Just what the hell do you think you are playing at?" he asked in a voice that rang with cold fury. Garry's happy grin faded.

"And I'm glad to see you also." Garry's tone was mild, but his eyes sparkled with annoyance behind his spectacles.

Sean reached down and seized the front of Garry's shirt. With one clean jerk, he lifted his brother out of the canvas chair. It was a feat of brute strength, for Garry was a big, solidly built man.

"Let me tell you a little secret," Sean said. "I spend four days getting into position for a shot at the only decent bull I've seen all season. At the critical moment you come barging in like von Richthofen and rev the hell out of us!"

"Look, Sean, I didn't—" Garry tried to placate him, but Sean wasn't even listening.

"You goddam pen-pushing office wallah. You soft-arsed tourist playing tough guy. Who the hell are you trying to impress?"

"Sean." Garry held up both hands, palms open. "Come on, be reasonable. How was I to know?"

"Reasonable? When you shoot up my concession and chase the hell out of my jumbo? Reasonable? When you screw up my best client and the last shot we will get at a big bull this safari?"

"I said I'm sorry."

"If you're sorry now, just think how sorry you're going to be five minutes from now," said Sean. With his left hand still gripping Garry's shirt, he shoved him backward. Instinctively Garry resisted. Instantly Sean reversed the pressure, and it took Garry by surprise.

Sean did not cock his right hand. He threw the punch only five inches, but the full power of his broad muscled shoulders was behind it and Garry was moving into it. Garry's teeth clicked together in his jaw. As he staggered backward his spectacles spun from his head. The camp chair caught him at the back of his knees; he went over backward, falling heavily and awkwardly.

"Damn it, that felt good," said Sean, clenching and unclenching his right hand as he moved around the overturned chair to reach him again.

"Sean!" Isabella recovered from her shock. "Stop it, Sean! Leave him alone!" She ran forward to interpose herself between her brothers, but Shasa caught her arm to restrain her. Although she struggled to be free, he held her easily.

Garry struggled into a sitting position. His expression was dazed. A little trail of blood crept out of one nostril, and he tried to sniff it back. Then he lifted his hand and smeared it across his upper lip. He held the bloodied hand close to his myopic eyes and inspected it with disbelief.

"Come on, big shot." Sean was standing over him. "Get on your feet. I've been saving up for this."

"Leave him alone, Sean. Please!" Isabella hated the violence and the blood and this terrifying anger between two people she loved so dearly. "Stop it! Stop it!"

"Quiet, Bella!" Her father shook her sharply. "Keep out of this."

Still sitting in the dust, Garry shook himself like a great St. Bernard dog.

"Come on, Mr. bloody chairman of the board," Sean taunted him. "Get on your feet, Mr. businessman of the sodding year. Let's see your style, Mr. *Fortune* magazine five hundred."

"Leave them, Bella." Shasa still held her. "This had to come. It's been brewing for twenty years. Let them work it out." Suddenly Isabella understood. Sean's choice of jibes was an expression of the envy and resentment he had accumulated over a lifetime.

Sean was the firstborn, the golden princeling, the pick of the litter. All those honors and titles should have been his. He should have been the prime recipient of his father's favor and approbation, and yet he had lost it all. It had been stolen away from him by the runt.

"Piss-bed," said Sean. "Four-eyes." Those were childhood insults. Isabella had a vivid memory of the lordly superiority of the elder brother. She remembered how in the Cape winters of their childhood, when the snow lay thick on the Hottentots Holland mountains, Sean would turn Garry out of bed in the dawn and send him to sit on the toilet to warm the seat for him. She remembered a hundred other episodes of humiliation and casual bullying by which Sean had reinforced his domination over the weakling.

Garry came to his feet. He had applied twenty years of unremitting labor to building up the sickly body he had been born with. Now his chest was a barrel of muscle, and coarse body hair curled out of the $V$ of his shirtfront. His limbs were almost grotesquely overdeveloped. However, he stood almost four inches shorter than his elder brother as they confronted each other.

"That," he said quietly, "is the last time. It will never happen again. Do you understand?"

"No." Sean shook his head, his anger contained behind a mocking smile. "I don't understand, Piss-bed. You are going to have to explain it to me."

The German client and his two nubile nurses had climbed down from the Toyota and followed Sean into the *boma*. Now they were watching with delighted anticipation.

Without his glasses Garry blinked like an owl, but his teeth clenched so hard that humps of muscles like walnuts bulged on the hinges of his jaw below his ears. Sean leaned forward, balanced on the balls of his feet and slapped Garry's cheek lightly, still smiling mockingly. Garry went for him.

He was fast for such a heavy man, the way a bull buffalo is fast, the way an old mugger crocodile is fast, but Sean was fast as a leopard. He ducked under Garry's rush and threw a left-hander into his belly just below the sternum of his ribs. It was like throwing a brick at a battle tank. Garry did not even grunt. He merely hunched his shoulders and came in again.

Sean weaved and danced ahead of him, the insolent grin still on his lips. He was letting Garry come to him and counter-punching with the rushes. His blows thudded on rubbery muscle as though he were beating a truck tire with a baseball bat.

The German nurses were squealing with happy horror. The camp servants came running from the kitchen lines. Their heads bobbed up in a row along the low *boma* wall, their eyes wide with fascination.

"Stop them, Daddy," Isabella pleaded, but Shasa was assessing his sons with a calculating eye. So far this was the way he would have expected it to go.

Sean was all flash and style, tossing back his glossy locks after each exchange, taking a moment to glance at his audience, especially the blond nurses.

Garry, on the other hand, was plugging away solidly, making Sean dance and weave to keep out of range of those massive arms. He was obviously willing to take all the body shots Sean could throw at him. However, it was surprisingly difficult for Sean to land on Garry's head. Garry had a trick of hunching his muscled shoulders at the final instant and deflecting Sean's fists.

He was also very quick with his arms, and some of Sean's best punches to the head were caught by Garry's heavy biceps or on his hairy forearms.

At first Garry's rushes seemed to be without purpose. Then Shasa realized he was remorselessly driving Sean back into the corner wall of the *boma*, attempting to pin and grapple him there. Each time, Sean managed to break clear and Garry would begin all over again. He was as patient as a sheepdog, working him into the position he wanted, grimly accepting the punishment Sean was inflicting. Blood from his nostril was running into his mouth and dripping from his chin onto the front of his khaki bush shirt.

By this time Sean's mocking grin was becoming a little strained, and the flow of taunts had long since dried up. His movements were no longer so crisp. On the other hand, Garry moved with the same ponderous rhythm and momentum, pushing Sean back, back, always back. Sean's punches were losing their snap, and he threw them less prolifically.

Then Garry blocked him as he tried to pirouette away to the right, anticipating his move precisely. Sean backpedaled quickly to regain poise and felt the thatch of the wall touch his back. He ducked to go under Garry's outstretched arm, and Garry let his first punch fly.

All the spectators gasped, and one of the nurses squeaked shrilly. Garry's punch was a thunderbolt with two hundred pounds of muscle and bone and determination driving it. It hissed through the air and, although Sean caught it on his guard, it drove on through. It crashed against the curved dome of his skull, high above the hairline, with a force that made his long shining hair swirl and flicker as though a gust of wind had caught it.

For an instant Sean's eyes rolled fully backward in their sockets, giving him a blind white stare. His knees buckled and sagged under him. Then he partially recovered, but his face was frosted with pain and his mouth was twisted with panic as he tried to avoid the next bearlike rush.

Garry charged in, eagerly seizing the moment for which he had worked so doggedly. His arms were spread as though to welcome an old friend or a lover. Suddenly he kicked and spurted like a long-distance runner hearing the bell for the final lap. He had fooled them all, including Sean. They had thought those ponderous rushes were all the speed he had, but suddenly there was more, much more.

In the same fashion a buffalo bull charges in for the kill, crabbing across the front of his victim, lulling him, making him doubt that he is really the focus of all that mountainous aggression. Then at the last moment he turns with bewildering speed to hook and gore and trample.

Half stunned, Sean could not avoid him. Garry's arms snapped around him in a murderous hug, and the momentum of his charge carried them both onward into the dining tent. The bar table went over in a shower of ancient spirits, noble wines and precious crystal. They trampled the glittering splinters underfoot, and a heady cloud of fumes enveloped them for a moment before they barged onward.

The long dining table spread with Madeira lace crashed over. The Rosenthal dinner service burst into ten thousand expensive splinters. As they went out through the back of the tent, they ripped out the guy ropes and the canvas sagged into weary folds. The servants scattered with cries of alarm and excitement and encouragement.

In a ferocious waltz, they whirled each other in erratic circles. Garry's grip was unshakable. He had double-locked his wrists behind his brother's back. His arms convulsed, rippling with muscle as they tightened like a python crushing its prey.

One of Sean's arms was trapped in that deadly circle. With his free fist, he beat wildly at Garry's head, but he lacked purchase and the blows had no sting. Although one caught Garry in the mouth and split his lip, it left his big white teeth intact. He merely ducked his head, slitted his eyes and squeezed and squeezed.

With an approving roar from the black audience and feminine squeals from Sean's admirers, they lunged into the far side of the thatched *boma* wall and it burst open.

The two of them, still locked together, came storming back onto the central stage. One of the nurses was not quick enough to avoid them. She was knocked over in a tangle of long tanned legs, flaring skirts and lacy underwear that might have stopped any lesser show. Nobody even glanced at her.

Garry was trying to swing Sean off his feet, lifting him high with each turn. Although Sean's face was swelling and darkening with blood from the constriction of his chest and breathing, he managed like a cat to come down on his feet after each wild swing until Garry steered him into the middle of the campfire. Sean's legs were bare, and the flames licked at them, frizzling the hair off his calves, scorching the thin kudu-skin *velskoen*.

Sean let out a howl of anguish and bounded high in his brother's arms. He managed to jump clear of the fire, but Garry's grip was inexorable. Grunting with the effort, he forced Sean slowly backward, bending him like a longbow. Sean's scorched legs buckled, and he sank lower and lower. His knees touched the ground, and Garry bent over him and grunted again as he tightened the circle of his arms another inch.

The air was forced from Sean's lungs in a long hollow groan, and his face suffused with dark blood. Garry grunted again, and his grip tightened another notch, remorseless as a mechanical steel press. Sean's eyes began to bulge from their sockets, and his jaw fell open. His tongue lolled out between his teeth.

"Garry! You are killing him!" Isabella screamed, her concern moving from one brother to the other. Her father held her, and Garry showed no sign of having heard her. He grunted yet again and squeezed.

This time they heard Sean's ribs crack like green twigs. He cried out and went slack as a half-empty bag of wheat in Garry's arms. Garry dropped him and stood back, breathing heavily. His own face was flushed and swollen with the effort.

Sean tried to sit up, but the pain of the cracked ribs lanced him and he moaned again and clutched his chest. Garry

301

smoothed back his hair with both hands, but the unruly crest at the crown of his scalp sprang up again immediately.

"Right," said Garry calmly. "From now on you will behave yourself. Do you hear me?"

Sean managed to push himself up onto his knees with one hand, clutching his chest with the other.

"Do you hear me?" Garry asked again, standing over him.

"Screw you," Sean whispered. The effort hurt his chest.

Garry leaned over and prodded his injured chest with a thick, hard thumb.

"Do you hear me?"

"Okay, okay!" Sean yelped. "I hear you!"

"Good." Garry nodded and turned to the hovering nurses. "Fräulein," he said in passable German, "I think we have need of your professional services."

They rushed forward clucking. One on each side of him, they raised Sean to his feet and led him away to his tent.

Shasa released Isabella's arm.

"Well," he murmured. "That seems to have sorted that out at last." Then he glanced at the shambles of the dining tent.

"I do hope that wasn't the last bottle of Chivas."

Garry sat on the camp bed stripped to the waist while Isabella anointed his bruises with arnica salve from the first-aid box. Hectic blotches left by Sean's fists covered his arms and upper body like the dappling of a giraffe's hide. His nose was swollen, and his lip was lumped and crusted with fresh scab.

"I think it's an improvement," Isabella told him. "Before your face was only half nose, now it is all nose."

Garry chuckled and pinched the end of it gingerly. "We have taken care of Master Sean. Now it seems as though you are next on the list to be taught a little respect."

She kissed the top of his head where the tuft stood up from his crown. "Teddy Bear," she said. "You know, Garry, Holly is a lucky girl; you are one hell of a man." He blushed; he actually blushed, and her love for him was confirmed and strengthened. He was no longer comical, even with the bloated nose and thick upper lip.

Sean groaned again, theatrically, and Otto Heider threw back his head and laughed.

"Here!" He poured another three fingers of whisky into the tumbler that stood on the bedside table. "This is for the pain, like chloroform."

Sean leaned across to take the glass and tossed back the whisky. "I've been jumped on by buffalo and kicked by jumbo, but this one— Hey, Trudi, take it easy."

Trudi paused with the surgical tape in her hand and kissed him full on the lips.

"Be quiet," she said. "I am fixing you." She had a sexy German lisp and soft red lips.

"You are a great little fixer," he admitted. She tinkled with laughter and resumed work on his injured chest, passing the tape under his armpit to Erica, who sat behind Sean on his king-size bed.

"No more *humsen* for you." Erica smiled severely. "Not for many long times." And she passed the tape under his other armpit, back to Trudi.

Otto Heider laughed again. "Are you going to retire injured and leave me to take care of these two little vixen all on my own?" Otto was amazingly generous to his friends, and Sean was an old friend. Otto shared with his friends. The four of them—Otto, Trudi, Erica and Sean—had done more than merely hunt together. It had been a fun safari. Except for the elephant that Garry had messed up, they had all enjoyed themselves immensely.

"You no good anymore. But your brother—he strong like a bull." Trudi slanted her eyes wickedly. "He fight good. You think he *bumsen* good?"

Sean stared at her thoughtfully for a moment. Then he began to grin. "My brother is a prude, a prig. He was almost certainly a virgin when he married that po-faced wench of his. I doubt he would know what to do with a good piece of *bumsen* if you waved it under his nose."

"We show him what to do with it," Trudi promised. "Me and Erica, we show him good."

"What do you think, Otto?" Sean looked across at his client. "Can I borrow the ladies tonight? It shouldn't take long? I'll have them back at your tent by midnight."

Otto shook his head with admiration. "My friend, you are one funny man. You always make such good jokes. Hey, girls, you like it? What you think? It's a funny joke, hey?"

Sean was laughing with them, holding his injured ribs to cushion them. However, there was a vindictive gleam in his eyes.

Sean understood better than any of them what had happened that day. It had been much more than another brotherly brawl that he had provoked. It had been the ultimate territorial contest of two young bulls in a final battle for dominance and rank. He had lost, and the defeat rankled deeply.

He knew that he could never seriously challenge again. Garry had beaten him in every sphere, from the boardroom to the physical arena. Garry was at last unassailable. All Sean could do now was adulterate his power. He wanted to lay in a little insurance against the stormy days he was sure lay ahead.

Garry was having a dream. It was extraordinarily vivid and real. He was being pursued across an open meadow by a horde of dancing wood nymphs, and his legs were lead beneath him. Each pace was an effort, as though he were wading through a swamp of hot treacle.

He could see Holly and the children standing at the far side of the meadow. She was holding the baby in her arms, and the other children crowded about her legs, clinging to her skirts. Holly was calling something to him, although he could not hear the words. Tears poured from those lovely bicolored eyes of hers.

He tried to reach her, but he felt the soft warm hands of the nymphs on his body, holding him back. He tried to shrug off the hands, but the effort was unconvincing. In despair he saw Holly and the children turn away from him. She gathered the little ones closer around her, and they faded away into the woods beyond the meadow.

He tried to call them to wait, but his own thoughts and feelings were confused. The hands on him were exciting. Suddenly his own arousal was overpowering. He no longer wanted to escape. He didn't want the dream to end, for even in his sleep he realized it was a dream.

He let himself flow with the fantasy, and there were smooth warm bodies pressing close around him. The smell of excited young womanhood was sweet and irresistible in his nostrils. He heard their laughter muffled by his own flesh and the startling sensation of their hot lubricious mouths upon him.

Holly and the children were gone; he had forgotten them, their images erased by his lust. He felt himself surrendering to it completely.

Then suddenly he was wide awake and he realized it was not a dream. His bed was filled with squirming bodies. They swarmed over him. He did not know how many hands were stroking and pressing and tugging and caressing him. Silky hair washed over his face like seawater. Hot wet little tongues licked and probed at him. Long smooth limbs wrapped and enveloped him.

For a moment longer he lay quiescent. Then he let out a cry and sprang upright. Moonlight poured into his tent. The naked feminine bodies glowed like opals as they clung to him.

His elder brother was sitting on the end of his bed. Sean's chest was wrapped in white tape, but there was a boyish grin on his face. "You have won first prize, Garry, old fruit. To the victor the spoils. Enjoy, lad, enjoy!"

"You bastard!" Garry reached for him.

But Sean was gone with an alacrity that disregarded the injuries to his chest. The two girls scrambled out of the rumpled bed in a confusion of limbs and bouncing bosoms and bobbing white buttocks.

Garry grabbed them, one under each arm, and lifted them as easily as he would a pair of kittens. He carried them out of his tent. They squealed and kicked ineffectually in the air.

He saw his father in the doorway of his tent belting his dressing gown.

"I say, old chap, what's going on?"

"My darling brother put a bunch of vermin in my bed. Just getting rid of them," Garry told him politely.

"Pity," said Shasa. "Awful waste." But Garry marched on. Shasa sauntered along behind him, hands in the pockets of his dressing gown, grinning with amusement.

Isabella was in a short lace nightie, wide-eyed with sleep as she stumbled out of her tent. "Garry, what on earth have you got there?"

"I should have thought that was fairly obvious."

"Two, Garry? Isn't that a bit greedy?"

"Ask Sean. It was his idea."

"What are you going to do with them? May I come along?"

"Delighted. You and Pater can report to Holly for me."

Garry led the small procession out of the camp, across the glade and down to the edge of the water hole. It was a cold night, and frost crunched under their feet. The approach to the water hole had been trampled into a greasy black porridge by the hoofs of the game that drank from it.

"Please, we make little joke," Trudi trilled from under Garry's arm, wriggling weakly.

"It is joke," Erica agreed tearfully. "Please to let go." She had slipped around and hung headdown in Garry's grip. Her bare bottom flashed in the light of the moon, and she bicycled her legs in the air.

"Me, too," Garry told them. "I make little joke. I think my joke better than your little joke."

His first throw was not his best, a mere twenty feet. But, then, Erica was the plumper and heavier of the two and she classed as a ranging shot. His second throw was much better, all of thirty feet, and Trudi shrieked in flight. The sound was cut off abruptly as she plunged below the icy water.

Both girls came up spluttering and wailing miserably under a coat of glistening black mud.

"Now, that," said Garry, "is what I call a real joke."

# 25

Sean was late for breakfast. He paused in the entrance to the dining tent, and his eyes narrowed as he glanced around.

The servants had made good most of the damage. The broken furniture had been repaired by the camp handyman during the night. Isaac had put together a scratch dinner service to replace the breakages. Trudi and Erica had washed off most of the mud, but their hair was still drying in colored plastic curlers. However, none of this held Sean's attention.

He looked at his place at the end of the long table. It was his camp, and that seat was his by tradition and custom. Everybody knew that. His name was printed on the canvas back of the chair.

Garry was sitting in his chair. The swelling of his nose had subsided considerably, and he had repaired the side frame of his damaged spectacles. His hair was still wet from the shower. He looked big and cocky and self-satisfied, and he was sitting in Sean's chair.

He looked up at Sean from his hunter's breakfast of impala liver and onions and scrambled eggs. "Morning, Sean," he said cheerfully. "Get me a cup of coffee while you're up."

There was a sudden silence at the table. Every one of them

watched Sean for his reaction. Slowly Sean's scowl faded and he smiled.

"How many sugars?" he asked as he went to the sideboard and took the coffeepot out of Isaac's hands.

"Two will do." Garry resumed eating, and an audible ripple of relief ran down the table. Everybody started talking again at the same time.

Sean brought his younger brother the coffee mug, and Garry nodded. "Thanks, Sean. Sit down." He indicated the empty chair beside him. "We have got a few things to discuss."

Isabella wanted desperately to listen to the conversation, but the two German girls were giggling and chattering, flirting with Shasa and Otto indiscriminately. She knew Garry was setting out the program of meetings that would be taking place in this camp over the next few days. The names of the visitors and every detail about them would be important to her, and to Nicky.

"What about this Italian woman? You've had her as a client before. What's she like?" she heard Garry ask.

Sean shrugged. "Elsa Pignatelli? Swiss Italian. She shoots well, when you can get her to shoot. Never takes a chance, but when she pulls that trigger something falls down. I've never seen her miss."

Garry thought about that for a moment, then nodded. "Anything else?"

"She's bloody-minded. Wants things done her way, and you can't slip anything over on her—eyes in the back of her head. I tried to pad the bill a little. She picked it up right away."

Garry nodded. "Doesn't surprise me. She's one of the richest women in Europe. Pharmaceuticals and chemicals. Heavy engineering, jet engines, armaments. She has run the show since her husband died seven years ago. She has a tough reputation."

"Last season we took a full-out charge from a wounded jumbo in thick Jesse bush. She stood her ground and put him down with a frontal brain shot at twenty paces. Then she turned on me and chewed me up. Accused me of firing at her elephant. She's tough, all right."

"Anything else? Any weaknesses? Liquor?" Garry asked.

Sean shook his head. "One glass of champagne every evening. Fresh bottle of Dom Pérignon each time. She drinks one glass and sends the rest away. Fifty dollars a bottle."

"Anything else?" Garry stared at him through his thick spectacles.

Sean grinned. "Come on, Garry. She's an old aunty—must be all of fifty."

"Actually, she is forty-two," Garry contradicted him.

Sean sighed. "Okay, you want to know if we played hide-the-sausage together. Look, I made the offer. Hell, it's expected of me. That's part of the service. She laughed. She said she didn't want to be arrested for child abuse." He shook his head. Sean didn't like admitting to sexual failure.

"Pity! We have to do business with her," Garry pointed out. "I need any leverage I can lay my hands on."

"I'll bring her in at five this afternoon," Sean promised. "Then she's all yours, and the best of British luck to you."

They all drove out to the airstrip to give Otto and his nurses a send-off. The mood was gay.

Not only had the German girls forgiven Garry for their midnight dunking, he seemed to have won their esteem and piqued their interest by his forthright refusal of their offer. They made a huge fuss over him, kissing and hugging him and ruffling his hair until he blushed again.

"Next time we make good jokes again," they promised him. They waved furiously through the side windows as the Beechcraft roared down the airstrip and flashed into the air. Half a mile out and two hundred feet high, Sean threw the aircraft into a maximum-rate turn and came diving back on them, flashing barely twenty feet over their heads. The girls in the backseat were still waving.

"Cowboy!" gruffed Garry as he climbed behind the wheel of the Toyota. "Are you coming, Bella?"

"I'll drive back with Pater," she called. She knew it would be easier for her to pump her father than her brother. She ran to the second truck and jumped up into the seat beside Shasa.

They were halfway back to the camp before she got her chance.

"So who is Elsa Pignatelli?" she asked sweetly. "And why haven't I heard of her before?"

Shasa looked startled. "How did you find out about her?"

"Don't you trust me, Pater? I am your personal assistant, aren't I?" Cunningly she saddled him with guilt, and immediately he began trying to exonerate himself. "Forgive me, Bella. It's not that I don't trust you. It's all rather hush-hush."

"She is the main reason for us all being here, isn't that so?"

But Shasa was still being evasive.

"Elsa Pignatelli is an avid huntress, a veritable Diana. She has hunted with Sean for the last three seasons. Her passion is hunting cats—lion and leopard. You know that Sean has a reputation for bringing in big cats."

"We haven't come to watch her kill cats," Isabella pressed him. Shasa shook his head and relented. "Amongst the Pignatelli assets are a number of chemical factories—pharmaceuticals, agricultural fertilizers and pesticides, plastics and paints. They hold certain patents that we are interested in."

"So why didn't Garry fly to Geneva or Rome, or wherever she lives?"

"Lausanne, actually."

"So why didn't he go to her, or why didn't she send one of her people to meet him in Johannesburg, instead of this Tarzan setting in the jungle? What precisely is all the mystery?"

Shasa slowed the truck and gave all his attention to negotiating the rocky ford of the river. He did not reply until they were climbing the steep opposite bank in four-wheel drive.

"Forgive me for not letting you in on it. I was going to tell you. Our interests are not confined entirely to agricultural pesticides. There would be a lot of unfriendly people out there in the big wide world who would be very interested in any discussions between Pignatelli Industries and the chairman of Armscor."

"Ah, you are wearing your Armscor hat, so it must be armaments or weapons."

Shasa glanced across at her speculatively. She had a brightly colored scarf bound around her like a turban, and the wind had rouged her cheeks. She was very lovely, and Shasa felt a prickle of guilt that he should have mistrusted her. She was part of him; he should trust her as he did his own self.

"You and I have discussed the weapons of last resort," he murmured.

"Not nuclear weapons?" Isabella said. "You have the bomb already. All that fuss over Operation Skylight."

"No, not nuclear weapons," he sighed. "Something just as nasty, I'm afraid. You know that I share your distaste for weapons of mass indiscriminate destruction. However, such weapons are not intended ever to be used. Their effectiveness lies in their mere existence."

"If they exist, then sooner or later some madman is going to use them," she said flatly.

Again Shasa shook his head. "We've been over this before, my darling. But the bare fact remains that I have been entrusted with the job of providing our nation with all possible means of protecting itself. I have not been given the option of deciding which weapons are morally acceptable."

"Do we really need some other nastiness?" she insisted.

"There is a groundswell of hatred running against our little country. It is being cunningly orchestrated by a small, vicious group of our enemies. They are brainwashing an entire generation of young people around the world to regard us as monsters who must be destroyed at all costs. Very soon these young people will be in positions of authority and command. They are the decision makers of tomorrow. One day we could see an American naval task force blockading our coast. We could face a military invasion of, say, Indian troops backed by Australia and Canada and all the members of the Commonwealth."

"Oh, Papa, that is farfetched. Isn't it?"

"Still remote," Shasa agreed. "But you met influential members of the British Labor Government while we were in London. You spoke to members of the American Democratic Party—Teddy Kennedy for one. Do you remember what he told you?"

"Yes, I remember," said Isabella, and the memory subdued her.

"We must make absolutely certain that no nation—not even one of the superpowers—can ever with impunity consider armed intervention in our internal affairs."

"We already have the bomb," she pointed out.

"Nuclear weapons are expensive, difficult to deliver and impossible to limit or control in their effects. There are other effective deterrents."

"Elsa Pignatelli is going to provide an alternative? Why should she help us?"

"Signora Pignatelli is a sympathizer. She is a member of the Italian South Africa Society. She knows and understands Africa. She is a huntress, and she has other ties with this continent. Her father was on General de Bono's staff when he invaded Abyssinia in 1935. Her husband fought in the Western Desert under Rommel and was captured at Benghazi. He spent three years as a POW in South Africa and developed an affection for the country that lasted his lifetime. He transmitted those feelings to her. She visits Africa regularly, either to hunt or to do business. She understands the problems we face and rejects, as we do, the simplistic solutions the rest of the world would try to force upon us. This meeting was arranged at her suggestion."

Isabella wanted to ask questions, but she knew it was wiser to let him come to it in his own time.

She sat silently staring at the rutted track, barely noticing the herd of impala that crossed ahead of the vehicle in a series of lithe bounds. They were lovely but insubstantial as smoke blown through the forest.

"Only four people know about this meeting, Bella. Signora Pignatelli has not trusted her own staff. Apart from Garry and I, only the prime minister is aware of the subject of our meeting."

Isabella suppressed the sickening sense of treachery that lay at the pit of her stomach. She wanted to warn him not to tell. Then she thought of Nicholas and she sat quietly.

"Five years ago, NATO contracted with two chemical companies in Western Europe to develop a nerve gas that could be used under battlefield conditions. Last autumn the contracts were canceled, mostly due to pressure from the socialist governments of Scandinavia and Holland. However, much work had already been done on the development of these weapons, and one company had produced and tested a gas that met all the original criteria."

"That company was Pignatelli Chemicals?" Isabella asked. When Shasa nodded, she went on, "What were the criteria that NATO laid down?"

"The weapon has to be safe to store and transport. Pignatelli developed two separate substances, each on its own absolutely inert and harmless. They can be transported in bulk tankers by road or by rail without any risk whatsoever. But when they combine they form a heavier-than-air gas which is approximately eleven times more toxic than the cyanide gas used in American execution chambers."

Shasa pulled off the track and parked the truck on the verge beneath the outspread branches of a flowering kigelia tree, the lovely sausage tree, with its gigantic pods the size and shape of polonies.

He lifted Sean's double-barreled .577 Gibbs rifle off the rack behind the driver's seat and loaded it with two fat brass cartridges from the bandolier.

"Let's go down to the hippo pool," he suggested.

Isabella followed him down the footpath to the deep green pool of the river. The rifle was insurance, for hippos have killed more human beings in Africa than all the snakes and lions and buffalo combined.

Yet they did not look dangerous as they wallowed under the bank, only their backs exposed like great black river boulders. Then a bull opened his jaws in a pink, cavernous gape, showing the curved ivory tusks that could scythe papyrus reeds or guillotine a full-grown ox into pieces. He turned his piggy eyes upon them and regarded them with bloodshot malevolence.

They sat side by side on a dead log, and Shasa propped the

rifle close at hand. After a moment the bull hippo closed his jaws and sank back below the surface so that only his eyes and the tips of his small round ears were exposed. Shasa stared back at him just as balefully.

"Eleven times more toxic than cyanide gas," he repeated. "It is terrifying stuff."

"Then, why, Pater? It is heinous. Why do it?"

He shrugged. "To protect ourselves from hatred." He picked up a pebble from between his feet and lobbed it at the hippo. The pebble splashed twenty feet short, but the bull submerged completely. Shasa went on speaking.

"The gas is code-named Cyndex 25, and it has other desirable properties apart from his ability to deal swift and silent death."

"How heartening," Isabella murmured. "What are they?"

"It is odorless. There is no warning; death comes unannounced. However, it can be given a signature, any signature one chooses—the smell of ripe apples, or jasmine, or even Chanel Number Five if you so wish."

"That's macabre, Pater. Not your usual style."

He did not respond to the rebuke. "It is also highly unstable. Decay time is a mere three hours after mixing. Thereafter it is absolutely harmless. This is extremely advantageous. You can gas an opposing army and then move your own troops in to occupy the area three hours later."

"Charming," Isabella whispered. "I have no doubt the political possibilities have not entirely escaped the prime minister. Say, if a million blacks went on the rampage."

Shasa sighed. "It doesn't bear thinking of."

"But you have thought of it, haven't you, Pater?" He was silent, acquiescing. "You say that NATO canceled the contracts. Only Pignatelli Chemicals is manufacturing this Cyndex 25?"

"No. They manufactured and tested the gas. It was the twenty-fifth prototype, hence the numerical designation. But when the NATO contract was canceled they discontinued production and allowed the original stocks to degenerate."

Isabella glanced sideways at him. "Degenerate?"

"As I said before, it is a highly unstable product. It has a very short storage life—six months. New stocks have to be constantly manufactured to replace those that deteriorate."

"Lucrative for Capricorn Chemicals," Isabella pointed out.

Shasa ignored the remark. "Signora Pignatelli will be able to supply us with blueprints for the plant; it is a complicated manufacturing procedure with very delicate manufacturing tolerances.''

"When will you begin to manufacture?" Isabella asked.

Shasa chuckled. "Hold your horses, young lady. It isn't even certain that Signora Pignatelli can be persuaded to sell us the blueprints and the formula. That is what we are going to chat about now." He glanced at his wristwatch. "Almost lunchtime, and we are still half an hour from camp."

Sean called on the camp radio on the "unmanned airfield" frequency when he was still forty minutes out. So they were waiting on the airstrip when the Beechcraft slanted in toward the field that evening.

Shading his eyes against the low lying sun, Shasa made out the head of Sean's passenger through the windscreen as she sat in the right-hand seat. He felt an electric tickle down the back of his neck that was more than simple curiosity. It was extraordinary that he and Elsa Pignatelli had never met, for they came from the same world, that exclusive world of wealth and rank and privilege that knows no national boundaries. They had literally dozens of mutual friends and acquaintances, and he was aware that on several occasions over the years they had been within a few minutes or kilometers of meeting each other. Shasa had been on friendly terms with her husband.

The two men had skied in the same party one afternoon at Klosters and had run the notorious Wang together, that terrible ice wall that hangs above the village. At the time Bruno Pignatelli had apologized for his wife's absence but explained that she had flown to Rome that weekend to visit her elderly mother. She and Shasa must have passed each other at Zurich Airport, traveling in different directions.

On another occasion, during Shasa's tenure at the embassy in London, they were invited separately to a dinner at the Swiss embassy. He learned afterward that they would have been table companions, but Elsa Pignatelli had been obliged to cancel for family reasons only days before the engagement.

Since then Shasa had heard Elsa Pignatelli's name mentioned and discussed in detail at many a society dinner or weekend house party, often spitefully and vindictively but often with admiration and open envy. He had seen her photograph in the glossy women's fashion magazines to which Centaine and Isabella subscribed religiously. Courtney Industries had dealt with Pignatelli interests for twenty years to the benefit and satisfaction of both parties. In the weeks since this meeting had been

**313**

arranged Shasa had studied the considerable information about her contained in the file that Special Services had provided.

Sean taxied the Beechcraft to the hard stand of compacted red clay and switched off the engines. Elsa Pignatelli stepped out on to the wing, then jumped down to earth. She moved with the supple grace of a young gymnast, yet she was tall and long-limbed. Shasa knew she had modeled for Yves St.-Laurent before marrying Bruno Pignatelli.

Although he felt he knew her, Shasa was unprepared for his reaction to her physical presence. The electric tickle spread from his neck to the back of his arms, and he felt the hair there come erect as she looked around. Her dark gaze swept over Garry and Isabella and the servants and fastened directly on him.

Her hair was very dark, with an almost bluish gloss in the late-afternoon sunlight. It was drawn back severely and secured behind her head in a neat, tight coil. This emphasized her fine bone structure, the high, slightly domed forehead and vaulted cheekbones. And yet her features were full and feminine. Her lips looked soft, and her mouth was wide.

"Shasa Courtney," she said as she came toward him with a free hip-swinging model's gait. She smiled, and he saw her jaw-line was clean. He knew the following year in July she would celebrate her forty-third year. However, her skin was flawless and lovingly cared for under light natural-toned makeup.

"Signora Pignatelli." He took her hand. It was cool and firm with long, narrow bones. Her grip was swift but strong, the kind of hand that could hold a racket handle or the reins of a thoroughbred.

He regretted that the contact had been so fleeting, but her eyes were compensation. They were starred with rays of brown and gold that radiated from the central pupil. They were bright, intelligent eyes, and the lashes were long and black and curled.

"It is my regret that we have not met sooner," Shasa said in awkward Italian.

She smiled and answered in faultless English, tinged with only an intriguing hint of an accent, "Oh, but we have." Her teeth were startlingly white, but one incisor was just crooked enough to suggest that they were her own and not some orthodontist's artifice.

"Where?" Sean was surprised.

"Windsor Park. The Guards' Polo Club." She was amused by his confusion. "You were playing number two for the Duke of Edinburgh's invitation team."

"My goodness, that was ten years ago."

"Eleven," she said. "We were never introduced, but we met for approximately three seconds at the buffet after the match. You offered me a smoked-salmon sandwich."

"You have a marvelous memory," he said, admitting defeat. "Did you accept the sandwich?"

"How ungallant of you not to remember," she teased. Then she turned to the others. "You must be Garrick Courtney?" And Shasa hastened to introduce first Garry and then Isabella.

The servants were loading Signora Pignatelli's luggage into one of the trucks. It was heavy leather luggage with brass-bound corners, and there was plenty of it. Only people who flew in their own jets and were not subjected to the caprices of the commercial airlines' regulations could afford that type and quantity of luggage. Among it were four long gun cases.

"You'll ride with me, signora." Sean tossed back his hair and called to her as he stepped up into the high driver's seat of his hunting vehicle. She ignored the suggestion and fell in naturally beside Shasa as he crossed to the second truck.

Isabella started to follow them, but Garry caught her hand and steered her toward the seat in Sean's truck that Elsa had refused.

"Come on, Bella, wise up!" Garry murmured. "Three's a crowd."

Isabella started. It hadn't occurred to her—not Pater and the widow! Then she leaned briefly against Garry's arm.

"I didn't realize that you included matchmaking among your many talents."

At sundowner time, Isaac brought Elsa Pignatelli a seething tulip-shaped glass of Dom Pérignon from a freshly opened bottle without being ordered to do so. He knew all the foibles of each of their regular clients.

While they sat in the half circle around the campfire, keeping above the drift of blue smoke, Sean called his two trackers to the evening conference. This ritual was mainly for the benefit of the client, for everything of importance had been discussed previously and well out of earshot. However, the average client, and especially the first-timers, were impressed by the flow of Swahili between Sean and his trackers. In addition, being included in the ritual gave them a sense of being part of the hunt, not merely excess baggage.

The trackers, both of whom had been with Sean since he had been an apprentice in Kenya at the time of the Mau Mau rebellion, were natural actors and hammed it up splendidly. They squatted respectfully on either side of Sean's camp chair and called him Bwana Mkubwa, or Big Chief. They mimed the animals they were discussing and drew their spoor in the dust between their feet. They rolled their eyes and shook their heads, then hawked and spat into the fire for emphasis.

They were an oddly assorted pair. One was a tall, taciturn Samburu with shaved head, classical Nilotic features and Maria Theresa silver dollars set in the enlarged lobes of his ears. The other was a gnome with a puckish face and bright beady eyes.

Matatu was one of the few surviving members of the forest Ndorobo tribe, a people famous for their magical bushcraft, adepts of forest lore who had unfortunately been unable to withstand the impact of progress that had destroyed their forests and contaminated them with all civilization's ailments and diseases from tuberculosis to alcoholism and venereal disease.

Sean had named him Matatu, or Number Three, because his tribal name was not pronounceable and because he was the third tracker Sean had hired. The other two had not lasted longer than a week each. Matatu had been with Sean more than half Sean's lifetime.

Matatu said, "Ngwi," and rolled his eyes as he drew a perfect imprint of a leopard's spoor in the dust. Sean questioned him in sonorous Swahili, to which Matatu replied in his piping lyrical voice, at the end spitting explosively in the fire. Sean turned to Elsa Pignatelli to translate.

" 'A week ago I hanged five leopard baits, two on the river and the others along the rim overlooking the national park.' "

Elsa nodded; she knew the area well from her previous trips.

" 'We had one strike a few days ago. An old tabby that came out of the park. She fed only once, then left it, and we tracked her back into the park. Since then it has been quiet.' "

Sean turned back and asked Matatu another question. The little Ndorobo answered at length, obviously enjoying the attention.

"Matatu checked the baits today while I was fetching you from Salisbury. You are in luck, signora. We have had another strike on one of the river baits. Matatu says it's a good tom. He ate well last night. The impala bait has been hanging for a week, and even with the cool weather it has ripened nicely. If he feeds again tonight, then we'll sit up for him tomorrow evening."

"*Si.*" Elsa nodded. "That's good."

"So tomorrow morning we can check the bait and shoot a few more impala, just in case we need them. After lunch we'll

**316**

have an hour's liedown and then we'll go into the hide around three o'clock tomorrow afternoon."

"You check the bait. You shoot the impala," Elsa told him. "Tomorrow morning I have a meeting to attend." She smiled at Shasa in the chair beside her. "We have much to discuss."

The discussion took up most of the morning. Garry had made the arrangements with deceptive simplicity. He had sent Isabella off in the Toyota with Sean to check the leopard baits and had then ordered Isaac and his staff to set up three chairs and a folding table under a msasa tree at the edge of the glade, well away from the camp itself.

Under the msasa tree, three of them, Garry, Shasa and Elsa Pignatelli, were as secure from eavesdropping as at any spot on the planet. It was bizarre, Shasa thought, to be discussing such a terrifying subject in such tranquil and beautiful surroundings.

On the other hand, the negotiations did not follow the course Shasa and Garry had hoped for. Although Elsa Pignatelli had with her a handsome pigskin attaché case, it remained locked and unopened while they delicately circled around the central issue.

Almost immediately it became obvious that Elsa had not yet made up her mind to proceed with the Cyndex 25 enterprise. On the contrary, she was obviously having serious doubts and misgivings, and would need a great deal of persuasion.

"It is a hideous thing to let loose in the world," she said at one point. "My relief when NATO rescinded the original contract and ordered us to allow the existing stocks to degrade and to dismantle the plant was immense. I cannot imagine what possessed me even to consider equipping another plant, especially one over which I would have no direct control."

All that morning, Shasa and Garry worked to allay her fears. Between them they tried to devise some arrangement that would satisfy her demands on control and the ultimate rules of engagement under which Cyndex could be used.

"If you were to begin manufacturing, any NATO expert who ever inspected the plant and analyzed a sample of the gas would know immediately where the technology was obtained," she pointed out. "If that happened and it was traced back to Pignatelli . . ."

She did not finish the sentence, merely spread her long, graceful hands in an expressive Italian gesture. Gradually, as the discussion continued, Elsa moved around in her chair to face Shasa. She began to direct all her remarks and questions to him alone.

Subtly, almost subconsciously, she excluded Garry from the exchanges. Beneath his bluff exterior Garry was an intuitive and sensitive negotiator. Even before they themselves had realized it, he had detected the currents that ran between these two. He recognized that, belonging to the same generation and the same caste, they shared values and understood a special code he could not comprehend.

He sensed that Elsa Pignatelli wanted to be reassured not by him, but by the man to whom she was inexorably being drawn. Tactfully he withdrew into silence and watched them fall in love with each other without realizing what was happening to them.

The hum of the engine of the returning Toyota startled them. Shasa glanced at his watch with disbelief.

"Good gracious, it's lunchtime already, and we have settled nothing."

"We have two weeks in which to talk," Elsa pointed out. She rose to her feet. "We can pick up again from here tomorrow morning."

As the three of them came back into the *boma*, Sean was already at the bar table mixing Pimm's No. I in a crystal jug. He prided himself on his personal recipe.

"Good news, signora," he called. "Can I wheedle you into a festive Pimm's?"

She smiled a refusal. "I'll have my usual Badoit water with a slice of lemon. Now, tell me the good news."

"The leopard fed again last night. Judging by the sign, he came in early, half an hour before sunset. So he's starting to get careless and bold, and he's huge. He's got paws on him like snowshoes."

"Thank you, Sean. You always find good cats for me, but never so soon. This is the first day of safari."

"Take a nap after lunch, just to settle your nerves, and we'll go into the hide around three this afternoon."

Isaac offered Elsa her mineral water on a silver tray, then distributed the tall glasses of Pimm's to the musical accompaniment of tinkling ice. Sean gave them a toast.

"To a big old tom leopard death at the base of the tree." The professional hunter's horror was a cat down from the tree, waiting wounded in the tall grass.

They all drank the toast, and immediately afterward Shasa and Elsa fell into a quiet but intent conversation that excluded the younger Courtneys. Garry seized on the opportunity to take his elder brother's arm and gently lead him out of earshot.

318

"How are you feeling, Sean?" he asked.

"Fine. Never better." Sean was puzzled by this uncustomary brotherly concern.

"You don't look fine to me." Garry shook his head. "In fact, it is fairly obvious that you are sickening for a go of malaria, and those ribs—"

"What sort of crap is this?" Sean was getting annoyed. "There's nothing wrong with my ribs that a couple of codeine won't fix."

"You won't be able to hunt with Signora Pignatelli this evening."

"The hell I won't. I've set up this cat, and he's a beaut"

"You will stay in your tent this evening with a bottle of chloroquine tablets beside your bed, and if anybody asks, you have a temperature of a hundred and four in the shade."

"Listen, big shot, you've screwed up my elephant already. You're not going to do the same with my leopard."

"Pater will hunt with the client," Garry said firmly. "You are staying in camp."

"Pater?" Sean stared at him for a moment before he started to grin. "The randy old dog! Pater has the hots for the widow, has he?"

"Why do you always make it sound so vulgar?" Garry asked mildly. "We are trying to do business with Signora Pignatelli, and Pater needs to develop the relationship to a point of mutual trust. That's all there is to it."

"And when those two geriatric nymphos mess up the leopard, old Sean will be the one who has to go in to clean up."

"You told me Signora Pignatelli never misses, and Pater is as good a hunter as you any day. Besides which, you aren't frightened of a wounded leopard, not the fearless Sean Courtney— surely not?"

Sean scowled at the jibe, then bit back his response. "I'll go set it up for them," he agreed. Then he smiled. "To answer your question—no, Garry, I'm not frightened of a wounded leopard—or of anything else. Bear that in mind, old son."

Shasa lay stretched out on his camp bed with a book. The safari camp was one of the few places in his existence where he had the opportunity to read for pleasure rather than for business or political necessity. He was reading Alan Moorehead's *White Nile* for the fourth time and savoring every word of it when Garry popped his head into the tent.

"We have a little problem, Pater. Sean's having a go of malaria."

Shasa sat up and dropped the book with alarm. "How bad?" He knew Sean never took malarial suppressants such as Paludrine or Maloprim. Sean preferred to build up his immunity to the disease and treated only symptoms. Shasa knew also that there had recently appeared along the Zambezi a new strain of *P. falciparum* that was resistant to the usual drugs, and that had a dangerous tendency to mutate into the pernicious cerebral form. "I should go to him."

"Don't worry. It's responding to chloroquine already, and he's asleep. So you shouldn't disturb him."

Shasa looked relieved, and Garry went on smoothly, "But somebody will have to hunt with Signora Pignatelli this evening, and you have more experience than I do."

The hide was in the lower branches of a wild ebony tree, only ten feet above ground level. Sean had raised it not to protect the hunter, for a leopard could climb the tree and be in it with him before he drew breath, but rather to provide a wider field of view across the narrow stream to the bait tree.

Sean had chosen the bait tree with infinite care, and Shasa nodded approval as he surveyed it. Most important, it was above the prevailing easterly evening breeze, so the hunter's scent would be wafted away. Also, it was surrounded by dense shoulder-high riverine bush, which would give the leopard confidence in its approach.

The main trunk leaned out over the riverbed at a slight angle to give the cat an easy climb to the horizontal branch, twenty feet above the ground, from which the carcass of an impala was suspended by a short length of chain. The foliage of the ebony tree was dense and green. That would also give the leopard confidence to climb. However, the horizontal branch was open, with a window of blue sky beyond it that would silhouette the leopard as it stretched out and reached down to pull the stinking bait up to him.

The hide was exactly sixty-five yards from the bait tree. Sean had measured it with a builder's tape, while earlier that afternoon Elsa Pignatelli had sighted and fired her rifle on the marked range behind the main camp. Shasa had set up a target at precisely sixty-five yards, and she had put three shots into the bull's-eye, forming a perfect cloverleaf pattern with the three bulletholes slightly overlapping each other.

The hide was built of mopane poles and thatch, and was a

comfortable little tree house. Inside were two camp chairs facing the firing apertures in the thatch wall. Matatu and the Samburu tracker laid out blankets and sleeping bags, a tucker-box with snacks and a thermos filled with hot coffee.

Their vigil might last until the dawn, so they were provided with a powerful flashlight that drew power from a twelve-volt car battery, a handheld two-way radio to communicate with the trackers, and even a china chamberpot with a tasteful floral pattern to allow them to last out the night without discomfort.

When Matatu had set up the furnishings of the hide to his satisfaction, he scrambled down the ladder, and he and Shasa had a last brief conference beside the Toyota.

"I think that he will come before dark," Matatu said in Swahili. "He is a cheeky devil and he gorges like a pig. I think he will be hungry tonight, and he will not be able to withstand his greed."

"If he does not come, we will wait through until the dawn. Do not return here until I call for you on the radio. Go in peace now, Matatu."

"Stay in peace, *Bwana*. Let us pray that the memsahib kills cleanly. I do not want this spotted devil to feast on my liver."

The trackers waited until the hunters had climbed into the hide and settled down before they drove the Toyota away. They would park on the crest of the valley two miles distant and wait for the sound of gunfire or a call on the two-way radio.

Shasa and Elsa sat side by side in the two camp chairs. Their elbows were almost, but not quite, touching. The sleeping bags were spread over the chair backs, ready to draw over their shoulders when the temperature began to drop. There were rugs over their laps. Both of them wore leather jackets, some protection not only against the cold, but also, in an emergency, against sharp curling claws.

Elsa had her long rifle barrel thrust through the firing aperture, ready to raise the butt to her shoulder with the minimum of movement. It was a 7-millimeter Remington magnum loaded with a 175-grain Nosler bullet that would cover the sixty-five yards to the bait tree at three thousand feet per second. Shasa had the big eight-bore shotgun as a backup weapon. Designed for shooting wild geese at long range, it was a devastating weapon in close work.

As the beat of the Toyota engine faded, the silence of the bushveld descended on the river valley. It was a silence that whispered with intimate sounds: the gentle sigh of the breeze in the leaves above their heads, the stir of a bird in the undergrowth along the river, the far-off booming shout of a bull baboon that echoed faintly along the rocky cliffs at the head of the valley, the tiny ticking sounds of the termite legions gnawing away at the dry mopane poles on which they sat.

Both of them had brought books to while away the hours until dusk, but neither of them opened them. They sat very close to each other, and they were vitally aware of each other's proximity. Shasa felt as comfortable and companionable in her presence as though they were old and trusted friends. He smiled at the fancy. He turned his head surreptitiously to glance at Elsa. She had anticipated this and was smiling at him already.

She turned the hand that lay on the arm of the chair between them palm uppermost. He took the hand in his own and was surprised by the smooth warm feel of her skin and by the sharp emotion her touch evoked. He hadn't felt like that for many a long year. They sat side by side holding hands like a pair of teenagers on their first date and waited for the leopard to come.

Although all his senses were tuned to the subtle sounds and signs of the wilderness, Shasa's mind was free to wander through the junkroom of memory. He thought about many things in those quiet hours as the sun turned across the blue dome of sky and sank toward the jagged line of hills. He thought about the other women he had known. There had been many of those. He had no way of knowing how many; the passage of time had rendered most of them faceless and nameless. Just a very few would remain with him forever.

The first had been a sly-faced little harlot. When Centaine had caught them at it, she had scrubbed him in a scalding tub of Lysol and carbolic soap that had taken the skin off his most tender parts. He smiled at that far-off memory.

The other that stood out in his memory was Tara, mother of all his children. They had been antagonists from the very beginning. He had always thought of her as the beloved enemy. Then love had wrested the upper hand, and for a time they had been happy together. Finally they had become enemies again, true enemies. Their enmity had been inflamed rather than mitigated by that brief illusory period of happiness.

After Tara there had been fifty or a hundred others—it did not really matter how many. Not one of them had been able to give him what he sought, nor had they been able to alleviate the loneliness.

Recently, in middle age, he had even fallen into the age-old trap of seeking immortality in young feminine bodies in the flower of their youth. Though the flesh was sweet and firm, he had found no contact of the mind and could no longer match their energy. Sadly he had left them to their booming mindless music and their frenetic search for they knew not what. He had walked on alone.

He thought of loneliness then, as he did so often these days. Over the years, he had learned that it was the most corrosive and destructive of all man's ills. Most of his life he had been alone. Although there had been a half brother, he had never known him as a sibling, and Centaine had raised Shasa as an only child.

In all the multitude of humankind that had filled his life, the servants and business associates, the acquaintances and syco-phants, even his own children, there had been only one person with whom he had been able to share all the triumphs and di-sasters of his life, only one who had been constant in her en-couragement and understanding and love.

However, Centaine was seventy-six years old and aging fast. He was sick to his soul of loneliness and afraid of the greater loneliness that he knew lay ahead.

At that moment the woman who sat beside him tightened her grip on his hand as though she empathized with his despair. When he turned his head and looked into her honey-golden eyes, she was no longer smiling. Her expression was serious, and she held his gaze without shift or embarrassment. The sense of aloneness faded, and he felt calm and at peace as he seldom had in all his fifty-odd years.

Outside their little tree house, the light mellowed and flared into the soft glow of the African twilight. It was a time of mag-ical stillness, in which the world held its breath and all the forest colors were richer and deeper. The sun sagged like a dying gladiator and bowed its bloody head below the forest top. The light went with it, and the outlines of the forest trunks and branches faded and softened and receded.

A francolin called in the gloom. Shasa leaned forward in his seat and looked through the firing aperture in the thatch wall. He saw the dark partridgelike bird perched on a dead branch on the far side of the river. Its bare cheeks were bright scarlet, and it cocked its head and looked down from its perch and made that creaking sound like a rusty hinge that was a special warn-ing: "Beware! I see a killer cat."

Elsa also heard the call, and because she too knew the African wild and understood the meaning of it, she squeezed Shasa's hand briefly, then released it. Slowly she reached forward for the pistol grip of the rifle and achingly slowly lifted the rifle to

**323**

her shoulder. The tension in the hide was a palpable charge that held them both in its thrall. The leopard was out there, silent and secretive as a dappled golden shadow.

They were both adepts in the art of the hunter. Neither of them moved except to blink their eyes to keep their vision clear in the failing light. They drew and released each breath with infinite care and heard the pulse of their racing hearts beat in their eardrums.

The light was going faster, while the unseen leopard circled the bait tree. Shasa could imagine him in his mind's eye, each deliberate stealthy step, one paw raised and held aloft, then laid down again softly, the yellow eyes endlessly turning and darting, the round black-tipped ears flicking to catch the faintest sound of danger.

The outline of the bait tree receded; the carcass of the impala hanging on its chain was a dark, amorphous blob. The open window of sky above the bare branch dulled and bruised to the shade of tarnished lead. Still the leopard prowled and circled in the dark thicket.

Shooting light was almost gone, night came on apace, and then suddenly the leopard was in the tree. There was no sound or warning. The abruptness of it was a little miracle that stopped both their hearts, then sent them racing away at a mad pace.

The leopard was standing on the branch. However, he was only a darker shape in the darkness, and even as Elsa laid her cheek to the polished walnut wood of the buttstock the darkness was complete and the shape of the leopard was swallowed up by the night.

Shasa felt rather than saw Elsa lower the rifle. He stared through the aperture, but there was nothing to see, and he turned his head and laid his lips against Elsa's ear.

"We must wait until morning," he breathed, and she touched his cheek in agreement.

Out in the darkness they heard the clink of the chain links. Shasa imagined the leopard lying belly down on the branch, reaching down with one front paw to hook the carcass and draw it up, holding it with both front feet, sniffing the putrefying flesh hungrily, thrusting its head into the belly cavity to reach the lungs and liver and heart.

In the silence they heard the tearing sound of fangs in flesh, the grating and splintering of rib bone, the ripping of wet hide, as the leopard began to feed.

The night was long, and Shasa could not sleep. As the hunter, his was the responsibility of monitoring each of the leopard's movements. After the first few hours, Elsa's head sagged against his shoulder. Moving stealthily, he slipped his arm around her, pulled her down-filled sleeping bag up snugly over her shoulders, and held her close while she slept.

She slept quietly, like a tired child. Her breathing was light and warm against his cheek. Even though his arm went dead and numb, he did not wish to disturb her. He sat happy and virtuous in his discomfort.

The leopard fed at intervals during the night, the chain tinkling and bones grating and cracking. Then there were long periods of silence when Shasa feared it had left, before the sounds began again.

Of course, he could easily have turned the powerful spotlight on the tree and lit the leopard for her. It would have probably sat bemused, blinking those huge yellow eyes into the blinding beam. The idea never even occurred to him, and he would have been bitterly disappointed if Elsa had even contemplated such an unfair tactic.

Deep down Shasa disliked the technique of baiting for the great cats. He had personally never killed one of them on a bait. Although in Rhodesia it was perfectly legal, Shasa's own sporting ethic could never come to terms with luring them into a prepared position to offer a carefully staged broadside shot to a hidden marksman shooting from a dead rest.

Every lion and leopard he had ever taken, he had tracked down on foot, often in the thickest cover, and the animal had been alert and aware of his presence. In consequence he had experienced a hundred failures and not more than a dozen kills in all his years as a hunter. However, each success had been a peak of the hunting experience, a memory to last his lifetime.

He did not despise Elsa or any of the other clients who took their cats over bait. They were not Africans, as he was, and their time in the bushveld was limited to a few short days. They were paying huge sums of money for the privilege, and much of that money was channeled back into the protection and conversation of the species they hunted. Therefore they were entitled to the best possible chance of success. He did not resent this, but it was not his way.

Sitting beside her in the dark hide, he realized suddenly that his own hunting of the cats was over forever. Like so many old hunters, he had had his surfeit of blood. He loved the hunting game as much as, probably more than, he ever had, but it was enough. He had killed his last elephant and lion and leopard. The thought made him glad and at the same time sad, a kind of sweet warm melancholy that mingled well with the new emotion he had conceived for the lovely lady who slept on his shoulder. He thought how he would in future take his pleasure in the hunt through her, the way he was doing now. He dreamed happily of traveling with her to the hunting fields of the world: Russia for the sheep of Marco Polo, Canada for the polar bear, Brazil for the spotted jaguar, Tanzania for the great Cape buffalo with a horn spread over fifty inches wide. These vicarious pleasures sustained him through the long night.

Then a pair of Heughlin's robins chorused a duet from the undergrowth along the river, a melodious entreaty that sounded like "Don't do it! Don't do it!" repeated over and over, at first softly and then rising to an excited crescendo.

After this certain harbinger of the dawn, Shasa glanced upward and made out the uppermost branches of the ebony tree against the lightening sky. It would be shooting light in fifteen minutes. Dawn comes on swiftly in Africa.

He touched Elsa's cheek to wake her, and immediately she snuggled against him. He realized she must have been feigning sleep for some time. She had come awake so secretly he had not realized it. Since then she had been lying against him and savoring their intimate contact, just as he had been doing.

"Is the leopard still there?" she asked, a breath of a whisper close to his ear.

"Don't know," he answered as softly. It was almost two hours since he last had heard it feeding. Perhaps it had left already. "Be ready," he warned her.

She straightened in her chair and leaned forward to where the rifle was propped in the forked rest. Although they were no longer touching, he felt very close to her and his arm tingled with the flow of returning blood, which her head on his shoulder had impeded.

The light strengthened. Vaguely he could make out the open window through the foliage of the ebony tree. He blinked his eyes and stared into it. The outline of the branch formed out of the gloom. The branch appeared bare, and he felt a swoop of disappointment for her. The leopard was gone.

He turned his head slowly to tell her, but he never took his eyes off the branch. He checked the words on his lips and stared harder, feeling tiny ants of excitement crawl along his nerve ends. The outline of the branch was better defined, but it was strangely thickened and misshapen.

Now he could just make out the blob of the dangling impala carcass. Most of it had been devoured, and it was a ravaged

326

bundle of bare bones and torn skin. But there was something else hanging from the branch, a long, snakelike ribbon. He could not decide what it was until it curled and swung lazily. Then he realized.

"The tail, the leopard's tail." Like a hidden creature in a puzzle picture, the whole thing jumped into focus.

The leopard was still draped on the branch, lying flat, its neck outstretched. Its chin was propped against the rough bark. It was sluggish with the weight of meat in its belly, too lazy to move from its perch. Only its long tail swung down.

He felt Elsa stiffen beside him as she also made out the shape of the leopard. He reached across gently to restrain her. The light was still too poor; they must wait it out. As he touched her arm, he felt the tension in her through his fingertips. She seemed to vibrate like the strings of a violin lightly touched with a bow.

The light bloomed. The shape of the leopard hardened. Its hide turned to buttery gold studded with black rosettes. Its tail swung gently like a metronome set to the slowest beat. It lifted its head slightly and pricked its ears. The light caught its eyes, a flare of yellow, like a distant flash of sheet lightning. It looked toward them and blinked sleepily in regal indolence, so beautiful that Shasa felt his chest squeezing for breath.

It was time to make the kill. He touched Elsa, a light, imperative tap on her upper arm. She settled down behind the telescopic sight of the rifle. Shasa braced himself for the shot and stared at the leopard, willing the bullet into its heart, hoping to see it topple and tumble lifeless from the high branch.

The seconds drew out, each of them an age. The shot did not come.

The leopard rose to its full height, standing easily erect on the narrow branch. It stretched, arching its back deeply, digging its extended claws into the bark.

"Now!" Shasa commanded her silently. "Shoot it now!"

The leopard yawned. Its pink tongue curled out between its gaping fangs. Its thin black lips drew back into a fierce rictus.

"Now!" With telepathic effort Shasa tried to force her to make the shot. He dared not reinforce the command with a word or touch for fear he would disturb her concentration in the very act of firing.

The leopard straightened and flicked its tail over its back. Then, without further warning, it launched itself into flight and dropped from the branch to the soft mulched floor of the forest, twenty feet below. It was a leap so controlled and graceful that

327

there was no sound as it landed. The undergrowth swallowed it instantly.

They sat for almost a minute in total silence. At last Elsa set the safety catch with a click, lowered the unfired rifle and turned her head toward him. In the dawn light, tears shone like seed pearls on the long curled lashes of her lower lids. "He was so beautiful," she whispered. "I could not kill him, not today, not on this day."

He understood instantly. This day was their day, their very first day together as lovers. She had declined to desecrate it.

"I dedicate the leopard to you," she said.

"You do me too much honor," he replied, and kissed her. Their embrace was strangely innocent, almost childlike, devoid as yet of sexual passion. It was a thing of the spirit rather than of the body. There would be time for that later, all the time in the world, but not today, not on this blessed day.

Sean had made a miraculous recovery from his malaria and was waiting eagerly at the *boma* gate to welcome the returning hunters. The reputation of a safari company is built upon the quality of trophies it produced for its clients, especially its important clients.

As the Toyota pulled up he glanced hopefully into the back, but his mouth tightened with disappointment. He spoke first to Matatu, and the little Ndorobo tracker shook his head gloomily. "The devil came late and left early."

"I'm sorry, signora." Sean turned to her and handed her down from the truck.

"That is hunting," she murmured. He had never seen her so philosophical before. Usually she was as angry and as impatient with failure as he was.

"Your shower is ready, hot like you like it. Breakfast will be waiting as soon as you have cleaned up."

The rest of the party were full of condolences when Shasa and Elsa appeared in the dining tent, both of them showered and dressed in freshly laundered and crisply ironed khaki. Shasa was shaved and redolent of after-shave lotion.

"Bad luck, Pater. So sorry, signora," they chorused, and were puzzled that the couple looked smug and self-satisfied and fell on their breakfast with as much gusto as if there were a world-record leopard in the skinning shed.

"We can continue our meeting after breakfast," Garry suggested over coffee.

"And I'll renew the baits this morning." Sean came in. "Matatu says the leopard was never alarmed or spooked. We can try again tonight. This time I'll hunt with you, signora. It takes the touch of the master.''

Instead of accepting the suggestions immediately, Elsa glanced across at Shasa, then lowered her eyes demurely to her coffee cup.

''Well, actually,'' Shasa began, ''to tell the truth, we rather thought, that is, Elsa and I, rather Signora Pignatelli and I . . .'' As Shasa floundered for words, all three of his brood stared at him in astonishment. Was this the master of savoir-faire? Was this Mr. Cool himself speaking?

''Your father has promised to show me the Victoria Falls,'' Elsa said, coming to his rescue.

Shasa looked relieved and rallied gamely. ''We'll take the Beechcraft,'' he agreed briskly. ''Signora Pignatelli has never seen the falls. This seems like a good opportunity.''

The other members of the family recovered from their confusion as rapidly as Shasa had. ''That's a lovely idea,'' Isabella enthused. ''It's the most awe-inspiring spectacle, signora. You'll adore it.''

Garry nodded. ''It's only an hour's flight. You could have lunch at the Vic Falls Hotel and be back here for tea.''

''And you can still be ready to go into the leopard hide at four this afternoon,'' Sean agreed. He waited expectantly for his client to agree.

Once again Elsa glanced at Shasa, who drew a deep breath. ''Actually, we may stay over at the Vic Falls Hotel for a day or two.''

Slowly various degrees of comprehension dawned on the three young faces.

Isabella recovered first. ''Quite right. You'll need time. You'll want to walk in the rain forest, perhaps take a raft trip down the gorge below the falls.''

''Bella is right; you'll need three or four days. So many interesting things to do and see.''

''That, Garry old boy, is the understatement of the week,'' Sean drawled, and both Garry and Isabella glared at him furiously.

# 26

In the cool, clean air, not yet sullied by the smoke of the bush
fires of the late winter season, the spray cloud of the Victoria
Falls was visible at sixty miles' distance. It rose two thousand
feet into the sky, a silver mountain as brilliant as an alp of snow.

Shasa shed altitude as they approached. Ahead of them the
great Zambezi glinted in the sun, broad and tranquil, studded
by islands on which stood forests of graceful, giraffe-necked
ivory nut palms.

Then the main gorge opened beneath them and they peered
down in wonder as they watched the great river, well over a mile
wide, tumble over the sheer edge of the chasm and fall three
hundred and fifty feet in a welter of foaming waters and blown
spray. Along the brink of the chasm, black rock castles split the
flow of the river. Over it all towered the immense spray cloud,
shot through with rainbows of astonishing color.

Below the falls the flood of the river, a staggering thirty-eight
thousand cubic feet a second, was trapped between vertical cliffs
of rock. Raging at this restraint, it charged madly into the narrow throat of the gorge.

Shasa banked the aircraft into a tight right-hand turn, pointing
one wing into the abyss, so that Elsa could gaze down with her
view unobstructed.

With each circuit he allowed the Beechcraft to drop lower
until they were in danger of being engulfed by the splendid chaos
of rock and water. The silver, leaping spray blew over the canopy, blinding them for an instant before they burst once more
into sunlight and rainbows garlanded the sky around them.

Shasa landed at the small private airfield of Sprayview on the
outskirts of the village and taxied to the hard stand. He switched
off the engines and turned to Elsa. The wonder of it was still in

her eyes, and her expression was solemn with an almost religious awe.

"Now you have worshiped in the cathedral of Africa," Shasa told her softly. "The one place that truly embodies all of the grandeur and mystery and savagery of this continent."

They were fortunate enough to find the Livingstone Suite at the hotel vacant.

The building was in the style and dimensions of a bygone era. The walls were thick and the rooms were immense, but cool and comfortable. The suite was decorated with prints of the drawings the old explorer Thomas Baines had made of the falls only a few years after David Livingstone had first discovered them. From the windows of their sitting room they could see across the gorge and the railway bridge that spanned it. The steelwork of the arched bridge seemed delicate as lace, and the entire structure was light and graceful as the wing of an eagle in flight.

They left the suite and wandered down the pathway to the brink of the gorge. They walked hand in hand through the rain forest, where spray fell in an eternal soaking rain and the vegetation was green and luxuriant. The rock trembled beneath their feet, and the air was filled with the thunder of falling water. Spray soaked their clothing and their hair and ran down their faces, and they laughed together with the joy of it.

They followed the rim of the gorge downstream, out of the spray cloud. The bright sunshine dried their hair and clothing almost as swiftly as the spray had drenched them. They found a rocky perch on the very edge and sat side by side, dangling their legs over the terrifying chasm while the mad waters churned into green whirlpools far below.

"Look!" Shasa cried, pointing upward as a small bird of prey stooped out of the sun and fell on whistling knife-blade wings into the flock of black swifts that swirled along the cliff face below them.

"A Taita falcon," Shasa exulted. "One of the rarest birds in Africa."

The falcon struck one of the swifts in flight, killing it instantly in a burst of feathers. Then, binding to its prey, it fell into the void and disappeared from their view in the gloom far below.

That evening they dined on steaks of crocodile tail, which tasted like lobster, but when they went up to their suite they were suddenly both shy and nervous. Shasa drank a cognac in the sitting room. When finally he went into the bedroom, Elsa was already propped up on the pillows. Her hair was down on the shoulders of her lace nightdress, thick and black and glossy.

Shasa was overcome by a sense of panic. He was no longer young, and there had been one or two occasions recently with other women that had shaken his confidence.

She smiled and lifted her arms to him in invitation. He need not have worried. She manned him as no other woman ever had. In the morning, when they awoke in each other's arms, the sun was streaming in through the high windows.

She sighed and smiled with a slow and languorous contentment and said, "My man." And kissed him.

Their illicit honeymoon drew out from one day to the next. They did things together, silly little things for which Shasa had had neither the time nor the inclination for many years.

They slept late each morning, then spent the rest of it loafing in their swimming costumes beside the pool. They read for hours in companionable silence, stretched out in the sunlight. At intervals they anointed each other with suntan oil, making it a fine excuse to touch and examine each other in leisurely detail.

Elsa was lean and smooth and tanned. The condition and tone of her muscle and skin were the rewards of endless hours of aerobics and calisthenics and beauty care. She was obviously proud of her body. Shasa came to share that pride as he compared her to the other seminaked bodies sunning themselves under the msasa trees on the green lawns.

Only up very close were the stigmata that life and childbirth had left upon her visible. Shasa found even those small blemishes appealing. They emphasized her maturity and bespoke her experience and understanding of life. She was a woman, ripe and complete.

This was made even more apparent when they talked. They talked for hours at a time, lazy contented conversations during which they explored each other's minds in the same way they were exploring each other's bodies in the double bed upstairs in the Livingstone Suite.

She told him about herself with an engaging candor. She described her husband Bruno's slow, cruel death as the crab of cancer had eaten him alive, and her own agony as she watched helplessly. She spoke of the loneliness that had followed, seven long years of it. She did not have to tell him that she hoped it was now behind her. She merely reached out and touched his hand, and it was understood.

She told him of her children: a son, also named Bruno, and

three daughters. The elder two girls were married, the youngest was at university in Milan, and Bruno junior had an MBA from Harvard and was now working for Pignatelli Industries in Rome.

"He does not have his father's fire," she told Shasa frankly. "I do not think he will ever fill those shoes; they are many sizes too large for him."

She made Shasa think of his owns sons. They spoke of the heartaches and disappointments their children had brought them and of the rare joys some of them had bestowed on them.

Together they explored their love of horses and hunting, of music and art and fine things lovingly crafted, of books and music and theater. Finally they spoke of power and money, openly admitting their addictions to all these things

They held nothing back, and at one point Elsa regarded him solemnly. "It is too early to be absolutely certain, but I think that you and I will be good together."

"I believe that also," he replied as gravely, and it was as though they had made a vow and a commitment.

They danced together in the balmy African nights. They laid their cheeks together, still hot and brown from the sun, and swayed to the beat of the steel band.

After midnight, they at last climbed the broad stairway, hand in hand, to their suite and the wide soft bed.

"Good Lord!" Shasa said with genuine amazement one morning. "It's Thursday. We have been here four days. The kids will be wondering what on earth has happened to us." They were eating brunch on the open terrace.

"I think they will guess." Elsa looked up from the mango she was peeling for him and smiled. "And I don't think that 'kids' is the correct description for that rumbustious litter of yours."

"Van Wyk will be arriving at Chiwewe tomorrow," Shasa pointed out.

"I know," she sighed. "I hate the thought of ending this, but we must be there to meet him."

Sir Clarence Van Wyk was one of those extraordinary creatures that African evolution sometimes throws up.

He was a pure-bred Afrikaner. His father had been chief justice of South Africa while it was still part of the British Empire, and he had received his hereditary title while it was still permissible for a South African to accept that honor.

Sir Clarence was a product of Eton and Sandhurst. He had been an officer in a famous Guards regiment and was heir to the considerable family estates in the Cape of Good Hope. He was also the minister in Ian Smith's government specifically charged with funding the debilitating guerrilla warfare in which Rhodesia was engaged, and in evading the comprehensive sanctions the British Labor Government, the United States and the United Nations had placed on these perpetrators of unilateral independence.

Garry and Shasa had arranged this meeting during their stopover in Salisbury on the way to Chiwewe. Sir Clarence was an avid big game hunter, and they had promised him a bit of sport in the intervals between their deliberations.

Sir Clarence arrived at Chiwewe in a Rhodesian air force helicopter. He had with him two of his aides and a pair of bodyguards, all of whom threatened to put a strain on the safari camp. The staff and facilities were geared to entertaining a much smaller number of guests. However, Sean had been given plenty of notice, and additional equipment, staff and stores had been sent down from Salisbury by truck.

The conference table under the msasa tree was extended and additional chairs were set out for Sir Clarence and his team. Isabella joined them as her father's personal assistant. From the beginning Sir Clarence made no attempt to conceal his interest in her.

At six foot five inches, Sir Clarence towered above even Shasa or Sean. He was a most impressive figure of a man whose plummy upperclass English accent and classical features belied his Afrikaner origins. He had a brilliant financial and political brain and a reputation as a lady's man.

Under the msasa tree, they negotiated the marketing and transportation of a nation's wealth and produce, and the commissions and handling fees due to each of them.

Rhodesia was a primary producer, which simplified these deliberations considerably. Her small-scale mines, which worked narrow quartz reefs, nevertheless turned out a considerable gold production. This did not concern them, for gold was anonymous. There was no "Made in Rhodesia" stamp on it, and its high value-to-bulk ratio made it readily transportable and disposable.

It was different with the other primary products of the country: tobacco and rare metals, chiefly chromium. These had to be transported in bulk, their country of origin had to be concealed and then they had to be disseminated to the markets of the world.

From Rhodesia, the railways ran southward to the harbors of

Durban and Cape Town in the Republic of South Africa. That was the natural route for these treasures to take. For years now, ever since the Smith government's declaration of independence, Garry Courtney and Courtney Enterprises had played a leading role in helping Rhodesia evade the sanctions campaign against it.

Now there was to be an ambitious new strategy. After carefully studying the Pignatelli group of industries, Garry and Sir Clarence were offering Elsa Pignatelli the lucrative opportunity of taking part in these antisanctions activities.

Pignatelli Industries owned the second-largest tobacco company in Europe, after the British American Tobacco Company. In addition, it had a controlling interest in Winnipeg Mining in Canada and operated a stainless-steel mill and vanadium refinery in southern Italy near Taranto.

All this dovetailed neatly with Rhodesia's need to find a market for her products, but there was hard bargaining to come.

Although it was conducted in a superficially civilized and friendly atmosphere, these were all shrewd and merciless financial predators locked in a contest of minds and wills. Isabella watched them with awe. Her brother used his bluff, almost bumbling manner, his myopic ingenuous gaze and hearty laugh, to conceal his steely, calculating mind.

Elsa Pignatelli, poised and beautiful, shamelessly exploited her looks and her charms and used the feminine rapier against their masculine cutlasses. She matched and met them with ease.

Sir Clarence was suave, his manners courtly. He held the line like the Guardsman he was and made them pay dearly for every inch he was forced to yield. Then he counterattacked with consummate timing.

Shasa sat aloof at his end of the table, leaving most of the bargaining to Garry. However, when he spoke his comments were pithy and apposite and very often served to break a logjam in the negotiations and to propose an equitable compromise.

The sums of money they were discussing were of numbing magnitude. While Isabella recorded the minutes of this conference, she amused herself by calculating 2½ percent of three billion dollars. That would be Courtney Enterprises' share of the loot in the coming twelve months alone, all of it earned without any additional capital investment on their part. When she had the total worked out, she looked at her brother with renewed respect.

At noon the conference adjourned for an elaborate lunch. Sir Clarence had brought with him a selected baron of the finest

Rhodesian beef. Sean and his chef had passed the morning in barbecuing it to golden-brown perfection over a fire of mopane coals. They cleared their palates with a glass of Dom Pérignon while they watched Sean carve pink slices from the joint, the juices spurting and sizzling from around the blade.

During the luncheon, Sir Clarence demonstrated as great a skill and finesse as he had at the conference table in his attempts to cut Isabella out of the herd and put his brand on her.

Isabella was flattered by his attentions and more than a little tempted. He was a superior man, a dominant herd bull. Power is a wonderful aphrodisiac for any woman. In addition, he had thick, wavy dark hair with just a touch of grey at the temples. She liked his eyes. He was so tall, and he amused her with his urbane wit.

She found herself smiling at his sallies, and once she glanced down at his feet. They must be size fourteen in those gleaming handmade chukka boots, she thought, smiling again. Perhaps that was a fallacy, but nevertheless the possibility was intriguing.

She could almost hear Nanny's rebuke ring in her ears. "All the Courtneys got hot blood. You must be careful, missy, and remember you are a lady."

She knew he was married, but it seemed a long time since she had taken comfort from a man's body, and he was so big and powerful. Perhaps if Sir Clarence continued to demonstrate the requisite amount of class and stamina—then perhaps, just perhaps, he stood a chance.

After lunch they returned to the conference table. It seemed to Isabella that their minds had been stimulated rather than dulled by the Dom Pérignon.

At four o'clock Garry glanced at his watch. "If we aren't to miss the evening flight, I suggest we adjourn until tomorrow morning."

They drove down to the pools in both trucks to shoot the evening flight of ring-necked doves coming in to drink.

Without making it too obvious, Sir Clarence had contrived to seat himself beside Isabella in the leading truck. However, at the last moment, just as they were about to pull away, she jumped down and ran back to sit beside Garry in the second truck. She didn't want to make it too easy for Sir C. She sensed that he would enjoy the chase as much as the kill. Garry was in an ebullient mood. As he drove he slipped one arm around her shoulders and squeezed her.

"God, I love it," he exulted. "I love Harold Wilson and

James Callaghan and all those sanctimonious little bleeding hearts in the General Assembly of the United Nations. I love being a sanctions-buster. It's exciting and romantic. It makes me feel like Al Capone or Captain Blood. Yo-ho-ho and a bottle of rum! It gives me a fine feeling of patriotism and the opportunity to make a telling political statement, while at the same time I can pocket seventy-five million pounds in lovely hard cash that the taxman will never see. It's beautiful. I love all sanctioneers and prohibitionists.''

"You are incorrigible." She laughed at him. "Isn't there any limit to your appetite for riches?''

At that he sobered and removed his arm from her shoulders. "You think I'm avaricious?'' he asked. "It's not so, Bella. The truth is that I am a player in the great game. I don't play for the monetary prize, I play for the thrill of winning. I was a loser for too much of my life. Now I must be a winner.''

"Is that all there is to it?'' She was also serious now. "You are playing with the wealth and well-being of millions of little people to gratify your ego.''

"When I win, those little people win. The sanctioneers seek to inflict starvation and misery upon millions of ordinary people in order to enforce their particular political vision. That, in my view, is a crime against humanity. When I frustrate their efforts, I strike a powerful blow for the little people.''

"Oh, Garry, you aren't a white knight. Don't pretend to be one—please!''

"Oh, yes, I am," he contradicted her. "I am one of the white knights of the capitalist system. Don't you see that? The only way out of our dilemma in southern Africa is through the education and upliftment of the people, particularly the blacks, and by the creation of wealth. We must steer for a society based not on class or caste or race or creed, but on merit. A society in which every person can pull his full weight and be rewarded in proportion to that effort—that is the capitalistic way.''

"Garry, I have never heard you speak like that before, like a liberal.''

"Not a liberal, a capitalist. Apartheid is a primitive feudal system. As a capitalist, I abhor it as much as or more than any of the sanctioneers. Capitalism destroyed the ancient feudalism of medieval Europe. Capitalism cannot coexist with a system that reserves power and privilege to a hereditary minority, a system that suppresses the free-market principles of labor and goods. Capitalism will destroy apartheid if it is allowed to do so. The sanctioneers would deny and inhibit that process. By

**337**

their well-intentioned but misguided actions they bolster apart-heid and they play into the hands of its perpetrators.''

She stared at him. "I've never thought about it that way be-fore."

"Poverty leads to repression. It is easy to oppress the poor. It is almost impossible to oppress an educated and prosperous people forever."

"So you will point the way to freedom through the economic rather than the political kingdom."

"Precisely." Garry nodded. Then he boomed out his big laugh. "And I'll set a fine capitalistic example by making my-self seventy-five million pounds a year in the process."

He braked the truck and turned off the track, following the leading Toyota, with Sean at the wheel, down to the pools in the mopane forest.

These were shallow depressions, known in Africa as "pans," filled with a muddy grey water. They were warmed by the sun and heavily laced with the pungent urine of the elephant herds that regularly bathed and drank in them. Despite the temperature and flavor of the water, the flocks of doves preferred them to the clear running water of the river only two miles distant.

The birds came in the hour before sunset in flocks that filled the air like blue-grey smoke. In their tens of thousands they winged in along established flight lanes.

Sean set up his guns on these lanes, five or six hundred meters from the water. He did not wish to prevent the birds from drink-ing by placing the guns over the pans. Instead he forced them to run the gauntlet to reach the water. As a matter of honor, each gun was expected to observe strictly a daily bag limit of fifty birds, and to attempt only the difficult, challenging shots at high, swiftly flying doves.

The guns were placed in pairs, not merely for company, but also to check each other and see that fair play was done, and to provide an appreciative audience for a finely taken double or a beautifully led shot at a blue streak passing a hundred feet over-head at seventy miles an hour.

Quite naturally, Elsa paired with Shasa, and their cries of *"Bello! Molto bello!"* and "Jolly good shot! Well done!" rang through the mopane as they encouraged each other.

Garry and Sean made a pair on the west side of the pans. Deliberately they placed themselves behind a tall stand of timber so that the doves were forced high and hurtled into their view over the treetops without warning, presenting a shot so fleeting as to call for lightning reflexes and instinctive calculation of lead.

Once Sean missed his bird, shooting two or three feet behind it. Garry swiveled with the long Purdy mounting to his shoulder and brought the escaping dove tumbling down on a trail of loose feathers. He looked across at his older brother with his spectacles glinting gleefully and boomed with laughter. Sean tossed back his hair and tried to ignore him, but his face darkened with fury.

Isabella was left with Sir Clarence at the south end of a grassy glen, out of sight of the rest of the party. She was shooting the gold-engraved 20-gauge Holland & Holland her father had given her. However, she had not fired it for almost a year, and her lack of practice showed in her shooting

She clean missed the first three birds in succession and then pricked one. She said, "Damn! Double damn!" She hated to wound them.

Sir Clarence took an accomplished double, then set his shotgun against the trunk of a mopane tree and crossed to where she stood.

"I say, do you mind if I give you a few tips?" he asked.

When she smiled at him over her shoulder he came up behind her. "You are allowing your right hand to overpower the gun." He folded her in his arms and took her hands in his huge fists. "Remember, your left hand must always dominate. The right hand is there only to pull the trigger."

He mounted the gun to her shoulder for her and squeezed her left hand onto the forestock for emphasis.

"Head up," he said. "Both eyes open. Watch the bird, not the gun." He smelled masculine. The perfume of his after-shave lotion did not entirely conceal the odor of fresh male sweat. His arms around her felt very agreeable.

"Oh," she said. "You mean like this?" And she pushed backward gently with her hard round buttocks as she aimed over the barrels.

"Precisely." There was a catch in his voice. "You have got it exactly right."

"Goodness gracious me!" She used one of Nana's cherished expressions to herself. "He is size fourteen all over." She had to work hard to keep herself from giggling like a schoolgirl.

Sir Clarence was warming rapidly to his self-appointed task as tutor, and Isabella told herself firmly, "That's enough already. We don't want to spoil him." And she gently freed herself from his embrace.

"Let me try it," she said, and she shot the next dove so cleanly that it did not even flutter a wing.

"You are a natural," he murmured. She turned her head away to conceal her smile at the double entendre.

"I understand from your brother that you are also a first-class horsewoman," he pursued relentlessly, not waiting for her reply. "I have recently purchased a magnificent Arab stallion. I doubt there is another like him in Africa. I'd love to show him to you."

"Oh?" she asked with a feigned lack of interest, concentrating on loading the shotgun. "Where is he?"

"On my ranch at Rusape. We could have the Alouette drop us off there on the way back to Salisbury tomorrow afternoon."

"I might enjoy that," she agreed. "I'd like to meet your wife. I've heard that she is a delightful lady."

He fielded it without a blink. "Alas, my wife is in Europe at the moment. She'll be away for another month at the least. You'd have to put up with me alone." He gave the last sentence a subtle emphasis, and this time she could not prevent herself smiling.

"I'll have to think about that, Sir Clarence," she said. "I imagine that you are rather a large handful to put up with."

This time his grave expression cracked and he smiled back at her. "Nothing that you couldn't handle, my dear."

She wondered what the reward from her mysterious masters would be if she could present them with not only the antisanctions strategy but also the complete Rhodesian order of battle. "All in the line of duty," she assured herself.


"Full bag!" Shasa called across to Elsa. He broke open his shotgun and placed it across the crook of his arm. He called to the two black children who had come along, "Pakamisa! Pick them up!"

They scampered away to pick up the last two doves. Shasa and Elsa sauntered back to where the trucks were parked beyond the pan. The sun was almost on the treetops, and the thin stratum of cloud above it was gilded to brightest gold—the color of a wedding ring, Shasa decided for no apparent reason.

"All right," Elsa said suddenly, as though she had reached a difficult decision.

"Forgive me"—he was puzzled—"what is all right?"

"I trust you," she said. "There will be conditions attached, but I will give you the blueprint for the plant and the formula for Cyndex 25."

He drew a slow breath. "I will try to be worthy of your trust."

340

That evening, as they sat at the campfire withdrawn from the rest of the party, she set down the conditions.

"You will give me your personal guarantee that Cyndex will never be used except on the express authority of the prime minister or his successors in office."

Shasa glanced across the flames to make certain they were not being overheard. "I swear that to you. I will obtain the prime minister's written agreement."

"Now, as to the rules of engagement, Cyndex will never be used on any section of the South African people," Elsa went on carefully. "It will never be used in internal political or civil conflict. It will never be used to quell an uprising of the populace or in a future civil war."

"I agree."

"It may be used only to repel a military invasion by troops of a foreign power, and then only when the use of conventional arms fails."

"I agree."

"There is one other condition—a little more personal."

"Name it."

"You will come to Lausanne personally to arrange the details."

"That will be my particular pleasure."

It was the last morning of safari. The guests had packed and were ready to leave Chiwewe. Their luggage was stacked outside each tent, ready for the camp staff to collect.

The business was done, the contracts signed. Elsa Pignatelli had agreed to assist with the marketing of Rhodesian tobacco and chrome—for a princely fee—while Garry Courtney had undertaken to provide shipping and false documentation for these materials from South African ports. His rewards for these services would include extension of the Chiwewe hunting concessions as well as his monetary commissions.

The entire party was due to be ferried back to Salisbury in the Rhodesian air force helicopter. The helicopter had already been in radio contact with the camp when it was airborne and only a hundred nautical miles out. They had expected it to land in the glade in front of the camp thirty minutes before. It was overdue, and they were worried.

In small groups they stood around the campfire in the *boma* sipping a final Pimm's No. I. Instinctively they kept glancing to the sky and listening for the sound of the Alouette's rotors.

Sean and Bella were together. "When are you coming to Cape Town?" she asked her eldest brother.

"I'll try to get down at the end of the season, if you promise to line up some crumpet for me."

"Whenever did you need help?" she asked.

Sean grinned and kissed her. "I'm not as bad as Pater," he protested. "Look at the old dog. He's off to Europe with the widow, I hear."

They both looked across at Elsa and Shasa.

"It's puke-making at their age," Sean teased.

Isabella came loyally to her father's defense. "Daddy is one of the most attractive—"

"Cool it, Bella." He squeezed her arm. "Worry about Sir C. You'll be lucky to escape with your virtue. They don't call him Cantering Clarence for nothing."

As if in response to his name, Sir Clarence drifted across to Isabella and quietly spirited her aside.

"We'll drop the others off at Salisbury," he murmured, leaning over her solicitiously. "Then the helicopter can take the two of us on to my ranch. We don't have to make a fuss about our little excursion, do we?"

"Of course not," Isabella agreed sweetly. "We don't want my papa—or Lady Van Wyk—spoiling our innocent interlude of horse appreciation."

"Exactly," he agreed. "Some things are best—" He broke off as the radio in Sean's tent crackled urgently and burst into life.

Sean bounded from the *boma* and disappeared into his tent. More than any of them, he had been worried by the overdue helicopter. They heard him acknowledging his call sign from the approaching helicopter.

"Tugboat, this is Big Foot. Go ahead."

"Big Foot, we have a change of plan. Please inform the minister that this flight is being diverted to hot-pursuit operations. We will pick you up with your recce team in sixteen minutes. I have ten Scouts on board. Alternative arrangements will be made for ministerial transport as soon as possible. Over."

"Roger, Tugboat. We will be ready for pickup. Standing by."

"War is such a damned nuisance," Sir Clarence sighed. They had overheard every word of the radio exchange. "We will have to sit around here until they can send another chopper to fetch us."

"What has happened?" Isabella demanded.

"Terrorist action," Sir Clarence explained. "Probably an attack on a white farm somewhere. Our helicopter is being diverted. The pursuit takes precedence over all other traffic. Can't let these murderous swine get away with it—have to keep the morale of the farmers up.''

He didn't mention how desperately short of military helicopters the Rhodesian air force was, but shrugged instead.

"It does look as though the fates are conspiring against us."

"Perhaps we'll just have to postpone our little arrangements—" Isabella broke off as Sean came out of the tent, shrugging on his light pursuit harness with its canvas pockets for ammunition and grenades and water bottles. His FN rifle was slung over one shoulder.

"Matatu, come on, you skinny little bugger," he bellowed. "We've got real work to do now. Hot pursuit."

The diminutive Ndorobo tracker appeared like a grinning black jack-in-the-box.

"Hili, Bwana,'' he piped in Swahili. "We will roast some ZANLA testicles on the campfire tonight."

"You bloodthirsty little devil. You love it, don't you?" Sean grinned with his own fierce joy, then turned to the others clustered in the center of the boma.

"Sorry, folks. Have to leave you to make your own way back to Salisbury. Matatu and I have a date." He singled out Garry in the group. "Why don't you ferry them up to Salisbury in the Beechcraft? With all that luggage it will take you a couple of trips, but it's better than sitting around waiting for the chopper to be free."

He broke off and cocked his head to listen. "Here she comes now."

He moved quickly among them, shaking hands in brief farewell.

"Will we see you again next season, signora? Next time, I promise you a big leopard . . .

"Sorry to bump you off the flight, Sir Clarence.

"Cheerio, Dad. Keep out of mischief . . .'' This with a wink and a glance at Elsa Pignatelli.

" 'Bye, little sister.'' He kissed Isabella, and she clung to him for a moment.

"Be careful, Sean. Please don't let anything happen to you."

He hugged her and laughed at the absurdity of the idea. "You are in more danger of receiving incoming fire from Sir C," he chuckled.

He looked up at the sky. The helicopter was a black insect shape above the trees.

He crossed to shake his younger brother's hand. "Damn it, Garry, who wants your job—when I can be doing this?"

While they waited for the helicopter to settle, Sean stood in the gateway of the *boma* with Matatu.

Isabella felt her throat close up and tears prickle her eyes. They made such an incongruous pair, the tall, heroic figure of her brother with his flowing locks and tanned muscular limbs and the wizened black gnome at his side. As she watched, Sean dropped one hand onto the little man's shoulder in an affectionate embrace, an affirmation of the trust bred between them in a hundred desperate adventures and a mark of the special bond between these two warrior-hunters.

Then they were racing forward into the blown dust cloud of the hovering helicopter, ducking low under the spinning blur of the rotors and scrambling into the open hatchway.

Immediately the machine rose and went boring away into the southeast, keeping low over the treetops, not wasting a moment in the climb for altitude.

## 27

The ten Scouts were seated along the benches in the main cabin of the helicopter, each of them heavily pregnant with his body harness and pack, draped with belts of ammunition and grenades and water bottles, bare arms and legs blackened. Only their teeth sparkled in faces that were either smeared with camouflage cream or were naturally dark. At least half the Ballantyne Scouts were loyal Matabele.

It was well known that blacks and whites fighting together as comrades tended to bring out the best qualities in each other as warriors. The Ballantyne Scouts were the crack unit of Rhodesia's fighting forces, although the Selous Scouts and the Special Air Services and the Rhodesian Regiment would split your crust if they heard you say it.

As Sean clambered into the cabin, he recognized every man of them and greeted them by name. They returned the greeting with a laconic economy of words that belied their awe and respect. Sean and Matatu were already a living legend in the Scouts. The two of them had trained most of these tough young veterans in the subtle skills of bushcraft.

Roland Ballantyne, the founder and commanding colonel of the Scouts, had tried every ruse to inveigle Sean in as his second-in-command—so far without success. In the meantime he called on Sean and Matatu whenever there was a heavy contact in the offing.

Now Sean dropped onto the seat beside him, and snapped on his seat belt. While he began rubbing camouflage cream into his face he shouted above the clatter of the rotors, "Greetings, Skipper. What's the rumble?"

"Bunch of terrs hit a tobacco farm outside Karoi yesterday evening. They ambushed the farmer at the homestead gate. Shot him down as his wife came out on the veranda to welcome him. She held them off alone all night in the farmhouse—even under rocket fire. Gutsy bird. Some time after midnight they pulled out and gapped it."

"How many?"

"Twenty plus."

"Which way?"

"North into the valley."

"Contact?"

"Not yet." Roland shook his head. Even under the camo cream he was lantern-jawed and impressive. He was probably five years older than Sean. Like Sean, he had built a hell of a reputation in the few short years since the bush war had begun.

"Local unit is following up but making heavy weather, losing ground every hour. The gooks are running hard."

"They'll bombshell and try to lose themselves amongst the local black population in the Tribal Trust area," Sean predicted as he bound a grubby scrap of camouflage net over his shining shoulder-length locks. "Get us to the follow-up unit, Skipper."

"We'll be in radio contact any minute—" Roland broke off as the flight engineer beckoned him to the radio handset. "Come on." He unbuckled his safety belt and led the way down the vibrating, bucking aisle between the benches. Sean followed him. He stood beside Roland, bracing himself against the bulkhead and craning his head to listen to the tinny, disembodied voice in the speaker. "Bushbuck, this is Striker One," Roland said into the mouthpiece. "Do you have contact?"

"Striker One, this is Bushbuck. Negative. I say again, negative on contact."

"Are you on the spoor, Bushbuck?"

"Affirmative, but chase has bombshelled." That meant that the terrorist gang had split up to hinder pursuit.

"Roger, Bushbuck. As soon as you hear our engines, give us yellow smoke."

"Confirm yellow smoke, Striker One."

Forty-five minutes later, the helicopter pilot picked out the smoke signal, a canary yellow feather drifting over the dark green roof of the forest. The helicopter dropped toward it and hovered above the grass tops in an open glade between the trees standing in the tree line. They saw the police unit that had pushed the pursuit thus far. It was obvious at a glance that these were not elite bush fighters but garrison troops from Karoi. They were townies and reserves doing their monthly call-up duties and not enjoying the chase one little bit.

Sean and Matatu exited together, jumping the six feet to earth and landing like a pair of cats, in balance with hot guns. They spread out swiftly and took cover while the helicopter soared and hovered two hundred feet above them.

It took them fifteen seconds to make certain that the police had the drop area secure. Then Sean ran across to the leader of the pursuit unit.

"Okay, Sergeant," he snapped crisply, "hit your bottle. Drink, man, drink."

The sergeant was red-faced, burnt by the sun, and overweight. Even in the valley heat, he had stopped sweating. The sweat had dried on his shirt in irregular white rings of salt. He didn't know enough to keep himself from dehydrating. Another hour and he would be a casualty.

"Water is finished." The sergeant's voice was hoarse. Sean tossed him a precious water bottle, and while the man drank he asked, "What's the line of spoor?"

The sergeant pointed to the earth ahead of him, but already Matatu had picked up the sign left by the fleeing gang. He scampered along it, cocking his head to study the fine details that were invisible to any but the truly talented eye. He followed it for a mere fifty paces, then doubled back to where Sean waited.

"Five of them," he chirped. "One wounded in the left leg . . ."

"The farmer's widow must have given them a good run."

". . . but the spoor is cold. We must play the spring hare."

Sean nodded. The "spring hare" was a technique he and Matatu had worked out between them. It could be effective only with a tracker of Matatu's caliber. They had to be able to guess where the chase was heading. They had to have a good idea of the line and rate of march before they could leapfrog—or spring-hare—down the line.

Here there was no doubt. The band of terrorists would have to keep northward toward the Zambezi and the Tribal Trust lands, where they could expect to find food and shelter and some rudimentary medical treatment for their wounded. There were many sympathizers among the black Shona and Batonka tribesmen who lived along the valley rim. Those who would not co-operate willingly would be forced to do so at the muzzle of an AK-47 assault rifle.

All right, so they would keep on northward. However, the wilderness ahead was vast. There was hard going and broken terrain, rocky valleys and jumbled granite kopjes. If the fleeing band turned only a few degrees off the obvious line of march, they could disappear without trace.

Sean ran out into the open glade and signaled the circling Alouette, holding his arms in a crucifix. The helicopter responded instantly.

"Okay, Sergeant," Sean called, jumping up into the helicopter, "Keep after them. We'll go ahead and try to cut the spoor. Maintain radio contact—and remember to drink."

"Right on, sir!" The sergeant grinned. The brief meeting had given him and his men fresh heart. They all knew who Sean was. He and Matatu were legend.

"Give them hell, sir!" he yelled up at Sean, who waved from the open hatch of the Alouette as they soared away.

Sean swallowed half a dozen codeine tablets for his ribs, which were beginning to ache, and washed them down with a swig from his spare water bottle. He and Matatu crouched together in the opening of the hatchway, peering down at the canopy of the forest five hundred feet below. Only at moments like these, when the hunt was running hot and hard, could Matatu subdue his terror of flying.

Now he leaned so far out of the hatch that Sean had to keep an arm around his waist to keep him from falling. Matatu was positively shivering in his grip, the way a good gundog shivers with the scent of the bird in his nostrils.

Suddenly he pointed, and Sean yelled to the flight engineer, "Turn ten degrees left."

Over the intercom the engineer relayed the change of course to the pilot in the high cockpit.

Sean could see no possible reason for Matatu's turn to the west. Below them the forest was amorphous and featureless.

The rocky kopjes that broke the leafy monotony were miles apart, random and indistinguishable one from the other.

Two minutes later Matatu pointed again, and Sean interpreted for him. "Turn back five degrees right."

The Alouette banked obediently. Matatu was performing his special magic. He was actually tracking the fugitives from five hundred feet above the canopy of trees, not by sight or sign, but by a weird intuitive sense that Sean would not have credited if he had not seen it happen on a hundred other chases over the years.

Matatu quivered in Sean's grip and turned his face up to his master's. He was grinning wickedly, his lips trembling with excitement. The blast of the slipstream had filled his eyes with tears, which were streaming down his cheeks.

"Down!" he yelped, and pointed again.

"Down!" Sean yelled at the flight engineer. As the helicopter dropped, Sean looked across at Roland Ballantyne.

"Hot guns!" he warned, and Roland signaled his men. They straightened up on the hard benches and leaned forward like hunting dogs on a leash. As one man they raised their weapons, muzzles high, and with a metallic clatter that carried above the roar of the turbo engines they locked and loaded.

The helicopter checked and hovered six feet above the baked dry earth. Sean and Matatu jumped together, and cleared the drop zone.

As soon as they were clear they went down into cover, facing outward. Sean's FN was at his shoulder as he scanned the bush around him. The Scouts came boiling out of the hatchway and scattered to adopt a defensive perimeter. The helicopter climbed away empty.

The second they were in position Roland Ballantyne signaled across to Sean with a clenched fist: "Go!"

Well separated, Sean and Matatu went forward. The Scouts spread out and covered them, eyes glinting, restless trigger fingers cocked. Matatu had brought them down into a bottleneck where a series of steep rocky ridges formed a funnel. The apex of the $V$ was cut through by a dry riverbed. Over the millennia storm water had sculpted a natural staircase that climbed the ridge, and the elephant herds that used this natural pass had worn down the contours and leveled the gradients.

Would the fleeing band have traded time for stealth? Would they have chosen the elephant highway, rather than toil up the jagged rocky ridge at another, less obvious point?

Matatu flicked his fingers underhand, signaling Sean to cast the eastern approach to the pass. Sean was as good a tracker as any white man alive. To save precious time, Matatu would trust him with such a simple cast as this.

Sean moved across the sun, so that the indentation of the spoor threw a rim of shadow apparent to his eye. It was the old tracker's trick to highlight the spoor. He concentrated all his attention on the earth, trusting the hovering Scouts to cover his back. They were all good men; he had trained them himself.

He felt a little electric thrill as he picked it up. It was close in against the cliff face. One of the round water-worn river boulders had been displaced. It was sitting a quarter of an inch askew in the natural dish of earth that had held it. He touched it with a fingertip just to check. He would not call Matatu and risk his scorn until he was certain.

"Little bugger will mock me for a week if I make a bum call."

The boulder was the size of his head, and it moved slightly under his finger. Yes, it had been recently dislodged. Sean whistled, and Matatu appeared at his side like the genie of the lamp. Sean did not have to point it out. Matatu saw it instantly and nodded his approbation.

The file of fugitives was antitracking skilfully. They had moved up the watercourse in Indian file, keeping in close under the precipitous rocky side. They had used the river boulders as stepping-stones to hide their tracks, but this one had been slightly dislodged by the weight of the men passing over it.

Matatu darted forward. A hundred or so paces farther on he found a spot where the wounded terrorist's foot had slipped off one of the stepping-stones and touched the soft white sand, leaving a brush mark. Only a highly trained eye would have noticed the faint shade of color difference between the surface grains and the freshly exposed grains of sand from below.

Matatu knelt over it and studied the faint scuff mark. Then he blew gently on the surrounding sand to gauge its friability. He rocked back on his heels while he pondered the factors that had effected the color difference in the grains—the moisture content of the sand, the angle of the sun, the strength of the breeze and, most important, the time elapsed since the sand had been disturbed.

"Two hours," he said with finality. Sean accepted his judgment without question.

"Two hours behind them," Sean reported to Roland Ballantyne.

"How does he do it?" Roland shook his head in wonder.

"He brought us straight here, and now he gives us the exact time. He's gained us eight hours in fifteen minutes. How does he do it, Sean?"

"Beats me," Sean admitted. "He's just a chocolate-coated miracle."

"Can he spring-hare us again?" Roland demanded. He spoke no Swahili, so Sean had to translate.

"Spring-hare, Matatu?"

"*Ndio*, Bwana." Matatu nodded happily and preened under the patent admiration of the colonel.

"Leave four men to follow up on the ground," Sean advised. "Tell them to follow the watercourse and there's a good chance they will pick up the spoor at the top."

Roland gave the orders, and the four Scouts moved away up the funnel in good order. Sean called down the helicopter, and they scrambled aboard.

They flew on into the north. However, they had not been airborne for more than ten minutes before Matatu wriggled in Sean's grip and yelped, "Turn! Turn back!"

Under Sean's direction the helicopter made a wide circle. Matatu was leaning halfway out of the hatch, and his head swung quickly from side to side as he peered downward. For the first time he seemed uncertain.

"Down!" he cried suddenly, pointing to a long streak of darker green vegetation that filled a shallow kidney-shaped depression in the terrain ahead of them.

The Alouette descended gently, warily. Matatu pointed out a landing zone at the far side of the depression.

The scrub below them was dense and thorny, and the ground was studded with ant heaps. These were bare, concretelike towers, hard red clay each as high as a man's shoulder, standing like headstones in a cemetery. They would make the landing difficult and dangerous.

Little bugger is taking us into the worst possible LZ, Sean thought bitterly. Why does he have to choose this particular spot?

The helicopter checked in midair, and Sean turned his head and yelled at Roland, "Hot guns, man!" Then he followed Matatu. They landed side by side and scurried forward, dropping into cover behind one of the ant heaps.

He did not turn his head to watch the other Scouts come out of the hatch. He was watching the tangled thorn scrub out ahead, sweeping his flanks with a darting penetrating scrutiny, holding the FN leveled and his thumb on the safety. Although it was a million-to-one chance that there was a terrorist within five miles of the LZ, still the landing drill was second nature to all of them.

"No gooks here," Sean assured himself. Then, incredibly, stunningly, they were under fire.

From the thorn scrub on their left flank AK fire raked them. The sharp, distinctive rattle of the fusillades swept over them. Dust and chips of red clay flew from the side of the ant heap only inches in front of Sean's face. He reacted instantly. He rolled and realigned, and as he brought the FN to bear he glimpsed a grisly little cameo of death from the corner of his eye.

One of the Scouts, the last man out of the hatch, had been hit. As his feet touched the ground, a burst of AK fire caught him across the belly. It doubled him over and drove him backward three sharp paces. The bullets exiting from his back pulled his body out of shape. They sucked half his guts out of him and blew them through the stark sunlit air in a misty pink streak. Then he was down and gone into the scrub.

As Sean returned fire, the realization flashed upon him: Matatu has dropped us into direct contact. He punctuated his thoughts with short measured bursts of the FN. The little bugger has been too bloody good this time, he thought. He has dropped us right on their heads.

At the same time he was assessing the contact. Obviously the gang had been taken as unaware as they themselves had been. They had not been able to prepare any kind of defense, nor had they had time to set up an ambush. Probably they had heard the roar of the approaching helicopter, and then only seconds later the Scouts had begun dropping among them.

Surprise, Sean thought, shooting at the muzzle flashes of an AK that were fluttering the leaves of a thorn bush only thirty paces ahead.

From experience he had learned that the Shona guerrillas facing him were first-class soldiers, doughty and brave and dedicated. They had two weaknesses, however. First, their fire control was poor; they believed that sheer weight of fire made up for inaccuracy. Their other weakness was an inability to react swiftly to surprise. Sean knew that for another minute or so the terrorists in the scrub in front of him would be disorganized and flustered.

Hit them now, he thought, snatching a phosphorus grenade from his webbing. As he pulled the pin from the grenade he opened his mouth to yell at Roland Ballantyne, "Come on, Roland. Sweep line! Charge the sods before they settle down."

Roland beat him to it. The same thoughts must have raced through his mind. "Take them, boys! Sweep line—on the charge!"

Sean leaped to his feet and in the same movement hurled the grenade in a high, arcing trajectory. It fell thirty yards ahead of him, and the thorn scrub erupted in a blinding white cloud of phosphorus smoke. Flaming fragments, burning with a dazzling white radiance, showered over the area.

Sean raced forward, conscious of the small dark shape that ran at his heels. Matatu was his shadow. Other grenades were exploding across the front, and the thorn scrub was thrashed by the blasts and lashed by the sheets of automatic fire the Scouts threw down as they charged.

The gang broke before them. One of them ducked out of the bush ten paces ahead of Sean, a teenager in tattered blue jeans and a soft camouflage cap. Burning globules of phosphorus had adhered to his upper body. They sizzled and flared, leaving smoking black spots on his arms and torso. The smoke smelling like barbecueing meat.

Sean shot him, but the burst was low. It broke his left hip, and the boy dropped. The AK rifle flew from his grip, and he rolled onto his back and held his hands in front of his face.

"No, *Mambo!*" he screamed in English. "Don't kill me! I am a Christian—for the love of God, spare me!"

"Matatu," Sean snapped without checking or looking round. *"Kufa!"*

He jumped over the maimed guerrilla. The magazine of his FN was half empty. He could not afford to waste a single round, and Matatu had his skinning knife. He spent hours each day honing the blade. If he had been a section leader, Sean might have saved him for interrogation, but Matatu could cut this one's throat. Cannon fodder like him was of no use to them, and medical attention was expensive.

The Scouts swept the bush, and it was over in less than two minutes. It was no contest. It was like pitting Pekinese puppies against a pack of wild dogs. The Scouts charged through and then whirled and came back.

"Secure the area," Roland Ballantyne ordered. He was standing less than twenty yards from Sean. He held the muzzle of his rifle pointed at the sky, and the heated metal distorted the air around it in a watery mirage. "Well done, Sean. That little black devil of yours is a charm." He glanced across at Matatu.

Matatu was straightening up from the corpse of the hip-shot

terrorist. He had slit his throat with a single stroke, across the side of the throat and up under the ear to catch the carotid artery.

He was wiping the blade of his skinning knife on his thigh as he scurried back to his rightful place at Sean's side, but he grinned an acknowledgment at Roland Ballantyne. Both of them were distracted, still heady with the euphoria of violence and blood.

The corpse of one of the other guerrillas lay in the scrub between them. The flesh and clothing still smoldered with burned-out phosphorus, and the man's clothing was splattered with bright blood from his gunshot wounds. Roland Ballantyne walked past him with barely a glance. It was impossible the terrorist could have survived such terrible injuries.

The terrorist rolled over abruptly. He had been concealing a Tokarev pistol under his shattered chest. With a last flutter of life he lifted the Tokarev. He was close enough to touch Roland with the muzzle.

"Roland!" Sean screamed a warning, and although Roland reacted instantly it was too late. The shot would take him in the spine from a range of three feet.

Sean did not have time to raise the FN to his shoulder. He fired from the hip, aiming instinctively. The bullet caught the terrorist in the face. His head burst like an overripe watermelon hit with a pick handle, and he flopped over onto his back. The Tokarev slipped unfired from his nerveless fingers.

Roland Ballantyne straightened up slowly, and for a long moment he stared down at the corpse. The man's legs were kicking and trembling convulsively. Roland contemplated his own mortality and saw the agony of his own death reflected in the man's bulging eyeballs.

He tore his gaze away and looked across at Sean.

"I owe you one," he said curtly. "You can collect anytime." And he turned away to shout orders at his Scouts to gather the kill. There were green plastic body bags in the hovering Alouette.

# 28

Le Morne Brabant was a jagged mountain of black volcanic lava that seemed to tower over them threateningly, even though they were almost four miles out on the oceanic stream.

The sapphire currents that eddied around the toe of the island of Mauritius created an enrichment of marine life that big game anglers around the world recognized as a "hot spot." There were other famous grounds such as those off the ribbons of the Great Barrier Reef, at Cabo San Lucas on the Californian peninsula or in the lee of the island of Nova Scotia. At all these points the concentrations of vast shoals of bait fish attracted the ocean predators—the giant marlin and the tuna species. The sports anglers of the world came to pit their skill and their strength against these sleek monsters.

Shasa Courtney always insisted on chartering the same boat and the same island crew. Each boat sets up its own individual vibration in the water, a combination of engine and propeller and hull configuration that is as unique to that boat as a fingerprint is to a man. That vibration either attracts or repels fish.

*Le Bonheur* was a lucky boat. She pulled fish, and her skipper had eyes like a gannet. He could spot the flash of a single seabird diving on a school of bait fish on the horizon, or at a mile's distance pick out the sickle-shaped dorsal fin of a cruising marlin and estimate the fish's weight to within ten kilos.

Today, however, they were desperate for a bait. They had been out for almost two hours without putting a bait on the outriggers.

Everywhere they looked there were shoals of bait fish. The Indian Ocean seemed to swarm with their multitudes. They darkened the surface of the water like patches of cloud shadow, and dense flocks of seabirds circled over them, screaming and diving in avaricious hysteria. Every few minutes a volley of leaping bonito would burst through the surface and arc through the brilliant tropical sunshine in glittering silver parabolas.

They were being panicked and driven up by the great pelagic fish that circled in the depths below the shoals. It was one of those crazy days that occur all too seldom in a fisherman's life when there are simply too many fish. The ravenous predators were harrying the shoals so viciously that they were unable to feed. All their energy was diverted to avoiding the voracious charging monsters that were tearing through the shoals. They ignored the small finger-length feather lures with which the crew of *Le Bonheur* was trying to tempt them.

Standing on the flying bridge fifteen feet above the deck, Shasa could see deep into the limpid blue waters. He could clearly make out the hordes of bonito, like fat cigars as long as his forearm, dodging and ducking through *Le Bonheur*'s wake. They almost touched the feather jigs as they darted past them.

"We need one—just one bait," Shasa groaned. "On a day like this it's an ironclad guarantee of a marlin."

Elsa Pignatelli leaned over the bridge rail beside him. She wore only a tiny flaming scarlet bikini, and she was tanned and smooth as a loaf of honey bread crisp from the oven.

"Look!" she cried. Shasa whirled just in time to see a marlin come out of the water alongside *Le Bonheur*. It was driven high into the air by the speed and power of its charge as it split a shoal of bonito. Its eyes were the size of tennis balls, and its spike was the length and thickness of a baseball bat. Water streamed from its flanks in silver cascades, and it wagged its great head in the air. In the excitement of the feeding frenzy it had changed color, like a chameleon, and it burned with bands of electric blue and lilac that turned the tropical blue of the sky pale in contrast.

"A grander!" Shasa shouted the colloquial name for a fish that would push the scale beyond the mystic thousand-pound mark.

The marlin fell back and hit the water flat on its side with a report like a shot of cannon.

"A bait!" cried Shasa, clutching his brow like a Shakespearian tragedian. "My kingdom for a bait!"

The other half-dozen boats of the Black River fleet that they could see scattered toward the horizon were suffering the same agonies. They could hear the frustrated lamentations of their skippers on the ship's radio. Nobody had bait, while out there the marlin were waiting to commit suicide.

"What can *I* do?" Elsa demanded. "Do you want me to propound a little of my witchcraft and weave a spell for you?"

"I don't know if that would be strictly ethical." Shasa grinned back at her. "But I'm willing to try anything. Weave away, my lovely witch!"

Elsa opened her purse and found her lipstick. "Tom Thumb, Thomas à Becket, Rumpelstiltskin!" she intoned solemnly, and drew a scarlet hieroglyph on his naked chest that had a distinctly phallic outline. "I diddle you! I fiddle you! I doddle you! I doodle you!"

"Oh yes. I love it," Shasa laughed out loud. "I could get seriously hooked on your type of magic."

"You have to believe in it," she warned him, "or else it just won't work."

"I believe," said Shasa fervently. "Oh, how I believe in doodling you!"

Down on the deck below them one of the crew squealed suddenly, and they heard the tinny whir of the ratchet on one of the small bait rods.

Shasa's laughter was cut off abruptly. For an instant he stared at her with awe. "Damn me! You really are a witch," he muttered, and he dived for the ladder and slid down to the deck.

The deckhand brought a skipjack bonito over the side and cradled it lovingly in his arms. The fish quivered and struggled, but he cushioned its fat round body against his chest. It was a pretty metallic blue and silver, with a pointed snout and sharp-bladed tail fins. Its lower body was laced with lateral lines of black. Shasa saw with relief that it was lightly hooked in the hinge of the jaw. There was no damage to its gills.

He slipped the small hook from its jaw and ordered the deckie, "Turn him!" The deckie inverted the bonito, and immediately its struggles ceased. Holding it upside down was a trick that disorientated and quieted it.

Shasa had his bait instruments laid out like those of a surgeon. He selected the long crochet hook and worked it carefully into the front of the bonito's eye socket. The blunt steel tip pushed the eyeball aside and did not damage it in the least. He steered the needle into the canal through the bone of the fish's skull. The tip emerged from the same spot in the opposite eye socket. The fish showed no sign of distress and lay quietly in the deckie's arms.

Shasa hooked a loop of 120-pound Dacron line over the steel crochet hook and gently drew the line back through the wound. He dropped the crochet hook and snatched up the huge 12/0 marlin hook. With a series of quick deft turns he attached the hook firmly between the bonito's eyes. The fish was still alive and virtually unharmed. Its eyesight was unimpaired.

Shasa stood back and nodded to the deckie. He knelt on the gunwale and lowered the bonito over the side, solicitous as a nursemaid. As soon as it was released, the fish darted away, drawing the heavy steel trace and the attached Dacron line behind it. It disappeared almost instantly into the blue depths.

Shasa stood beside the fighting chair. The stubby rod was set into the gimbal. The Fin-Nor Tycoon reel was made of gold-anodized marine-grade aluminium alloy. Even so, it weighed over five kilos and held over a kilometer of the braided Dacron line. The line hissed softly as it streamed off the reel. Shasa adjusted the tension on it with a light touch of his fingertips.

He had marked the line with wraps of silk thread at intervals of fifty yards. He let out a measured hundred yards before he tightened the drag lever of the reel.

The deckie was already lowering the halyard of one of the twenty-foot outriggers that protruded like whippy steel antennae from each side of the hull. The purpose of the outrigger was to hold the lines separated and to allow the slack bight of line to drop back when the marlin struck.

"No." Shasa stopped him. "I will hold it myself."

This was a more precise method of determining the depth of the bait and amount of drop-back. However, it required patience, experience and fortitude to handhold the line rather than merely to loll in the chair and leave it in the clip of the outrigger.

Carefully Shasa stripped a hundred feet of line off the big Fin-Nor and coiled it on the deck. Then he perched on the stern of *Le Bonheur* and called to the skipper, *"Allez!"*

The skipper engaged the gear lever, and the propeller began to turn lazily. The diesel engine was ticking over at idling revs and *Le Bonheur* began to inch forward against the scend of the swells.

Slowly she built up to a leisurely walking speed. The tension on the line in Shasa's hand increased. He could feel the weight of the bonito on the other end. The fish began to follow the boat like a dog on a leash. Shasa judged the depth of the bait by the angle at which the line entered the water. He could tell the condition and liveliness of the bonito by the faint vibration of its tail and the intermittent tugs and jerks it gave as it attempted to turn or dive.

Within minutes Shasa's arm was numb and cramping, but he

357

ignored the discomfort and called up to Elsa on the bridge, "How about a little more of your 'fiddle me, diddle me' magic?"

She shook her head. "It only works once. From here on you are on your own."

At slow speed *Le Bonheur* rolled sluggishly over the swells, and at Shasa's order it began a wide and gentle turn up into the north.

Halfway through the turn, the line went slack in Shasa's hand. He stood up quickly from his seat on the gunwale.

"What is it?" Elsa called down eagerly.

"Probably nothing," he grunted, but all his concentration was on the feel of the line.

It came taut again, but now the bonito's movements were altered. He could feel its frantic struggles transmitted through his fingertips. It ducked and dived and tried to turn, but the gentle progress of *Le Bonheur* drew it forward remorselessly.

"*Attention!*" Shasa alerted the crew.

"What's happening?" Elsa asked again.

"Something is frightening the bonito," he answered. "It's seen something down there."

He could imagine the terror of the small fish as a gigantic shadow circled it stealthily in the blue underworld of the ocean. The marlin would be wary, for the bonito was behaving unnaturally; it should have darted away instantly. The marlin was stalking the bonito gingerly, but soon its appetite would exceed its caution. Shasa waited a minute and another minute, crouched over the transom, rigid with excitement.

Suddenly the line was plucked from his fingers, but for an instant he felt the mighty weight and majesty of the marlin as it struck the bonito with the broad blunt edge of its spike.

"Strike!" Shasa howled, holding both arms above his head. "Stop engines!"

Obediently the skipper slipped the gear lever into neutral, and *Le Bonheur* wallowed dead in the water. Shasa picked up the line again and held it with the lightest pressure of his fingertips. It was slack; no sign of life. The bonito had been killed instantly by that massive blow.

Vividly he imagined what was happening in those mysterious blue depths. The marlin had killed, and now it was circling again. It might lose interest or become alarmed by the unnatural movement of the carcass. It was essential that no movement or drift on the line scare it off.

The seconds dripped like treacle, slow and sticky.

"He is making another circle," Shasa said, trying to encourage himself. Still nothing happened.

"*Il est parti,*" the skipper announced lugubriously. "*Il a refusé.*"

"I'll kick your pessimistic butt if you wish it on me," Shasa told him furiously. "He hasn't bloody well *parti*-ed. He's coming around for another circle."

The line twitched in his fingers, and Shasa let out a shout of relief.

"*Le voilà!* There he is!"

Elsa clapped her hands. "Eat, fish. Smell that lovely sweet flesh. Eat it," she implored.

The line jiggled and tugged softly, and Shasa let a few inches slide through his fingers. He could imagine the marlin picking up the carcass in its horny beak and turning it headfirst to swallow it down.

"Don't let him feel the hook," Shasa whispered. The loop of line should allow the point of the hook to lie flat against the bonito's head as it slid down the marlin's gaping maw. If, however, the loop had twisted or hung up—Shasa did not want to think about that.

There was another long pause. Then the line came taut again and began to move off with a sedate but purposeful momentum.

"He's swallowed it," Shasa exulted, and let the line flow through his fingers; coil after coil unwound from the deck and slipped away over the transom.

Shasa leaped to the swivel chair and swung himself into the seat. He clipped the harness to the rings on top of the glittering Fin-Nor reel. The harness formed a hammocklike sling around his lower back and buttocks and was attached directly to the reel.

Only the ignorant or the deliberately misinformed believed the angler was buckled into the chair like a fighter pilot and that this gave him some sort of unsporting advantage. The only thing that kept him in the chair was his own strength and balance. If he made a mistake, the fish, weighing over a thousand pounds, and as fast and powerful as a marine diesel engine, could pluck him and the rod effortlessly over the side and give him a swift trip down to the five-hundred-fathom mark.

As Shasa settled behind the rod and engaged the brake, the line came up short against the spool and the rod tip bowed over, as though it were kowtowing to the fish's brute strength.

Shasa thrust his feet against the footboard and took the strain with his legs.

*"Allez!"* he yelled at Martin the skipper. "Go!"

The diesel bellowed as Martin opened the throttle wide and a dense cloud of oily black diesel smoke belched from the exhausts. *Le Bonheur* leaped forward and crashed her shoulder into the swell.

No man had the strength to drive the point of the huge Mustad hook into the iron-hard mouth of the marlin. Shasa was using the power and speed of the boat to set the hook, to bury the barb deep in the horny beak. The spool of the reel hummed against its own massive brake pads, and the line streamed away in a white blur.

Shasa judged that the hook was in. *"Arrêtez-vous!* Stop!" he cried, and Martin closed the throttle.

They stopped and hung in the water. The rod was arched over as though the line were attached to the bottom of the ocean, but the reel was still, held by the brake.

Then the fish shook its head, and the power of it crashed the butt of the rod back and forth in its gimbal as though it were a twig in a high wind.

"Here he goes!" Shasa howled. The fish had been taken aback by the unexpected drag of the line, but even *Le Bonheur* had been unable to move its massive body against the drag of the water.

Now at last the marlin realized that something was seriously wrong, and it made its first mad run. Once again the line poured off the reel in a molten blur, and Shasa was lifted high off the seat like a jockey pushing for the post. So great was the friction in the massive Fin-Nor reel that it began to smoke. The grease on the bearings melted and boiled, bubbling and spurting from the casing in steaming jets.

Leaning back with the full weight of his body, Shasa kept both hands well clear of the humming reel. The Dacron line was as dangerous as the blade of a butcher's band saw. It could take off a finger effortlessly or slash skin and flesh and muscle to the bone.

The fish ran as though there were no restraint upon him. The line on the spool melted away, three hundred yards were gone, then four. In seconds half a kilometer of line had gone over the side.

"He's a goddam Chinaman and he's going home to daddy!" Shasa yelled. "He's never going to stop!"

Abruptly the ocean parted in a maelstrom of white water, and the fish came out. Such was its girth and mass that it gave the illusion of moving in slow motion. It rose into the air, and the

360

water poured from its body as though from the hull of a surfacing submarine. It came all the way out and, though it was five hundred yards from *Le Bonheur*, it seemed to blot out half the sky.

"*Qu'il est grand!*" shrieked Martin. "*Je n'ai jamais vu un autre comme ça!*" And Shasa knew it was true—he had never seen a fish to match this one, not by half. It seemed to light the heavens with a reflected blue radiance like a flash of distant lightning.

Then, like a steeplechaser taking a fence, the fish reached the zenith of its leap and curved back to the surface of the ocean. It opened to its bulk in a shock wave, and then it was gone, leaving them all shaken by the memory of its majesty.

The line was blurring from the reel. Though Shasa had the brake dangerously heavy, pushing the drag up near the 120-pound breaking strain, it still streamed away as though there were no check upon it.

"*Tournez-vous!* Turn!" There was an edge of panic in Shasa's voice as he yelled at the skipper, "Turn and chase him!"

With full rudder and opposite engine thrust Martin spun the boat on its heel and they roared away in pursuit of the fish. *Le Bonheur* was rushing into wind and current, and the swells battered her. She dug her nose into them, and was bursting them open in white spray. Then as she leaped over the crests she was almost airborne, and she came pounding down into the troughs on her belly.

In the chair Shasa was thrown around mercilessly. He hung on to the arms of the chair and rode the swells with his legs, his backside not touching the seat. The rod was bent like a longbow at full stretch. Even though *Le Bonheur* was running at full throttle, he was still losing line. The marlin was outrunning them by ten knots. The line on the reel wasted away, and Shasa watched helplessly as the spool seemed to shrink.

"Shasa!" Elsa shrieked from the bridge. "He has turned!" She was so excited that she spoke in Italian. Shasa had by now had enough practice with the language to understand her warning.

"Stop! *Arrêtez!*" he howled at the skipper.

For no apparent reason the marlin had suddenly turned completely about and was charging back toward the boat.

This was not yet apparent from the direction that the line was running into the water. The marlin had thrown a half-mile loop in the line, which was potentially catastrophic. The side drag of the loop in the water could snap the heavy line like cotton when the marlin came up tight on it. Elsa had spotted the turn in the very nick of time.

Shasa had to pick up that loop before the marlin passed under the boat. He pumped with his legs in a powerful mechanical rhythm, coming up to gain a foot of line, sinking down to give himself slack to take it onto the reel with two quick turns of the handle. Up and down he bobbed, grunting for air with each cycle, legs and arms working together, the wet line coming onto the spool under such tension that a fine haze of droplets sprayed from the braid. The line was cutting sideways through the water, slicing a tiny feather from the surface. The loop was shrinking. The fish passed under the boat. The line began to straighten.

Shasa pumped with a frantic rhythm, getting the last few turns of line onto the reel.

"Turn now!" he gasped. Sweat was pouring down his naked chest. It mingled with the lipstick design Elsa had drawn, running down to stain the waistband of his shorts. "Turn quickly! Quickly!"

The fish was tearing away in the opposite direction, and the skipper got *Le Bonheur* around just as the line came up tight again. The full weight of the fish came down on the rod tip, and it whipped over like a willow tree struck by a gale of wind. Shasa was levered up out of the chair to the full stretch of his legs, and the strain on the line was ounces short of snapping it.

He thumbed off the brake, releasing the tension, and the line crackled off the spool at fifty miles an hour. With despair he watched as the precious feet of line that he had won back with so much effort blurred effortlessly over the side.

"Chase him!" he blurted, and *Le Bonheur* pounded after the fish.

It was exquisite teamwork now. No single man could subdue a fish like this alone and unaided. The handling of the boat was critical, each turn and run and backup had to be quick and precise.

Precious seconds before it was apparent to the men on the deck below, Elsa called out to warn of each new, wild evolution of the great fish. For an hour those irresistible rushes never ceased. Every second of that time the thin strand of Dacron was under immense pressure, and Shasa stood in the chair and used his weight against it, pumping the rod and churning the reel. He took turn after agonizing turn onto the spool, then watched it dissipate again as the fish made another charge.

One of the deckhands spilled seawater from a bucket over his shoulders to cool him. The salt burned the abrasions around his waist where the nylon straps of the harness had rubbed through his skin. Blood seeped from the injuries and stained his shorts a watery pink. Every time the fish ran, the harness cut in a little deeper.

The second hour was bad. The fish showed no sign of weakening. Shasa was streaming with sweat, and his hair was sodden as if he were standing under a shower. The galls made by the harness around his middle were bleeding freely. The working of the boat hammered his thighs against the arms of the chair, and he was bruising extensively. Elsa came down from the bridge and tried to pack a cushion between the harness and his torn flesh. She gave him a handful of salt tablets and made him drink two cans of Coca-Cola, holding them to his mouth while he gulped them down.

"Tell me something." He grinned crookedly at her with agony in his single eye. "What the hell am I doing this for?"

"Because you are a crazy macho man. And there are some things a man must do." She toweled the sweat off his face and kissed him with a fierce, protective pride.

Sometime during the third hour Shasa got his second wind. Twenty years ago it would have come sooner and lasted longer. The second wind was an extraordinary sensation. The pain of the galling harness receded, the cramps in his arms and legs smoothed away, he felt light-headed and invincible. His legs stopped juddering under him, and he planted his feet more firmly on the footboard.

"All right, fish," he said softly. "You have had your innings. Now it's my turn." He leaned back with all his weight against the rod and felt the fish give.

It was only a tiny check on the rod, a shudder of movement, but down there in the blue depths the great fish had stumbled slightly.

"Yes, fish," Shasa whispered as his spirits soared, "it's hurting you, too, now, isn't it?" He pumped with legs that were once more strong beneath him and laid four tight white coils of line on the reel—and he knew that they would stay there this time. The fish was coming at last.

By the end of the fourth hour the fish had no more wild dashing runs to make. It was fighting deep and dogged, making slow, almost sedate circles three hundred feet below the drifting boat. It was working on its side, offering as much resistance as possible to the pressure of rod and line. It was almost four feet across the shoulder, and it weighed nearly three quarters of a ton. The great half-moon of its tail swept back and forth to a stately beat, and its enormous eyes glowed like opals in the semidark. Waves of lilac and azure flame rippled across its body like the aurora of the Arctic skies. Around it went, and around again in steady sweeping circles.

Shasa Courtney was crouched in the fighting chair, bowed over the rod like a hunchback. All the euphoria of the second wind had evaporated. He bent and straightened his legs with the deliberate agony of an arthritic, and every muscle and nerve screamed in protest at the movement.

Fish and man had established a dreadful pattern in this final phase of the struggle. The fish went out on the far lap of its circle, and the man hung on grimly, his sinews strained to the same pitch as the Dacron line. Then the fish swung through the circle and came back in under the boat; for a few moments the tension on the line abated and the arc in the rod straightened.

Shasa took two quick turns of line, then hung on again as the fish swung onto the outward leg. With each circle he recovered a few feet of line, but he paid a price for it in sweat and pain. Shasa knew he was coming to the end of his endurance. He thought about the risk of doing permanent damage to his body. He could feel his heart pulsing like a swollen fragile sac in his chest, and his spine was shot through with fire. Soon something must snap or burst inside him, but he pulled with all his remaining strength and felt the fish give again.

"Please," he whispered to it. "You are killing us both. Just give up now. Please."

He gathered himself and pulled again—and the fish broke. It rolled like a waterlogged tree trunk and succumbed to the pressure of the rod. It came up, sluggish and heavy, and thrust its head through the surface so close to the stern of the boat that it seemed to Shasa that he could reach out and touch one of its great glowing eyes with the tip of the rod.

It stood on its tail, pointed its nose spike to the sky and shook its head the way a spaniel coming ashore shakes the water from its ears. The heavy steel trace whipped and whistled around its head, and the rod was battered and slammed from side to side. The butt clattered and banged in the gimbal, and the line flashed and looped and traced sweeping designs in the air.

Still the fish stood in the water and opened its mighty triangular beak wide and kept shaking its head, and Shasa was helpless in the face of such power. He could not control it. The rod was jerked back and forth in his grip, and he watched the steel trace flog like the lash of a bullwhip.

With a sense of despair he saw the long shank of the hook

twist and flick in the hinge of the open jaw. The gyrations of the fish were working it loose from the bone.

"Stop it!" he gasped at the fish, and tried to haul it over on its side. He felt the hook come loose and slip and skid across the bone before it caught again. The fish gaped at him, and he saw the hook still holding lightly on to the very lip of the iron black beak. One more shake of the head and the hook would be catapulted away on the swinging steel trace.

Shasa rose up in the chair and gathered the last of his strength. He hauled the marlin backward, and it toppled and crashed back into the sea in a smother of foam.

"The trace," he croaked at the deckie. "Get the trace." A direct pull on the steel wire trace would bring the fish under control.

During all four hours of the struggle, no person other than the angler had been permitted to touch the rod or the line to assist in the capture. Those were the rules of the sporting ethic laid down by the International Game Fishing Association.

Now, with the fish played out and lying beaten on the surface, the crew was permitted to handle the thirty-foot steel trace, which was attached to the end of the line, and to hold the fish with it while the flying gaff was driven into its flesh.

"Trace!" Shasa pleaded as the deckie, wearing heavy leather gloves, reached out over the stern and tried to get a hand to the top swivel of the trace. It was just beyond his fingertips.

The marlin wallowed on the surface, rolling and pitching like a dead log in the swells.

"One more time." Shasa rose up and braced himself behind the rod. He pulled with a steady, even pressure. The hook was holding only by its needle point, the barb was not buried—the slightest twist or jerk could free it.

The second deckhand stood ready with the flying gaff, a massive stainless-steel hook on the end of a detachable pole. Once that hook was plunged into the marlin's shoulder, the struggle would be over.

The top swivel of the trace was six inches from the fingertips of the gloved hand, and the marlin fanned its tail, a last exhausted effort. The tip of the rod gave a little nod, almost as though approving the gallant spirit of the fish—and the hook came free.

The rod snapped straight and the hook flicked through the air and clattered against *Le Bonheur*'s gunwale. Shasa fell back into the chair with a crash. Only forty feet away the marlin lay on the surface with its back and tall dorsal fin exposed. It was free but too spent to swim away; its tail made only spasmodic, convulsive movements.

They all stared at it until Martin the skipper recovered his wits. He slipped *Le Bonheur* into reverse and backed her up on the wallowing monster.

"*On l'aura!* We will have him!" he yelled at the gaff man as the marlin bumped against the stern. The deckhand sprang to the transom and raised the gleaming hook high to drive the point into the fish's unprotected hump.

Shasa tumbled from the chair, his legs buckling weakly under him. Only just in time did he manage to seize the deckie's shoulder and arrest the blow before it was struck.

"No," he croaked. "No." He wrested the gaff from the man's hand and flung it onto the deck. The crew stared at him in astonishment and chagrin. They had worked almost as hard as Shasa had for this fish.

It did not matter. He would explain to them later that it was unethical to free-gaff a fish. The moment the marlin threw the hook, the contest was over. The fish had won. To kill him now would be a deadly offense to all the ethics of sportsmanship.

Shasa's legs could no longer support his weight. He collapsed across the transom. The fish still lay on the surface beneath the stern. He reached down and touched the colossal dorsal fin. The edge was sharp as a broadsword's.

"Well done, fish," Shasa whispered, and his eyes stung with the salt of his own sweat and with other things. "It was a hell of a fight. Good for you, fish."

He stroked the fin as though it were the body of a lovely woman. His touch seemed to galvanize the marlin. The strokes of its tail became stronger and more regular. His gill plates opened and closed like a bellows as he breathed, and he began to move away slowly.

They followed him for almost half a mile as he swam upon the surface with his fin standing in the blue like a tall tower. Shasa and Elsa stood hand in hand at the rail in silence and watched the strength and vigor return to the great fish.

Faster beat his tail, and he steadied in the water and pressed against the swells with all his former majesty. Gradually the tall fin sank below the surface, and they saw the long dark shape of his body recede into the depths. There was one last flash of light like the reflection from a mirror deep in the blue water, and then the fish was gone.

On the long run back to port, Shasa and Elsa sat very close together. They watched the lovely emerald gem of the island

366

grow before them, and once or twice they smiled at each other in quiet and perfect accord.

When *Le Bonheur* ran into the Black River harbor and came into the dock, the other boats of the fleet were already tied up alongside. On the scaffold in front of the clubhouse hung the carcasses of two dead marlin. Neither of them was half the size of the fish Shasa had lost. A small admiring crowd was gathered around them. The successful anglers were posing with their rods. Their names and the marlin's weights were chalked on the glory board. An Indian photographer from Port Louis was crouched over his tripod recording their moment of triumph.

"Don't you wish your fish was hanging there?" Elsa asked softly as they paused to watch the scene.

"How beautiful a marlin is when he is alive," Shasa murmured. "And how ugly he is when he is dead." He shook his head. "My fish deserves better than that."

"And so do you," she said, and led him to the bar in the clubhouse. He moved stiffly, like a very old man, but his bruises gave him a strange, masochistic pride.

Elsa ordered him a Green Island rum and lime.

"That should give you strength to get you home, old man," she teased him lovingly.

"Home" was Maison des Alizés, the House of the Trade Winds. It was a rambling old plantation house built a hundred years before by one of the French sugar barons. Shasa's architects had renovated it and restored it in authentic detail.

It sat like a glistening wedding cake in twenty acres of its own gardens. The old French baron had begun a collection of tropical plants, and Shasa had added to those over the years. The pride of the collection was the Royal Victoria water lilies, whose leaves floated on the gleaming fish ponds. The leaves were four feet across and curled at the edges like enormous platters, and the blooms were the size of a man's head.

Maison des Alizés was situated below the massif of Le Morne Brabant, only twenty minutes' drive from the clubhouse at Black River harbor. This was the main reason Shasa had purchased it. He referred to it as his fishing shack.

As they drove up under the spreading canopy of ficus trees, Shasa remarked, "Well, it looks as though the rest of the party has arrived safely."

Half a dozen cars were parked along the curve of the driveway in front of the main portals of the house. Elsa's pilot had ferried two engineers from Zurich in her personal jet. They were the technical directors of Pignatelli Chemicals, who had developed the process and designed the plant for manufacturing Cyndex 25. Shasa had met Werner Stolz, the German director, during the delicate preliminary discussions in Europe. These had gone smoothly, under Elsa's skillful direction.

The technical directors and engineers of Capricorn Chemical Industries had come in from Johannesburg to attend this conference. Capricorn Chemical Industries was a fully owned subsidiary of Courtney Industrial Holdings. Under Garry's chairmanship, Capricorn was the largest manufacturer of agricultural fertilizers and pesticides on the African continent.

The company had its main plant near the town of Germiston in the industrial triangle of the Transvaal. The existing plant already incorporated a high-security section that manufactured highly toxic pesticides. There was adequate space available to double this facility. The Cyndex plant could be set up without any fuss or undue public speculation.

The technical representatives of Pignatelli and Capricorn had come together here to discuss the blueprints and the specifications for the new plant. For obvious reasons, it would have been unwise to conduct this meeting on the site in South Africa. In fact, Elsa had insisted that none of her staff should ever visit the plant or have any connection with the enterprise that could be traced back to Pignatelli.

Mauritius had offered a perfect venue for this meeting. Shasa had owned Maison des Alizés for over ten years. He and his family and their guests were frequent visitors. Their presence here was unremarkable, and Shasa was on excellent terms with the Mauritian government and most of the influential figures on the island. The Mauritians treated the family as honored and privileged guests.

Before his illness Bruno Pignatelli had also been a keen big game angler who visited Mauritius regularly, so Elsa was also well known and respected on the island. Nobody was going to pry into her affairs or make awkward inquiries about her reasons for being at Maison des Alizés with a team of her engineers and consultants.

Shasa and Elsa were still keeping up appearances and exercising elaborate decorum, even to the extent of occupying separate, but connecting, suites on the top floor of Maison des Alizés. The family thought this little charade was hilarious. They were all waiting for the two of them in the gazebo on the lawn above the fish pools when they came down for evening cocktails.

Elsa had bathed Shasa and anointed his bruises and scrapes so that he looked very dapper and refreshed and limped only slightly as they strolled down the front steps together. He was dressed in a cream-colored tropical silk suit with a crisp new eye patch, and she wore a full-length gauzy chiffon with a frangipani spray in her hair.

"Look at the little devils. Do you really believe they are just jolly good pals?" Garry demanded with a twinkle in his eye, and Isabella and Holly had to cling to each other for support. Even Centaine covered her smile with her Japanese fan and turned away to speak to one of the engineers.

Isabella had every reason to be at Maison des Alizés even though the Senate was in session. She was on the board of directors of Capricorn Chemicals. Since the trip to Chiwewe concession, when she had first learned of the Cyndex project, Isabella had shown a sudden interest in CCI. She had succeeded in having herself appointed to the Senate standing committee on agriculture, and after that it had required only a few subtle hints to get Garry to offer her a seat on the CCI board. She had rapidly become an active and valuable addition to the management team of Capricorn and had never missed a meeting of the board. She had taken a particular interest in the Cyndex project, and Garry had naturally included her in this gathering.

Garry had also seized the opportunity of bringing Holly and the children along for an unscheduled holiday. Although he would be heavily occupied with the technical discussions, he hoped to be able to spend some time with his family each day. Holly had been complaining recently that they saw so little of him, and the children were growing up so quickly that he was missing a big slice of their childhood. These days Centaine Courtney-Malcomess never missed a chance to be with her great-grandchildren, and she had insisted on boarding the Lear when it took off from Lanseria private airport outside Johannesburg.

Indeed, so large had been the family contingent and the weight of their luggage that the other Capricorn directors had been obliged to catch the next commercial flight.

Maison des Alizés was bursting at the seams. Every bed was occupied and they had set up two extra cots in the nursery for the babies. Centaine had borrowed extra trained staff from La Pirogue, the five-star beach resort just down the coast at Flic and Flac, to deal with the invasion. Then she had sent the Lear back to Johannesburg to bring in supplies of such essentials as Imperial caviar, and vintage Krug, fresh fruit and baby foods that were unobtainable on the island.

The Krug was flowing freely now as Shasa and Elsa joined the party under the frivolous fretwork roof of the gazebo. There

369

was an exuberant orgy of kisses and handshakes and back-slapping and happy cries of greeting.

Elsa had been presented to Centaine only briefly the previous evening, when the old lady had arrived at Maison des Alizés. Even though Centaine had been tired by the long jet flight, they had warmed to each other immediately. Centaine had squinted at her in that particular way she had when she was concentrating deeply. Then her eyes had straightened and she had smiled and held out her hand.

"Shasa has told me many good things about you, but I suspect that's not half of it," she had said in Italian. Elsa had smiled with pleasure at the compliment and at Centaine's command of her language.

"I did not know you spoke Italian, Signora Courtney-Malcomess."

Centaine nodded. "There is still much we have to learn about each other."

"I look forward to that," Elsa replied. They had recognized kindred spirits, and now, under the gazebo, Elsa moved naturally to Centaine's side and kissed her cheek.

Well, Centaine thought complacently as she took Elsa's arm, Shasa took long enough to find this one, but she was well worth waiting for.

Garry's children were chasing each other around the gazebo, their shrieks and howls detracting a little from the sophisticated ambience of the gathering.

"I must admit," Shasa remarked as he regarded his grand-children balefully, "that I'm becoming more like Henry the Eighth every day—I prefer small children in the abstract."

"As I recall, at that age you were every bit as bad," Centaine said immediately, rallying to the defense of her brood of great-grandchildren. But at that moment a particularly piercing squeal made Shasa wince.

"For that one alone you would have boiled me in oil. Mater, you are in danger of becoming a doting great-granny."

"They'll soon have enough of it." Centaine smiled down on them fondly.

"Not before I do, I assure you," he muttered, and went off to where Isabella was chatting with the Pignatelli engineers.

Isabella had set out to be charming to the German director, and by this time he was throwing off sparks. For Isabella there was a bizarre sense of unreality about the scene. She felt like an actress in a Franco Zeffirelli movie. The gleaming ivory house, the weird shapes of the trees and tropical plants, the gigantic fronds of the Royal Victoria water lilies floating on the ponds and the shoals of multicolored ornamental carp sailing beneath them, all contributed to a fantastic dreamlike setting. The laughter, the disjointed, enigmatic conversations in different languages and the cries of the children were all so inconsequential when set against the true reason for this gathering.

There was Nana holding court like a dowager empress, and Holly and Elsa Pignatelli wearing precious chiffons and silks that would cost a working man's wages for a year, while somewhere far away her little Nicholas dressed in combat camouflage and played with the ghastly weapons of war, with soldiers and terrorists for companions.

Here she was flirting with this balding middle aged man who looked like a grocer or a barman, but who was in reality the purveyor of death in one of its least attractive guises. Here she was smiling at her big teddy bear of a brother and linking arms with her beloved father while she conspired to betray them both, and her country to boot. Here was the shell, the beautiful, groomed, intelligent, successful young woman, fully in control of her destiny and the world around her, while within was a terrified, confused creature, suffering and bereaved, a pawn of powerful, shadowy forces in a game she did not understand.

"One day at a time," she warned herself. "One step at a time." And the next step would be the Cyndex 25 project.

Perhaps this would be the ultimate endeavor that Ramón had promised her. Once she had given them the Cyndex project, perhaps they would be able to escape from the web—she, Ramón and Nicholas. Perhaps then the nightmare would end.

# 29

The conference began the following morning in the dining room of Maison des Alizés. They sat beneath the revolving fans at the long walnut table that extended to seat thirty persons and talked about death. They discussed the mechanics and the chemical structure of death. They argued about the packaging and the quality control and the cost-efficiency of death, as though they were talking about manufacturing potato crisps or face cream.

Isabella steeled herself to show no reaction to the things she heard discussed at the long table. She had learned never to underestimate the powers of observation of her brother Garry. Behind the horn-rimmed spectacles and bluff, genial façade he missed very little. She knew he would pick up any sign of horror or revulsion she showed, and that would probably be the end of her involvement in the project.

The Pignatelli technicians had prepared a dossier. The copies were contained in untitled but handsome pigskin folders placed on the dining room table in front of each of them. The dossier was exhaustive and covered every aspect of the problem of manufacturing, storing and deploying the nerve gas.

Werner Stolz, the technical director, took them through the dossier a paragraph at a time. As horror unfolded on horror, read out in Werner's clipped sibilant German accent, Isabella found she had to exercise all her self-control to keep her expression neutral and businesslike.

"Cyndex 25 is a volatile gas consisting of an organophosphorus compound of the alkylphosphonic fluoridic acid group. Gases of this composition are known as G agents and include Sarin and Soman.

"However, Cyndex 25 has desirable features that differ distinctly from these older types of nerve gas . . ." As he enumerated these features, Isabella was appalled by his choice of the adjective "desirable," but she nodded thoughtfully and kept her eyes on the dossier.

"Cyndex 25 has a unique and highly aggressive combination of properties. These are high toxicity, rapid action and percutaneous effectiveness as well as absorption through the lungs and mucous membranes of the human body. Other advantages are high cost-effective ratios. By reason of its dual chemical structure, it is safe to manufacture, store and handle. Once the two agents which make up Cyndex 25 are mixed, the gas becomes highly unstable and has an extremely short effective life span. Thus it is more readily controlled in the field. After the elimination of the threatened population, the treated terrain can more swiftly be taken under friendly control."

He beamed benignly down the table at them. "I would like now to discuss each of these properties in greater detail. Let us take the question of toxicity. Cyndex in either vapor or aerosol

372

form absorbed through the lungs has an $LD^{50}$ dosage"—he smiled apologetically—"which means that it will kill fifty percent of the threatened population of moderately active adult men in two minutes, and a hundred percent of the population in ten minutes. This is not significantly more rapid than Sarin, but it is in its percutaneous effect that Cyndex comes into its own. It is absorbed much more rapidly through the skin, the eyes, the nose, the throat, and the digestive system than Sarin is. One microliter of Cyndex—and I remind you that is a millionth part of a liter—applied to naked skin will incapacitate a man in two minutes and kill in fifteen minutes. This is approximately four times more potent than Sarin. Although atropine injected intravenously within thirty seconds may inhibit the process and reduce some of the symptoms, it will not arrest spontaneous collapse of the respiratory system and subsequent death by suffocation. I will come later to the specific symptoms of exposure to the agent, but let us now discuss the cost of manufacture. Please turn to page twelve of the dossier."

They obeyed like schoolchildren, and Werner Stolz went on, "You will see from the bottom line of our estimate that at this point in time the plant will cost in the region of twenty million U.S. dollars and the direct cost of manufacture will amount to twenty dollars per kilo."

Isabella wondered, even in the stress of listening to these horrific details, why the use of newspeak clichés such as "bottom line" and "this point in time" annoyed her so. I wish he would speak plain English, she thought, as if that would somehow make the facts more palatable. Werner was still speaking.

"Translated into comparative terms, that means that the entire plant would cost the same as a single Harrier jet fighter from British Aerospace, and the cost of manufacture of a stock of Cyndex sufficient to ensure the defense of the country for twelve months would be equivalent to the purchase of fifty Sidewinder air-to-air missiles . . ."

"That's an offer we just can't refuse," Garry chuckled. Isabella felt a stab of hatred for him that shocked her with its intensity.

How can he joke about something like this? she thought. She dared not look up at him; he might read her thoughts. Werner nodded and smiled agreement with Garry.

"Of course, Cyndex needs no special vehicle for dissemination. Ordinary crop-sprayer aircraft such as those in day-to-day use in agricultural situations can be readily adapted for the purpose. The gas may also be delivered by artillery projectile. The new G5 long-range howitzer being developed at present by Armscor would be ideal.''

At noon they broke for a swim in the pool and a buffet lunch on the terrace. The discussion dwelled largely on Elsa and Shasa's recent visit to the Salzburg Festival, where Herbert von Karajan had directed the Berlin Philharmonic Orchestra. They went back into the dining room to listen to a description of the symptoms of Cyndex 25 poisoning.

''Although it has never been tested on human subjects, we have determined that the symptoms of moderate exposure to Cyndex aerosol will not differ greatly from other G agent nerve gases,'' Werner told them. ''These would commence with a sensation of tightness in the chest and difficulty in breathing, followed by copious running of the nose and a burning, stinging pain in the eyes and a dimming of vision.''

Isabella felt her own eyes begin to sting in sympathy, and she dabbed at them surreptitiously.

''As these symptoms become progressively more intense, there will be heavy salivation and frothing at the mouth, sweating and trembling, nausea and belching, sensations of heartburn and stomach cramps which swiftly lead to projectile vomiting and explosive diarrhea. These will be followed by involuntary urination and bleeding from the mucous membranes of the eyes, nose, mouth and genitalia. Trembling, twitching and giddiness and muscle cramps will lead to paralysis and convulsions.

''However, the immediate cause of death will be total collapse of the respiratory system. Cyndex owes its superior toxicity to the ease with which it penetrates the blood-brain barrier in the central nervous system.''

The others were silent and subdued for a full minute after Werner finished. Then Garry asked softly, ''If Cyndex has never been used on human subjects, how do you anticipate these symptoms?''

''Initially by extrapolation with the effects of other G agent nerve gases, Sarin in particular.'' Werner Stolz paused, for the first time showing some sign of embarrassment. ''Thereafter the gas was tested on primate subjects.'' He cleared his throat. ''Chimpanzees were used in laboratory tests.''

With an effort Isabella prevented herself making some gesture of disgust and outrage. However, her horror became almost uncontrollable as the director went on remorselessly, ''We found, however, that chimpanzees are extremely expensive laboratory animals. You are fortunate in that you have access to an almost unlimited supply of cheap and entirely satisfactory laboratory animals in the shape of *Papio ursinus*, the chacma baboon, which is indigenous to South Africa and still occurs there in large numbers.''

"We aren't going to test on live animals?" Isabella's voice was shrill even in her own ears. Immediately she regretted the outburst and tried to recover her poise. "I mean, is it really necessary?"

They were all staring at her now, and she flushed with anger at her lack of self-control. It was Garry who broke the silence.

He spoke lightly, but there was a steely glint behind the lenses of his spectacles. "The baboon is not my favorite animal. I have seen them kill newborn lambs at Camdeboo to eat the milk curds in their stomachs. Nana will tell you about their depredations on her roses and vegetable garden. I am sure we all share your distaste and your reluctance to see unnecessary suffering inflicted on any living thing." He paused. "However, in this instance we are considering the defense of the country, the safety of our nation—and the expenditure of many millions of Courtney money."

He looked across at Shasa, who nodded agreement.

"The short answer is, I am afraid, yes. We must test. Better that some animals should die than our own people. It is not a pretty thought, but it is essential. I'm sorry, Bella. If it offends you, then you don't have to have anything further to do with the project. You can resign your seat on the Capricorn board and we'll say no more about it. We will all understand and respect your feelings."

"No." She shook her head, "I understand the necessity. I'm sorry I raised the subject." She realized how close she had come to letting Nicholas and Ramón down. Their safety and freedom were worth any price she might be forced to pay. She forced herself to smile and said lightly, "You don't get rid of me that easily. I'll keep my seat, thank you very much."

Garry studied her face for a second longer. Then he nodded. "Good. I'm glad we have settled that." And he turned his full attention back to Werner Stolz.

Isabella composed her expression into one of polite attention and clasped her hands in her lap. "This is one project Red Rose will have no qualms about reporting," she promised herself.

Isabella sent the Red Rose dispatch three days after she arrived back in Cape Town.

Over the years a routine had developed between her and the

375

forces that controlled her. When she had information she sent a Red Rose telegram to the address in London, and usually within twenty-four hours she received instructions for a dead drop. These always took the same form. She was given the time and location at which to park her Porsche. The location was always a public carpark: sometimes the Parade at the old fort, or a drive-in cinema, or one of the large supermarkets in the suburbs.

She would write her message on sheets of the one-time pad and leave them in an envelope under the driver's seat with the door unlocked. When she would return to the Porsche half an hour or so later, the envelope would be missing. When they had a message or instructions for her the same method would be employed, except that when she returned to the Porsche there would be an envelope containing typed instructions under the driver's seat.

At the end of the conference at Maison des Alizés Garry had personally collected all the leather-covered dossiers and seen to the shredding of the contents. He was very concerned that no detail of the Cyndex project fall into unauthorized hands. Isabella had made a few careful notes during the discussions, but he had relieved her of these also.

"Don't you trust me, Teddy Bear?" She had made a joke of it, and though he chuckled he had been adamant.

"I don't even trust myself." And he had held out his hand for her notepad. "You want to remember any details, you come and ask me, Bella, but you don't write down anything—I mean *anything*."

She knew better than to make an issue of it.

Even though she had no notes to refer to, the Red Rose report that she sent was shaky only in the area of the chemical composition of Cyndex 25. She knew that it was an organophosphate of the G group of nerve gases but could not recall the exact atomic structure of the constituent parts or the sequence of manufacture. However, she gave the proposed location of the plant and the tentative timetable for construction. The forecast was that the plant would be in production within seven months.

At this stage the only ingredient that needed to be imported was a phosphate precursor—again she was uncertain of the exact chemical structure of this agent. However, she was able to report that the reason that this catalyst could not be manufactured in South Africa—at least, for the time being—was that the correct grade of stainless steel for the redoubt in which it was mixed was not obtainable locally. However, the state-owned ISCOR steel works would work on the production of this grade of steel, and it was anticipated they would be able to supply it within eighteen months. After that time Cyndex would be 100 percent locally manufactured. In the meantime the precursor would be supplied through a Pignatelli front company in Taipei, which was already holding stocks sufficient for the first year of operation of the Capricorn plant.

Apart from the problem with the supply of chemical-grade stainless steel, the other difficulty the conference had foreseen was the availability of skilled technicians to operate the plant. Pignatelli Chemicals had declined to provide any personnel. It was anticipated that these would be recruited in Britain or Israel. The conference had emphasized security clearance of any foreign technicians who were thus engaged.

The rest of Isabella's report covered the transportation, storage and dissemination of the gas in battlefield situations. Both Puma helicopters and Impala jet fighters of the South African air force could be adapted to serve as delivery vehicles. In addition, work would begin immediately on the design and testing of a shell for the G5 howitzer, which would be designated "155-mm CW (Chemical Warfare) ERFB Cargo." This shell would deliver eleven kilos of Cyndex 25 to a maximum range of thirty-five kilometers. The rotation of the shell in flight would centrifugally open valves in the cargo head and mix the two constituent ingredients of the gas prior to impact in the target area.

She was fully aware of the value of this information, so she was emboldened to add a final line to the twenty-six pages of her report.

"Red Rose requests access as soon as possible."

She waited anxiously for a reaction to her request after she had delivered it. There was none.

As time passed with no reply she understood that she was being punished for her impertinence, and at first she was defiant. Then as the weeks became months she started to become truly worried. At the end of the second month she sent an abject apology to the London accommodation address.

"Red Rose regrets importunate request for access. No insubordination was contemplated. Awaiting further orders."

It was another month before those orders came. She was instructed to use any means necessary to ensure that she was a member of the team from Capricorn Chemicals that would travel to London and Israel to interview and recruit personnel for the operation of the Cyndex plant.

Isabella had difficulty imagining how she could justify any

377

claim to being a member of the recruiting team. What possible reason could she give Garry that would not immediately arouse his suspicions as to her motives? She agonized over this for weeks before the next board meeting of CCI. Then, at the meeting itself, it all fell into place with an ease that amazed her.

The subject of recruitment came up at the meeting, even though it was not on the agenda, and Isabella saw her opportunity and gave her views on the subject in an impromptu but articulate and well-reasoned address.

When she finished, she saw she had impressed Garry, and he remarked in not entirely jocular fashion, "Perhaps we should send you to do the job, Dr. Courtney."

She shrugged, not to appear overeager. "Why not? I could fit in a little shopping—I need a few new frocks."

"Typical woman," Garry sighed, but six weeks later she found herself back in the Cadogan Square flat. The personnel manager of CCI was ensconced in the Berkeley Hotel, only a short walk from Cadogan Square. The two of them conducted the preliminary interviews in the dining room of the flat.

The night she arrived in London, there was an anonymous phone caller. She did not recognize the voice. The message was simple.

"Red Rose. Tomorrow you will interview Benjamin Afrika. Make certain that he is selected."

She couldn't place the name, so she looked up the application in her file. To her surprise she found that Benjamin Afrika had been born in Cape Town. This, however, seemed to be his strongest claim to the job on offer. Despite the fact that his academic qualifications were good, he was really too young—only twenty-four years of age. He had four A levels and a B.S. in chemical engineering from Leeds University with two years' experience as a scientific assistant with Imperial Chemical Industries at one of their factories near Liverpool. At the salary they were offering she could have found a hundred applicants with similar or better qualifications in South Africa.

She could not squeeze him into any of the vacant senior posts. There were, however, two more junior positions to fill.

Benjamin Afrika was the third interviewee on the morning's list. He walked into the Cadogan Square dining room at eleven o'clock in the morning, and Isabella felt herself go ice cold with panic.

Benjamin Afrika was a colored man, but this was not what caused her consternation. Benjamin Afrika was her half brother, the man whom she knew as Ben Gama, bastard son of her mother and the notorious terrorist and black revolutionary Moses Gama.

So great was the shock of seeing him that she was unable to utter a word. A host of turbulent thoughts tumbled in confusion through her mind as she stared at Benjamin. She thought about how his name, and the name of Tara Courtney, their mother, were never mentioned at Weltevreden—even after all these years the scandal and tragedy surrounding them cast a dark shadow over the family. How would it be possible for her to secure employment for Benjamin in one of the Courtney companies? Nana would have a hernia, and Pater would throw a blue fit. Then there was Garry . . .

Fortunately for Isabella, the CCI personnel manager was also evincing symptoms of acute distress, but the source of his concern was much more straightforward than Isabella's. It was merely the color of Benjamin's skin. In the long pregnant pause that followed Benjamin's entry, Isabella was able to take control of herself again and bring some order to her jumbled emotions. Benjamin had shown no sign of recognition, and she took her lead from him.

Abruptly the CCI manager leaped to his feet. To compensate for his initial reaction, he now became overeffusive and ducked around the desk to seize Benjamin's hand.

"I'm David Meekin, head of personnel at CCI. I'm delighted to meet you, young man," he babbled enthusiastically, pulling out a chair for Benjamin. "We have been studying your credentials, and your CV. Very impressive—I mean truly impressive."

He seated Benjamin and offered him a cigarette. "This is Dr. Courtney, who is a director of CCI," Meekin introduced them.

Benjamin half rose from his seat and made a small bow. "How do you do, ma'am."

Isabella did not trust herself to speak. She nodded and then gave all her attention to Benjamin's letter of application while Meekin began the interview.

He asked the usual questions about the work Benjamin had done at CCI and his reasons for wanting this job, but clearly his heart was not in the task. He wanted to get it over with. Meanwhile, Isabella was working out her own plans. If she had not recognized Ben's name, Afrika, it was highly unlikely that anyone else at home would do so, either. Apart from Michael, no other member of the family, as far as she knew, had ever met Ben. There was no reason why they ever should. He would be a junior employee in one of a hundred factories in a town over

379

a thousand miles from Weltevreden. Michael, of course, could be relied on to support her and Ben completely.

David Meekin had no more questions to ask, and he glanced at Isabella inquiringly.

"I see you were born in Cape Town, Mr. Afrika," she said, speaking for the first time. "Do you still have South African citizenship? You haven't taken naturalized British citizenship?"

"No, Dr. Courtney." Ben shook his head. "I am still a South African. I have a passport issued by South Africa House here in London."

"Good. Can you tell us something about your family? Do they still live in Cape Town?"

"Both my father and my mother were schoolteachers. They were killed in a motor accident in Cape Town in 1969."

"I'm sorry." She glanced down at her file. It was possible that Tara, their mother, had tried to conceal the facts of Ben's birth by contriving a false birth certificate. She could check that easily enough. She looked up again.

"I hope you will forgive my next question, Mr. Afrika. It may sound impertinent. However, Capricorn Chemicals is a defense contractor to Armscor, and all its employees are vetted by the South African security police. It would be best if you tell us now if you are, or have ever been, a member of any political organization."

Ben smiled softly. He really was a good-looking young man. By some fortunate chance he seemed to have inherited the best features from both sides of his racial ancestry.

"You want to know if I am a member of the ANC?" he asked.

Isabella's mouth tightened with annoyance. "Or any other radical political organization," she said curtly.

"I am not a political creature, Dr. Courtney. I am a scientist and an engineer. I am a member of the Society of Engineers, but of no other body."

So he was not interested in politics? She remembered the bitter political argument they had become embroiled in at their last meeting—when was that? Almost eight years ago, she realized with surprise. Of course, the Red Rose instructions that she had received gave the lie to his protests. Nonetheless, she had to cover herself.

"Again you must pardon the personal nature of my questions, but your frank replies now may save us all a great deal of embarrassment later. You must be aware of the racial situation in South Africa. As a colored person you will not be allowed to vote, and furthermore you will be subject to a body of legislation and a policy known as apartheid, which, to say the least, restricts many of the freedoms which you will have taken as your natural right here in England."

"Yes, I know all about apartheid," Ben agreed.

"Then why would you want to give up what you have here and return to a country where you will be treated as a second-class citizen, and where your prospects of advancement will be limited by your skin tone?"

"I am an African, Dr. Courtney. I want to go home. I think I can be of service to my country and my people. I believe I can make a good life for myself in the land of my birth."

They stared at each other for long seconds. Then Isabella said softly, "I can find no fault with those sentiments, Mr. Afrika. Thank you for coming to talk to us. We have your address and telephone number. We will contact you one way or the other, just as soon as we are able to do so."

When Ben had left neither she nor Meekin spoke for a while. Isabella stood up and moved to the window. Looking down into the square, she saw Ben leave the front door of the building. As he buttoned his overcoat he glanced up and saw her in the second-floor window. He lifted one hand in farewell, then set off toward Pont Street and turned the corner.

"Well," said David Meekin beside her, "we can cross that one off the list."

"For what reason?" Isabella asked. Meekin was flustered. He had expected her to agree immediately. "His qualifications. His experience—"

"The color of his skin?" Isabella suggested.

"That, too," Meekin nodded. "He would be in a position at Capricorn where he might have to give orders to white employees. He might actually have white females under him. It would cause ill feelings."

"There are at least a dozen black and colored managers in other Courtney companies," Isabella pointed out.

"Yes, I know," Meekin acceded hurriedly, "but they have coloreds and blacks under them, not whites."

"My father and my brother are both very eager to advance blacks and coloreds to managerial positions. My brother in particular feels that bringing all sections of our community to prosperity and responsibility is the only recipe for long-term peace and harmony in our country."

"I would agree with that one hundred percent."

"I found Mr. Afrika a most personable young man. I agree

381

that he is a little young and lacking in experience for either of the senior posts. However—''

Meekin changed tack, like the corporate survivor he was. ''I'd like to suggest that we short-list Afrika for the post of technical assistant to the director.''

''I agree with your suggestion wholeheartedly.'' Isabella smiled her sweetest, most winning smile. Her estimate had been correct. David Meekin's most firmly held principles were subject to negotiation.

They finished the interview with the last candidate at four that afternoon. As soon as Meekin had left Cadogan Square to return to the Berkeley Hotel, Isabella telephoned her mother.

''The Lord Kitchener Hotel, good afternoon.'' She recognized her mother's voice.

''Hello, Tara. It's Isabella.'' And then, for emphasis, ''Isabella Courtney, your daughter.''

''Bella, my baby. It's been ever so long. Let's see now—eight years at least. I thought you'd forgotten your old mamma.'' She always made Isabella feel guilty, and she made a lame excuse.

''I'm sorry, Tara. The pace of life—I don't seem to have time for anything . . .''

''Yes, Mickey tells me that you have been ever so successful and clever. He says that you are Dr. Courtney now, and a senator,'' Tara gushed on. ''Mind you, Bella, how can you bring yourself to have anything to do with that bunch of racist bigots that call themselves the National Party? In any civilized society, John Vorster would have been sent to the gallows years ago.''

''Tara, is Ben there?'' Isabella cut her off.

''I thought it was too good to be true that my own daughter wanted to talk to me.'' Tara's tone was martyred and long-suffering. ''I'll call Ben.''

''Hello, Bella.'' He came on the phone almost immediately.

''We must talk,'' she told him.

''Where?'' he asked.

She thought swiftly. ''Hatchards.''

''The bookshop in Piccadilly? Okay. When?''

''Tomorrow, ten in the morning.''

Ben was in the African fiction section, thumbing through a Nadine Gordimer novel. She stood beside him and picked a book at random from the shelves.

''Ben, I don't know what this is about.''

''I'm applying for a job, Bella. It's as simple as that.'' He smiled easily.

"I don't want to know, either," she went on quickly. "Just tell me—do you really have valid papers in the name of Afrika?"

"Tara registered my birth in the name of a colored couple, friends of hers. She was never married to my father—and of course their relationship was illegal. She could have been imprisoned for being in love with Moses Gama and giving birth to me." His tone was easy; there was even a light smile on his lips. She looked for some sign of bitterness or anger but found none. "Officially my name is Benjamin Afrika. I have a birth certificate and South African passport in that name."

"I have to warn you, Ben, there is terrible bitterness and hatred in the Courtney side of the family. Your father was convicted of murdering Nana's second husband, I mean Centaine Courtney Malcomess's husband."

"Yes, I know."

"You and I will never be able to acknowledge each other in South Africa."

"I understand."

"If Nana, if my grandmother or my father ever found out about you—well, I just don't know what the consequences would be."

"They won't find out about it from me."

"If it was up to me, I would not—" She broke off and lowered her voice. "Ben, be careful. We have never had a chance to become close; a chasm divides us. Nevertheless, you are my brother. I don't want anything to happen to you."

"Thank you, Bella." He was still smiling softly, and she knew she could never penetrate the curtain.

She went on quietly, "I will warn Michael that you are coming home. Please believe me that I will help you in any way I can. If you need me, let Michael know. It would be best if we do not contact each other once you arrive in the country."

Impulsively she dropped the book she was holding and embraced him.

"Oh, Ben, Ben! What a terrible world we live in. We are brother and sister, and yet . . . It's cruel and inhuman—I hate it."

"Perhaps we can help to change the world." He returned her embrace quickly, then they drew apart.

"There are many things that I can never tell you, Ben. Forces beyond our control. If we try to oppose them, we will be crushed. They are too powerful for us."

"Still, some of us must try."

"Oh, God, Ben. You terrify me when you speak like that."

"Good-bye, Bella," he said sadly. "I think we might have been good for each other—if only things had been ordained differently." He placed the Gordimer novel back on the shelf and without looking back walked out into Piccadilly.

# 30

Over the years it had become traditional that whenever Isabella was in Johannesburg she stayed with Garry and Holly.

Before she had given up her career to become a full-time wife and mother, Holly had been one of the leading architects in the country. Her designs had won international awards. When they had come to build their own home, Garry, who was never one to stint, had given her an open budget and egged her on to design her final masterpiece. She had managed to combine opulence and space with such good taste and invention that their home was Isabella's favorite retreat. She preferred it even to Weltevreden.

As always the family breakfasted on the man-made island in the center of the miniature lake. On a morning such as this, when the highveld sunshine decked the world in splendor, the roof of the pagoda had been rolled back by its electrically powered machinery and was open to the sky. The flocks of pink flamingo on the lake shore were free-ranging birds, persuaded to interrupt their continental migrations by this jewellike stretch of open water.

The older children were in school uniform, ready to leave for their daily penance. Isabella was feeding the latest addition to Garry's family, her year-old goddaughter—an exercise they both enjoyed immensely. It aroused all Isabella's frustrated maternal instincts.

Garry, in his shirtsleeves and broad, brightly colored braces at the head of the breakfast table, had just lit his first cigar of the day.

"Who was the one that accused me of being squeamish?" Isabella demanded of him as she shoveled a teaspoonful of egg into her goddaughter's mouth, then scraped up the overspill as it trickled down her chin.

"It's not a case of squeamishness at all," Garry protested too loudly. "I've got five meetings this morning and Holly's charity ball this evening. Give me a break, Bella."

"You could have canceled any one of those meetings," Isabella pointed out. "Or all of them."

"Look, Mavourneen, there'll be so many politicians and generals crowding the place that there is nothing I could add to the proceedings."

"Don't come over all Irish with me, begorrah. You are funking it, Teddy Bear, and we both know it."

Garry let out one of his evasive guffaws and turned to Holly. "What time do we have to be there this evening, lover?" But Holly was on Isabella's side.

"Why are you making Bella go through with this awful business?" she demanded.

"I am doing no such thing." Garry was unconvincingly indignant. "It's her decision entirely." He glanced at his wristwatch, then growled with theatrical menace at his children.

"You monsters are going to be late for school. Get out of it!" They showed not the least sign of terror as they lined up to kiss him good-bye, then clattered off over the bridge like a squadron of cavalry.

"Me, too." Bella wiped her goddaughter's face and stood up, but Garry stopped her.

"Look, Bella, I apologize. I know I hinted that you couldn't take it. You are as tough as any man I know. You don't have to prove it."

"So you admit you are chickening out, then?" she asked.

"All right," he capitulated. "Hell, I don't want to watch it. You don't have to, either."

"I am a director of Capricorn," she said, gathering up her handbag and briefcase. "I'll see you at eight."

As she climbed into the Porsche she felt a twinge of guilt. The true reason for her determination to witness the Cyndex 25 tests was not one of duty, not even to demonstrate her toughness. The last Red Rose communiqué she had received had promised her access to Nicholas as soon as she reported that the tests had been successfully carried out.

The drive down to Germiston took her a little over an hour on the new highway. Holly had designed the Capricorn Chemicals plant, and her taste and touch were distinctive. It did not look like a factory. There were lawns and trees, and a cunning exploitation of the terrain so that the least pleasing features of the industrial buildings were disguised or concealed. Those buildings that she had been able to clothe in glass and natural stone were given prominence. The various units were scattered over many hundreds of acres.

The prancing goat figure of the Capricorn logo surmounted the main entrance gateway. Isabella pressed her electronic keycard into the lock and the gates trundled open. The uniformed guards saluted her as she drove through.

All the visitors' slots in the carpark behind the main administration block were filled. Most of the visiting vehicles were black limousines sporting ministerial number plates or military pennants on the bonnet.

She rode up in the lift, and as she stepped into the director's suite she surveyed the room swiftly. It was a small, almost intimate gathering. Not more than twenty persons were present, and she was the only woman. The politicals and the civil servants were in regulation dark suits, and the military were in uniform. All branches of the service were represented, including the security police, and all those present were of staff or general rank.

She knew more than half of those present, including the cabinet minister and the two deputy ministers. A refreshment table had been laid out, including alcohol, but nobody was drinking anything stronger than coffee. The conversations were exclusively in Afrikaans, and she was struck once again by the major differences between the two white races. The English section was preoccupied with luxury and material possessions, with finance and commerce, while the Afrikaners lived in the halls of political and military power. Here were gathered some of the most powerful men in the land. Though financial paupers compared to the Courtneys, their political influence dominated the entire society. Compared to them the Courtneys were of little account. Within the citadel of power the military men, rather like their Russian equivalents, formed a caste of their own before whose strength even the state president bowed his head.

Within seconds she had singled out the most influential men in the room and made her way toward them, exchanging greetings and handshakes and smiles with the others as she passed. In this patriarchal society she had carved an unusual niche for herself. They accepted her as almost an equal.

"I'm a sort of honorary male." She smiled to herself and

386

shook hands with the minister of defense, then turned to his deputy with a controlled and friendly smile.

"Good morning, General De La Rey," she greeted him in fluent colloquial Afrikaans. Lothar De La Rey had been the first grand passion of her life. They had lived together for six months before he had dropped her and gone off to marry a good Afrikaner girl of the Dutch Reformed faith. If he had not, he would not now be a deputy minister and a man who, it was whispered, had no ceiling on his political future.

"Good morning, Dr. Courtney." He was as polite, but he could not keep his eyes on her face. They slid over her body in swift appreciation.

Go ahead, lover boy, she thought, knowing she had never looked better in her life. Eat your heart out—then go home to your fat little farm girl.

Despite her lingering resentment she had to admit to herself that he also was looking good. So many Afrikaners put on weight once their rugby-playing days were over. Lothar was as lean and hard and clean-cut as he had been ten years before. He was probably just about ripe for a little fling, she thought, and he would certainly have some interesting pillow talk.

I'd love to have my revenge on you, she thought. She had once contemplated committing suicide over him. It would give her pleasure to place him on the list of Red Rose's informers. Then quite suddenly she thought of Ramón, her Ramón, and her physical interest in Lothar subsided.

Only in the line of duty, she decided—and at that moment the Capricorn general manager caught her eye.

She made a short welcoming address to the company and apologized for the absence of the chairman. Then she invited them into the projection room for the presentation.

The videotape Capricorn had prepared was of high professional quality. It included computer-generated simulations and artist's impressions of the deployment and dissemination of Cyndex 25 under combat and battlefield conditions. As the video ran, Isabella glanced round the semidarkened room. She could see that all the military men were passionately excited by this new weapon. They watched the screen with deadly concentration, and when the tape came to an end they broke into animated discussion among themselves.

When Paul Searle, the Israeli technical director whom Isabella had recruited in Tel Aviv, stood up and called for comment, they bombarded him with searching questions. Isabella noticed that up to this time there had been no sign of Ben. His brown face had been discreetly kept in a back room somewhere. Inevitably one of the generals asked the question Isabella had been dreading. He put it bluntly.

"Has this gas ever been used on a human population? If so, can you give us details?"

"Perhaps the general can provide us with a few surplus Cuban POWs from Angola?" the director asked. They laughed delightedly at the graveyard humor.

"Seriously, General, the answer to your question is no. However, it has been tested extensively overseas under laboratory conditions with excellent results. In fact, we have arranged for you to witness our own first test today."

The pesticide and poisons division of Capricorn Chemicals was situated half a mile from the administrative block. The party drove down in a convoy with the minister of defense's black Cadillac in the lead. Isabella sat beside him in the backseat and pointed out features of the Capricorn plant.

"This section here is the uranium enrichment plant. You see how we have made it appear to be merely an extension of the main bulk phosphate refinery . . ."

The minister of defense had the reputation of possessing a fiery temper. However, she had always gotten on well with him, and she respected him for his dedication and political acumen. They chatted in friendly fashion during the short drive until they drew up at the front gate of the pesticide and agricultural poisons plant. This was a separate compound within the main complex.

It was surrounded by a twelve-foot diamond-mesh fence. There were prominent warning notices placed at intervals along the fence. These featured red skull-and-crossbones designs with warnings in three languages: "Danger! *Gevaar! Ingozi!*"

The guards at the main gate had Rottweiler guard dogs on leads. The plant was screened by a grove of trees. The building was long and low, the walls were of natural stone and all the external windows were of smoked one-way glass. There was a further security check at the entrance, and even the minister was asked to pass through the electronic scanner.

The Israeli director led them down a series of carpeted corridors, each separated by steel fire and gasproof doors, until finally they entered the new Cyndex extension. The building was still so new that it smelled of raw concrete. They assembled in a small entrance lobby. The gas doors closed behind them, and the director addressed them.

"Strict safety procedures are in force in this section of the building. You will notice the air-conditioning." He gestured at

388

the panels in the walls. "The quality of air in the building is strictly monitored at all times. In the highly unlikely event of a leak developing, the air can be pumped out and changed within ten seconds." For a few minutes more he elaborated on the building's safety features. "However, for your further safety, before entering the main plant you will be required to don protective suits."

There were separate changing rooms for the sexes. In the women's room a colored female attendant assisted Isabella to strip to her underwear and then hung her suit in one of the lockers for her. She helped Isabella into the one-piece white protective overall that had been laid out for her. There were white plastic boots and gloves, and she showed Isabella how to place the helmet over her head and switch on the compressed air supply. There was a clear plastic visor, and the air cylinder was contained in a neat backpack that formed part of the helmet attachment. There were built-in headphones that permitted normal conversation.

Isabella returned to the lobby and rejoined the rest of the party.

"If we are all ready, my lady and gentlemen?" The director turned to the door in the far wall. It slid open, and they trooped through. There were four technicians to welcome them. Isabella noticed that while the visitors wore white suits, the four technicians were in chrome yellow and the director's suit was tomato red for easy identification.

One of the yellow-suited technicians ushered them down yet another short corridor. As they went, he fell in beside Isabella.

"Good morning, Dr. Courtney," he said softly.

With a small shock she recognized his voice, and she looked into his visor. "Hello, Mr. Afrika," she murmured. "How are you enjoying your job with Capricorn?" It was the first time she had seen him since London.

"It is very interesting, thank you." That was all that passed between them before they entered the test room, but Lothar De La Rey had been watching her. As they seated themselves in the row of padded leather armchairs Lothar took the seat beside Isabella and asked, "*Wie is die kaffir?* Who is the nigger?"

"His name is Afrika. He has a degree in chemical engineering."

"How do you know him?" Lothar insisted.

"I was on the selection committee that recruited him."

"He has security clearance, of course?"

"Of course. He was cleared by your own department," she

added artlessly. He nodded, and they turned their attention back to the director.

"These are the test cubicles." At the end of the room were four windows that looked in on separate chambers; each was the size of a telephone booth—or a toilet cabinet would be a better description, Isabella decided.

"The windows are of double armored glass," the director pointed out. "And you will notice the monitors above each." He pointed to the electronic panels on which vital life functions were displayed in green LED printout.

Behind the windows, strapped to bare white plastic chairs, were four small humanoid figures. For a moment Isabella thought they were children. Then the director explained.

"The test subjects are baboons of the genus *Papio ursinus*. They may seem unfamiliar to you, because they have been shaved to resemble human subjects more closely. You will notice that number one is almost completely unprotected."

The naked, shaved body strapped to the chair in the first cubicle was pathetically vulnerable-looking. The infant's disposable diaper that was its only garment added to the poignancy.

"Number two is wearing clothing that resembles normal military uniform."

This baboon was dressed in a miniature suit of combat fatigues, but its arms and head were unprotected.

"Number three is fully covered except for eyes, mouth and nose." The animal wore gloves and a soft plastic hood that left only its face bare.

"Number four is equipped with a fully protective suit, similar to those which have been issued to you. These will be worn by friendly forces when handling or disseminating Cyndex 25." He paused. "I may add that subjects one, two and three have been sedated. There will be physical symptoms apparent upon application of the test agent, but these are reflexive reactions of the central nervous system and should not be construed as indicating the degree of suffering that the animal is undergoing."

Isabella felt her stomach muscles tightening, and despite the filtered air she was breathing her chest felt tight and constricted.

"Cyndex 25 is colorless and odorless. However, for safety reasons we have added the scent of almonds to our gas. There will be no aerosol mist or any other indication of its application, except via the monitoring equipment. The readout will show parts of Cyndex 25 in one hundred thousand parts of air." He paused and cleared his throat. "Now, gentlemen—and my lady— if you are ready, we will proceed with the demonstration."

The minister nodded his helmeted head, and the director gave a terse order into the microphone on his desk. Isabella imagined Ben or one of the other technicians adjusting the controls in the back room.

For a few seconds nothing happened. The breathing and the heartbeats of the four baboons continued sedately tracing regular luminous green patterns on the screens.

Then the panel registering the concentration of Cyndex 25 in the inflowing air flickered and moved up from 0 to 5—five parts of nerve gas in one hundred thousand parts of air.

Within seconds the displays began to alter—all except for the one above the fully suited baboon. The heartbeats accelerated swiftly, the breathing became rapid and deep. The changes were most violent on the display panel above the naked ape.

Isabella stared at it in horror. She saw its eyelids flicker and tears begin to run down the shaven face. It mouthed the air, its tongue lolling and rolling between its lips. Strings of silver saliva drooled down onto its chest.

"Fifteen seconds," intoned the director. "Subject number one is now incapacitated. Number four is unaffected, two and three are registering medium to acute symptoms."

The naked baboon began to writhe and struggle against the retaining straps. Isabella tasted bitter bile rising in the back of her throat and swallowed it.

Suddenly the baboon opened its mouth wide and shrieked. The thin, agonized cry carried to them even through the double-glazed windows. It ripped along Isabella's nerve endings. She clenched her fists and felt a cold sickly sweat break out beneath the clinging white suit. Beside her she felt Lothar De La Rey stir, and all around her the other men made small instinctive gestures of revulsion and discomfort. They were soldiers and policemen hardened to atrocity and suffering, yet they shuffled their feet, clenched gloved hands or made ducking, twisting movements of their heads.

All three of the exposed animals were twitching and kicking, rolling their heads, arching their spines in spasmodic convulsions. The mucous linings of their tongues and of their open screaming mouths turned a bright boiled scarlet, their fluttering streaming eyeballs glazed over with a network of bloodshot veins. They began to vomit. The diaper the first baboon wore was soiled by a spreading stain of urine and feces.

Isabella fought down the waves of nausea that rose to engulf her. She wanted to scream, to run, to hide from the horror of it.

"One minute, five seconds. Number one, all vital life signs terminated." The pathetic childlike corpse hung against the straps. Its shaven nakedness was aberrant and obscene.

"Two minutes, fifteen seconds. Number two terminated."

"Three minutes, eight seconds. Number three terminated."

"You will notice that number four is totally unaffected. The suit has afforded complete protection."

Isabella rose to her feet. "Excuse me," she blurted. She had been determined to outlast any of the men in the room. Her vow was forgotten now. She fled down the corridor and burst into the women's changing room.

She ripped the helmet from her head, dropped onto her knees and clutched the cold porcelain of the toilet bowl with both hands. She choked and sobbed, and her horror and pity and guilt shot up her throat in a thick bitter acid stream and spewed into the bowl.

After what she had just experienced Isabella could not bring herself to return to the blissful domestic environment of Garry and Holly's home.

She left the Capricorn plant without seeing the minister or Lothar or any of the other officials. She drove without attention to her surroundings. She drove fast, too fast, pushing the Porsche up near its top speed. She was trying to expurgate her shame in the elemental and purifying sensation of speed. The attempt was not successful. After an hour she turned back toward Johannesburg and slowed the Porsche to a more moderate pace.

The fuel tank was almost empty, and she pulled into the next service station that she reached. While the attendant refueled her tank she realized she had lost track of her whereabouts. This was not her home town. She knew only that she was somewhere in the network of roads and the maze of residential suburbs that surround the huge industrial and mining complex of the city of Johannesburg.

She asked the attendant which was the quickest route from here back to Sandton. As soon as he explained where she was, she realized that fate or her own subconscious had guided her. She was only two or three miles from Michael's home. A few years previously, Michael had bought himself a smallholding of fifty acres on which stood a dilapidated farmhouse. It was close enough to the offices of the *Golden City Mail* for him to commute to work. Michael had set about renovating the house on a do-it-yourself basis. He had planted a hundred or so fruit trees, much to the delight of the birds and locusts and aphids, and he kept a flock of chickens that wandered into the kitchen and defecated on the sink and down the refrigerator door.

"Well, it's their home, too," Michael had explained to her when she remonstrated. "A turd or two never hurt anybody." Although Michael's original intention had been to convert the birds into an endless series of poulet roti and coq au vin, he had so far not been able to bring himself to chop off a single head. Some of the birds had already died of old age.

"Michael!" Isabella felt her spirits lighten, and she checked her wristwatch. It was after six. He should be home by now. "Michael is exactly the person I need right now."

As she drove along the winding track through the scraggly blue gum plantation that marked the boundary of Michael's estate, she saw his Volkswagen Kombi parked in front of the house. Michael's old Valiant had finally passed away. She smiled as she remembered Michael's description of how an electrical short circuit had self-ignited in rush hour traffic and the ancient vehicle had given itself a Viking's funeral, creating a five-mile traffic jam as its cortege of mourners. She noted that the Kombi, acquired secondhand, seemed not to be in much better shape.

One half of the tin roof of Michael's home was painted in fresh sparkling apple green, but the other half was rusted red. He had lost heart in the middle of the renovations.

Michael had also cleared a landing strip down one boundary of his property and had registered it as a private airfield with the directorate of civil aviation. He kept his old Cessna Centurion aircraft in a hangar at the far end of his fruit orchard. The building was constructed with secondhand corrugated iron sheets that Michael had purchased cheaply from a scrapyard. The resulting edifice was very much in keeping with Michael's usual style.

She found him in the hangar working in the interior of the blue and white aircraft. She tugged at the leg of his overalls, and he crawled out backward and registered surprise and pleasure. They hadn't seen each other for almost a year.

After he had kissed her, he fetched a bottle of wine from the rusty old refrigerator in the corner and filled two tumblers. Only then did Isabella notice that he seemed nervous and distracted. He kept glancing at his watch and going to the door of the hangar. She was hurt and disappointed.

"You are expecting somebody," she said. "I'm sorry, Mickey. I should have phoned you beforehand. I hope I haven't put you out."

"No, of course not. Not at all," he assured her, but he stood up with alacrity and obvious relief. "But . . . well, to tell the truth . . ." his voice trailed off, and once again he glanced over her head toward the door.

One of his lovers, she thought bitterly. He's worried I will meet his latest fancy boy. She resented him not being available when she needed him so badly, and she cut short their farewells.

She watched him in the rearview mirror as she drove back through the trees. He looked lonely and vulnerable, and her anger at him evaporated.

Poor dear Mickey, she thought. You are as lost and unhappy as I am.

She checked the Porsche at the gate to the property, then pulled out and turned eastward on to the main tarmac highway heading back toward Sandton. Another vehicle was approaching, a nondescript grey van. As it drew level, she casually glanced sideways at the driver and immediately straightened up in the seat. The driver was her brother Ben. He had not noticed her and was in conversation with the black man who sat in the passenger seat beside him. The passenger was much darker-skinned than Ben, a full-blooded Zulu or Xhosa, with striking features and a smoldering expression. It was not the kind of face one would readily forget.

She slowed the Porsche and watched the departing vehicle in her rearview mirror. Suddenly the rear brake lights of the van glowed red, then the turning indicator began to flick on and off. The van turned into the track leading to Michael's house and disappeared among the blue gums.

"Mystery solved," Isabella muttered, and she accelerated the Porsche. "Although I don't understand why Michael didn't want me to see Ben. He knows I arranged the job at Capricorn for him." She considered it for a moment longer. "It must be the man with Ben. That's a face to remember. I wonder who he is?"

It was almost eight and the sun had already set when she pulled into the garage under Garry's house in Sandton.

"Damn it," Garry greeted her as she entered the living room. "Where the hell have you been? Do you know what the time is?" Both Garry and Holly were in evening dress. It was not often she saw Garry angry.

"Oh my God! The ball! I'm sorry."

Then Garry saw her face, and immediately his anger smoothed away. "Poor Bella. You look as though you have had a lousy day. We'll wait while you change."

"No, no," she protested. "Go ahead. I'll follow you."

For Isabella the evening was a disaster. The partner Holly had arranged for her was a university professor and a total bore.

Because she was a senator he wanted to discuss politics all evening.

"Don't you think I get enough of that?" she asked tartly, and he sulked at the rebuke. She left early. The rest of the night was troubled and nightmare-ridden. She dreamed of a shaven ape dressed in military battle dress and strapped into a white chair.

Somewhere in her dreams the tortured creature changed identity and became her own little Nicholas in his camouflage suit. She woke in a cold trembling welter of sweat and horror.

She could not risk sleep again, nor the fantasies that sleep might bring. She sat in a chair and read until dawn defined the outline of the windows. She ran a bath, but before she could step into it there was a knock at the door of her suite. When she opened it, Garry stood on the threshold in a silk dressing gown. His hair was in disarray and his eyes were bleary and swollen with sleep.

"I have just had a call from Pater at Weltevreden," he told her.

"At this hour? Is everything all right? Is it Nana?"

"No. He told me to tell you that both of them are well."

"Then what did he want?"

"He wants you and me to fly down to Weltevreden immediately."

"Both of us?"

"Yes. You and me. Immediately."

"What on earth for?"

"He wouldn't say. Just that it's a matter of life and death."

She stared at Garry. "What can it be?"

"How soon can you be ready to leave—half an hour?"

"Yes, of course."

"I'll ring Lanseria Airport and tell them to have the Lear ready and the pilots standing by." He checked his watch. "We can be in Cape Town before ten o'clock."

When they landed at Cape Town's D. F. Malan Airport, Klonkie the chauffeur was waiting for them. He drove them directly to Weltevreden.

Shasa and Centaine were waiting for them in the gun room. By family tradition the gun room was where the most dire and unpleasant subjects were addressed and thrashed out, both figuratively and literally. For it was here, across the big leather armchair, that Shasa had administered corporal punishment to his three sons. A summons to the gun room was never taken lightly, and Isabella felt a prickle of apprehension as she and Garry entered.

Nana and Shasa stood shoulder to shoulder behind the old desk, and their expressions were so bleak that Isabella stopped dead in her tracks and Garry bumped into her from behind. She hardly felt it.

"What is it?" she asked fearfully. Then she realized that Nanny was also in the room, standing in front of the stone fireplace. The old colored woman had been weeping. Her face was swollen with grief, and her eyes were bloodshot. She clutched a sodden handkerchief in one hand.

"Oh, Miss Bella," she sobbed. "I'm so sorry, child. I had to do it—for your sake . . ."

"What on earth are you talking about, Nanny?" Isabella started toward her to comfort her—and then stopped again.

A dreadful sense of disaster overwhelmed her as she realized what lay on the desk in front of Nana and Shasa.

"What have you done, Nanny?" she whispered, chilled and stricken with despair. "You've destroyed us."

On the desk was her leather-bound journal. Nanny had been into her safe.

"You have destroyed me and my baby. Oh, Nanny, how could you do this to us?"

The journal was open at the page that contained the lock of Nicholas's hair. On the desk top beside it lay his knitted baby bootee and the copy of his birth certificate.

"Oh, you stupid prying old woman." Isabella's anger boiled over. "You'll never know what harm you have done. You've killed my Nicky. I'll never forgive you for this, never."

Nanny wailed with despair, then covered her mouth with her wet handkerchief and fled from the room.

"She did it because she loves you, Bella," Shasa told her sternly. "She did what you should have done eight years ago."

"It was none of her business. It's nothing to do with any of you. You don't understand. If you meddle with this, you will put Nicky and Ramón in terrible danger."

She ran to the desk, snatched up the journal and clutched it to her chest. "This is mine. You have no right to interfere."

"What is happening here?" Garry stepped up beside Isabella. "Come on, Bella. If you are in trouble, then it concerns all of us. We are a family. We stand together."

"Yes, Bella, Garry is right. We stand together."

"If only you had come to us right away—" Centaine broke off and sat down behind the desk. "Recriminations will not help us now. We have to work this out—all of us together. Sit down, Bella. We can guess most of it. You must tell us the rest of it. Tell us about Nicky and Ramón, all of it.''

Isabella swayed on her feet, confused and torn by the torment of her emotions. Garry wrapped a thick muscular arm around her shoulders to steady her.

''It's okay, Bella. We are all here behind you now. Who is Nicky? Who is Ramón?''

''Nicky is my son. Ramón is his father,'' she said softly, and buried her face against the great comforting barrel of his chest.

They let her cry for a while, then Centaine lifted the telephone. ''I'll call Doc Saunders. He can give her a shot to calm her.''

Isabella spun toward her. ''No, Nana. I don't need anything. I'll be all right. Just give me a minute.''

Centaine set the telephone back on its cradle, and Garry led Isabella to the buttoned-leather sofa and sat beside her. Shasa came to sit on her other side, and they held her between them.

''All right,'' Centaine said at last. ''That's enough. You can weep later. Now we've got work to do.''

Isabella straightened up, and Shasa handed her the handkerchief from his breast pocket.

''Tell us how it happened,'' Centaine ordered.

Isabella took a deep breath. ''I met Ramón at the Rolling Stones concert in Hyde Park when Daddy and I were living in London,'' she whispered. Her voice strengthened as she went on. She spoke for almost half an hour. She told them why she and Ramón had been unable to marry and how they had gone to Spain for Nicholas's birth.

''I was going to bring him here to Weltevreden. Ramón and I planned to be married here just as soon as he was free.''

She told them how Ramón and Nicholas had been abducted. She told them of the water torture of the infant she had been forced to witness and the nightmare of her existence since then.

''What did they want from you, these mysterious people? What price did you have to pay for Ramón and Nicky's safety? What did you have to give them in exchange for the chance to visit Nicky?'' Shasa demanded harshly.

Centaine thumped her cane on the wooden floor. ''That is not important at the moment. We'll deal with that later.''

''No.'' Isabella shook her head. ''I don't mind answering. They wanted nothing from me. I think they were forcing Ramón to perform some service for them. They rewarded him by allowing me to visit the two of them, Ramón and Nicholas.''

''You are lying, Bella,'' Shasa accused her harshly. ''Ramón

**397**

Machado is using you. You are being forced to work for him and his masters.''

"No." She was appalled that he had seen through her lies so easily. "Ramón is as helpless as I am. We are being threatened and blackmailed—''

"Stop it, Bella,'' Shasa cut her short. "You are the one being forced to pay the price. Nicholas is the hostage. Ramón is the evil puppet master who pulls the strings.''

She cried out in anguish. "No! You are wrong! Ramón is—''

"I'll tell you who Ramón de Santiago y Machado is. Yes, you provided us with his family tree and his full names and date of birth,'' Shasa pointed out. Isabella clutched the journal protectively. "You know that I have friends in Israel. One of them is the director of Mossad. I telephoned him. He ran Ramón's name through their computer. It links into the CIA computer. Our own security forces also have an open file on Ramón de Santiago y Machado. In the three days since Nanny brought your journal to us, I have been able to discover quite a few interesting facts about your Ramón." He jumped up from the sofa and crossed to his desk. He pulled open one of the drawers and returned with a thick file that he slammed down on the coffee table in front of her. Press cuttings, photographs, documents and reams of computer sheets spilled out from between the bulging covers.

"This came in last night in the Israeli diplomatic bag from Tel Aviv. I didn't call you until I had studied it. It makes interesting reading." Shasa picked out a photograph from the pile. "Fidel Castro's victorious entry into Havana in January 1959. Those are Che Guevara and Ramón together in the second jeep." He flipped over another glossy black and white print. "The Congo, 1965. Patrice Lumumba Brigade. Ramón is the second white man from the left. The corpses are executed Simba rebels." He picked out another. "Ramón with his cousin Fidel Castro after the Bay of Pigs. Apparently Ramón was instrumental in gathering the advance intelligence of the landing." He scuffled through the pack of photographs. "This one is fairly recent. Colonel-General Ramón de Santiago y Machado, head of the African section of the Fourth Directorate of the KGB, receiving the award of the Order of Lenin from General Secretary Brezhnev. Very handsome in his uniform, isn't he, Bella? Look at all those medals."

She cringed away from the photograph as though her father were holding a black mamba.

Garry leaned across and took the photograph out of Shasa's

hand. "Is this Ramón?" he demanded of her, holding it before her face. She dropped her eyes but would not answer.

"Come on, Bella. You must tell us. Is this your Ramón?"

Still she refused to reply. Shasa had to shock her into acceptance. "It is all an elaborate deception. He probably singled you out as his victim. He almost certainly arranged the abduction and the water torture of your son. He has been toying with you ever since then. Did you know that his nickname is El Zorro Dorado? It seems that Castro himself selected the name: the Golden Fox."

Isabella's head jerked up. She remembered the remark made by José, the paratrooper, that had puzzled her at the time. "Pele is the cub of the fox, El Zorro." Somehow that was the last tiny detail that forced her to face the truth.

"El Zorro—yes." Her expression hardened. The first gleam of burning hatred showed in her eyes. She looked instinctively toward her grandmother.

"What are we going to do, Nana?" she asked.

"Well, the first thing we are going to do is rescue Nicholas," Centaine said briskly.

"You don't know what you are saying, Nana," Garry objected. His expression was stunned.

"I always know what I'm saying," Centaine Courtney-Malcomess told him firmly. "I'm putting you in charge, Garry. This takes precedence over everything else. You can have whatever you need. I don't mind what it costs. Just get me that child. That's all that counts. Do I make myself clear, young man?"

Garry's bemused expression cleared slowly. He began to grin.

"Yes, Nana, you make yourself abundantly clear."

Garry converted the gun room at Weltevreden into his operations room.

He could have chosen any of a dozen better-equipped facilities in one of the Courtney conference centers or boardrooms. Somehow none of these had the secure family atmosphere of this room, which for so long had been the center of their lives. None of the others queried his choice.

"This is restricted to the family. We bring in nobody from outside until it is absolutely necessary," he warned them.

He set up two large boards on easels, one each side of the desk. On one he hung a large-scale map of Africa south of the Sahara. The second board he left blank for the time being, except for a photograph that he pinned at the top.

It was one that Isabella had taken of Nicholas on the beach.

He was in bathing trunks, his hair tousled by sea salt and wind as he laughed into the camera.

"That's to remind me what this is all about," Garry told them. "I want to imprint that face on my mind. As Nana has said—from now on that is all that counts. That face. That child."

He scowled at it. "All right, young Nicky, where are you?"

He turned to Isabella, who was seated at the desk, and placed the heavy volume of *Jane's All the World's Aircraft* in front of her.

"Okay, Bella. Let's presume that it was a Russian military freighter that flew you from Lusaka to this base where you met Nicky. Let's find what type it was." He opened the book in front of her and began turning the pages.

"That's it," she said, stabbing at one of the illustrations.

"Are you certain?" he demanded, leaning over her shoulder.

"Ilyushin Il-76. NATO reporting name Candid," he read aloud. "*Jane's* lists its estimated cruise speed as seven hundred fifty to eight hundred kilometers an hour."

He jotted it down on his navigation pad. "Okay, you say the course was three hundred degrees magnetic and the flying time was two hours, fifty-six minutes. We know it was on the Atlantic coast—let's mark that up on the chart."

He went to the map and set to work with the dividers and protractor.

"Garry"—Isabella was worried—"just because Nicky was there last year does not mean that he will still be there, does it?"

"Of course not," he agreed without looking around from the chart. "However, from what you tell us, Nicky seemed to be settled at that camp. He was in school and had been there long enough to make friends and build a reputation as a soccer player—Pele?" He turned and beamed at her through his spectacles like a friendly goldfish. "We know from both Israeli and South African intelligence reports that your friend El Zorro is still operating in Angola. He was spotted in Luanda by a CIA agent as recently as fourteen days ago. And we have to start planning somewhere. Until we find out for sure that Nicky is not there, we'll presume he is."

He stepped back from the map. "There we go," he muttered. "It looks like somewhere north of Luanda and south of the Zaire border. There are five, no, six river mouths in that general area within a hundred miles of each other. Crosswinds could have made a ten-degree deviation in the Candid's course either way."

He came back to the desk and picked up the large sheet of art paper on which Isabella had sketched from memory a map of the airstrip and river mouth. He studied it dubiously, then shook his head. "It could be any one of the six rivers shown on the map." He peered closely at the map. "They are the Tabi, the Ambriz, the Catacanha, the Chicamba, the Mabubas and the Quicabo. Do any of those names ring a bell, Bella?"

She shook her head. "Nicky called the base Tercio."

"That is probably a code name," said Garry. He pinned her sketch map beside Nicky's photograph on the second board. "Any comments so far?" He looked across at Centaine and Shasa. "What about it, Pater?"

"It's a thousand kilometers from the Namibian border, which is our nearest friendly territory. We can forget about any over land attempt to reach Nicky.

"Helicopters?" Centaine asked. Both men shook their heads simultaneously.

"Out of range without refueling," Garry said.

Shasa agreed. "We'd be flying over a battle zone. According to our latest intelligence the Cubans have a solid radar chain covering the Namibian border and at least a squadron of MiG-23 fighters based just north of the border at Lubango."

"What about using the Lear?" Centaine insisted. Both men laughed.

"We can't outrun a MiG, Nana," said Garry. "And they've got more guns than we have."

"Yes, but you can circle around them, fly 'way out over the Atlantic and come back in behind them. I know fighters can't fly very far, and the Lear can go to Mauritius."

They stopped laughing and looked at each other. "You think she got rich by being stupid?" Garry asked. Then he addressed her directly.

"Supposing we could get there in the Lear, then what? We can't land or take off—the Lear needs a thousand-meter runway. From what Bella tells us, it's a short strip and a guerrilla training base with South American or, more likely, Cuban paratroopers guarding it. They aren't going to hand Nicky over to us, not without an argument."

"Yes. I expect we'll have to fight," Centaine nodded. "So now it's time to send for Sean."

"Sean?" Shasa blinked. "Of course!"

"Nana, I love you," said Isabella, and picked up the telephone. "International, I want to put an urgent call through to Ballantyne Barracks at Bulawayo in Rhodesia."

The call took almost two hours to come through, by which

time Garry had telephoned the airport and spoken to his pilots. The Lear was already on its way to Bulawayo when Sean finally came on the line.

Garry said, "Let me talk to him," and took the telephone out of Isabella's hand. They argued for less than a minute, then Garry snarled, "Don't give me that crap, Sean. The Lear will be at Bulawayo airport within the next hour to pick you up. I want your hairy arse on board, but pronto. I'll phone General Walls or Ian Smith if necessary. We need you here. The family needs you."

He hung up and looked at Centaine. "Sorry, Nana."

"I have heard the expression before," she murmured. "And sometimes a little strong language works wonders."

# 31

Major Sean Courtney of the Ballantyne Scouts stood before the makeshift situation board in the Weltevreden gun room and studied the photograph of his nephew. His promotion to major and second-in-command of the Scouts was only three months old. Roland Ballantyne had finally maneuvered him into a full-time billet with the regiment.

"You can see he's Bella's boy. Takes after her. Ugly little brat." Sean grinned at her. "No wonder she's been keeping him up her sleeve."

She stuck out her tongue at him. He was good for her; he gave her hope again. He was so hard and competent and tough-looking, he brimmed with such sublime confidence in his own strength and immortality that she had to believe in it, too.

"When will they let you see Nicky again?" he asked. She thought for a second. She could not tell him about their promise to give her access as soon as the Cyndex 25 tests were completed. That would mean admitting to all of them that she was a traitress.

"I think it will be soon. I haven't seen Nicky for almost a year. It must be soon. Days rather than weeks from now."

"You won't go," Garry cut in. "We aren't going to give you into their clutches again."

"Oh, shut up, Garry," Sean snapped. "Of course she has to go. How the hell will we know where they are holding Nicky if she doesn't?"

"I thought—" Garry began, his face flushing with anger.

"Okay, matey. Let's make a bargain here. I run the actual operation—you are responsible for all the logistics and backup. How about it?"

"Good!" Centaine cut in. "That's the way we'll do it. Go on, Sean. Tell us how you'll carry out the rescue."

"Okay. In broad outline, this is it. We'll work out the details later. First of all, we have to accept that it's a fully offensive operation. We are sure as hell going to run into heavy opposition. They are going to try to kill us—we've got to kill them first. We are not going to mess around. If we want Nicky, we have to fight for him. However, if things go wrong, we might have to face a political and legal storm both here and abroad. We might be deemed guilty of anything from terrorism to murder. Are we prepared to accept that?"

He looked around the circle of attentive faces. They all nodded without hesitation.

"Good. That's settled. Now for practicalities. We assume Nicky is being held in northern Angola at this coastal base. Bella goes in as she did last time. Once she is in position with Nicky she calls us in."

"How?" Garry demanded.

"That's your problem. You have Courtney Communications at your beck and call. Get them to come up with some kind of miniature radio or even a transponder. As soon as she is in position, Bella will activate it and give us a fix."

"Okay," Garry agreed. "We have those electronic position markers that we use for flagging aerial geological surveys. We should be able to adapt one of those. How will Bella smuggle it in?"

"Again, that's your problem," Sean told him brusquely. "Let's get on with it. So Bella is in the target area. She gives us a fix. We go in—"

"How?" Garry asked again.

"There is only one way—from the sea." Sean swept his hand across the map of the southern Atlantic and down to the nose of the African continent.

"We've got the trawling and canning factory at Walvis Bay. One of those new long-range trawlers of yours, Garry, the ones you send down to Veema Seamount. They'll do nearly thirty knots and have a range of four thousand miles."

"Damn it, yes!" Garry beamed. "*Lancer* has just finished a major refit in Cape Town docks. She is at sea at this very moment, on her way back to Walvis Bay. I'll tell them to hold her there, fully refueled and ready for sea. Van Der Berg, the skipper, is a first-class seaman."

"Tell them to unload the nets and all the other heavy items we won't need," Sean added.

"Right. I'll also arrange extra war and all-risks cover on the insurance policy. I know the way you bang up equipment." Garry was becoming indignant. "Hell, you went through four Landcruisers last year."

"That's enough squabbling." Centaine brought them firmly back on track. "Tell us, Sean. Are you going to sail *Lancer* into this river?"

"No, Nana. We'll use landing craft to run into the beach, inflatables with outboard motor. Do you know anybody at Simonstown naval base?"

"I know the minister of defense," Bella cut in. "And Admiral Keyter."

"Beauty!" Sean nodded. "If you get the boats, see if you can also get permission for a dozen or so boat handlers to volunteer for a little extra-curricular fun and games. Those naval commandos are hot babies, and they will fall over themselves for a chance at a good barney. Play up the fact that it's an ANC training base that we are going to hose down and that we'll be doing them a good turn."

"I also know the minister. I will go with Bella to see him," Centaine agreed. "I guarantee you all the special equipment you need. Just give me a list, Sean."

"I'll have it ready by tomorrow morning."

"What about weapons—and men?"

"Scouts," Sean told them. "They don't come any better. I trained them myself. I'll need about twenty men. I know exactly who I want. I'll talk to Roland Ballantyne right away. Things are pretty quiet up there in Rhodesia at the moment, the rainy season. He'll let me have them. I might have to break one of his legs, but he'll let me have them. They'll need a couple of days of boat training, but they'll be ready to go by the end of next week." He looked across at Isabella. "It all depends on you now, Bella. You are our hunting dog. Lead us to them, lass."

Eleven days after she sent the Red Rose coded confirmation that Capricorn Chemicals had successfully tested Cyndex 25, Isabella received permission and instructions for a visit to Nicholas. She was instructed to take the South African Airways flight to London that refueled in Kinshasa on the Congo River and to disembark at this stopover instead of continuing on to London.

She would be met at Kinshasa Airport.

"It's looking good." Sean was jubilant as he placed his finger on the map. "Here's Kinshasa. It's within three or four hundred kilometers of the expected target area. They are going to pick you up on the doorstep, not the roundabout route via Nairobi and Lusaka that they sent you on last time." He looked across at Isabella. "So they want you to take next Friday's flight? If it works out, that means you will probably be in position on Saturday, or Sunday at the very latest. We will sail from Walvis Bay in *Lancer* just as soon as I can get up there. The boys have finished their training, and all the equipment is on board *Lancer*. They have been sitting around doing nothing for almost a week— they'll be glad to be on their way."

He studied the map, then punched his calculator. "We can be in position one hundred nautical miles off the mouth of the Congo River by Monday the twelfth. How does that suit you, Garry?"

Garry stood up and went to the map. "I'll be waiting with the Lear at Windhoek Airport—here. I will make my first flyover on the night of Monday the twelfth. I'll have to head out to sea at least five hundred miles before I can turn back. That's the estimated range of the Cuban radar net in southern Angola. Five hundred miles is well beyond the operational range of the MiG squadron at Lubango." He touched the Cuban base on the map. "All right, then I'll hit the coast at the mouth of the Congo here and fly south down the coast until I pick up the signal of Bella's transponder."

"Hold on, Garry," Shasa intervened. "How's that working out?"

"The boys at Courtney Communications have done a damn fine job in the short time they had available." He opened his briefcase. "This is it!"

"A bicycle pump?" Shasa asked.

"Apparently Nicky is a soccer star. He asked Bella to bring him a new ball, and he complained that they had to keep pumping his old ball. The pump is a natural accessory to go with the ball. It should arouse no suspicion. This one is in perfect working order." He demonstrated a few strokes of the pump, and the air hissed out in a satisfactory manner.

"The transponder is fitted into the handle of the pump. It has a thirty-day battery life. It is activated simply by twisting the handle like this." He showed them. "There is one drawback. We have had to make the transponder small enough to fit into the handle, and in the process we have been forced to reduce the power of the signal. It has a range of less than twelve kilometers, even with the very sensitive antenna that we have fitted into the Lear. I'll have to fly in that close before I pick up the signal."

"What about Cuban fighters in the north?" Shasa asked anxiously.

"According to South African intelligence, the nearest squadron is based at Saurimo. I will make one quick run down the coast. As soon as I pick up Bella's signal, I'll head back out to sea. I've worked it out on paper; even if Cuban radar picked me up as I enter Angolan airspace and they immediately scramble a flight of MiGs from Saurimo, I should be able to turn out and run for it before they can catch me."

"What about SAMs?" Shasa persisted.

"Intelligence reports the Cuban SAM regiments are all in the south."

"And if Intelligence is wrong?"

"Come on, Pater! Sean's running a hell of a lot more risk than I am."

"This kind of thing is Sean's job, and he has not got a wife and a flock of kids."

"Do we want to get Nicky out—or what?" Garry turned his back on his father, ending the exchange. "All right, where was I? Yes, I pick up Bella's signal. I turn out to sea and make radio contact with *Lancer* as she lies off the Congo mouth. I give them the fix on the base, and then I just come on home."

"I rather think," Shasa drawled nonchalantly, "that I'll go along with you for the ride, Garry!"

"Come on, Pater, you're Battle of Britain vintage. Act your age."

"I taught you to fly, my boy, and I can still fly circles around you any day of the week."

Garry glanced across at Nana for support. Her expression was stony. He threw his hands in the air and began to grin.

"Welcome aboard, Skipper," he acquiesced.

* * *

"Good-bye, Nana." Isabella hugged the old lady with a sudden despairing strength. "Pray for us."

"You just bring my great-grandson here to me, missy. He and I have got a lot of catching up to do."

Isabella turned to her father. "I love you, Daddy."

"Not as much as I love you."

"I have been so stupid. I should have trusted you. I should have come to you right in the beginning." She gulped. "I've done terrible things, Daddy. Things I haven't told you about yet. I wonder if you'll ever be able to forgive me."

"You are my girl." His voice was husky. "My very special, my only girl. Come back safely—and bring your baby with you."

She kissed him and held him hard. Then she whirled and almost ran through the international departures gate of Jan Smuts Airport.

Centaine and Shasa stood staring after her long after she had disappeared. Overhead the airport loudspeaker system was already calling her flight.

"This is the final call for all passengers traveling on the South African Airways SA 516 to Kinshasa and London."

Centaine turned away and took Shasa's arm. She limped heavily on her cane. Her leg always seemed to get worse when she was worried or under unusual strain.

The chauffeur had the car parked at the main entrance, although one of the traffic constables was trying to move him on. Shasa settled Centaine in the backseat, then went around to the other door and climbed in beside her.

"There is something we haven't talked about yet." Centaine took his hand.

"Yes," Shasa agreed. "I know what you are going to ask. What have they extorted from Bella? What price have they made her pay?"

"She's been working for them for years, ever since the birth of that child. That is obvious now."

"I don't want to think about it." Shasa sighed. "But I know we'll have to face it, sooner or later. This bastard who has tied her up is a general in the KGB—so we know who Bella's masters are."

"Shasa." Centaine hesitated. Then her voice firmed. "You recall the Skylight scandal?"

"I'll never forget it."

"There was a leak—a traitor," Centaine pressed on doggedly.

"Bella knew nothing about Skylight. I was very careful to keep her out of it," Shasa said hotly.

"Do you remember the Israeli nuclear scientist who came down to Dragon's Fountain? What was his name—Aaron somebody? Bella had a little fling with him. You told me that her name was in the security register at Pelindaba. She spent the night with him."

"Mother, you aren't suggesting—?" Shasa broke off. "My God, do you realize what information she has had access to over the years? As a senator, and as my assistant, most of the sensitive Armscor projects have passed over her desk!"

"The Cyndex project at Capricorn," Centaine nodded. "She was at the tests only a few weeks back. Why is she being allowed to see Nicholas now? Has she given them some special piece of information, do you think?"

They were silent for a long time. Then Shasa asked softly, "Where does loyalty to the family and to one of our children end—and loyalty and patriotic duty to our country begin?"

"I think that you and I will have to face that question very soon." She sighed. "But let's see this other business through first."

*Lancer* was tied up at the hospital jetty alongside the Courtney canning factory in Walvis Bay. She was a 250-foot stern trawler but had the sleek lines of a modern cruise liner. She had been built to work in any fishery in any ocean, to get there fast, stay at sea for months at a time and then get back to port just as fast.

Sean stood on the jetty and looked her over. He did not like her bright yellow paintwork; it was much too visible. On the other hand, her stern chute would make for easy launching and recovery of the landing boats. Anyway, it was much too late to do anything about the paintwork now, he decided.

Half the Scouts were lining the rail of the trawler, and as soon as they recognized him they launched into a chorus of "Why Was He Born So Beautiful?"

Sean gave them the finger. "No goddamn respect," he lamented, and ran up the gangway. They were delighted to see him and crowded around him to shake his hand. Much of their enthusiasm was a symptom of boredom; for these highly trained fighting men, a week of inactivity had been almost insupportable.

They were all dressed like trawlermen in worn and faded jeans, tattered woolen jerseys and an assortment of caps and balaclava helmets.

Sergeant Major Esau Gondele was a full-blooded Matabele, an old comrade in a dozen desperate contacts and battles. He saluted Sean, then grinned as Sean punched his arm.

"You're out of uniform, Esau. Take it easy, brother."

Twelve of the twenty Scouts that Sean had chosen were Matabele; the others were young white Rhodesians—nearly all of them the sons of ranchers and game wardens and miners who had been brought up in the bush.

In the Scouts there was no awareness of color. As Esau Gondele had once remarked to Sean, "The best cure for racism is to have somebody shoot at you. Man, it does not matter then what color the arse is that comes to save yours—black or white, you're ready to give it a lily fat kiss."

Sean had worried about the naval commandos from Simonstown who were handling the inflatables. They were all tough young Afrikaners. They might have trouble fitting into this multiracial team.

"How are you getting on with the rock spiders?" Sean asked Esau Gondele, using the pejorative slang for an Afrikaner.

"Some of them are my best friends already, but still I wouldn't want one of them to marry my sister." He chuckled. "No, seriously, Sean, they're all right. They know their job. I told them they don't have to call me Baasie, and they saw the joke."

"Okay, Sergeant Major, we are leaving port at nightfall. It's unlikely that there'll be anybody here taking an interest in us. But we'll take no chances. You and I are going to check equipment before we sail, and then we'll brief the boys as soon as we cast off."

The crew accommodation was cramped and spartan. The Scouts and the six commandos crowded into the mess, perched on the table and the bunks. Within minutes the air was fogged with cigarette smoke and *Lancer* was pitching and rolling heavily to the thrust of the cold green Benguela current.

All the Scouts Sean had chosen were proven sailors who had done boat patrols on the choppy waters of Lake Kariba. *Mal de mer* was the reason he had not sent for Matatu. The little Ndorobo would have been puking his heart out by now. It felt strange going into an operation without Matatu at his side, like going on a journey without a St. Christopher medal. Matatu was his good luck charm. He put that thought out of his mind and looked around the crowded mess.

"Can you all see?" Sean had tacked the maps up on the bulkhead. There was a chorus of assent.

"We are heading up here." He prodded the map. "And the mission is to pick up two prisoners, a woman and a child."

There were groans and raspberries of mock disappointment, and Sean grinned.

"It's okay, don't panic. There'll be plenty of gooks. It's hot guns all the way, gentlemen, and open season."

The groans turned to ironic cheers, and Sean waited for them to settle down.

"This is a sketch map of the target area. As you can see, it's pretty rough, but it gives you some idea of what to expect. I expect to find the prisoners being held in this compound here, near the beach. Probably in this hut. I will lead the rescue party. We will go in with three of the boats."

He noticed Esau Gondele squatting on one of the bunks with a South African naval commando squashed up on each side of him. The three of them were sharing a cigarette, passing the butt from hand to hand as they listened to his briefing. "What price apartheid now?" Sean smiled to himself, and went on.

"If there is going to be any serious trouble, it's going to come down this road alongside the river from the terrorist camp near the airstrip, here and here. Sergeant Major Gondele will lead the support unit up the river in the other three boats and set up a roadblock to prevent any gooks coming through. You will have to hold there for thirty minutes after you hear the first shot fired. That will give us time to spring the prisoners. Then you pull out and get back downriver and hotfoot out to sea to RZ with *Lancer*. It's simple, and it must be quick. We aren't going to hang around a second longer than necessary, but if you can sort out a few of the uglies while you are about it nobody is going to complain. Okay, now we'll go over it again in detail and tomorrow we'll practice launching the boats and recovering them again in rough water. We'll do that every day, plus weapons drill and equipment checks—you aren't going to have much time to write home before we hit the beach on the night of Tuesday the thirteenth. Keep that date open. Write it down."

The commercial flight landed at Kinshasa in the middle of a tropical downpour. Rainwater cascaded down the windows as the aircraft taxied to its berth, and Isabella was soaked in the few seconds that it took to leave the aircraft and board the airport bus.

As she had been promised, there was someone to meet her as she came through the Customs and Immigration barrier. He was a good-looking young pilot in plain khaki flying overalls without any insignia or rank. When he greeted her in Spanish she was able to detect a Cuban accent, now that she knew to listen for it.

He insisted on carrying her suitcase and the box of gifts for Nicholas and flirted with her brazenly in the ramshackle taxi that drove them from the main airport building down to the private and charter section of the airfield.

By the time they got there, the rain had stopped. Although heavy clouds still covered the sky, it was stiflingly hot and humid. He loaded her luggage into the back compartment of a small single-engine aircraft. She did not recognize the type. It carried no insignia other than an enigmatic number and was painted an overall drab sandy color.

"Are we going to fly in this weather?" she asked him. "Isn't it dangerous?"

"Ah, señora, if you die you will die in my arms—what a glorious passing!"

As soon as they were airborne he placed his hand on her thigh, the better to point out the passing scenery.

"Keep your hands on the wheel. Keep your eyes on the road." She lifted his hand and gave it back to him. He flashed his teeth and his eyes and laughed as though he had made a conquest.

She could not remain angry for long. Every minute they kept on this heading confirmed the fact that she was being taken to the base where last she had seen Nicholas. Two hours later she made out the grey expanse of the Atlantic beneath the lowering cloud banks ahead.

The pilot turned south along the coast, and then she sat up straight in the seat and her spirits took wing. She recognized the oxbow in the river and the open mouth to the sea. The pilot pulled on flap and lined up for a landing on the red clay strip.

Nicky, she thought. Soon now, my baby. Soon we'll be free again.

As they taxied in, she saw him. He was standing on the front seat of the jeep. He had shot up at least another two inches, and his legs seemed too gawky and coltish for his body. His hair was longer than she remembered and curled out from under his camo cap, but his eyes were the same, that marvelous clear green that sparkled even at this distance. As soon as he recognized her behind the windscreen, he waved both hands over his head, and his teeth flashed in his darkly tanned and beautiful face.

In the jeep with him were the driver and José, the Cuban

411

paratrooper. They were grinning as widely as Nicky as she climbed out of the front seat of the aircraft.

Nicky jumped out of the jeep and ran to meet her. For a heady moment she thought he might rush into her arms. Then he got control of himself and offered her his hand.

"Welcome, Mamma." She thought the strength of her love might choke her. "It is good to see you again."

"Hello, Nicky." Her voice was husky. "You have grown so much I hardly recognized you. You are becoming a man now."

It was the right thing to say. He hooked his thumbs into his belt and called imperiously to José and the driver, "Come and take my mother's luggage."

"Right away, General Pele." José gave him a mock salute, then said to Isabella, "Greetings, Señora. We have been looking forward to your visit."

I'm everybody's favorite aunt now, Isabella thought cynically.

From her box of goodies she gave José and the driver each a 200-pack of Marlboro cigarettes, and her popularity was enhanced a hundredfold. In Angola, Western cigarettes were hard currency.

As Nicholas drove them down to the beach he chattered happily, and though she showed a flattering interest in everything he had done and achieved since their last meeting, she was checking her surroundings with a much more businesslike eye than she had previously. She realized she had made serious errors in the sketch map she had drawn for Sean. The training base had been enlarged since her last visit. There must now be several thousand soldiers here, and she saw some kind of artillery parked under camouflage nets. They looked like long-barreled antiaircraft guns. Farther on she noticed parked trucks with dish-shaped radar antennae pointed skyward, and she thought of her father and Garry bringing the Lear in overhead. There was no way to warn them of these changes.

When they reached the beach compound, Isabella checked the distance registered on the odometer. It was only 3.6 kilometers from the airstrip to the beach, much closer than she had estimated. She wondered just how this might endanger the rescue operation. Reinforcements could be rushed in more swiftly than Sean had allowed for.

José carried her luggage into the guardhouse. Waiting for her were the same two women who had met her before. However, their attitude was friendlier and more informal.

"I have brought you a gift," Isabella greeted them, and gave them each a bottle of perfume that she had chosen for size rather than for subtle aroma. They were delighted and sprayed themselves so liberally that the air in the room was difficult to breathe. It was some minutes before they could get around to searching Isabella's luggage.

This time the camera was passed without comment, though they lingered longingly over her cosmetics. Isabella invited them to try a little of her lipstick, and they accepted with alacrity and admired the results in the mirror of Isabella's compact. The atmosphere was more that of a gathering of old friends than of a security screening.

By the time they came to examine the box of gifts for Nicholas, their hearts were obviously no longer in the task. One of them picked out the deflated soccer ball. "Ah, Pele will like this," she cried. Isabella's nerves prickled with tension as she handled the pump.

"For the ball," she explained.

"*Sí.* I know, to pump air." The woman gave it a few desultory strokes, then dropped it back into the box.

"I am sorry to have inconvenienced you, señora. We only do our duty."

"Of course. I understand," Isabella agreed.

"You will stay with us two weeks. That is good. Pele has been very excited that you are coming. He is a good boy. Everybody likes him very much. Everybody is very proud of him."

She helped Isabella to carry her cases across to the same hut they had given her on her last visit.

Nicholas was sitting on her bed, already in his swimming trunks.

"Come, Mamma, we will go for a swim now. I will race you out to the reef."

He swam like an otter, and she was hard pressed to keep up with him.

That evening, when just the two of them were alone in her hut, she gave him his gifts from the box. Although the soccer ball was the greatest hit, he also enjoyed her choice of books and clothes. She had brought a selection of colorful surfer's baggies and T-shirts that delighted him. There was also a Sony cassette player and a box of music cassettes. His favorites were Creedence Clearwater Revival and the Beatles.

"Can you rock 'n' roll?" she asked. "I'll show you." And she put a Johnny Halliday tape on the player.

They gyrated around the hut in their bathing suits, shrieking with laughter, until Adra called them for dinner. Adra was as taciturn and withdrawn as ever, and Isabella ignored her and

**413**

concentrated all her attention on Nicholas. She had stored up a selection of elephant jokes for him.

"How do you know an elephant has been in the refrigerator? You see his footprints in the butter." He loved that one. In return he told her a joke he had heard from José the paratrooper. It left her gasping.

"Do you know what that means?" she asked in nervous trepidation.

"Of course," he told her. "One of the big girls at school showed me." And Isabella thought it prudent not to pursue the subject.

After they had seen him to bed, Adra walked with her to the hut and Isabella whispered, "Where is Ramón, the marqués? Is he here?"

Adra looked around carefully before replying. "No. He will come soon. I think tomorrow or the next day. He says he will come to you. He says to tell you he loves you."

Alone in her hut, Isabella found she was trembling at the prospect of meeting Ramón again, now that she knew him for what he was. She doubted whether she would be able to act naturally toward him. The thought of making love to him terrified her. Surely he would sense the change in her feelings toward him. He might take Nicholas away or have her imprisoned.

"Please, God, let Sean reach me before Ramón does. Keep him away until Sean comes." She lay awake that night, cold with dread that Ramón would suddenly appear out of the darkness and she would have to take him into her bed.

As before, she and Nicholas spent the next two days swimming and fishing and playing with Twenty-six on the beach. The puppy had grown into a lanky, long-tailed, cross-eyed, floppy-eared dog that Nicholas adored. It shared his bed with him; Isabella did not have the authority to forbid it, even though Nicholas's long legs were speckled with flea bites.

On Monday night, while she watched Nicholas prepare for bed, she reached up casually and took down the bicycle pump from the shelf above his bed on which the new soccer ball held pride of place. She twisted the handle and heard the faint internal click as the transponder switched on. She replaced the pump on the shelf just as Nicholas came back from the bathroom smelling of the peppermint toothpaste she had brought for him from Cape Town.

As she leaned over the bed to tuck in the mosquito net, he reached up unexpectedly and threw both arms around her neck. "I love you, Mamma," he whispered shyly, and she kissed him.

His mouth was soft and moist and warm and tasted of tooth-paste, and she thought her heart would burst with love of him. Quickly embarrassed by his own display, Nicholas rolled over, pulled the sheet up to his chin, closed his eyes tightly and made ostentatious snoring sounds.

"Sleep well, Nicky. I love you, too—with all my heart," she whispered.

As she walked back to her own hut, thunder growled and lightning flickered across the night sky. As she looked up, a heavy drop of warm rain struck her on the center of her forehead.

# 32

It was very quiet in the cockpit of the Lear. They were at forty thousand feet, almost service ceiling, as high as they could get for maximum endurance and speed.

"Enemy coast ahead," Shasa said softly.

Garry chuckled. "Come on, Pater. People only say things like that in World War Two movies."

They were high above the cloud mass in a world of enchanted silver moonlight. The cloud below them shone with the peculiar brilliance of an alpine snowfield.

"One hundred nautical miles to run to the mouth of the Congo River." Shasa checked their position on the screen of the satellite nav system. "We should be almost exactly overhead *Lancer*'s station."

"Better give them a call," Garry suggested.

Shasa switched radio frequencies.

"Hello, Donald Duck. This is the Magic Dragon. Do you read?"

"Hello, Dragon. This is the Duck. Reading you ten and ten." The reply was immediate, and Shasa smiled with relief as he recognized his eldest son's voice. "Sean must have had his thumb

415

on the button," he murmured, then keyed his microphone. "Stand by, Duck. We are heading for Disneyland."

"Have a nice trip. Duck is standing by."

Shasa swiveled in the copilot's seat and looked back into the Lear's passenger cabin. The two technicians from Courtney Communications were crouched over their equipment. It had taken them ten days to install all the special electronics. Much of it was state-of-the-art equipment that was still under test with Armscor and had not yet been issued to the air force. It was not built into the Lear's body but strapped and screwed to the cabin floor. Their intent faces were painted a witch's green by the glow from the display panel, and the enormous headphones distorted the shape of their heads.

Shasa switched to the intercom. "How you doing, Len?"

The head engineer glanced up at him. "No radar lash. We are receiving normal radio traffic from Luanda, Kinshasa and Brazzaville. No signal from the target."

"Carry on." Shasa turned. He knew the new frequency-search equipment was skipping through the bands. It should pick up any military traffic from Luanda or Saurimo military bases. The antenna mounted under the Lear's belly would warn them if they were detected by hostile radar. Len, the radio engineer, had been chosen for his command of Spanish. He would be able to monitor any Cuban radio traffic.

"Okay, Garry." Shasa touched his arm. "We are overhead the Congo mouth. Your new heading is one seventy-five."

"New heading one seventy-five." Garry stood the Lear on one wing tip as they turned southeast to run parallel with the coastline.

By some freak of wind and weather, a deep hole opened in the cloud mass beneath them. The moon was directly overhead and only two days from its full. Its light beamed down into the chasm, and forty thousand feet below they saw the platinum gleam of water and the dark shape of the African coast.

"Ambriz River mouth in four minutes," Shasa warned.

"We have initiated search for target signal," Len confirmed in his headphones.

"Overhead Ambriz," Shasa intoned.

"No target signal received."

"Catacanha River mouth in six minutes," Shasa said.

He hadn't really expected the Ambriz to yield results. It was the outer limit of their search cone. He looked ahead and grimaced. Directly in their track a gigantic mountain of menacing black cloud rose hammer-headed into the stratosphere.

He estimated its height at sixty or seventy thousand feet, way above the Lear's ceiling.

"How do you like that Charlie Bravo?" he asked. Garry shook his head and looked down at the screen of the weather radar set. The enormous tropical thunderstorm showed up as a lurid and ferocious crimson cancer on the screen.

"Ninety-six miles ahead, and it's a real lulu. Looks like it's sitting right over one of our target river mouths, the Chicamba."

"If it is, it will wipe out any signal from Bella's transponder." Shasa was looking worried.

"We wouldn't be able to fly through that anyway," Garry growled.

"Overhead the Catacanha, Len. Are you picking up anything from our target?"

"Negative, Mr. Courtney." Then his voice changed. "Hold on! Oh, shit! Somebody is hitting us with radar lash."

"Garry"—Shasa reached across to shake his shoulder— "they've picked us up on radar."

"Switch to the international frequency," Garry said, "and listen."

They sat frozen in their seats, listening to the static of that great turbulent storm ahead.

Suddenly the carrier band hissed and a voice cut in clearly. "Unidentified aircraft. This is Luanda control. You are in restricted airspace. Identify yourself immediately. I say again, you are in restricted airspace."

"Luanda control, this is British Airways flight BA 051. We have an engine malfunction. Request a position fix." Shasa began a garbled delaying argument with Luanda. Every second he could gain was crucial. He asked them for a clearance to land at Luanda and pretended not to be receiving or understanding their refusals and urgent orders to vacate national airspace.

"They haven't fallen for it, Mr. Courtney," Len warned him as he swept the military frequencies. "They have scrambled a flight of MiGs from Saurimo airfield. They are vectoring them in on us."

"How long before we cross the Chicamba River mouth?" Garry demanded.

"Fourteen minutes," Shasa snapped back.

"Well, Lordy, Lordy!" Garry grinned. "We are on a head-on course with those MiGs. They are coming in at Mach 2. This is going to be fun."

They sped southward into the silver moonlight.

"Mr. Courtney, we have more radar lash. I think the MiGs have got us on their attack radar."

"Thank you, Len. Chicamba River in one minute, thirty seconds."

"Mr. Courtney!" There was a strident tone to Len's voice. "The MiG leader is reporting target acquisition. They are onto us, sir. The attack radar lash is increasing. The MiG leader is requesting weapons-free."

"I thought you said they couldn't intercept us," Shasa said mildly to Garry. "I thought we were out of their operational range."

"Hell, Dad, anyone can make a mistake."

"Mr. Courtney!" Len's voice was a shriek. "I have the target signal, weak and intermittent. About six kilometers. Dead ahead!"

"Are you sure, Len?"

"It's our transponder for sure!"

"The Chicamba River mouth. Bella is at the Chicamba!" Shasa shouted. "Let's get the hell out of here."

"Mr. Courtney, the MiGs are weapons-free and attacking. Radar lash is very strong and increasing."

"Hold on!" Garry called. "Grab your hats!"

He rolled the Lear wingover into a dive.

"What the hell are you doing?" Shasa shouted as he was pressed back into the copilot's seat by the G force. "Turn and get out to sea."

"They'd nail us before we'd gone a mile." Garry held the Lear in the dive.

"Christ, Garry, you'll tear the wings off us."

The airspeed indicator revolved swiftly up toward the "never exceed" barrier.

"Take your choice, Pater. We tear the wings off her—or the MiGs shoot the arse off us."

"Mr. Courtney, the MiG leader reports missile lock." Len was stuttering with terror.

"What are you going to do, Garry?" Shasa grabbed Garry's arm.

"I'm going in there." Garry pointed at the soaring moon-washed mountain of the thunderstorm. It was a sheer precipice of turbulent cloud that obscured the heavens ahead of them. The cloud banks boiled and seethed with the great winds and air currents within. Lightning flashed and glowed deep in the belly of the storm.

"You are crazy," Shasa whispered.

"No MiG will follow us in," Garry said. "No missile will hold its lock with all that energy and electrical discharge burning around us."

"Mr. Courtney, MiG leader has fired a missile—and another. Two missiles running . . ."

"Pray for us sinners," Garry said, and he held the Lear down in its death dive; the airspeed needle went through the "never exceed" barrier.

"I think this is it." Shasa's voice was matter-of-fact, and as he said it something struck the Lear a crashing blow. She flipped over onto her back, the ball of the flight director spun like a top in its cage, and then they were into the storm.

All visibility was wiped out instantly and thick grey cloud like wet cotton wool engulfed them. They were thrown onto their safety harnesses as the storm attacked the Lear. It was a ravening beast that clawed and lashed them.

The Lear tumbled and swirled like a dead leaf in a whirlwind. The instruments on the control panel spun and toppled, the altimeter yo-yo'd as they dropped into the void, then hit a vicious updraught that hurled them up two thousand feet and twisted them wing over wing.

Suddenly the cloud was lit by internal lightning. It dazzled them and rumbled through their heads, drowning out the agonized shriek of the Lear's jets. Blue fire danced on the metal skin of the aircraft as though she were aflame. They hit the bottom of another hole with a force that plunged them against the padding of their seats and buckled their spines. Then they were hurled aloft only to plunge once again. All around them the bodywork of the Lear creaked and groaned as the storm tried to rip her apart.

Garry was helpless. He knew better than to fight the wheel and rudders and increase the brutal stress on her control surfaces. The Lear was fighting for her life. He whispered encouragement to her and held the control wheel with a light and loving touch, trying to ease her nose up out of the graveyard spiral.

"Courage, darling," he whispered. "Come on, baby. You can do it."

Shasa was clinging to the armrests of his seat and staring at the altimeter. They were down to fifteen thousand feet and still dropping. None of the other instruments was making any sense. They jerked and wavered and kicked.

He concentrated on the altimeter. It unwound jerkily. Ten thousand, seven, four thousand. The strength of the storm increased; their heads were whipped back and forth, threatening

419

to snap their spines. The shoulder straps cut painfully into their flesh.

Something in the fuselage broke with a tearing crash. Shasa ignored it and tried to focus on the altimeter. His vision was starred and disorientated by the Lear's vicious plunges.

Two thousand feet, one thousand—zero. They should have hit the ground, but the tremendous changes of barometric pressure within the swirling body of the storm had thrown out the reading.

Suddenly the Lear steadied and the turbulence abated. Garry pressed on rudder and stick, and she responded. The flight director stabilized and rotated toward vertical as the Lear rolled back onto even keel and they burst out of the cloud.

The change was stunning. The noise of the storm gave way to the low hum of the jets. Moonlight flooded into the cockpit, and Shasa gasped with shock.

They were almost on the surface of the sea, skimming over it like a flying fish rather than a bird. A drop of another hundred feet would have plunged them beneath the green Atlantic rollers.

"Cutting it a little fine, son." Shasa's voice was hoarse, and he tried to grin, but his eye patch had been shaken loose and hung down under his ear. He adjusted it with trembling fingers.

"Come on, Navigator." Garry chuckled unconvincingly. "Give me a course to fly."

"New course is two six zero degrees. How is she handling?"

"Like a breeze." Garry turned gently onto the new heading. The Lear came around serenely and sped out into the Atlantic, leaving the dark continental mass astern.

"Len." Shasa turned in the seat and looked back into the cabin. The technicians' faces were pale and lightly washed with the sweat of terror. "What do you make of the MiGs?"

Len stared at him like an owl as he tried to adjust to the shock of still being alive.

"Pull yourself together, man!" Shasa snapped.

Len stooped quickly to his control panel. "Yes, we still have contact. MiG leader is reporting target destroyed. He is short of fuel and returning to base."

"Farewell, Fidel. Thank the Lord that you are a lousy shot," Garry murmured, and he kept the Lear low down in the surface clutter where the shore radar would have difficulty picking them up. "Where is *Lancer*?"

"Should be dead ahead." Shasa thumbed the microphone. "Donald Duck, this is the Magic Dragon."

"Go ahead, Dragon."

"It's the Chicamba. I repeat, the Chicamba. Do you copy that? Over."

"Roger. Chicamba. I say again, Chicamba. Did you have any trouble? We heard pom-pom jet traffic southeast of here. Over."

"Nothing to it. It was a Sunday school picnic. Now it's your turn to visit Disneyland. Over."

"We are on our way, Dragon."

"Break a leg, Duck. Over and out."

It was half past five on Tuesday morning when Garry put the Lear down on the tarmac at Windhoek Airport. They climbed down stiffly and stood in a group at the foot of the steps, overcome by a sense of anticlimax. Then Garry walked to the nearest engine, which was softly crackling and pinging as it cooled.

"Pater," he called. "Come and have a look at this."

Shasa stared at the alien object that had buried itself in the metal fuselage below the pod of the Garrett turbofan engine. It was painted a harsh industrial yellow, a long-finned arrowlike tube that protruded six feet from the torn metal skin of the Lear.

"What the hell is that?" Shasa asked.

"That, Mr. Courtney," said Len, who had come up behind him, "is a Soviet ATOLL air-to-air missile that failed to explode."

"Well, Garry," Shasa murmured, "Fidel wasn't such a lousy shot after all."

"Bless Russian workmanship," Garry said. "Perhaps it's a little early, Dad, but could you stand a glass of champagne?"

"What a splendid idea," said Shasa.


"The Chicamba River." Shoulder to shoulder, Sean and Esau Gondele leaned over the chart table. "There she is."

Sean laid his finger on the insignificant nick in the outline of the continent. "Just south of Catacanha." He looked up at the trawler skipper. Van Der Berg was built like a sumo wrestler, squat and heavy, with a leathery skin burnt and desiccated by sun and wind.

"What do you know about it, Van?" he asked.

Van shrugged. "Never been in that close. Just another piss-willy little river. But I'll get you as close as you want to go."

"A mile off the reef will do very nicely."

"You've got it," Van promised. "When?"

"I want you to keep below the horizon all of tomorrow, then at nightfall you can take us in at 0200 hours."

For the Scouts, the witching hour was always two hours after

421

midnight. It was then that the enemy would be at his lowest ebb, both physically and mentally.

At one in the morning Sean held his final briefing in the crew mess of *Lancer*. He checked each man separately. They were all dressed in navy blue fisherman's jerseys and jeans and black canvas rubber-soled combat boots. On their heads were knitted black woolen caps, and all their faces and hands were black, either naturally or with camo cream.

The only uniform item they wore was their webbing, all of it supplied by the South African defense force from Cuban equipment captured in the south of Angola. Their weapons were Soviet AKM assault rifles, Tokarev pistols and Bulgarian M75 antipersonnel grenades. Three men in Esau Gondele's section would carry RPG 7 antitank rocket launchers. Part of the agreement made with the South Africans in return for their cooperation was that nothing would ever be traced back to them.

One at a time, they stepped up to the table and handed over all their personal items—signet rings, dog tags, pay books, wallets, wristwatches and any other form of identification. Esau Gondele sealed them in separate envelopes and issued each of them an identical black waterproof digital wristwatch to replace his own.

While this was happening the trawler captain called on the intercom from the bridge, "We are seven nautical miles off the river mouth. Bottom is shoaling nice and gently. I'll have you in position a few minutes before time."

"Good on you," Sean told him. Then he turned back to the ring of black faces. "Very well, gentlemen, you know what we are after. Just a few airy thoughts to occupy those busy little minds of yours—if you are going to cull anybody, just make sure that you don't take out the woman or the child. She's my sister." He let that sink in for a moment. "Thought number two. The sketch maps I have shown you are more fantasy than fact. Don't rely on them. Thought number three. Don't get left behind on the beach when we pull out. Chicamba is no place to spend a holiday. The food and the accommodations are rotten." He picked up his rifle from the bunk. "So, my children, let's go and do it."

*Lancer* groped toward the shore by radar and depth sounder. All her running lights were extinguished. Her engines were ticking over so she barely maintained steerage. In the darkness ahead Sean could make out the intermittent luminous flare of the surf breaking on the outer reef. There were no lights ashore.

The land itself had been absorbed by the night. The cloud over-head was unbroken. No glimmer of star or moon came through.

Van Der Berg straightened up from the radar hood. "One mile off," he said quietly. "Water is six fathoms and shoaling." He glanced across at the dark figure of his colored helmsman. "Stop engines."

The tremble of the engines through the deck beneath their feet ceased, and *Lancer* wallowed like a log.

"Thanks, Van," Sean said. "I'll bring you back a nice pres-ent." He ran lightly down the companionway to the main deck.

They were waiting in the stern, each team standing by its own black rubber landing boat. Sean smelled a musky odor in the air and grimaced. He didn't like it, but the use of "boom" before a contact had become a tradition in the Scouts.

"It's an old African custom," he consoled himself. "The mad Mahdi's fuzzy-wuzzies smoked it before they revved old Kitchener at Khartoum."

"Sergeant Major, the smoking light is out," he grated, and he heard them shuffle in the darkness as they rubbed out their cannabis cigarettes on the deck. Sean realized that the smoke dulled the edge of their fear and bolstered the reckless bravado that was part of the Scout tradition, but he himself had never used it. He relished the sensation of fear; it throbbed in his blood and beat in his brain. He was never more alive than at a time like this, going into battle and mortal danger. He would not wish to shade that pure clean flame of fear.

One at a time the flexible rubber hulls, laden with men and equipment, slid down the stern chute of the trawler and splashed softly onto the water. The boatmen started the Toyota outboards and they burbled gently in the night. Even on a still and windless night like this, the sound would not carry a hundred yards.

They formed up into a long black snake, a boat's length be-tween them. Sean was in the leading inflatable with three of his best men. The boatman shone a hooded penlight over the stern to keep the boats that followed on station. They moved off qui-etly toward land.

Sean was standing in the stern. On a lanyard around his neck was a small luminous compass, but he relied mainly on his nightscope to bring them in to shore. It was a Zeiss image en-hancer. It looked like a large pair of plastic-coated binoculars.

Ahead of him the breaking surf flared green fire in the lens, and he made out clearly the dark spot in the line that marked the river mouth. He touched the boatman's shoulder to redirect him. The next wave lifted and shoved them as it slid by under

**423**

the hull, and they heard its hoarse susurration on either hand as they ran through the pass into the calmer waters of the lagoon.

Through the Zeiss lens he saw the shaggy tops of the palms silhouetted against the cloud banks and the open throat of the river ahead. He flicked the penlight, and Esau Gondele's boat moved up alongside.

"There she is." He leaned over to whisper to the big Matabele and pointed out the river mouth.

"I see it." Esau had his own nightscope held to his eyes.

"Tear their nuts out!" The pod of three attack boats moved off together, and Sean watched them disappear into the river and merge with the loom of the land.

He whispered to the boatman and they turned parallel with the beach. As they ran down the lagoon, Sean scanned the shore through the Zeiss lens. Half a mile from the mouth he made out in the gloom of a palm grove the square outline of a hut and then beyond it a second. "It fits with Bella's description," he decided.

They ran toward the beach. Now he saw the gleam of metal above the nearest hut. It was the tall Christmas-tree antenna and dish of a satellite communications center.

"That's it."

Sand grated softly beneath the keel of the inflatable and they leaped over the side into blood-warm water that reached to their knees. Sean led them ashore. The beach sand was so white he could see little ghost crabs scuttling away ahead of them. The men raced to the edge of the palm grove and dropped into cover below the high-water ridge.

Sean took a few moments to check his bearings. According to Isabella's description of her first visit, the communications center was where they had received and searched her. She had told him there were two or three female radio operators running the center. In addition, she had counted approximately twenty para guards, who were billeted in the barracks beyond the wire.

The gate to the compound was always locked at sunset. She had warned him of that. There was always a sentry posted there. He patrolled the wire, and they changed the guard every four hours.

"Here he comes now," Sean murmured as he saw the dark shape of the sentry moving along the barbed-wire fence. He lowered the nightscope and whispered to the Scout who lay beside him, "Twenty paces ahead, Porky. He's moving left to right."

"Got him." Porky Soaves was a Portuguese Rhodesian whose

specialty was the slingshot. He could hit a dove on the wing at fifty meters. At ten meters he could drive a steel ball bearing clean through the bone of a man's skull.

He slid forward like a night adder, and as the Cuban sentry came level he rose onto one knee and drew like a longbow man. The double surgical rubber strands of the slingshot snapped, and the sentry collapsed without a sound into the fluffy white sand.

"Go!" said Sean softly, and the second Scout ran forward with the heavy wire cutters. The strands of barbed wire made little musical pinging sounds as they parted. Sean ran to the opening.

As each of the Scouts slipped through the hole in the wire, he slapped their shoulders and pointed them to their targets. He sent two of them to the main gate to take the sentries there, two to shut down the communications center and the rest of them to hose down the barracks at the rear of the compound and to cull the garrison guards.

If the arrangements were the same as last time, the first hut on the right of the radio room should be Isabella's. Nicky would be in the second one with his Cuban nursemaid. Isabella called her Adra. From Sean's estimate of the situation, the nursemaid was one of the uglies. She would have to go. He would cull her at the first opportunity.

Sean ran toward the line of huts, but before he reached them a woman in the communications hut started to scream. The sharp hysterical bursts of sound raked Sean's nerve endings. The screams were cut off by a short burst of automatic fire.

Here we go! Sean thought, and the night erupted with gunfire and flame and the mortal thrill of combat.

# 33

Isabella slept fitfully and woke a little before midnight to the sound of thunder and of jet engines passing overhead.

She threw aside the mosquito net and ran out into the night.

The wind generated by a mighty thunderstorm that was moving up from the south flapped the skirts of her nightdress around her bare legs and rattled the palm fronds.

The sound of jet engines rose and fell as wind and cloud blanketed it. It seemed to her that there was more than one aircraft up there above the cloud. She hoped that one of them was the Lear with her father and Garry aboard.

"Have you picked up the signal?" she wondered as she strained her eyes into the black heavens. "Can you hear me, Daddy? Do you know I'm here?"

She saw nothing, not even the shine of a single star, and the sound of engines overhead faded and left only the soughing of the wind and the rumble and crash as the thunderstorm fired its opening broadsides.

The rain began to fall again, and she ran back into the hut. She dried her hair and her bare feet and stood at the window looking down toward the beach.

"Please, God. Let them know we are here. Help Sean to find us."

At breakfast, Nicholas said to her, "I haven't had a chance to try out my new soccer ball."

"But we've played with it every day, Nicky."

"Yes, but . . . I mean, with good players." Then, realizing what he had said, "You are a good player—for a girl. I think you would make an excellent goalkeeper—with some more practice. But, Mamma, I would like some of my friends from school."

426

"I don't know." Isabella looked at Adra. "Are your friends allowed here?"

Adra did not look around from the wood stove. "Ask José," she said. "Perhaps it will be allowed."

That afternoon José and Nicholas arrived at the compound with a jeepload of small black boys. The soccer match on the beach was noisy and passionately contested. On three occasions Isabella and José had to untangle a knot of punching and kicking bodies. After each battle, play was resumed as though nothing had happened.

Isabella was selected as goalkeeper for the Sons of the Revolution. But after she had let through five goals Nicholas, the team captain, came to her tactfully, "I think you are tired, Mamma, and would like to rest now." And she was sent to the sidelines.

The Sons of the Revolution beat the Angolan Tigers twenty-six goals to five, and Isabella felt very guilty about those five. After the final whistle Isabella produced a two-kilo bag of toffees and chocolates from her gift box, and her lack of athletic prowess was immediately forgiven by her captain and both teams.

At dinner Nicholas chatted easily, and Isabella tried to act naturally, but her eyes kept straying to the window of the hut and the beach. If Sean were coming, he would come tonight. She noticed Adra watching her thoughtfully. She made another effort to follow Nicholas's conversation, but she was thinking about Adra now.

Could they take her with them? she pondered. Would she want to come? Adra was such a reticent and secretive person that she could never even guess at her true feelings, except her love for Nicholas—that was all that was certain.

Could she trust her enough to warn her of the rescue? she wondered. Should she give Adra the choice of coming away or remaining? In fairness, could she take Nicholas from her after all these years of devotion to him? Surely it would break her heart, and yet could she trust her enough to tell her? Could she risk their freedom, hers and Nicholas's, and could she risk the lives of her brother and all those other gallant young men who were attempting to rescue them? More than once during the meal she was on the point of speaking to Adra, but each time she shied away from it at the last moment.

When she tucked Nicholas into bed he lifted his face to her, and she kissed him quite naturally. He held her tightly for a moment.

"Do you have to go away again, Mamma?" he asked.

"Would you come with me, if you could?" she countered.

"And leave Padre and Adra?" He lapsed into silence. It was the first time he had ever spoken to her of Ramón, and it troubled her deeply. Was it respect or fear she had detected in his voice? She could not be certain.

On an impulse she began, "Nicky, tonight—if anything happens, don't be afraid."

"What will happen?" He sat up with interest.

"I don't know. Probably nothing." He looked disappointed and dropped back onto the pillow.

"Good night, Nicky," she whispered.

Adra was waiting for her in the darkness between the huts. It was the opportunity Isabella had waited for.

"Adra," she whispered. "I have to talk to you. Tonight—" she broke off.

"Tonight?" Adra prompted her, and when she still hesitated Adra went on, "Yes, tonight he will come. He says to expect him. He could not come before, but tonight he will come to you."

Isabella felt panic rise to wash reason away. "Oh, God—are you sure?" Then she caught herself. "That is wonderful. I have waited so long."

All thoughts of warning Adra of the rescue attempt were wiped from her mind. How could she face Ramón now that she realized what a cruel and evil monster he truly was? How could she let him touch her without trembling?

"I must go now," Adra whispered, and she slipped away into the darkness, leaving Isabella alone with her terror. She had planned to wear jeans and a jersey beneath her nightdress so as to be ready to leave when Sean came, but she dared not do that now.

She lay so long alone in the darkness beneath the mosquito net that at last she began to hope that Sean would come to her before Ramón did, or at least that dawn would save her.

Then suddenly she knew he was in the hut with her. She smelled him before she heard him, the faint but distinctive odor of his body that had always aroused her so readily. Her nostrils and every nerve in her body jumped tight. Her breathing seized up in her throat.

She heard the whisper of his feet across the floor of the hut and then his touch on the bed.

"Ramón." Her breath escaped in an explosive gust.

"Yes, it is me." His voice struck her like a blow in the face. She felt him lift the mosquito net and she lay rigid. His fin-

**428**

gertips brushed her face, and she thought she might scream. She did not know how to act, what to say to him. "He will know." She realized she was panicking. She dared not move or speak.

"Bella?" he said, and she heard the first suspicion in his tone. In sudden inspiration she reached up and seized him.

"Don't talk," she whispered fiercely. "I cannot wait another moment—don't say anything. Take me now, Ramón."

She knew she was not acting out of character. Often in that distant, happy past she had been like this—urgent, wild with desire, brooking not an instant's delay.

She sat up and began to tear at his clothing. I have to keep him from talking, from asking any questions, she thought desperately. I have to quieten and reassure him that nothing has changed.

With terror in her heart and the smell of him filling her head she let his hands lift her nightdress, and then the hard smooth naked length of him slid into the bed beside her.

"Bella," he whispered harshly. "I have wanted you too much for too long." And his mouth covered hers. It felt as though he were sucking out her very being from between her lips, the way he might suck the juice and flesh from a ripe orange.

With shame at the perversity and treachery of her own body she felt herself overwhelmed by raw sexual passion. She was making love to a sleek and beautiful animal, something inhuman and cruel and infinitely dangerous. Fear mingled with lust to spur and goad her. She felt like that doomed creature in the bullring of Granada whose tragic struggle and lingering death had moved her so when long ago she and her love had been fresh and young.

At last when they were spent together, he lay on top of her as though he were dead. She could not move; her guilt and his weight threatened to suffocate her. She hated herself almost as much as she hated him.

"It was never like that before," he whispered. "You never did that to me before."

She could not trust herself to reply. She could not know what might come out once she began to speak. She realized she was on the verge of a terrible destructive madness—and yet when he lay beside her and he stroked her and gently touched the most intimate parts of her body her thighs fell apart and she felt her flesh melt and her bones soften.

He began to speak softly. He told her how he loved her. He spoke about the future, when the three of them would be safe and happy in some secure and secret place. His lies were beautiful; they conjured up wonderful pictures in her mind. Although she knew they were false, she wanted desperately to believe them.

When at last he fell asleep with his face pressed between her naked breasts, she stroked the crisp, springing curls of his head with a terrible regret and a longing for things she knew did not exist. So deep was her distress that it had driven all other thoughts from her consciousness, until abruptly and shockingly the night was ripped through by the screams of a woman and the sound of gunfire.

She felt Ramón come awake and at the same instant spring from the bed, naked and lithe as a jungle cat. She heard the metallic snick of a firearm as he snatched the pistol from the holster that lay on the floor beside the bed. The night was lit by flame and explosion. She saw Ramón silhouetted against the light from the window. He held the pistol at the level of his eyes, pointed at the roof, ready for instant use.

Then she heard Sean's beloved voice, shouting for her in the darkness beyond the window: "Bella, where are you?"

She saw Ramón's dark shape dart to the window, and the pistol glinted in the light of an exploding grenade as he leveled it.

"Look out, Sean!" she screamed. "Man with a gun!"

Ramón fired twice, changing position after each shot. There was no answering fire from beyond the window. She realized that Sean dared not fire for fear of hitting her or Nicholas.

She rolled from the bed and dropped to the floor on hands and knees. Frantically she crawled toward the door. She wanted to get to Nicholas, she had to get to Nicholas.

Halfway across the hut she felt Ramón's muscular bare arm whipped around her neck from behind, and he forced her to her feet. With the last of her breath, she screamed, "Sean! He has got me!"

"Bitch!" Ramón hissed in her ear. "Treacherous bitch." And then he raised his voice. "I'll kill her!" he shouted. "I'll blow her head off."

He dragged her to the door and forced her down the steps. "Move, bitch," he grated. "Keep moving. I know who Sean is. He won't fire—not with you as a shield. Move!"

The pressure on her throat was choking her. She could not resist it. He ran with her toward Nicholas's hut. The communications hut was in flames. From its thatched roof flame and sparks towered into the night sky. It was as bright as a stage.

The serpentine shadows of palm trunks writhed upon the pale sandy earth.

They burst into Nicholas's hut. Adra and the child were crouched in the center of the floor. Adra was covering Nicholas with her body.

"Padre!" Nicholas shrieked.

"Come with Adra!" Ramón snapped at him. "Keep close to her. Follow me."

In a tight group they left the hut and moved toward the carpark. Ramón held Isabella from behind; with his free hand he pressed the pistol to her head.

"I'll blow her head off!" he called into the dancing shadows. "Keep your distance!"

"Please, Padre, do not hurt Mamma," Nicholas wailed.

"Keep quiet, boy!" Ramón snarled at him. Then, raising his voice again, "Call your dogs off, Sean. Unless you want your sister and her son to die."

After a moment, Sean's voice bellowed out of the shadows, "Hold your fire, Scouts! Back off, Scouts!"

Ramón kept them moving toward one of the jeeps. Isabella was choking for breath; the muzzle of the pistol was pressed so hard into her ear that the tender skin tore and a drop of blood ran down her neck.

"Please, you're hurting me," Isabella gasped.

"Don't hurt Mamma," Nicholas cried, and twisted out of Adra's grip. He ran to Isabella's side, and for a moment Adra was isolated, offering a clear shot.

In the darkness beyond the firelight a yellow flower of gun flame bloomed, and a single bullet whiplashed across twenty yards of open ground.

The side of Adra's head dissolved in a liquid red smear. She was snatched over backward and hit the earth with her arms flung wide open.

"Adra!" Nicholas screamed, but before he could run to her Ramón grabbed him around the waist.

"No, leave Adra," he snapped. "Stay close to me now, Nicky."

The three of them were in the center of a brightly lit stage. There was no other living soul in view. The corpse of one of the Cuban woman signalers lay curled against the wall of the burning building, and two dead paratroopers lay at the gate to the compound.

Ramón called out an order in Spanish to any of his paratroopers who might still be alive, but he knew it was a vain effort. He knew the quality of the attackers. He had recognized the name of Isabella's brother the instant she had called it out. Sean's shouted order addressed to the Scouts had confirmed it. He guessed that his men were all dead. They had probably died in that first storm of gunfire.

These were the notorious Ballantyne Scouts, he was certain of that, but how they had gotten here eluded him. He knew only that Isabella had somehow managed to call them in. They were out there in the shadows, and they would strike the same way they had killed Adra, swiftly and with deadly accuracy, if he gave them the faintest chance.

The only advantage he had on his side now was time. He knew Raleigh Tabaka would have heard the gunfire and would be leading a relief column of his guerrillas down from the airfield. They would be here in minutes. He backed toward the nearest of the three parked jeeps in the motor pool.

Sean watched them over the sights of the AKM. He lay at the base of one of the palms, the outline of his head broken by a pile of dead fronds. At this range of forty yards the assault rifle with the rate-of-fire selector on single shot was accurate enough only to put a bullet into a two-inch circle. He had aimed for the bridge of Adra's nose and hit her in the left eye. The bullet had sheared off the side of her skull.

That kind of accuracy was not sufficient to risk a shot at Ramón Machado. The man was good. He was using his two hostages for maximum cover, ducking and weaving like a boxer so that Sean could never hold a steady bead on his head.

To Sean, his sister's naked body was disconcerting and shocking in the yellow firelight. Her breasts were very pale and tender-looking; the stark black triangle stood out clearly at the base of her belly. He knew his Scouts were watching her.

Even in the stress of battle, the way Ramón Machado held her against his own naked body infuriated Sean and threatened to impair his judgment. He was tempted to risk a shot. His finger on the trigger lacked only an ounce of pressure, but Ramón ducked his head behind Isabella's shoulder as they reached the jeep.

Ramón slid into the driver's seat and dragged Isabella and the child in with him. The engine started with a bellow, and sand spun from beneath the rear wheels as Ramón accelerated toward the gate.

Sean fired a low burst at the nearest back wheel and saw a bullet strike sparks from the spinning steel hub. Then the jeep crashed into the barrier gate and ripped out one of the poles.

The gate crumpled before its rush, and the vehicle bounced through the wreckage and roared down the track, dragging a tangle of wire and fence poles behind it like a sleigh.

Sean leaped to his feet and raced to the second jeep. Four of his Scouts were pelting for the same vehicle, and they piled into the back of it as Sean started the engine. He spun it in a wide circle and then gunned it through the ruined gate. They jolted over the mangled frame, then roared in pursuit of Ramón and his hostages.

If Isabella's sketch map was accurate, this track would take them down along the river toward the airstrip and Esau Gondele's roadblock.

Esau would hose down anything that came down the track, from either direction. An RPI-7 rocket would turn Isabella and her son to mincemeat.

Sean thrust the palm of his hand down on the horn ring and blew a long wailing blast. He hoped Esau Gondele might understand the warning and hold his fire, but he knew it was a forlorn hope. Smoked up with boom, the Scouts would be hot and quick on the trigger.

He had to overtake them. He shoved the pedal flat and roared into the wall of white dust left standing on the narrow track by the vehicle ahead of him. The track turned right abruptly, and for a second he lost it and slewed over the verge. The jeep canted over on its outside wheels and they crashed and tore through the light brush before he got her back onto the track.

The angle of the breeze altered as they turned, and the dust was blown aside. Only fifty yards ahead he saw the taillights of the escaping vehicle, and he hit it with the full beam of his headlights.

In the front seat Ramón Machado was driving with one hand. His other arm was locked around Isabella's shoulders, holding her in an awkward cramped position. Her head was twisted around on the long column of her neck. Her hair fluttered and rippled in the wind, and her eyes were dark and wide with terror in the pale oval of her face. She was shouting something at Sean, but the words were whipped away by the wind.

Nicholas was clutching the back of Isabella's seat. He was dressed in a white T-shirt and shorts. He was also looking back at the pursuing jeep, and even in these desperate moments Sean was struck by the resemblance of the child to the mother. His fury at the man who was threatening them smoked in his brain and armed him with reckless courage.

Then he realized that the other jeep was down on one side.

**433**

The burst of fire he had given it had ripped the near-side rear tire. Long tattered shreds of black rubber peeled from the spinning rim. The tangle of fencing wire and the crumpled pipe frame of the gate dragged behind the damaged vehicle like a drogue, tearing up a spray of sand and dust from the track and slowing it down.

He was gaining on them rapidly. The track had turned away from the beach and was running alongside the steep bank of the river. The mangrove trees loomed in the headlights of the two racing vehicles, and between their trunks the dark water glinted sullenly.

Ramón glanced back over his shoulder and realized the other jeep was only three feet from his tailgate. He ducked his head and released his grip on Isabella. He snatched the pistol from his lap and twisted around to aim at Sean's face. The range was under twelve feet, but both jeeps were pounding and swerving over the rough track. The bullet struck the side post of the windscreen and ricocheted away into the darkness.

One of the Scouts thrust his rifle forward to return fire, but Sean struck the barrel upward.

"Hold your fire!" he shouted, and he drove into the back of the other jeep with a ringing clash of metal.

The impact snapped their heads backward, and Nicholas was thrown over the seat with his legs kicking in the air as he struggled to regain his balance.

"Jump!" Sean howled at Isabella, but before she could react Ramón grabbed her again and pulled her close.

Once again Sean butted his jeep into the back of the other vehicle. It crushed in the tailgate and slewed it half off the track.

Ramón was struggling one-handedly to hold it on the road. The back end was swinging wildly. Dust boiled out from the rear wheels in a cloud, half blinding Sean. Isabella was screaming, and Nicholas scrambled up and crouched on the rear seat again. His face was white and terrified.

Another bend in the track flung the leading vehicle up onto the verge. While Ramón tried desperately to control it, Sean saw his chance and gunned his own jeep up alongside it. For a second they were racing side by side like a team in harness.

Ramón Machado and Sean Courtney looked into each other's eyes at a distance of six feet, and hatred flashed between them like a discharge of electricity. It was a primeval emotion, a deep atavistic understanding, as two dominant males met and recognized that one must kill the other.

Sean spun the wheel hard left and swerved into him, forcing his far wheels off the track. The bole of a palm tree wiped off the paintwork and smeared the metal down the length of the vehicle. Ramón swerved back and hit Sean as hard.

Then Ramón released his grip on Isabella. He snatched the pistol from his naked lap and thrust it into Sean's face, reaching out between the speeding jeeps. His face was a dark mask of fury and hatred.

Isabella threw herself sideways and grabbed the steering wheel. As Ramón fired she wrenched it over with all her strength. The bullet flew away into the night, and the jeep whipped into a murderous skid and plunged over the river-bank.

In the instant before it disappeared Sean saw both Isabella and Ramón hurled head first against the windscreen, and from the backseat Nicholas's small form was catapulted high into the darkness. Then Sean was past, braking hard, wrestling with the wheel as the jeep slewed into a broadside skid. The moment he had it under control, he snapped the gear lever into reverse and roared backward to the point where the other vehicle had disappeared.

Dust still hung in the air, and the earth at the crest of the bank had been torn by the spinning tires. Sean leaped from the driver's seat and ran to the top of the bank. The jeep was in the river below him. The headlights were still burning beneath the surface, like two drowned moons. It had capsized, and its rear wheels were spinning in a froth of white foam. Nicholas's small, crumpled body lay on the bank at the water's edge.

Sean launched himself down the bank. Sliding and slipping, he kept his footing like a cat and used his momentum to carry him out in a long clean racing dive. He hit the water flat like an Olympic racer.

He drove himself down deep. The headlights burned through the murk, and his underwater vision was blurred and distorted. He reached the carcass of the submerged jeep and pulled himself down under it. The air in the rear fuel tank was holding it just clear of the muddy bottom, and he wriggled into the opening.

Something pale loomed in front of him, and he reached out and touched a naked body. Quickly he ran his hands over it and touched large smooth breasts. He reached up, seized a handful of long floating hair and dragged Isabella out from under the wreck.

He surfaced with her in his arms and found with relief that

**435**

she was choking and gasping and struggling weakly. He dragged her to the bank. One of the Scouts had shown enough presence of mind to drive the jeep to the lip of the bank so that the beam of the headlights shone down and gave them light.

Isabella crawled naked and running with water to where Nicky lay and drew him into her lap. He began to struggle and kick.

"My father," he wailed. *"Mi padre!"*

Knee deep in mud, Sean peered down into the water. Water had flooded the engine of the jeep and stalled it, but the lights still burned in the depths.

Swiftly he weighed the need for haste against his desire to find Ramón Machado. He knew that reinforcements must even now be on the way from the guerrilla camp. They had only minutes in hand. He was about to turn away and go to help Isabella, to get her and the child up the bank, when he saw a flash of movement in the water. A shadow passed as though a shark had swum between him and the submerged headlights.

Bastard! he thought, and shouted to his men on the bank above him: "Bring me my rifle."

One of them came sliding down the bank. Before he could reach Sean and hand him the AKM, there was a swirl in the muddy water. It was far out in the river at the edge of the light. Ramón's head burst through.

"Get him!" roared Sean. "Nail the bastard!"

Ramón's hair was slicked down over his eyes, and water streamed down his face as he gasped wildly for air. One of the Scouts on the bank fired a short burst, and the bullets flickered a spray of water from the surface around Ramón's head. Ramón drew another breath and ducked under. For a moment his bare feet showed above the surface, kicking in the air, and then he was gone.

"Bastard! Bastard!" Sean swore, and he snatched his own AKM from the hands of his Scout as the man reached him. He fired a long, angry, frustrated burst into the river, and the bullets chopped up a patch of dancing froth on the spot where Ramón had disappeared.

Then he checked his fury and waited for Ramón's head to show again, but the tide was ripping downstream, carrying everything with it. Out there were dark and twisted mangroves behind which Ramón could shelter, and beyond the beams of the headlights the waters were dark and obscure.

After another minute he knew he had lost him. He had to let him go. He crushed down his frustration and his hatred and

**436**

turned back to Isabella. She was wet and smeared with mud. The edge of the windscreen had opened a cut in her hairline, and a trickle of blood diluted by river water was spreading down her face.

Sean shrugged out of his sodden jersey and helped her into it.

As she thrust her arms through the sleeves she gasped, "What happened to Ramón?"

"The bastard gapped it." Sean hauled her to her feet. "Time is wasting. We're out of here."

Nicholas broke from his mother's grip and darted to the edge of the water.

"My father—I will not leave my father."

Sean grabbed him by one arm. "Come on, Nicky." Nicholas whirled and sank his small white teeth into Sean's wrist.

"You little swine." Sean clouted him open-handed across the side of his head, almost knocking him off his feet. "No more of your little dago tricks, matey."

He picked him up, kicking and fighting, and slung him over his shoulder.

"I will not go. I want to stay with *mi padre*."

Sean grabbed Isabella's hand and, carrying Nicholas easily, he pulled her up the bank. There were other figures around the jeep, and for a moment Sean did not recognize them. He dropped Isabella's hand and lifted the AKM by the pistol grip.

"Hold it, Sean," Esau Gondele cautioned him as he ran forward.

"Where did you spring from?"

"You almost ran into our ambush," Esau told him. "You were just one second away from getting an RPG rocket up your backside. We are back there." He pointed up the tracks.

"Where are your boats?"

"Two hundred yards upriver."

"Pull your men out—we'll hitch a ride back with you." He broke off and cocked his head.

"Douse those lights," Esau Gondele snapped at one of his men, who leaned into the parked jeep and hit the switch. The headlights faded.

They stood listening in the darkness.

"Trucks coming fast from the direction of the airstrip." They all heard them clearly in the stillness.

"More gooks," Esau agreed.

"Take us to the boats," Sean ordered. "*Tout de suite*—and the tooter the sweeter."

437

They ran in a group, keeping to the track. A hundred yards along, Esau Gondele whistled, the sharp double flute of a night-flying dikkop, one of the Scouts' recognition signals. The whistle was repeated from the darkness just ahead, and Sean stumbled over the dead palm trunks that they had dragged across the track as a roadblock.

"Come on," Esau Gondele called them off the track. "The boats are this way."

As he spoke they saw headlights moving through the trees ahead. A convoy of vehicles was speeding down the track toward them from the direction of the airstrip.

Nicholas was still kicking and struggling in Sean's grip, and Isabella was trying desperately to reassure him.

"It will be all right, Nicky darling. These people are our friends. They are taking us home to a safe place."

"This is my home—I want my father. They killed Adra. I hate them! I hate you! I hate them!" he screamed in Spanish.

Sean shook him violently. "One more peep out of you, my old China, and I'll knock your cocky little head right off your shoulders."

"This way." Esau Gondele led them at a run away from the roadblock. Within fifty yards they reached the riverbank where the boats were moored.

Sean glanced back and saw the convoy of trucks come rumbling around a bend in the road. The beams of their headlights swept overhead, but they were hidden from them by the angle of the riverbank. In the lights Sean saw that the back of each truck was crowded with armed men.

Sean lifted Isabella into the nearest inflatable boat. She tripped on the wet folds of the jersey that hung around her legs and sprawled in the bilges.

"Clumsy bint," he grunted, and threw Nicholas into the boat after her. It was a mistake.

Nicholas rebounded like a rubber ball, and as Sean tried to grab him he ducked under his arm and shot up the bank.

"You little devil!" Sean whirled and went after him.

"My baby!" Isabella cried, and she jumped out of the boat. She sloshed through the mud and raced up the bank in pursuit of the two of them.

"Come back, Nicky—oh, please, come back."

Nicholas was running toward the approaching convoy. Like a hare he ducked and dodged through the brush ahead of Sean. He was twenty feet short of the track when Sean dived and caught him by the ankle. Seconds later Isabella tripped over them and sprawled full-length on the soft sandy earth.

The headlights of the convoy swept over them, but the three of them were lying behind a clump of low bush, concealed from the men in the cab of the leading truck. Nicholas screamed again and tried to crawl away, but Sean pinned him down and covered his mouth with the palm of one hand.

The trucks bore down upon them, then braked as they saw the palm trunks that blocked the road. The leading truck in the convoy drew up only twenty feet from where they lay in darkness.

Still smothering Nicholas under him, Sean reached out and pushed Isabella's face down to the earth. A white face shines like a mirror.

From the cab of the truck a man jumped down and ran forward to inspect the roadblock. Then he turned and shouted an order. A dozen guerrillas in combat camouflage swarmed from the back of the truck and seized the tree trunks.

As they lifted and dragged them clear, the headlights lit the face of the officer who commanded them. Isabella lifted her head and saw his features clearly. She recognized him immediately. It was not a face ever to forget. The last time she had seen this man he had been a passenger in the van driven by her half brother, Ben Afrika. The two of them had been on their way to a rendezvous with Michael Courtney. He was probably the finest-looking black man she had ever seen, tall, regal and fierce as a hawk.

He turned his head and for a moment seemed to stare directly at her. Then he turned again to watch his men roll the logs aside. The moment the road was clear he strode to the cab of the truck and vaulted into it. He slammed the door, and the truck roared forward.

The troop convoy followed it. As the last pair of headlights swept past them, Sean tucked Nicholas under his arm, pulled Isabella to her feet and hurried her back toward the riverbank.

Sean kept a firm grip on the scruff of Nicholas's neck in the leading boat as the flotilla ran back downriver. The glow from the burning huts lit the underbelly of the clouds, and even above the sound of the outboard motors they could hear shouts and the sound of automatic gunfire.

"What are they shooting at?" Isabella asked as she huddled against Sean for warmth.

"Probably at shadows—or at each other." He chuckled softly.

"Nothing quite like a nervous gook with a rifle in his hand for burning up ammo."

The outgoing tide sped them through the mouth into the lagoon. Through his nightscope Esau Gondele picked up the wake of the other flotilla of inflatables heading back from the beach. They came together as they reached the pass in the reef and lined up to head out into the open sea.

*Lancer* in her bright yellow paint showed up through the lens of the nightscope at half a mile distance.

As soon as they had recovered the last inflatable through the stern chute of the trawler, she opened up her engines and ran for the open Atlantic.

Sean turned to Esau Gondele. "What was the butcher bill, Sergeant Major Gondele?"

"We lost one man, Major Courtney," he replied as formally. "Jeremiah Masoga. We brought him back with us." The Scouts always retrieved their dead.

Sean felt that familiar sickening pang; another good man gone. Jeremiah was only nineteen years old. Sean had already decided to give him his second stripe. He wished now that he had done it before this. You can never make amends to the dead.

"Three wounded; nothing bad enough to make them miss the party tonight."

"Put Jeremiah in the refrigerated hold," Sean ordered. "We'll ship him home as soon as we reach Cape Town. He'll get a regimental burial with full honors."

When they were still two hundred nautical miles from Table Bay, Centaine Courtney sent out a Courtney helicopter to pick up Sean, and Isabella and Nicholas. The old lady could not wait any longer to meet her great-grandson.

# 34

Ramón clung to the roots of one of the mangrove trees to steady himself against the drag of the outgoing tide as it funneled through the river mouth. The razor-edged shells of the fresh-water mussels that covered the stem cut into his hand, but he hardly felt the pain. He was staring out across the river.

The reflection from the flames of the burning compound flecked the surface of the water with sovereigns of gold.

The boats passed within fifty feet of where he crouched chin deep in the mud and slime of the mangroves. Their motors buzzed softly in the stillness of the night. Their outlines were indistinct, three dark hippo shapes that passed swiftly on the tide heading for the mouth and the open sea—but he imagined that one of the figures in the leading boat was smaller than the others and wore a pale T-shirt.

It was only then, in the moment of losing Nicholas, that he realized that he was, after all, just another father. For the first time in his life he acknowledged his love and his dependence on that love. He loved his son, and he was losing him. He groaned in anguish.

Then rage boiled up in him and burned away all other feel-ing. It was a consuming anger against all those who had inflicted this loss upon him. He stared into the empty darkness that had swallowed his son, and a fire of vengeance burned through every fiber of his being. He wanted to shout this fury after them. He wanted to rail against the woman, he wanted to curse and scream out his frustration, but he caught himself. That was not his way. He must be cold and sharp as steel now. He must think clearly and with icy purpose.

The first thought that came into his mind was that he had lost his hold on Red Rose. She was no longer of any value to him or the cause. Now she was the sacrifice. He knew how to destroy her and all those around her. The hilt of the weapon was in his head; it only remained to unsheathe it.

He pushed off from the mangrove and let the tide sweep him into the curve of the river, swimming across it with an easy breaststroke. The bottom shelved gently under him, and he touched sand and waded ashore.

Raleigh Tabaka was waiting for him beside the burnt-out ruins of the communications center. Ramón dressed hastily in borrowed trousers and jacket; his hair was still damp and matted with river mud.

Smoke from the smoldering buildings hazed the first grey light of dawn. Raleigh Tabaka's men were recovering the corpses and laying them out in a long row under the palms. In rigor mortis they were locked into the attitudes in which they had met their deaths. It was a grotesque charade.

José, the paratrooper, had one arm thrown over his face as though protecting his eyes. His chest was mangled by grenade shrapnel. Adra's arms were extended as though she were hanging on a crucifix, and half her head was missing. Ramón glanced at her without particular interest, as he might at a worn-out article of clothing that no longer had any utility for him.

"How many?" he asked Raleigh Tabaka.

"Twenty-six," Tabaka replied. "All of them. There were no survivors. Whoever it was, they did a thorough job. Who were they? Do you have any idea?"

"Yes." Ramón nodded. "I have a very good idea." And before Raleigh could speak again Ramón told him, "I am taking over the Cyndex project—personally."

"Comrade General"—Raleigh frowned with affront—"that has been my operation from the very beginning. I have controlled the two brothers."

"Yes," Ramón agreed implacably. "You have done very well. You will receive all the recognition you deserve. But I am taking over the direction of the project. I will leave for the south as soon as an aircraft is available. You will accompany me."

"It doesn't end here, Bella," Shasa said gravely. "We cannot just pretend that nothing else happened. I did not want to complicate the rescue attempt by considering the full murky depths of this whole dreadful business. However, now Nicholas is safe here at Weltevreden we are forced to do so. Many people, including the members of your family, risked their lives for you and Nicholas. One gallant young man, a stranger,

442

a trooper of Sean's regiment, died to save you. Now you owe us the truth.''

They were assembled in the gun room once again, and Isabella was on trial before the family.

Her grandmother sat in the chair to one side of the fireplace. She sat very straight. Her hand on the ivory head of her cane was blue-veined beneath the thin parchment of skin. Her hair, once a thick, unmanageable bush, was now the purest silver cap washed with a hint of blue. Her expression was severe.

''We want to hear it all, Isabella. You will not leave this room until you have told every detail.''

''Nana, I am so ashamed. I had no choice.''

''I did not ask for excuses and self-abasement missy. I want the truth.''

''You must understand, Bella. We know that you have done terrible damage to the national interest, to the family, to yourself. Now it is our duty to contain and control that damage.'' Shasa stood in front of the fireplace with his hands clasped under the tails of his blazer. His tone had moderated. ''We want to help you, but we must know the truth before we can do so.''

Isabella looked up at him with a hunted expression. ''Can I talk to you and Nana alone?'' She glanced at her brothers. Garry lolled in the armchair under the window with thumbs hooked in his gaudy braces. He rolled an unlit cigar from one side of his mouth to the other. Sean sat on the windowsill, his legs thrust straight out in front of him. His bare arms, tanned and sleek with muscle, were crossed over his chest.

''No,'' said Centaine firmly. ''The boys have risked their lives for you and Nicky. If you have stored up more trouble for yourself and the family, they are the ones who will be called upon to bail you out. No, you don't get out of it that easily. They deserve to hear everything you have to tell us. Don't leave anything out. Do you hear me?''

Slowly Isabella lowered her face into her hands. ''They gave me the code name Red Rose.''

''Speak up, girl. Don't mumble.'' Centaine banged her cane on the floor between her feet, and Isabella started and looked up.

''I did everything they told me to,'' she said, looking the old lady in the face. ''When Nicky was still an infant, just over a month old, they made a film and showed it to me. They almost drowned my baby. They held him by the feet and ducked him—'' She broke off, then drew a deep breath to steady herself. ''They warned me that in the next film they would cut off parts of his body and then send them to me—his fingers, his toes, his arms and legs and then"—she choked on the word—"and then his head."

They were all silent and appalled until Centaine spoke.

"Go on."

"They told me I must work for Daddy, I must inveigle myself into his Armscor work." Shasa winced, and Isabella twisted her fingers together. "I'm sorry, Daddy. They told me that I must enter politics, stand for Parliament, use the family connection."

"I should have suspected your sudden political aspirations," Centaine said bitterly.

"I'm sorry, Nana."

"Don't keep saying you're sorry!" Centaine snapped. "It does not contribute anything worthwhile and it is damnably irritating. Just get on with it, child."

"For a while they asked nothing of me—for almost two years. Then the orders started to come. The first was the Siemens radar chain."

Shasa grunted and was about to speak. Then he checked himself and reached for the handkerchief in the breast pocket of his blazer.

"Then they wanted more and more."

"The Skylight project?" Shasa asked. When she nodded he glanced at Centaine.

"You were right, Mater." He looked back at his daughter. "You will have to write it all down. Everything you ever gave them. I want a list—dates, documents, meetings, everything. We must know everything that is compromised."

"Daddy—" Isabella began. For a moment she could not go on.

"Spit it out, missy," Centaine ordered.

"Cyndex 25," Isabella said.

"Oh God—no!" Shasa breathed.

"That was why they gave me access to Nicky this last time—the Cyndex specifications and Ben."

"Ben?" Garry straightened up in his chair. "Who is Ben?"

"Ben Gama," Centaine said harshly. "Tara's little black bastard, the son of Moses Gama. The man that killed my Blaine, the man that disgraced this family." She looked at Isabella for confirmation.

"Yes, Nana. My half brother, Ben." She looked at her brothers. "Your half brother, too, only he doesn't call himself Ben Gama now, he calls himself Benjamin Afrika."

"Why do I know that name?" Garry asked.

"Because he works for you," Isabella said. "They made me arrange a job for him. I recruited him for Capricorn when I was in London. He works for Capricorn Chemicals as a laboratory technician, in the poisons division."

"In the Cyndex plant?" Shasa asked with disbelief. "You didn't get him in there?"

"Yes, Pater, I did." She was about to apologize again but then looked at her grandmother's face.

Garry leaped out of his chair and strode to the desk. He seized the telephone and spoke to the operator on the Weltevreden exchange.

"Get me a call to Capricorn Chemicals—you've got the number, haven't you? I want to speak to the managing director immediately. It's urgent, very urgent. Call me back here the moment you have him on the line."

He replaced the telephone. "We'll have to have him, Ben, we'll have to have him taken in for questioning right away. If they placed him in the plant, it was for some good or, rather, for some nefarious reason."

"He is one of them," Centaine burst out. None of them had ever heard such bitterness in her tone or seen such hatred on her face. They all stared at her in horror. "He is one of the revolutionaries, the destroyers. With that black Satan as his father and Tara to poison his mind over all the years, he must be one of them. God grant that we can prevent whatever terrible thing they are planning."

They were all of them subdued by the horror of their imaginings.

The telephone split the silence, and Garry snatched up the receiver. "I have the managing director of Capricorn on the line."

"Good. Put him on. Hello, Paul. Thank God I got you. Hold on one second." He pressed the "conference" key on the telephone so that they could all hear the conversation.

"Listen, Paul. You have an employee in the poisons division. In the new pesticide plant. Benjamin Afrika."

"Yes, Mr. Courtney. I don't know him personally, but the name is vaguely familiar. Hold on, let me get the computer printout on him. Yes, here we go. Benjamin Afrika. He joined us in April."

"Okay, Paul. I want him arrested and held by the company security guards. He is to be held completely incommunicado,

445

do you understand that? No phone calls. No lawyers. No press. Nothing.''

"Can we do that, Mr. Courtney?''

"I can do anything I want to, Paul. Bear that in mind. Give the order for his arrest now. I'll hold on while you do it.''

"It will take two seconds," the managing director agreed. They heard his voice in the background as he spoke to security over the internal circuit.

"All right, Mr. Courtney. They are on their way to get Afrika.''

"Now, listen, Paul. What is the position with the Cyndex manufacturing program? Have you started to ship to the army yet?''

"Not yet, Mr. Courtney. The first shipment is due to go out next Tuesday. The ordnance are sending their own trucks.''

"Okay, Paul. What stocks are you holding at the moment?''

"Let me check the computer." Paul's voice was starting to betray his agitation. "At the moment in the five-kilo artillery canisters we have six hundred and thirty-five each of Formula A and B, in the fifty-kilo aerial cylinders we have twenty-six of each of both formulas. They will go to the air force at the end of next week—''

Garry cut him off. "Paul, I want a physical count of every canister and cylinder. I want some of your senior men in the storage area right away to check the serial numbers of each piece against the plant manifest—and I want it done within the next hour.''

"Is something wrong, Mr. Courtney?''

"I'll tell you that when you have the results of your stocktake for me. I'll be waiting at this number. Come back to me as soon as you can—or come back a damned sight sooner than that.''

As he hung up Sean demanded, "How soon can you get us to Capricorn?''

"The Lear is out of action. DCA want a full overhaul of the airframe and a new airworthiness certificate after that missile strike.''

"How soon, Garry?" Sean insisted.

Garry thought for a second. "The Queen Air is so slow, but it will be quicker than waiting for the scheduled flight to Johannesburg. At least we will be able to fly directly to the airstep at the Capricorn plant. If we leave in the next hour, we could be there early this afternoon.''

"Shouldn't we notify the police?" Shasa asked.

Centaine banged her stick imperiously. "No police. Not yet—not ever, if we can help it. Grab Tara's black bastard and beat the truth out of him if we have to, but we must try to keep this in the family." She broke off as the telephone rang.

Garry picked it up and listened for a few seconds. Then he said, "I see. Thank you, Paul. I'm flying up right away. I should be at the Capricorn strip by one this afternoon." He hung up and looked around their anxious faces. "The little brown bird has flown. Benjamin Afrika hasn't showed up at the plant for the last four days. Nobody has heard from him. Nobody knows where he is."

"What about the stocks of Cyndex?" Shasa demanded.

"They are checking them. They'll have the results when we land at Capricorn." Garry told him. "Pater and Nana must stay here at Weltevreden to liaise at this end. If you need to get a message to us while we are in the air, you can telephone Information at Jan Smuts Airport control and get them to relay." He looked across at his brother.

"Sean will come with me. I might need some muscle."

Sean sauntered across to his father and held out his hand. "Keys of the gun safe, please, Pater."

Shasa handed them over, and Sean turned the lock on the heavy steel door and swung it open. He stepped into the safe and studied the rack of revolvers and pistols for a moment before he selected a .357-magnum Smith & Wesson revolver. He took down a packet of ammunition from the shelf above it and thrust the revolver into the belt of his jeans.

"I'd better take one as well." Garry went to the safe.

"Garry," Isabella called after him, "I'm coming with you and Sean."

"Forget it, Mavourneen." Garry didn't even look at her as he selected a Heckler & Koch 9-millimeter parabellum from the rack. "There is nothing further that you can contribute."

"Yes, there is. You don't know what Ben looks like. I can recognize him—and there is something else I haven't told you yet."

"What is it?"

"I'll tell you when we are in the air."

Garry levelled the twin-engine Beechcraft Queen Air onto a northerly heading and turned in his seat to beckon to Isabella where she sat in the main passenger cabin.

She unfastened her seat belt, went up to the cockpit, and leaned over the back of Garry's seat.

447

"Okay, Bella. Let's hear it. What else can you tell us?"

She looked across at Sean in the copilot's seat.

"Do you remember the night at the Chicamba River when Nicky tried to escape and you and I ran back to catch him?"

Sean nodded and she went on, "You remember the guerrilla officer in the first truck, the one who supervised the clearing of the roadblock? Well, I got a really good look at him and I knew I had seen him before. I was absolutely certain of it, but it didn't make any sense, not until now."

"When and were had you seen him?"

"He was with Ben—and they were going into Michael's farm at Firgrove."

"Michael?" Garry cut in. "Our Michael?"

"Yes," she confirmed. "Michael Courtney."

"You think Michael is mixed up in this?"

"Well, don't you think so? Otherwise what would he be doing with that ANC terrorist commander—and Ben?"

They were all silent thinking about it for a while. Then Isabella went on, "Garry, you obviously suspect that Ben has stolen a cylinder or two of Cyndex. If he's mixed up with terrorists, how do you think they would use it? Spray it from an aircraft, perhaps?"

"Yes, that it is the most likely way."

"Michael has a plane at Firgrove."

"Oh, shit," Garry whispered. "Please don't let it be true. Not Mickey—please, not Mickey."

"Michael has been publishing that commie rag of his for years," Sean pointed out grimly. "And he's got very chummy with a lot of the uglies in the process."

Nobody answered him. Garry said, "Bella, get us each a Coke, please."

She went back to the refrigerator in the bar and brought two cans. They drank, and Sean lowered the can and belched softly. "The Rand Easter Show opened this morning," he said.

Garry looked at him. "What the hell has that got to do with it?"

"Nothing." Sean grinned at him wickedly. "The Rand Easter Show—the biggest, glitziest show in the country. Half a million people all in one place. All of industry showing its products—the farmers, the businessmen, every goddam tinker, tailor and Indian chief will be there. The grand opening this evening at eight o'clock, the fireworks display, and the military tattoo and the stock car racing and the show jumping. The prime minister making a speech, and all the big shots in their dark suits and carnation buttonholes. Hell, of course, it means nothing.''

"Don't fool around, Sean," Garry grated at him.

"You're absolutely right, Garry." Sean kept on grinning. "I mean, at heart the ANC are really decent, civilized fellows. Just because they left off a few car bombs and put burning motorcar tires around people's necks doesn't mean they don't have beautiful souls. Hell, don't let's judge them too harshly. A Russian limpet mine in a crowded supermarket is one thing, but they'd never dream of spraying the Rand Easter Show with Cyndex 25. Would they?''

"No." Garry shook his head. "I mean, Ben and Mickey are our own brothers. They wouldn't—no . . ." His voice trailed off. Then he said angrily, "Damn it, if only we had the Lear, we'd be there by now."

The radio squawked, and Garry adjusted his headphones.

"Charlie Sierra X ray, this is Jan Smuts Information. I have a relay for you from Capricorn. Are you ready to copy?''

"Go head, Information.''

"Message reads: 'All stocks and serial numbers tally.' Message ends.''

"Thank God," Garry breathed.

"Tell them to check what's inside the cylinders," Sean suggested mildly.

Garry's expression altered. "Information, please relay to Capricorn. Message reads: 'Take samples from all containers.' Message ends.''

Garry removed his headphones. "I want so badly for it not to be true," he said. "But you're right, Sean. They aren't idiots. It would be simple enough to stamp a couple of empty cylinders with false numbers and substitute them in the stockroom.''

"How much longer?''

Garry checked his navigation. "Another hour. Thank the Lord for this tailwind.''

Sean looked around at his sister. "Do me a big favor, sweetheart. Next time you fancy a little bit of nooky, pick somebody a mite tamer—like Jack the Ripper.''

The Capricorn airstrip was marked by the gigantic figure of a goat laid out artistically in white quartz. It stood out clearly on the brown veld from a distance of five miles. Garry touched down smoothly and taxied to the hangar building, where four vehicles and a group of Capricorn employees headed by Paul, the managing director, were waiting to receive them.

As Garry and Sean jumped down from the Queen Air and turned to give Isabella a hand, Paul rushed forward.

"Mr. Courtney, you were right. Two of the small canisters contain only carbon dioxide gas. Somebody has switched them. There are ten kilos of Cyndex 25 out there somewhere!"

They stared at him in total horror. Ten kilos could wipe out an army.

"It's time to call in the police. They've got to pick up Ben Afrika. Do we have his address?" Sean asked.

"I have already sent somebody to his home," Paul cut in. "He isn't there. His landlady says she hasn't seen him for the last few days. He hasn't eaten or slept there."

"Firgrove," Isabella said softly.

"Right," Garry snapped. "Sean you'd better get out there right away. Take Bella with you to show you the way and to identify Ben if you run into him. I'll run things from this end. I'll be in the boardroom. Call me as soon as you get to Firgrove. I'll get police backup for you and raise hell all around. We've got to get hold of those missing canisters."

Sean turned to Paul. "I need a car—a fast one."

"Take mine." He pointed to a new BMW parked next to the hangar. "The tank is full. Here are the keys."

"Come on, Bella. Let's go." They ran to the BMW.

"Don't get stopped by the traffic cops, Fangio," Isabella warned him as he pushed the BMW hard along the highway. "We should have sent the cops out to Firgrove before we left Cape Town. God, it's three o'clock already."

"We couldn't do anything until we were sure that someone had ripped off a couple of Cyndex tanks," Sean pointed out.

He leaned across and switched the car radio on. Isabella glanced at him inquiringly.

"Three o'clock news," he explained and turned to Radio Highveld. It was the third item on the newscast.

"Since this morning record crowds have been passing through the gates of the Rand Easter Show. Today is the opening day. A spokesman for the show committee stated that by noon today more than two hundred thousand visitors had already entered the grounds."

Sean switched off the set and slammed his clenched fist against the dashboard of the BMW.

"Michael!" he shouted. "It's always the bleeding hearts that are capable of the wildest excesses. How many innocents have been tortured and murdered in the name of God, peace and the

450

fellowship of men?'' He hit the dashboard again, and Bella reached across to touch his arm.

"Slow down, Sean. You take the next exit right." Bella hung on to the door handle as he swung the BMW into the bend.

"How much farther?"

"Only a couple of miles."

Sean pulled back the tail of his coat and drew the Smith & Wesson from his belt. With his thumb he spun the chambers.

"What are you going to do with that?'' Isabella asked nervously. "Ben and Mickey—"

"Ben and Mickey have got nice friends," he said, slipping the revolver into his belt.

"There it is." Isabella leaned forward in the seat and pointed ahead. "That's the gate in Mickey's place."

Sean slowed the BMW and turned off onto the dirt track. He drove sedately through the blue gum plantation until they glimpsed the buildings ahead. Then he stopped and reversed the BMW across the track.

"Why are you doing that?'' Isabella asked.

"I'm going in on foot," Sean told her. "No point in announcing my arrival."

"But why are you parking across the road?"

"To stop anybody trying to leave in a hurry." He pulled the keys from the ignition and jumped out. "You wait here. No, not in the car. Hide in the trees over there, and don't even stick your head up until I call you out, do you hear?"

"Yes, Sean."

"And don't slam the door," he told her as she slipped out of the passenger seat. "Now, give it to me. Where does Mickey keep his plane?"

"Behind the house at the end of the orchard." She pointed. "You can't see it from here, but you won't miss it. It's a big corrugated tin shed, all rusty and ramshackle."

"Sounds like our Mickey," Sean muttered. "Now, remember what I told you. Stay out of the way." He began to run.

He stayed off the track and kept the trees of the orchard and the chicken shed between him and the buildings. It was only a few hundred yards to the veranda of the main house. There were chickens clucking and scratching around his feet as he crouched behind the wall and quickly surveyed the building. The front door and all the windows were wide open, but there was no sign of the occupants.

Sean vaulted easily over the wall and slipped through the front door. The sitting room and kitchen were empty, al-

451

though dirty dishes and glasses were piled in the sink. There were three bedrooms, and all of them had been recently occupied. The beds were unmade, and there was discarded clothing on the floor and men's toilet items in the bathrooms and on the dressing tables.

Sean picked up a shirt and turned the collar. A name tag embroidered in red thread was stitched into the inside of it: B. AFRIKA.

He dropped the shirt and ran back silently to the kitchen door. It stood open to the orchard of scraggly insect-ravaged fruit trees. Beyond them rose the corrugated iron roof of a large shed, and from a stubby roof mast a sad-looking wind sock drooped like a used condom.

Sean darted into the orchard and dodged between the fruit trees until he reached the wall of the shed. He flattened himself against it and laid his ear to the thin corrugated galvanized sheet. Through it he heard the murmur of men's voices, too indistinct to understand the words. He checked the revolver in his belt, making certain the butt was at hand for a quick draw, and eased himself along the back wall of the shed toward the small green wooden door.

Before he reached it, the door swung open and two men stepped out into the sunlight.

Ben Afrika was good with his hands and prided himself on the quality of his workmanship. He knelt on the pilot's seat of the Cessna Centurion aircraft and tightened the final bolts that held the twin cylinders to the deck in front of the right-hand passenger seat.

He had drilled the bolt holes with care so as not to damage any of the control cables that ran under the floorboards. Of course, he could have let the cylinders lie loose on the cabin floor, but that would have offended his engineering sense. There was always a danger of air turbulence in flight that might damage the valve or the tubing. He had positioned the steel bottles so that, while in flight, either the pilot or his passenger could reach the valve handle readily.

The bottle that contained element A was painted in a black and white checkered pattern with three red rings around the middle. Element B was in a crimson bottle with a single black ring. Each bottle was stamped with a unique serial number.

It had taken all Ben's skill to forge two ordinary medical oxygen bottles to exactly the same exterior appearance. He had engraved the serial numbers by hand. The bottles were small enough to be smuggled in and out of the Capricorn plant in pockets specially sewn into his overcoat. It had called for ingenuity and immaculate timing to get them through the security check at the main gate of the plant.

The bottles were joined by a stainless-steel T-piece that screwed into the special left-hand thread in the necks. Ben had turned the fittings on the small secondhand lathe in the rear of the hangar. To operate them, the taps on each bottle were screwed open, and after that a half turn on the swinging valve handle of the T-piece allowed the twin elements to mingle and become active. From there the nerve gas flowed under pressure into the flexible armored hose. The hose led back between the front seats into the rear luggage compartment.

Ben had drilled a three-centimeter hole clean through both the floorboards of the compartment and the outer metal skin of the Centurion. The end of the gas hose passed out of this hole and protruded ten centimeters below the fuselage. He had fixed the hose in place and sealed the narrow gap where it passed through the fuselage with Pratleys putty, which dried as hard as iron.

The gas would spray from below the aircraft well behind the line of the front seats, and would be carried back in the slipstream without any danger of reaching the occupants of the Centurion. However, as an added protection they would wear safety suits and breathe bottled oxygen during the release of the gas.

The suits hung on the hangar wall, ready to be donned in minutes. They were commercially marketed full-length protection suits approved by the fire department for use by proto rescue teams in the gold mines.

For a second time Ben put a spanner on each of the hose connections and the joints of the T-piece to satisfy himself that there were no leaks. At last he grunted with satisfaction and backed out of the open cabin door. He wiped his hands on a piece of cotton waste and went across to the workbench against the nearest wall.

The other two men were leaning over the bench studying the map. Ben came up behind Michael Courtney and draped his arm affectionately over his brother's shoulders.

"All set, Mickey," he said in his incongruous south London accent.

He then gave his full attention to Ramón Machado. Ben hero-worshiped this man. When he was alone with Michael he often discussed him with the awe of an acolyte discussing the omnipotence of the Pope. Michael, on the other hand, realized the hideous nature of their mission, and it had taken many months of soul-searching for him to convince himself that this was something that had to be done if the struggle was to succeed.

Ramón seemed to sense his lingering reluctance and turned to him now. "Michael, I want you to ring Met and get a final weather forecast for this evening."

Michael picked up the telephone from the bench in front of him. He dialed the number of the weather information services at Jan Smuts Airport and listened to the prerecorded announcement.

"Wind is still two nine zero degrees at five knots," he repeated. "No change since this morning. Weather is settled. Barometric pressure steady."

"Very well." Ramón picked up his red marker pencil and circled the position of the showgrounds on the large-scale aeronautical map. Then he marked in the wind direction.

"Okay. This will be your line of approach, about a mile upwind of the target. Try to maintain a thousand feet above ground level. Open the gas valve as you pass the water towers. They are very prominently lit with navigational warning lights."

"Yes," Michael said. "I flew over the area yesterday. The stadium will be floodlit, and there will be a laser show—I can't possibly miss it."

"Well done, comrade." Ramón gave him one of his rare, irresistible smiles. "Your preparations have been excellent."

Michael looked down, and Ben interjected, "I heard on the one o'clock news that by noon more than two hundred thousand visitors had already passed through the showground turnstiles. It will be more like half a million by the time Vorster starts his official opening speech. What a blow we'll strike for freedom today."

"Vorster's speech is scheduled to start at seven P.M." Ramón picked up one of the advertising brochures issued by the show committee. He studied the opening program. "But it might be a few minutes late. We must allow for that. He will probably talk for between forty minutes and an hour. The military tattoo begins at eight P.M. When will you take off?"

"If we take off from here at 1845 hours,"—Michael worked it out—"it's about forty-eight minutes' flying. I timed it yesterday. That will get me over the target at thirty-three minutes past seven."

"That would be about right," Ramón agreed. "Vorster should

454

still be speaking. You will make two passes across the range. A thousand feet above ground level, one mile upwind. After the second pass you turn west and head directly for the Botswana border. What is your estimated flying time to the rendezvous with Raleigh Tabaka?''

"Three hours fifteen minutes," Michael replied. "That gets me there approximately eleven o'clock tonight. By that time any residual gas will have degraded."

"Raleigh Tabaka will light the airstrip with flares. As soon as you land, remove all the gas equipment and set fire to the plane. From there it's up to Raleigh to get you out to Zambia and Tercio base."

Ramón studied their faces. "That's it, then. I know that we've gone over it a dozen times, but are there any questions?''

The brothers shook their heads, and Ramón smiled wryly. Despite the difference in the color of their skins and the texture of their hair, there was a strong resemblance.

The revolution could never go forward without this kind of obedience and unquestioning faith, Ramón thought, and he felt an unaccustomed envy of such uncomplicated trust. Let them believe that this single act would change the world and herald the perfect dawn of universal socialism and brotherly love. Ramón knew that nothing was so simple.

He envied them their faith, but he wondered if they truly had the stomach to live through the stark reality of the slaughter of half a million lambs and the Red Terror that must follow the successful onslaught of the revolution. Sublime belief in the ultimate rightness of their action might permit them to turn the valve on a pair of innocent-looking steel bottles, but could they endure the reality of half a million corpses twisted and contorted in piles of hideous death? He wondered.

Only the steel men survived. These two were not of that temper. The Red Terror would claim them as it did all weaklings. After tonight their usefulness would be reduced. They would be expendable.

He touched Michael's shoulder gently. He knew Michael liked to be touched by another man. He let the touch become a caress.

"You have done wonderfully well. Now you must eat and rest. I will leave you before you take off this evening. I salute you both."

They walked in a group to the door in the rear of the shed, but before they reached it Michael stopped.

"I want to look at Ben's installation of the bottles and go over my own checks," he said diffidently. "I want to be absolutely certain."

"You are right to want everything perfect, comrade," Ramón agreed. "We'll have something for you to eat when you come up to the house."

They watched him climb into the cockpit of the Centurion and begin checking the instruments before they walked together to the door.

Ramón threw open the small back door in the rear wall of the hangar. As he and Ben stepped through into the sunlight together Sean Courtney was crouched against the side wall on their left-hand side, staring at them.

Only six feet separated Ramón and Sean, and their mutual recognition was instantaneous. Sean reached under his coat and plucked out the big magnum revolver. The double-action pull on the trigger delayed the shot a fleeting part of a second, and Ramón seized Ben Afrika's arm and pulled him forward between them. With a muzzle-flash that was bright even in the sunlight, Sean's shot crashed into Ben's body.

The hollow-point bullet struck him on the tip of the left elbow and mushroomed instantly. It plowed through his arm and into his flank. The entry wound into his body was the size of an egg cup. The bullet struck his last rib and began to break up. Some fragments were deflected into his lung; others tore through his entrails. A splinter of the copper jacket cut between the vertebrae of the spine and half severed his spinal cord.

Ben was flung sideways by the impact and he slid down the wall, leaving a bright smear of his blood across the rusty corrugated iron. Ramón Machado ducked back into the hangar before Sean could bring the revolver down from the head-high recoil. He kicked the door closed behind him and snatched the Tokarev automatic from his shoulder holster.

He snapped two quick shots through the thin wall, aiming for where he judged Sean was standing. Sean had anticipated this, and had dropped flat and flipped over twice. He estimated Ramón's stance from the sound of the shots and the angle of the bullets cutting through the corrugated iron wall. He fired double-handed, and the heavy bullet punched a hole through the wall and missed Ramón's head by a foot.

Ramón ducked behind a drum of Avgas and shouted across the hangar at Michael as he sat at the controls of the aircraft.

"Start up!"

Michael had been frozen with shock in the pilot seat of the Centurion, but at Ramón's order he recovered and flipped on both master switches and both magnetos and turned the key. The Centurion's engine fired and caught. He pushed the throttle open, and she roared eagerly and strained against the wheel brakes.

"Get her rolling!" Ramón shouted, and fired two more shots through the wall at random.

The Centurion moved forward toward the open hangar door, gathering speed swiftly. Ramón raced after her, ducked under the wing and jerked open the passenger door.

"Where is Ben?" Michael shouted at him as he scrambled into the seat.

"Ben is finished," Ramón shouted back. "Keep going."

"What do you mean, *finished*?" Michael twisted in the seat and closed the throttle. "We can't leave him."

"Ben is dead, man." Ramón caught his hand on the throttle. "Ben has been shot. He's finished. We have to get out of here."

"Ben—"

"Keep her going."

Michael pushed the throttle open once again and swung the Centurion onto the runway. His face was twisted with grief.

"Ben," he whispered, and he let the speed build up until the Centurion was taxiing tail up along the strip. They reached the end, and he used brake and engine to swing her around, facing back down the runway into the wind.

"The engine is cold," he said. "She hasn't had a chance to warm up."

"We've got to chance it," Ramón told him. "The police are going to be swarming in. They're onto us; somehow they've tumbled to it."

"Ben?"

"Forget about Ben!" Ramón snapped. "Get us into the air."

"Where are we going—Botswana?" Michael still hesitated.

"Yes," Ramón told him. "But first we are going to finish this operation. Head for the showgrounds."

"But—but you say the police are onto us," Michael protested.

"How can they stop us now? It will take an hour to get an air force Impala into the air—go, man, go!"

Michael pushed the pitch fully fine and opened the throttle wide. The Centurion bounded down the strip.

As the speed built up they saw a figure run out from behind the hangar. Michael recognized his brother.

"Sean!" he exclaimed.

"Keep going," Ramón told him.

457

Sean dropped onto one knee at the verge of the runway, and as the Centurion raced toward him he thrust out both arms toward it in the classic double-handled grip and fired three deliberate shots. Each time the heavy recoil threw the muzzle of the revolver toward the sky.

The last shot struck the windscreen, and they both ducked instinctively. It left a silver cobweb in the Perspex pane, and then Michael rotated the Centurion's nose and they skimmed over the boundary fence and bore up into the clear blue highveld sky.

At two hundred feet the cold motor stuttered and coughed. Then it caught again and ran smoothly.

"Head for the showgrounds," Ramón repeated. "We won't get Vorster, but it's still a good target. There are two hundred thousand of them."

Michael leveled out at a thousand feet and turned onto his track.

As the Centurion soared overhead, Sean emptied the revolver, blazing up at its belly. He saw no sign of his bullets striking, and the landing wheels of the Centurion retracted as she rose unharmed into the sky.

Sean jumped to his feet and sprinted into the hangar. He saw the telephone on the workbench.

"Thank God!" He ran to the bench and snatched it up.

As he dialed the Capricorn number, he noticed the open map under his hands and the Rand Easter Show brochure. The red-marked notations on the map ringed the location of the showgrounds, and a broad arrow indicated the wind direction and speed.

The operator on the switchboard answered on the third ring. "Capricorn Chemical Industries, good day. How may I help you?"

"Get me Mr. Garry Courtney in the boardroom. I'm his brother. This is an emergency."

"He is expecting your call. You are going straight through."

As he waited Sean glanced quickly around the hangar. He saw the safety suits hanging on the wall beside the door.

"Is that you, Sean?" Garry's voice was strained.

"Yes, it's me. I'm at Firgrove. It's as bad as we feared. Michael and Ben and the Fox. The target is the showgrounds."

"Did you stop them, Sean?"

"No. Michael and the Fox are airborne. They took off two

minutes ago. They are almost certainly heading for the showgrounds."

"Are you sure, Sean?"

"Of course I'm bloody sure. I'm in Mickey's hangar and I'm looking at a map right now. The showgrounds are marked and the wind speed and direction. There are smokeproof suits hanging on the wall—they didn't have a chance to get into them."

"I'll warn the police, the air force."

"Don't be a prick, Garry. It will take an order from the chief of the defense force and the minister before they'll send up a fighter or a helicopter gunship. That could take a month of Sundays. By then two hundred thousand people will be dead."

"What must we do, Sean?" At last the administrator deferred to the man of action.

"Take the Queen Air," Sean told him. "She's faster and bigger and more powerful than the little Centurion. You have to intercept them and force them down before they reach the show."

"Describe Mickey's Centurion," Garry ordered crisply.

"Blue on top. White belly. Her markings are ZS-RRW, Romeo Romeo Whisky. You know the location of Firgrove and their course to reach the show."

"I'm on my way," said Garry. The connection clicked and went dead.

Sean picked up the Smith & Wesson from the bench top where he had dropped it and spilled the empty cases from the chambers. From his pocket he pulled a box of ammunition and reloaded swiftly. He ran back to the door and with the revolver held ready he stood clear and kicked it open. Immediately he dropped into a gunfighter's crouch and aimed through the doorway.

Ben had dragged his paralyzed legs only a few yards before he collapsed. He lay in a huddle at the foot of one of the peach trees. He was bleeding copiously; bright arterial blood had soaked his shirt and the tops of his trousers. His left arm hung by a tatter of mangled flesh. The shattered bone spiked through the meat like a skewer.

Sean straightened up and safed the Smith & Wesson. He walked through the door and stood looking down at Ben.

Ben was still alive. He rolled over painfully to look up at Sean. His eyes were brown as burnt sugar and filled with a dreadful anguish.

459

"They got away, didn't they?" he whispered. "They will succeed. You cannot stop us. The future belongs to us."

Isabella came running through the trees. She saw Sean and swerved toward him.

"I told you to keep out of the way," he growled at her. "Why can't you ever do as you're told?"

She saw Ben lying at his feet and stopped short.

"It's Ben. Oh, God, what have you done to him?"

She started forward again and dropped to her knees beside the prostrate body. Carefully she lifted Ben's head into her lap, but the movement tore something in his injured lung and he began to cough. A mouthful of blood spilled between his open lips and poured down his chin.

"Oh, God, Sean. You've killed him!" Isabella sobbed.

"I hope so," Sean said softly. "With all my heart, I hope so."

"Sean, he's your brother."

"No," said Sean. "He's not my brother. He's just a lump of shit."

As Garry Courtney started the engines of the Queen Air, he was calculating furiously.

Capricorn was almost sixty miles closer to the showgrounds than Firgrove was, and in addition the Queen Air was seventy or eighty knots faster than the Centurion at the cruise. It was seven minutes since Sean had called him, nine minutes since Mickey had taken off.

It was all running very close. He dared not try to guess where to intercept the Centurion and try to cut its track. There was only one sure course open to him. He had to fly directly to the showgrounds, then turn and head back on the reciprocal of Michael's heading. He had to risk everything on a head-on interception.

As he opened the throttles and ran the Queen Air out onto the runway, he found with mild surprise that he still had a half-smoked cigar between his teeth. In the panic of getting to the aircraft he had forgotten all about it. As he lifted the big twin-engined machine into the air, he drew deeply on the cigar. It was the very best Havana, and he smiled at the irony. The fragrant smoke calmed his nerves a little.

"I'm not as good at this as Sean is," he said to himself. "Give me a hectic day on the stock exchange or a nice bloody takeover deal any day." He pushed the Queen Air right over the manual, squeezing an extra fifteen knots out of her.

He picked out the showgrounds from almost seven miles out. A pod of giant balloons floated above it like colorful whales. The vast carparks were aglitter with sunlight reflected from thousands of vehicles.

He turned back onto a direct heading for Firgrove and leaned forward in his seat, peering ahead through the windscreen and puffing on the fat cigar. He was still running calculations of speed and time and distance through his head.

"If I'm going to meet them, it should be five or six minutes—" He broke off as a beam of sunlight reflecting from something ahead and below caught his eye. He pushed his horn-rimmed spectacles up onto his nose, once again hating his weak myopic eyes, and peered fitfully down, trying to find it again.

He had left the built-up residential areas behind and was flying over open countryside studded with small villages and criss-crossed with roads. The patterns of plowed lands and plantations of trees disturbed his eye and threw up a hundred decoys and optical tricks to confuse him. He searched frantically, sweeping the open sky briefly and then concentrating on the earth below. He expected the Centurion to be well under him.

He saw the shadow first. It flitted and jumped like a grass-hopper across the fields. A moment later he saw the tiny blue aircraft. It was a thousand feet below him and two miles directly ahead. He pushed the nose of the Queen Air down into a dangerous altitude and dived to intercept.

The two aircraft were converging at almost five hundred knots, and before Garry could get the Queen Air down to the same altitude as the Centurion it had passed like a blue flash below him.

Garry hauled up one wing into a maximum-rate turn and came around behind the Centurion. He used the Queen Air's superior speed and the dive to overhaul the smaller aircraft.

"We'll be there in about ten minutes," Michael warned Ramón. "You'd better get ready."

Ramón leaned forward and reached down to the gaudily painted cylinders bolted to the floorboards between his feet. Carefully he opened the tap on the neck of each of the bottles. He felt the rush of internal pressure that was checked immediately by the gate of the main valve in the connecting T-piece.

Now all that was needed was only to thumb the valve lever across, half a turn in a counterclockwise direction, to send the mixed and activated gas hissing into the long hose and spraying out through the nozzle under the Centurion's belly.

Ramón straightened up and glanced across at Michael in the pilot's seat beside him.

"All set—" he began. Then he broke off and stared with astonishment through the side window beside Michael's head.

An enormous silver fuselage filled the entire frame of the window. Another aircraft was flying wing tip to wing tip with them, and the pilot peered across at them. He was a large baby-faced man with dark horn-rimmed glasses and the stub of a cigar clamped in one corner of his mouth.

"Garry!" shouted Michael in consternation. Garry lifted his right hand and stabbed downward with his thumb, an unmistakable gesture.

Instinctively Michael flung the Centurion into a tight descending turn and dropped away toward the earth like a stone. He leveled out just above the treetops.

He glanced in his rearview mirror and saw the Queen Air's round silver nose a hundred yards from his tail and closing rapidly. He hauled the Centurion up and around hard, but the moment he leveled out the silver machine loomed up beside him. Garry had always been a far better pilot than he was, and the Queen Air had the wings to outfly him.

"I can't get away from him."

"Fly straight for the target," Ramón ordered brusquely. "There is nothing he can do."

Michael had hoped that Ramón would abandon the operation now, but reluctantly he turned back onto his original track. He was down to two hundred feet above the tops of the tallest trees. Garry followed him around and came up alongside him. Their wing tips were only a yard apart.

Once again Garry signaled him to land. Instead Michael snatched up the microphone of his radio, knowing that Garry would be tuned to 118.7 megahertz.

"I'm sorry, Garry," he cried. "I have to do it. I'm sorry."

Garry's voice boomed through the radio speaker into the cabin. "Land immediately, Mickey. It's not too late. We can still get you out of this. Don't be a fool, man."

Michael shook his head vehemently and pointed ahead.

Garry's expression hardened. He dropped back, and before Michael could react he slid in sideways and thrust the Queen Air's wing tip under the Centurion's tail. Then he came back hard on the control wheel and flicked the smaller plane's tail up, so she tumbled forward into an almost vertical dive.

The Centurion was too low and the dive too steep for Michael to recover before he hit the top branches of a tall blue gum tree.

Michael threw up his hands as he saw it coming, but a dry branch as thick as a man's arm stabbed through the windscreen, which had been weakened by Sean's bullet. The point of the branch caught Michael at the base of his throat. It found the notch between his collarbones and went through with the ease of a hypodermic needle, transfixing his upper torso and coming out between his shoulder blades.

The momentum of the falling aircraft snapped the branch off, and the jagged butt protruded from his throat like an ugly, twisted lance.

The Centurion drove on, crashing and crackling through the treetops. First one wing, then the other, were ripped away, braking the aircraft's speed, until it fell clear of the trees and the wingless fuselage hit the ground and bounced and skidded to rest at the edge of a field of standing maize stalks.

Ramón Machado dragged himself upright in the seat, amazed he was still alive. He looked across at Michael. Michael's mouth was wide open in a silent shriek; the jagged branch stuck out of his throat, and a fountain of his blood spurted over the remains of the shattered windscreen.

Ramón released the catch of his seat belt and tried to lift himself out of his seat. He found himself anchored, and he looked down. His left leg was broken. It was twisted like a piece of boiled spaghetti between the seat and gas cylinders. The leg of his trousers was ripped up to the knee, and the stainless steel valve handle was buried deeply in the flesh of his calf.

As he stared at it, he became aware of the faint hiss of escaping gas. His leg had twisted the valve handle into the open position. Cyndex 25 was spurting into the hose and spraying from the nozzle under the fuselage.

Ramón grabbed at the door handle and threw all his weight upon it. It was jammed solid. He placed both hands under the knee of his injured leg and hauled on it, trying to pull it free. The leg elongated, and he heard the ends of shattered bone shards grate together deep in his flesh, but the stainless-steel valve handle held it as inexorably as a bear trap.

Suddenly he smelled the odor of almonds, and his nostrils began to burn and sting. Silver mucus flooded from both nostrils and drooled over his lips and down his chin. His eyes turned to coals of fire in their sockets and his vision dimmed.

In the darkness the agony assailed him. It surpassed any conception he had ever had of pain. He began to scream. He screamed and screamed, sitting in a puddle of his own urine and feces, until at last his lungs collapsed and he could scream no more.

# 35

Centaine Courtney-Malcomess sat on a fallen log at the edge of the forest and watched the puppy and the child at play.

The puppy was the pick of the last litter Dandy Lass of Weltevreden had had before Centaine had been forced to have the gallant old bitch put down. The puppy had inherited all her mother's best points. She would be a champion also, Centaine was convinced of it.

Nicholas was working her with an old silk stocking stuffed with guinea-fowl feathers. He learned as quickly as the puppy. He seemed to have a way with dogs and horses.

It's in his blood, Centaine thought complacently. He's a true Courtney, despite the name and the fancy Spanish title.

She went on to think of her other Courtneys.

Tomorrow Shasa and Elsa Pignatelli were marrying in the little slave church that Centaine had so lovingly restored. It would be one of the biggest weddings to be held in the Cape of Good Hope for at least a decade. Guests were coming from England and Europe and Israel and America.

There would have been a time not so many years ago when Centaine would have wanted to make all the plans and supervise all the preparations for the wedding herself. Now she was content to leave it all to Isabella and Elsa Pignatelli.

"Let them get on with it," she told herself firmly. "I've got my hands full with my roses and my dogs and Nicky."

She thought about Isabella. She was contrite and chastened, but Centaine was not satisfied that it was enough. She had debated long and hard with herself and with Shasa before at last agreeing to cover for the girl and shield her from the full consequences of her treason and the righteous fury of the law.

Still, she has a penance to perform, thought Centaine, grimly justifying her leniency. Isabella will dedicate the rest of her life to making amends. She owes a lifetime of service to every member of this family and to all the people of this wonderful land of ours whom she betrayed. I'll see to it that she pays all her debts in full, she thought purposefully. Then she turned to watch the puppy find the feather bag that Nicholas had hidden in the reeds down by the stream, the puppy's long silky tail waving like a triumphant banner as she came to deliver it to her young master.

At last the boy and the dog came to sit at her feet together, and Nicholas put one tanned bare arm around the puppy's neck and hugged her.

"Have you decided on a name for her yet?" Centaine asked. It had taken her almost two years to break down the child's resistance to her, but she felt that now she had at last won him over from his memories of Adra and his previous life.

"Yes, Nana. I want to call her Twenty-six." The boy's English had improved vastly since she had enrolled him at Western Province Junior School.

"That's an unusual name. Why did you choose it?"

"I had another dog once—he was called Twenty-six." And yet his memories of that other time had almost faded.

"Well, that is an excellent reason—and it's a fine name. Dandy Twenty-six of Weltevreden."

"Yes! Yes!" Nicholas hugged the puppy's neck. "Dandy Twenty-six."

Centaine looked down on him fondly. He was still a mixed-up and confused little boy, but he was a thoroughbred with the blood of champions in his veins.

Give us time, she thought. Just give me a little more time with him.

"Shall I tell you a story, Nicholas?" she asked. She had the most wonderful family stories, of elephant hunts and lions, of wars with Boers and Zulus and Germans, of lost diamond mines and of fighter planes and a thousand other things to thrill the soul of a small boy.

So now she told him a story of shipwreck and of a castaway on a burning shore. She told him of a journey through a cruel desert with little yellow pixies as companions—and he walked every step of the enchanted way beside them.

465

At last she looked at her wristwatch and said, "That's enough for today, young master Nicholas. Your mother will be wondering whatever has become of us."

Nicholas sprang up to help her to her feet, and the two of them walked down the hill toward the big house with the puppy gamboling around them.

They walked quite slowly, because Nana had a sore leg, and Nicholas took her hand to help her over the rough places.

Internationally bestselling author
# WILBUR SMITH
*never fails to deliver nonstop action and thrills.*
Experience the excitement.
Published by Fawcett Books.

Call toll free 1-800-733-3000 to order by phone and use your major
credit card. Or use this coupon to order by mail.

| | | |
|---|---|---|
| __THE ANGELS WEEP | 449-20497-9 | $5.95 |
| __THE BURNING SHORE | 449-21189-4 | $5.99 |
| __DARK OF THE SUN | 449-21555-5 | $4.95 |
| __THE DIAMOND HUNTERS | 449-21614-4 | $4.95 |
| __FLIGHT OF THE FALCON | 449-20271-2 | $5.95 |
| __THE LEOPARD HUNTS IN DARKNESS | 449-20725-0 | $4.95 |
| __MEN OF MEN | 449-20496-0 | $5.95 |
| __POWER OF THE SWORD | 449-21414-1 | $5.95 |
| __RAGE | 449-21613-6 | $4.99 |
| __SHOUT AT THE DEVIL | 449-21554-7 | $5.95 |
| __THE SOUND OF THUNDER | 449-14819-X | $5.99 |
| __THE SUNBIRD | 449-14825-4 | $5.99 |
| __A TIME TO DIE | 449-14761-4 | $5.99 |
| __WHEN THE LION FEEDS | 449-21553-9 | $5.95 |

Name_____
Address _____
City_____State_____Zip_____

Please send me the FAWCETT BOOKS I have checked above.
I am enclosing                                              $_____
  plus
Postage & handling*                                        $_____
Sales tax (where applicable)                               $_____
Total amount enclosed                                      $_____

*Add $2 for the first book and 50¢ for each additional book.

Send check or money order (no cash or CODs) to Fawcett Mail Sales,
400 Hahn Road, Westminster, MD 21157.

Prices and numbers subject to change without notice.
Valid in the U.S. only.
All orders subject to availability.                        WSMITH